THE DELUGE

Vol. II.

THE DELUGE.

An Historical Novel

OF

POLAND, SWEDEN, AND RUSSIA.

A SEQUEL TO

"WITH FIRE AND SWORD."

BY

HENRYK SIENKIEWICZ.

AUTHORIZED AND UNABRIDGED TRANSLATION FROM THE POLISH BY

JEREMIAH CURTIN.

IN TWO VOLUMES.
Vol. II.

Fredonia Books
Amsterdam, The Netherlands

The Deluge
An Historical Novel of Poland, Sweden and Russia.
Vol. II

by
Henryk Sienkiewicz

Authorized and unabridged translation from the Polish by Jeremiah Curtin.

ISBN 1-58963-019-X

Reprinted from the 1925 edition

Fredonia Books
Amsterdam, The Netherlands
http://www.FredoniaBooks.com

THE DELUGE.

CHAPTER I.

THE war with cannon was no bar to negotiations, which the fathers determined to use at every opportunity. They wished to delude the enemy and procrastinate till aid came, or at least severe winter. But Miller did not cease to believe that the monks wished merely to extort the best terms.

In the evening, therefore, after that cannonading, he sent Colonel Kuklinovski again with a summons to surrender. The prior showed Kuklinovski the safeguard of the king, which closed his mouth at once. But Miller had a later command of the king to occupy Boleslav, Vyelunie, Kjepits, and Chenstohova.

"Take this order to them," said he to Kuklinovski; "for I think that they will lack means of evasion when it is shown them." But he was deceived.

The prior answered: "If the command includes Chenstohova, let the general occupy the place with good fortune. He may be sure that the cloister will make no opposition; but Chenstohova is not Yasna Gora, of which no mention is made in the order."

When Miller heard this answer he saw that he had to deal with diplomats more adroit than himself; reasons were just what he lacked, — and there remained only cannon.

A truce lasted through the night. The Swedes worked with vigor at making better trenches; and on Yasna Gora they looked for the damages of the previous day, and saw with astonishment that there were none. Here and there roofs and rafters were broken, here and there plaster had dropped from the walls, — that was all. Of the men, none had fallen, no one was even maimed. The prior, going around on the walls, said with a smile to the soldiers, —

"But see, this enemy with his bombarding is not so terrible as reported. After a festival there is often more harm done. God's care is guarding you; God's hand protects you; only let us endure, and we shall see greater wonders."

Sunday came, the festival of the offering of the Holy Lady. There was no hindrance to services, since Miller was waiting for the final answer, which the monks had promised to send after midday.

Mindful meanwhile of the words of Scripture, how Israel bore the ark of God around the camp to terrify the Philistines, they went again in procession with the monstrance.

The letter was sent about one o'clock, not to surrender; but to repeat the answer given Kuklinovski, that the church and the cloister are called Yasna Gora, and that the town Chenstohova does not belong to the cloister at all. "Therefore we implore earnestly his worthiness," wrote the prior Kordetski, "to be pleased to leave in peace our Congregation and the church consecrated to God and His Most Holy Mother, so that God may be honored therein during future times. In this church also we shall implore the Majesty of God for the health and success of the Most Serene King of Sweden. Meanwhile we, unworthy men, while preferring our request, commend ourselves most earnestly to the kindly consideration of your worthiness, confiding in your goodness, from which we promise much to ourselves in the future."

There were present at the reading of the letter, Sadovski; Count Veyhard; Horn, governor of Kjepitsi; De Fossis, a famous engineer; and the Prince of Hesse, a man young and very haughty, who though subordinate to Miller, was willing to show his own importance. He laughed therefore maliciously, and repeated the conclusion of the letter with emphasis, —

"They promise much to themselves from your kindness; General, that is a hint for a contribution. I put one question, gentlemen: Are the monks better beggars or better gunners?"

"True," said Horn, "during these first days we have lost so many men that a good battle would not have taken more."

"As for me," continued the Prince of Hesse, "I do not want money; I am not seeking for glory, and I shall freeze off my feet in these huts. What a pity that we did not go to Prussia, a rich country, pleasant, one town excelling another."

Miller, who acted quickly but thought slowly, now first understood the sense of the letter; he grew purple and said, —

"The monks are jeering at us, gracious gentlemen."

"They had not the intention of doing so, but it comes out all the same," answered Horn.

"To the trenches, then! Yesterday the fire was weak, the balls few."

The orders given flew swiftly from end to end of the Swedish line. The trenches were covered with blue clouds; the cloister answered quickly with all its energy. But this time the Swedish guns were better planted, and began to cause greater damage. Bombs, loaded with powder, were scattered, each drawing behind it a curl of flame. Lighted torches were hurled too, and rolls of hemp steeped in rosin.

As sometimes flocks of passing cranes, tired from long flying, besiege a high cliff, so swarms of these fiery messengers fell on the summit of the church and on the wooden roofs of the buildings. Whoso was not taking part in the struggle, was near a cannon, was sitting on a roof. Some dipped water from wells, others drew up the buckets with ropes, while third parties put out fire with wet cloths. Balls crashing rafters and beams fell into garrets, and soon smoke and the odor of burning filled all the interior of buildings. But in garrets, too, defenders were watching with buckets of water. The heaviest bombs burst even through ceilings. In spite of efforts more than human, in spite of wakefulness, it seemed that, early or late, flames would embrace the whole cloister. Torches and bundles of hemp pushed with hooks from the roofs formed burning piles at the foot of the walls. Windows were bursting from heat, and women and children confined in rooms were stifling from smoke and exhalations. Hardly were some missiles extinguished, hardly was the water flowing in broken places, when there came new flocks of burning balls, flaming cloths, sparks, living fire. The whole cloister was seized with it. You would have said that heaven had opened on the place, and that a shower of thunders was falling; still it burned, but was not consumed; it was flaming, but did not fall into fragments; what was more, the besieged began to sing like those youths in the fiery furnace ; for, as the day previous, a song was now heard from the tower, accompanied by trumpets. To the men standing on the walls and working at the guns, who at each moment might think that all was blazing and falling to ruins behind their shoulders, that song was like healing balsam, announcing continually that the church was standing, that the cloister was standing, that so far flames had not vanquished the efforts of men. Hence it became a custom to sweeten with such harmony the suffering of the siege, and to keep removed from the ears of women the terrible shouts of raging soldiery.

But in the Swedish camp that singing and music made no small impression. The soldiers in the trenches heard it at first with wonder, then with superstitious dread.

"How is it," said they to one another, "we have cast so much fire and iron at that hen-house that more than one powerful fortress would have flown away in smoke and ashes, but they are playing joyously? What does this mean?"

"Enchantment!" said others.

"Balls do not harm those walls. Bombs roll down from the roofs as if they were empty kegs! Enchantment, enchantment!" repeated they. "Nothing good will meet us in this place."

The officers in fact were ready to ascribe some mysterious meaning to those sounds. But others interpreted differently, and Sadovski said aloud, so that Miller might hear : "They must feel well there, since they rejoice; or are they glad because we have spent so much powder for nothing?"

"Of which we have not too much," added the Prince of Hesse.

"But we have as leader Poliorcetes," said Sadovski, in such a tone that it could not be understood whether he was ridiculing or flattering Miller. But the latter evidently took it as ridicule, for he bit his mustache.

"We shall see whether they will be playing an hour later," said he, turning to his staff.

Miller gave orders to double the fire, but these orders were carried out over-zealously. In their hurry, the gunners pointed the cannons too high, and the result was they carried too far. Some of the balls, soaring above the church and the cloister, went to the Swedish trenches on the opposite side, smashing timber works, scattering baskets, killing men.

An hour passed; then a second. From the church tower came solemn music unbroken.

Miller stood with his glass turned on Chenstohova. He looked a long time. Those present noticed that the hand with which he held the glass to his eyes trembled more and more; at last he turned and cried, —

"The shots do not injure the church one whit!" And anger, unrestrained, mad, seized the old warrior. He hurled the glass to the earth, and it broke into pieces. "I shall go wild from this music!" roared he.

At that moment De Fossis, the engineer, galloped up. "General," said he, "it is impossible to make a mine. Under a layer of earth lies rock. There miners are needed."

Miller used an oath. But he had not finished the imprecation when another officer came with a rush from the Chenstohova entrenchment, and saluting, said, —

"Our largest gun has burst. Shall we bring others from Lgota?"

Fire had slackened somewhat; the music was heard with more and more solemnity. Miller rode off to his quarters without saying a word. But he gave no orders to slacken the struggle; he determined to worry the besieged. They had in the fortress barely two hundred men as garrison; he had continual relays of fresh soldiers.

Night came, the guns thundered unceasingly; but the cloister guns answered actively, — more actively indeed than during the day, for the Swedish camp-fires showed them ready work. More than once it happened that soldiers had barely sat around the fire and the kettle hanging over it, when a ball from the cloister flew to them out of the darkness, like an angel of death. The fire was scattered to splinters and sparks, the soldiers ran apart with unearthly cries, and either sought refuge with other comrades, or wandered through the night, chilled, hungry, and frightened.

About midnight the fire from the cloister increased to such force that within reach of a cannon not a stick could be kindled. The besieged seemed to speak in the language of cannons the following words: "You wish to wear us out, — try it! We challenge you!"

One o'clock struck, and two. A fine rain began to fall in the form of cold mist, but piercing, and in places thickened as if into pillars, columns and bridges seeming red from the light of the fire. Through these fantastic arcades and pillars were seen at times the threatening outlines of the cloister, which changed before the eye; at one time it seemed higher than usual, then again it fell away as if in an abyss. From the trenches to its walls stretched as it were ill-omened arches and corridors formed of darkness and mist, and through those corridors flew balls bearing death; at times all the air above the cloister seemed clear as if illumined by a lightning flash; the walls, the lofty works, and the towers were all outlined in brightness, then again they were quenched. The soldiers looked before them with superstitious and gloomy dread. Time after time one pushed another and whispered, —

"Hast seen it? This cloister appears and vanishes in turn. That is a power not human."

"I saw something better than that," answered the other. "We were aiming with that gun that burst, when in a moment the whole fortress began to jump and quiver, as if some one were raising and lowering it. Fire at such a fortress; hit it!"

The soldier then threw aside the cannon brush, and after a while added, —

"We can win nothing here! We shall never smell their treasures. Brr, it is cold! Have you the tar-bucket there? Set fire to it; we can even warm our hands."

One of the soldiers started to light the tar by means of a sulphured thread. He ignited the sulphur first, then began to let it down slowly.

"Put out that light!" sounded the voice of an officer. But almost the same instant was heard the noise of a ball; then a short cry, and the light was put out.

The night brought the Swedes heavy losses. A multitude of men perished at the camp-fires; in places regiments fell into such disorder that they could not form line before morning. The besieged, as if wishing to show that they needed no sleep, fired with increasing rapidity.

The dawn lighted tired faces on the walls, pale, sleepless, but enlivened by feverishness. Kordetski had lain in the form of a cross in the church all night; with daylight he appeared on the walls, and his pleasant voice was heard at the cannon, in the curtains, and near the gates.

"God is forming the day, my children," said he. "Blessed be His light. There is no damage in the church, none in the buildings. The fire is put out, no one has lost his life. Pan Mosinski, a fiery ball fell under the cradle of your little child, and was quenched, causing no harm. Give thanks to the Most Holy Lady ; repay her."

"May Her name be blessed," said Mosinski; "I serve as I can."

The prior went farther.

It had become bright day when he stood near Charnyetski and Kmita. He did not see Kmita; for he had crawled to the other side to examine the woodwork, which a Swedish ball had harmed somewhat. The prior asked straightway, —

"But where is Babinich? Is he not sleeping?"

"I, sleep in such a night as this!" answered Pan Andrei, climbing up on the wall. "I should have no conscience. Better watch as an orderly of the Most Holy Lady."

"Better, better, faithful servant!" answered Kordetski.

Pan Andrei saw at that moment a faint Swedish light gleaming, and immediately he cried, —

"Fire, there, fire! Aim! higher! at the dog-brothers!"

Kordetski smiled, seeing such zeal, and returned to the cloister to send to the wearied men a drink made of beer with pieces of cheese broken in it.

Half an hour later appeared women, priests, and old men of the church, bringing steaming pots and jugs. The soldiers seized these with alacrity, and soon was heard along all the walls eager drinking. They praised the drink, saying, —

"We are not forgotten in the service of the Most Holy Lady. We have good food."

"It is worse for the Swedes," added others. "It was hard for them to cook food the past night; it will be worse the night coming."

"They have enough, the dog-faiths. They will surely give themselves and us rest during the day. Their poor guns must be hoarse by this time from roaring continually."

But the soldiers were mistaken, for the day was not to bring rest. When, in the morning, officers coming with the reports informed Miller that the result of the night's cannonading was nothing, that in fact the night had brought the Swedes a considerable loss in men, the general was stubborn and gave command to continue cannonading. "They will grow tired at last," said he to the Prince of Hesse.

"This is an immense outlay of powder," answered that officer.

"But they burn powder too?"

"They must have endless supplies of saltpetre and sul-

phur, and we shall give them charcoal ourselves, if we are
able to burn even one booth.   In the night I went near the
walls, and in spite of the thunder, I heard a mill clearly,
that must be a powder-mill."

"I will give orders to cannonade as fiercely as yesterday,
till sunset.   We will rest for the night.   We shall see if an
embassy does not come out."

"Your worthiness knows that they have sent one to
Wittemberg ? "

"I know; I will send too for the largest cannons.   If it
is impossible to frighten the monks or to raise a fire inside
the fortress, we must make a breach."

"I hope, your worthiness, that the field-marshal will approve the siege."

"The field-marshal knows of my intention, and he has
said nothing," replied Miller, dryly.   "If failure pursues
me still farther, the field-marshal will give censure instead
of approval, and will not fail to lay all the blame at my
door.   The king will say he is right, — I know that.   I have
suffered not a little from the field-marshal's sullen humor,
just as if 't is my fault that he, as the Italians state, is consumed by *mal francese.*"

"That they will throw the blame on you I doubt not,
especially when it appears that Sadovich is right."

"How right ?   Sadovich speaks for those monks as if he
were hired by them.   What does he say ? "

"He says that these shots will be heard through the
whole country, from the Carpathians to the Baltic."

"Let the king command in such case to tear the skin
from Count Veyhard and send it as an offering to the
cloister; for he it is who instigated to this siege."

Here Miller seized his head.

"But it is necessary to finish at a blow.   It seems to me,
something tells me, that in the night they will send some
one to negotiate; meanwhile fire after fire ! "

The day passed then as the day previous, full of thunder,
smoke, and flames.   Many such were to pass yet over Yasna
Gora.   But the defenders quenched the conflagrations and
cannonaded no less bravely.   One half the soldiers went to
rest, the other half were on the walls at the guns.

The people began to grow accustomed to the unbroken
roar, especially when convinced that no great damage was
done.   Faith strengthened the less experienced; but among
them were old soldiers, acquainted with war, who per-

formed their service as a trade. These gave comfort to the villagers.

Soroka acquired much consideration among them; for, having spent a great part of his life in war, he was as indifferent to its uproar as an old innkeeper to the shouts of carousers. In the evening when the guns had grown silent he told his comrades of the siege of Zbaraj. He had not been there in person, but he knew of it minutely from soldiers who had gone through that siege and had told him.

"There rolled on Cossacks, Tartars, and Turks, so many that there were more under-cooks there than all the Swedes that are here. And still our people did not yield to them. Besides, evil spirits have no power here; but there it was only Friday, Saturday, and Sunday that the devils did not help the ruffians; the rest of the time they terrified our people whole nights. They sent Death to the breastworks to appear to the soldiers and take from them courage for battle. I know this from a man who saw Death himself."

"Did he see her?" asked with curiosity peasants gathering around the sergeant.

"With his own eyes. He was going from digging a well; for water was lacking, and what was in the ponds smelt badly. He was going, going, till he saw walking in front of him some kind of figure in a black mantle."

"In a black, not in a white one?"

"In black; in war Death dresses in black. It was growing dark, the soldier came up. 'Who is here?' inquired he — no answer. Then he pulled the mantle, looked, and saw a skeleton. 'But what art thou here for?' asked the soldier. 'I am Death,' was the answer; 'and I am coming for thee in a week.' The soldier thought that was bad. 'Why,' asked he, 'in a week, and not sooner? Art thou not free to come sooner?' The other said: 'I can do nothing before a week, for such is the order.'"

"The soldier thought to himself: 'That is hard; but if she can do nothing to me now, I'll pay her what I owe.' Winding Death up in the mantle, he began to beat her bones on the pebbles; but she cried and begged: 'I'll come in two weeks!' 'Impossible.' 'In three, four, ten, when the siege is over; a year, two, fifteen — ' 'Impossible.' 'I'll come in fifty years.' The soldier was pleased, for he was then fifty, and thought: 'A hundred years is enough; I'll let her go.' The man is living this minute, and well; he goes to a battle as to a dance, for what does he care?"

"But if he had been frightened, it would have been all over with him?"

"The worst is to fear Death," said Soroka, with impor tance. "This soldier did good to others too; for after he had beaten Death, he hurt her so that she was fainting for three days, and during that time no one fell in camp, though sorties were made."

"But we never go out at night against the Swedes."

"We have n't the head for it," answered Soroka.

The last question and answer were heard by Kmita, who was standing not far away, and he struck his head. Then he looked at the Swedish trenches. It was already night. At the trenches for an hour past deep silence had reigned. The wearied soldiers were seemingly sleeping at the guns.

At two cannon-shots' distance gleamed a number of fires; but at the trenches themselves was thick darkness.

"That will not enter their heads, nor the suspicion of it, and they cannot suppose it," whispered Kmita to himself.

He went straight to Charnyetski, who, sitting at the gun carriage, was reading his rosary, and striking one foot against the other, for both feet were cold.

"Cold," said he, seeing Kmita; "and my head is heavy from the thunder of two days and one night. In my ears there is continual ringing."

"In whose head would it not ring from such uproars? But to-day we shall rest. They have gone to sleep for good. It would be possible to surprise them like a bear in a den; I know not whether guns would rouse them."

"Oh," said Charnyetski, raising his head, "of what are you thinking?"

"I am thinking of Zbaraj, how the besieged inflicted with sorties more than one great defeat on the ruffians."

"You are thinking of blood, like a wolf in the night."

"By the living God and his wounds, let us make a sortie! We will cut down men, spike guns! They expect no attack."

Charnyetski sprang to his feet.

"And in the morning they will go wild. They imagine, perhaps, that they have frightened us enough and we are thinking of surrender; they will get their answer. As I love God, 't is a splendid idea, a real knightly deed! That should have come to my head too. But it is needful to tell all to Kordetski, for he is commander."

They went.

Kordetski was taking counsel in the chamber with Zamoyski. When he heard steps, he raised his voice and pushing a candle to one side, inquired, —

"Who is coming? Is there anything new?"

"It is I, Charnyetski," replied Pan Pyotr, "with me is Babinich; neither of us can sleep. We have a terrible odor of the Swedes. This Babinich, father, has a restless head and cannot stay in one place. He is boring me, boring; for he wants terribly to go to the Swedes beyond the walls to ask them if they will fire to-morrow also, or give us and themselves time to breathe."

"How is that?" inquired the prior, not concealing his astonishment. "Babinich wants to make a sortie from the fortress?"

"In company, in company," answered Charnyetski, hurriedly, "with me and some others. They, it seems, are sleeping like dead men at the trenches; there is no fire visible, no sentries to be seen. They trust over much in our weakness."

"We will spike the guns," said Kmita.

"Give that Babinich this way!" exclaimed Zamoyski; "let me embrace him! The sting is itching, O hornet! thou wouldst gladly sting even at night. This is a great undertaking, which may have the finest results. God gave us only one Lithuanian, but that one an enraged and biting beast. I applaud the design; no one here will find fault with it. I am ready to go myself."

Kordetski at first was alarmed, for he feared bloodshed, especially when his own life was not exposed; after he had examined the idea more closely, he recognized it as worthy of the defenders.

"Let me pray," said he. And kneeling before the image of the Mother of God, he prayed a while, with outspread arms, and then rose with serene face.

"Pray you as well," said he; "and then go."

A quarter of an hour later the four went out and repaired to the walls. The trenches in the distance were sleeping. The night was very dark.

"How many men will you take?" asked Kordetski of Kmita.

"I?" answered Pan Andrei, in surprise. "I am not leader, and I do not know the place so well as Pan Charnyetski. I will go with my sabre, but let Charnyetski lead the men, and me with the others; I only wish to have my Soroka go, for he can hew terribly."

This answer pleased both Charnyetski and the prior, for they saw in it clear proof of submission. They set about the affair briskly. Men were selected, the greatest silence was enjoined, and they began to remove the beams, stones, and brick from the passage in the wall.

This labor lasted about an hour. At length the opening was ready, and the men began to dive into the narrow jaws. They had sabres, pistols, guns, and some, namely peasants, had scythes with points downward, — a weapon with which they were best acquainted.

When outside the wall they organized; Charnyetski stood at the head of the party, Kmita at the flank; and they moved along the ditch silently, restraining the breath in their breasts, like wolves stealing up to a sheepfold.

Still, at times a scythe struck a scythe, at times a stone gritted under a foot, and by those noises it was possible to know that they were pushing forward unceasingly. When they had come down to the plain, Charnyetski halted, and, not far from the enemy's trenches, left some of his men, under command of Yanich, a Hungarian, an old, experienced soldier; these men he commanded to lie on the ground. Charnyetski himself advanced somewhat to the right, and having now under foot soft earth which gave out no echo, began to lead forward his party more swiftly. His plan was to pass around the intrenchment, strike on the sleeping Swedes from the rear, and push them toward the cloister against Yanich's men. This idea was suggested by Kmita, who now marching near him with sabre in hand, whispered, —

"The intrenchment is extended in such fashion that between it and the main camp there is open ground. Sentries, if there are any, are before the trenches and not on this side of it, so that we can go behind freely, and attack them on the side from which they least expect attack."

"That is well," said Charnyetski; "not a foot of those men should escape."

"If any one speaks when we enter," continued Pan Andrei, "let me answer; I can speak German as well as Polish; they will think that some one is coming from Miller, from the camp."

"If only there are no sentries behind the intrench-ments."

"Even if there are, we shall spring on in a moment; before they can understand who and what, we shall have them down."

"It is time to turn, the end of the trench can be seen," said Charnyetski; and turning he called softly, "To the right, to the right!"

The silent line began to bend. That moment the moon lighted a bank of clouds somewhat, and it grew clearer. The advancing men saw an empty space in the rear of the trench.

As Kmita had foreseen, there were no sentries whatever on that space; for why should the Swedes station sentries between their trenches and their own army, stationed in the rear of the trenches. The most sharp-sighted leader could not suspect danger from that side.

At that moment Charnyetski said in the lowest whisper: "Tents are now visible. And in two of them are lights. People are still awake there, — surely officers. Entrance from the rear must be easy."

"Evidently," answered Kmita. "Over that road they draw cannon, and by it troops enter. The bank is already at hand. Have a care now that arms do not clatter."

They had reached the elevation raised carefully with earth dug from so many trenches. A whole line of wagons was standing there, in which powder and balls had been brought.

But at the wagons, no man was watching; passing them, therefore, they began to climb the embankment without trouble, as they had justly foreseen, for it was gradual and well raised.

In this manner they went right to the tents, and with drawn weapons stood straight in front of them. In two of the tents lights were actually burning; therefore Kmita said to Charnyetski, —

"I will go in advance to those who are not sleeping. Wait for my pistol, and then on the enemy!" When he had said this, he went forward.

The success of the sortie was already assured; therefore he did not try to go in very great silence. He passed a few tents buried in darkness; no one woke, no one inquired, "Who is there?"

The soldiers of Yasna Gora heard the squeak of his daring steps and the beating of their own hearts. He reached the lighted tent, raised the curtain and entered, halted at the entrance with pistol in hand and sabre down on its strap.

He halted because the light dazzled him somewhat; for on the camp table stood a candlestick with six arms, in which bright lights were burning.

At the table were sitting three officers, bent over plans. One of them, sitting in the middle, was poring over these plans so intently that his long hair lay on the white paper. Seeing some one enter, he raised his head, and asked in a calm voice, —

"Who is there ? "

"A soldier," answered Kmita.

That moment the two other officers turned their eyes toward the entrance.

"What soldier, where from ? " asked the first, who was De Fossis, the officer who chiefly directed the siege.

"From the cloister," answered Kmita. But there was something terrible in his voice.

De Fossis rose quickly and shaded his eyes with his hand. Kmita was standing erect and motionless as an apparition; only the threatening face, like the head of a predatory bird, announced sudden danger.

Still the thought, quick as lightning, rushed through the head of De Fossis, that he might be a deserter from Yasna Gora; therefore he asked again, but excitedly, —

"What do you want ? "

"I want this ! " cried Kmita; and he fired from a pistol into the very breast of De Fossis.

With that a terrible shout and a salvo of shots was heard on the trench. De Fossis fell as falls a pine-tree struck by lightning; another officer rushed at Kmita with his sword, but the latter slashed him between the eyes with his sabre, which gritted on the bone; the third officer threw himself on the ground, wishing to slip out under the side of the tent; but Kmita sprang at him, put his foot on his shoulder, and nailed him to the earth with a thrust.

By this time the silence of night had turned into the day of judgment. Wild shouts : "Slay, kill ! " were mingled with howls and shrill calls of Swedish soldiers for aid. Men bewildered from terror rushed out of the tents, not knowing whither to turn, in what direction to flee. Some, without noting at once whence the attack came, ran straight to the enemy, and perished under sabres, scythes, and axes, before they had time to cry "Quarter ! " Some in the darkness stabbed their own comrades; others unarmed, half-dressed, without caps, with hands raised upward, stood motionless on one spot; some at last dropped on the earth among the overturned tents. A small handful wished to defend themselves; but a blinded throng bore them away, threw them down, and trampled them.

Groans of the dying and heart-rending prayers for quarter increased the confusion.

When at last it grew clear from the cries that the attack had come, not from the side of the cloister, but from the rear, just from the direction of the Swedish army, then real desperation seized the attacked. They judged evidently that some squadrons, allies of the cloister, had struck on them suddenly.

Crowds of infantry began to spring out of the intrenchment and run toward the cloister, as if they wished to find refuge within its walls. But soon new shouts showed that they had come upon the party of the Hungarian, Yanich, who finished them under the very fortress.

Meanwhile the cloister-men, slashing, thrusting, trampling, advanced toward the cannons. Men with spikes ready, rushed at them immediately; but others continued the work of death. Peasants, who would not have stood before trained soldiers in the open field, rushed now a handful at a crowd.

Valiant Colonel Horn, governor of Kjepitsi, endeavored to rally the fleeing soldiers; springing into a corner of the trench, he shouted in the darkness and waved his sword. The Swedes recognized him and began at once to assemble; but in their tracks and with them rushed the attackers, whom it was difficult to distinguish in the darkness.

At once was heard a terrible whistle of scythes, and the voice of Horn ceased in a moment. The crowd of soldiers scattered as if driven apart by a bomb. Kmita and Charnyetski rushed after them with a few people, and cut them to pieces.

The trench was taken.

In the main camp of the Swedes trumpets sounded the alarm. Straightway the guns of Yasna Gora gave answer, and fiery balls began to fly from the cloister to light up the way for the home-coming men. They came panting, bloody, like wolves who had made a slaughter in a sheepfold; they were retreating before the approaching sound of musketeers. Charnyetski led the van, Kmita brought up the rear.

In half an hour they reached the party left with Yanich; but he did not answer their call · he alone had paid for the sortie with his life, for when he rushed after some officer, his own soldiers shot him.

The party entered the cloister amid the thunder of cannon and the gleam of flames. At the entrance the prior was waiting, and he counted them in order as the heads were pushed in through the opening. No one was missing save Yanich.

Two men went out for him at once, and half an hour later they brought his body; for Kordetski wished to honor him with a fitting burial.

But the quiet of night, once broken, did not return till white day. From the walls cannon were playing; in the Swedish positions the greatest confusion continued. The enemy not knowing well their own losses, not knowing whence the aggressor might come, fled from the trenches nearest the cloister. Whole regiments wandered in despairing disorder till morning, mistaking frequently their own for the enemy, and firing at one another. Even in the main camp were soldiers and officers who abandoned their tents and remained under the open sky, awaiting the end of that ghastly night. Alarming news flew from mouth to mouth. Some said that succor had come to the fortress, others asserted that all the nearer intrenchments were captured.

Miller, Sadovski, the Prince of Hesse, Count Veyhard, and other superior officers, made superhuman exertions to bring the terrified regiments to order. At the same time the cannonade of the cloister was answered by balls of fire, to scatter the darkness and enable fugitives to assemble. One of the balls struck the roof of the chapel, but striking only the edge of it, returned with rattling and crackling toward the camp, casting a flood of flame through the air.

At last the night of tumult was ended. The cloister and the Swedish camp became still. Morning had begun to whiten the summits of the church, the roofs took on gradually a ruddy light, and day came.

In that hour Miller, at the head of his staff, rode to the captured trench. They could, it is true, see him from the cloister and open fire; but the old general cared not for that. He wished to see with his own eyes all the injury, and count the slain. The staff followed him; all were disturbed, — they had sorrow and seriousness in their faces. When they reached the intrenchment, they dismounted and began to ascend. Traces of the struggle were visible everywhere; lower down than the guns were the overthrown tents; some were still open, empty, silent. There were piles of bodies, especially among the tents; half-naked corpses, mangled, with staring eyes, and with terror stiffened in their dead eyeballs, presented a dreadful sight. Evidently all these men had been surprised in deep sleep; some of them were barefoot; it was a rare one who grasped his rapier in his dead hand; almost no one wore a helmet or a cap. Some were lying in tents, especially at the side of the entrance; these, it was apparent, had barely succeeded in waking; others, at the sides of tents, were caught by death at the moment when they were seeking safety in flight. Everywhere there were many bodies, and in places such piles that it might be thought some cataclysm of nature had killed those soldiers; but the deep wounds in their faces and breasts, some faces blackened by shots, so near that all the powder had not been burned, testified but too plainly that the hand of man had caused the destruction.

Miller went higher, to the guns; they were standing dumb, spiked, no more terrible now than logs of wood; across one of them lay hanging on both sides the body of a gunner, almost cut in two by the terrible sweep of a scythe. Blood had flowed over the carriage and formed a broad pool beneath it. Miller observed everything minutely, in silence and with frowning brow. No officer dared break that silence. For how could they bring consolation to that aged general, who had been beaten like a novice through his own want of care? That was not only defeat, but shame; for the general himself had called that fortress a hen-house, and promised to crush it between his fingers, for he had nine thousand soldiers, and there were two hundred men in the garrison; finally, that general was a soldier, blood and bone, and against him were monks.

That day had a grievous beginning for Miller.

Now the infantry came up and began to carry out bodies. Four of them, bearing on a stretcher a corpse, stopped before the general without being ordered.

Miller looked at the stretcher and closed his eyes.

"De Fossis," said he, in a hollow voice.

Scarcely had they gone aside when others came; this time Sadovski moved toward them and called from a distance, turning to the staff, —

"They are carrying Horn!"

But Horn was alive yet, and had before him long days of atrocious suffering. A peasant had cut him with the very point of a scythe; but the blow was so fearful that it opened the whole framework of his breast. Still the wounded man retained his presence of mind. Seeing Miller and the staff, he smiled, wished to say something, but instead of a sound there came through his lips merely rose-colored froth; then he began to blink, and fainted.

"Carry him to my tent," said Miller, "and let my doctor attend to him immediately."

Then the officers heard him say to himself, —

"Horn, Horn, — I saw him last night in a dream, — just in the evening. A terrible thing, beyond comprehension!"

And fixing his eyes on the ground, he dropped into deep thought; all at once he was roused from his revery by the voice of Sadovski, who cried: "General! look there, there — the cloister!"

Miller looked and was astonished. It was broad day and clear, only fogs were hanging over the earth; but the sky was clear and blushing from the light of the morning. A white fog hid the summit itself of Yasna Gora, and according to the usual order of things ought to hide the church; but by a peculiar phenomenon the church, with the tower, was raised, not only above the cliff, but above the fog, high, high, — precisely as if it had separated from its foundations and was hanging in the blue under the dome of the sky. The cries of the soldiers announced that they too saw the phenomenon.

"That fog deceives the eye!" said Miller.

"The fog is lying under the church," answered Sadovski.

"It is a wonderful thing; but that church is ten times higher than it was yesterday, and hangs in the air," said the Prince of Hesse.

"It is going yet! higher, higher!" cried the soldiers. "It will vanish from the eye!"

In fact the fog hanging on the cliff began to rise toward the sky in the form of an immense pillar of smoke; the church planted, as it were, on the summit of that pillar, seemed to rise higher each instant; at the same time when it was far up, as high as the clouds themselves, it was veiled more and more with vapor; you would have said that it was melting, liquefying; it became more indistinct, and at last vanished altogether.

Miller turned to the officers, and in his eyes were depicted astonishment and a superstitious dread.

"I acknowledge, gentlemen," said he, "that I have never seen such a thing in my life, altogether opposed to nature : it must be the enchantment of papists."

"I have heard," said Sadovski, "soldiers crying out, 'How can you fire at such a fortress?' In truth I know not how."

"But what is there now?" cried the Prince of Hesse. "Is that church in the fog, or is it gone?"

"Though this were an ordinary phenomenon of nature, in any event it forebodes us no good. See, gentlemen, from the time that we came here we have not advanced one step."

"If," answered Sadovski, "we had only not advanced; but to tell the truth, we have suffered defeat after defeat, and last night was the worst. The soldiers losing willingness lose courage, and will begin to be negligent. You have no idea of what they say in the regiments. Besides, wonderful things take place ; for instance, for a certain time no man can go alone, or even two men, out of the camp ; whoever does so is as if he had fallen through the earth, as if wolves were prowling around Chenstohova. I sent myself, not long since, a banneret and three men to Vyelunie for warm clothing, and from that day, no tidings of them."

"It will be worse when winter comes; even now the nights are unendurable," added the Prince of Hesse.

"The mist is growing thinner!" said Miller, on a sudden.

In fact a breeze rose and began to blow away the vapors. In the bundles of fog something began to quiver; finally the sun rose and the air grew transparent. The walls of the cloister were outlined faintly, then out came the church and the cloister. Everything was in its old place. The fortress was quiet and still, as if people were not living in it.

"General," said the Prince of Hesse, with energy, "try negotiations again, it is needful to finish at once."

"But if negotiations lead to nothing, do you, gentlemen, advise to give up the siege?" asked Miller, gloomily.

The officers were silent. After a while Sadovski said,—

"Your worthiness knows best that it will come to that."

"I know," answered Miller, haughtily, "and I say this only to you, that I curse the day and the hour in which I came hither, as well as the counsellor who persuaded me to this siege [here he pierced Count Veyhard with his glance]

You know, however, after what has happened, that I shall not withdraw until I turn this cursed fortress into a heap of ruins, or fall myself."

Displeasure was reflected in the face of the Prince of Hesse. He had never respected Miller over-much; hence he considered this mere military braggadocio ill-timed, in view of the captured trenches, the corpses, and the spiked cannon. He turned to him then and answered with evident sarcasm, —

"General, you are not able to promise that; for you would withdraw in view of the first command of the king, or of Marshal Wittemberg. Sometimes also circumstances are able to command not worse than kings and marshals."

Miller wrinkled his heavy brows, seeing which Count Veyhard said hurriedly, —

"Meanwhile we will try negotiations. They will yield; it cannot be otherwise."

The rest of his words were drowned by the rejoicing sound of bells, summoning to early Mass in the church of Yasna Gora. The general with his staff rode away slowly toward Chenstohova; but had not reached headquarters when an officer rushed up on a foaming horse.

"He is from Marshal Wittemberg!" said Miller.

The officer handed him a letter. The general broke the seal hurriedly, and running over the letter quickly with his eyes, said with confusion in his countenance, —

"No! This is from Poznan. Evil tidings. In Great Poland the nobles are rising, the people are joining them. At the head of the movement is Krishtof Jegotski, who wants to march to the aid of Chenstohova."

"I foretold that these shots would be heard from the Carpathians to the Baltic," muttered Sadovski. "With this people change is sudden. You do not know the Poles yet; you will discover them later."

"Well! we shall know them," answered Miller. "I prefer an open enemy to a false ally. They yielded of their own accord, and now they are taking arms. Well! they will know our weapons."

"And we theirs," blurted out Sadovski. "General, let us finish negotiations with Chenstohova; let us agree to any capitulation. It is not a question of the fortress, but of the rule of his Royal Grace in this country."

"The monks will capitulate," said Count Veyhard. "To-day or to-morrow they will yield."

So they conversed with one another; but in the cloister after early Mass the joy was unbounded. Those who had not gone out in the sortie asked those who had how everything had happened. Those who had taken part boasted greatly, glorifying their own bravery and the defeat they had given the enemy.

Among the priests and women curiosity became paramount. White habits and women's robes covered the wall. It was a beautiful and gladsome day. The women gathered around Charnyetski, crying " Our deliverer! our guardian!" He defended himself particularly when they wanted to kiss his hands, and pointing to Kmita, said, —

"Thank him too. He is Babinich,[1] but no old woman. He will not let his hands be kissed, for there is blood on them yet; but if any of the younger would like to kiss him on the lips, I think that he would not flinch."

The younger women did in fact cast modest and at the same time enticing glances at Pan Andrei, admiring his splendid beauty; but he did not answer with his eyes to those dumb questions, for the sight of these maidens reminded him of Olenka.

"Oh, my poor girl!" thought he, "if you only knew that in the service of the Most Holy Lady I am opposing those enemies whom formerly I served to my sorrow!"

And he promised himself that the moment the siege was over he would write to her in Kyedani, and hurry off Soroka with the letter. " And I shall send her not empty words and promises; for now deeds are behind me, which without empty boasting, but accurately, I shall describe in the letter. Let her know that she has done this, let her be comforted."

And he consoled himself with this thought so much that he did not even notice how the maidens said to one another, in departing, —

"He is a good warrior; but it is clear that he looks only to battle, and is an unsocial grumbler."

---

[1] This name is derived from *baba* an old woman

CHAPTER II.

ACCORDING to the wish of his officers, Miller began negotiations again. There came to the cloister from the Swedish camp a well-known Polish noble, respected for his age and his eloquence. They received him graciously on Yasna Gora, judging that only in seeming and through constraint would he argue for surrender, but in reality would add to their courage and confirm the news, which had broken through the besieged wall, of the rising in Great Poland ; of the dislike of the quarter troops to Sweden ; of the negotiations of Yan Kazimir with the Cossacks, who, as it were, seemed willing to return to obedience ; finally, of the tremendous declaration of the Khan of the Tartars, that he was marching with aid to the vanquished king, all of whose enemies he would pursue with fire and sword.

But how the monks were mistaken ! The personage brought indeed a large bundle of news,— but news that was appalling, news to cool the most fervent zeal, to crush the most invincible resolution, stagger the most ardent faith.

The priests and the nobles gathered around him in the council chamber, in the midst of silence and attention ; from his lips sincerity itself seemed to flow, and pain for the fate of the country. He placed his hand frequently on his white head as if wishing to restrain an outburst of despair ; he gazed on the crucifix ; he had tears in his eyes, and in slow, broken accents, he uttered the following words :—

"Ah, what times the suffering country has lived to ! All help is past : it is incumbent to yield to the King of the Swedes. For whom in reality have you, revered fathers, and you lords brothers, the nobles, seized your swords ? For whom are you sparing neither watching nor toil, nor suffering nor blood ? For whom, through resistance,— unfortunately vain,— are you exposing yourselves and holy places to the terrible vengeance of the invincible legions of Sweden ? Is it for Yan Kazimir ? But he has already disregarded our kingdom. Do you not know that he has already made his choice, and preferring wealth, joyous feasts, and peaceful delights to a troublesome throne,

has abdicated in favor of Karl Gustav ? You are not willing
to leave him, but he has left you; you are unwilling to break
your oath, he has broken it ; you are ready to die for
him, but he cares not for you nor for any of us. Our lawful
king now is Karl Gustav ! Be careful, then, lest you draw
on your heads, not merely anger, vengeance, and ruin, but
sin before heaven, the cross, and the Most Holy Lady ; for
you are raising insolent hands, not against invaders, but
against your own king."

These words were received in silence, as though death
were flying through that chamber. What could be more
terrible than news of the abdication of Yan Kazimir ? It
was in truth news monstrously improbable ; but that old
noble gave it there in presence of the cross, in presence of
the image of Mary, and with tears in his eyes.

But if it were true, further resistance was in fact madness. The nobles covered their eyes with their hands, the
monks pulled their cowls over their heads, and silence, as
of the grave, continued unbroken ; but Kordetski, the prior,
began to whisper earnest prayer with his pallid lips, and
his eyes, calm, deep, clear, and piercing, were fixed on the
speaker immovably.

The noble felt that inquiring glance, was ill at ease and
oppressed by it; he wished to preserve the marks of importance, benignity, compassionate virtue, good wishes, but
could not; he began to cast restless glances on the other
fathers, and after a while he spoke further : —

"It is the worst thing to inflame stubbornness by a long
abuse of patience. The result of your resistance will be the
destruction of this holy church, and the infliction on you —
God avert it ! — of a terrible and cruel rule, which you will
be forced to obey. Aversion to the world and avoidance of its
questions are the weapons of monks. What have you to do
with the uproar of war, — you, whom the precepts of your
order call to retirement and silence ? My brothers, revered
and most beloved fathers ! do not take on your hearts, do
not take on your consciences, such a terrible responsibility.
It was not you who built this sacred retreat, not for you
alone must it serve ! Permit that it flourish, and that it
bless this land for long ages, so that our sons and grandsons
may rejoice in it."

Here the traitor opened his arms and fell into tears. The
nobles were silent, the fathers were silent ; doubt had
seized all. Their hearts were tortured, and despair was at

hand; the memory of baffled and useless endeavors weighed on their minds like lead.

"I am waiting for your answer, fathers," said the venerable traitor, dropping his head on his breast.

Kordetski now rose, and with a voice in which there was not the least hesitation or doubt, spoke as if with the vision of a prophet, —

"Your statement that Yan Kazimir has abandoned us, has abdicated and transferred his rights to Karl Gustav, is a calumny. Hope has entered the heart of our banished king, and never has he toiled more zealously than he is toiling at this moment to secure the salvation of the country, to secure his throne, and bring us aid in oppression."

The mask fell in an instant from the face of the traitor; malignity and deceit were reflected in it as clearly as if dragons had crept out at once from the dens of his soul, in which till that moment they had held themselves hidden.

"Whence this intelligence, whence this certainty?" inquired he.

"Whence?" answered the prior, pointing to a great crucifix hanging on the wall. "Go! place your finger on the pierced feet of Christ, and repeat what you have told us."

The traitor began to bend as if under the crushing of an iron hand, and a new dragon, terror, crawled forth to his face.

Kordetski, the prior, stood lordly, terrible as Moses; rays seemed to shoot from his temples.

"Go, repeat!" said he, without lowering his hand, in a voice so powerful that the shaken arches of the council chamber trembled and echoed as if in fear, — "Go, repeat!"

A moment of silence followed; at last the stifled voice of the visitor was heard, —

"I wash my hands — "

"Like Pilate!" finished Kordetski.

The traitor rose and walked out of the room. He hurried through the yard of the cloister, and when he found himself outside the gate, he began to run, almost as if something were hunting him from the cloister to the Swedes.

Zamoyski went to Charnyetski and Kmita, who had not been in the hall, to tell them what had happened.

"Did that envoy bring any good?" asked Charnyetski; "he had an honest face."

"God guard us from such honest men!" answered Zamoyski; "he brought doubt and temptation."

"What did he say?" asked Kmita, raising a little the lighted match which he was holding in his hand.

"He spoke like a hired traitor."

"That is why he hastens so now, I suppose," said Charnyetski. "See! he is running with almost full speed to the Swedish camp. Oh, I would send a ball after him!"

"A good thing!" said Kmita, and he put the match to the cannon.

The thunder of the gun was heard before Zamoyski and Charnyetski could see what had happened. Zamoyski caught his head.

"In God's name!" cried he, "what have you done? — he was an envoy."

"I have done ill!" answered Kmita; "for I missed. He is on his feet again and hastens farther. Oh! why did it go over him?" Here he turned to Zamoyski. "Though I had hit him in the loins, they could not have proved that we fired at him purposely, and God knows I could not hold the match in my fingers; it came down of itself. Never should I have fired at an envoy who was a Swede, but at sight of Polish traitors my entrails revolt."

"Oh, curb yourself; for there would be trouble, and they would be ready to injure our envoys."

But Charnyetski was content in his soul; for Kmita heard him mutter, "At least that traitor will be sure not to come on an embassy again."

This did not escape the ear of Zamoyski, for he answered: "If not this one, others will be found; and do you, gentlemen, make no opposition to their negotiations, do not interrupt them of your own will; for the more they drag on, the more it results to our profit. Succor, if God sends it, will have time to assemble, and a hard winter is coming, making the siege more and more difficult. Delay is loss for the enemy, but brings profit to us."

Zamoyski then went to the chamber, where, after the envoy's departure, consultation was still going on. The words of the traitor had startled men; minds and souls were excited. They did not believe, it is true, in the abdication of Yan Kazimir; but the envoy had held up to their vision the power of the Swedes, which previous days of success had permitted them to forget. Now it confronted their minds with all that terror before which towns and fortresses not such as theirs had been frightened, — Poznan, Warsaw, Cracow, not counting the multitude of castles which had opened their gates to the conqueror; how could Yasna Gora defend itself in a general deluge of defeats?

"We shall defend ourselves a week longer, two, three," thought to themselves some of the nobles and some of the monks; "but what further, what end will there be to these efforts?"

The whole country was like a ship already deep in the abyss, and that cloister was peering up like the top of a mast through the waves. Could those wrecked ones, clinging to the mast, think not merely of saving themselves, but of raising that vessel from under the ocean?

According to man's calculations they could not, and still, at the moment when Zamoyski re-entered the hall, Kordetski was saying, —

"My brothers! if you sleep not, neither do I sleep. When you are imploring our Patroness for rescue, I too am praying. Weariness, toil, weakness, cling to my bones as well as to yours; responsibility in like manner weighs upon me — nay, more perhaps, than upon you. Why have I faith while you seem in doubt? Enter into yourselves; or is it that your eyes, blinded by earthly power, see not a power greater than the Swedes? Or think you that no defence will suffice, that no hand can overcome that preponderance? If that is the case your thoughts are sinful, and you blaspheme against the mercy of God, against the all-might of our Lord, against the power of that Patroness whose servants you call yourselves. Who of you will dare to say that that Most Holy Queen cannot shield us and send victory? Therefore let us beseech her, let us implore night and day, till by our endurance, our humility, our tears, our sacrifice of body and health, we soften her heart, and pray away our previous sins."

"Father," said one of the nobles, "it is not a question for us of our lives or of our wives and children; but we tremble at the thought of the insults which may be put on the image, should the enemy capture the fortress by storm."

"And we do not wish to take on ourselves the responsibility," added another.

"For no one has a right to take it, not even the prior," added a third.

And the opposition increased, and gained boldness, all the more since many monks maintained silence. The prior, instead of answering directly, began to pray.

"O Mother of Thy only Son!" said he, raising his hands and his eyes toward heaven, "if Thou hast visited us so that in Thy capital we should give an example to others of endurance, of bravery, of faithfulness to Thee, to the country, to the king, — if Thou hast chosen this place in order to rouse by it the consciences of men and save the whole country, have mercy on those who desire to restrain, to stop the fountain of Thy grace, to hinder Thy miracles, and resist Thy holy will." Here he remained a moment in ecstasy, and then turned to the monks and nobles: "What man will take on his shoulders this responsibility, — the responsibility of stopping the miracles of Mary Her grace, Her salvation for this kingdom and the Catholic faith?"

"In the name of the Father, Son, and Holy Ghost!" answered a number of voices, "God preserve us from that!"

"Such a man will not be found!" cried Zamoyski.

And those of the monks in whose hearts doubt had been plunging began to beat their breasts, for no small fear had now seized them; and none of the councillors thought of surrender that evening.

But though the hearts of the older men were strengthened, the destructive planting of that hireling had given forth fruits of poison.

News of the abdication of Yan Kazimir and the improbability of succor went from the nobles to the women, from the women to the servants; the servants spread it among the soldiers, on whom it made the very worst impression. The peasants were astonished least of all; but experienced soldiers, accustomed to calculate the turns of war in soldier fashion only, began to assemble and explain to one another the impossibility of further defence, complaining of the stubbornness of monks, who did not understand the position; and, finally, to conspire and talk in secret.

A certain gunner, a German of suspected fidelity, proposed that the soldiers themselves take the matter in hand, and come to an understanding with the Swedes touching the surrender of the fortress. Others caught at this idea; but there were those who not only opposed the treason resolutely, but informed Kordetski of it without delay.

Kordetski, who knew how to join with the firmest trust in the powers of heaven the greatest earthly adroitness and caution, destroyed the secretly spreading treason in its inception.

First of all he expelled from the fortress the leaders of the treason, and at the head of them that gunner, having no fear whatever of what they could inform the Swedes regarding the state of the fortress and its weak sides; then, doubling the monthly wages of the garrison, he took from them an oath to defend the cloister to the last drop of their blood.

But he redoubled also his watchfulness, resolving to look with more care to the paid soldiers, as well as the nobles, and even his own monks. The older fathers were detailed to the night choirs; the younger, besides the service of God, were obliged to render service on the walls.

Next day a review of the infantry was held. To each bastion one noble with his servants, ten monks and two reliable gunners were detailed. All these were bound to watch, night and day, the places confided to them.

Pan Mosinski took his place at the northeastern bastion; he was a good soldier, the man whose little child had survived in a miraculous manner, though a bomb fell near its cradle. With him Father Hilary Slavoshevski kept guard. On the western bastion was Father Myeletski, of the nobles Pan Mikolai Kryshtoporski, a man surly and abrupt in speech, but of unterrified valor. The southeastern bastion was occupied by Charnyetski and Kmita, and with them was Father Adam Stypulski, who had formerly been a hussar. He, when the need came, tucked up his habit, aimed cannon, and took no more heed of the balls flying over his head than did the old sergeant Soroka. Finally, to the southwestern bastion were appointed Pan Skorjevski and Father Daniel Ryhtalski, who were distinguished by this, that both could abstain from sleep two and three nights in succession without harm to their health or their strength.

Fathers Dobrosh and Malahovski were appointed over the sentries. Persons unfitted for fighting were appointed to the roofs. The armory and all military implements Father Lyassota took under his care; after Father Dobrosh, he took also the office of master of the fires. In the night he had to illuminate the walls so that infantry of the enemy might not approach them. He arranged sockets and iron-holders on the towers, on which flamed at night torches and lights.

In fact, the whole tower looked every night like one gigantic torch. It is true that this lightened cannonading for the Swedes; but it might serve as a sign that the fortress was holding out yet, if, perchance, some army should march to relieve the besieged.

So then not only had designs of surrender crept apart into nothing, but the besieged turned with still greater zeal to defence. Next morning the prior walked along the walls, like a shepherd through a sheepfold, saw that everything was right, smiled kindly, praised the chiefs and the soldiers, and coming to Charnyetski, said with radiant face, —

"Our beloved leader, Pan Zamoyski, rejoices equally with me, for he says that we are now twice as strong as at first. A new spirit has entered men's hearts, the grace of the Most Holy Lady will do the rest; but meanwhile I will take to negotiations again. We will delay and put off, for by such means the blood of people will be spared."

"Oh, revered father!" said Kmita, "what good are negotiations? Loss of time! Better another sortie to-night, and we will cut up those dogs."

Kordetski (for he was in good humor) smiled as a mother smiles at a wayward child; then he raised a band of straw lying near the gun, and pretended to strike Pan Andrei with it on the shoulders: "And you will interfere here, you Lithuanian plague; you will lap blood as a wolf, and give an example of disobedience; here it is for you, here it is for you!"

Kmita, delighted as a schoolboy, dodged to the right and to the left, and as if teasing purposely, repeated: "Kill the Swedes! kill, kill, kill!"

And so they gave comfort to one another, having ardent souls devoted to the country. But Kordetski did not omit negotiations, seeing that Miller desired them earnestly and caught after every pretext. This desire pleased Kordetski, for he divined, without trouble, that it could not be going well with the enemy if he was so anxious to finish.

Days passed then, one after another, in which guns and muskets were not indeed silent, but pens were working mainly. In this way the siege was prolonged, and winter was coming harsher and harsher. On the Carpathian summits clouds hatched in their precipitous nests storms, frost, and snows, and then came forth on the country, leading their icy descendants. At night the Swedes cowered around fires, choosing to die from the balls of the cloister rather than freeze.

A hard winter had rendered difficult the digging of trenches and the making of mines. There was no progress

in the siege. In the mouths not merely of officers, but of
the whole army, there was only one word, — "negotiations."

The priests feigned at first a desire to surrender. Father
Dobrosh and the learned priest Sebastyan Stavitski came to
Miller as envoys. They gave him some hope of agreement.
He had barely heard this when he opened his arms and was
ready to seize them with joy to his embraces.   It was no
longer a question of Chenstohova, but of the whole country.
The surrender of Yasna Gora would have removed the last
hope of the patriots, and pushed the Commonwealth finally
into the arms of the King of Sweden ; while, on the contrary,
resistance, and that a victorious resistance, might change
hearts and call out a terrible new war.   Signs were not
wanting.   Miller knew this, felt what he had undertaken,
what a terrible responsibility was weighing on him ; he knew
that either the favor of the king, with the baton of a marshal,
honors, a title, were waiting for him, or final fall.   Since
he had begun to convince himself that he could not crack
this "nut," he received the priests with unheard-of honor, as
if they were embassadors from the Emperor of Germany or
the Sultan.   He invited them to a feast, he drank to their
honor, and also to the health of the prior and Pan Zamoyski ;
he gave them fish for the cloister ; finally, he offered conditions of surrender so gracious that he did not doubt for a moment that they would be accepted in haste.

The fathers thanked him humbly, as beseemed monks ;
they took the paper and went their way. Miller promised
the opening of the gates at eight of the following morning.
Joy indescribable reigned in the camp of the Swedes. The
soldiers left the trenches, approached the walls, and began
to address the besieged.

But it was announced from the cloister that in an affair of
such weight the prior must consult the whole Congregation ;
the monks therefore begged for one day's delay. Miller consented without hesitation. Meanwhile they were counselling
in the chamber till late at night.

Though Miller was an old and trained warrior, though
there was not, perhaps, in the whole Swedish army a general
who had conducted more negotiations with various places
than that Poliorcetes, still his heart beat unquietly when next
morning he saw two white habits approaching his quarters.

They were not the same fathers. First walked Father
Bleshynski, a reader of philosophy, bearing a sealed
letter: after him came Father Malahovski, with hands

crossed on his breast, with drooping head and a face slightly pale.

The general received them surrounded by his staff and all his noted colonels; and when he had answered politely the submissive bow of Father Bleshynski, he took the letter from his hand hastily and began to read.

But all at once his face changed terribly: a wave of blood flew to his head; his eyes were bursting forth, his neck grew thick, and terrible anger raised the hair under his wig. For a while speech was taken from him; he only indicated with his hand the letter to the Prince of Hesse, who ran over it with his eyes, and turning to the colonels, said calmly, —

"The monks declare only this much, that they cannot renounce Yan Kazimir before the primate proclaims a new king; or speaking in other words, they will not recognize Karl Gustav."

Here the Prince of Hesse laughed. Sadovski fixed a jeering glance on Miller, and Count Veyhard began to pluck his own beard from rage. A terrible murmur of excitement rose among those present.

Then Miller struck his palms on his knees and cried, —

"Guards, guards!"

The mustached faces of four musketeers showed themselves quickly in the door.

"Take those shaven sticks," cried the general, "and confine them! And Pan Sadovski, do you trumpet for me under the cloister, that if they open fire from one cannon on the walls, I will hang these two monks the next moment."

The two priests were led out amid ridicule and the scoffing of soldiers. The musketeers put their own caps on the priests' heads, or rather on their faces to cover their eyes, and led them of purpose to various obstacles. When either of the priests stumbled or fell, an outburst of laughter was heard in the crowds; but the fallen man they raised with the butts of muskets, and pretending to support, they pushed him by the loins and the shoulders. Some threw horse-dung at the priests; others took snow and rubbed it on their shaven crowns, or let it roll down on their habits. The soldiers tore strings from trumpets, and tying one end to the neck of each priest, held the other, and imitating men taking cattle to a fair, called out the prices.

Both fathers walked on in silence, with hands crossed on

their breasts and prayers on their lips. Finally, trembling from cold and insulted, they were enclosed in a barn; around the place guards armed with muskets were stationed.

Miller's command, or rather his threat, was trumpeted under the cloister walls.

The fathers were frightened, and the troops were be-numbed from the threat. The cannon were silent; a council was assembled, they knew not what to do. To leave the fathers in cruel hands was impossible; and if they sent others, Miller would detain them as well. A few hours later he himself sent a messenger, asking what the monks thought of doing.

They answered that until the fathers were freed no negotiations could take place; for how could the monks believe that the general would observe conditions with them if, despite the chief law of nations, he imprisoned envoys whose sacredness even barbarians respect?

To this declaration there was no ready answer; hence terrible uncertainty weighed on the cloister and froze the zeal of its defenders.

The Swedish army dug new trenches in haste, filled baskets with earth, planted cannon; insolent soldiers pushed forward to within half a musket-shot of the walls. They threatened the church, the defenders; half-drunken soldiers shouted, raising their hands toward the walls, "Surrender the cloister, or you will see your monks hanging!"

Others blasphemed terribly against the Mother of God and the Catholic faith. The besieged, out of respect to the life of the fathers, had to listen with patience. Rage stopped the breath in Kmita's breast. He tore the hair on his head, the clothing on his breast, and wringing his hands, said to Charnyetski, —

"I asked, 'Of what use is negotiation with criminals?' Now stand and suffer, while they are crawling into our eyes and blaspheming! O Mother of God, have mercy on me, and give me patience! By the living God, they will begin soon to climb the walls! Hold me, chain me like a murderer. for I shall not contain myself."

But the Swedes came ever nearer, blaspheming more boldly.

Meanwhile a fresh event brought the besieged to despair. Stefan Charnyetski in surrendering Cracow had obtained the condition of going out with all his troops, and remaining with them in Silesia till the end of the war. Seven hundred infantry of those troops of the royal guard, under command of Colonel Wolf, were near the boundary, and trusting in stipulations, were not on their guard. Count Veyhard persuaded Miller to capture those men.

Miller sent Count Veyhard himself, with two thousand cavalry, who crossing the boundary at night attacked those troops during sleep, and captured them to the last man. When they were brought to the Swedish camp, Miller commanded to lead them around the wall, so as to show the priests that that army from which they had hoped succor would serve specially for the capture of Chenstohova.

The sight of that brilliant guard of the king dragged along the walls was crushing to the besieged, for no one doubted that Miller would force them first to the storm.

Panic spread again among the troops of the cloister; some of the soldiers began to break their weapons and exclaim that there was help no longer, that it was necessary to surrender at the earliest. Even the hearts of the nobles had fallen; some of them appeared before Kordetski again with entreaties to take pity on their children, on the sacred place, on the image, and on the Congregation of monks. The courage of the prior and Pan Zamoyski was barely enough to put down this movement.

But Kordetski had the liberation of the imprisoned fathers on his mind first of all, and he took the best method; for he wrote to Miller that he would sacrifice those brothers willingly for the good of the church. Let the general condemn them to death; all would know in future what to expect from him, and what faith to give his promises.

Miller was joyful, for he thought the affair was approaching its end. But he did not trust the words of Kordetski at once, nor his readiness to sacrifice the monks. He sent therefore one of them, Father Bleshynski, to the cloister, binding him first with an oath to explain the power of the Swedes and the impossibility of resistance. The monk repeated everything faithfully, but his eyes spoke something else, and concluding he said, —

"But prizing life less than the good of the Congregation, I am waiting for the will of the council; and whatsoever you decide I will lay before the enemy most faithfully."

They directed him to say: "The monks are anxious to treat, but cannot believe a general who imprisons envoys." Next day the other envoy of the fathers came to the cloister, and returned with a similar answer.

After this both heard the sentence of death. The sentence

was read at Miller's quarters in presence of the staff and distinguished officers. All observed carefully the faces of the monks, curious to learn what impression the sentence would make; and with the greatest amazement they saw in both a joy as great, as unearthly, as if the highest fortune had been announced to them. The pale faces of the monks flushed suddenly, their eyes were filled with light, and Father Malahovski said with a voice trembling from emotion, —

"Ah! why should we not die to-day, since we are predestined to fall a sacrifice for our Lord and the king?"

Miller commanded to lead them forth straightway. The officers looked at one another. At last one remarked: "A struggle with such fanaticism is difficult."

The Prince of Hesse added: "Only the first Christians had such faith. Is that what you wish to say?" Then he turned to Count Veyhard. "Pan Veyhard," said he, "I should be glad to know what you think of these monks?"

"I have no need to trouble my head over them," answered he, insolently; "the general has already taken care of them."

Then Sadovski stepped forward to the middle of the room, stood before Miller, and said with decision: "Your worthiness, do not command to execute these monks."

"But why not?"

"Because there will be no talk of negotiations after that; for the garrison of the fortress will be flaming with vengeance, and those men will rather fall one upon the other than surrender."

"Wittemberg will send me heavy guns."

"Your worthiness, do not do this deed," continued Sadovski, with force; "they are envoys who have come here with confidence."

"I shall not have them hanged on confidence, but on gibbets."

"The echo of this deed will spread through the whole country, will enrage all hearts, and turn them away from us."

"Give me peace with your echoes; I have heard of them already a hundred times."

"Your worthiness will not do this without the knowledge of his Royal Grace?"

"You have no right to remind me of my duties to the king."

"But I have the right to ask for permission to resign

from service, and to present my reasons to his Royal Grace. I wish to be a soldier, not an executioner."

The Prince of Hesse issued from the circle in the middle of the room, and said ostentatiously, —

" Give me your hand, Pan Sadovski ; you are a gentleman, a noble, and an honest man."

" What does this mean ? " roared Miller, springing from his seat.

" General," answered the Prince of Hesse, " I permit myself to remark that Pan Sadovski is an honorable man, and I judge that there is nothing in this against discipline."

Miller did not like the Prince of Hesse; but that cool, polite, and also contemptuous manner of speaking, special to men of high rank, imposed on him, as it does on many persons of low birth. Miller made great efforts to acquire this manner, but had no success. He restrained his outburst, however, and said calmly, —

" The monks will be hanged to-morrow."

" That is not my affair," answered the Prince of Hesse ; " but in that event let your worthiness order an attack on those two thousand Poles who are in our camp, for if you do not they will attack us. Even now it is less dangerous for a Swedish soldier to go among a pack of wolves than among their tents. This is all I have to say, and now I permit myself to wish you success." When he had said this he left the quarters.

Miller saw that he had gone too far. But he did not withdraw his orders, and that same day gibbets were erected in view of the whole cloister. At the same time the soldiers, taking advantage of the truce, pushed still nearer the walls, not ceasing to jeer, insult, blaspheme, and challenge. Whole throngs of them climbed the mountain, stood as closely together as if they intended to make an assault.

That time Kmita, whom they had not chained as he had requested, did not in fact restrain himself, and thundered from a cannon into the thickest group, with such effect that he laid down in a row all those who stood in front of the shot. That was like a watchword ; for at once, without orders, and even in spite of orders, all the cannons began to play, muskets and guns thundered.

The Swedes, exposed to fire from every side, fled from the fortress with howling and screaming, many falling dead on the road.

Charnyetski sprang to Kmita: "Do you know that for that the reward is a bullet in the head?"

"I know, all one to me. Let me be —"

"In that case aim surely."

Kmita aimed surely; soon, however, he missed. A great movement rose meanwhile in the Swedish camp, but it was so evident that the Swedes were the first to violate the truce, that Miller himself recognized in his soul that the besieged were in the right.

What is more, Kmita did not even suspect that with his shots he had perhaps saved the lives of the fathers; but Miller, because of these shots, became convinced that the monks in the last extremity were really ready to sacrifice their two brethren for the good of the church and the cloister.

The shots beat into his head this idea also, that if a hair were to fall from the heads of the envoys, he would not hear from the cloister anything save similar thunders; so next day he invited the two imprisoned monks to dinner, and the day after he sent them to the cloister.

Kordetski wept when he saw them, all took them in their arms and were astonished at hearing from their mouths that it was specially owing to those shots that they were saved. The prior, who had been angry at Kmita, called him at once and said, —

"I was angry because I thought that you had destroyed the two fathers; but the Most Holy Lady evidently inspired you. This is a sign of Her favor, be rejoiced."

"Dearest, beloved father, there will be no more negotiations, will there?" asked Kmita, kissing Kordetski's hands.

But barely had he finished speaking, when a trumpet was heard at the gates, and an envoy from Miller entered the cloister.

This was Pan Kuklinovski, colonel of the volunteer squadron attached to the Swedes. The greatest ruffians without honor or faith served in that squadron, in part dissidents such as Lutherans, Arians, Calvinists, — whereby was explained their friendship for Sweden; but a thirst for robbery and plunder attracted them mainly to Miller's army. That band, made up of nobles, outlaws, fugitives from prison and from the hands of a master, of attendants, and of gallows-birds snatched from the rope, was somewhat like Kmita's old party, save in this, that Kmita's men fought as do lions, and those preferred to plunder, offer violence to noble women, break open stables and treasure chests. But Kuklinovski himself had less resemblance to Kmita. Age had mixed gray with his hair. He had a face dried, insolent, and shameless. His eyes, which were unusually prominent and greedy, indicated violence of character. He was one of those soldiers in whom, because of a turbulent life and continuous wars, conscience had been burned out to the bottom. A multitude of such men strolled about in that time, after the Thirty Years' War, through all Germany and Poland. They were ready to serve any man, and more than once a mere simple incident determined the side on which they were to stand.

Country and faith, in a word all things sacred, were thoroughly indifferent to them. They recognized nothing but war, and sought in it pleasure, dissipation, profit, and oblivion of life. But still when they had chosen some side they served it loyally enough, and that through a certain soldier-robber honor, so as not to close the career to themselves and to others. Such a man was Kuklinovski. Stern daring and immeasurable stubbornness had won for him consideration among the disorderly. It was easy for him to find men. He had served in various arms and services. He had been ataman in the Saitch; he had led regiments in Wallachia; in Germany he had enlisted volunteers in the Thirty Years' War, and had won a certain fame as a leader of cavalry. His crooked legs, bent in bow fashion, showed that he had spent the greater part of his life on horseback. He was as thin as a splinter, and somewhat bent from profligacy. Much blood, shed not in war only, weighed upon him. And still he was not a man wholly wicked by nature; he felt at times nobler influences. But he was spoiled to the marrow of his bones, and insolent to the last degree. Frequently had he said in intimate company, in drink: "More than one deed was done for which the thunderbolt should have fallen, but it fell not."

The effect of this impunity was that he did not believe in the justice of God, and punishment, not only during life, but after death. In other words, he did not believe in God; still, he believed in the devil, in witches, in astrologers, and in alchemy. He wore the Polish dress, for he thought it most fitting for cavalry; but his mustache, still black, he trimmed in Swedish fashion, and spread at the ends turned upward. In speaking he made every word diminutive, like a child; this produced a strange impression when heard from the mouth of such a devil incarnate and such a cruel ruffian, who was ever gulping human blood. He talked much and boastingly; clearly he thought himself a celebrated personage, and one of the first cavalry colonels on earth.

Miller, who, though on a broader pattern, belonged himself to a similar class, valued him greatly, and loved specially to seat him at his own table. At that juncture Kuklinovski forced himself on the general as an assistant, guaranteeing that he would with his eloquence bring the priests to their senses at once.

Earlier, when, after the arrest of the priests, Pan Zamoyski was preparing to visit Miller's camp and asked for a hostage, Miller sent Kuklinovski; but Zamoyski and the prior would not accept him, as not being of requisite rank.

From that moment, touched in his self-love, Kuklinovski conceived a mortal hatred for the defenders of Yasna Gora, and determined to injure them with all his power. Therefore he chose himself as an embassy, — first for the embassy itself, and second so as to survey everything and cast evil seed here and there. Since he was long known to Charnyetski he approached the gate guarded by him; but Charnyetski was sleeping at the time, — Kmita, taking his place, conducted the guest to the council hall.

Kuklinovski looked at Pan Andrei with the eye of a specialist, and at once he was pleased not only with the form but the bearing of the young hero, which might serve as a model.

"A soldier," said he, raising his hand to his cap, "knows at once a real soldier. I did not think that the priests had such men in their service. What is your rank, I pray?"

In Kmita, who had the zeal of a new convert, the soul revolted at sight of Poles who served Swedes; still, he remembered the recent anger of Kordetski at his disregard of negotiations; therefore he answered coldly, but calmly, —

"I am Babinich, former colonel in the Lithuanian army, but now a volunteer in the service of the Most Holy Lady."

"And I am Kuklinovski, also colonel, of whom you must have heard; for during more than one little war men mentioned frequently that name and this sabre [here he struck at his side], not only here in the Commonwealth, but in foreign countries."

"With the forehead." said Kmita. "I have heard."

"Well, so you are from Lithuania, and in that land are famous soldiers. We know of each other, for the trumpet of fame is to be heard from one end of the world to the other. Do you know there, worthy sir, a certain Kmita?"

The question fell so suddenly that Pan Andrei was as if fixed to the spot. "But why do you ask of him?"

"Because I love him, though I know him not, for we are alike as two boots of one pair; and I always repeat this, with your permission, 'There are two genuine soldiers in the Commonwealth, — I in the kingdom, and Kmita in Lithuania,' — a pair of dear doves, is not that true? Did you know him personally?"

"Would to God that you were killed!" thought Kmita; but, remembering Kuklinovski's character of envoy, he answered aloud: "I did not know him personally. But now come in, for the council is waiting."

When he had said this, he indicated the door through which a priest came out to receive the guest. Kuklinovski entered the chamber with him at once, but first he turned to Kmita: "It would please me," said he, "if at my return you and none other were to conduct me out."

"I will wait here," answered Kmita. And he was left alone. After a while he began to walk back and forth with quick steps; his whole soul was roused within him, and his heart was filled with blood, black from anger.

"Pitch does not stick to a garment like evil fame to a man," muttered he. "This scoundrel, this wretch, this traitor calls me boldly his brother, and thinks he has me as a comrade. See to what I have come! All gallows-birds proclaim me their own, and no decent man calls me to mind without horror. I have done little yet, little! If I could only give a lesson to this rascal! It cannot be but that I shall put my score on him."

The council lasted long in the chamber. It had grown dark. Kmita was waiting yet.

At last Kuklinovski appeared. Pan Andrei could not see the colonel's face, but he inferred from his quick panting, that the mission had failed, and had been also displeasing, for the envoy had lost desire for talk. They walked on then for some time in silence. Kmita determined meanwhile to get at the truth, and said with feigned sympathy, —

"Surely, you are coming with nothing. — Our priests are stubborn; and, between you and me, they act ill, for we can-not defend ourselves forever."

Kuklinovski halted and pulled him by the sleeve. "And do you think that they act ill? You have your senses; these priests will be ground into bran, — I guarantee that! They are unwilling to obey Kuklinovski; they will obey his sword."

"You see, it is not a question of the priests with me," said Kmita, "but of this place, which is holy, that is not to be denied, but which the later it is surrendered the more severe must the conditions be. Is what men say true, that through the country tumults are rising, that here and there they are slashing the Swedes, and that the Khan is marching with aid? If that is true, Miller must retreat."

"I tell you in confidence, a wish for Swedish broth is rising in the country, and likely in the army as well; that is true. They are talking of the Khan also. But Miller will not retreat; in a couple of days heavy artillery will come. We'll dig these foxes out of their hole, and then what will be will be! — But you have sense."

"Here is the gate!" said Kmita; "here I must leave you, unless you wish me to attend you down the slope?"

"Attend me, attend me! A couple of days ago you fired after an envoy."

"Indeed! What do you mean?"

"Maybe unwillingly. But better attend me; I have a few words to say to you."

"And I to you."

"That is well."

They went outside the gate and sank in the darkness. Here Kuklinovski stopped, and taking Kmita again by the sleeve, began to speak, —

"You, Sir Cavalier, seem to me adroit and foreseeing, and besides I feel in you a soldier, blood and bone. What the devil do you stick to priests for, and not to soldiers? Why be a serving lad for priests? There is a better and a pleasanter company with us, — with cups, dice, and women. Do you understand?"

Here he pressed Kmita's arm with his fingers. "This house," continued he, pointing with his finger to the fortress, "is on fire, and a fool is he who flees not from a house when 't is burning. Maybe you fear the name of traitor? Spit on those who would call you that! Come to our company; I, Kuklinovski, propose this. Obey, if you like; if you don't like, obey not — there will be no offence. General

Miller will receive you well, I guarantee that; you have
touched my heart, and I speak thus from good wishes.
Ours is a joyous company, joyous! A soldier's freedom is
in this, — to serve whom he likes. Monks are nothing to
you! If a bit of virtue hinders you, then cough it out.
Remember this also, that honest men serve with us. How
many nobles, magnates, hetmans! What can be better?
Who takes the part of our little Kazimir? No man save
Sapyeha alone, who is bending Radzivill."

Kmita grew curious: "Did you say that Sapyeha is bending Radzivill?"

"I did. He is troubling him terribly there in Podlyasye,
and is besieging him now in Tykotsin. But we do not disturb him."

"Why is that?"

"Because the King of Sweden wants them to devour one
another. Radzivill was never reliable; he was thinking of
himself. Besides, he is barely breathing. Whoever lets
himself be besieged is in a fix, he is finished."

"Will not the Swedes go to succor him?"

"Who is to go? The king himself is in Prussia, for
there lies the great question. The elector has wriggled out
hitherto; he will not wriggle out this time. In Great Poland is war, Wittemberg is needed in Cracow, Douglas has
work with the hill-men; so they have left Radzivill to himself. Let Sapyeha devour him. Sapyeha has grown, that
is true; but his turn will come also. Our Karl, when he
finishes with Prussia, will twist the horns of Sapyeha.
Now there is no power against him, for all Lithuania
stands at his side."

"But Jmud?"

"Pontus de la Gardie holds that in his paws, and heavy
are the paws; I know him."

"How is it that Radzivill has fallen, he whose power was
equal to that of kings?"

"It is quenching already, quenching — "

"Wonderful are the ordinances of God!"

"The wheel of war changes. But no more of this.
Well, what? Do you make up your mind to my proposition? You'll not be sorry! Come to us. If it is too
hurried to-day, think till to-morrow, till the day after, before the heavy artillery comes. These people here trust
you evidently, since you pass through the gate as you do
now. Or come with letters and go back no more."

" You attract others to the Swedish side, for you are an envoy of Sweden," said Kmita; " it does not beseem you to act otherwise, though in your soul who knows what you think ? There are those who serve the Swedes, but wish them ill in their hearts."

" Word of a cavalier ! " answered Kuklinovski, " that I speak sincerely, and not because I am filling the function of an envoy. Outside the gate I am no longer an envoy ; and if you wish I will remove the office of envoy of my own will, and speak to you as a private man. Throw that vile fortress to the devil ! "

" Do you say this as a private man ? "

" Yes."

" And may I give answer to you as to a private man ? "

" As true as life I propose it myself."

" Then listen, Pan Kuklinovski." Here Kmita inclined and looked into the very eyes of the ruffian. " You are a rascal, a traitor, a scoundrel, a crab-monger, an arch-cur ! Have you enough, or shall I spit in your eyes yet ? "

Kuklinovski was astounded to such a degree that for a time there was silence.

" What is this ? How is this ? Do I hear correctly ? "

" Have you enough, you cur ? or do you wish me to spit in your eyes ? "

Kuklinovski drew his sabre ; but Kmita caught him with his iron hand by the wrist, twisted his arm, wrested the sabre from him, then slapped him on the cheek so that the sound went out in the darkness ; seized him by the other side, turned him in his hand like a top, and kicking him with all his strength, cried, —

" To a private man, not to an envoy ! "

Kuklinovski rolled down like a stone thrown from a ballista. Pan Andrei went quietly to the gate.

The two men parted on the slope of the eminence ; hence it was difficult to see them from the walls. But Kmita found waiting for him at the gate Kordetski, who took him aside at once, and asked, —

" What were you doing so long with Kuklinovski."

" I was entering into confidence with him," answered Pan Andrei.

" What did he say ? "

" He said that it was true concerning the Khan."

" Praise be to God, who can change the hearts of pagans and make friends out of enemies."

"He told me that Great Poland is moving."

"Praise be to God!"

"That the quarter soldiers are more and more unwilling
to remain with the Swedes; that in Podlyasye, the voevoda
of Vityebsk, Sapyeha, has beaten the traitor Radzivill, and
that he has all honest people with him. As all Lithuania
stands by him, except Jmud, which De la Gardie has
taken."

"Praise be to God! Have you had no other talk with
each other?"

"Yes; Kuklinovski tried afterward to persuade me to
go over to the Swedes."

"I expected that," said the prior; "he is a bad man.
And what did you answer?"

"You see he told me, revered father, as follows: 'I put
aside my office of envoy, which without that is finished beyond the gates, and I persuade you as a private man.' And
I to make sure asked, 'May I answer as to a private man?'
He said, 'Yes' — then —"

"What then?"

"Then I gave it to him in the snout, and he rolled down
hill."

"In the name of the Father, Son, and Holy Ghost!"

"Be not angry, father; I acted very carefully, and that
he will not say a word about the matter to any man is
certain."

The priest was silent for a time, then said; "That you
acted honestly, I know. I am only troubled at this, that
you have gained a new enemy. He is a terrible man."

"One more, one less!" said Kmita. Then he bent to
the ear of the priest. "But Prince Boguslav, he at least
is an enemy! What is such a Kuklinovski? I don't even
look back at him."

CHAPTER III.

Now the terrible Arwid Wittemberg made himself heard. A famous officer brought his stern letter to the cloister, commanding the fathers to surrender the fortress to Miller. "In the opposite event," wrote Wittemberg, "if you do not abandon resistance, and do not yield to the said general, you may be sure that a punishment awaits you which will serve others as an example. The blame for your suffering lay to yourselves."

The fathers after receiving this letter determined in old fashion to procrastinate, and present new difficulties daily. Again days passed during which the thunder of artillery interrupted negotiations, and the contrary.

Miller declared that he wished to introduce his garrison only to insure the cloister against bands of freebooters. The fathers answered that since their garrison appeared sufficient against such a powerful leader as the general himself, all the more would it suffice against bands of freebooters. They implored Miller, therefore, by all that was sacred, by the respect which the people had for the place, by God and by Mary, to go to Vyelunie, or wherever it might please him. But the patience of the Swedes was exhausted. That humility of the besieged, who implored for mercy while they were firing more and more quickly from cannons, brought the chief and the army to desperation.

At first Miller could not get it into his head why, when the whole country had surrendered, that one place was defending itself; what power was upholding them; in the name of what hopes did these monks refuse to yield, for what were they striving, for what were they hoping ?

But flowing time brought more clearly the answer to that question. The resistance which had begun there was spreading like a conflagration. In spite of a rather dull brain, the general saw at last what the question with Kordetski was; and besides, Sadovski had explained incontrovertibly that it was not a question of that rocky nest, nor of Yasna Gora, nor of the treasures gathered in the cloister, nor of the safety of the Congregation, but of the fate of the whole Commonwealth. Miller discovered that that silent priest knew what he was doing, that he had knowledge of his mission, that he had risen as a prophet to enlighten the land by example, — to call with a mighty voice to the east and the west, to the north and the south, *Sursum corda!* (Raise your hearts) in order to rouse, either by his victory or his death and sacrifice, the sleeping from their slumber, to purify the sinful, to bring light into darkness.

When he had discovered this, that old warrior was simply terrified at that defender and at his own task. All at once that "hen-house" of Chenstohova seemed to him a giant mountain defended by a Titan, and the general seemed small to himself; and on his own army he looked, for the first time in his life, as on a handful of wretched worms. Was it for them to raise hands against that mysterious and heaven-touching power? Therefore Miller was terrified, and doubt began to steal into his heart. Seeing that the fault would be placed upon him, he began himself to seek the guilty, and his anger fell first on Count Veyhard. Disputes rose in the camp, and dissensions began to inflame hearts against one another; the works of the siege had to suffer therefrom.

Miller had been too long accustomed to estimate men and events by the common measure of a soldier, not to console himself still at times with the thought that at last the fortress would surrender. And taking things in human fashion, it could not be otherwise. Besides, Wittemberg was sending him six siege guns of the heaviest calibre, which had shown their force at Cracow.

"Devil take it!" thought Miller; "such walls will not stand against guns like these, and if that nest of terrors, of superstitions, of enchantment, winds up in smoke, then things will take another turn, and the whole country will be pacified."

While waiting for the heavier guns, he commanded to fire from the smaller. The days of conflict returned. But in vain did balls of fire fall on the roofs, in vain did the best gunners exert superhuman power. As often as the wind blew away the sea of smoke, the cloister appeared untouched, imposing as ever, lofty, with towers piercing calmly the blue of the sky. At the same time things happened which spread superstitious terror among the besiegers. Now balls flew over the whole mountain and struck soldiers on the other side; now a gunner, occupied in aiming a gun, fell on a sudden ; now smoke disposed itself in terrible and strange forms ; now powder in the boxes exploded all at once, as if fired by some invisible hand.

Besides, soldiers were perishing continually who alone, in twos or in threes, went out of the camp. Suspicion fell on the Polish auxiliary squadrons, which, with the exception of Kuklinovski's regiment, refused out and out every co-operation in the siege, and showed daily more menacing looks. Miller threatened Colonel Zbrojek with a court-martial, but he answered in presence of all the officers : " Try it, General."

Officers from the Polish squadrons strolled purposely through the Swedish camp, exhibiting contempt and disregard for the soldiers, and raising quarrels with the officers. Thence it came to duels, in which the Swedes, as less trained in fencing, fell victims more frequently. Miller issued a severe order against duels, and finally forbade the Poles entrance to the camp. From this it came that at last both armies were side by side like enemies, merely awaiting an opportunity for battle.

But the cloister defended itself ever better. It turned out that the guns sent by Pan Myaskovski were in no wise inferior to those which Miller had, and the gunners through constant practice arrived at such accuracy that each shot threw down an enemy. The Swedes attributed this to enchantment. The gunners answered the officers that with that power which defended the cloister it was no business of theirs to do battle.

A certain morning a panic began in the southwestern trench, for the soldiers had seen distinctly a woman in a blue robe shielding the church and the cloister. At sight of this they threw themselves down on their faces. In vain did Miller ride up, in vain did he explain that mist and smoke had disposed themselves in that form, in vain besides was his threat of court-martial and punishment. At the first moment no one would hear him, especially as the general himself was unable to hide his amazement.

Soon after this the opinion was spread through the whole army that no one taking part in the siege would die his own death. Many officers shared this belief, and Miller was not free from fears ; for he brought in Lutheran ministers and enjoined on them to undo the enchantment. They walked through the camp whispering, and singing psalms ; fear,

however, had so spread that more than once they heard
from the mouths of the soldiers: "Beyond your power,
beyond your strength!"

In the midst of discharges of cannon a new envoy from
Miller entered the cloister, and stood before the face of
Kordetski and the council.

This was Pan Sladkovski, chamberlain of Rava, whom
Swedish parties had seized as he was returning from
Prussia. They received him coldly and harshly, though he
had an honest face and his look was as mild as the sky;
but the monks had grown accustomed to see honest faces on
traitors. He was not confused a whit by such a reception;
combing briskly his yellow forelock with his fingers, he
began : —

"Praised be Jesus Christ!"

"For the ages of ages!" answered the Congregation, in a
chorus.

And Kordetski added at once: "Blessed be those who
serve him."

"I serve him," answered Sladkovski, "and that I serve
him more sincerely than I do Miller will be shown soon.
H'm! permit me, worthy and beloved fathers, to cough, for I
must first spit out foulness. Miller then — tfu! sent me,
my good lords, to you to persuade you — tfu! — to surrender. But I accepted the office so as to say to you: Defend yourselves, think not of surrender, for the Swedes are
spinning thin, and the Devil is taking them by the eye."

The monks and the laity were astonished at sight of such
an envoy. Pan Zamoyski exclaimed at once: "As God is
dear to me, this is an honest man!" and springing to him
began to shake his hand; but Sladkovski, gathering his
forelock into one bunch, said, —

"That I am no knave will be shown straightway. I have
become Miller's envoy so as to tell you news so favorable
that I could wish, my good lords, to tell it all in one breath.
Give thanks to God and His Most Holy Mother who chose
you as instruments for changing men's hearts. The country,
taught by your example and by your defence, is beginning
to throw off the yoke of the Swedes. What's the use in
talking? In Great Poland and Mazovia the people are
beating the Swedes, destroying smaller parties, blocking
roads and passages. In some places they have given the
enemy terrible punishment already. The nobles are
mounting their horses, the peasants are gathering in crowds,

and when they seize a Swede they tear straps out of him.
Chips are flying, tow is flying! This is what it has come
to. And whose work is this? — yours."

"An angel, an angel is speaking!" cried monks and
nobles, raising their hands toward heaven.

"Not an angel, but Sladkovski, at your service. This is
nothing! — Listen on. The Khan, remembering the kindness
of the brother of our rightful king, Yan Kazimir, to whom
may God give many years! is marching with aid, and has
already passed the boundary of the Commonwealth. The
Cossacks who were opposed he has cut to pieces, and is
moving on with a horde of a hundred thousand toward
Lvoff, and Hmelnitski *nolens volens* is coming with him."

"For God's sake, for God's sake!" repeated people,
overcome as it were by happiness.

But Pan Sladkovski, sweating and waving his hand, with
still more vigor cried, —

"That is nothing yet! Pan Stefan Charnyetski, with
whom the Swedes violated faith, for they carried captive
his infantry under Wolf, feels free of his word and is
mounting. Yan Kazimir is collecting troops, and may return any day to the country and the hetmans. Listen further,
the hetmans, Pototski and Lantskoronski, and with them
all the troops, are waiting only for the coming of the king
to desert the Swedes and raise sabres against them. Meanwhile they are coming to an understanding with Sapyeha
and the Khan. The Swedes are in terror; there is fire in
the whole country, war in the whole country — whosoever
is living is going to the field!"

What took place in the hearts of the monks and the
nobles is difficult of description. Some wept, some fell on
their knees, other repeated, "It cannot be, it cannot be!"
Hearing this, Sladkovski approached the great crucifix
hanging on the wall and said, —

"I place my hands on these feet of Christ pierced with a
nail, and swear that I declare the pure and clean truth. I
repeat only: Defend yourselves, fail not; trust not the
Swedes; think not that by submission and surrender you
could insure any safety for yourselves. They keep no
promises, no treaties. You who are closed in here know not
what is passing in the whole country, what oppression has
come, what deeds of violence are done, — murdering of
priests, profanation of sanctuaries, contempt of all law. They
promise you everything, they observe nothing. The whole

kingdom is given up as plunder to a dissolute soldiery. Even those who still adhere to the Swedes are unable to escape injustice. Such is the punishment of God on traitors, on those who break faith with the king. Delay! — I, as you see me here, if only I survive, if I succeed in slipping away from Miller, will move straightway to Silesia, to our king. I will fall at his feet and say: Gracious King, save Chenstohova and your most faithful servants! But, most beloved fathers, stand firm, for the salvation of the whole Commonwealth is depending upon you."

Here Sladkovski's voice trembled, tears appeared on his eyelids, but he spoke further. "You will have grievous times yet: siege guns are coming from Cracow, which two hundred infantry are bringing. One is a particularly dreadful cannon. Terrible assaults will follow. But these will be the last efforts. Endure yet these, for salvation is coming already. By these red wounds of God, the king, the hetmans, the army, the whole Commonwealth will come to rescue its Patroness. This is what I tell you: rescue, salvation, glory is right here — not distant."

The worthy noble now burst into tears, and sobbing became universal.

Ah! still better news was due to that wearied handful of defenders, to that handful of faithful servants, and a sure consolation from the country.

The prior rose, approached Sladkovski, and opened wide his arms. Sladkovski rushed into them, and they embraced each other long; others following their example began to fall into one another's arms, embrace, kiss, and congratulate one another as if the Swedes had already retreated. At last the prior said, —

"To the chapel, my brethren, to the chapel!"

He went in advance, and after him the others. All the candles were lighted, for it was growing dark outside; and the curtains were drawn aside from the wonder-working image, from which sweet abundant rays were scattered at once round about. Kordetski knelt on the steps, farther away the monks, the nobles, and common people; women with children were present also. Pale and wearied faces and eyes which had wept were raised toward the image; but from behind the tears was shining on each face a smile of happiness. Silence continued for a time; at last Kordetski began, —

"Under thy protection we take refuge, Holy Mother of God — "

Further words stopped on his lips, weariness, long suffer-ing, hidden alarms, together with the gladsome hope of rescue, rose in him like a mighty wave ; therefore sobbing shook his breast, and that man, who bore on his shoulders the fate of the whole country, bent like a weak child, fell on his face, and with weeping immeasurable had strength only to cry : " O Mary, Mary, Mary ! "

All wept with him, but the image from above cast brightest rays.

It was late at night when the monks and the nobles went each his own way to the walls ; but Kordetski remained all night lying in the chapel in the form of a cross. There were fears in the cloister that weariness might overpower him ; but next morning he appeared on the bastions, went among the soldiers and the garrison, glad and refreshed, and here and there he repeated, —

"Children, the Most Holy Lady will show again that she is mightier than siege guns, and then will come the end of your sorrows and torments."

That morning Yatsek Bjuhanski, an inhabitant of Chensto-hova, disguised as a Swede, approached the walls to confirm the news that great guns were coming from Cracow, but also that the Khan with the horde was approaching. He de-livered a letter from Father Anton Pashkovski, of the mon-astery at Cracow, who, describing the terrible cruelty and robbery of the Swedes, incited and implored the fathers of Yasna Gora to put no trust in the promises of the enemy, but to defend the sacred place patiently against the inso-lence of the godless.

"There is no faith in the Swedes," wrote Father Pash-kovski, " no religion. Nothing divine or human is sa-cred and inviolate for them. It is not their custom to respect anything, though guarded by treaties or public declarations."

That was the day of the Immaculate Conception. Some tens of officers and soldiers of the allied Polish squadrons besought with most urgent requests Miller's permission to go to the fortress for divine service. Perhaps Miller thought that they would become friendly with the garrison, carry news of the siege guns and spread alarm ; perhaps he did not wish by refusing to cast sparks on inflammable ele-ments, which without that made relations between the Poles and the Swedes more and more dangerous : 't is enough that he gave the permission.

With these quarter soldiers went a certain Tartar of the Polish Mohammedan Tartars. He, amid universal astonishment, encouraged the monks not to yield their holy place to vile enemies, considering with certainty that the Swedes would soon go away with shame and defeat. The quarter soldiers repeated the same, confirming completely the news brought by Sladkovski. All this taken together raised the courage of the besieged to such a degree that they had no fear of those gigantic cannons, and the soldiers made sport of them among themselves.

After services firing began on both sides. There was a certain Swedish soldier who had come many times to the wall, and with a trumpet-like voice had blasphemed against the Mother of God. Many a time had the besieged fired at him, but always without result. Kmita aimed at him once, but his bow-string broke; the soldier became more and more insolent, and roused others by his daring. It was said that he had seven devils in his service who guarded and shielded him.

He came this day again to blaspheme ; but the besieged, trusting that on the day of the Immaculate Conception enchantments would have less effect, determined to punish him without fail. They fired a good while in vain ; at last a cannon ball, rebounding from an ice wall, and tripping along the snow like a bird, struck him straight in the breast and tore him in two. The defenders comforted themselves with this and cried out : " Who will blaspheme against Her another time ? " Meanwhile the revilers had rushed down to the trenches, in panic.

The Swedes fired at the walls and the roofs ; but the balls brought no terror to the besieged.

The old beggarwoman, Konstantsia, who dwelt in a cranny of the cliff, used to go, as if in ridicule of the Swedes, along the whole slope, gathering bullets in her apron, and threatening from time to time the soldiers with her staff. They, thinking her a witch, were afraid she would injure them, especially when they saw that bullets did not touch her.

Two whole days passed in vain firing. They hurled on the roof ship ropes very thickly steeped in pitch ; these flew like fiery serpents ; but the guards, trained in a masterly manner, met the danger in time. A night came with such

darkness that, in spite of the fires, tar barrels, and the fire-
works of Father Lyassota, the besieged could see nothing.

Meanwhile some uncommon movement reigned among the
Swedes. The squeak of wheels was heard, men's voices, at
times the neighing of horses, and various other kinds of uproar. The soldiers on the walls guessed the cause easily.

" The guns have come surely," said some.

The officers were deliberating on a sortie which Charnyetski advised; but Zamoyski opposed, insisting, with reason,
that at such important works the enemy must have secured
themselves sufficiently, and must surely hold infantry in
readiness. They resolved merely to fire toward the north
and south, whence the greatest noise came. It was impossible to see the result in the darkness.

Day broke at last, and its first rays exposed the works of
the Swedes. North and south of the fortress were intrenchments, on which some thousands of men were employed.
These intrenchments stood so high that to the besieged the
summits of them seemed on a line with the walls of the
fortress. In the openings at the top were seen great jaws
of guns, and the soldiers standing behind them looked at a
distance like swarms of yellow wasps.

The morning Mass was not over in the church when unusual thunder shook the air; the window-panes rattled; some of
them dropped out of the frames from shaking alone, and were
broken with a sharp shiver on the stone floor; and the whole
church was filled with dust which rose from fallen plaster.

The great siege guns had spoken.

A terrible fire began, such as the besieged had not experienced. At the end of Mass all rushed out on the walls
and roofs. The preceding storms seemed innocent play in
comparison with this terrible letting loose of fire and iron.

The smaller pieces thundered in support of the siege
guns. Great bombs, pieces of cloth steeped in pitch,
torches, and fiery ropes were flying. Balls twenty-six
pounds in weight tore out battlements, struck the walls
of buildings; some settled in them, others made great holes,
tearing off plaster and bricks. The walls surrounding the
cloister began to shake here and there and lose pieces,
and struck incessantly by new balls threatened to fall.
The buildings of the cloister were covered with fire.

The trumpeters on the tower felt it totter under them.
The church quaked from continuous pounding, and candles
fell out of the sockets at some of the altars.

Water was poured in immense quantities on the fires that had begun, on the blazing torches, on the walls, on the fire balls; and formed, together with the smoke and the dust, rolls of steam so thick that light could not be seen through them. Damage was done to the walls and buildings. The cry, "It is burning, it is burning!" was heard oftener amid the thunder of cannon and the whistle of bullets. At the northern bastion the two wheels of a cannon were broken, and one injured cannon was silent. A ball had fallen into a stable, killed three horses, and set fire to the building. Not only balls, but bits of grenades, were falling as thickly as rain on the roofs, the bastions, and the walls.

In a short time the groans of the wounded were heard. By a strange chance three young men fell, all named Yan. This amazed other defenders bearing the same name; but in general the defence was worthy of the storm. Even women, children, and old men came out on the walls. Soldiers stood there with unterrified heart, in smoke and fire, amid a rain of missiles, and answered with determination to the fire of the enemy. Some seized the wheels and rolled the cannon to the most exposed places; others thrust into breaches in the walls stones, beams, dung, and earth.

Women with dishevelled hair and inflamed faces gave an example of daring, and some were seen running with buckets of water after bombs which were still springing and ready to burst right there, that moment. Ardor rose every instant, as if that smell of powder, smoke, and steam, that thunder, those streams of fire and iron, had the property of rousing it. All acted without command, for words died amid the awful noise. Only the supplications which were sung in the chapel rose above the voices of cannon.

About noon firing ceased. All drew breath; but before the gate a drum was sounded, and the drummer sent by Miller, approaching the gate, inquired if the fathers had had enough, and if they wished to surrender at once. Kordetski answered that they would deliberate over the question till morning. The answer had barely reached Miller when the attack began anew, and the artillery fire was redoubled.

From time to time deep ranks of infantry pushed forward under fire toward the mountain, as if wishing to try an assault; but decimated by cannon and muskets, they returned each time quickly and in disorder under their own batteries. As a wave of the sea covers the shore and when it retreats

leaves on the sand weeds, mussels, and various fragments
broken in the deep, so each one of those Swedish waves
when it sank back left behind bodies thrown here and
there on the slope.

Miller did not give orders to fire at the bastions, but at
the wall between them, where resistance was least. Indeed,
here and there considerable rents were made, but not large
enough for the infantry to rush through.

Suddenly a certain event checked the storm.

It was well toward evening when a Swedish gunner
about to apply a lighted match to one of the largest guns
was struck in the very breast by a ball from the cloister.
The ball came not with the first force, but after a third
bound from the ice piled up at the intrenchment; it merely
hurled the gunner a number of yards. He fell on an open
box partly filled with powder. A terrible explosion was
heard that instant, and masses of smoke covered the trench.
When the smoke fell away it appeared that five gunners
had lost their lives; the wheels of the cannon were injured,
and terror seized the soldiers. It was necessary to cease fire
for the time from that intrenchment, since a heavy fog had
filled the darkness; they also stopped firing in other places.

The next day was Sunday. Lutheran ministers held
services in the trenches, and the guns were silent. Miller
again inquired if the fathers had had enough. They answered that they could endure more.

Meanwhile the damage in the cloister was examined and
found to be considerable. People were killed and the wall
was shaken here and there. The most formidable gun was
a gigantic culverin standing on the north. It had broken
the wall to such a degree, torn out so many stones and
bricks, that the besieged could foresee that should the fire
continue two days longer a considerable part of the wall
would give away.

A breach such as the culverin would make could not be
filled with beams or earth. The prior foresaw with an eye
full of sorrow the ruin which he could not prevent.

Monday the attack was begun anew, and the gigantic gun
widened the breach. Various mishaps met the Swedes,
however. About dusk that day a Swedish gunner killed
on the spot Miller's sister's son, whom the general loved as
though he had been his own, and intended to leave him all
that he had, — beginning with his name and military
reputation and ending with his fortune. But the heart of

the old warrior blazed up with hatred all the more from this loss.

The wall at the northern bastion was so broken that preparations were made in the night for a hand-to-hand assault. That the infantry might approach the fortress with less danger, Miller commanded to throw up in the darkness a whole series of small redoubts, reaching the very slope. But the night was clear, and white light from the snow betrayed the movements of the enemy. The cannons of Yasna Gora scattered the men occupied in making those parapets formed of fascines, fences, baskets, and timbers.

At daybreak Charnyetski saw a siege machine which they had already rolled toward the walls. But the besieged broke it with cannon fire without difficulty; so many men were killed on that occasion that the day might have been called a day of victory for the besieged, had it not been for that great gun which shook the wall incessantly with irrestrainable power.

A thaw came on the following days, and such dense mists settled down that the fathers attributed them to the action of evil spirits. It was impossible to see either the machines of war, the erection of parapets, or the work of the siege. The Swedes came near the very walls of the cloister. In the evening Charnyetski, when the prior was making his usual round of the walls, took him by the side and said in a low voice, —

"Bad, revered father! Our wall will not hold out beyond a day."

"Perhaps these fogs will prevent them from firing," answered Kordetski; "and we meanwhile will repair the rents somehow."

"The fogs will not prevent the Swedes, for that gun once aimed may continue even in darkness the work of destruction; but here the ruins are falling and falling."

"In God and in the Most Holy Lady is our hope."

"True! But if we make a sortie? Even were we to lose men, if they could only spike that dragon of hell."

Just then some form looked dark in the fog, and Babinich appeared near the speakers.

"I saw that some one was speaking; but faces cannot be distinguished three yards away," said he. "Good evening, revered father! But of what is the conversation?"

"We are talking of that gun. Pan Charnyetski advises a

sortie. These fogs are spread by Satan; I have commanded
an exorcism."

"Dear father," said Pan Andrei, "since that gun has
begun to shake the wall, I am thinking of it, and something
keeps coming to my head. A sortie is of no use. But let
us go to some room; there I will tell you my plans."

"Well," said the prior, "come to my cell."

Soon after they were sitting at a pine table in Kordetski's
modest cell. Charnyetski and the priest were looking
carefully into the youthful face of Babinich, who said, —

"A sortie is of no use in this case. They will see it and
repulse it. Here one man must do the work."

"How is that?" asked Charnyetski.

"One man must go and burst that cannon with powder;
and he can do it during such fogs. It is best that he go in
disguise. There are jackets here like those worn by the
enemy. As it will not be possible to do otherwise, he will
slip in among the Swedes; but if at this side of the trench
from which the gun is projecting there are no soldiers, that
will be better still."

"For God's sake! what will the man do?"

"It is only necessary to put a box of powder into the
mouth of the gun, with a hanging fuse and a thread to be
ignited. When the powder explodes, the gun — devil I
wanted to say — will burst."

"Oh, my son! what do you say? Is it little powder
that they thrust into it every day, and it does not
burst?"

Kmita laughed, and kissed the priest on the sleeve of his
habit. "Beloved father, there is a great heart in you,
heroic and holy —"

"Give peace now!" answered the prior.

"And holy," repeated Kmita; "but you do not understand cannon. It is one thing when powder bursts in the
butt of the cannon, for then it casts forth the ball and the
force flies out forward, but another if you stop the mouth
of a gun with powder and ignite it, — no cannon can stand
such a trial. Ask Pan Charnyetski. The same thing will
take place if you fill the mouth of a cannon with snow
and fire it; the piece will burst. Such is the villanous
power of powder. What will it be when a whole box of
it explodes at the mouth? Ask Pan Charnyetski."

"That is true. These are no secrets for soldiers,"
answered Charnyetski.

"You see if this gun is burst," continued Kmita, "all the rest are a joke."

"This seems impossible to me," said Kordetski; "for, first, who will undertake to do it?"

"A certain poor fellow," said Kmita; "but he is resolute, his name is Babinich."

"You!" cried the priest and Charnyetski together.

"Ai, father, benefactor! I was with you at confession, and acknowledged all my deeds in sincerity; among them were deeds not worse than the one I am now planning; how can you doubt that I will undertake it? Do you not know me?"

"He is a hero, a knight above knights," cried Charnyetski. And seizing Kmita by the neck, he continued: "Let me kiss you for the wish alone; give me your mouth."

"Show me another remedy, and I will not go," said Kmita; "but it seems to me that I shall manage this matter somehow. Remember that I speak German as if I had been dealing in staves, wainscots, and wall plank in Dantzig. That means much, for if I am disguised they will not easily discover that I am not of their camp. But I think that no one is standing before the mouth of the cannon; for it is not safe there, and I think that I shall do the work before they can see me."

"Pan Charnyetski, what do you think of this?" asked the prior, quickly.

"Out of one hundred men one might return from such an undertaking; but *audaces fortuna juvat* [fortune favors the bold]."

"I have been in hotter places than this," said Kmita: "nothing will happen to me, for such is my fortune. Ai, beloved father, and what a difference! Ere now to exhibit myself, and for vainglory, I crawled into danger; but this undertaking is for the Most Holy Lady. Even should I have to lay down my head, which I do not foresee, say yourself could a more praiseworthy dea'h be wished to any man than down there in this cause?"

The priest was long silent, and then said at last, —

"I should try to restrain you with persuasion, with prayers and imploring, if you wished to go for mere glory; but you are right: this is a question affecting the honor of the Most Holy Lady, this sacred place, the whole country! And you, my son, whether you return safely or win the palm of glory, you will gain the supreme happiness, —

salvation. Against my heart then I say, Go ; I do not detain you. Our prayers, the protection of God, will go with you."

"In such company I shall go boldly and perish with joy."

"But return, soldier of God, return safely ; for you are loved with sincerity here. May Saint Raphael attend you and bring you back, cherished son, my dear child ! "

"Then I will begin preparations at once," said Pan Andrei, joyfully pressing the priest. " I will dress in Swedish fashion with a jacket and wide-legged boots. I will fill in the powder, and do you, father, stop the exorcisms for this night ; fog is needful to the Swedes, but also to me."

" And do you not wish to confess before starting ? "

" Of course, without that I should not go ; for the devil would have approach to me."

" Then begin with confession."

Charnyetski went out of the cell, and Kmita knelt down near the priest and purged himself of his sins. Then, gladsome as a bird, he began to make preparations.

An hour or two later, in the deep night, he knocked again at the prior's cell, where Pan Charnyetski also was waiting.

The two scarcely knew Pan Andrei, so good a Swede had he made himself. He had twirled his mustaches to his eyes and brushed them out at the ends ; he had put his hat on one side of his head, and looked precisely like some cavalry officer of noted family.

" As God lives, one would draw a sabre at sight of him," said Charnyetski.

" Put the light at a distance," said Kmita ; " I will show you something."

When Father Kordetski had put the light aside quickly, Pan Andrei placed on a table a roll, a foot and a half long and as thick as the arm of a sturdy man, sewn up in pitched linen and filled firmly with powder. From one end of it was hanging a long string made of tow steeped in sulphur.

" Well," said he, " when I put this flea-bane in the mouth of the cannon and ignite the string, then its belly will burst."

" Lucifer would burst ! " cried Pan Charnyetski. But he remembered that it was better not to mention the name of the foul one, and he slapped his own mouth.

" But how will you set fire to the string ? " asked Kordetski.

"In that lies the whole danger, for I must strike fire. I have good flint, dry tinder, and steel of the best; but there will be a noise, and they may notice something. The string I hope will not quench, for it will hang at the beard of the gun, and it will be hard to see it, especially as it will hide itself quickly in burning; but they may pursue me, and I cannot flee straight toward the cloister."

"Why not?" asked the priest.

"For the explosion would kill me. The moment I see the spark on the string I must jump aside with all the strength in my legs, and when I have run about fifty yards, must fall to the ground under the intrenchment. After the explosion I shall rush toward the cloister."

"My God, my God, how many dangers!" said the prior, raising his eyes to heaven.

"Beloved father, so sure am I of returning that even emotion does not touch me, which on an occasion like this ought to seize me. This is nothing! Farewell, and pray the Lord God to give me luck. Only conduct me to the gate."

"How is that? Do you want to go now?" asked Charnyetski.

"Am I to wait till daylight, or till the fog rises? Is not my head dear to me?"

But Pan Andrei did not go that night, for just as they came to the gate, darkness, as if out of spite, began to grow light. Some movement too was heard around the great siege gun.

Next morning the besieged were convinced that the gun was transferred to another place.

The Swedes had received apparently some report of a great weakness in the wall a little beyond the bend near the southern bastion, and they determined to direct missiles to that spot. Maybe too the prior was not a stranger to the affair, for the day before they had seen old Kostuha (Konstantsia) going out of the cloister. She was employed chiefly when there was need of giving false reports to the Swedes. Be that as it may, it was a mistake on their part; for the besieged could now repair in the old place the wall so greatly shaken, and to make a new breach a number of days would be needed.

The nights were clear in succession, the days full of uproar. The Swedes fired with terrible energy. The spirit of doubt began again to fly over the fortress. Among the besieged were nobles who wished to surrender; some of the monks too had lost heart. The opposition gained strength

and importance. The prior made head against it with unrestrained energy, but his health began to give way. Meanwhile came reinforcements to the Swedes and supplies from
Cracow, especially terrible explosive missiles in the form
of iron cylinders filled with powder and lead. These caused
more terror than damage to the besieged.

Kmita, from the time that he had conceived the plan
of bursting the siege gun, secreted himself in the fortress.
He looked every day at the roll, with heart-sickness. On
reflection he made it still larger, so that it was almost an
ell long and as thick as a boot-leg. In the evening he cast
greedy looks toward the gun, then examined the sky like an
astrologer. But the bright moon, shining on the snow continually, baffled his plan.

All at once a thaw came ; clouds covered the horizon, and
the night was dark, — so dark that even strain your eyes
you could see nothing. Pan Andrei fell into such humor as
if some one had given him the steed of the Sultan ; and midnight had barely sounded when he stood before Charnyetski
in his cavalry dress, the roll under his arm.

"I am going!" said he.

"Wait, I will speak to the prior."

"That is well. Kiss me, Pan Pyotr, and go for the prior."

Charnyetski kissed him with feeling, and turned away.
He had hardly gone thirty steps when Kordetski stood
before him in white. He had guessed that Kmita was
going, and had come there to bless him.

"Babinich is ready ; he is only waiting for your reverence."

"I hurry, I hurry!" answered the priest. "O Mother of
God, save him and aid him !"

After a while both were standing at the opening where
Charnyetski left Kmita, but there was no trace of him.

"He has gone!" said the prior, in amazement.

"He has gone!" repeated Charnyetski.

"But, the traitor!" said the prior, with emotion, "I intended to put this little scapular on his neck."

Both ceased to speak ; there was silence around, and as
the darkness was dense there was firing from neither side.
On a sudden Charnyetski whispered eagerly, —

"As God is dear to me, he is not even trying to go in
silence! Do you hear steps crushing the snow ? "

"O Most Holy Lady, guard thy servant!" said the prior.

Both listened carefully for a time, till the brisk steps and
the noise on the snow had ceased.

"Do you know, your reverence, at moments I think that he will succeed, and I fear nothing for him. The strange man went as if he were going to an inn to drink a glass of liquor. What courage he has in him! Either he will lay down his head untimely, or he will be hetman. H'm! if I did not know him as a servant of Mary, I should think that he has — God give him success, God grant it to him! for such another cavalier there is not in the Commonwealth."

"It is so dark, so dark!" said Kordetski; "but they are on their guard since the night of your sortie. He might come upon a whole rank before he could see it."

"I do not think so. The infantry are watching, that I know, and watch carefully; but they are in the intrenchment, not before the muzzles of their own cannon. If they do not hear the steps, he can easily push under the intrenchment, and then the height of it alone will cover him — Uf!"

Here Charnyetski puffed and ceased speaking; for his heart began to beat like a hammer from expectation and alarm, and breath failed him.

Kordetski made the sign of the cross in the darkness.

A third person stood near the two. This was Zamoyski.

"What is the matter?" asked he.

"Babinich has gone to blow up the siege gun."

"How is that? What is that?"

"He took a roll of powder, cord, and flint, and went."

Zamoyski pressed his head between his hands.

"Jesus, Mary! Jesus, Mary! All alone?"

"All alone."

"Who let him go? That's an impossible deed!"

"I. For the might of God all things are possible, even his safe return," said Kordetski.

Zamoyski was silent. Charnyetski began to pant from emotion.

"Let us pray," said the prior.

The three knelt down and began to pray. But anxiety raised the hair on the heads of both knights. A quarter of an hour passed, half an hour, an hour as long as a lifetime.

"There will be nothing now!" said Charnyetski, sighing deeply.

All at once in the distance a gigantic column of flame burst forth, and a roar as if all the thunders of heaven had been hurled to the earth; it shook the walls, the church, and the cloister.

"He has burst it, he has burst it!" shouted Charnyetski.

New explosions interrupted further speech of his.

Kordetski threw himself on his knees, and raising his hands, cried to heaven, "O Most Holy Mother, Guardian, Patroness, bring him back safely!"

A noise was made on the walls. The garrison, not knowing what had happened, seized their arms. The monks rushed from their cells. No one was sleeping. Even women sprang forth. Questions and answers crossed one another like lightnings.

"What has happened?"

"An assault!"

"The Swedish gun has burst!" cried one of the cannoneers.

"A miracle, a miracle!"

"The largest gun is burst!"

"That great one!"

"Where is the prior?"

"On the wall. He is praying; he did this."

"Babinich burst the gun!" cried Charnyetski.

"Babinich, Babinich! Praise to the Most Holy Lady! They will harm us no longer."

At the same time sounds of confusion rose from the Swedish camp. In all the trenches fires began to shine. An increasing uproar was heard. By the light of the fires masses of soldiers were seen moving in various directions without order, trumpets sounded, drums rolled continually; to the walls came shouts in which alarm and amazement were heard.

Kordetski continued kneeling on the wall.

At last the night began to grow pale, but Babinich came not to the fortress.

CHAPTER IV.

WHAT had happened to Pan Andrei, and in what way had
he been able to carry out his plan ?

After leaving the fortress he advanced some time with a
sure and wary step. At the very end of the slope he halted
and listened. It was silent around, — so silent in fact that
his steps were heard clearly on the snow. In proportion as
he receded from the walls, he stepped more carefully. He
halted again, and again listened. He was somewhat afraid
of slipping and falling, and thus dampening his precious
roll; he drew out his rapier therefore and leaned on it. That
helped him greatly. Thus feeling his way, after the course
of half an hour he heard a slight sound directly in front.

" Ah ! they are watching. The sortie has taught them
wariness," thought he.

And he went farther now very slowly. He was glad that
he had not gone astray, for the darkness was such that he
could not see the end of the rapier.

" Those trenches are considerably farther : I am advancing well then ! " whispered he to himself.

He hoped also not to find men before the intrenchment;
for, properly speaking, they had nothing to do there, especially at night. It might be that at something like a hundred or fewer yards apart single sentries were stationed;
but he hoped to pass them in such darkness. It was joyous in his soul.

Kmita was not only daring but audacious. The thought
of bursting the gigantic gun delighted him to the bottom
of his soul, — not only as heroism, not only as an immortal
service to the besieged, but as a terrible damage to the
Swedes. He imagined how Miller would be astounded,
how he would gnash his teeth, how he would gaze in helplessness on those walls ; and at moments pure laughter
seized him.

And as he had himself said, he felt no emotion, no fear,
no unquiet. It did not even enter his head to what an
awful danger he was exposing himself. He went on as
a school-boy goes to an orchard to make havoc among

apples. He recalled other times wnen he harried Hovanski, stole up at night to a camp of thirty thousand with two hundred such fighters as himself.

His comrades stood before his mind: Kokosinski, the gigantic Kulvyets-Hippocentaurus, the spotted Ranitski, of senatorial stock, and others; then for a moment he sighed after them. "If they were here now," thought he, "we might blow up six guns." Then the feeling of loneliness oppressed him somewhat, but only for a short while; soon memory brought before his eyes Olenka. Love spoke in him with immeasurable power. He was moved to tenderness. If she could see him, the heart would rejoice in her this time. Perhaps she thinks yet that he is serving the Swedes. He is serving them nicely! And soon he will oblige them! What will happen when she learns of all these perils? What will she think? She will think surely, "He is a whirlwind, but when it comes to a deed which no other can do, he will do it; where another dares not go, he will go. Such a man is that Kmita!"

"Another such deed I shall never accomplish," said Pan Andrei; and boastfulness seized him completely. Still, in spite of these thoughts he did not forget where he was, whither he was going, what he intended to do; and he began to advance like a wolf on a night pasture. He looked behind once and a second time. No church, no cloister! All was covered with thick, impenetrable gloom. He noted, however, by the time, that he must have advanced far already, and that the trench might be right there.

"I am curious to know if there are sentries," thought he.

But he had not advanced two steps after giving himself this question, when, in front of him, was heard the tramp of measured steps and a number of voices inquired at various distances, —

"Who goes?"

Pan Andrei stood as if fixed to the earth. He felt hot.

"Ours," answered a number of voices.

"The watchword!"

"Upsala."

"The counter-sign!"

"The crown."

Kmita saw at this moment that there was a change of sentries. "I'll give you Upsala and a crown!" And he rejoiced. This was really for him a very favorable circumstance, for he might pass the line of guards at the moment of changing sentries, when the tramp of the soldiers drowned his own steps.

In fact, he did so without the least difficulty, and went after the returning soldiers rather boldly up to the trench itself. There they made a turn to go around it; but he pushed quickly into the ditch and hid in it.

Meanwhile objects had become somewhat more visible; Pan Andrei thanked Heaven, for in the previous darkness he could not by feeling have found the gun sought for. Now, by throwing back his head and straining his vision, he saw above him a black line, indicating the edge of the trench, and also the black outlines of the baskets between which stood the guns.

He could indeed see their jaws thrust out a little above the trench. Advancing slowly in the ditch, he discovered the great gun at last. He halted and began to listen. From the intrenchment a noise came, — a murmur; evidently the infantry were near the guns, in readiness. But the height of the intrenchment concealed Kmita; they might hear him, they could not see him. Now he had only to rise from below to the mouth of the gun, which was high above his head.

Fortunately the sides of the ditch were not too steep; and besides the embankment freshly made, or moist with water, had not frozen, since for some time there had been a thaw.

Taking note of all this, Kmita began to sink holes quietly in the slope of the intrenchment and to climb slowly to the gun. After fifteen minutes' work he was able to seize the opening of the culverin. Soon he was hanging in the air, but his uncommon strength permitted him to hold himself thus till he pushed the roll into the jaws of the cannon.

"Here's dog sausage for thee!" muttered he; "only don't choke with it!"

Then he slipped down and began to look for the string, which, fastened to the inner side of the roll, was hanging to the ditch. After a while he felt it with his hand. But then came the greatest difficulty, for he had to strike fire and ignite the string.

Kmita waited for a moment, thinking that the noise would increase somewhat among the soldiers in the breastworks. At last he began to strike the flint lightly with the steel. But that moment above his head was heard in German the question, —

"Who is there in the ditch?"

"It is I, Hans!" answered Kmita, without hesitation; "the devils have taken my ramrod into the ditch, and I am striking fire to find it."

"All right, all right," said the gunner. "It is your luck there is no firing, for the wind would have taken your head off."

"Ah!" thought Kmita, "the gun besides my charge has still its own, — so much the better."

At that moment the sulphur-string caught, and delicate little sparks began to run upward along its dry exterior.

It was time to disappear. Kmita hurried along the ditch with all the strength in his legs, not losing an instant, not thinking overmuch of the noise he was making. But when he had run twenty yards, curiosity overcame in him the feeling of his terrible danger.

"The string has gone out, there is moisture in the air!" thought he; and he stopped. Casting a look behind, he saw a little spark yet, but much higher than he had left it.

"Eh, am I not too near?" thought he; and fear hurried him forward.

He pushed on at full speed; all at once he struck a stone and fell. At that moment a terrible roar rent the air; the earth trembled, pieces of wood, iron, stones, lumps of ice and earth, whistled about his ears, and here his sensations ended.

After that were heard new explosions in turn. These were powder-boxes standing near the cannon which exploded from the shock.

But Kmita did not hear these; he lay as if dead in the ditch. He did not hear also how, after a time of deep silence, the groans of men were heard, cries and shouts for help; how nearly half the army, Swedish and allied, assembled.

The confusion and uproar lasted long, till from the chaos of testimony the Swedish general reached the fact that the siege-gun had been blown up of purpose by some one. Search was ordered immediately. In the morning the searching soldiers found Kmita lying in the ditch.

It appeared that he was merely stunned from the explosion. He had lost, to begin with, control of his hands and feet. His powerlessness lasted the whole ensuing day. They nursed him with the utmost care. In the evening he had recovered his power almost completely.

He was brought then by command before Miller, who occupied the middle place at the table in his quarters; around him sat the Prince of Hesse, Count Veyhard, Sadovski, all the noted officers of the Swedes, of the Poles, Zbrojek, Kalinski, and Kuklinovski. The last at sight of Kmita became blue, his eyes burned like two coals, and his mustaches began to quiver. Without awaiting the question of the general, he said, —

"I know this bird. He is from the Chenstohova garrison. His name is Babinich."

Kmita was silent; pallor and weariness were evident on his face, but his glance was bold and his countenance calm.

"Did you blow up the siege-gun?" asked Miller.

"I did."

"How did you do it?"

Kmita stated all briefly, concealed nothing. The officers looked at one another in amazement.

"A hero!" whispered the Prince of Hesse to Sadovski.

But Sadovski inclined to Count Veyhard. "Count Veyhard," asked he, "how are we to take a fortress with such defenders? What do you think, will they surrender?"

"There are more of us in the fortress ready for such deeds," said Kmita. "You know not the day nor the hour."

"I too have more than one halter in the camp," said Miller.

"We know that. But you will not take Yasna Gora while there is one man alive there."

A moment of silence followed. Then Miller inquired, —

"Is your name Babinich?"

Pan Andrei thought that after what he had done, and in presence of death, the time had come in which he had no need to conceal his name. Let people forget the faults and transgressions bound up with it; let glory and devotion shine over them.

"My name is not Babinich," said he, with a certain pride, "my name is Andrei Kmita; I was colonel of my own personal squadron in the Lithuanian contingent."

Hardly had Kuklinovski heard this when he sprang up as if possessed, stuck out his eyes, opened his mouth, and began to strike his sides with his hands. At last he cried, —

"General, I beg for a word without delay, without delay."

A murmur rose at the same time among the Polish officers, which the Swedes heard with wonder, since for them the name Kmita meant nothing. They noted at once that this must be no common soldier, for Zbrojek rose, and approaching the prisoner said, —

"Worthy colonel, in the straits in which you are I cannot help you; but give me your hand, I pray."

Kmita raised his head and began to snort.

"I will not give a hand to traitors who serve against their country!"

Zbrojek's face flushed. Kalinski, who stood right behind him, withdrew. The Swedish officers surrounded them at once, asking what man this Kmita was whose name had made such an impression. During this time Kuklinovski had squeezed Miller up to the window, and said, —

"For your worthiness the name Kmita is nothing; but he is the first soldier, the first colonel, in the whole Commonwealth. All know of him, all know that name; once he served Radzivill and the Swedes; now it is clear that he has gone over to Yan Kazimir. There is not his equal among soldiers, save me. He was the only man who could go alone and blow up that gun. From this one deed you may know him. He fought Hovanski, so that a reward was put on his head. He with two or three hundred men kept up the whole war after the defeat at Shklov, until others were found who, imitating him, began to tear at the enemy. He is the most dangerous man in all the country — "

"Why do you sing his praises to me?" inquired Miller. "That he is dangerous I know to my own irreparable loss."

"What does your worthiness think of doing with him?"

"I should give orders to hang him; but being a soldier myself, I know how to value daring and bravery. Besides, he is a noble of high birth, — I will order him shot, and that to-day."

"Your worthiness, it is not for me to instruct the most celebrated soldier and statesman of modern times; but I permit myself to say that that man is too famous. If you shoot him, Zbrojek's squadron and Kalinski's will withdraw at the latest this very day, and go over to Yan Kazimir."

"If that is true, I'll have them cut to pieces before they go!" cried Miller.

"Your worthiness, a terrible responsibility! for if that becomes known, — and the cutting down of two squadrons is hard to hide, — the whole Polish army will leave Karl Gustav; at present their loyalty is tottering, as you know. The hetmans are not reliable. Pan Konyetspolski with six

thousand of the best cavalry is at the side of our king. That
force is no trifle. God defend us if these too should turn
against us, against the person of his Royal Grace ! Besides,
this fortress defends itself ; and to cut down the squadrons
of Zbrojek and Kalinski is no easy matter, for Wolf is here
too with his infantry. They might come to an agreement
with the garrison of the fortress."

" A hundred horned devils ! " cried Miller ; " what do you
want, Kuklinovski ? do you want me to give Kmita his life ?
That cannot be."

" I want," answered Kuklinovski, " you to give him to me."

" What will you do with him ? "

" Ah, I — will tear him alive from his skin."

" You did not know even his real name, you do not know
him. What have you against him ? "

" I made his acquaintance first in the fortress, where I
have been twice as an envoy to the monks."

" Have you reasons for vengeance ? "

" Your worthiness, I wished privately to bring him to
our camp. He, taking advantage of the fact that I laid
aside my office of envoy, insulted me, Kuklinovski, as no
man in life has insulted me."

" What did he do to you ? "

Kuklinovski trembled and gnashed his teeth. " Better
not speak of it. Only give him to me. He is doomed to
death anyhow, and I would like before his end to have a
little amusement with him, — all the more because he is
the Kmita whom formerly I venerated, and who repaid me
in such fashion. Give him to me ; it will be better for you.
If I rub him out, Zbrojek and Kalinski and with them all
the Polish knighthood will fall not upon you, but upon me,
and I 'll help myself. There will not be anger, wry faces,
and mutiny. It will be my private matter about Kmita's
skin, of which I shall have a drum made."

Miller fell to thinking ; a sudden suspicion flashed over
his face.

" Kuklinovski," said he, " maybe you wish to save him ? "

Kuklinovski smiled quietly, but that smile was so terrible
and sincere that Miller ceased to doubt.

" Perhaps you give sound advice," said he.

" For all my services I beg this reward only."

" Take him, then."

Now both returned to the room where the rest of the
officers were assembled. Miller turned to them and said. —

"In view of the services of Pan Kuklinovski I place at his absolute disposal this prisoner."

A moment of silence followed; then Pan Zbrojek put his hands on his sides, and asked with a certain accent of contempt, —

"And what does Pan Kuklinovski think to do with the prisoner?"

Kuklinovski bent, straightened himself quickly, his lips opened with an ill-omened smile, and his eyes began to quiver.

"Whoso is not pleased with what I do to the prisoner, knows where to find me." And he shook his sabre.

"Your promise, Pan Kuklinovski," said Zbrojek.

"Promise, promise!"

When he had said this he approached Kmita. "Follow me, little worm; come after me, famous soldier. Thou 'rt a trifle weak; thou needst swathing, — I 'll swathe thee."

"Ruffian!" said Kmita.

"Very good, very good, daring soul! Meanwhile step along."

The officers remained in the room; Kuklinovski mounted his horse before the quarters. Having with him three soldiers, he commanded one of them to lead Kmita by a lariat; and all went together toward Lgota, where Kuklinovski's regiment was quartered.

On the way Kmita prayed ardently. He saw that death was approaching, and he committed himself with his whole soul to God. He was so sunk in prayer and in his own doom that he did not hear what Kuklinovski said to him; he did not know even how long the road was.

They stopped at last before an empty, half-ruined barn, standing in the open field, at some distance from the quarters of Kuklinovski's regiment. The colonel ordered them to lead Kmita in, and turning himself to one of the soldiers, said, —

"Hurry for me to the camp, bring ropes and a tar bucket!"

The soldier galloped with all the breath in his horse, and in quarter of an hour returned at the same pace, with a comrade. They had brought the requisite articles.

"Strip this spark naked!" ordered Kuklinovski; "tie his hands and feet behind him with a rope, and then fasten him to a beam."

"Ruffian!" said Kmita.

"Good, good! we can talk yet, we have time!"

Meanwhile one of the soldiers climbed up on the beam, and the others fell to dragging the clothes from Kmita. When he was naked the three executioners placed Pan Andrei with his face to the ground, bound his hands and feet with a long rope, then passing it still around his waist they threw the other end to the soldier sitting on the beam.

"Now raise him, and let the man on the beam pull the rope and tie it!" said Kuklinovski.

In a moment the order was obeyed.

"Let him go!"

The rope squeaked. Pan Andrei was hanging parallel with the earth, a few ells above the threshing-floor. Then Kuklinovski dipped tow in the burning tar-bucket, walked up to him, and said, —

"Well, Pan Kmita, did not I say that there are two colonels in the Commonwealth? — only two, I and thou! And thou didst not wish to join company with Kuklinovski, and kicked him! Well, little worm, thou art right! Not for thee is the company of Kuklinovski, for Kuklinovski is better. Hei! a famous colonel is Pan Kmita, and Kuklinovski has him in his hand, and Kuklinovski is roasting his sides!"

"Ruffian!" repeated Kmita, for the third time.

"This is how he will roast his sides!" finished Kuklinovski, and he touched Kmita's side with the burning tow; then he said, —

"Not too much at first; we have time."

Just then the tramp of horses was heard near the barn-door.

"Whom are the devils bringing?" asked Kuklinovski.

The door squeaked and a soldier entered. "General Miller wishes to see your grace at once!"

"Ah! that is thou, old man?" asked Kuklinovski. "What business? What devil?"

"The general asks your grace to come to him straightway."

"Who came from the general?"

"There was a Swedish officer; he has ridden off already. He had almost driven the breath out of his horse."

"I'll go," said Kuklinovski. Then he turned to Kmita: "It was hot for thee; cool off now, little worm. I'll come again soon, we'll have another talk."

"What shall be done with the prisoner?" asked one of the soldiers.

"Leave him as he is. I shall return directly. Let one go with me."

The colonel went out, and with him that soldier who had sat on the beam at first. There remained only three, but soon three new ones entered the barn.

"You may go to sleep," said he who had reported Miller's order to Kuklinovski, "the colonel has left the guard to us."

"We prefer to remain," replied one of the first three soldiers, "to see the wonder; for such a — "

Suddenly he stopped. A certain unearthly sound was wrested from his throat like the call of a strangled cock. He threw out his arms and fell as if struck by lightning.

At the same moment the cry of "Pound" was heard through the barn, and two of the newly arrived rushed like leopards on the two remaining soldiers. A terrible, short struggle surged up, lighted by the gleams of the burning tar-bucket. After a moment two bodies fell in the straw, for a moment longer were heard the gasps of the dying, then that voice rose which at first seemed familiar to Kmita.

"Your grace, it is I, Kyemlich, and my sons. We have been waiting since morning for a chance, we have been watching since morning." Then he turned to his sons: "Now out, rogues, free the colonel in a breath, — quickly!"

And before Kmita was able to understand what was taking place there appeared near him the two bushy forelocks of Kosma and Damian, like two gigantic distaffs. The ropes were soon cut, and Kmita stood on his feet. He tottered at first; his stiffened lips were barely able to say, —

"That is you ? — I am thankful."

"It is I!" answered the terrible old man. "O Mother of God ! Oh — let his grace dress quickly. You rogues — " And he began to give Kmita his clothes.

"The horses are standing at the door," said he. "From here the way is open. There are guards; maybe they would let no one in, but as to letting out, they will let out. We know the password. How does your grace feel ? "

"He burned my side, but only a little. My feet are weak — "

"Drink some gorailka."

Kmita seized with eagerness the flask the old man gave him, and emptying half of it said, —

"I was stiff from the cold. I shall be better at once."

"Your grace will grow warm on the saddle. The horses are waiting."

"In a moment I shall be better," repeated Kmita. "My side is smarting a little — that's nothing! — I am quite well." And he sat on the edge of a grain-bin.

After a while he recovered his strength really, and looked with perfect presence of mind on the ill-omened faces of the three Kyemliches, lighted by the yellowish flame of the burning pitch. The old man stood before him.

"Your grace, there is need of haste. The horses are waiting."

But in Pan Andrei the Kmita of old times was roused altogether.

"Oh, impossible!" cried he, suddenly; "now I am waiting for that traitor."

The Kyemliches looked amazed, but uttered not a word, — so accustomed were they from former times to listen blindly to this leader.

The veins came out on his forehead; his eyes were burning in the dark, like two stars, such was the hate and the desire of vengeance that gleamed in them. That which he did then was madness, he might pay for it with his life; but his life was made up of a series of such madnesses. His side pained him fiercely, so that every moment he seized it unwittingly with his hand; but he was thinking only of Kuklinovski, and he was ready to wait for him even till morning.

"Listen!" said he; "did Miller really call him?"

"No," answered the old man. "I invented that to manage the others here more easily. It would have been hard for us three against five, for some one might have raised a cry."

"That was well. He will return alone or in company. If there are any people with him, then strike at once on them. Leave him to me. Then to horse! Has any one pistols?"

"I have," said Kosma.

"Give them here! Are they loaded, is there powder in the pan?"

"Yes."

"Very well. If he comes back alone, when he enters spring on him and shut his mouth. You can stuff his own cap into it."

"According to command," said the old man. "Your grace permits us now to search these? We are poor men."

He pointed to the corpses lying on the straw.

"No! Be on the watch. What you find on Kuklinovski will be yours."

"If he returns alone," said the old man, "I fear nothing. I shall stand behind the door; and even if some one from the quarters should come, I shall say that the colonel gave orders not to admit."

"That will do. Watch!"

The tramp of a horse was heard behind the barn. Kmita sprang up and stood in the shadow at the wall. Kosma and Damian took their places near the door, like two cats waiting for a mouse.

"He is alone," said the old man.

"Alone," repeated Kosma and Damian.

The tramp approached, was right there and halted suddenly.

"Come out here, some one, — hold the horse!"

The old man jumped out quickly. A moment of silence followed, then to those waiting in the barn came the following conversation, —

"Is that you, Kyemlich? What the thunder! art mad, or an idiot? It is night, Miller is asleep. The guard will not give admission; they say that no officer went away. How is that?"

"The officer is waiting here in the barn for your grace. He came right away after you rode off; he says that he missed your grace."

"What does all this mean? But the prisoner?"

"Is hanging."

The door squeaked, and Kuklinovski pushed into the barn; but before he had gone a step two iron hands caught him by the throat, and smothered his cry of terror. Kosma and Damian, with the adroitness of genuine murderers, hurled him to the ground, put their knees on his breast, pressed him so that his ribs began to crack, and gagged him in the twinkle of an eye.

Kmita came forward, and holding the pitch light to his eyes, said, —

"Ah! this is Pan Kuklinovski! Now I have something to say to you!"

Kuklinovski's face was blue, the veins were so swollen that it seemed they might burst any moment; but in his eyes, which were coming out of his head and bloodshot, there was quite as much wonder as terror.

"Strip him and put him on the beam !" cried Kmita.

Kosma and Damian fell to stripping him as zealously as if they wished to take the skin from him together with his clothing.

In a quarter of an hour Kuklinovski was hanging by his hands and feet, like a half goose, on the beam. Then Kmita put his hands on his hips and began to brag terrribly.

"Well, Pan Kuklinovski," said he, " who is better, Kmita or Kuklinovski ? " Then he seized the burning tow and took a step nearer. "Thy camp is distant one shot from a bow, thy thousand ruffians are within call, there is thy Swedish general a little beyond, and thou art hanging here from this same beam from which 't was thy thought to roast me. — Learn to know Kmita ! Thou hadst the thought to be equal to Kmita, to belong to his company, to be compared with him ? Thou cut-purse, thou low ruffian, terror of old women, thou offscouring of man, Lord Scoundrel of Scoundrelton ! Wry-mouth, trash, slave ! I might have thee cut up like a kid, like a capon ; but I choose to roast thee alive as thou didst think to roast me."

Saying this, he raised the tow and applied it to the side of the hanging, hapless man ; but he held it longer, until the odor of the burned flesh began to spread through the barn.

Kuklinovski writhed till the rope was swinging with him. His eyes, fastened on Kmita, expressed terrible pain and a dumb imploring for pity ; from his gagged lips came woful groans ; but war had hardened the heart of Pan Andrei, and there was no pity in him, above all, none for traitors.

Removing at last the tow from Kuklinovski's side, he put it for a while under his nose, rubbed with it his mustaches, his eyelashes, and his brows ; then he said, —

"I give thee thy life to meditate on Kmita. Thou wilt hang here till morning, and now pray to God that people find thee before thou art frozen."

Then he turned to Kosma and Damian. "To horse ! " cried he, and went out of the barn.

Half an hour later around the four riders were quiet hills, silent and empty fields. The fresh breeze, not filled with smoke of powder, entered their lungs. Kmita rode ahead, the Kyemliches after him. They spoke in low voices. Pan

Andrei was silent, or rather he was repeating in silence the morning "Our Father," for it was not long before dawn.

From time to time a hiss or even a low groan was rent from his lips, when his burned side pained him greatly. But at the same time he felt on horseback and free ; and the thought that he had blown up the greatest siege gun, and besides that had torn himself from the hands of Kukli- novski and had wrought vengeance on him, filled Pan Andrei with such consolation that in view of it the pain was nothing.

Meanwhile a quiet dialogue between the father and the sons turned into a loud dispute.

"The money belt is good," said the greedy old man ; "but where are the rings ?   He had rings on his fingers ; in one was a stone worth twenty ducats."

"I forgot to take it," answered Kosma.

"I wish you were killed ! Let the old man think of everything, and these rascals have n't wit for a copper ! You forgot the rings, you thieves ?   You lie like dogs !"

"Then turn back, father, and look," muttered Damian.

"You lie, you thieves ! You hide things.   You wrong your old father, — such sons !   I wish that I had not begot- ten you.   You will die without a blessing."

Kmita reined in his horse somewhat.   "Come this way !" called he.

The dispute ceased, the Kyemliches hurried up, and they rode farther four abreast.

"And do you know the road to the Silesian boundary ? " asked Pan Andrei.

"O Mother of God ! we know, we know," answered the old man.

"There are no Swedish parties on the road ? "

"No, for all are at Chenstohova, unless we might meet a single man ; but God give us one !"

A moment of silence followed.

"Then you served with Kuklinovski ? " asked Kmita.

"We did, for we thought that being near we might serve the holy monks and your grace, and so it has happened. We did not serve against the fortress, — God save us from that ! we took no pay unless we found something on Swedes."

"How on Swedes ? '

"For we wanted to serve the Most Holy Lady even outside the walls ; therefore we rode around the camp at

nfght or in the daytime, as the Lord God gave us ; and
when any of the Swedes happened alone, then we — that is
— O Refuge of sinners ! — we — ”

"Pounded him !" finished Kosma and Damian.

Kmita laughed. "Kuklinovski had good servants in you.
But did he know about this ? "

" He received a share, an income. He knew, and the
scoundrel commanded us to give a thaler a head. Otherwise he threatened to betray us. Such a robber, — he
wronged poor men ! And we have kept faith with your
grace, for not such is service with you. Your grace adds
besides of your own ; but he, a thaler a head, for our toil,
for our labor. On him may God — ”

" I will reward you abundantly for what you have done,"
said Kmita. " I did not expect this of you."

The distant sound of guns interrupted further words.
Evidently the Swedes had begun to fire with the first dawn.
After a while the roar increased. Kmita stopped his horse ;
it seemed to him that he distinguished the sound of the
fortress cannon from the cannon of the Swedes ; therefore
he clinched his fist, and threatening with it in the direction
of the enemies' camp said, —

"Fire away, fire away ! Where is your greatest gun
now ? ”

CHAPTER V.

THE bursting of the gigantic culverin had really a crushing effect upon Miller, for all his hopes had rested hitherto
on that gun.   Infantry were ready for the assault, ladders
and piles of fascines were collected ; but now it was necessary to abandon all thought of a storm.

The plan of blowing up the cloister by means of mines
came also to nothing.   Miners brought in previously from
Olkush split, it is true, the rock, and approached on a diago-
nal to the cloister ; but work progressed slowly.   The work-
men, in spite of every precaution, fell frequently from the
guns of the church, and labored unwillingly.   Many of
them preferred to die rather than aid in the destruction of
a sacred place.

Miller felt a daily increasing opposition.   The frost took
away the remnant of courage from his unwilling troops,
among whom terror was spreading from day to day with a
belief that the capture of the cloister did not lie within
human power.

Finally Miller himself began to lose hope, and after the
bursting of the gun he was simply in despair ; a feeling of
helplessness and impotence took possession of him.   Next
morning he called a council, but he called it with the secret
wish to hear from officers encouragement to abandon the
fortress.

They began to assemble, all wearied and gloomy.   In
silence they took their places around a table in an enormous and cold room, in which the steam from their breaths
stood before their faces, and they looked from behind it as
from behind a cloud.   Each one felt in his soul exhaustion
and weariness ; each one said to himself : "There is no counsel to give save one, which it is better for no man to be the
first to give."   All waited for what Miller would say.   He
ordered first of all to bring plenty of heated wine, hoping
that under the influence of warm drink it would be easier
to obtain a real thought from those silent figures, and
encouragement to retreat from the fortress.

At last, when he supposed that the wine had produced its
effect, he spoke in the following words : —

"Have you noticed, gentlemen, that none of the Polish colonels have come to this council, though I summoned them all?"

"It is known of course to your worthiness that servants of the Polish squadron have, while fishing, found silver belonging to the cloister, and that they fought for it with our soldiers. More than ten men have been cut down."

"I know; I succeeded in snatching a part of that silver from their hands, indeed the greater part. It is here now, and I am thinking what to do with it."

"This is surely the cause of the anger of the Polish colonels. They say that if the Poles found the silver, it belongs to the Poles."

"That's a reason!" cried Count Veyhard.

"For my mind, it is a strong reason," said Sadovski; "and I think that if you had found the silver you would not feel bound to divide it, not only with the Poles, but even with me, a Cheh."

"First of all, my dear sir, I do not share your good will for the enemies of our king," answered the count, with a frown.

"But we, thanks to you, must share with you shame and disgrace, not being able to succeed against a fortress to which you have brought us."

"Then have you lost all hope?"

"But have you any yourself to give away?"

"Just as if you knew; and I think that these gentlemen share more willingly with me in my hope, than with you in your fear."

"Do you make me a coward, Count Veyhard?"

"I do not ascribe to you more courage than you show."

"And I ascribe to you less."

"But I," said Miller, who for some time had looked on the count with dislike as the instigator of the ill-starred undertaking, "shall have the silver sent to the cloister. Perhaps kindness and graciousness will do more with these surly monks than balls and cannon. Let them understand that we wish to possess the fortress, not their treasures."

The officers looked on Miller with wonder, so little accustomed were they to magnanimity from him. At last Sadovski said, —

"Nothing better could be done, for it will close at once the mouths of the Polish colonels who lay claim to the silver. In the fortress it will surely make a good impression."

"The death of that Kmita will make the best impression," answered Count Veyhard. "I hope that Kuklinovski has already torn him out of his skin."

"I think that he is no longer alive," said Miller. "But that name reminds me of our loss, which nothing can make good. That was the greatest gun in the whole artillery of his grace. I do not hide from you, gentlemen, that all my hopes were placed on it. The breach was already made, terror was spreading in the fortress. A couple of days longer and we should have moved to a storm. Now all our labor is useless, all our exertions vain. They will repair the wall in one day. And the guns which we have now are no better than those of the fortress, and can be easily dismounted. No larger ones can be had anywhere, for even Marshal Wittemberg has n't them. The more I ponder over it, the more the disaster seems dreadful. And to think that one man did this, — one dog! one Satan! I shall go mad! To all the horned devils!"

Here Miller struck the table with his fist, for unrestrained anger had seized him, the more desperately because he was powerless. After a while he cried, —

"But what will the king say when he hears of this loss?" After a while he added: "And what shall we do? We cannot gnaw away that cliff with our teeth. Would that the plague might strike those who persuaded me to come to this fortress!"

Having said this, he took a crystal goblet, and in his excitement hurled it to the floor so that the crystal was broken into small bits.

This unbecoming frenzy, more befitting a peasant than a warrior holding such a high office, turned all hearts from him, and soured good-humor completely.

"Give counsel, gentlemen!" cried Miller.

"It is possible to counsel, but only in calmness," answered the Prince of Hesse.

Miller began to puff and blow out his anger through his nostrils. After a time he grew calm, and passing his eyes over those present as if encouraging them with a glance, he said, —

"I ask your pardon, gentlemen, but my anger is not strange. I will not mention those places which, when I had taken command after Torstenson, I captured, for I do not wish, in view of the present disaster, to boast of past fortune. All that is done at this fortress simply passes reason. But still it is necessary to take counsel. For that purpose I have summoned you. Deliberate, then, and what the majority of us determine at this council will be done."

"Let your worthiness give us the subject for deliberation," said the Prince of Hesse. "Have we to deliberate only concerning the capture of the fortress, or also concerning this, whether it is better to withdraw?"

Miller did not wish to put the question so clearly, or at least he did not wish the "either — or," to come first from his mouth; therefore he said, —

"Let each speak clearly what he thinks. It should be a question for us of the profit and praise of the king."

But none of the officers wished more than Miller to appear first with the proposition to retreat, therefore there was silence again.

"Pan Sadovski," said Miller after a while, in a voice which he tried to make agreeable and kind, "you say what you think more sincerely than others, for your reputation insures you against all suspicion."

"I think, General," answered the colonel, "that Kmita was one of the greatest soldiers of this age, and that our position is desperate."

"But you were in favor of withdrawing from the fortress?"

"With permission of your worthiness, I was only in favor of not beginning the siege. That is a thing quite different."

"Then what do you advise now?"

"Now I give the floor to Count Veyhard."

Miller swore like a pagan.

"Count Veyhard will answer for this unfortunate affair," said he.

"My counsels have not all been carried out," answered the count, insolently. "I can boldly cast responsibility from myself. There were men who with a wonderful, in truth an inexplicable, good-will for the priests, dissuaded his worthiness from all severe measures. My advice was to hang those envoy priests, and I am convinced that if this had been done terror would have opened to us before this time the gates of that hen-house."

Here the count looked at Sadovski; but before the latter had answered, the Prince of Hesse interfered: "Count, do not call that fortress a hen-house, for the more you decrease its importance the more you increase our shame."

"Nevertheless I advised to hang the envoys. Terror and always terror, that is what I repeated from morning till night; but Pan Sadovski threatened resignation, and the priests went unharmed."

"Go, Count, to-day to the fortress," answered Sadovski, "blow up with powder their greatest gun as Kmita did ours, and I guarantee that, that will spread more terror than a murderous execution of envoys."

The count turned directly to Miller: "Your worthiness I thought we had come here for counsel and not for amusement."

"Have you an answer to baseless reproaches?" asked Miller.

"I have, in spite of the joyousness of these gentlemen, who might save their humor for better times."

"Oh, son of Laertes, famous for stratagems!" exclaimed the Prince of Hesse.

"Gentlemen," answered the count, "it is universally known that not Minerva but Mars is your guardian deity; but since Mars has not favored you, and you have renounced your right of speech, let me speak."

"The mountain is beginning to groan, and soon we shall see the small tail of a mouse," said Sadovski.

"I ask for silence!" said Miller, severely. "Speak, Count, but keep in mind that up to this moment your counsels have given bitter fruit."

"Which, though it is winter, we must eat like mouldy biscuits," put in the Prince of Hesse.

"This explains why your princely highness drinks so much wine," said Count Veyhard; "and though it does not take the place of native wit, it helps you to a happy digestion of even disgrace. But no matter! I know well that there is a party in the fortress which is long desirous of surrender, and that only our weakness on one side and the superhuman stubbornness of the prior on the other keep it in check. New terror will give this party new power; for this purpose we should show that we make no account of the loss of the gun, and storm the more vigorously."

"Is that all?"

"Even if it were all, I think that such counsel is more in accordance with the honor of Swedish soldiers than barren jests at cups, or than sleeping after drinking-bouts. But that is not all. We should spread the report among our soldiers, and especially among the Poles, that the men at work now making a mine have discovered the old underground passage leading to the cloister and the church."

"That is good counsel," said Miller.

"When this report is spread among the soldiers and the Poles, the Poles themselves will persuade the monks to surrender, for it is a question with them as with the monks, that that nest of superstitions should remain intact."

"For a Catholic that is not bad!" muttered Sadovski.

"If he served the Turks he would call Rome a nest of superstitions," said the Prince of Hesse.

"Then, beyond doubt, the Poles will send envoys to the priests," continued Count Veyhard, — "that party in the cloister, which is long anxious for surrender will renew its efforts under the influence of fear; and who knows but its members will force the prior and the stubborn to open the gates?"

"The city of Priam will perish through the cunning of the divine son of Laertes," declaimed the Prince of Hesse.

"As God lives, a real Trojan history, and he thinks he has invented something new!" said Sadovski.

But the advice pleased Miller, for in very truth it was not bad. The party which the count spoke of existed really in the cloister. Even some priests of weaker soul belonged to it. Besides, fear might extend among the garrison, including even those who so far were ready to defend it to the last drop of blood.

"Let us try, let us try!" said Miller, who like a drowning man seized every plank, and from despair passed easily to hope. "But will Kuklinovski or Zbrojek agree to go again as envoys to the cloister, or will they believe in that passage, and will they inform the priests of it?"

"In every case Kuklinovski will agree," answered the count; "but it is better that he should believe really in the existence of the passage."

At that moment they heard the tramp of a horse in front of the quarters.

"There, Pan Zbrojek has come!" said the Prince of Hesse, looking through the window.

A moment later spurs rattled, and Zbrojek entered, or rather rushed into the room. His face was pale, excited;

and before the officers could ask the cause of his excitement the colonel cried, —

"Kuklinovski is no longer living!"

"How? What do you say? What has happened?" exclaimed Miller.

"Let me catch breath," said Zbrojek, "for what I have
seen passes imagination."

"Talk more quickly. Has he been murdered?" cried all.

"By Kmita," answered Zbrojek.

The officers all sprang from their seats, and began to look
at Zbrojek as at a madman; and he, while blowing in quick
succession bunches of steam from his nostrils, said, —

"If I had not seen I should not have believed, for that is
not a human power. Kuklinovski is not living, three soldiers are killed, and of Kmita not a trace. I knew that he
was a terrible man. His reputation is known in the whole
country. But for him, a prisoner and bound, not only to
free himself, but to kill the soldiers and torture Kuklinovski to death, — that a man could not do, only a devil!"

"Nothing like that has ever happened; that's impossible of belief!" whispered Sadovski.

"That Kmita has shown what he can do," said the Prince
of Hesse. "We did not believe the Poles yesterday when
they told us what kind of bird he was; we thought they
were telling big stories, as is usual with them."

"Enough to drive a man mad," said the count.

Miller seized his head with his hands, and said nothing.
When at last he raised his eyes, flashes of wrath were crossing in them with flashes of suspicion.

"Pan Zbrojek," said he, "though he were Satan and not
a man, he could not do this without some treason, without
assistance. Kmita had his admirers here; Kuklinovski his
enemies, and you belong to the number."

Zbrojek was in the full sense of the word an insolent soldier; therefore when he heard an accusation directed against
himself, he grew still paler, sprang from his place, approached
Miller, and halting in front of him looked him straight in
the eyes.

"Does your worthiness suspect me?" inquired he.

A very oppressive moment followed. The officers present
had not the slightest doubt were Miller to give an affirmative
answer something would follow terrible and unparalleled in
the history of camps. All hands rested on their rapier hilts.
Sadovski even drew his weapon altogether.

But at that moment the officers saw before the window a yard filled with Polish horsemen. Probably they also had come with news of Kuklinovski, but in case of collision they would stand beyond doubt on Zbrojek's side. Miller too saw them, and though the paleness of rage had come on his face, still he restrained himself, and feigning to see no challenge in Zbrojek's action, he answered in a voice which he strove to make natural, —

"Tell in detail how it happened."

Zbrojek stood for a time yet with nostrils distended, but he too remembered himself; and then his thoughts turned in another direction, for his comrades, who had just ridden up, entered the room.

"Kuklinovski is murdered!" repeated they, one after another. "Kuklinovski is killed! His regiment will scatter! His soldiers are going wild!"

"Gentlemen, permit Pan Zbrojek to speak; he brought the news first," cried Miller.

After a while there was silence, and Zbrojek spoke as follows, —

"It is known to you, gentlemen, that at the last council I challenged Kuklinovski on the word of a cavalier. I was an admirer of Kmita, it is true; but even you, though his enemies, must acknowledge that no common man could have done such a deed as bursting that cannon. It behooves us to esteem daring even in an enemy; therefore I offered him my hand, but he refused his, and called me a traitor. Then I thought to myself, 'Let Kuklinovski do what he likes with him.' My only other thought was this: 'If Kuklinovski acts against knightly honor in dealing with Kmita, the disgrace of his deed must not fall on all Poles, and among others on me.' For that very reason I wished surely to fight with Kuklinovski, and this morning taking two comrades, I set out for his camp. We come to his quarters; they say there, 'He is not at home.' I send to this place, — he is not here. At his quarters they tell us, 'He has not returned the whole night.' But they are not alarmed, for they think that he has remained with your worthiness. At last one soldier says, 'Last evening he went to that little barn in the field with Kmita, whom he was going to burn there.' I ride to the barn; the doors are wide open. I enter; I see inside a naked body hanging from a beam. 'That is Kmita,' thought I; but when my eyes have grown used to the darkness, I see that the body is some thin and bony one, and Kmita looked like a Hercules. It is a wonder to me that he could shrink so much in one night. I draw near — Kuklinovski!"

"Hanging from the beam?" asked Miller.

"Exactly! I make the sign of the cross, — I think, 'Is it witchcraft, an omen, deception, or what?' But when I saw three corpses of soldiers, the truth stood as if living before me. That terrible man had killed these, hung Kuklinovski, burned him like an executioner, and then escaped."

"It is not far to the Silesian boundary," said Sadovski.

A moment of silence followed. Every suspicion of Zbrojek's participation in the affair was extinguished in Miller's soul. But the event itself astonished and filled him with a certain undefined fear. He saw dangers rising around, or rather their terrible shadows, against which he knew not how to struggle; he felt that some kind of chain of failures surrounded him. The first links were before his eyes, but farther the gloom of the future was lying. Just such a feeling mastered him as if he were in a cracked house which might fall on his head any moment. Uncertainty crushed him with an insupportable weight, and he asked himself what he had to lay hands on.

Meanwhile Count Veyhard struck himself on the forehead. "As God lives," said he, "when I saw this Kmita yesterday it seemed as if I had known him somewhere. Now again I see before me that face. I remember the sound of his voice. I must have met him for a short time and in the dark, in the evening; but he is going through my head, — going —" Here he began to rub his forehead with his hand.

"What is that to us?" asked Miller; "you will not mend the gun, even should you remember; you will not bring Kuklinovski to life."

Here he turned to the officers. "Gentlemen, come with me, whoso wishes, to the scene of this deed."

All wished to go, for curiosity was exciting them. Horses were brought, and they moved on at a trot, the general at the head. When they came to the little barn they saw a number of tens of Polish horsemen scattered around that building, on the road, and along the field.

"What men are they?" asked Miller of Zbrojek.

"They must be Kuklinovski's; I tell your worthiness that those ragamuffins have simply gone wild."

Zbrojek then beckoned to one of the horsemen, —

"Come this way, come this way. Quickly!"

The soldier rode up.

"Are you Kuklinovski's men?"

"Yes."

"Where is the rest of the regiment?"

"They have run away. They refused to serve longer against Yasna Gora."

"What does he say?" asked Miller.

Zbrojek interpreted the words.

"Ask him where they went to."

Zbrojek repeated the question.

"It is unknown," said the soldier. "Some have gone to Silesia. Others said that they would serve with Kmita, for there is not another such colonel either among the Poles or the Swedes."

When Zbrojek interpreted these words to Miller, he grew serious. In truth, such men as Kuklinovski had were ready to pass over to the command of Kmita without hesitation. But then they might become terrible, if not for Miller's army, at least for his supplies and communication. A river of perils was rising higher and higher around the enchanted fortress.

Zbrojek, into whose head this idea must have come, said, as if in answer to these thoughts of Miller: "It is certain that everything is in a storm now in our Commonwealth. Let only such a Kmita shout, hundreds and thousands will surround him, especially after what he has done."

"But what can he effect?" asked Miller.

"Remember, your worthiness, that that man brought Hovanski to desperation, and Hovanski had, counting the Cossacks, six times as many men as we. Not a transport will come to us without his permission, the country houses are destroyed, and we are beginning to feel hunger. Besides, this Kmita may join with Jegotski and Kulesha; then he will have several thousand sabres at his call. He is a grievous man, and may become most harmful."

"Are you sure of your soldiers?"

"Surer than of myself," answered Zbrojek, with brutal frankness.

"How surer?"

"For, to tell the truth, we have all of us enough of this siege."

"I trust that it will soon come to an end."

"Only the question is: How? But for that matter to capture this fortress is at present as great a calamity as to retire from it."

Meanwhile they had reached the little barn. Miller dismounted, after him the officers, and all entered. The soldiers had removed Kuklinovski from the beam, and covering him with a rug laid him on his back on remnants of straw. The bodies of three soldiers lay at one side, placed evenly one by the other.

"These were killed with knives."

"But Kuklinovski?"

"There are no wounds on Kuklinovski, but his side is roasted and his mustaches daubed with pitch. He must have perished of cold or suffocation, for he holds his own cap in his teeth to this moment."

"Uncover him."

The soldier raised a corner of the rug, and a terrible face was uncovered, swollen, with eyes bursting out. On the remnants of his pitched mustaches were icicles formed from his frozen breath and mixed with soot, making as it were tusks sticking out of his mouth. That face was so revolting that Miller, though accustomed to all kinds of ghastliness, shuddered and said, —

"Cover it quickly. Terrible, terrible!"

Silence reigned in the barn.

"Why have we come here?" asked the Prince of Hesse, spitting. "I shall not touch food for a whole day."

All at once some kind of uncommon exasperation closely bordering on frenzy took possession of Miller. His face became blue, his eyes expanded, he began to gnash his teeth, a wild thirst for the blood of some one had seized him; then turning to Zbrojek, he screamed, —

"Where is that soldier who saw that Kuklinovski was in the barn? He must be a confederate!"

"I know not whether that soldier is here yet," answered Zbrojek. "All Kuklinovski's men have scattered like oxen let out from the yoke."

"Then catch him!" bellowed Miller, in fury.

"Catch him yourself!" cried Zbrojek, in similar fury.

And again a terrible outburst hung as it were on a spider-web over the heads of the Swedes and the Poles. The latter began to gather around Zbrojek, moving their mustaches threateningly and rattling their sabres.

During this noise the echoes of shots and the tramp of horses were heard, and into the barn rushed a Swedish officer of cavalry.

'General!" cried he. "A sortie from the cloister!

The men working at the mine have been cut to pieces!
A party of infantry is scattered!"

"I shall go wild!" roared Miller, seizing the hair of his
wig. "To horse!"

In a moment they were all rushing like a whirlwind
toward the cloister, so that lumps of snow fell like
hail from the hoofs of their horses. A hundred of Sadovski's cavalry, under command of his brother, joined
Miller and ran to assist. On the way they saw parties of
terrified infantry fleeing in disorder and panic, so fallen
were the hearts of the Swedish infantry, elsewhere unrivalled. They had left even trenches which were not
threatened by any danger. The oncoming officers and
cavalry trampled a few, and rode finally to within a furlong of the fortress, but only to see on the height as clearly
as on the palm of the hand, the attacking party returning
safely to the cloister; songs, shouts of joy, and laughter
came from them to Miller's ears.

Single persons stood forth and threatened with bloody
sabres in the direction of the staff. The Poles present at
the side of the Swedish general recognized Zamoyski himself, who had led the sortie in person, and who, when he
saw the staff, stopped and saluted it solemnly with his cap.
No wonder he felt safe under cover of the fortress cannon.

And, in fact, it began to smoke on the walls, and iron
flocks of cannon balls were flying with terrible whistling
among the officers. Troopers tottered in their saddles, and
groans answered whistles.

"We are under fire. Retreat!" commanded Sadovski.

Zbrojek seized the reins of Miller's horse. "General,
withdraw! It is death here!"

Miller, as if he had become torpid, said not a word, and
let himself be led out of range of the missiles. Returning
to his quarters, he locked himself in, and for a whole day
would see no man. He was meditating surely over his
fame of Poliorcetes.

Count Veyhard now took all power in hand, and began
with immense energy to make preparations for a storm.
New breastworks were thrown up; the soldiers succeeding
the miners broke the cliff unweariedly to prepare a mine.
A feverish movement continued in the whole Swedish
camp. It seemed that a new spirit had entered the besiegers, or that reinforcements had come. A few days
later the news thundered through the Swedish and allied

Polish camps that the miners had found a passage going under the church and the cloister, and that it depended now only on the good-will of the general to blow up the whole fortress.

Delight seized the soldiers worn out with cold, hunger, and fruitless toil. Shouts of: "We have Chenstohova! We'll blow up that hen-house!" ran from mouth to mouth. Feasting and drinking began.

The count was present everywhere; he encouraged the soldiers, kept them in that belief, repeated a hundred times daily the news of finding the passage, incited to feasting and frolics.

The echo of this gladness reached the cloister at last. News of the mines dug and ready to explode ran with the speed of lightning from rampart to rampart. Even the most daring were frightened. Weeping women began to besiege the prior's dwelling, to hold out to him their children when he appeared for a while, and cry, —

"Destroy not the innocent! Their blood will fall on thy head!"

The greater coward a man had been, the greater his daring now in urging Kordetski not to expose to destruction the sacred place, the capital of the Most Holy Lady.

Such grievous, painful times followed, for the unbending soul of our hero in a habit, as had not been till that hour. It was fortunate that the Swedes ceased their assaults, so as to prove more convincingly that they needed no longer either balls or cannon, that it was enough for them to ignite one little powder fuse. But for this very reason terror increased in the cloister. In the hour of deep night it seemed to some, the most timid, that they heard under the earth certain sounds, certain movements; that the Swedes were already under the cloister. Finally, a considerable number of the monks fell in spirit. Those, with Father Stradomski at the head of them, went to the prior and urged him to begin negotiations at once for surrender. The greater part of the soldiers went with them, and some of the nobles.

Kordetski appeared in the courtyard, and when the throng gathered around him in a close circle, he said, —

"Have we not sworn to one another to defend this holy place to the last drop of our blood? In truth, I tell you that if powder hurls us forth, only our wretched bodies, only the temporary covering, will fall away and return to the earth, but the souls will not return, — heaven will open above them, and they will enter into rejoicing and happiness, as into a sea without bounds. There Jesus Christ will receive them, and that Most Holy Mother will meet them, and they like golden bees will sit on her robe, and will sink in light and gaze on the face of the Lord."

Here the reflection of that brightness was gleaming on his face. He raised his inspired eyes upward, and spoke on with a dignity and a calm not of earth: —

"O Lord, the Ruler of worlds, Thou art looking into my heart, and Thou knowest that I am not deceiving this people when I say that if I desired only my own happiness I would stretch out my hands to Thee and cry from the depth of my soul: O Lord! let powder be there, let it explode, for in such a death is redemption of sins and faults, for it is eternal rest, and Thy servant is weary and toil-worn over-much. And who would not wish a reward of such kind, for a death without pain and as short as the twinkle of an eye, as a flash in the heavens, after which is eternity unbroken, happiness inexhaustible, joy without end. But Thou hast commanded me to guard Thy retreat, therefore it is not permitted me to go. Thou hast placed me on guard, therefore Thou hast poured into me Thy strength, and I know, O Lord, I see and feel that although the malice of the enemy were to force itself under this church, though all the powder and destructive saltpetre were placed there, it would be enough for me to make the sign of the cross above them and they would never explode."

Here he turned to the assembly and continued: "God has given me this power, but do you take fear out of your hearts. My spirit pierces the earth and tells you: Your enemies lie, there are no powder dragons under the church. You, people of timid hearts, you in whom fear has stifled faith, deserve not to enter the kingdom of grace and repose to-day. There is no powder under your feet then! God wishes to preserve this retreat, so that, like Noah's ark, it may be borne above the deluge of disasters and mishap; therefore, in the name of God, for the third time I tell you, there is no powder under the church. And when I speak in His name, who will make bold to oppose me, who will dare still to doubt?"

When he had said this he was silent and looked at the throng of monks, nobles, and soldiers. But such was the unshaken faith, the conviction and power in his voice that they were silent also, and no man came forward. On the contrary,

solace began to enter their hearts, till at last one of the soldiers, a simple peasant, said, —

"Praise to the name of the Lord! For three days they
say they are able to blow up the fortress; why do they not
blow it up?"

"Praise to the Most Holy Lady! Why do they not blow
it up?" repeated a number of voices.

Then a wonderful sign was made manifest. Behold all
about them on a sudden was heard the sound of wings, and
whole flocks of small winter birds appeared in the court of
the fortress, and every moment new ones flew in from the
starved country-places around. Birds such as gray larks,
ortolans, buntings with yellow breasts, poor sparrows, green
titmice, red bulfinches, sat on the slopes of the roofs, on the
corners over the doors, on the church; others flew around
in a many-colored crown above the head of the prior, flap-
ping their wings, chirping sadly as if begging for alms, and
having no fear whatever of man. People present were
amazed at the sight; and Kordetski, after he had prayed for
a while, said at last, —

"See these little birds of the forest. They come to the
protection of the Mother of God, but you doubt Her power."

Consolation and hope had entered their hearts; the monks,
beating their breasts, went to the church, and the soldiers
mounted the walls.

Women scattered grain to the birds, which began to pick
it up eagerly.

All interpreted the visit of these tiny forest-dwellers as a
sign of success to themselves, and of evil to the enemy.

"Fierce snows must be lying, when these little birds, caring neither for shots nor the thunder of cannon, flock to our
buildings," said the soldiers.

"But why do they fly from the Swedes to us?"

"Because the meanest creature has the wit to distinguish
an enemy from a friend."

"That cannot be," said another soldier, "for in the Swedish camp are Poles too; but it means that there must be
hunger there, and a lack of oats for the horses."

"It means still better," said a third, "that what they say
of the powder is downright falsehood."

"How is that?" asked all, in one voice.

"Old people say," replied the soldier, "that if a house is
to fall, the sparrows and swallows having nests in spring
under the roof, go away two or three days in advance; every

creature has sense to feel danger beforehand. Now if powder were under the cloister, these little birds would not fly
to us."

"Is that true?"

"As true as Amen to 'Our Father!'"

"Praise to the Most Holy Lady! it will be bad for the
Swedes."

At this moment the sound of a trumpet was heard at the
northwestern gate; all ran to see who was coming.

It was a Swedish trumpeter with a letter from the camp.
The monks assembled at once in the council hall. The letter
was from Count Veyhard, and announced that if the fortress
were not surrendered before the following day it would be
hurled into the air. But those who before had fallen under
the weight of fear had no faith now in this threat.

"Those are vain threats!" said the priests and the nobles
together.

"Let us write to them not to spare us; let them blow us
up!"

And in fact they answered in that sense.

Meanwhile the soldiers who had gathered around the
trumpeter answered his warnings with ridicule.

"Good!" said they to him. "Why do you spare us? We
will go the sooner to heaven."

But the man who delivered the answering letter to the
messenger said, —

"Do not lose words and time for nothing. Want is gnawing you, but we lack nothing, praise be to God! Even the
birds fly away from you."

And in this way Count Veyhard's last trick came to nothing. And when another day had passed it was shown with
perfect proof how vain were the fears of the besieged, and
peace returned to the cloister.

The following day a worthy man from Chenstohova, Yatsek Bjuhanski, left a letter again giving warning of a storm;
also news of the return of Yan Kazimir from Silesia, and the
uprising of the whole Commonwealth against the Swedes.
But according to reports circulating outside the walls, this
was to be the last storm.

Bjuhanski brought the letter with a bag of fish to the
priests for Christmas Eve, and approached the walls disguised
as a Swedish soldier. Poor man! — the Swedes saw him
and seized him. Miller gave command to stretch him on the
rack; but the old man had heavenly visions in the time of his

torture, and smiled as sweetly as a child, and instead of pain unspeakable joy was depicted on his face. The general was present at the torture, but he gained no confession from the martyr; he merely acquired the despairing conviction that nothing could bend those people, nothing could break them.

Now came the old beggarwoman Kostuha, with a letter from Kordetski begging most humbly that the storm be delayed during service on the day of Christ's birth. The guards and the officers received the beggarwoman with insults and jeers at such an envoy, but she answered them straight in the face, —

"No other would come, for to envoys you are as murderers, and I took the office for bread, — a crust. I shall not be long in this world; I have no fear of you : if you do not believe, you have me in your hands."

But no harm was done her. What is more, Miller, eager to try conciliation again, agreed to the prior's request, even accepted a ransom for Bjuhanski, not yet tortured quite out of his life; he sent also that part of the silver found with the Swedish soldiers. He did this last out of malice to Count Veyhard, who after the failure of the mine had fallen into disfavor again.

At last Christmas Eve came. With the first star, lights great and small began to shine all around in the fortress. The night was still, frosty, but clear. The Swedish soldiers, stiffened with cold in the intrenchments, gazed from below on the dark walls of the unapproachable fortress, and to their minds came the warm Scandinavian cottages stuffed with moss, their wives and children, the fir-tree gleaming with lights ; and more than one iron breast swelled with a sigh, with regret, with homesickness, with despair. But in the fortress, at tables covered with hay, the besieged were breaking wafers. A quiet joy was shining in all faces, for each one had the foreboding, almost the certainty, that the hours of suffering would be soon at an end.

"Another storm to-morrow, but that will be the last," repeated the priests and the soldiers. "Let him to whom God will send death give thanks that the Lord lets him be present at Mass, and thus opens more surely heaven's gates, for whoso dies for the faith on the day of Christ's birth must be received into glory."

They wished one another success, long years, or a heavenly crown ; and so relief dropped into every heart, as if suffering were over already.

But there stood one empty chair near the prior; before it a plate on which was a package of white wafers bound with a blue ribbon. When all had sat down, no one occupied that place. Zamoyski said, —

" I see, revered father, that according to ancient custom there are places for men outside the cloister."

"Not for men outside," said Father Agustine, "but as a remembrance of that young man whom we loved as a son, and whose soul is looking with pleasure upon us because we keep him in eternal memory."

"As God lives," replied Zamoyski, "he is happier now than we. We owe him due thanks."

Kordetski had tears in his eyes, and Charnyetski said, —

" They write of smaller men in the chronicles. If God gives me life, and any one asks me hereafter, who was there among us the equal of ancient heroes, I shall say Babinich."

" Babinich was not his name," said Kordetski.

" How not Babinich ? "

" I long knew his real name under the seal of confession; but when going out against that cannon, he said to me: ' If I perish, let men know who I am, so that honorable repute may rest with my name, and destroy my former misdeeds.' He went, he perished; now I can tell you that he was Kmita ! "

" That renowned Lithuanian Kmita ? " cried Charnyetski, seizing his forelock.

" The same. How the grace of God changes hearts ! "

" For God's sake. Now I understand why he undertook that work; now I understand where he got that daring, that boldness, in which he surpassed all men. Kmita, Kmita, that terrible Kmita whom Lithuania celebrates."

"Henceforth not only Lithuania, but the whole Commonwealth will glorify him in a different manner."

" He was the first to warn us against Count Veyhard."

" Through his advice we closed the gates in good season, and made preparations."

" He killed the first Swede with a shot from a bow."

" And how many of their cannon did he spoil! Who brought down De Fossis ? "

" And that siege gun! If we are not terrified at the storm of to-morrow, who is the cause ? "

" Let each remember him with honor, and celebrate his name wherever possible, so that justice be done," said Kordetski; "and now may God give him eternal rest."

"And may everlasting light shine on him," answered one chorus of voices.

But Pan Charnyetski was unable for a long time to calm himself, and his thoughts were continually turning to Kmita.

"I tell you, gentlemen, that there was something of such kind in that man that though he served as a simple soldier, the command of itself crawled at once to his hand, so that it was a wonder to me how people obeyed such a young man unwittingly. In fact, he was commander on the bastion, and I obeyed him myself. Oh, had I known him then to be Kmita!"

"Still it is a wonder to me," said Zamoyski, "that the Swedes have not boasted of his death."

Kordetski sighed. "The powder must have killed him on the spot."

"I would let a hand be cut from me could he be alive again," cried Charnyetski. "But that such a Kmita let himself be blown up by powder!"

"He gave his life for ours," said Kordetski.

"It is true," added Zamoyski, "that if that cannon were lying in the intrenchment, I should not think so pleasantly of to-morrow."

"To-morrow God will give us a new victory," said the prior, "for the ark of Noah cannot be lost in the deluge."

Thus they conversed with one another on Christmas Eve, and then separated; the monks going to the church, the soldiers, some to quiet rest, and others to keep watch on the walls and at the gates. But great care was superfluous, for in the Swedish camp there reigned unbroken calm. They had given themselves to rest and meditation, for to them too was approaching a most serious day.

The night was solemn. Legions of stars twinkled in the sky, changing into blue and rosy colors. The light of the moon changed to green the shrouds of snow stretching between the fortress and the hostile camp. The wind did not howl, and it was calm, as from the beginning of the siege it had not been near the cloister.

At midnight the Swedish soldiers heard the flow of the mild and grand tones of the organ; then the voices of men were joined with them; then the sounds of bells, large and small. Joy, consolation, and great calm were in those sounds; and the greater was the doubt, the greater the feeling of helplessness which weighed down the hearts of the Swedes.

The Polish soldiers from the commands of Zbrojek and Kalinski, without seeking permission, went up to the very walls. They were not permitted to enter through fear of some snare; but they were permitted to stand near the walls. They also collected together. Some knelt on the snow, others shook their heads pitifully, sighing over their own lot, or beat their breasts, promising repentance; and all heard with delight and with tears in their eyes the music and the hymns sung according to ancient usage.

At the same time the sentries on the walls who could not be in the church, wishing to make up for their loss, began also to sing, and soon was heard throughout the whole circuit of the walls the Christmas hymn: —

> " He is lying in the manger;
> Who will run
> To greet the little stranger? "

In the afternoon of the following day the thunder of guns drowned again every other sound. All the intrenchments began to smoke simultaneously, the earth trembled in its foundations; as of old there flew on the roof of the church heavy balls, bombs, grenades, and torches fixed in cylinders, pouring a rain of melted lead, and naked torches, knots and ropes. Never had the thunder been so unceasing, never till then had such a river of fire and iron fallen on the cloister; but among the Swedish guns was not that great gun, which alone could crush the wall and make a breach necessary for assault.

But the besieged were so accustomed to fire that each man knew what he had to do, and the defence went in its ordinary course without command. Fire was answered with fire, missile with missile, but better aimed, for with more calmness.

Toward evening Miller went out to see by the last rays of the setting sun the results; and his glance fell on the tower outlined calmly on the background of the sky.

"That cloister will stand for the ages of ages!" cried he, beside himself.

"Amen!" answered Zbrojek, quietly.

In the evening a council was assembled again at headquarters, still more gloomy than usual. Miller opened it himself.

"The storm of to-day," said he, "has brought no result. Our powder is nearly consumed; half of our men are lost, the rest discouraged: they look for disasters, not victory. We have no supplies; we cannot expect reinforcements."

"But the cloister stands unmoved as on the first day of the siege," added Sadovski.

"What remains for us?"

"Disgrace."

"I have received orders," said the general, "to finish quickly or retreat to Prussia."

"What remains to us?" repeated the Prince of Hesse.

All eyes were turned to Count Veyhard, who said: "To save our honor!"

A short broken laugh, more like the gnashing of teeth, came from Miller, who was called Poliorcetes. "The Count wishes to teach us how to raise the dead," said he.

Count Veyhard acted as though he had not heard this.

"Only the slain have saved their honor," said Sadovski.

Miller began to lose his cool blood. "And that cloister stands there yet, that Yasna Gora, that hen-house! I have not taken it! And we withdraw. Is this a dream, or am I speaking in my senses?"

"That cloister stands there yet, that Yasna Gora!" repeated word for word the Prince of Hesse, "and we shall withdraw, — defeated!"

A moment of silence followed; it seemed as though the leader and his subordinates found a certain wild pleasure in bringing to mind their shame and defeat.

Now Count Veyhard said slowly and emphatically: "It has happened more than once in every war that a besieged fortress has ransomed itself from the besiegers, who then went away as victors; for whoso pays a ransom, by this same recognizes himself as defeated."

The officers, who at first listened to the words of the speaker with scorn and contempt, now began to listen more attentively.

"Let that cloister pay us any kind of ransom," continued the count; "then no one will say that we could not take it, but that we did not wish to take it."

"Will they agree?" asked the Prince of Hesse.

"I will lay down my head," answered Count Veyhard, "and more than that, my honor as a soldier."

"Can that be!" asked Sadovski. "We have enough of this siege, but have they enough? What does your worthiness think of this?"

Miller turned to Veyhard · "Many grievous moments, the

most grievous of my life, have I passed because of your counsels, Sir Count; but for this last advice I thank you, and will be grateful."

All breasts breathed more freely. There could be no real question but that of retreating with honor.

On the morrow, the day of Saint Stephen, the officers assembled to the last man to hear Kordetski's answer to Miller's letter, which proposed a ransom, and was sent in the morning.

They had to wait long. Miller feigned joyousness, but constraint was evident on his face. No one of the officers could keep his place. All hearts beat unquietly. The Prince of Hesse and Sadovski stood under the window conversing in a low voice.

" What do you think?" asked the first; " will they agree?"

" Everything indicates that they will agree. Who would not wish to be rid of such terrible danger come what may, at the price of a few tens of thousands of thalers, especially since monks have not worldly ambition and military honor, or at least should not have? I only fear that the general has asked too much."

" How much has he asked?"

" Forty thousand from the monks, and twenty thousand from the nobles; but in the worst event they will try to reduce the sum."

" Let us yield, in God's name, let us yield. If they have not the money, I would prefer to lend them my own, if they will let us go away with even the semblance of honor. But I tell your princely highness that though I recognize the count's advice this time as good, and I believe that they will ransom themselves, such a fever is gnawing me that I would prefer ten storms to this waiting."

" Uf! you are right. But still this Count Veyhard may go high."

" Even as high as the gibbet," said the other.

But the speakers did not foresee that a worse fate than even the gibbet was awaiting Count Veyhard.

That moment the thunder of cannon interrupted further conversation.

" What is that? firing from the fortress!" cried Miller. And springing up like a man possessed, he ran out of the room.

All ran after him and listened. The sound of regular salvos came indeed from the fortress.

"Are they fighting inside, or what?" cried Miller; "I don't understand."

"I will explain to your worthiness," said Zbrojek; "this is Saint Stephen's Day, and the name's day of the Zamoyskis, father and son; the firing is in their honor."

With that shouts of applause were heard from the fortress, and after them new salvos.

"They have powder enough," said Miller, gloomily. "That is for us a new indication."

But fate did not spare him another very painful lesson.

The Swedish soldiers were so discouraged and fallen in spirit that at the sound of firing from the fortress the detachments guarding the nearest intrenchments deserted them in panic.

Miller saw one whole regiment, the musketeers of Smaland, taking refuge in disorder at his own quarters; he heard too how the officers repeated among themselves at this sight, —

"It is time, it is time, it is time to retreat!"

But by degrees everything grew calm; one crushing impression remained. The leader, and after him the subordinates, entered the room and waited, waited impatiently; even the face of Count Veyhard, till then motionless, betrayed disquiet.

At last the clatter of spurs was heard in the antechamber, and the trumpeter entered, all red from cold, his mustaches covered with his frozen breath.

"An answer from the cloister!" said he, giving a large packet wound up in a colored handkerchief bound with a string.

Miller's hands trembled somewhat, and he chose to cut the string with a dagger rather than to open it slowly. A number of pairs of eyes were fixed on the packet; the officers were breathless. The general unwound one roll of the cloth, a second, and a third, unwound with increasing haste till at last a package of wafers fell out on the table. Then he grew pale, and though no one asked what was in the package, he said. "Wafers!"

"Nothing more?" asked some one in the crowd.

"Nothing more!" answered the general, like an echo.

A moment of silence followed, broken only by panting; at times too was heard the gritting of teeth, at times the rattling of rapiers.

"Count Veyhard!" said Miller, at last, with a terrible and ill-omened voice.

"He is no longer here!" answered one of the officers.
Again silence followed.

That night movement reigned in the whole camp. Scarcely
was the light of day quenched when voices of command were
heard, the hurrying of considerable divisions of cavalry, the
sound of measured steps of infantry, the neighing of horses,
the squeaking of wagons, the dull thump of cannon, with the
biting of iron, the rattle of chains, noise, bustle, and turmoil.

"Will there be a new storm in the morning?" asked the
guards at the gates.

But they were unable to see, for since twilight the sky
was covered with clouds, and abundant snow had begun to
fall. Its frequent flakes excluded the light. About five
o'clock in the morning all sounds had ceased, but the snow
was falling still more densely. On the walls and battlements it had created new walls and battlements. It covered the whole cloister and church, as if wishing to hide them
from the glance of the enemy, to shelter and cover them
from iron missiles.

At last the air began to grow gray, and the bell commenced
tolling for morning service, when the soldiers standing guard
at the southern gate heard the snorting of a horse.

Before the gate stood a peasant, all covered with snow;
behind him was a low, small wooden sleigh, drawn by a thin,
shaggy horse. The peasant fell to striking his body with his
arms, to jumping from one foot to the other, and to crying, —

"People, but open here!"

"Who is alive?" they asked from the walls.

"Your own, from Dzbov. I have brought game for the
benefactors."

"And how did the Swedes let you come?"

"What Swedes?"

"Those who are besieging the church."

"Oho, there are no Swedes now!"

"Praise God, every soul! Have they gone?"

"The tracks behind them are covered."

With that, crowds of villagers and peasants blackened the
road, some riding, others on foot, there were women too,
and all began to cry from afar, —

"There are no Swedes! there are none! They have gone
to Vyelunie. Open the gates! There is not a man in the
camp!"

"The Swedes have gone, the Swedes have gone!" cried
men on the walls; and the news ran around like lightning.

Soldiers rushed to the bells, and rang them all as if for an alarm. Every living soul rushed out of the cells, the dwellings, and the church.

The news thundered all the time. The court was swarming with monks, nobles, soldiers, women, and children. Joyful shouts were heard around. Some ran out on the walls to examine the empty camp; others burst into laughter or into sobs. Some would not believe yet; but new crowds came continually, peasants and villagers.

They came from Chenstohova, from the surrounding villages, and from the forests near by, noisily, joyously, and with singing. New tidings crossed one another each moment. All had seen the retreating Swedes, and told in what direction they were going.

A few hours later the slope and the plain below the mountain were filled with people. The gates of the cloister were open wide, as they had been before the siege; and all the bells were ringing, ringing, ringing, — and those voices of triumph flew to the distance, and then the whole Commonwealth heard them.

The snow was covering and covering the tracks of the Swedes.

About noon of that day the church was so filled with people that head was as near head as on a paved street in a city one stone is near another. Father Kordetski himself celebrated a thanksgiving Mass, and to the throng of people it seemed that a white angel was celebrating it. And it seemed to them also that he was singing out his soul in that Mass, or that it was borne heavenward in the smoke of the incense, and was expanding in praise to the Lord.

The thunder of cannon shook not the walls, nor the glass in the windows, nor covered the people with dust, nor interrupted prayer, nor that thanksgiving hymn which amid universal ecstasy and weeping, the holy prior was intoning —

"Te Deum laudamus."

CHAPTER VI.

THE horses bore Kmita and the Kyemliches swiftly to-ward the Silesian boundary. They advanced with caution to avoid meeting Swedish scouts, for though the cunning Kyemliches had "passes," given by Kuklinovski and signed by Miller, still soldiers, though furnished with such documents, were usually subjected to examination, and examination might have an evil issue for Pan Andrei and his comrades. They rode, therefore, swiftly, so as to pass the boundary in all haste and push into the depth of the Emperor's territory. The boundaries themselves were not free from Swedish ravagers, and frequently whole parties of horsemen rode into Silesia to seize those who were going to Yan Kazimir. But the Kyemliches, during their stay at Chenstohova, occupied continually with hunting individual Swedes, had learned through and through the whole region, all the boundary roads, passages, and paths where the chase was most abundant, and were as if in their own land.

Along the road old Kyemlich told Pan Andrei what was to be heard in the Commonwealth; and Pan Andrei, having been confined so long in the fortress, forgetting his own pain, listened to the news eagerly, for it was very unfavorable to the Swedes, and heralded a near end to their domination in Poland.

"The army is sick of Swedish fortune and Swedish company," said old Kyemlich; "and as some time ago the soldiers threatened the hetmans with their lives if they would not join the Swedes, so now the same men entreat Pototski and send deputations asking him to save the Commonwealth from oppression, swearing to stand by him to the death. Some colonels also have begun to attack the Swedes on their own responsibility."

"Who began first?"

"Jegotski, the starosta of Babimost, and Pan Kulesha. These began in Great Poland, and annoy the Swedes notably. There are many small divisions in the whole country, but it is difficult to learn the names of the leaders, for

they conceal them to save their own families and property
from Swedish vengeance. Of the army that regiment rose
first which is commanded by Pan Voynillovich."

"Gabryel? He is my relative, though I do not know
him."

"A genuine soldier. He is the man who rubbed out
Pratski's party, which was serving the Swedes, and shot
Pratski himself; but now he has gone to the rough mountains beyond Cracow; there he cut up a Swedish division,
and secured the mountaineers from oppression."

"Are the mountaineers fighting with the Swedes already?"

"They were the first to rise; but as they are stupid
peasants, they wanted to rescue Cracow straightway with
axes. General Douglas scattered them, for they knew nothing of the level-country; but of the parties sent to pursue
them in the mountains, not a man has returned. Pan
Voynillovich has helped those peasants, and now has gone
himself to the marshal at Lyubovlya, and joined his
forces."

"Is Pan Lyubomirski, the marshal, opposed to the
Swedes?"

"Reports disagreed. They said that he favored this side
and that; but when men began to mount their horses
throughout the whole country he went against the Swedes.
He is a powerful man, and can do them a great deal of
harm. He alone might war with the King of Sweden.
People say too that before spring there will not be one
Swede in the Commonwealth."

"God grant that!"

"How can it be otherwise, your grace, since for the siege
of Chenstohova all are enraged against them? The army is
rising, the nobles are fighting already wherever they can,
the peasants are collecting in crowds, and besides, the Tartars are marching; the Khan, who defeated Hmelnitski
and the Cossacks, and promised to destroy them completely
unless they would march against the Swedes, is coming in
person."

"But the Swedes have still much support among magnates and nobles?"

"Only those take their part who must, and even they are
merely waiting for a chance. The prince voevoda of Vilna
is the only man who has joined them sincerely, and that act
has turned out ill for him."

Kmita stopped his horse, and at the same time caught his side, for terrible pain had shot through him.

"In God's name!" cried he, suppressing a groan, "tell me what is taking place with Radzivill. Is he all the time in Kyedani?"

"O Ivory Gate!" said the old man; "I know as much as people say, and God knows what they do not say. Some report that the prince voevoda is living no longer; others that he is still defending himself against Pan Sapyeha, but is barely breathing. It is likely that they are struggling with each other in Podlyasye, and that Pan Sapyeha has the upper hand, for the Swedes could not save the prince voevoda. Now they say that, besieged in Tykotsin by Sapyeha, it is all over with him."

"Praise be to God! The honest are conquering traitors! Praise be to God! Praise be to God!"

Kyemlich looked from under his brows at Kmita, and knew not himself what to think, for it was known in the whole Commonwealth that if Radzvill had triumphed in the beginning over his own troops and the nobles who did not wish Swedish rule, it happened, mainly, thanks to Kmita and his men. But old Kyemlich did not let that thought be known to his colonel, and rode farther in silence.

"But what has happened to Prince Boguslav?" asked Pan Andrei, at last.

"I have heard nothing of him, your grace," answered Kyemlich. "Maybe he is in Tykotsin, and maybe with the elector. War is there at present, and the King of Sweden has gone to Prussia; but we meanwhile are waiting for our own king. God give him! for let him only show himself, all to a man will rise, and the troops will leave the Swedes straightway."

"Is that certain?"

"Your grace, I know only what those soldiers said who had to be with the Swedes at Chenstohova. They are very fine cavalry, some thousands strong, under Zbrojek, Kalinski, and other colonels. I may tell your grace that no man serves there of his own will, except Kuklinovski's ravagers; they wanted to get the treasures of Yasna Gora. But all honorable soldiers did nothing but lament, and one quicker than another complained: 'We have enough of this Jew's service! Only let our king put a foot over the boundary, we will turn our sabres at once on the Swedes; but while he is not here, how can we begin, whither can we go?' So they complain; and in the other regiments which are under the hetmans it is still worse. This I know certainly, for deputations came from them to Pan Zbrojek with arguments, and they had secret talks there at night; this Miller did not know, though he felt that there was evil about him."

"But is the prince voevoda of Vilna besieged in Tykotsin?" asked Pan Andrei.

Kyemlich looked again unquietly on Kmita, for he thought that surely a fever was seizing him if he asked to have the same information repeated; still he answered, —

"Besieged by Pan Sapyeha."

"Just are Thy judgments, O God!" said Kmita. "He who might compare in power with kings! Has no one remained with him?"

"In Tykotsin there is a Swedish garrison. But with the prince only some of his trustiest attendants have remained."

Kmita's breast was filled with delight. He had feared the vengeance of the terrible magnate on Olenka, and though it seemed to him that he had prevented that vengeance with his threats, still he was tormented by the thought that it would be better and safer for Olenka and all the Billeviches to live in a lion's den than in Kyedani, under the hand of the prince, who never forgave any man. But now when he had fallen his opponents must triumph by the event; now when he was deprived of power and significance, when he was lord of only one poor castle, in which he defended his own life and freedom, he could not think of vengeance; his hand had ceased to weigh on his enemies.

"Praise be to God! praise be to God!" repeated Kmita.

He had his head so filled with the change in Radzivill's fortunes, so occupied with that which had happened during his stay in Chenstohova, and with the question where was she whom his heart loved, and what had become of her, that a third time he asked Kyemlich: "You say that the prince is broken?"

"Broken completely," answered the old man. "But are you not sick?"

"My side is burned. That is nothing!" answered Kmita.

Again they rode on in silence. The tired horses lessened their speed by degrees, till at last they were going at a walk. That monotonous movement lulled to sleep Pan Andrei, who was mortally wearied, and he slept long, nodding in the saddle. He was roused only by the white light of day. He looked around with amazement, for in the first moment it seemed to him that everything through which he had passed in that night was merely a dream; at last he inquired, —

"Is that you, Kyemlich? Are we riding from Chenstohova?"

"Of course, your grace."

"But where are we?"

"Oho, in Silesia already. Here the Swedes will not get us."

"That is well!" said Kmita, coming to his senses completely. "But where is our gracious king living?"

"At Glogov."

"We will go there then to bow down to our lord, and offer him service. But listen, old man, to me."

"I am listening, your grace."

Kmita fell to thinking, however, and did not speak at once. He was evidently combining something in his head; he hesitated, considered, and at last said: "It cannot be otherwise!"

"I am listening, your grace," repeated Kyemlich.

"Neither to the king nor to any man at the court must you mutter who I am. I call myself Babinich, I am faring from Chenstohova. Of the great gun and of Kuklinovski you may talk, so that my intentions be not misconstrued, and I be considered a traitor, for in my blindness I aided and served Prince Radzivill; of this they may have heard at the court."

"I may speak of what your grace did at Chenstohova — "

"But who will show that 't is true till the siege is over?"

"I will act at your command."

"The day will come for truth to appear at the top," added Kmita, as it were to himself, "but first our gracious lord must convince himself. Later he also will give me his witness."

Here the conversation was broken. By this time it had become perfect day. Old Kyemlich began to sing matins, and Kosma and Damian accompanied him with bass voices. The road was difficult, for the frost was cutting, and besides, the travellers were stopped continually and asked for news, especially if Chenstohova was resisting yet. Kmita answered that it was resisting, and would take care of itself; but there was no end to questions. The roads were swarming with travellers, the inns everywhere filled. Some people were seeking refuge in the depth of the country from the neighboring parts of the Commonwealth before Swedish oppression; others were pushing toward the boundary for news. From time to time appeared nobles, who, having had enough of the Swedes, were going, like Kmita, to offer their services to the fugitive king. There were seen, also, attendants of private persons; at times smaller or larger parties of soldiers, from armies, which either voluntarily or in virtue of treaties with the Swedes had passed the boundaries, — such, for instance, as the troops of Stefan Charnyetski. News from the Commonwealth had roused the hope of those "exiles," and many of them were making ready to come home in arms. In all Silesia, and particularly in the provinces of Ratibor and Opol, it was boiling as in a pot; messengers were flying with letters to the king and from the king; they were flying with letters to Charnyetski, to the primate, to Pan Korytsinski, the chancellor; to Pan Varshytski, the castellan of Cracow, the first senator of the Commonwealth, who had not deserted the cause of Yan Kazimir for an instant.

These lords, in agreement with the great queen, who was unshaken in misfortune, were coming to an understanding with one another, with the country, and with the foremost men in it, of whom it was known that they would gladly resume allegiance to their legal lord. Messengers were sent independently by the marshal of the kingdom, the hetmans, the army, and the nobles, who were making ready to take up arms.

It was the eve of a general war, which in some places had broken out already. The Swedes put down these local outbursts either with arms or with the executioner's axe, but the fire quenched in one place flamed up at once in another. An awful storm was hanging over the heads of the Scandinavian invaders; the ground itself, though covered with snow, began to burn their feet; threats and vengeance surrounded them on all sides; their own shadows alarmed them.

They went around like men astray. The recent songs of triumph died on their lips, and they asked one another in the greatest amazement, "Are these the same people who yesterday left their own king, and gave up without fighting a battle?" Yes, lords, nobles, army, — an example unheard of in history, — passed over to the conqueror; towns and castles threw open their gates; the country was occupied.

Never had a conquest cost fewer exertions, less blood. The Swedes themselves, wondering at the ease with which they had occupied a mighty Commonwealth, could not conceal their contempt for the conquered, who at the first gleam of a Swedish sword rejected their own king, their country, provided that they could enjoy life and goods in peace, or acquire new goods in the confusion. What in his time Count Veyhard had told the emperor's envoy, Lisola, the king himself, and all the Swedish generals repeated : "There is no manhood in this nation, there is no stability, there is no order, no faith, no patriotism ! It must perish."

They forgot that that nation had still one feeling, specially that one whose earthly expression was Yasna Gora. And in that feeling was rebirth.

Therefore the thunder of cannon which was heard under the sacred retreat found an echo at once in the hearts of all magnates, nobles, town-dwellers, and peasants. An outcry of awe was heard from the Carpathians to the Baltic, and the giant was roused from his torpor.

"That is another people !" said the amazed Swedish generals.

And all, from Arwid Wittemberg to the commandants of single castles, sent to Karl Gustav in Prussia tidings filled with terror.

The earth was pushing from under their feet; instead of recent friends, they met enemies on all sides; instead of submission, hostility; instead of fear, a wild daring ready for everything; instead of mildness, ferocity; instead of long-suffering, vengeance.

Meanwhile from hand to hand were flying in thousands throughout the whole Commonwealth the manifestoes of Yan Kazimir, which, issued at first in Silesia, had found no immediate echo. Now, on the contrary, they were seen in castles still free of the enemy. Wherever the Swedish hand was not weighing, the nobles assembled in crowds large and small, and beat their breasts, listening to the lofty words of the fugitive king, who, recounting faults and sins, urged them not to lose hope, but hasten to the rescue of the fallen Commonwealth.

"Though the enemy have already advanced far, it is not too late," wrote Yan Kazimir, "for us to recover the lost provinces and towns, give due praise to God, satisfy the profaned churches with the blood of the enemy, and restore the former liberties, laws and ancient enactments of

Poland to their usual circuit; if only there is a return of
that ancient Polish virtue, and that devotion and love of
God peculiar to your ancestors, virtues for which our great-
grandfather, Sigismund I., honored them before many nations.   A return to virtue has already diminished these recent transgressions.   Let those of you to whom God and
His holy faith are dearer than aught else rise against the
Swedish enemy.   Do not wait for leaders or voevodas, or for
such an order of things as is described in public law.   At
present the enemy have brought all these things to confusion
among you; but do you join, the first man to a second, a
third to these two, a fourth to the three, a fifth to the four,
and thus farther, so that each one with his own subjects may
come, and when it is possible try resistance.   Afterward you
will select a leader.   Join yourselves one party to another,
and you will form an army.   When the army is formed
and you have chosen a known chief over it, wait for our
person, not neglecting an occasion wherever it comes to defeat the enemy.   If we hear of the occasion, and your readiness and inclination, we will come at once and lay down our
life wherever the defence of the country requires it."

This manifesto was read even in the camp of Karl Gustav,
in castles having Swedish garrisons, in all places wherever
Polish squadrons were found.   The nobles shed tears at
every word of the king their kind lord, and took an oath on
crosses, on pictures of the Most Holy Lady, and on scapu-
lars to please him.   To give a proof of their readiness, while
ardor was in their hearts and their tears were not dry, they
mounted here and there without hesitation, and moved on
while hot against the Swedes.

In this way the smaller Swedish parties began to melt
and to vanish.   This was done in Lithuania, Mazovia, Great
and Little Poland.   More than once nobles who had assembled at a neighbor's house for a christening, a name's day,
a wedding or a dance, without any thought of war, finished
the entertainment with this, that after they had taken a
good share of drink they struck like a thunderbolt and cut
to pieces the nearest Swedish command.   Then, amid songs
and shouts, they assembled for the road.   Those who wished
to "hunt" rode farther, changed into a crowd greedy for
blood, from a crowd into a " party " which began steady war.
Subject peasants and house-servants joined the amusement
in throngs; others gave information about single Swedes or
small squads disposed incautiously through the villages.

And the number of "balls" and "masquerades" increased
with each day. Joyousness and daring personal to the
people were bound up with these bloody amusements.

They disguised themselves gladly as Tartars, the very
name of which filled the Swedes with alarm; for among
them were current marvellous accounts and fables touching
the ferocity, the terrible and savage bravery of those sons
of the Crimean steppes, with whom the Scandinavians had
never met hitherto. Besides, it was known universally that
the Khan with about a hundred thousand of the horde was
marching to succor Yan Kazimir; and the nobles made a
great uproar while attacking Swedish commands, from which
wonderful disorder resulted.

The Swedish colonels and commandants in many places
were really convinced that Tartars were present, and retreated in haste to larger fortresses and camps, spreading
everywhere erroneous reports and alarm. Meanwhile the
neighborhoods which were freed in this manner from the
enemy were able to defend themselves, and change an unruly
rabble into the most disciplined of armies.

But more terrible for the Swedes than "masquerades"
of nobles, or than the Tartars themselves, were the movements of the peasants. Excitement among the people began with the first day of the siege of Chenstohova; and
ploughmen hitherto silent and patient began here and there
to offer resistance, here and there to take scythes and flails
and help nobles. The most brilliant Swedish generals
looked with the greatest alarm at these crowds, which
might at any moment turn into a genuine deluge and
overwhelm beyond rescue the invaders.

Terror seemed to them the most appropriate means by
which to crush in the beginning this dreadful danger.
Karl Gustav cajoled still, and retained with words of kindness those Polish squadrons which had followed him to
Prussia. He had not spared flattery on Konyetspolski, the
celebrated commander from Zbaraj. This commander stood
at his side with six thousand cavalry, which at the first hostile meeting with the elector spread such terror and destruction among the Prussians that the elector abandoning
the fight agreed as quickly as possible to the conditions.

The King of Sweden sent letters also to the hetmans, the
magnates, and the nobles, full of graciousness, promises,
and encouragement to preserve loyalty to him. But at
the same time he issued commands to his generals and

commandants to destroy with fire and sword every opposition within the country, and especially to cut to pieces peasant parties. Then began a period of iron military rule. The Swedes cast aside the semblance of friendship. The sword, fire, pillage, oppression, took the place of the former pretended good will. From the castles they sent strong detachments of cavalry and infantry in pursuit of the "masqueraders." Whole villages, with churches and priests' dwellings, were levelled to the earth. Nobles taken prisoners, were delivered to the executioner; the right hands were cut from captured peasants, then they were sent home.

These Swedish detachments were specially savage in Great Poland, which, as it was the first to surrender, was also the first to rise against foreign dominion. Commandant Stein gave orders on a certain occasion to cut the hands from more than three hundred peasants. In towns they built permanent gibbets, which every day were adorned with new victims. Pontus de la Gardie did the same in Lithuania and Jmud, where the noble villages took up arms first, and after them the peasants. Because in general it was difficult for the Swedes in the disturbance to distinguish their friends from their enemies, no one was spared.

But the fire put down in blood, instead of dying, grew without ceasing, and a war began which was not on either side a question merely of victory, castles, towns, or provinces, but of life or death. Cruelty increased hatred, and they began not to struggle, but to exterminate each the other without mercy.

CHAPTER VII.

THIS war of extermination was just beginning when Kmita, with the three Kyemliches, reached Glogov, after a journey which was difficult in view of Pan Andrei's shaken health. They arrived in the night. The town was crowded with troops, lords, nobles, servants of the king and of magnates. The inns were so occupied that old Kyemlich with the greatest trouble found lodgings for his colonel outside the town at the house of a rope-maker.

Pan Andrei spent the whole first day in bed in pain and fever from the burn. At times he thought that he should be seriously and grievously ill; but his iron constitution gained the victory. The following night brought him ease, and at daybreak he dressed and went to the parish church to thank God for his miraculous escape.

The gray and snowy winter morning had barely dissipated the darkness. The town was still sleeping, but through the church door lights could be seen on the altar, and the sounds of the organ came forth.

Kmita went to the centre of the church. The priest was celebrating Mass before the altar; there were few worshippers so far. At benches some persons were kneeling with their faces hidden in their hands; but besides these Pan Andrei saw, when his eyes had grown used to the darkness, a certain figure lying in the form of a cross in front of the pews on a carpet. Behind him were kneeling two youths with ruddy and almost angelic childish faces.

This man was motionless, and only from his breast moving continually with deep sighs could it be known that he was not sleeping, but praying earnestly and with his whole soul. Kmita himself became absorbed in a thanksgiving prayer; but when he had finished his eyes turned involuntarily to the man lying as a cross, and could not leave him; something fastened them to him. Sighs deep as groans, audible in the silence of the church, shook that figure continually. The yellow rays of the candles burning before the altar, together with the light of day, whitening in the windows, brought it out of the gloom, and made it more and more visible.

Pan Andrei conjectured at once from the dress that he must be some noted person, besides all present, not excepting the priest celebrating Mass, looked on him with honor and respect. The unknown was dressed entirely in black velvet bound with sable, but on his shoulders he had, turned down, a white lace collar, from under which peeped the golden links of a chain; a black hat with feathers of like color lay at his side; one of the pages kneeling beyond the carpet held gloves and a sword enamelled in blue. Kmita could not see the face of the unknown, for it was hidden by the folds of the carpet, and besides, the locks of an unusually thick wig scattered around his head concealed it completely.

Pan Andrei pressed up to the front pew to see the face of the unknown when he rose. Mass was then drawing to an end. The priest was singing *Pater noster*. The people who wished to be at the following Mass were coming in through the main entrance. The church was filled gradually with figures with heads shaven at the sides, dressed in cloaks with long sleeves, in military burkas, in fur cloaks, and in brocade coats. It became somewhat crowded. Kmita then pushed with his elbow a noble standing at his side, and whispered, —

"Pardon, your grace, that I trouble you during service, but my curiosity is most powerful. Who is that?" He indicated with his eyes the man lying in the form of a cross.

"Have you come from a distance, that you know not?" asked the noble.

"Certainly I come from a distance, and therefore I ask in hope that if I find some polite man he will not begrudge an answer."

"That is the king."

"As God lives!" cried Kmita.

But at that moment the king rose, for the priest had begun to read the Gospel.

Pan Andrei saw an emaciated face, yellow and transparent, like church wax. The eyes of the king were moist, and his lids red. You would have said that all the fate of the country was reflected in that noble face, so much was there in it of pain, suffering, care. Sleepless nights divided between prayer and grief, terrible deceptions, wandering, desertion, the humiliated majesty of that son, grandson, and great-grandson of powerful kings, the gall which his own subjects had given him to drink so bountifully, the ingratitude of that country for which he was ready to devote his blood and life, — all this could be read in that face as in a book, and still it expressed not only resignation, obtained through faith and prayer, not only the majesty of a king and an anointed of God, but such great, inexhaustible kindness that evidently it would be enough for the greatest renegade, the most guilty man, only to stretch out his hands to that father, and that father would receive him, forgive him, and forget his offences.

It seemed to Kmita at sight of him that some one had squeezed his heart with an iron hand. Compassion rose in the ardent soul of the young hero. Compunction, sorrow, and homage straitened the breath in his throat, a feeling of immeasurable guilt cut his knees under him so that he began to tremble through his whole body, and at once a new feeling rose in his breast. In one moment he had conceived such a love for that suffering king that to him there was nothing dearer on earth than that father and lord, for whom he was ready to sacrifice blood and life, bear torture and everything else in the world. He wished to throw himself at those feet, to embrace those knees, and implore forgiveness for his crimes. The noble, the insolent disturber, had died in him in one moment, and the royalist was born, devoted with his whole soul to his king.

"That is our lord, our unhappy king," repeated he to himself, as if he wished with his lips to give witness to what his eyes saw and what his heart felt.

After the Gospel, Yan Kazimir knelt again, stretched out his arms, raised his eyes to heaven, and was sunk in prayer. The priest went out at last, there was a movement in the church, the king remained kneeling.

Then that noble whom Kmita had addressed pushed Pan Andrei in the side.

"But who are you?" asked he.

Kmita did not understand the question at once, and did not answer it directly, so greatly were his heart and mind occupied by the person of the king.

"And who are you?" repeated that personage.

"A noble like yourself," answered Pan Andrei, waking as if from a dream.

"What is your name?"

"What is my name? Babinich; I am from Lithuania, from near Vityebsk."

"And I am Pan Lugovski, of the king's household. Have you just come from Lithuania, from Vityebsk?"

"No; I come from Chenstohova."

Pan Lugovski was dumb for a moment from wonder.

"But if that is true, then come and tell us the news. The king is almost dead from anxiety because he has had no certain tidings these three days. How is it? You are perhaps from the squadron of Zbrojek, Kalinski, or Kuklinovski, from near Chenstohova."

"Not from near Chenstohova, but directly from the cloister itself."

"Are you not jesting? What is going on there, what is to be heard? Does Yasna Gora defend itself yet?"

"It does, and will defend itself. The Swedes are about to retreat."

"For God's sake! The king will cover you with gold. From the very cloister do you say that you have come? How did the Swedes let you pass?"

"I did not ask their permission; but pardon me, I cannot give a more extended account in the church."

"Right, right!" said Pan Lugovski. "God is merciful! You have fallen from heaven to us! It is not proper in the church, — right! Wait a moment. The king will rise directly; he will go to breakfast before high Mass. To-day is Sunday. Come stand with me at the door, and when the king is going out I will present you. Come, come, there is no time to spare."

He pushed ahead, and Kmita followed. They had barely taken their places at the door when the two pages appeared, and after them came Yan Kazimir slowly.

"Gracious King!" cried Pan Lugovski, "there are tidings from Chenstohova."

The wax-like face of Yan Kazimir became animated in an instant.

"What tidings? Where is the man?" inquired he.

"This noble; he says that he has come from the very cloister."

"Is the cloister captured?" cried the king.

That moment Pan Andrei fell his whole length at the feet of the king. Yan Kazimir inclined and began to raise him by the arms.

"Oh, ceremony another time, another time!" cried he. "Rise, in God's name, rise! Speak quickly! Is the cloister taken?"

Kmita sprang up with tears in his eyes, and cried with animation, —

"It is not, and will not be taken, Gracious Lord. The Swedes are beaten. The great gun is blown up. There is fear among them, hunger, misery. They are thinking of retreat."

"Praise, praise to Thee, Queen of the Angels and of us!" said the king. Then he turned to the church door, removed his hat, and without entering knelt on the snow at the door. He supported his head on a stone pillar, and sank into silence. After a while sobbing began to shake him. Emotion seized all, and Pan Andrei wept loudly. The king, after he had prayed and shed tears, rose quieted, with a face much clearer. He inquired his name of Kmita, and when the latter had told his assumed one, said, —

"Let Pan Lugovski conduct you at once to our quarters. We shall not take our morning food without hearing of the defence."

A quarter of an hour later Kmita was standing in the king's chamber before a distinguished assembly. The king was only waiting for the queen, to sit down to breakfast. Marya Ludvika appeared soon. Yan Kazimir barely saw her when he exclaimed, —

"Chenstohova has held out! The Swedes will retreat! Here is Pan Babinich, who has just come, and he brings the news."

The black eyes of the queen rested inquiringly on the youthful face of the hero, and seeing its sincerity, they grew bright with joy; and he, when he had made a profound obeisance, looked also at her boldly, as truth and honesty know how to look.

"The power of God!" said the queen. "You have taken a terrible weight from our hearts, and God grant this is the beginning of a change of fortune. Do you come straight from near Chenstohova?"

"Not from near Chenstohova, he says, but from the cloister itself, — one of the defenders!" exclaimed the king. "A golden guest! God grant such to come daily; but let him begin. Tell, brother, tell how you defended yourselves, and how the hand of God guarded you."

"It is sure, Gracious King and Queen, that nothing saved us but the guardianship of God and the miracles of the Most Holy Lady, which I saw every day with my eyes."

Here Kmita was preparing for his narrative, when new

dignitaries appeared. First came the nuncio of the Pope; then the primate, Leshchynski; after him Vydjga, a golden-mouthed preacher, who was the queen's chancellor, later bishop of Varmia, and finally primate. With him came the chancellor of the kingdom, Pan Korytsinski, and the Frenchman De Noyers, a relative of the queen, and other dignitaries who had not deserted the king in misfortune, but chose to share with him the bitter bread of exile rather than break plighted faith.

The king was eager to hear; therefore he ceased eating, every moment, and repeated, "Listen, gentlemen, listen; a guest from Chenstohova! Good news; hear it! From Yasna Gora itself!"

Then the dignitaries looked with curiosity on Kmita, who was standing as it were before a court; but he, bold by nature and accustomed to intercourse with great people, was not a whit alarmed at sight of so many celebrated persons; and when all had taken their places, he began to describe the whole siege.

Truth was evident in his words; for he spoke with clear-ness and strength, like a soldier who had seen everything, touched everything, passed through everything. He praised to the skies Pan Zamoyski and Pan Charnyetski; spoke of Kordetski, the prior, as of a holy prophet; exalted other fathers; missed no one save himself; but he ascribed the whole success of the defence, without deviation, to the Most Holy Lady, to Her favor and miracles.

The king and the dignitaries listened to him in amaze-ment. The archbishop raised his tearful eyes to heaven. Father Vydjga interpreted everything hurriedly to the nuncio; other great personages caught their heads; some prayed, or beat their breasts.

At last, when Kmita came to the recent storms, — when he began to relate how Miller had brought heavy guns from Cracow, and among them one against which not only the walls of Chenstohova, but no walls in the world could stand, — such silence began as though some one were sow-ing poppy seeds, and all eyes rested on Pan Andrei's lips.

But he stopped suddenly, and began to breathe quickly; a clear flush came out on his face; he frowned, raised his head, and spoke boldly: "Now I must speak of myself, though I should prefer to be silent. And if I say aught which seems praise, God is my witness that I do so not for rewards, for I do not need them, since the greatest reward for me is to shed my blood for majesty."

"Speak boldly, I believe you," said the king. "But that great gun?"

"That great gun — I, stealing out in the night from the fortress, blew into fragments with powder."

"O loving God!" cried the king.

But after this cry was silence, such astonishment had seized each person. All looked as at a rainbow at the young hero, who stood with flashing eyes, with a flush on his face, and with head proudly erect. And so much was there in him at that moment of a certain terribleness and wild courage that the thought came to each one unwittingly, such a man might dare such a deed. After silence of a moment the primate said, —

"This man looks like that!"

"How did you do it?" asked the king.

Kmita explained how he did it.

"I cannot believe my ears," said Pan Korytsinski, the chancellor.

"Worthy gentlemen," answered the king, with dignity, "you do not know whom we have before us. There is yet hope that the Commonwealth has not perished while it gives such cavaliers and citizens."

"This man might say of himself, ' *Si fractus illabatur orbis, impavidum ferient ruinæ* (If the broken firmament should fall the ruins would strike him unterrified)!'" said Father Vydjga, who loved to quote authors at every opportunity.

"These are almost impossible things," said the chancellor again. "Tell, Cavalier, how you brought away your life, and how you passed through the Swedes."

"The explosion stunned me," said Kmita, "and next day the Swedes found me in the ditch lying as if lifeless. They judged me at once, and Miller condemned me to death."

"Then did you escape?"

"A certain Kuklinovski begged me of Miller, so that he might put me to death, for he had a fierce animosity against me."

"He is a well-known disturber and murderer; we have heard of him," said the castellan of Kjyvinsk. "His regiment is with Miller at Chenstohova. That is true!"

"Previously Kuklinovski was an envoy from Miller to the cloister, and once tried to persuade me in secret to treason when I was conducting him to the gate. I struck him in the face and kicked him. For that insult he was enraged against me."

"Ah, this I see is a noble of fire and sulphur!" cried the king, amused. "Do not go into such a man's road. Did Miller then give you to Kuklinovski?"

"He did, Gracious Gentlemen. Kuklinovski shut me with himself and some men in an empty little barn. There he had me tied to a beam with ropes; then he began to torture me and to burn my sides with fire."

"By the living God!"

"While doing this he was called away to Miller; when he was gone three nobles came, certain Kyemliches, his soldiers, who had served with me previously. They killed the guards, and unbound me from the beam—"

"And you fled! Now I understand," said the king.

"No, your Royal Grace. We waited for the return of Kuklinovski. Then I gave command to tie him to that same beam, and I burned him better with fire."

When he had said this, Kmita, roused by remembrance, became red again, and his eyes gleamed like those of a wolf. But the king, who passed easily from grief to joy, from seriousness to sport, began to strike the table with his hand, and exclaim with laughter,—

"That was good for him! that was good for him! Such a traitor deserved nothing better!"

"I left him alive," continued Kmita, "but he must have perished from cold before morning."

"That's a deed; he does not give away his own. We need more of such!" cried the king, now completely delighted. "Did you come hither with those soldiers? What are their names?"

"They are Kyemlich, a father and two sons."

"My mother is from the house of Kyemlich," said Father Vydjga.

"It is evident that there are great and small Kyemliches," answered Kmita, smiling; "these are not only small persons, but robbers; they are fierce soldiers, however, and faithful to me."

Meanwhile the chancellor, who had been whispering for a time in the ear of the Archbishop of Gnyezno, said at last,—

"Many come here who for their own praise or for an expected reward are glad to raise dust. They bring false and disturbing news, and are frequently sent by the enemy."

This remark chilled all present. Kmita's face became purple.

"I do not know the office of your grace," said he, "which, I think, must be considerable, therefore I do not wish to offend you; but there is no office, as I think, which would empower any one to give the lie to a noble, without reason."

"Man! you are speaking to the grand chancellor of the kingdom," said Lugovski.

"Whoso gives me the lie, even if he is chancellor, I answer him, it is easier to give the lie than to give your life, it is easier to seal with wax than with blood!"

Pan Korytsinski was not angry; he only said: "I do not give you the lie, Cavalier; but if what you say is true, you must have a burned side."

"Come to another place, your great mightiness, to another room, and I will show it to you!" roared Kmita.

"It is not needful," said the king; "I believe you without that."

"It cannot be, your Royal Grace," exclaimed Pan Andrei; "I wish it myself, I beg it as a favor, so that here no one, even though I know not how worthy, should make me an exaggerator. My torment would be an ill reward; I wish belief."

"I believe you," answered the king.

"Truth itself was in his words," added Marya Ludvika. "I am not deceived in men."

"Gracious King and Queen, permit. Let some man go aside with me, for it would be grievous for me to live here in suspicion."

"I will go," said Pan Tyzenhaus, a young attendant of the king. So saying, he conducted Kmita to another room, and on the way said to him, "I do not go because I do not believe you, for I believe; but to speak with you. Have we met somewhere in Lithuania? I cannot remember your name, for it may be that I saw you when a youth, and I myself was a youth then?"

Kmita turned away his face somewhat to hide his sudden confusion.

"Perhaps at some provincial diet. My late father took me with him frequently to see public business."

"Perhaps. Your face is surely not strange to me, though at that time it had not those scars. Still see how *memoria fragilis est* (weak memory is); also it seems to me you had a different name."

"Years dull the memory," answered Pan Andrei.

They went to another room. After a while Tyzenhauz returned to the royal pair.

"He is roasted, Gracious King, as on a spit," said he; "his whole side is burned."

When Kmita in his turn came back, the king rose, pressed his head, and said, —

"We have never doubted that you speak the truth, and neither your pain nor your services will pass unrewarded."

"We are your debtors," added the queen, extending her hand to him.

Pan Andrei dropped on one knee and kissed with reverence the hand of the queen, who stroked him on the head like a mother.

"Be not angry with the chancellor," said the king. "In this place there are really not a few traitors, or, if not traitors, men who are unwise, that wind three after three, and it belongs to the chancellor's office to discover truth touching public affairs."

"What does my poor anger mean for such a great man?" answered Pan Andrei. "And I should not dare to murmur against a worthy senator, who gives an example of loyalty and love of country to all."

The chancellor smiled kindly and extended his hand. "Well, let there be peace! You spoke ill to me of wax; but know this, that the Korytsinskis have sealed often with blood, not with wax only."

The king was rejoiced. "This Babinich has pleased us," said he to the senators, "has touched our heart as few have. We will not let you go from our side, and God grant that we shall return together soon to our beloved country."

"Oh, Most Serene King," cried Kmita, with ecstasy; "though confined in the fortress of Yasna Gora, I know from the nobles, from the army, and even from those who, serving under Zbrojek and Kalinski, besieged Chenstohova, that all are waiting for the day and the hour of your return. Only show yourself, Gracious Lord, and that day all Lithuania, Poland, and Russia will stand by you as one man! The nobles will join; even insignificant peasants will go with their lord to resist. The army under the hetmans is barely breathing from eagerness to move against the Swedes. I know this, too, that at Chenstohova deputies came from the hetmans' troops to arouse Zbrojek, Kalinski, and Kuklinovski, against the Swedes. Appear on the boundary to-day, and in a week there will not be a Swede; only appear, only show yourself, for we are there like sheep without a shepherd."

Sparks came from Kmita's eyes while he was speaking, and such great ardor seized him that he knelt in the middle of the hall. His enthusiasm was communicated even to the queen herself, who, being of fearless courage, had long been persuading the king to return.

Therefore, turning to Yan Kazimir, she said with energy and determination: "I hear the voice of the whole people through the mouth of this noble."

"That is true, that is true, Gracious Lady, our Mother!" exclaimed Kmita.

But certain words in what Kmita had said struck the chancellor and the king.

"We have always been ready," said the king, "to sacrifice our health and life, and hitherto we have been waiting for nothing else but a change in our subjects."

"That change has taken place already," said Marya Ludvika.

"*Majestas infracta malis* (Majesty unbroken by misfortune)!" said Father Vydjga, looking at her with homage.

"It is important," said the archbishop, "if, really, deputations from the hetmans went to Chenstohova."

"I know this from my men, those Kyemliches," answered Pan Andrei. "In the squadrons of Zbrojek and Kalinski all spoke openly of this, paying no attention to Miller and the Swedes. These Kyemliches were not enclosed in the fortress; they had relations with the world, with soldiers and nobles, — I can bring them before your Royal Grace and your worthinesses; let them tell how it is seething in the whole country as in a pot. The hetmans joined the Swedes from constraint only; the troops wish to return to duty. The Swedes beat nobles and priests, plunder, violate ancient liberties; it is no wonder then that each man balls his fist and looks anxiously at his sabre."

"We, too, have had news from the troops," said the king; "there were here, also, secret envoys who told us of the general wish to return to former loyalty and honor."

"And that agrees with what this cavalier tells," said the chancellor. "But if deputations are passing among the regiments it is important, for it means that the fruit is already ripe, that our efforts were not vain, that our work is accomplished, that the time is at hand."

"But Konyetspolski," said the king, "and so many others who are still at the side of the invader, who look into his eyes and give assurances of their devotion?"

Then all grew silent, the king became gloomy on a sudden, and as when the sun goes behind a cloud a shadow covers at once the whole world, so did his face grow dark. After a time he said, —

"God sees in our heart that even to-day we are ready to move, and that not the power of Sweden detains us, but the unhappy fickleness of our people, who, like Proteus, take on a new form every moment. Can we believe that this change is sincere, this desire not imagined, this readiness not deceitful? Can we believe that people who so recently deserted us, and with such light hearts joined the invader against their own king, against their own country, against their own liberties? Pain straitens our heart, and we are ashamed of our own subjects! Where does history show such examples? What king has met so many treasons, so much ill-will? Who has been so deserted? Call to mind, your kindnesses, that we in the midst of our army, in the midst of those who were bound to shed their blood for us, — it is a danger and a terror to tell it, — we were not sure of our life. And if we left the country and had to seek an asylum, it is not from fear of the Swedish enemy, but of our own subjects, to save our own children from the terrible crime of king murder and parricide."

"Gracious Lord!" exclaimed Kmita; "our people have sinned grievously; they are guilty, and the hand of God is punishing them justly; but still, by the wounds of Christ, there has not been found among that people, and God grant that there will never be found, a man who would raise his hand on the sacred person of the anointed of God."

"You do not believe, because you are honest," said the king, "but we have letters and proofs. The Radzivills have paid us badly for the kindness with which we have covered them; but still Boguslav, though a traitor, was moved by conscience, and not only did he not wish to lend a hand to such a deed, but he was the first to warn us of it."

"What deed?" asked the astonished Kmita.

"He informed us," said the king, "that there was a man who offered for one hundred gold ducats to seize us and deliver us, living or dead, to the Swedes."

A shiver passed through the whole assembly at these words of the king, and Kmita was barely able to groan out the question, "Who was that man? — who was he?"

"A certain Kmita," answered the king.

A wave of blood suddenly struck Pan Andrei in the head, it grew dark in his eyes, he seized his forelock, and with a terribly wandering voice said: "That is a lie! Prince Boguslav lies like a dog! Gracious King, believe not that traitor; he did that of purpose to bring infamy on an enemy, and to frighten you, my king. He is a traitor! Kmita would not have done such a deed."

Here Pan Andrei turned suddenly where he was standing. His strength, exhausted by the siege, undermined by the explosion of powder in the great gun, and through the torture given by Kuklinovski, left him altogether, and he fell without consciousness at the feet of the king.

They bore him into the adjoining room, where the king's physician examined him. But in the assembly of dignitaries they knew not how to explain why the words of the king had produced such a terrible impression on the young man.

"Either he is so honest that horror alone has thrown him off his feet, or he is some relative of that Kmita," said the castellan of Cracow.

"We must ask him," replied the chancellor. "In Lithuania nobles are all related one to another, as in fact they are with us."

"Gracious Lord," said Tyzenhauz, "God preserve me from wishing to speak evil of this young man; but we should not trust him at present too much. That he served in Chenstohova is certain, — his side is burned; this the monks would not have done in any event, for they as servants of God must have every clemency, even for prisoners and traitors; but one thing is coming continually to my head and destroying trust in him, that is, I met him somewhere in Lithuania, — still a youth, at a diet or a carnival, — I don't remember — "

"And what of that?" asked the king.

"And it seems to me always that his name was not Babinich."

"Do not tell every little thing," said the king; "you are young and inattentive, and a thing might easily enter your head. Whether he is Babinich or not, why should I not trust him? Sincerity and truth are written on his lips, and evidently he has a golden heart. I should not trust myself, if I could not trust a soldier who has shed his blood for us and the country."

"He deserves more confidence than the letter of Prince

Boguslav," said the queen, suddenly, "and I recommend this to the consideration of your worthinesses, there may not be a word of truth in that letter. It might have been very important for the Radzivills of Birji that we should lose courage completely, and it is easy to admit that Prince Boguslav wished also to ruin some enemy of his, and leave a door open to himself in case of changed fortune."

"If I were not accustomed," said the primate, "to hear wisdom itself coming from the mouth of the gracious queen, I should be astonished at the quickness of these words, worthy of the ablest statesman — "

"*Comasque gerens, animosque viriles* (Though wearing tresses, she has the courage of a man)," interrupted Father Vydjga, in a low voice.

Encouraged by these words, the queen rose from her chair and began to speak : "I care not for the Radzivills of Birji, for they, as heretics, listen easily to the whispers of the enemy of the human race ; nor of the letter of Prince Boguslav, which may touch private affairs. But I am most pained by the despairing words of my lord and husband, the king, spoken against this people. For who will spare them if their own king condemns them ? And still, when I look through the world, I ask in vain, where is there another such people in which the praise of God endures with the manner of ancient sincerity and increases continually ? In vain do I look for another people in which such open candor exists. Where is there another State in which no one has heard of those hellish blasphemies, subtle crimes, and never-ending feuds with which foreign chronicles are filled. Let people skilled in the history of the world show me another kingdom where all the kings died their own quiet deaths. You have no knives or poisons here ; you have no protectors, as among the English. It is true that this nation has grown grievously guilty, has sinned through frivolity and license. But where is the nation that never errs, and where is the one which, as soon as it has recognized its offence, begins penance and reformation ? Behold they have already taken thought, they are now coming, beating their breasts to your majesty, ready to spill their blood, to yield their lives, to sacrifice their fortune for you. And will you reject them ; will you not forgive the penitent ; will you not trust those who have reformed, those who are doing penance ; will you not return the affection of a father to children who have erred ? Trust them, since they are yearning for their

Yagyellon blood, and for your government, which is of their
fathers. Go among them; I, a woman, fear no treason, for
I see love, I see sorrow for sins and restoration of this
kingdom to which they called you after your father and
your brother. It does not seem to me likely that God will
destroy such a great commonwealth, in which the light of
the true faith is burning. For a short period God's justice
has stretched forth the rod to chastise, not to ruin its children, and soon will the fatherly love of that heavenly Lord
receive them an cherish them. But do not contemn them,
O king, and fear not to confide in their sonly discretion, for
in this way alone can you turn evil into good, suffering into
comfort, defeat into triumph.'

When she had said this, the queen sat down, with fire
still in her eyes, and heaving breast; all looked at her with
veneration, and her chancellor, Vydjga, began to speak with
a resonant voice, —

> " Nulla sors longa est, dolor et voluptas,
> Invicens cedunt.
> Ima permutat brevis hora summis."

> (No fortune is long, pain and pleasure
> Yield in turn.
> A short hour changes the lowest with the highest.)

But no one heard what he said, for the ardor of the heroic
lady was communicated to every heart. The king himself
sprang up, with a flush on his sallow face, and said, —

"I have not lost the kingdom yet, since I have such a
queen. Let her will be done, for she spoke with prophetic
inspiration. The sooner I move and appear in my realms
the better."

To this the primate answered with seriousness: "I do
not wish to oppose the will of my gracious king and queen,
nor to turn them from an undertaking in which there is
hazard, but in which there may be also salvation. Still I
should consider it a wise thing to assemble in Opol, where
a majority of the senators are tarrying, and there listen to
the ideas of all; these may develop and explain the affair
more clearly and broadly."

"Then to Opol!" exclaimed the king, "and afterward to
the road, and what God will give!"

"God will give a happy return and victory!" said the
queen.

"Amen!" said the primate.

CHAPTER VIII.

PAN ANDREI fretted in his lodgings like a wounded wild-cat. The hellish revenge of Boguslav Radzivill brought him almost to madness. Not enough that that prince had sprung out of his hands, killed his men, almost deprived him of life; he had put upon him besides shame such as no one, not merely of his name, but no Pole from the beginning of the world, had ever groaned under.

There were moments when Kmita wished to leave everything — the glory which was opening before him, the service of the king — and fly away to avenge himself on that magnate whom he wanted to eat up alive.

But on the other hand, in spite of all his rage and the whirlwind in his head, he remembered that while the prince lived revenge would not vanish; and the best means, the only way to hurl back his calumny and lay bare all the infamy of his accusation, was precisely the service of the king; for in it he could show the world that not only had he not thought of raising his hand against the sacred person of Yan Kazimir, but that among all the nobles of Lithuania and Poland no person more loyal than Kmita could be found.

But he gnashed his teeth and was boiling like a stew; he tore his clothing, and long, long was it before he could calm himself. He gloated over the thought of revenge. He saw this Radzivill again in his hands; he swore by the memory of his father, that he must reach Boguslav even if death and torments were awaiting him therefor. And though the prince was a mighty lord whom not only the revenge of a common noble, but even the revenge of a king, could not easily touch; still, whoso knew that unrestrained soul better, would not have slept calmly, and more than once would have trembled before his vows.

And still Pan Andrei did not know yet that the prince had not merely covered him with shame and robbed him of repute.

Meanwhile the king, who from the first had conceived a great love for the young hero, sent Pan Lugovski to him that same day, and on the morrow commanded Kmita to accompany his majesty to Opol, where at a general assembly of the senators it was intended to deliberate on the return of the king to the country. Indeed there was something over which to deliberate. Lyubomirski, the marshal of the kingdom, had sent a new letter, announcing that everything in the country was ready for a general war, and urging earnestly the return. Besides this, news was spread of a certain league of nobles and soldiers formed for the defence of the king and the country, concerning which men had really been thinking for some time, but which, as appeared afterward, was concluded a little later, under the name of the Confederation of Tishovtsi.

All minds were greatly occupied by the news, and immediately after a thanksgiving Mass they assembled in a secret council, to which, at the instance of the king, Kmita too was admitted, since he had brought news from Chenstohova.

They began then to discuss whether the return was to take place at once, or whether it were better to defer it till the army, not only by wish, but by deed, should abandon the Swedes.

Yan Kazimir put an end to these discussions by saying: "Do not discuss, your worthinesses, the return, or whether it is better to defer it awhile, for I have taken counsel already concerning that with God and the Most Holy Lady. Therefore I communicate to you that whatever may happen we shall move in person these days. Express your ideas therefore, your worthinesses, and be not sparing of counsel as to how our return may be best and most safely accomplished."

Opinions were various. Some advised not to trust too greatly to the marshal of the kingdom, who had once shown hesitation and disobedience, when, instead of giving the crown to the emperor for safe keeping, according to the order of the king, he had carried it to Lyubovlya. "Great," said they, "is the pride and ambition of that lord, and if he should have the person of the king in his castle, who knows what he might do, or what he would ask for his services; who knows that he would not try, or wish to seize the whole government in his own hands, and become the protector, not only of the entire country, but of the king?"

These advised the king therefore to wait for the retreat

of the Swedes and repair to Chenstohova, as to the place from which grace and rebirth had spread over the Commonwealth. But others gave different opinions, —

"The Swedes are yet at Chenstohova, and though by the grace of God they will not capture the place, still there are no unoccupied roads. All the districts about there are in Swedish hands. The enemy are at Kjepitsi, Vyelunie, Cracow; along the boundary also considerable forces are disposed. In the mountains near the Hungarian border, where Lyubovlya is situated, there are no troops save those of the marshal; the Swedes have never gone to that distance, not having men enough nor daring sufficient. From Lyubovlya it is nearer to Russia, which is free of hostile occupation, and to Lvoff, which has not ceased to be loyal, and to the Tartars, who, according to information, are coming with succor; all these are waiting specially for the decision of the king."

"As to Pan Lyubomirski," said the Bishop of Cracow, "his ambition will be satisfied with this, that he will receive the king first in his starostaship of Spij, and will surround him with protection. The government will remain with the king, but the hope itself of great services will satisfy the marshal. If he wishes to tower above all others through his loyalty, then, whether his loyalty flows from ambition or from love to the king and the country, his majesty will always receive notable profit."

This opinion of a worthy and experienced bishop seemed the most proper; therefore it was decided that the king should go through the mountains to Lyubovlya, and thence to Lvoff, or whithersoever circumstances might indicate.

They discussed also the day of returning; but the voevoda of Lenchytsk, who had just come from his mission to the emperor for aid, said that it was better not to fix the date, but to leave the decision to the king, so that the news might not be spread and the enemy forewarned. They decided only this, that the king would move on with three hundred dragoons, under command of Tyzenhauz, who, though young, enjoyed already the reputation of a great soldier.

But still more important was the second part of the deliberations, in which it was voted unanimously that on his arrival in the country, government and the direction of the war should pass into the hands of the king, whom nobles, troops, and hetmans were to obey in all things. They spoke besides of the future, and touched upon the causes of those sudden misfortunes which, as a deluge, had covered the whole land in such a brief period. And the primate himself gave no other cause for this than the disorder, want of obedience, and excessive contempt for the office and majesty of the king.

He was heard in silence, for each man understood that it was a question here of the fate of the Commonwealth, and of great, hitherto unexampled changes in it, which might bring back the ancient power of the State, and which was long desired by the wise queen who loved her adopted country.

From the mouth of the worthy prince of the church there came words like thunderbolts, and the souls of the hearers opened to the truth, almost as flowers open to the sun.

"Not against ancient liberties do I rise," said the primate, "but against that license which with its own hands is murdering the country. In very truth men have forgotten in this Commonwealth the distinction between freedom and license; and as excessive pleasure ends in pain, so freedom unchecked has ended in slavery. You have descended to such error, citizens of this illustrious Commonwealth, that only he among you passes for a defender of liberty who raises an uproar, who breaks diets and opposes the king, not when it is needful, but when for the king it is a question of saving the country. In our treasury the bottom of the chest can be seen; the soldier unpaid seeks pay of the enemy; the diets, the only foundation of this Commonwealth, are dissolved after having done nothing, for one disorderly man, one evil citizen, for his own private purpose may prevent deliberation. What manner of liberty is that which permits one man to stand against all? If that is freedom for one man, then it is bondage for all others. And where have we gone with the use of this freedom which seemed such sweet fruit? Behold one weak enemy, against whom our ancestors gained so many splendid victories, now *sicut fulgur exit ab occidente et poret usque ad orientem* (flashes like lightning from the west, and goes as far as the east). No one opposes him, traitorous heretics aided him, and he seized possession of all things; he persecutes the faith, he desecrates churches, and when you speak of your liberties he shows you the sword. Behold what your provincial diets have come to, what your veto has come to, what your license has come to, your degradation of the king at every step. Your king, the natural defender of the country, you have rendered, first of all, powerless, and then you complain that he does not defend you. You did not want your own government, and now the enemy is governing. And who, I ask, can save us in this fall, who can bring back ancient glory to this Commonwealth, if not he who has spent so much of his life and time for it; when the unhappy domestic war with the Cossacks tore it, who exposed his consecrated person to dangers such as no monarch in our time has passed through; who at Zborovo, at Berestechko, and at Jvanyets fought like a common soldier, bearing toils and hardships beyond his station of king? To him now we will confide ourselves; to him, with the example of the ancient Romans, we will give the dictatorship, and take counsel ourselves how to save in time coming this fatherland from domestic enemies, from vice, license, disorder, disobedience, and restore due dignity to the government and the king."

So spoke the primate; and misfortune with the experience of recent times had changed his hearers in such a degree that no man protested, for all saw clearly that either the power of the king must be strengthened, or the Commonwealth must perish without fail. They began therefore to consider in various ways how to bring the counsels of the primate into practice. The king and queen listened to them eagerly and with joy, especially the queen, who had labored long and earnestly at the introduction of order into the Commonwealth.

The king returned then to Glogov glad and satisfied, and summoning a number of confidential officers, among whom was Kmita, he said, —

" I am impatient, my stay in this country is burning me, I could wish to start even to-morrow; therefore I have called you, as men of arms and experience, to provide ready methods. It is a pity that we should lose time, when our presence may hasten considerably a general war."

" In truth," said Lugovski, "if such is the will of your Royal Grace, why delay? The sooner the better."

" While the affair is not noised about and the enemy do not double their watchfulness," added Colonel Wolf.

" The enemy are already on their guard, and have taken possession of the roads so far as they are able," said Kmita.

" How is that?" asked the king.

" Gracious Lord, your intended return is no news for the Swedes. Almost every day a report travels over the whole Commonwealth, that your Royal Grace is already on the road, or even now in your realms, *inter regna.* Therefore it is necessary to observe the greatest care, and to hurry by through narrow places stealthily, for Douglas's scouts are waiting on the roads."

" The best carefulness," said Tyzenhauz, looking at Kmita, "is three hundred faithful sabres; and if my gracious lord gives me command over them, I will conduct him in safety, even over the breasts of Douglas's scouts."

" You will conduct if there are just three hundred, but suppose that you meet six hundred or a thousand, or come upon a superior force waiting in ambush, what then ? "

" I said three hundred," answered Tyzenhauz, " for three hundred were mentioned. If however that is too small a party, we can provide five hundred and even more."

" God save us from that. The larger the party, the more noise will it make," said Kmita.

" I think that the marshal of the kingdom will come out to meet us with his squadrons," put in the king.

" The marshal will not come out," answered Kmita, " for he will not know the day and the hour, and even if he did know some delay might happen on the road, as is usual ; it is difficult to foresee everything."

" A soldier says that, a genuine soldier ! " said the king. " It is clear that you are not a stranger to war."

Kmita laughed, for he remembered his attacks on Hovanski. Who was more skilled than he in such actions ? To whom could the escort of the king be entrusted with more judgment ?

But Tyzenhauz was evidently of a different opinion from the king, for he frowned and said with sarcasm against Kmita, " We wait then for your enlightened counsel."

Kmita felt ill will in the words ; therefore he fixed his glance on Tyzenhauz and answered, —

" My opinion is that the smaller the party the easier it will pass."

" How is that ? "

" The will of your Royal Grace is unfettered," said Kmita, " and can do what it likes, but my reason teaches me this : Let Pan Tyzenhauz go ahead with the dragoons, giving out purposely that he is conducting the king ; this he will do to attract the enemy to himself. His affair is to wind out, to escape from the trap safely. And we with a small band in a day or two will move after him with your Royal Grace ;

and when the enemy's attention is turned in another direction it will be easy for us to reach Lyubovlya."

The king clapped his hands with delight. "God sent us
this soldier!" cried he. "Solomon could not judge better. I
give my vote for this plan, and there must not be another.
They will hunt for the king among the dragoons, and the king
will pass by under their noses. It could not be better!"

"Gracious King," cried Tyzenhauz, "that is pastime."

"Soldier's pastime!" said the king. "But no matter, I
will not recede from that plan."

Kmita's eyes shone from delight because his opinion had
prevailed, but Tyzenhauz sprang from his seat.

"Gracious Lord!" said he, "I resign my command from
the dragoons. Let some one else lead them."

"And why is that?"

"For if your Royal Grace will go without defence, exposed to the play of fortune, to every destructive chance
which may happen, I wish to be near your person to expose
my breast for you and to die should the need be."

"I thank you for your sincere intention," answered Yan
Kazimir; "but calm yourself, for in just such a way as
Babinich advises shall I be least exposed."

"Let Pan Babinich, or whatever his name may be, take
what he advises on his own responsibility! It may concern
him that your Royal Grace be lost in the mountains. I take
as witness God and my companions here present that I advised against it from my soul."

Scarcely had he finished speaking when Kmita sprang up,
and standing face to face with Tyzenhauz asked, "What do
you mean by these words?"

Tyzenhauz measured him haughtily with his eyes from
head to foot, and said, "Do not strain your head, little man,
toward mine, the place is too high for you."

To which Kmita with lightning in his eyes replied, "It is
not known for whom it would be too high if —"

"If what?" asked Tyzenhauz, looking at him quickly.

"If I should reach higher people than you."

Tyzenhauz laughed. "But where would you seek them?"

"Silence!" said the king suddenly, with a frown. "Do
not begin a quarrel in my presence."

Yan Kazimir made an impression of such dignity on all
surrounding him, that both young men were silent and confused, remembering that in the presence of the king un-
seemly words had escaped them. But the king added, —

"No one has the right to exalt himself above that cavalier who burst the siege gun and escaped from Swedish hands, even though his father lived in a village, which, as I see, was not the case, for a bird from his feathers, and blood from deeds are easily known. Drop your offences." Here the king turned to Tyzenhauz. "You wish it; then remain with our person. We may not refuse that. Wolf or Denhoff will lead the dragoons. But Babinich too will remain, and we will go according to his counsel, for he has pleased our heart."

"I wash my hands!" said Tyzenhauz.

"Only preserve the secret, gentlemen. Let the dragoons go to Ratibor to-day, and spread as widely as possible the report that I am with them. And then be on the watch, for you know not the day nor the hour — Go, Tyzenhauz, give the order to the captain of the dragoons."

Tyzenhauz went out wringing his hands from anger and sorrow; after him went other officers.

That same day the news thundered through all Glogov that the king had already gone to the boundaries of the Commonwealth. Even many distinguished senators thought that the departure had really taken place. Couriers, sent purposely, took the report to Opol and to the roads on the boundary.

Tyzenhauz, though he had declared that he washed his hands, did not give up the affair as lost; as attendant of the king, he had access to the person of the monarch every moment made easy. That very day therefore, after the dragoons had gone, he stood before the face of Yan Kazimir, or rather before both royal persons, for Marya Ludvika was present.

"I have come for the order," said he; "when do we start?"

"The day after to-morrow, before dawn."

"Are many people to go?"

"You will go; Lugovski with the soldiers. The castellan of Sandomir goes also with me. I begged him to take as few men as possible; but we cannot dispense with a few trusty and tried sabres. Besides, his holiness the nuncio wishes to accompany me; his presence will add importance, and will touch all who are faithful to the true church. He does not hesitate therefore to expose his sacred person to hazard. Do you have a care that there are not more than forty horses, for that is Babinich's counsel."

"Gracious Lord!" said Tyzenhauz.

"And what do you wish yet?"

"On my knees I implore one favor. The question is settled, the dragoons have gone, — we shall travel without defence, and the first scouting party of a few tens of horses may capture us. Listen, your Royal Grace, to the prayer of your servant, on whose faithfulness God is looking, and do not trust in everything to that noble. He is an adroit man, since he has been able in so short a time to steal into your heart and favor; but —"

"Do you envy him?" interrupted the king.

"I do not envy him, Gracious Lord; I do not wish even to suspect him of treason positively; but I would swear that his name is not Babinich. Why does he hide his real name? Why is it somehow inconvenient to tell what he did before the siege of Chenstohova? Why specially has he insisted upon dragoons going out first, and that your Royal Grace should go without an escort?"

The king thought awhile, and began, according to his custom, to pout his lips repeatedly.

"If it were a question of collusion with the Swedes," said he at last, "what could three hundred dragoons do? What power would they be, and what protection? Babinich would need merely to notify the Swedes to dispose a few hundred infantry along the roads, and they could take us as in a net. But only think if there can be a question of treason here. He would have had to know beforehand the date of our journey, and to inform the Swedes in Cracow; and how could he do so, since we move the day after to-morrow? He could not even guess that we would choose his plan; we might have gone according to your suggestion or that of others. It was at first decided to go with the dragoons; then if he wished to talk with the Swedes this special party would have confused his arrangements, for he would have to send out new messengers and give fresh notice. All these are irrefragable reasons. And besides he did not insist at all on his opinion, as you say; he only offered, as did others, what seemed to him best. No, no! Sincerity is looking forth from the eyes of that noble, and his burned side bears witness that he is ready to disregard even torture."

"His Royal Grace is right," said the queen, on a sudden; "these points are irrefragable, and the advice was and is good."

Tyzenhauz knew from experience that when the queen gave her opinion it would be vain for him to appeal to the king, Yan Kazimir had such confidence in her wit and penetration. And it was a question now with the young man only that the king should observe needful caution.

"It is not my duty," answered he, "to oppose my king and queen. But if we are to go the day after to-morrow, let this Babinich not know of it till the hour of departure."

"That may be," said the king.

"And on the road I will have an eye on him, and should anything happen he will not go alive from my hands."

"You will not have to act," said the queen. "Listen; not you will preserve the king from evil happenings on the road, from treason, and snares of the enemy; not you, not Babinich, not the dragoons, not the powers of earth, but the Providence of God, whose eye is turned continually on the shepherds of nations and the anointed of the Lord. It will guard him. It will protect him and bring him safely; and in case of need, send him assistance, of which you do not even think, you who believe in earthly power only."

"Most Serene Lady!" answered Tyzenhauz, "I believe, too, that without the will of God not a hair will fall from the head of any man; but to guard the king's person through fear of traitors is no sin for me."

Marya Ludvika smiled graciously. "But you suspect too hastily, and thus cast shame on a whole nation, in which, as this same Babinich has said, there has not yet been found one to raise his hand against his own king. Let it not astonish you that after such desertion, after such a breaking of oaths and faith as the king and I have experienced, I say still that no one has dared such a terrible crime, not even those who to-day serve the Swedes."

"Prince Boguslav's letter, Gracious Lady?"

"That letter utters untruth," said the queen, with decision. "If there is a man in the Commonwealth ready to betray even the king, that man is Prince Boguslav, for he in name only belongs to this people."

"Speaking briefly, do not put suspicion on Babinich," said the king. "As to his name, it must be doubled in your head. Besides, we may ask him; but how can we say to him here, how inquire, 'If you are not Babinich, then what is your name?' Such a question might pain an honest man terribly, and I'll risk my head that he is an honest man."

"At such a price, Gracious Lord, I would not convince myself of his honesty."

"Well, well, we are thankful for your care. To-morrow for prayer and penance, and the day after to the road, to the road!"

Tyzenhauz withdrew with a sigh, and in the greatest secrecy began preparations that very day for the journey. Even dignitaries who were to accompany the king were not all informed of the time. But the servants were ordered to have horses in readiness, for they might start any day for Ratibor.

The king did not show himself the entire following day, even in the church; but he lay in the form of a cross in his own room till night, fasting and imploring the King of kings for aid, not for himself, but for the Commonwealth.

Marya Ludvika, together with her ladies-in-waiting, was also in prayer.

Then the following night freshened the strength of the wearied ones; and when in darkness the Glogov church-bell sounded to matins, the hour had struck for the journey.

CHAPTER IX.

THEY rode through Ratibor, merely stopping to feed the horses. No one recognized the king, no one paid much attention to the party, for all were occupied with the recent passage of the dragoons, among whom, as all thought, was the King of Poland. The retinue was about fifty in number, for several dignitaries accompanied the king; five bishops alone, and among others the nuncio, ventured to share with him the toils of a journey not without peril. The road within the boundary of the empire, however, presented no danger. At Oderberg, not far from the junction of the Olsha with the Odra, they entered Moravia.

The day was cloudy, and snow fell so thickly that it was not possible to see the road a few steps ahead. But the king was joyous and full of courage, for a sign had been manifested which all considered most favorable, and which contemporary historians did not neglect to insert in their chronicles. Behold, just as the king was departing from Glogov, a little bird, entirely white, appeared before his horse and began to circle round, rising at times in the air, at times coming down to the head of the king, chirping and twittering joyously meanwhile. They remembered that a similar bird, but black, had circled over the king when he was retreating from Warsaw before the Swedes.

But this was white, exactly of the size and form of a swallow; which fact roused the greater wonder, because it was deep winter, and swallows were not thinking yet of return. But all were rejoiced, and the king for the first few days spoke of nothing else, and promised himself the most successful future. It appeared from the beginning, too, how sound was Kmita's advice to travel apart.

Everywhere in Moravia people were telling of the recent passage of the King of Poland. Some stated that they had seen him with their own eyes, all in armor, with a sword in his hand and a crown on his head. Various stories, also, were current of the forces which he had with him, and in general the number of his dragoons was exaggerated to the fabulous. There were some who had seen ten thousand,

and who could not wait till the last horses, men, gunners, and flags had passed.

"Surely," said they, "the Swedes will spring before them, but what they will do with such a force is unknown."

"Well," asked the king of Tyzenhauz, "was not Babinich right?"

"We are not in Lyubovlya yet, Gracious Lord," replied the young magnate.

Babinich was satisfied with himself and with the journey. Generally he went ahead of the king's party with the three Kyemliches, examining the road; sometimes he rode with the rest, entertaining the king with narratives of single incidents in the siege of Chenstohova, of which the king never had enough. And almost every hour that young hero, cheerful, mettlesome, eagle-like, drew nearer the heart of the king. Time passed for the monarch now in prayer, now in pious meditation on eternal life, now in discussing the coming war and the aid hoped from the emperor, and finally in looking at knightly amusements with which the attendant soldiers endeavored to shorten the time of the journey. For Yan Kazimir had this in his nature, that his mind passed easily from seriousness almost to frivolity, from hard labor to amusements, to which, when there was leisure, he gave himself with his whole soul, as if no care, no grief had pressed him at any time.

The soldiers then exhibited themselves, each with what he could do; the Kyemliches, Kosma, and Damian, immense and awkward figures, amused the king by breaking horse-shoes, which they broke like canes; he paid them a thaler apiece, though his wallet was empty enough, for all his money, and even the diamonds and "parafanaly" (paraphernalia) of the queen, had been spent on the army.

Pan Andrei exhibited himself by throwing a heavy hatchet, which he hurled upward with such force that it was barely visible, and then he sprang under the instrument with his horse and caught it by the handle as it fell. At sight of this the king clapped his hands.

"I saw that done," said he, "by Pan Slushka, brother of the vice-chancellor's wife, but he threw not so high by half."

"This is customary with us in Lithuania," said Pan Andrei; "and when a man practises it from childhood he becomes skilful."

"Whence have you those scars across the lip?" asked the king of him once, pointing to Kmita's scars. "Some one went through you well with a sabre."

"That is not from a sabre, Gracious Lord, but from a bullet. I was fired at by a man who put the pistol to my mouth."

"An enemy or one of ours?"

"One of ours; but an enemy whom I shall yet call to account, and till that happens it is not proper for me to speak of it."

"Have you such animosity as that?"

"I have no animosity, Gracious Lord, for on my head I bear a still deeper scar from a sabre, through which cut my soul almost left me; but since an honorable man did it I harbor no offence against him." Kmita removed his cap and showed the king a deep furrow, the white edges of which were perfectly visible. "I am not ashamed of this wound," said he, "for it was given me by such a master that there is not another like him in the Commonwealth."

"Who is such a master?"

"Pan Volodyovski."

"For God's sake! I know him. He did wonders at Zbaraj. And I was at the wedding of his comrade, Skshetuski, who was the first to bring me news of the besieged. Those are great cavaliers! And with them was a third, him the whole army glorified as the greatest of all. A fat noble, and so amusing that we almost burst our sides from laughter."

"That is Pan Zagloba, I think!" said Kmita; "he is a man not only brave, but full of wonderful stratagems."

"Do you know what they are doing now?"

"Volodyovski used to lead dragoons with the voevoda of Vilna."

The king frowned. "And is he serving the Swedes now with the prince voevoda?"

"He! The Swedes? He is with Pan Sapyeha. I saw myself how, after the treason of the prince, he threw his baton at his feet."

"Oh, he is a worthy soldier!" answered the king. "From Pan Sapyeha we have had news from Tykotsin, where he is besieging the voevoda. God give him luck! If all were like him, the Swedish enemy would regret their undertaking."

Here Tyzenhauz, who had been listening to the conversation, asked suddenly, "Then were you with Radzivill at Kyedani?"

Kmita was somewhat confused, and began to throw up his hatchet. "I was," answered he.

"Give peace to your hatchet," said Tyzenhauz. "And what were you doing at the prince's house?"

"I was a guest," answered Kmita, impatiently, "and I ate his bread, until I was disgusted with his treason."

"And why did you not go with other honorable soldiers to Pan Sapyeha?"

"Because I had made a vow to go to Chenstohova, which you will more easily understand when I tell you that our Ostra Brama was occupied by the Northerners."

Tyzenhauz began to shake his head and smack his lips; this attracted the attention of the king, so that he looked inquiringly at Kmita. The latter, made impatient, turned to Tyzenhauz and said, —

"My worthy sir! Why do I not inquire of you where you have been, and what you have been doing?"

"Ask me," replied Tyzenhauz; "I have nothing to conceal."

"Neither am I before a court; and if I shall ever be, you will not be my judge. Leave me, then, that I lose not my patience."

When he had said this, he hurled the hatchet so sharply that it grew small in the height; the king raised his eyes after it, and at that moment he was thinking of nothing save this, would Babinich catch it in its fall, or would he not catch it?

Babinich put spurs to his horse, sprang forward, and caught it. That same evening Tyzenhauz said to the king, —

"Gracious Lord, this noble pleases me less and less."

"But me more and more," answered the king, pursing his lips.

"I heard to-day one of his people call him colonel; he only looked threateningly, and straightway confused the man. There is something in that."

"And it seems to me sometimes that he does not wish to tell everything," added the king; "but that is his affair."

"No, Gracious Lord," exclaimed Tyzenhauz, forcibly, "it is not his affair, it is our affair, and that of the whole Commonwealth. For if he is some traitor who is planning the death or captivity of your Royal Grace, then with your person will perish all those who at this moment have taken arms; the whole Commonwealth will perish, which you alone are competent to save."

"I will ask him myself to-morrow."

"God grant that I be a false prophet, but nothing good looks out of his eyes. He is too smart, too bold, too daring; and such people are ready for anything."

The king looked troubled. Next morning, when they moved on their journey, he beckoned Kmita to approach him.

"Where were you, Colonel?" asked the king, suddenly.

A moment of silence followed.

Kmita struggled with himself; the wish was burning him to spring from his horse, fall at the feet of the king, and throw off the burden he was bearing, — tell the whole truth at once. But he thought of the fearful impression which the name Kmita would make, especially after the letter of Prince Boguslav Radzivill. How could he, who had been the right hand of Radzivill, who had maintained the preponderance of Prince Yanush, who had aided him in scattering his disobedient squadrons, who supported him in treason; how could he, accused and suspected of the most terrible crime, — an attack on the person of the king, — succeed in convincing the king, the bishops, and senators, that he had corrected himself, that he was transformed? With what could he show the sincerity of his intentions? What proofs could he bring save naked words? His former offences pursue him unceasingly, unsparingly, as furious dogs a wild beast in the forest. He determined on silence. But he felt also unspeakable disgust and hatred of subterfuge. Must he throw dust in the eyes of the king, whom he loved with all the power of his soul, and deceive him with fictitious tales?

He felt that strength failed him for this; therefore he said, after a while: "Gracious King, the time will come, perhaps soon, in which I shall open my whole soul to your Royal Grace as in confession to a priest. But I wish deeds to vouch for me, for my sincere intention, for my loyalty and my love of majesty, not words simply. I have offended against you, my Gracious Lord, and the country, and I have repented too little yet; therefore I am seeking service in which I can find reparation more easily. Besides, who has not offended? Who in the whole Commonwealth does not need to beat his breast? It may be that I have offended more grievously than others, but I was the first also to bethink myself. Do not inquire, Gracious Lord, about anything until the present service will convince you concerning me; do not ask, for I cannot answer without closing the road of salvation to myself, for God is the witness, and the Most Holy Lady, our Queen, that I had no evil intent, that I am ready to give the last drop of my blood for you."

Here Pan Andrei's eyes grew moist, and such sincerity and sorrow appeared on his face that his countenance defended him with greater power than his words.

"God is looking at my intentions," said he, " and will account them to me at judgment. But, Gracious Lord, if you do not trust me, dismiss me, remove me from your person. I will follow at a distance, so as to come in time of difficulty, even without being called, and lay down my life for you. And then, Gracious Lord, you will believe that I am not a traitor, but one of that kind of servants of whom you have not many, even among those who cast suspicion on others."

"I believe you to-day," said the king. "Remain near our person as before, for treason does not speak in such fashion."

"I thank your Royal Grace," answered Kmita; and reining in his horse somewhat, he pushed back among the last ranks of the party.

But Tyzenhauz did not limit himself to conveying suspicions to the king. The result was that all began to look askance at Kmita. Audible conversation ceased at his approach, and whispers began. Every movement of his was followed, every word considered. Kmita noticed this, and was ill at ease among these men.

Even the king, though he did not remove confidence from him, had not for Pan Andrei such a joyful countenance as before. Therefore the young hero lost his daring, grew gloomy, sadness and bitterness took possession of his heart. Formerly in front, among the first, he used to make his horse prance ; now he dragged on many yards behind the cavalcade, with hanging head and gloomy thoughts.

At last the Carpathians stood white before the travellers. Snow lay on their slopes, clouds spread their unwieldy bodies on the summits ; and when an evening came clear at sunset, those mountains put on flaming garments from which marvellously bright gleams went forth till quenched in the darkness embracing the whole world. Kmita gazed on those wonders of nature which to that time he had never seen; and though greatly grieved, he forgot his cares from admiration and wonder.

Each day those giants grew greater, more mighty, till at last the retinue of the king came to them and entered a pass which opened on a sudden, like a gate.

"The boundary must be near," said the king, with emotion.

Then they saw a small wagon, drawn by one horse, and in the wagon a peasant. The king's men stopped him at once.

"Man," said Tyzenhauz, "are we in Poland?"

"Beyond that cliff and that little river is the emperor's boundary, but you are standing on the king's land."

"Which way is it then to Jivyets?"

"Go straight ahead; you will come to the road." And the mountaineer whipped his horse.

Tyzenhauz galloped to the retinue standing at a distance.

"Gracious Lord," cried he, with emotion, "you are now *inter regna*, for at that little river your kingdom begins."

The king said nothing, only made a sign to hold his horse, dismounted, and throwing himself on his knees, raised his eyes and his hands upward.

At sight of this, all dismounted and followed his example. That king, then a wanderer, fell after a moment in the form of a cross on the snow, and began to kiss that land, so beloved and so thankless, which in time of disaster had refused refuge to his head.

Silence followed, and only sighs interrupted it.

The evening was frosty, clear; the mountains and the summits of the neighboring fir-trees were in purple, farther off in the shadow they had begun to put on violet; but the road on which the king was lying turned as it were into a ruddy and golden ribbon, and rays fell on the king, bishops, and dignitaries.

Then a breeze began from the summits, and bearing on its wings sparks of snow, flew to the valley. Therefore the nearer fir-trees began to bend their snow-covered heads, bow to their lord, and to make a joyous and rustling sound, as if they were singing that old song, "Be welcome to us, thou dear master!"

Darkness had already filled the air when the king's retinue moved forward. Beyond the defile was spread out a rather roomy plain, the other end of which was lost in the distance. Light was dying all around; only in one place the sky was still bright with red. The king began to repeat *Ave Maria;* after him the others with concentration of spirit repeated the pious words.

Their native land, unvisited by them for a long time; the mountains which night was now covering; the dying twilight, the prayer, — all these caused a solemnity of heart and mind; hence after the prayer the king, the dignitaries, and the knights rode on in silence. Night fell, but in the east the sky was shining still more redly.

"Let us go toward that twilight," said the king, at last; "it is a wonder that it is shining yet."

Then Kmita galloped up. "Gracious Lord, that is a fire!" cried he.

All halted.

"How is that?" asked the king; "it seems to me that 't is the twilight."

"A fire, a fire! I am not mistaken!" cried Kmita.

And indeed, of all of the attendants of the king he knew most in that matter. At last it was no longer possible to doubt, since above that supposed twilight were rising as it were red clouds, rolling now brighter, now darker in turn.

"It is as if Jivyets were burning!" cried the king; "maybe the enemy is ravaging it."

He had not finished speaking when to their ears flew the noise of men, the snorting of horses, and a number of dark figures appeared before the retinue.

"Halt, halt!" cried Tyzenhauz.

These figures halted, as if uncertain what to do farther.

"Who are you?" was asked from the retinue.

"Ours!" said a number of voices. "Ours! We are escaping with our lives from Jivyets. The Swedes are burning Jivyets, and murdering people."

"Stop, in God's name! What do you say? Whence have they come?"

"They were waiting for our king. There is a power of them, a power! May the Mother of God have the king in Her keeping!"

Tyzenhauz lost his head for a moment. "See what it is to go with a small party!" cried he to Kmita; "would that you were killed for such counsel!"

Yan Kazimir began to inquire himself of the fugitives. "But where is the king?"

"The king has gone to the mountains with a great army. Two days ago he passed through Jivyets; they pursued him,

and were fighting somewhere near Suha. We have not heard
whether they took him or not; but to-day they returned to
Jivyets, and are burning and murdering."

"Go with God!" said Yan Kazimir.

The fugitives shot past quickly.

"See what would have met us had we gone with the
dragoons!" exclaimed Kmita.

"Gracious King!" said Father Gembitski, "the enemy
is before us. What are we to do?"

All surrounded the monarch, as if wishing to protect him
with their persons from sudden danger. The king gazed
on that fire which was reflected in his eyes, and he was
silent; no one advanced an opinion, so difficult was it to
give good advice.

"When I was going out of the country a fire lighted
me," said Yan Kazimir, at last; "and when I enter, another
gives light."

Again silence, only still longer than before.

"Who has any advice?" inquired Father Gembitski,
at last.

Then the voice of Tyzenhauz was heard, full of bitterness,
and insult: "He who did not hesitate to expose the king's
person to danger, who said that the king should go without
a guard, let him now give advice."

At this moment a horseman pushed out of the circle.
It was Kmita.

"Very well!" said he. And rising in the stirrups he
shouted, turning to his attendants standing at some distance, "Kyemliches, after me!"

Then he urged his horse to a gallop, and after him shot
the three horsemen with all the breath that was in the
breasts of their horses.

A cry of despair came from Tyzenhauz: "That is a conspiracy!" said he. "These traitors will give us up surely.
Gracious King, save yourself while there is time, for the
enemy will soon close the pass! Gracious King, save
yourself! Back! back!"

"Let us return, let us return!" cried the bishops and
dignitaries, in one voice.

Yan Kazimir became impatient, lightnings flashed from
his eyes; suddenly he drew his sword from its sheath and
cried, —

"May God not grant me to leave my country a second
time. Come what may, I have had enough of that!" And

he put spurs to his horse to move forward; but the nuncio himself seized the reins.

"Your Royal Grace," said he, seriously, "you bear on your shoulders the fate of the Catholic Church and the country, therefore you are not free to expose your person."

"Not free," repeated the bishops.

"I will not return to Silesia, so help me the Holy Cross!" answered Yan Kazimir.

"Gracious Lord! listen to the prayers of your subjects," said the castellan of Sandomir. "If you do not wish to return to the emperor's territory, let us go at least from this place and turn toward the Hungarian boundary, or let us go back through this pass, so that our return be not intercepted. There we will wait. In case of an attack by the enemy, escape on horses will remain to us; but at least let them not enclose us as in a trap."

"Let it be even so," said the king. "I do not reject prudent counsel, but I will not go wandering a second time. If we cannot appear by this road, we will by another. But I think that you are alarmed in vain. Since the Swedes looked for us among the dragoons, as the people from Jivyets said, it is clear proof that they know nothing of us, and that there is no treason or conspiracy. Just consider; you are men of experience. The Swedes would not have attacked the dragoons, they would not have fired a gun at them if they knew that we were following them. Be calm, gentlemen! Babinich has gone with his men for news, and he will return soon of a certainty."

When he had said this the king turned his horse toward the pass; after him his attendants. They halted on the spot where the first mountaineer had shown them the boundary.

A quarter of an hour passed, then a half-hour and an hour.

"Have you noticed, gentlemen," asked the voevoda of Lenchytsk on a sudden, "that the fire is decreasing?"

"It is going out, going out; you can almost see it die," said a number of voices.

"That is a good sign," said the king.

"I will go ahead with a few men," said Tyzenhauz. "We will halt about a furlong from here, and if the Swedes come we will detain them till we die. In every case there will be time to think of the safety of the king's person."

"Remain with the party; I forbid you to go!" said the king.

To which Tyzenhauz answered, —

"Gracious Lord, give command later to shoot me for disobedience, but now I will go, for now it is a question of you." And calling upon a number of soldiers in whom it was possible to trust in every emergency, he moved forward.

They halted at the other end of the defile which opened into the valley, and stood in silence, with muskets ready, holding their ears toward every sound. The silence lasted long; finally the sound of snow trampled by horses' feet came to them.

"They are coming!" whispered one of the soldiers.

"That is no party; only a few horses are to be heard," answered the other. "Pan Babinich is returning."

Meanwhile those approaching came in the darkness within a few tens of yards.

"Who is there?" cried Tyzenhauz.

"Ours! Do not fire there!" sounded the voice of Kmita.

At that moment he appeared before Tyzenhauz, and not knowing him in the darkness, inquired, —

"But where is the king?"

"At the end of the pass."

"Who is speaking, for I cannot see?"

"Tyzenhauz. But what is that great bundle which you have before you?" And he pointed to some dark form hanging before Kmita, on the front of the saddle.

Pan Andrei made no answer, but rode on. When he had reached the king's escort, he recognized the person of the king, for it was much clearer beyond the pass, and cried, —

"Gracious Lord, the road is open!"

"Are there no Swedes in Jivyets?"

"They have gone to Vadovitsi. That was a party of German mercenaries. But here is one of them, Gracious Lord; ask him yourself." And Pan Andrei pushed to the ground that form which he held before him, so that a groan was heard in the still night.

"Who is that?" asked the astonished king.

"A horseman!"

"As God is dear to me! And you have brought an informant! How is that? Tell me."

"Gracious Lord, when a wolf prowls in the night around a

flock of sheep it is easy for him to seize one; and besides, to tell the truth, this is not the first time with me."

The king raised his hands. "But this Babinich is a soldier, may the bullets strike him! I see that with such servants I can go even in the midst of Swedes."

Meanwhile all gathered around the horseman, who did not rise from the ground however.

"Ask him, Gracious Lord," said Kmita, not without a certain boastfulness in his voice; "though I do not know whether he will answer, for he is throttled a little and there is nothing here to burn him with."

"Pour some gorailka into his throat," said the king.

And indeed that medicine helped more than burning, for the horseman soon recovered strength and voice. Then Kmita, putting a sword-point to his throat, commanded him to tell the whole truth.

The prisoner confessed that he belonged to the regiment of Colonel Irlehorn, that they had intelligence of the passage of the king with dragoons, therefore they fell upon them near Suha, but meeting firm resistance they had to withdraw to Jivyets, whence they marched on to Vadovitsi and Cracow, for such were their orders.

"Are there other divisions of the Swedes in the mountains?" asked Kmita in German, while squeezing the throat of the horseman somewhat more vigorously.

"Maybe there are some," answered he in a broken voice. "General Douglas sent scouting-parties around, but they are all withdrawing, for the peasants are attacking them in passes."

"Were you the only ones in the neighborhood of Jivyets?"

"The only ones."

"Do you know that the King of Poland has passed?"

"He passed with those dragoons who fought with us at Suha. Many saw him."

"Why did you not pursue him?"

"We were afraid of the mountaineers.".

Here Kmita began again in Polish: "Gracious Lord, the road is open and you will find a night's lodging in Jivyets, for only a part of the place is burned."

But unconfiding Tyzenhauz was speaking at this time with the castellan of Voinik, and said: "Either that is a great warrior and true as gold, or a finished traitor. Consider, your worthiness, that all this may be simulated, from the taking of this horseman to his confederates. And if this is a trick, — if the Swedes are in ambush in Jivyets, — if the king goes and falls as into a net ? "

"It is safer to convince one's self," answered the castellan of Voinik.

Then Tyzenhauz turned to the king and said aloud: " Gracious Lord, permit me to go ahead to Jivyets and convince myself that what this cavalier says and what this trooper declares is true."

" Let it be so ! Permit them to go, Gracious Lord," said Kmita.

" Go," said the king; " but we will move forward a little, for it is cold."

Tyzenhauz rushed on at all speed, and the escort of the king began to move after him slowly. The king regained his good humor and cheerfulness, and after a while said to Kmita, —

" But with you it is possible to hunt Swedes as birds with a falcon, for you strike from above."

" That is my fashion," said Kmita. " Whenever your Royal Grace wishes to hunt, the falcon will always be ready."

" Tell how you caught him."

" That is not difficult. When a regiment marches there are always a few men who lag in the rear, and I got this one about half a furlong behind. I rode up to him; he thought that I was one of his own people, he was not on his guard, and before he could think I had seized and gagged him so that he could not shout."

" You said that this was not your first time. Have you then practised somewhere before ? "

Kmita laughed. " Oh, Gracious Lord, I have, and that of the best. Let your Royal Grace but give the order and I will go again, overtake them, for their horses are road-weary, take another man, and order my Kyemliches to take also."

They advanced some time in silence; then the tramp of a horse was heard, and Tyzenhauz flew up. " Gracious King," said he, " the road is free, and lodgings are ready."

" But did not I say so ? " cried Yan Kazimir. " You, gentlemen, had no need to be anxious. Let us ride on now, let us ride, for we have earned our rest."

All advanced at a trot, briskly, joyously; and an hour later the wearied king was sleeping a sleep without care on his own territory.

That evening Tyzenhauz approached Kmita. " Forgive

me," said he; "out of love for the king I brought you under suspicion."

Kmita refused his hand and said: "Oh, that cannot be! You made me a traitor and a betrayer."

"I would have done more, for I would have shot you in the head; but since I have convinced myself that you are an honest man and love the king, I stretch out my hand to you. If you wish, take it; if not, take it not. I would prefer to have no rivalry with you save that of attachment to the king; but I am not afraid of other rivalry."

"Is that your thought? H'm! perhaps you are right, but I am angry with you."

"Well, stop being angry. You are a strong soldier. But give us your lips, so that we may not lie down to sleep in hatred."

"Let it be so!" said Kmita.

And they fell into each other's arms.

CHAPTER X.

THE king's party arrived at Jivyets late in the evening, and paid almost no attention to the place, which was terrified by the recent attack of the Swedish detachment. The king did not go to the castle, which had been ravaged by the enemy and burned in part, but stopped at the priest's house. Kmita spread the news that the party was escorting the ambassador of the emperor, who was going from Silesia to Cracow.

Next morning they held on toward Vadovitsi, and then turned considerably to one side toward Suha. From this place they were to pass through Kjechoni to Yordanovo, thence to Novy Targ, and if it appeared that there were no Swedish parties near Chorshtyn to go to Chorshtyn; if there were, they were to turn toward Hungary and advance on Hungarian soil to Lyubovlya. The king hoped, too, that the marshal of the kingdom, who disposed of forces so considerable that no reigning prince had so many, would make the road safe and hasten forth to meet his sovereign. Only this could prevent, that the marshal knew not which road the king would take; but among the mountaineers there was no lack of trusty men ready to bear word to the marshal. There was no need even of confiding the secret to them, for they went willingly when told that it was a question of serving the king. These people, though poor and half wild, tilling little or not at all an ungrateful soil, living by their herds, pious, and hating heretics, were, in truth, given heart and soul to the sovereign. They were the first to seize their axes and move from the mountains when news of the taking of Cracow spread through the country, and especially when news came of the siege of Chenstohova, to which pious women were accustomed to go on pilgrimages. General Douglas, a well-known warrior, furnished with cannon and muskets, scattered them, it is true, on the plains, to which they were not accustomed; but the Swedes only with the greatest caution entered their special districts, in which it was not easy to reach them, and easy to suffer dis-

aster, — so that some smaller divisions, having needlessly
entered this labyrinth of mountains, were lost.

And now news of the king's passage with an army had
already done its own, for all had sprung up as one man to
defend him and accompany him with their axes, even
to the end of the world. Yan Kazimir might, if he had
only disclosed who he was, have surrounded himself in a
short time with thousands of half-wild " householders; " but
he thought justly that in such an event the news would be
carried about everywhere by all the whirlwinds through the
whole region, and that the Swedes might send out numerous
troops to meet him, therefore he chose to travel unknown
even to the mountaineers.

But in all places trusty guides were found, to whom it
was enough to say that they were conducting bishops and
lords who desired to preserve themselves from Swedish
hands. They were led, therefore, among snows, cliffs, and
whirlwinds, and over places so inaccessible that you would
have said: " A bird cannot fly through them."

More than once the king and the dignitaries had clouds
below them, and when there were not clouds their glances
passed over a shoreless expanse, covered with white
snows, ˙an expanse seemingly as wide as the whole country was wide; more than once they entered mountain
throats, almost dark, covered with snow, in which perhaps
only a wild beast might have its lair. But they avoided
places accessible to the enemy, shortening the road; and it
happened that a settlement, at which they expected to arrive
in half a day, appeared suddenly under their feet, and in it
they awaited rest and hospitality, though in a smoky hut
and a sooty room.

The king was in continual good humor; he gave courage to
others to endure the excessive toil, and he guaranteed that
by such roads they would surely reach Lyubovlya as safely
as unexpectedly.

" The marshal does not expect that we shall fall on his
shoulders ! " repeated the king, frequently.

" What was the return of Xenophon to our journey among
the clouds ? " asked the nuncio.

" The higher we rise, the lower will Swedish fortune fall,"
answered the king.

They arrived at Novy Targ. It seemed that all danger
was passed; still the mountaineers declared that Swedish
troops were moving about near Chorshtyn and in the

neighborhood. The king supposed that they might be the marshal's German cavalry, of which he had two regiments, or they might be his own dragoons sent in advance and mistaken for the enemy's scouts. Since in Chorshtyn the bishop of Cracow had a garrison, opinions were divided in the royal party. Some wished to go by the road to Chorshtyn, and then pass along the boundary to Spij; others advised to turn straight to Hungary, which came up in wedge-form to Novy Targ, and go over heights and through passes, taking guides everywhere who knew the most dangerous places.

This last opinion prevailed, for in that way meeting with the Swedes became almost impossible; and besides this "eagle" road over the precipices and through the clouds gave pleasure to the king.

They passed then from Novy Targ somewhat to the south and west, on the right hand of the Byaly Dunayets. The road at first lay through a region rather open and spacious, but as they advanced the mountains began to run together and the valleys to contract. They went along roads over which horses could barely advance. At times the riders had to dismount and lead; and more than once the beasts resisted, pointing their ears and stretching their distended and steaming nostrils forward toward precipices, from the depths of which death seemed to gaze upward.

The mountaineers, accustomed to precipices, frequently considered roads good on which the heads of unaccustomed men turned and their ears rang. At last they entered a kind of rocky chasm long, straight, and so narrow that three men could barely ride abreast in it. Two cliffs bounded it on the right side and the left. At places however the edges inclined, forming slopes less steep, covered with piles of snow bordered on the edges with dark pine-trees. Winds blew away the snow immediately from the bottom of the pass, and the hoofs of horses gritted everywhere on a stony road. But at that moment the wind was not blowing, and such silence reigned that there was a ringing in the ears. Above where between the woody edges a blue belt of sky was visible, black flocks of birds flew past from time to time, shaking their wings and screaming.

The king's party halted for rest. Clouds of steam rose from the horses, and the men too were tired.

"Is this Poland or Hungary?" inquired, after a time, the king of a guide.

"This is Poland."

"But why do we not turn directly to Hungary ? "

"Because it is impossible. At some distance this pass turns, beyond the turn is a cliff, beyond that we come out on the high-road, turn, then go through one more pass, and there the Hungarian country begins."

"Then I see it would have been better to go by the high-way at first," said the king.

"Quiet ! " cried the mountaineer, quickly. And springing to the cliff he put his ear to it.

All fixed their eyes on him ; his face changed in a moment, and he said : "Beyond the turn troops are coming from the water-fall ! For God's sake ! Are they not Swedes ? "

"Where ? How ? What ? " men began to ask on every side. "We hear nothing."

"No, for snow is lying on the sides. By God's wounds, they are near ! they will be here straightway ! "

"Maybe they are the marshal's troops," said the king.

In one moment Kmita urged his horse forward. "I will go and see ! " said he.

The Kyemliches moved that instant after him, like hunting-dogs in a chase; but barely had they stirred from their places when the turn of the pass, about a hundred yards distant, was made black by men and horses. Kmita looked at them, and the soul quivered within him from terror.

Swedes were advancing.

They were so near that it was impossible to retreat, especially since the king's party had wearied horses. It only remained to break through, to perish, or to go into captivity. The unterrified king understood this in a flash ; therefore he seized the hilt of his sword.

"Cover the king and retreat ! " cried Kmita.

Tyzenhauz with twenty men pushed forward in the twinkle of an eye ; but Kmita instead of joining them moved on at a sharp trot against the Swedes.

He wore the Swedish dress, the same in which he disguised himself when going out from the cloister. Seeing a horseman coming toward them in such a dress, the Swedes thought perhaps this was some party of their own belonging to the King of Sweden ; they did not hasten their pace, but the captain commanding pushed out beyond the first three.

"What people are you ? " asked he in Swedish, looking at the threatening and pale face of the young man approaching.

Kmita rode up to him so closely that their knees almost touched, and without speaking a word fired from a pistol directly into his ear.

A shout of terror was rent from the breasts of the Swedish cavalry; but still louder thundered the voice of Pan Andrei, "Strike!"

And like a rock torn from a cliff rolling down, crushing everything in its course, so did he fall on the first rank, bearing death and destruction. The two young Kyemliches, like two bears, sprang after him into the whirl. The clatter of sabres on mail and helmets was heard, like the sound of hammers, and was followed straightway by outcries and groans.

It seemed at the first moment to the astonished Swedes that three giants had fallen upon them in that wild mountain pass. The first three pushed back confused in the presence of the terrible man, and when the succeeding ones had extricated themselves from behind the bend of the pass, those in the rear were thrown back and confused. The horses fell to biting and kicking. The soldiers in the remoter ranks were not able to shoot, nor come to the assistance of those in front, who perished without aid under the blows of the three giants. In vain did they fall, in vain did they present their weapon points; here sabres were breaking, there men and horses fell. Kmita urged his horse till his hoofs were hanging above the heads of the steeds of his opponents, he was raging himself, cutting and thrusting. The blood rushed to his face, and from his eyes fire flashed. All thoughts were quenched in him save one, — he might perish, but he must detain the Swedes. That thought turned in him to a species of wild ecstasy; therefore his powers were trebled, his movements became like those of a leopard, mad, and swift as lightning. With blows of his sabre, which were blows beyond human, he crushed men as a thunderbolt crushes young trees; the twin Kyemliches followed, and the old man, standing a trifle in the rear, thrust his rapier out every moment between his sons, as a serpent thrusts out its bloody tongue.

Meanwhile around the king there rose confusion. The nuncio, as at Jivyets, seized the reins of his horse, and on the other side the bishop of Cracow pulled back the steed with all his force; but the king spurred him till he stood on his hind legs.

"Let me go!" cried the king. "As God lives! We shall pass through the enemy!"

"My Lord, think of the country!" cried the bishop of Cracow.

The king was unable to tear himself from their hands, especially since young Tyzenhauz with all his men closed the road. Tyzenhauz did not go to help Kmita; he sacrificed him, he wanted only to save the king.

"By the passion of our Lord!" cried he, in despair, "those men will perish immediately! Gracious Lord, save yourself while there is time! I will hold them here yet awhile!"

But the stubbornness of the king when once roused reckoned with nothing and no man. Yan Kazimir spurred his horse still more violently, and instead of retreating pushed forward.

But time passed, and each moment might bring with it final destruction.

"I will die on my own soil! Let me go!" cried the king.

Fortunately, against Kmita and the Kyemliches, by reason of the narrowness of the pass, only a small number of men could act at once, consequently they were able to hold out long. But gradually even their powers began to be exhausted. A number of times the rapiers of the Swedes had struck Kmita's body, and his blood began to flow. His eyes were veiled as it were by a mist. The breath halted in his breast. He felt the approach of death; therefore he wanted only to sell his life dearly. "Even one more!" repeated he to himself, and he sent down his steel blade on the head or the shoulder of the nearest horseman, and again he turned to another; but evidently the Swedes felt ashamed, after the first moment of confusion and fear, that four men were able to detain them so long, and they crowded forward with fury; soon the very weight of men and horses drove back the four men, and each moment more swiftly and strongly.

With that Kmita's horse fell, and the torrent covered the rider.

The Kyemliches struggled still for a time, like swimmers who seeing that they are drowning make efforts to keep their heads above the whirl of the sea, but soon they also fell. Then the Swedes moved on like a whirlwind toward the party of the king.

Tyzenhauz with his men sprang against them, and struck them in such fashion that the sound was heard through the mountains.

But what could that handful of men, led by Tyzenhauz, do against a detachment of nearly three hundred strong?

There was no doubt that for the king and his party the fatal hour of death or captivity must come.

Yan Kazimir, preferring evidently the first to the second, freed finally the reins from the hands of the bishops, and pushed forward quickly toward Tyzenhauz. In an instant he halted as if fixed to the earth.

Something uncommon had happened. To spectators it seemed as though the mountains themselves were coming to the aid of the rightful king.

Behold on a sudden the edges of the pass quivered as if the earth were moving from its foundations, as if the pines on the mountain desired to take part in the battle; and logs of wood, blocks of snow and ice, stones, fragments of cliffs, began to roll down with a terrible crash and roar on the ranks of the Swedes crowded in the pass. At the same time an unearthly howl was heard on each side of the narrow place.

Below in the ranks began seething which passed human belief. It seemed to the Swedes that the mountains were falling and covering them. Shouts rose, the lamentations of crushed men, despairing cries for assistance, the whining of horses, the bite and terrible sound of fragments of cliffs on armor.

At last men and horses formed one mass quivering convulsively, crushed, groaning, despairing, and dreadful. But the stones and pieces of cliffs ground them continually, rolling without mercy on the now formless masses, the bodies of horses and men.

"The mountaineers! the mountaineers!" shouted men in the retinue of the king.

"With axes at the dog-brothers!" called voices from the mountain.

And that very moment from both rocky edges appeared long-haired heads, covered with round fur caps, and after them came out bodies, and several hundred strange forms began to let themselves down on the slopes of the snow.

Dark and white rags floating above their shoulders gave them the appearance of some kind of awful birds of prey. They pushed down in the twinkle of an eye; the sound of their axes emphasized their wild ominous shouting and the groans of the Swedes.

The king himself tried to restrain the slaughter; some horsemen, still living, threw themselves on their knees, and raising their defenceless hands, begged for their lives. Nothing availed, nothing could stay the vengeful axes. A quarter of an hour later there was not one man living among the Swedes in the pass.

After that the bloody mountaineers began to hurry toward the escort of the king.

The nuncio looked with astonishment on those people, strange to him, large, sturdy, covered partly with sheepskin, sprinkled with blood, and shaking their still steaming axes.

But at sight of the bishops they uncovered their heads. Many of them fell on their knees in the snow.

The bishop of Cracow raising his tearful face toward heaven said, "Behold the assistance of God, behold Providence, which watches over the majesty of the king." Then turning to the mountaineers, he asked, "Men, who are you?"

"We are of this place," answered voices from the crowd.

"Do you know whom you have come to assist? This is your king and your lord, whom you have saved."

At these words a shout rose in the crowd. "The king! the king! Jesus, Mary! the king!" And the joyful mountaineers began to throng and crowd around Yan Kazimir. With weeping they fell to him from every side; with weeping, they kissed his feet, his stirrups, even the hoofs of his horse. Such excitement reigned, such shouting, such weeping that the bishops from fear for the king's person were forced to restrain the excessive enthusiasm.

And the king was in the midst of a faithful people, like a shepherd among sheep, and great tears were flowing down his face. Then his countenance became bright, as if some sudden change had taken place in his soul, as if a new, great thought from heaven by birth had flashed into his mind, and he indicated with his hand that he wished to speak; and when there was silence he said with a voice so loud that the whole multitude heard him, —

"O God, Thou who hast saved me by the hands of simple people, I swear by the suffering and death of Thy Son to be a father to them from this moment forward."

"Amen!" responded the bishops.

For a certain time a solemn silence reigned, then a new burst of joy. They inquired of the mountaineers whence they had come into the passes, and in what way they had appeared to rescue the king. It turned out that considerable parties of Swedes had been wandering about Chorshtyn, and, not capturing the castle itself, they seemed to seek some one and to wait. The mountaineers too had heard of a battle which those parties had delivered against troops among whom it was said that the king himself was advancing. Then they determined to push the Swedes into an ambush, and sending to them deceitful guides, they lured them into the pass.

"We saw," said the mountaineers, "how those four horsemen attacked those dogs; we wanted to assist the four horsemen, but were afraid to fall upon the dog-brothers too soon!"

Here the king seized his head. "Mother of Thy only Son!" cried he, "find Babinich for me! Let us give him at least a funeral! And he is the man who was considered a traitor, the one who first shed his own blood for us."

"It was I who accused him, Gracious Lord!" said Tyzenhauz

"Find him, find him!" cried the king. "I will not leave here till I look upon his face and put my blessing on him."

The soldiers and the mountaineers sprang to the place of the first struggle, and soon they removed from the pile of dead horses and men Pan Andrei. His face was pale, all bespattered with blood, which was hanging in large stiffened drops on his mustaches; his eyes were closed; his armor was bent from the blows of swords and horses' hoofs. But that armor had saved him from being crushed, and to the soldier who raised him it seemed as though he heard a low groan.

"As God is true, he is alive!" cried he.

"Remove his armor," called others.

They cut the straps quickly. Kmita breathed more deeply.

"He is breathing, he is breathing! He is alive!" repeated a number of voices.

But he lay a certain time motionless; then he opened his eyes. At that time one of the soldiers poured a little gorailka into his mouth; others raised him by the armpits.

Now the king, to whose hearing the cry repeated by several voices had come, rode up in haste. The soldiers drew into his presence Pan Andrei, who was hanging on them and slipping from their hands to the ground. Still, at sight of the king consciousness returned to him for a moment, a smile almost childlike lighted his face, and his pale lips whispered clearly, —

"My lord, my king, is alive — is free." And tears shone on his eyelashes.

"Babinich, Babinich! with what can I reward you?" cried the king.

"I am not Babinich; I am Kmita!" whispered the knight.

When he had said this he hung like a corpse in the arms of the soldiers.

CHAPTER XI.

SINCE the mountaineers gave sure information that on the road to Chorshtyn there was nothing to be heard of other Swedish parties, the retinue of the king turned toward the castle, and soon found themselves on the highway, along which the journey was easiest and least tiresome. They rode on amid songs of the mountaineers and shouts, "The king is coming! The king is coming!" and along the road new crowds of men joined them, armed with flails, scythes, forks, and guns, so that Yan Kazimir was soon at the head of a considerable division of men, not trained, it is true, but ready at any moment to go with him even to Cracow and spill their blood for their sovereign. Near Chorshtyn more than a thousand "householders" and half-wild shepherds surrounded the king.

Then nobles from Novy Sanch and Stary Sanch began to come in. They said that a Polish regiment, under command of Voynillovich, had defeated, that morning, just before the town of Novy Sanch, a considerable detachment of Swedes, of which almost all the men were either slain, or drowned in the Kamyenna or Dunayets.

This turned out to be really the fact, when soon after on the road banners began to gleam, and Voynillovich himself came up with the regiment of the voevoda of Bratslav.

The king greeted with joy a celebrated and to him well-known knight, and amidst the universal enthusiasm of the people and the army, he rode on toward Spij. Meanwhile men on horseback rushed with all breath to forewarn the marshal that the king was approaching, and to be ready to receive him.

Joyous and noisy was the continuation of the journey. New crowds were added continually. The nuncio, who had left Silesia filled with fear for the king's fate and his own, and for whom the beginning of the journey had increased this fear, was beside himself now with delight, for he was certain that the future would surely bring victory to the king, and besides to the church over heretics. The bishops shared his joy; the lay dignitaries asserted that the whole people, from the Carpathians to the Baltic, would grasp their weapons as these crowds had done. Voynillovich stated that for the greater part this had taken place already. And he told what was to be heard in the country, what a terror had fallen upon the Swedes, how they dared go no longer outside fortifications in small numbers, how they were leaving the smaller castles, which they burned, and taking refuge in the strongest.

"The Polish troops are beating their breasts with one hand, and are beginning to beat the Swedes with the other," said he. "Vilchkovski, who commands the hussar regiment of your Royal Grace, has already thanked the Swedes for their service, and that in such fashion that he fell upon them at Zakjevo, under the command of Colonel Altenberg, and slew a large number, — destroyed almost all. I, with the assistance of God, drove them out of Novy Sanch, and God gave a noted victory. I do not know whether one escaped alive. Pan Felitsyan Kohovski with the infantry of Navoi helped me greatly, and so they received pay for those dragoons at least whom they attacked two or three days ago."

"What dragoons?" asked the king.

"Those whom your Royal Grace sent ahead from Silesia. The Swedes fell on these suddenly, and though not able to disperse them, for they defended themselves desperately, they inflicted considerable loss. And we were almost dying of despair, for we thought that your Royal Grace was among those men in your own person, and we feared lest some evil might happen to majesty. God inspired your Royal Grace to send the dragoons ahead. The Swedes heard of it at once, and occupied the roads everywhere."

"Do you hear, Tyzenhauz?" asked the king. "An experienced soldier is talking."

"I hear, Gracious Lord," answered the young magnate.

"And what further, what further? Tell on!" said the king, turning to Voynillovich.

"What I know I shall surely not hide. Jegotski and Kulesha are active in Great Poland; Varshytski has driven Lindorm from the castle of Pilets; Dankoff is defending itself; Lantskoron is in our hands; and in Podlyasye, Sapyeha is gaining every day at Tykotsin. The Swedes are in greater straits in the castle, and with them is failing the prince voevoda of Vilna. As to the hetmans, they have moved already from Sandomir to Lyubelsk, showing clearly that they are breaking with the enemy. The voevoda of

Chernigov is with them, and from the region about is marching to them every living man who can hold a sabre in his hand. They say, too, that there is some kind of federation to be formed there against the Swedes, in which is the hand of Sapyeha as well as that of Stefan Charnyetski."

"Is Charnyetski now in Lyubelsk?"

"He is, your Royal Grace. But he is here to-day and there to-morrow. I have to join him, but where to find him I know not."

"There will be noise around him," said the king; "you will not need to inquire."

"So I think too," answered Voynillovich.

In such conversation was the road passed. Meanwhile the sky had grown perfectly clear, so that the azure was unspotted by even a small cloud. The snow was glittering in the sunlight. The mountains of Spij were extended gloriously and joyously before the travellers, and Nature itself seemed to smile on the king.

"Dear country!" said Yan Kazimir, "God grant me strength to bring thee peace before my bones rest in thy earth."

They rode out on a lofty eminence, from which the view was open and wide, for beyond, at the foot of it, was spread a broad plain. There they saw below, and at a great distance as it were, the movement of a human ant-hill.

"The troops of the marshal!" cried Voynillovich.

"Unless they are Swedes," said the king.

"No, Gracious Lord! The Swedes could not march from Hungary, from the south. I see now the hussar flag."

In fact a forest of spears soon pushed out in the blue distance, and colored streamers were quivering like flowers moved by the wind; above these flags spear-points were glittering like little flames. The sun played on the armor and helmets.

The throngs of people accompanying the king gave forth a joyous shout, which was heard at a distance, for the mass of horses, riders, flags, horse-tail standards, and ensigns began to move more quickly. Evidently they were moving with all speed, for the regiments became each moment more definite, and increased in the eye with incomprehensible rapidity.

"Let us stay on this height. We will await the marshal here," said the king.

The retinue halted; the men coming toward them moved

still more rapidly. At moments they were concealed from
the eye by turns of the road, or small hills and cliffs, scattered along the plain; but soon they appeared again, like a
serpent with a skin of splendid colors playing most beauti-
fully. At last they came within a quarter of a mile of the
height, and slackened their speed. The eye could take them
in perfectly, and gain pleasure from them. First advanced
the hussar squadron of the marshal himself, well armored,
and so imposing that any king might be proud of such troops.
Only nobles of the mountains served in this squadron,
chosen men of equal size; their armor was of bright squares
inlaid with bronze, gorgets with the image of the Most Holy
Lady of Chenstohova, round helmets with steel rims, crests
on the top, and at the side wings of eagles and vultures, on
their shoulders tiger and leopard skins, but on the officers
wolf skins, according to custom.

A forest of green and black streamers waved above them.
In front rode Lieutenant Victor; after him a janissary band
with bells, trumpets, drums, and pipes; then a wall of the
breasts of horses and men clothed in iron.

The king's heart opened at that lordly sight. Next to
the hussars came a light regiment still more numerous, with
drawn sabres in their hands and bows at their shoulders;
then three companies of Cossacks, in colors like blooming
poppies, armed with spears and muskets; next two hundred
dragoons in red jackets; then escorts belonging to different
personages visiting at Lyubovlya, attendants dressed as if
for a wedding, guards, haiduks, grooms, Hungarians, and
janissaries, attached to the service of great lords.

And all that changed in colors like a rainbow, and came
on tumultuously, noisily, amid the neighing of horses, the
clatter of armor, the thunder of kettle-drums, the roll of
other drums, the blare of trumpets, and cries so loud that it
seemed as though the snows would rush down from the
mountains because of them. In the rear of the troops were
to be seen closed and open carriages, in which evidently
were riding dignitaries of the church and the world.

The troops took position in two lines along the road, and
between them appeared, on a horse white as milk, the marshal of the kingdon, Pan Yerzy Lyubomirski. He flew on
like a whirlwind over that road, and behind him raced two
equerries, glittering in gold. When he had ridden to the
foot of the eminence, he sprang from his horse, and throwing the reins to one of the equerries, went on foot to the
king standing above.

He removed his cap, and placing it on the hilt of his sabre, advanced with uncovered head, leaning on a staff all set with pearls. He was dressed in Polish fashion, in military costume; on his breast was armor of silver plates thickly inlaid at the edges with precious stones, and so polished that he seemed to be bearing the sun on his bosom; over his left shoulder was hanging a cloak of Venetian velvet of dark color, passing into violet purple; it was fastened at the throat by a cord with a buckle of diamonds, and the whole cloak was embroidered with diamonds; in like manner a diamond was trembling in his cap, and these stones glittered like many-colored sparks around his whole person, and dazzled the eyes, such was the brightness which came from them.

He was a man in the vigor of life, of splendid form. His head was shaven around the temples; his forelock was rather thin, growing gray, and lay on his forehead in a shaggy tuft; his mustache, as black as the wing of a crow, drooped in fine points at both sides. His lofty forehead and Roman nose added to the beauty of his face, but the face was marred somewhat by cheeks that were too plump, and small eyes encircled with red lids. Great dignity, but also unparalleled pride and vanity were depicted on that face. You might easily divine that that magnate wished to turn to himself eternally the eyes of the whole Commonwealth, nay, of all Europe; and such was the case in reality.

Where Yerzy Lyubomirski could not hold the first place, where he could only share glory and merit with others, his wounded pride was ready to bar the way and corrupt and crush every endeavor, even when it was a question of saving the country.

He was an adroit and fortunate leader, but even in this respect others surpassed him immeasurably; and in general his abilities, though uncommon, were not equal to his ambition and desire of distinction. Endless unrest therefore was boiling in his soul, whence was born that suspiciousness, that envy, which later on carried him so far that he became more destructive to the Commonwealth than the terrible Yanush Radzivill. The black soul which dwelt in Prince Yanush was great also; it stopped before no man and no thing. Yanush wanted a crown, and he went toward it consciously over graves and the ruin of his country. Lyubomirski would have taken a crown if the hands of the nobles had placed it on his head; but having a smaller soul,

he dared not desire the crown openly and expressly. Radzivill was one of those men whom failure casts down to the
level of criminals, and success elevates to the greatness of
demigods ; Lyubomirski was a mighty disturber who was
always ready to ruin work for the salvation of the country,
in the name of his own offended pride, and to build up nothing in place of it.   He did not even dare to raise himself,
he did not know how.   Radzivill died the more guilty, Lyubomirski the more harmful man.

But at that hour, when in gold, velvet, and precious
stones he stood in front of the king, his pride was sufficiently satisfied.   For he was the first magnate to receive his
own king on his own land ; he first took him under a species
of guardianship, he had to conduct him to a throne which
had been overturned, and to drive out the enemy ; from
him the king and the country expected everything ; on him
all eyes were turned.   Therefore to show loyalty and service coincided with his self-love, in fact flattered it, he
was ready in truth for sacrifices and devotion, he was ready
to exceed the measure even with expressions of respect and
loyalty.   When therefore he had ascended one half of that
eminence on which the king was standing, he took his cap
from the sword-hilt and began, while bowing, to sweep the
snow with its diamond plume.

The king urged his horse somewhat toward the descent,
then halted to dismount, for the greeting.   Seeing this, the
marshal sprang forward to hold the stirrup with his worthy
hands, and at that moment grasping after his cloak, he
drew it from his shoulders, and following the example of
a certain English courtier, threw it under the feet of the
monarch.

The king, touched to the heart, opened his arms to the
marshal, and seized him like a brother in his embrace.
For a while neither was able to speak ; but at that exalted
spectacle the army, the nobles, the people, roared in one
voice, and thousands of caps flew into the air, all the guns,
muskets, and blunderbusses sounded, cannon from Lyubovlya answered in a distant bass, till the mountains trembled ; all the echoes were roused and began to course
around, striking the dark walls of pine woods, the cliffs
and rocks, and flew with the news to remoter mountains
and cliffs.

"Lord Marshal," said the king, "we will thank you for
the restoration of the kingdom !"

"Gracious Lord!" answered Lyubomirski, "my fortune, my life, my blood, all I have I place at the feet of your Royal Grace."

"Vivat! vivat Yoannes Casimirus Rex!" thundered the shouts.

"May the king live! our father!" cried the mountaineers.

Meanwhile the gentlemen who were riding with the king surrounded the marshal; but he did not leave the royal person. After the first greetings the king mounted his horse again; but the marshal, not wishing to recognize bounds to his hospitality and honor to his guest, seized the bridle, and going himself on foot, led the king through the lines of the army amid deafening shouts, till they came to a gilded carriage drawn by eight dapple-gray horses; in this carriage Yan Kazimir took his seat, together with Vidon, the nuncio of the Pope.

The bishops and dignitaries took seats in succeeding carriages, then they moved on slowly to Lyubovlya. The marshal rode at the window of the king's carriage, splendid, self-satisfied, as if he were already proclaimed father of the country. At both sides went a dense army, singing songs, thundering out in the following words: —

"Cut the Swedes, cut,
With sharpened swords.

"Beat the Swedes, beat,
With strong sticks.

"Roll the Swedes, roll,
Empale them on stakes.

"Torment the Swedes, torment,
And torture them as you can.

"Pound the Swedes, pound,
Pull them out of their skins.

"Cut the Swedes, cut,
Then there will be fewer.

"Drown the Swedes, drown,
If you are a good man!"

Unfortunately amidst the universal rejoicing and enthusiasm no one foresaw that later the same troops of Lyubomirski, after they had rebelled against their legal lord and king, would sing the same song, putting the **French** in place of the Swedes.

But now it was far from such a state. In Lyubovlya the cannon were thundering in greeting till the towers and battlements were covered with smoke, the bells were tolling as at a fire. At the part of the courtyard in which the king descended from the carriage, the porch and the steps were covered with scarlet cloth. In vases brought from Italy were burning perfumes of the East. The greater part of the treasures of the Lyubomirskis, — cabinets of gold and silver, carpets, mats, gobelin tapestry, woven wonderfully by Flemish hands, statues, clocks, cupboards, ornamented with precious stones, cabinets inlaid with mother-of-pearl and amber brought previously to Lyubovlya to preserve them from Swedish rapacity, were now arranged and hung up in display; they dazzled the eye and changed that castle into a kind of fairy residence. And the marshal had arranged all this luxury, worthy of a Sultan, in this fashion of purpose to show the king that though he was returning as an exile, without money, without troops, having scarcely a change of clothing, still he was a mighty lord, since he had servants so powerful, and as faithful as powerful. The king understood this intention, and his heart rose in gratitude; every moment therefore he took the marshal by the shoulder, pressed his head and thanked him. The nuncio, though accustomed to luxury, expressed his astonishment at what he beheld, and they heard him say to Count Apotyngen that hitherto he had had no idea of the power of the King of Poland, and now saw that the previous defeats were merely a temporary reverse of fortune, which soon must be changed.

At the feast, which followed a rest, the king sat on an elevation, and the marshal himself served him, permitting no one to take his place. At the right of the king sat the nuncio, at his left the prince primate, Leshchynski, farther on both sides dignitaries, lay and clerical, such as the bishops of Cracow, Poznan, Lvoff, Lutsk, Premysl, Helm; the archdeacon of Cracow; farther on keepers of the royal seal and voevodas, of whom eight had assembled, and castellans and referendaries; of officers, there were sitting at the feast Voynillovich, Viktor, Stabkovski, and Baldwin Shurski.

In another hall a table was set for inferior nobles, and there were large barracks for peasants, for all had **to be** joyful on the day of the king's coming.

At the tables there was no other conversation but touching the royal return, and the terrible adventures which had met them on the road, in which the hand of God had preserved the king. Yan Kazimir himself described the battle in the pass, and praised the cavalier who had held back the first Swedish onset.

"And how is he?" asked he of the marshal.

"The physician does not leave him, and guarantees his life; and besides, maidens and ladies in waiting have taken him in care, and surely they will not let the soul go from the body, for the body is shapely and young!" answered the marshal, joyously.

"Praise be to God!" cried the king. "I heard from his lips something which I shall not repeat to you, for it seems to me that I heard incorrectly, or that he said it in delirium; but should it come true you will be astonished."

"If he has said nothing which might make your Royal Grace gloomy."

"Nothing whatever of that nature," said the king; "it has comforted us beyond measure, for it seems that even those whom we had reason to hold our greatest enemies are ready to spill their blood for us if need be."

"Gracious Lord!" cried the marshal, "the time of reform has come; but under this roof your Royal Grace is among persons who have never sinned even in thought against majesty."

"True, true!" answered the king, "and you, Lord Marshal, are in the first rank."

"I am a poor servant of your Royal Grace."

At table the noise grew greater. Gradually they began to speak of political combinations; of aid from the emperor, hitherto looked for in vain; of Tartar assistance, and of the coming war with the Swedes. Fresh rejoicing set in when the marshal stated that the envoy sent by him to the Khan had returned just a couple of days before, and reported that forty thousand of the horde were in readiness, and perhaps even a hundred thousand, as soon as the king would reach Lvoff and conclude a treaty with the Khan. The same envoy had reported that the Cossacks through fear of the Tartars had returned to obedience.

"You have thought of everything," said the king, "in such fashion that we could not have thought it out better ourselves." Then he seized his glass and said: "To the health of our host and friend, the marshal of the kingdom!"

"Impossible, Gracious Lord!" cried the marshal; "no

man's health can be drunk here before the health of your Royal Grace."

All restrained their half-raised goblets; but Lyubomirski, filled with delight, perspiring, beckoned to his chief butler.

At this sign the servants who were swarming through the hall rushed to pour out Malvoisie again, taken with gilded dippers from kegs of pure silver. Pleasure increased still more, and all were waiting for the toast of the marshal.

The chief butler brought now two goblets of Venetian crystal of such marvellous work that they might pass for the eighth wonder of the world. The crystal, bored and polished to thinness during whole years, perhaps, cast real diamond light. On the setting great artists of Italy had labored. The base of each goblet was gold, carved in small figures representing the entrance of a conqueror to the Capitol. The conqueror rode in a chariot of gold on a street paved with pearls. Behind him followed captives with bound hands; with them a king, in a turban formed of one emerald; farther followed legionaries with eagles and ensigns. More than fifty small figures found room on each base, — figures as high as a hazel-nut, but made so marvellously that the features of the faces and the feelings of each one could be distinguished, the pride of the victors, the grief of the vanquished. The base was bound to the goblet with golden filigree, fine as hair bent with wondrous art into grape leaves, clusters, and various flowers. Those filigree were wound around the crystal, and joining at the top in one ring formed the edge of the goblet, which was set with stones in seven colors.

The head butler gave one such goblet to the king and the other to the marshal, both filled with Malvoisie. All rose from their seats; the marshal raised the goblet, and cried with all the voice in his breast, —

"Vivat Yoannes Casimirus Rex!"

"Vivat! vivat! vivat!"

At that moment the guns thundered again so that the walls of the castle were trembling. The nobles feasting in the second hall came with their goblets; the marshal wished to make an oration, but could not, for his words were lost in the endless shouts: "Vivat! vivat! vivat!"

Such joy seized the marshal, such ecstasy, that wildness was gleaming in his eyes, and emptying his goblet he shouted so that he was heard even in the universal tumult, —

"*Ego ultimus* (I am the last)!"

Then he struck the priceless goblet on his own head with such force that the crystal sprang into a hundred fragments, which fell with a rattle on the floor, and the head of the magnate was covered with blood. All were astonished, and the king said, —

"Lord Marshal, we regret not the goblet, but the head which we value so greatly."

"Treasures and jewels are nothing to me," cried the marshal, "when I have the honor of receiving your Royal Grace in my house. Vivat Yoannes Casimirus Rex!"

Here the butler gave him another goblet.

"Vivat! vivat!" shouted the guests without ceasing. The sound of broken glass was mingled with the shout. Only the bishops did not follow the example of the marshal, for their spiritual dignity forbade them.

The nuncio, who did not know of that custom of breaking glasses on the head, bent to the bishop of Poznan, sitting near him, and said, —

"As God lives, astonishment seizes me! Your treasury is empty, and for one such goblet two good regiments of men might be equipped and maintained."

"It is always so with us," answered the bishop; "when desire rises in the heart there is no measure in anything."

And in fact the desire grew greater each moment. Toward the end of the feast a bright light struck the windows of the castle.

"What is that?" asked the king.

"Gracious Lord, I beg you to the spectacle," answered the marshal. And tottering slightly, he conducted the king to the window. There a wonderful sight struck their eyes. It was as clear in the court as when there is daylight. A number of tens of pitch-barrels cast a bright yellow gleam on the pavement, cleared of snow and strewn with leaves of mountain-fern. Here and there were burning tubs of brandy which cast blue light; salt was sprinkled into some to make them burn red.

The spectacle began. First knights cut off Turkish heads, tilted at a ring and at one another; then the dogs of Liptovo fought with a bear; later, a man from the hills, a kind of mountain Samson, threw a millstone and caught it in the air. Midnight put an end to these amusements.

Thus did the marshal declare himself, though the Swedes were still in the land.

CHAPTER XII.

In the midst of feasting and the throng of new dignitaries, nobles, and knights who were coming continually, the kindly king forgot not his faithful servant who in the mountain-pass had exposed his breast to the Swedish sword with such daring; and on the day following his arrival in Lyubovlya he visited the wounded Pan Andrei. He found him conscious and almost joyful, though pale as death; by a lucky fortune the young hero had received no grievous wound, only blood had left him in large quantities.

At sight of the king, Kmita even rose in the bed to a sitting position, and though the king insisted that he should lie down again, he was unwilling to do so.

"Gracious Lord," said he, "in a couple of days I shall be on horseback, and with your gracious permission will go farther, for I feel that nothing is the matter with me."

"Still they must have cut you terribly. It is an unheard of thing for one to withstand such a number."

"That has happened to me more than once, for I think that in an evil juncture the sabre and courage are best. Ei, Gracious Lord, the number of cuts that have healed on my skin you could not count on an ox-hide. Such is my fortune."

"Complain not of fortune, for it is evident that you go headlong to places where not only blows but deaths are distributed. But how long do you practise such tactics? Where have you fought before now?"

A passing blush covered the youthful face of Kmita.

"Gracious Lord, I attacked Hovanski when all dropped their hands, and a price was set on my head."

"But listen," said the king, suddenly; "you told me a wonderful word in that pass. I thought that delirium had seized you and unsettled your reason. Now you say that you attacked Hovanski. Who are you? Are you not really Babinich? We know who attacked Hovanski!"

A moment of silence followed; at last the young knight raised his pale face, and said, —

"Not delirium spoke through me, but truth; it was I who battered Hovanski, from which war my name was heard throughout the whole Commonwealth. I am Andrei Kmita, the banneret of Orsha."

Here Kmita closed his eyes and grew still paler; but when the astonished king was silent, he began to speak farther, —

"I am, Gracious Lord, that outlaw, condemned by God and the judgments of men for killing and violence. I served Radzivill, and together with him I betrayed you and the country; but now, thrust with rapiers and trampled with horses' hoofs, unable to rise, I beat my breast, repeating, *Mea culpa, mea culpa!* (My fault, my fault!) and I implore your fatherly mercy. Forgive me, for I have cursed my previous acts, and have long since turned from that road which lies toward hell."

Tears dropped from the eyes of the knight, and with trembling he began to seek the hand of the king. Yan Kazimir, it is true, did not withdraw his hand; but he grew gloomy, and said, —

"Whoso in this land wears a crown should be unceasingly ready to pardon; therefore we are willing to forgive your offence, since on Yasna Gora and on the road you have served us with faithfulness, exposing your breast."

"Then forgive them, Gracious Lord! Shorten my torment."

"But one thing we cannot forget, — that in spite of the virtue of this people you offered Prince Boguslav to raise hands on majesty, hitherto inviolable, and bear us away living or dead, and deliver us into Swedish hands."

Kmita, though a moment before he had said himself that he was unable to rise, sprang from the bed, seized the crucifix hanging above him, and with the cuts on his face and fever in his flashing eyes, and breathing quickly, began to speak thus, —

"By the salvation of my father and mother, by the wounds of the Crucified, it is untrue! If I am guilty of that sin, may God punish me at once with sudden death and with eternal fires. If you do not believe me, I will tear these bandages, let out the remnant of the blood which the Swedes did not shed. I never made the offer. Never was such a thought in my head. For the kingdom of this world, I would not have done such a deed. Amen! on this cross, amen. amen!" And he trembled from feverish excitement.

"Then did the prince invent it?" asked the astonished king. "Why? for what reason?"

"He did invent it. It was his hellish revenge on me for what I did to him."

"What did you do to him?"

"I carried him off from the middle of his court and of his whole army. I wanted to cast him bound at the feet of your Royal Grace."

"It's a wonder, it's a wonder! I believe you, but I do not understand. How was it? You were serving Yanush, and carried off Boguslav, who was less guilty, and you wanted to bring him bound to me?"

Kmita wished to answer; but the king saw at that moment his pallor and suffering, therefore he said, —

"Rest, and later tell me all from the beginning. I believe you; here is our hand."

Kmita pressed the king's hand to his lips, and for some time was silent, for breath failed him; he merely looked at the king's face with immeasurable affection; at last he collected his strength, and said, —

"I will tell all from the beginning. I warred against Hovanski, but I was hard with my own people. In part I was forced to wrong them, and to take what I needed; I did this partly from violence, for the blood was storming within me. I had companions, good nobles, but no better than I. Here and there a man was cut down, here and there a house was burned, here and there some one was chased over the snow with sticks. An outcry was raised. Where an enemy could not touch me, complaint was made before a court. I lost cases by default. Sentences came one after another, but I paid no heed; besides, the devil flattered me, and whispered to surpass Pan Lashch, who had his cloak lined with judgments; and still he was famous, and is famous till now."

"For he did penance, and died piously," remarked the king.

When he had rested somewhat, Kmita continued: "Meanwhile Colonel Billevich — the Billeviches are a great family in Jmud — put off his transitory form, and was taken to a better world; but he left me a village and his granddaughter. I do not care for the village, for in continual attacks on the enemy I have gathered no little property, and not only have made good the fortune taken from me by the Northerners, but have increased it. I have still in Chenstohova enough to buy two such villages, and I need ask no one for bread. But when my party separated I went to winter quarters in the Lauda region. There the maiden, Billevich's granddaughter, came so near my heart that I forgot God's world. The virtue and honesty in this lady were such that I grew shamefaced in presence of my former deeds. She too, having an inborn hatred of transgression, pressed me to leave my previous manner of life, put an end to disturbances, repair wrongs, and live honestly."

" Did you follow her advice ? "

" How could I, Gracious Lord! I wished to do so, it is true, — God sees that I wished; but old sins follow a man. First, my soldiers were attacked in Upita, for which I burned some of the place."

" In God's name ! that is a crime," said the king.

" That is nothing yet. Later on, the nobles of Lauda slaughtered my comrades, worthy cavaliers though violent. I was forced to avenge them. I fell upon the village of the Butryms that very night, and took vengeance, with fire and sword, for the murder. But they defeated me, for a crowd of homespuns live in that neighborhood. I had to hide. The maiden would not look at me, for those homespuns were made fathers and guardians to her by the will. But my heart was so drawn to her that I could not help myself. Unable to live without her, I collected a new party and seized her with armed hand."

" Why, the Tartars do not make love differently."

" I own that it was a deed of violence. But God punished me through the hands of Pan Volodyovski, and he cut me so that I barely escaped with my life. It would have been a hundred times better for me if I had not escaped, for I should not have joined the Radzivills to the injury of the king and the country. But how could it be otherwise ? A new suit was begun against me for a capital offence; it was a question of life. I knew not what to do, when suddenly the voevoda of Vilna came to me with assistance."

" Did he protect you ? "

" He sent me a commission through this same Pan Volod-yovski, and thereby I went under the jurisdiction of the hetman, and was not afraid of the courts. I clung to Rad-zivill as to a plank of salvation. Soon I put on foot a squad-ron of men known as the greatest fighters in all Lithuania. There were none better in the army. I led them to Kyedani. Radzivill received me as a son, referred to our kinship through the Kishkis, and promised to protect me. He had his object. He needed daring men ready for all things, and I, simpleton, crawled as it were into bird-lime. Before his plans had come to the surface, he commanded me to swear on a crucifix that I would not abandon him in any straits. Thinking it a question of war with the Swedes or the Northerners, I took the oath willingly. Then came that terrible feast at which the Kyedani treaty was read. The treason was published. Other colonels threw their batons at the feet of the hetman, but the oath held me as a chain holds a dog, and I could not leave him."

"But did not all those who deserted us later swear loyalty?" asked the king, sadly.

"I, too, though I did not throw down my baton, had no wish to steep my hands in treason. What I suffered, Gracious Lord, God alone knows. I was writhing from pain, as if men were burning me alive with fire; and my maiden, though even after the seizure the agreement between us remained still unbroken, now proclaimed me a traitor, and despised me as a vile reptile. But I had taken oath not to abandon Radzivill. She, though a woman, would shame a man with her wit, and lets no one surpass her in loyalty to your Royal Grace."

"God bless her!" said the king. "I respect her for that."

"She thought to reform me into a partisan of the king and the country; and when that came to naught, she grew so steadfast against me that her hatred became as great as her love had been once. At that juncture Radzivill called me before him, and began to convince me. He explained, as two and two form four, that in this way alone could he save the falling country. I cannot, indeed, repeat his arguments, they were so great, and promised such happiness to the land. He would have convinced a man a hundred times wiser, much less me, a simple soldier, he such a statesman! Then, I say, your Royal Grace, that I held to him with both hands and my heart, for I thought that all others were blind; only he saw the truth, all others were sinning, only he was the just man. And I would have sprung into fire for him, as now I would for your Royal Grace, for I know not how to serve or to love with half a heart."

"I see that, this is true!" said Yan Kazimir.

"I rendered him signal service," continued Kmita, gloomily, "and I can say that had it not been for me his treason could not have yielded any poisonous fruits, for his own troops would have cut him to pieces with sabres. They were all ready for that. The dragoons, the Hungarian infantry, and the light squadrons were already slaying his Scots, when I sprang in with my men and rubbed them out in one twinkle. But there were other squadrons at various quarters; these I dispersed. Pan Volodyovski alone, who had come out from prison, led his Lauda men to Podlyasye by a wonder and by superhuman resolve, so as to join with Sapyeha. Those who escaped me assembled in Podlyasye in considerable numbers, but before they could do that many good soldiers perished through me. God alone can count them. I acknowledge the truth as if at confession. Pan Volodyovski, on his way to Podlyasye, seized me, and did not wish to let me live; but I escaped because of letters which they found on my person, and from which it transpired that when Volodyovski was in prison and Radzivill was going to shoot him, I interceded persistently and saved him. He let me go free then; I returned to Radzivill and served longer. But the service was bitter for me, the soul began to revolt within me at certain deeds of the prince, for there is not in him either faith, honesty, or conscience, and from his own words it comes out that he works as much for himself as for the King of Sweden. I began then to spring at his eyes. He grew enraged at my boldness, and at last sent me off with letters."

"It is wonderful what important things you tell," said the king. " At least we know from an eyewitness who *pars magna fuit* (took a great part) in affairs, how things happened there."

" It is true that *pars magna fui* (I took a great part)," answered Kmita. " I set out with the letters willingly, for I could not remain in that place. In Pilvishki I met Prince Boguslav. May God give him into my hands, to which end I shall use all my power, so that my vengeance may not miss him for that slander. Not only did I not promise him anything, Gracious Lord, not only is that a shameless lie, but it was just there in Pilvishki that I became converted when I saw all the naked deceit of those heretics."

" Tell quickly how it was, for we were told that Boguslav aided his cousin only through constraint."

" He? He is worse than Prince Yanush, and in his head was the treason first hatched. Did he not tempt the hetman first, pointing out a crown to him? God will decide at the judgment. Yanush at least simulated and shielded himself with *bono publico* (public good); but Boguslav, taking me for an arch scoundrel, revealed his whole soul to me. It is a terror to repeat what he said. 'The devils,' said he, 'must take your Commonwealth, it is a piece of red cloth, and we not only will not raise a hand to save it, but will pull besides, so that the largest piece may come to us. Lithuania,' said he, 'must remain to us, and after Yanush I will put on the cap of Grand Prince, and marry his daughter.'"

The king covered his eyes with his hands. "O passion of our Lord!" said he. "The Radzivills, Radzeyovski, Opalinski — how could that which happened not happen! — they must have crowns, even through rending what the Lord had united."

"I grew numb, Gracious Lord, I had water poured on my head so as not to go mad. The soul changed in me in one moment, as if a thunderbolt had shaken it. I was terrified at my own work. I knew not what to do, whether to thrust a knife into Boguslav or into myself. I bellowed like a wild beast, they had driven me into such a trap. I wanted service no longer with the Radzivills, but vengeance. God gave me a sudden thought: I went with a few men to the quarters of Prince Boguslav, I brought him out beyond the town, I carried him off and wanted to bring him to the confederates so as to buy myself into their company and into the service of your Royal Grace at the price of his head."

"I forgive you all!" cried the king, "for they led you astray; but you have repaid them! Kmita alone could have done that, no man besides. I overlook all and forgive you from my heart! But tell me quickly, for curiosity is burning me, did he escape?"

"At the first station he snatched the pistol from my belt and shot me in the mouth, —here is the scar. He killed my men and escaped. He is a famous knight, it would be hard to deny that; but we shall meet again, though that were to be my last hour."

Here Kmita began to tear at the blanket with which he was covered, but the king interrupted him quickly, —

"And through revenge he invented that letter against you?"

"And through revenge he sent that letter. I recovered from the wound, in the forest, but my soul was suffering more and more. To Volodyovski, to the confederates I could not go, for the Lauda men would have cut me to pieces with their sabres. Still, knowing that the hetman was about to march against them, I forewarned them to collect in a body. And that was my first good deed, for without that Radzivill would have crushed them out, squadron after squadron; but now they have overcome him and, as I hear, are besieging him. May God aid them and send punishment to Radzivill, amen!"

"That may have happened already; and if not it will happen surely," said the king. "What did you do further?"

"I made up my mind that, not being able to serve with the confederate troops of your Royal Grace, I would go to your person and there atone for my former offences with loyalty. But how was I to go? Who would receive Kmita, who would believe him, who would not proclaim him a traitor? Therefore I assumed the name Babinich, and passing through the whole Commonwealth, I reached Chenstohova. Whether I have rendered any services there, let Father Kordetski give witness. Day and night I was thinking only how to repair the injuries to the country, how to spill my blood for it, how to restore myself to repute and to honesty. The rest, Gracious Lord, you know already, for you have seen it. And if a fatherly kind heart incline you, if this new service has outweighed my old sins, or even equalled them, then receive me to your favor and your heart, for all have deserted me, no one comforts me save you. You alone see my sorrow and tears, — I am an outcast, a traitor, an oath-breaker, and still I love this country and your Royal Grace. God sees that I wish to serve both."

Here hot tears dropped from the eyes of the young man till he was carried away with weeping; but the king, like a loving father, seizing him by the head began to kiss his forehead and comfort him.

"Yendrek! you are as dear to me as if you were my own son. What have I said to you? That you sinned through blindness; and how many sin from calculation? From my heart I forgive you all, for you have wiped away your faults. More than one would be glad to boast of such services as yours. I forgive you and the country forgives; and besides, we are indebted to you. Put an end to your grieving."

"God give your Royal Grace everything good for this sympathy," said the knight, with tears. "But as it is I must do penance yet in the world for that oath to Radzivill; for though I knew not to what I was swearing, still an oath is an oath."

"God will not condemn you for that," said the king. "He would have to send half this Commonwealth to hell; namely, all those who broke faith with us."

"I think myself, Gracious King, that I shall not go to hell, for Kordetski assured me of that, though he was not certain that purgatory would miss me. It is a hard thing to roast for a hundred of years. But it is well even to go there! A man can endure much when the hope of salvation is lighting him; and besides prayers can help somewhat and shorten the torment."

"Do not grieve," said Yan Kazimir, "I will prevail on the nuncio himself to say Mass for your intention. With such assistance you will not suffer great harm. Trust in the mercy of God."

Kmita smiled through his tears. "Besides," said he, "God give me to return to strength, then I will shell the soul out of more than one Swede, and through that there will be not only merit in heaven, but it will repair my earthly repute."

"Be of good cheer and do not be troubled about earthly glory. I guarantee that what belongs to you will not miss you. More peaceful times will come; I myself will declare your services, which are not small, and surely they will be greater; and at the Diet, with God's help, I will have this question raised, and you will be restored soon to honor."

"Let that, Gracious Lord, give some comfort; but before then the courts will attack me, from which even the influence of your Royal Grace cannot shield me. But never mind! I will not yield while there is breath in my nostrils, and a sabre in my hand. I am anxious concerning the maiden. Olenka is her name, Gracious Lord; I have not seen her this long time, and I have suffered, oh, I have suffered a world without her and because of her; and though at times I might wish to drive her out of my heart and wrestle with love as with a bear, it's of no use, for such a fellow as he will not let a man go."

Yan Kazimir smiled good-naturedly and kindly: "How can I help you here, my poor man?"

"Who can help me if not your grace? That maiden is an inveterate royalist, and she will never forgive me my deeds at Kyedani, unless your Royal Grace will make intercession, and give witness how I changed and returned to the service of

the king and my country, not from constraint, not for profit,
but through my own will and repentance."

"If that is the question I will make the intercession; and
if she is such a royalist as you say, the intercession should
be effectual, — if the girl is only free, and if some mishap has
not met her such as are frequent in war-time."

"May angels protect her !"

"She deserves it. So that the courts may not trouble you,
act thus wise : Levies will be made now in haste. Since, as
you say, outlawry weighs on you, I cannot give you a commission as Kmita, but I will give you one as Babinich; you
will make a levy which will be for the good of the country,
for you are clearly a mettlesome soldier with experience.
You will take the field under Stefan Charnyetski; under
him death is easiest, but the chances of glory are easiest.
And if need comes you will attack the Swedes of yourself as
you did Hovanski. Your conversion and good deeds commenced with the day when you called yourself Babinich;
call yourself Babinich still further, and the courts will leave
you at rest. When you will be as bright as the sun, when
the report of your services will be heard through the Commonwealth, let men discover who this great cavalier is. This
and that kind of man will be ashamed to summon such a
knight to a court. At that time some will have died, you will
satisfy others. Not a few decisions will be lost, and I promise
to exalt your services to the skies, and will present them to
the Diet for reward, for in my eyes they deserve it."

"Gracious Lord ! how have I earned such favors ? "

"Better than many who think they have a right to them.
Well, well ! be not grieved, dear royalist, for I trust that
the royalist maiden will not be lost to you, and God grant
you to assemble for me more royalists soon."

Kmita, though sick, sprang quickly from the bed and fell
his whole length at the feet of the king.

"In God's name! what are you doing ? " cried the king.
" The blood will leave you! Yendrek! Hither, some one !"

In came the marshal himself, who had long been looking
for the king through the castle.

"Holy Yerzy! my patron, what do I see ? " cried he,
when he saw the king raising Kmita with his own hands.

"This is Babinich, my most beloved soldier and most
faithful servant, who saved my life yesterday," said the
king. " Help, Lord Marshal, to raise him to the couch."

CHAPTER XIII.

FROM Lyubovlya the king advanced to Dukla, Krosno, Lantsut, and Lvoff, having at his side the marshal of the kingdom, many dignitaries and senators, with the court squadrons and escorts. And as a great river flowing through a country gathers to itself all the smaller waters, so did new legions gather to the retinue of the king. Lords and armed nobles thronged forward, and soldiers, now singly, now in groups, and crowds of armed peasants burning with special hatred against the Swedes.

The movement was becoming universal, and the military order of things had begun to lead to it. Threatening manifestoes had appeared dated from Sanch: one by Constantine Lyubomirski, the marshal of the Circle of Knights; the other by Yan Vyelopolski, the castellan of Voinik, both calling on the nobles in the province of Cracow to join the general militia; those failing to appear were threatened with the punishments of public law. The manifesto of the king completed these, and brought the most slothful to their feet.

But there was no need of threats, for an immense enthusiasm had seized all ranks. Old men and children mounted their horses. Women gave up their jewels, their dresses; some rushed off to the conflict themselves.

In the forges gypsies were pounding whole nights and days with their hammers, turning the innocent tools of the ploughman into weapons. Villages and towns were empty, for the men had marched to the field. From the heaven-touching mountains night and day crowds of wild people were pouring down. The forces of the king increased with each moment. The clergy came forth with crosses and banners to meet the king; Jewish societies came with their rabbis; his advance was like a mighty triumph. From every side flew in the best tidings, as if borne by the wind.

Not only in that part of the country which the invasion of the enemy had not included did people rush to arms. Everywhere in the remotest lands and provinces, in towns, villages, settlements, and unapproachable wildernesses, the awful war of revenge and retaliation raised its flaming head. The lower the people had fallen before, the higher they raised their heads now; they had been reborn, changed in spirit, and in their exaltation did not even hesitate to tear open their own half-healed wounds, to free their blood of poisoned juices.

They had begun already to speak, and with increasing loudness, of the powerful union of the nobles and the army, at the head of which were to be the old grand hetman Revera Pototski and the full hetman Lantskoronski, Stefan Charnyetski and Sapyeha, Michael Radzivill, a powerful magnate anxious to remove the ill-fame which Yanush had brought on the house, and Pan Kryshtof Tyshkyevich, with many other senators, provincial and military officials and nobles.

Letters were flying every day between these men and the marshal of the kingdom, who did not wish that so noted a union should be formed without him. Tidings more and more certain arrived, till at last it was announced with authority that the hetmans and with them the army had abandoned the Swedes, and formed for the defence of the king and the country the confederation of Tyshovtsi.

The king knew of this first, for he and the queen, though far apart, had labored no little through letters and messengers at the formation of it; still, not being able to take personal part in the affair, he waited for the tenor of it with impatience. But before he came to Lvoff, Pan Slujevski with Pan Domashevski, judge of Lukoff, came to him bringing assurances of service and loyalty from the confederates and the act of union for confirmation.

The king then read that act at a general council of bishops and senators. The hearts of all were filled with delight, their spirits rose in thankfulness to God; for that memorable confederacy announced not merely that the people had come to their senses, but that they had changed; that people of whom not long before the foreign invader might say that they had no loyalty, no love of country, no conscience, no order, no endurance, nor any of those virtues through which nations and States do endure.

The testimony of all these virtues lay now before the king in the act of a confederation and its manifesto. In it was summed up the perfidy of Karl Gustav, his violation of oaths and promises, the cruelty of his generals and his

soldiers, such as are not practised by even the wildest of
people, desecration of churches, oppression, rapacity, robbery, shedding of innocent blood, and they declared against
the Scandinavian invasion a war of life or death. A manifesto terrible as the trumpet of the archangel, summoned
not only knights but all ranks and all people in the Commonwealth. Even *infames* (the infamous), *banniti* (outlaws),
and *proscripti* (the proscribed) should go to this war, said
the manifesto. The knights were to mount their horses
and expose their own breasts, and the land was to furnish
infantry, — wealthy holders more, the poorer less, according
to their wealth and means.

"Since in this state good and evil belong equally to all, it
is proper that all should share danger. Whoso calls himself a noble, with land or without it, and if one noble has a
number of sons, they should all go to the war against the
enemies of the Commonwealth. Since we all, whether of
higher or lower birth, being nobles, are eligible to all the
prerogatives of office, dignity, and profit in the country, so
we are equal in this, that we should go in like manner with
our own persons to the defence of these liberties and
benefits."

Thus did that manifesto explain the equality of nobles.
The king, the bishops, and the senators, who for a long time
had carried in their hearts the thought of reforming the
Commonwealth, convinced themselves with joyful wonder
that the people had become ripe for that reform, that they
were ready to enter upon new paths, rub the rust and mould
from themselves, and begin a new, glorious life.

"With this," explained the manifesto, "we open to each
deserving man of plebeian condition a place, we indicate
and offer by this our confederation an opportunity to reach
and acquire the honors, prerogatives, and benefits which
the noble estate enjoys — "

When this introduction was read at the royal council, a
deep silence followed. Those who with the king desired
most earnestly that access to rights of nobility should be
open to people of lower station thought that they would
have to overcome, endure, and break no small opposition;
that whole years would pass before it would be safe to give
utterance to anything similar; meanwhile that same nobility
which hitherto had been so jealous of its prerogatives, so
stubborn in appearance, opened wide the gate to the gray
crowds of peasants.

The primate rose, encircled as it were by the spirit of prophecy, and said, —

"Since you have inserted that *punctum* (paragraph), posterity will glorify this confederation from age to age, and when any one shall wish to consider these times as times of the fall of ancient Polish virtue, in contradicting him men will point to you."

Father Gembitski was ill; therefore he could not speak, but with hand trembling from emotion he blessed the act and the envoys.

"I see the enemy already departing in shame from this land!" said the king.

"God grant it most quickly!" cried both envoys.

"Gentlemen, you will go with us to Lvoff," said the king, "where we will confirm this confederation at once, and besides shall conclude another which the powers of hell itself will not overcome."

The envoys and senators looked at one another as if asking what power was in question; the king was silent, but his countenance grew brighter and brighter; he took the act again in his hand and read it a second time, smiled, and asked, —

"Were there many opponents?"

"Gracious Lord," answered Pan Domashevski, "this confederacy arose with unanimity through the efforts of the hetmans, of Sapyeha, of Pan Charnyetski; and among nobles not a voice was raised in opposition, so angry are they all at the Swedes, and so have they flamed up with love for the country and your majesty."

"We decided, moreover, in advance," added Pan Slujevski, "that this was not to be a diet, but that *pluralitas* (plurality) alone was to decide; therefore no man's *veto* could injure the cause; we should have cut an opponent to pieces with our sabres. All said too that it was necessary to finish with the *liberum veto*, since it is freedom for one, but slavery for many."

"Golden words of yours!" said the primate. "Only let a reform of the Commonwealth come, and no enemy will frighten us."

"But where is the voevoda of Vityebsk?" asked the king.

"He went in the night, after the signing of the manifesto, to his own troops at Tykotsin, in which he holds the voevoda of Vilna, the traitor, besieged. Before this time he must have taken him, living or dead."

"Was he so sure of capturing him?"

"He was as sure as that night follows day. All, even his most faithful servants, have deserted the traitor. Only a handful of Swedes are defending themselves there, and rein-forcements cannot come from any side. Pan Sapyeha said in Tyshovtsi, 'I wanted to wait one day, for I should have finished with Radzivill before evening! but this is more important than Radzivill, for they can take him without me; one squadron is enough.'"

"Praise be to God!" said the king. "But where is Charnyetski?"

"So many of the best cavaliers have hurried to him that in one day he was at the head of an excellent squadron. He moved at once on the Swedes, and where he is at this moment we know not."

"But the hetmans?"

"They are waiting anxiously for the commands of your Royal Grace. They are both laying plans for the coming war, and are in communication with Pan Yan Zamoyski in Zamost; meanwhile regiments are rolling to them every day with the snow."

"Have all left the Swedes then?"

"Yes, Gracious King. There were deputies also to the het-mans from the troops of Konyetspolski, who is with the person of Karl Gustav. And they too would be glad to re-turn to their lawful service, though Karl does not spare on them promises or flattery. They said too that though they could not *recedere* (withdraw) at once, they would do so as soon as a convenient time came, for they have grown tired of his feasts and his flattery, his eye-winking and clapping of hands. They can barely hold out."

"Everywhere people are coming to their senses, every-where good news," said the king. "Praise to the Most Holy Lady! This is the happiest day of my life, and a second such will come only when the last soldier of the enemy leaves the boundary of the Commonwealth."

At this Pan Domashevski struck his sword. "May God not grant that to happen!" said he.

"How is that?" asked the king, with astonishment.

"That the last wide-breeches should leave the boundaries of the Commonwealth on his own feet? Impossible, Gracious Lord! What have we sabres at our sides for?"

"Oh!" said the king, made glad, "that is bravery."

But Pan Slujevski, not wishing to remain behind Do-

mashevski, said : " As true as life we will not agree to
that, and first I will place a veto on it. We shall not be
content with their retreat; we will follow them ! "

The primate shook his head, and smiled kindly. " Oh,
the nobles are on horseback, and they will ride on and on !
But not too fast, not too fast ! The enemy are still within
the boundaries."

" Their time is short ! " cried both confederates.

" The spirit has changed, and fortune will change," said
Father Gembitski, in a weak voice.

" Wine ! " cried the king. " Let me drink to the change,
with the confederates."

They brought wine ; but with the servants who brought
the wine entered an old attendant of the king, who said, —

" Gracious Lord, Pan Kryshtoporski has come from Chenstohova, and wishes to do homage to your Royal Grace."

" Bring him here quickly ! " cried the king.

In a moment a tall, thin noble entered, with a frowning
look. He bowed before the king to his feet, then rather
haughtily to the dignitaries, and said, —

" May the Lord Jesus Christ be praised ! "

" For the ages of ages ! " answered the king. " What is
to be heard from the monastery ? "

" Terrible frost, Gracious Lord, so that the eyelids are
frozen to the eyeballs."

" But for God's sake ! tell us of the Swedes and not of the
frost ! " cried the king.

" But what can I say of them, Gracious Lord, when there
are none at Chenstohova ? " asked he, humorously.

" Those tidings have come to us," replied the king, " but
only from the talk of people, and you have come from the
cloister itself. Are you an eyewitness ? "

" I am, Gracious Lord, a partner in the defence and an eyewitness of the miracles of the Most Holy Lady."

" That was not the end of Her grace," said the king, raising his eyes to heaven, " but let us earn them further."

" I have seen much in my life," continued the noble ; " but
such evident miracles I have not seen, touching which the
prior Kordetski writes in detail in this letter."

Yan Kazimir seized hastily the letter handed him by the
noble, and began to read. At times he interrupted the reading to pray, then again turned to the letter. His face changed
with joyful feelings ; at last he raised his eyes to the noble.

" Father Kordetski writes me," said he, " that you have

lost a great cavalier, a certain Babinich, who blew up the
Swedish siege gun with powder ? "

" He sacrificed himself for all.   But some say he is alive,
and God knows what they have said ; not being certain, we
have not ceased to mourn him, for without his gallant deed
it would have been hard for us to defend ourselves."

" If that is true, then cease to mourn him.   Pan Babinich
is alive, and here with us.   He was the first to inform us
that the Swedes, not being able to do anything against the
power of God, were thinking of retreat.   And later he rendered such famous service that we know not ourselves how
to pay him."

" Oh, that will comfort the prior ! " cried the noble, with
gladness ; " but if Pan Babinich is alive, it is only because he
has the special favor of the Most Holy Lady.   How that
will comfort Father Kordetski !   A father could not love a
son as he loved him.   And your Royal Grace will permit me
to greet Pan Babinich, for there is not a second man of such
daring in the Commonwealth."

But the king began again to read, and after a while
cried, —

" What do I hear ?   After retreating they tried once again
to steal on the cloister ? "

" When Miller went away, he did not show himself again ;
but Count Veyhard appeared unexpectedly at the walls, trusting, it seems, to find the gates open.   He did, but the peasants
fell on him with such rage that he retreated shamefully.
While the world is a world, simple peasants have never
fought so in the open field against cavalry.   Then Pan
Pyotr Charnyetski and Pan Kulesha came up and cut him
to pieces."

The king turned to the senators.

" See how poor ploughmen stand up in defence of this
country and the holy faith."

" That they stand up, Gracious King, is true," cried the
noble.   " Whole villages near Chenstohova are empty, for
the peasants are in the field with their scythes.   There is
a fierce war everywhere ; the Swedes are forced to keep together in numbers, and if the peasants catch one of them
they treat him so that it would be better for him to go
straight to hell.   Who is not taking up arms now in the
Commonwealth ?   It was not for the dog-brothers to attack
Chenstohova.   From that hour they could not remain in
this country."

"From this hour no man will suffer oppression in this land who resists now with his blood," said the king, with solemnity; "so help me God and the holy cross!"

"Amen!" added the primate.

Now the noble struck his forehead with his hand. "The frost has disturbed my mind, Gracious Lord, for I forgot to tell one thing, that such a son, the voevoda of Poznan, is dead. He died, they say, suddenly."

Here the noble was somewhat ashamed, seeing that he had called a great senator "that such a son" in presence of the king and dignitaries; therefore he added, confused, —

"I did not wish to belittle an honorable station, but a traitor."

But no one had noticed that clearly, for all looked at the king, who said, —

"We have long predestined Pan Yan Leshchynski to be voevoda of Poznan, even during the life of Pan Opalinski. Let him fill that office more worthily. The judgment of God, I see, has begun upon those who brought this country to its decline, for at this moment, perhaps, the voevoda of Vilna is giving an account of his deeds before the Supreme Judge." Here he turned to the bishops and senators, —

"But it is time for us to think of a general war, and I wish to have the opinion of all of you, gentlemen, on this question."

CHAPTER XIV.

AT the moment when the king was saying that the voe-voda of Vilna was standing, perhaps, before the judgment of God, he spoke as it were with a prophetic spirit, for at that hour the affair of Tykotsin was decided.

On December 25 Sapyeha was so sure of capturing Tykotsin that he went himself to Tyshovtsi, leaving the further conduct of the siege to Pan Oskyerko. He gave command to wait for the final storm till his return, which was to follow quickly; assembling, therefore, his more prominent officers, he said, —

"Reports have come to me that among the officers there is a plan to bear apart on sabres the voevoda of Vilna immediately after capturing the castle. Now if the castle, as may happen, should surrender during my absence, I inform you, gentlemen, that I prohibit most strictly an attack on Radzivill's life. I receive letters, it is true, from persons of whom you gentlemen do not even dream, not to let him live when I take him. But I do not choose to obey these commands; and this I do not from any compassion, for the traitor is not worthy of that, but because I have no right over his life, and I prefer to bring him before the Diet, so that posterity may have in this case an example that no greatness of family, no office can cover such offence, nor protect him from public punishment."

In this sense spoke the voevoda of Vityebsk, but more minutely, for his honesty was equalled by this weakness: he esteemed himself an orator, and loved on every occasion to speak copiously, and listened with delight to his own words, adding to them the most beautiful sentences from the ancients.

"Then I must steep my right hand well in water," answered Zagloba, "for it itches terribly. But I only say this, that if Radzivill had me in his hands, surely he would not spare my head till sunset. He knows well who in great part made his troops leave him; he knows well who embroiled him with the Swedes. But even if he does, I know not why I should be more indulgent to Radzivill than Radzivill to me."

"Because the command is not in your hands and you must obey," said Sapyeha, with dignity.

"That I must obey is true, but it is well at times also to obey Zagloba. I say this boldly, because if Radzivill had listened to me when I urged him to defend the country, he would not be in Tykotsin to-day, but in the field at the head of all the troops of Lithuania."

"Does it seem to you that the baton is in bad hands ? "

"It would not become me to say that, for I placed it in those hands. Our gracious lord, Yan Kazimir, has only to confirm my choice, nothing more."

The voevoda smiled at this, for he loved Zagloba and his jokes.

"Lord brother," said he, "you crushed Radzivill, you made me hetman, and all this is your merit. Permit me now to go in peace to Tyshovtsi, so that Sapyeha too may serve the country in something."

Zagloba put his hands on his hips, thought awhile as if he were considering whether he ought to permit or not; at last his eye gleamed, he nodded, and said with importance, —

"Go, your grace, in peace."

"God reward you for the permission!" answered the voevoda, with a laugh.

Other officers seconded the voevoda's laugh. He was preparing to start, for the carriage was under the window; he took farewell of all, therefore, giving each instructions what to do during his absence; then approaching Volodyovski, he said, —

"If the castle surrenders you will answer to me for the life of the voevoda."

"According to order! a hair will not fall from his head," said the little knight.

"Pan Michael," said Zagloba to him, after the departure of the voevoda, "I am curious to know what persons are urging our Sapyo [1] not to let Radzivill live when he captures him."

"How should I know ? " answered the little knight.

"If you say that what another mouth does not whisper to your ear your own will not suggest, you tell the truth! But they must be some considerable persons, since they are able to command the voevoda."

[1] Sapyeha.

"Maybe it is the king himself."

"The king? If a dog bit the king he would forgive him that minute, and give him cheese in addition. Such is his heart."

"I will not dispute about that; but still, do they not say that he is greatly incensed at Radzivill?"

"First, any man will succeed in being angry, — for example, my anger at Radzivill; secondly, how could he be incensed at Radzeyovski when he took his sons in guardianship, because the father was not better? That is a golden heart, and I think it is the queen who is making requests against the life of Radzivill. She is a worthy lady, not a word against that, but she has a woman's mind; and know that if a woman is enraged at you, even should you hide in a crack of the floor, she will pick you out with a pin."

Volodyovski sighed at this, and said, —

"Why should any woman be angry with me, since I have never made trouble for one in my life?"

"Ah, but you would have been glad to do so. Therefore, though you serve in the cavalry, you rush on so wildly against the walls of Tykotsin with infantry, for you think not only is Radzivill there, but Panna Billevich. I know you, you rogue! Is it not true? You have not driven her out of your head yet."

"There was a time when I had put her thoroughly out of my head; and Kmita himself, if now here, would be forced to confess that my action was knightly, not wishing to act against people in love. I chose to forget my rebuff, but I will not hide this : if Panna Billevich is now in Tykotsin, and if God permits me a second time to save her from trouble, I shall see in that the expressed will of Providence. I need take no thought of Kmita, I owe him nothing; and the hope is alive in me that if he left her of his own will she must have forgotten him, and such a thing will not happen now as happened to me the first time."

Conversing in this way, they reached their quarters, where they found Pan Yan and Pan Stanislav, Roh Kovalski and the lord tenant of Vansosh, Jendzian.

The cause of Sapyeha's trip to Tyshovtsi was no secret, hence all the knights were pleased that so honorable a confederacy would rise in defence of the faith and the country.

"Another wind is blowing now in the whole Commonwealth," said Pan Stanislav, "and, thanks be to God, in the eyes of the Swedes."

"It began from Chenstohova," answered Pan Yan. "There was news yesterday that the cloister holds out yet, and repulses more and more powerful assaults. Permit not, Most Holy Mother, the enemy to put Thy dwelling-place to shame."

Here Jendzian sighed and said: "Besides the holy images how much precious treasure would go into enemies' hands; when a man thinks of that, food refuses to pass his throat!"

"The troops are just tearing away to the assault; we can hardly hold them back," said Pan Michael. "Yesterday Stankyevich's squadron moved without orders and without ladders, for they said, 'When we finish this traitor, we will go to relieve Chenstohova;' and when any man mentions Chenstohova all grit their teeth and shake their sabres."

"Why have we so many squadrons here when one half would be enough for Tykotsin?" asked Zagloba. "It is the stubbornness of Sapyeha, nothing more. He does not wish to obey me; he wants to show that without my counsel he can do something. As you see yourselves, how are so many men to invest one paltry castle? They merely hinder one another, for there is not room for them all."

"Military experience speaks through you, — it is impossible!" answered Pan Stanislav.

"Well, I have a head on my shoulders."

"Uncle has a head on his shoulders!" cried Pan Roh, suddenly; and straightening his mustaches, he began to look around on all present as if seeking some one to contradict him.

"But the voevoda too has a head," answered Pan Yan; "and if so many squadrons are here, there is danger that Prince Boguslav might come to the relief of his cousin."

"Then send a couple of light squadrons to ravage Electoral Prussia," said Zagloba; "and summon volunteers there from among common people. I myself would be the first man to go to try Prussian beer."

"Beer is not good in winter, unless warmed," remarked Pan Michael.

"Then give us wine, or gorailka, or mead," said Zagloba.

Others also exhibited a willingness to drink; therefore the lord tenant of Vansosh occupied himself with that business, and soon a number of decanters were on the table. Hearts were glad at this sight, and the knights began to drink to one another, raising their goblets each time for a new health.

"Destruction to the Swedes, may they not skin our bread very long!" said Zagloba. "Let them devour their pine cones in Sweden."

"To the health of his Royal Grace and the Queen!" said Pan Yan.

"And to loyal men!" said Volodyovski.

"Then to our own healths!"

"To the health of Uncle!" thundered Kovalski.

"God reward! Into your hands! and empty though your lips to the bottom. Zagloba is not yet entirely old! Worthy gentlemen! may we smoke this badger out of his hole with all haste, and move then to Chenstohova."

"To Chenstohova!" shouted Kovalski. "To the rescue of the Most Holy Lady."

"To Chenstohova!" cried all.

"To defend the treasures of Yasna Gora from the Pagans!" added Jendzian.

"Who pretend that they believe in the Lord Jesus, wishing to hide their wickedness; but in fact they only howl at the moon like dogs, and in this is all their religion."

"And such as these raise their hands against the splendors of Yasna Gora!"

"You have touched the spot in speaking of their faith," said Volodyovski to Zagloba, "for I myself have heard how they howl at the moon. They said afterward that they were singing Lutheran psalms; but it is certain that the dogs sing such psalms."

"How is that?" asked Kovalski. "Are there such people among them?"

"There is no other kind," answered Zagloba, with deep conviction.

"And is their king no better?"

"Their king is the worst of all. He began this war of purpose to blaspheme the true faith in the churches."

Here Kovalski, who had drunk much, rose and said: "If that is true, then as sure as you are looking at me, and as I am Kovalski, I'll spring straight at the Swedish king in the first battle, and though he stood in the densest throng, that is nothing! My death or his! I'll reach him with my lance, — hold me a fool, gentlemen, if I do not!"

When he had said this he clinched his fist and was going to thunder on the table. He would have smashed the glasses and decanters, and broken the table; but Zagloba caught him hastily by the arm and said, —

"Sit down, Roh, and give us peace. We will not think you a fool if you do not do this, but know that we will not stop thinking you a fool until you have done it. I do not understand, though, how you can raise a lance on the King of Sweden, when you are not in the hussars."

"I will join the escort and be enrolled in the squadron of Prince Polubinski; and my father will help me."

"Father Roh?"

"Of course."

"Let him help you, but break not these glasses, or I'll be the first man to break your head. Of what was I speaking, gentlemen? Ah! of Chenstohova. *Luctus* (grief) will devour me, if we do not come in time to save the holy place. *Luctus* will devour me, I tell you all! And all through that traitor Radzivill and the philosophical reasoning of Sapyeha."

"Say nothing against the voevoda. He is an honorable man," said the little knight.

"Why cover Radzivill with two halves when one is sufficient? Nearly ten thousand men are around this little booth of a castle, the best cavalry and infantry. Soon they will lick the soot out of all the chimneys in this region, for what was on the hearths they have eaten already."

"It is not for us to argue over the reasons of superiors, but to obey!"

"It is not for you to argue, Pan Michael, but for me; half of the troops who abandoned Radzivill chose me as leader, and I would have driven Karl Gustav beyond the tenth boundary ere now, but for that luckless modesty which commanded me to place the baton in the hands of Sapyeha. Let him put an end to his delay, lest I take back what I gave."

"You are only so daring after drink," said Volodyovski.

"Do you say that? Well, you will see! This very day I will go among the squadrons and call out, 'Gracious gentlemen, whoso chooses come with me to Chenstohova; it is not for you to wear out your elbows and knees against the mortar of Tykotsin! I beg you to come with me! Whoso made me commander, whoso gave me power, whoso had confidence that I would do what was useful for the country and the faith, let him stand at my side. It is a beautiful thing to punish traitors, but a hundred times more beautiful to save the Holy Lady, our Mother and the Patroness of this kingdom from oppression and the yoke of the heretic.'"

Here Zagloba, from whose forelock the steam had for some time been rising, started up from his place, sprang to a bench, and began to shout as if he were before an assembly, —

"Worthy gentlemen! whoso is a Catholic, whoso a Pole, whoso has pity on the Most Holy Lady, let him follow me! To the relief of Chenstohova!"

"I go!" shouted Roh Kovalski.

Zagloba looked for a while on those present, and seeing astonishment and silent faces, he came down from the bench and said, —

"I'll teach Sapyeha reason! I am a rascal if by tomorrow I do not take half the army from Tykotsin and lead it to Chenstohova."

"For God's sake, restrain yourself, father!" said Pan Yan.

"I'm a rascal, I tell you!" repeated Zagloba.

They were frightened lest he should carry out his threat, for he was able to do so. In many squadrons there was murmuring at the delay in Tykotsin; men really gnashed their teeth thinking of Chenstohova. It was enough to cast a spark on that powder; and what if a man so stubborn, of such immense knightly importance as Zagloba, should cast it? To begin with, the greater part of Sapyeha's army was composed of new recruits, and therefore of men unused to discipline, and ready for action on their own account, and they would have gone as one man without doubt after Zagloba to Chenstohova.

Therefore both Skshetuskis were frightened at this undertaking, and Volodyovski cried, —

"Barely has a small army been formed by the greatest labor of the voevoda, barely is there a little power for the defence of the Commonwealth, and you wish with disorder to break up the squadrons, bring them to disobedience. Radzivill would pay much for such counsel, for it is water to his mill. Is it not a shame for you to speak of such a deed?"

"I'm a scoundrel if I don't do it!" said Zagloba.

"Uncle will do it!" said Kovalski.

"Silence, you horseskull!" roared out Pan Michael.

Pan Roh stared, shut his mouth, and straightened himself at once.

Then Volodyovski turned to Zagloba: "And I am a scoundrel if one man of my squadron goes with you; you wish to ruin the army, and I tell you that I will fall first upon your volunteers."

"O Pagan, faithless Turk!" said Zagloba. "How is that? you would attack knights of the Most Holy Lady? Are you ready? Well, I know you! Do you think, gentlemen, that it is a question with him of an army or discipline? No! he sniffs Panna Billevich behind the walls of Tykotsin. For a private question, for your own wishes you would not hesitate to desert the best cause. You would be glad to flutter around a maiden, to stand on one foot, then the other, and display yourself. But nothing will come of this! My head for it, that better than you are running after her, even that same Kmita, for even he is no worse than you."

Volodyovski looked at those present, taking them to witness what injustice was done him; then he frowned. They thought he would burst out in anger, but because he had been drinking, he fell all at once into tenderness.

"This is my reward," said he. "From the years of a stripling I have served the country; I have not put the sabre out of my hand! I have neither cottage, wife, nor children; my head is as lone as a lance-point. The most honorable think of themselves, but I have no rewards save wounds in the flesh; nay, I am accused of selfishness, almost held a traitor."

Tears began to drop on his yellow mustaches. Zagloba softened in a moment, and throwing open his arms, cried, —

"Pan Michael, I have done you cruel injustice! I should be given to the hangman for having belittled such a tried friend!"

Then falling into mutual embraces, they began to kiss each other; they drank more to good understanding, and when sorrow had gone considerably out of his heart, Volodyovski said, —

"But you will not ruin the army, bring disobedience, and give an evil example?"

"I will not, Pan Michael, I will not for your sake."

"God grant us to take Tykotsin; whose affair is it what I seek behind the walls of the fortress? Why should any man jeer at me?"

Struck by that question, Zagloba began to put the ends of his mustaches in his mouth and gnaw them; at last he said: "Pan Michael, I love you as the apple of my eye, but drive that Panna Billevich out of your head."

" Why ? " asked Pan Michael, with astonishment.

" She is beautiful, *assentior* (I agree)," answered Zagloba, " but she is distinguished in person, and there is no proportion whatever between you. You might sit on her shoulder, like a canary-bird, and peck sugar out of her mouth. She might carry you like a falcon on her glove, and let you off against every enemy, for though you are little you are venomous like a hornet."

" Well, have you begun ? " asked Volodyovski.

" If I have begun, then let me finish. There is one woman as if created for you, and she is precisely that kernel — What is her name ? That one whom Podbipienta was to marry ? "

" Anusia Borzobogati ! " cried Pan Yan. "She is indeed an old love of Michael's."

" A regular grain of buckwheat, but a pretty little rogue; just like a doll," said Zagloba, smacking his lips.

Volodyovski began to sigh, and to repeat time after time what he always repeated when mention was made of Anusia : "What is happening to the poor girl ? Oh, if she could only be found ! "

" You would not let her out of your hands, for, God bless me, I have not seen in my life any man so given to falling in love. You ought to have been born a rooster, scratch the sweepings in a house-yard, and cry, ' Co, co, co,' at the top-knots."

" Anusia ! Anusia ! " repeated Pan Michael. " If God would send her to me — But perhaps she is not in the world, or perhaps she is married — "

" How could she be ? She was a green turnip when I saw her, and afterward, even if she ripened, she may still be in the maiden state. After such a man as Podbipienta she could not take any common fellow. Besides, in these times of war few are thinking of marriage."

" You did not know her well," answered Pan Michael. " She was wonderfully honest; but she had such a nature that she let no man pass without piercing his heart. The Lord God created her thus. She did not miss even men of lower station ; for example, Princess Griselda's physician, that Italian, who was desperately in love with her. Maybe she has married him and he has taken her beyond the sea."

" Don't talk such nonsense, Michael ! " cried Zagloba, with indignation. " A doctor, a doctor, — that the daughter of a noble of honorable blood should marry a man of such low estate! I have already said that that is impossible."

"I was angry with her myself, for I thought, 'This is without limit; soon she will be turning the heads of attorneys.'"

"I prophesy that you will see her yet," said Zagloba.

Further conversation was interrupted by the entrance of Pan Tokarzevich, who had served formerly with Radzivill, but after the treason of the hetman, left him, in company with others, and was now standard-bearer in Oskyerko's regiment.

"Colonel," said he to Volodyovski, "we are to explode a petard."

"Is Pan Oskyerko ready?"

"He was ready at midday, and he is not willing to wait, for the night promises to be dark."

"That is well; we will go to see. I will order the men to be ready with muskets, so that the besieged may not make a sortie. Will Pan Oskyerko himself explode the petard?"

"He will — in his own person. A crowd of volunteers go with him."

"And I will go!" said Volodyovski.

"And we!" cried Pan Yan and Pan Stanislav.

"Oh, 't is a pity that old eyes cannot see in the dark," said Zagloba, "for of a surety I should not let you go alone. But what is to be done? When dusk comes I cannot draw my sword. In the daytime, in the daytime, in the sunlight, then the old man likes to move to the field. Give me the strongest of the Swedes, if at midday."

"But I will go," said, after some thought, the tenant of Vansosh. "When they blow up the gate the troops will spring to the storm in a crowd, and in the castle there may be great wealth in plate and in jewels."

All went out, for it was now growing dark; in the quarters Zagloba alone remained. He listened for a while to the snow squeaking under the steps of the departing men, then began to raise one after another the decanters, and look through them at the light burning in the chimney to see if there was something yet in any of them.

The others marched toward the castle in darkness and wind, which rose from the north and blew with increasing force, howling, storming, bringing with it clouds of snow broken fine.

"A good night to explode a petard!" said Volodyovski.

"But also for a sortie," answered Pan Yan. "We must keep a watchful eye and ready muskets."

"God grant," said Pan Tokarzevich, "that at Chenstohova there is a still greater storm. It is always warmer for our men behind the walls. But may the Swedes freeze there on guard, may they freeze!"

"A terrible night!" said Pan Stanislav; "do you hear, gentlemen, how it howls, as if Tartars were rushing through the air to attack?"

"Or as if devils were singing a requiem for Radzivill!" said Volodyovski.

CHAPTER XV.

BUT a few days subsequent the great traitor in the castle was looking at the darkness coming down on the snowy shrouds and listening to the howling of the wind.

The lamp of his life was burning out slowly. At noon of that day he was still walking around and looking through the battlements, at the tents and the wooden huts of Sapyeha's troops; but two hours later he grew so ill that they had to carry him to his chambers.

From those times at Kyedani in which he had striven for a crown, he had changed beyond recognition. The hair on his head had grown white, around his eyes red rings had formed, his face was swollen and flabby, therefore it seemed still more enormous, but it was the face of a half corpse, marked with blue spots and terrible through its expression of hellish suffering.

And still, though his life could be measured by hours, he had lived too long, for not only had he outlived faith in himself and his fortunate star, faith in his own hopes and plans, but his fall was so deep that when he looked at the bottom of that precipice to which he was rolling, he would not believe himself. Everything had deceived him : events, calculations, allies. He, for whom it was not enough to be the mightiest lord in Poland, a prince of the Roman Empire, grand hetman, and voevoda of Vilna; he, for whom all Lithuania was less than what he desired and was lusting after, was confined in one narrow, small castle in which either Death or Captivity was waiting for him. And he watched the door every day to see which of these two terrible goddesses would enter first to take his soul or his more than half-ruined body.

Of his lands, of his estates and starostaships, it was possible not long before to mark out a vassal kingdom; now he is not master even of the walls of Tykotsin.

Barely a few months before he was treating with neighboring kings; to-day one Swedish captain obeys his commands with impatience and contempt, and dares to bend him to his will.

When his troops left him, when from a lord and a magnate who made the whole country tremble, he became a powerless pauper who needed rescue and assistance himself, Karl Gustav despised him. He would have raised to the skies a mighty ally, but he turned with haughtiness from the supplicant.

Like Kostka Napyerski, the foot-pad, besieged on a time in Chorshtyn, is he, Radzivill, besieged now in Tykotsin. And who is besieging him? Sapyeha, his greatest personal enemy. When they capture him they will drag him to justice in worse fashion than a robber, as a traitor.

His kinsmen have deserted him, his friends, his connections. Armies have plundered his property, his treasures and riches are blown into mist, and that lord, that prince, who once upon a time astonished the court of France and dazzled it with his luxury, he who at feasts received thousands of nobles, who maintained tens of thousands of his own troops, whom he fed and supported, had not now wherewith to nourish his own failing strength; and terrible to relate, he, Radzivill, in the last moments of his life, almost at the hour of his death, was hungry!

In the castle there had long been a lack of provisions; from the scant remaining supplies the Swedish commander dealt stingy rations, and the prince would not beg of him.

If only the fever which was devouring his strength had deprived him of consciousness; but it had not. His breast rose with increasing heaviness, his breath turned into a rattle, his swollen feet and hands were freezing, but his mind, omitting moments of delirium, omitting the terrible visions and nightmares which passed before his eyes, remained for the greater part of the time clear. And that prince saw his whole fall, all his want, all his misery and humiliation; that former warrior-victor saw all his defeat, and his sufferings were so immense that they could be equalled only by his sins.

Besides, as the Furies tormented Orestes, so was he tormented by reproaches of conscience, and in no part of the world was there a sanctuary to which he could flee from them. They tormented him in the day, they tormented him at night, in the field, under the roof; pride could not withstand them nor repulse them. The deeper his fall, the more fiercely they lashed him. And there were moments in which he tore his own breast. When enemies came against his country from every side, when foreign nations grieved over its hapless condition, its sufferings and bloodshed, he, the grand hetman, instead of moving to the field, instead of sacrificing the last drop of his blood, instead of astonishing the world like Leonidas or Themistocles, instead of pawning his last coat like Sapyeha, made a treaty with enemies against the mother, raised a sacrilegious hand against his own king, and imbrued it in blood near and dear to him. He had done all this, and now he is at the limit not only of infamy, but of life, close to his reckoning, there beyond. What is awaiting him?

The hair rose on his head when he thought of that. For he had raised his hand against his country, he had appeared to himself great in relation to that country, and now all had changed. Now he had become small, and the Commonwealth, rising from dust and blood, appeared to him something great and continually greater, invested with a mysterious terror, full of a sacred majesty, awful. And she grew, increased continually in his eyes, and became more and more gigantic. In presence of her he felt himself dust as prince and as hetman, as Radzivill. He could not understand what that was. Some unknown waves were rising around him, flowing toward him, with roaring, with thunder, flowing ever nearer, rising more terribly, and he understood that he must be drowned in that immensity, hundreds such as he would be drowned. But why had he not seen this awfulness and this mysterious power at first; why had he, mad man, rushed against it? When these ideas roared in his head, fear seized him in presence of that mother, in presence of that Commonwealth; for he did not recognize her features, which formerly were so kind and so mild.

The spirit was breaking within him, and terror dwelt in his breast. At moments he thought that another country altogether, another people, were around him. Through the besieged walls came news of everything that men were doing in the invaded Commonwealth, and marvellous and astonishing things were they doing. A war of life or death against the Swedes and traitors had begun, all the more terrible in that it had not been foreseen by any man. The Commonwealth had begun to punish. There was something in this of the anger of God for the insult to majesty.

When through the walls of Tykotsin came news of the siege of Chenstohova, Radzivill, a Calvinist, was frightened;

and fright did not leave his soul from that day, for then he perceived for the first time those mysterious waves which, after they had risen, were to swallow the Swedes and him; then the invasion of the Swedes seemed not an invasion, but a sacrilege, and the punishment of it inevitable. Then for the first time the veil dropped from his eyes, and he saw the changed face of the Commonwealth, no longer a mother, but a punishing queen.

All who had remained true to her and served with heart and soul, rose and grew greater and greater; whoso sinned against her went down. "And therefore it is not free to any one to think," said the prince to himself, "of his own elevation, or that of his family, but he must sacrifice life, strength, and love to her."

But for him it was now too late; he had nothing to sacrifice; he had no future before him save that beyond the grave, at sight of which he shuddered.

From the time of besieging Chenstohova, when one terrible cry was torn from the breast of an immense country, when as if by a miracle there was found in it a certain wonderful, hitherto unknown and not understood power, when you would have said that a mysterious hand from beyond this world rose in its defence, a new doubt gnawed into the soul of the prince, and he could not free himself from the terrible thought that God stood with that cause and that faith.

And when such thoughts roared in his head he doubted his own faith, and then his despair passed even the measure of his sins. Temporal fall, spiritual fall, darkness, nothingness, — behold to what he had come, what he had gained by serving self.

And still at the beginning of the expedition from Kyedani against Podlyasye he was full of hope. It is true that Sapyeha, a leader inferior to him beyond comparison, had defeated him in the field, and the rest of the squadrons left him, but he strengthened himself with the thought that any day Boguslav might come with assistance. That young eagle of the Radzivills would fly to him at the head of Prussian Lutheran legions, who would not pass over to the papists like the Lithuanian squadrons; and at once he would bend Sapyeha in two, scatter his forces, scatter the confederates, and putting themselves on the corpse of Lithuania, like two lions on the carcass of a deer, with roaring alone would terrify all who might wish to tear it away from them.

But time passed; the forces of Prince Yanush melted; even the foreign regiments went over to the terrible Sapyeha; days passed, weeks, months, but Boguslav came not.

At last the siege of Tykotsin began.

The Swedes, a handful of whom remained with Yanush, defended themselves heroically; for, stained already with terrible cruelty, they saw that even surrender would not guard them from the vengeful hands of the Lithuanians. The prince in the beginning of the siege had still the hope that at the last moment, perhaps, the King of Sweden himself would move to his aid, and perhaps Pan Konyetspolski, who at the head of six thousand cavalry was with Karl Gustav. But his hope was vain. No one gave him a thought, no one came with assistance.

"Oh, Boguslav! Boguslav!" repeated the prince, walking through the chambers of Tykotsin; "if you will not save a cousin, save at least a Radzivill!"

At last in his final despair Prince Yanush resolved on taking a step at which his pride revolted fearfully; that was to implore Prince Michael Radzivill of Nyesvyej for rescue. This letter, however, was intercepted on the road by Sapyeha's men; but the voevoda of Vityebsk sent to Yanush in answer a letter which he had himself received from Prince Michael a week before.

Prince Yanush found in it the following passage: —

"If news has come to you, gracious lord, that I intend to go with succor to my relative, the voevoda of Vilna, believe it not, for I hold only with those who endure in loyalty to the country and our king, and who desire to restore the former liberties of this most illustrious Commonwealth. This course will not, as I think, bring me to protect traitors from just and proper punishment. Boguslav too will not come, for, as I hear, the elector prefers to think of himself, and does not wish to divide his forces; and *quod attinet* (as to) Konyetspolski, since he will pay court to Prince Yanush's widow, should she become one, it is to his profit that the prince voevoda be destroyed with all speed."

This letter, addressed to Sapyeha, stripped the unfortunate Yanush of the remnant of his hope, and nothing was left him but to wait for the accomplishment of his destiny.

The siege was hastening to its close.

News of the departure of Sapyeha passed through the wall almost that moment; but the hope that in consequence

of his departure hostile steps would be abandoned were of
short duration, for in the infantry regiments an unusual
movement was observable.   Still some days passed quietly
enough, since the plan of blowing up the gate with a petard
resulted in nothing; but December 31 came, on which only
the approaching night might incommode the besiegers,
for evidently they were preparing something against the
castle, at least a new attack of cannon on the weakened
walls.

The day was drawing to a close.   The prince was lying
in the so-called "Corner" hall situated in the western part
of the castle.   In an enormous fireplace were burning whole
logs of pine wood which cast a lively light on the white and
rather empty walls.   The prince was lying on his back on a
Turkish sofa, pushed out purposely into the middle of the
room, so that the warmth of the blaze might reach it.
Nearer to the fireplace, a little in the shade, slept a page,
on a carpet; near the prince were sitting, slumbering in
arm-chairs, Pani Yakimovich, formerly chief lady-in-waiting
at Kyedani, another page, a physician, also the prince's
astrologer, and Kharlamp.

Kharlamp had not left the prince, though he was almost
the only one of his former officers who had remained.
That was a bitter service, for the heart and soul of the officer
were outside the walls of Tykotsin, in the camp of Sapyeha;
still he remained faithful at the side of his old leader.   From
hunger and watching the poor fellow had grown as thin as
a skeleton.   Of his face there remained but the nose, which
now seemed still greater, and mustaches like bushes.   He
was clothed in complete armor, breastplate, shoulder-pieces,
and morion, with a wire cape which came down to his shoulders.   His cuirass was battered, for he had just returned
from the walls, to which he had gone to make observations
a little while before, and on which he sought death every
day.   He was slumbering at the moment from weariness,
though there was a terrible rattling in the prince's breast as
if he had begun to die, and though the wind howled and
whistled outside.

Suddenly short quivering began to shake the gigantic body
of Radzivill, and the rattling ceased.   Those who were
around him woke at once and looked quickly, first at him
and then at one another.   But he said, —

"It is as if something had gone out of my breast; I feel
easier."

He turned his head a little, looked carefully toward the door, at last he said, "Kharlamp!"

"At the service of your highness!"

"What does Stahovich want here?"

The legs began to tremble under poor Kharlamp, for un-terrified as he was in battle he was superstitious in the same degree; therefore he looked around quickly, and said in a stifled voice, —

"Stahovich is not here; your highness gave orders to shoot him at Kyedani."

The prince closed his eyes and answered not a word.

For a time there was nothing to be heard save the doleful and continuous howling of the wind.

"The weeping of people is heard in that wind," said the prince, again opening his eyes in perfect consciousness. "But I did not bring in the Swedes; it was Radzeyovski."

When no one gave answer, he said after a short time, —

"He is most to blame, he is most to blame, he is most to blame."

And a species of consolation entered his breast, as if the remembrance rejoiced him that there was some one more guilty than he.

Soon, however, more grievous thoughts must have come to his head, for his face grew dark, and he repeated a number of times, —

"Jesus! Jesus! Jesus!"

And again choking attacked him; a rattling began in his throat more terrible than before. Meanwhile from without came the sound of musketry, at first infrequent, then more frequent; but amidst the drifting of the snow and the howl-ing of the whirlwind they did not sound too loudly, and it might have been thought that that was some continual knocking at the gate.

"They are fighting!" said the prince's physician.

"As usual!" answered Kharlamp. "People are freezing in the snow-drifts, and they wish to fight to grow warm."

"This is the sixth day of the whirlwind and the snow," answered the doctor. "Great changes will come in the kingdom, for this is an unheard of thing."

"God grant it!" said Kharlamp. "It cannot be worse."

Further conversation was interrupted by the prince, to whom a new relief had come.

"Kharlamp!"

"At the service of your highness!"

"Does it seem to me so from weakness, or did Oskyerko try to blow up the gate with a petard two days since?"

"He tried, your highness; but the Swedes seized the petards and wounded him slightly, and Sapyeha's men were repulsed."

"If wounded slightly, then he will try again. But what day is it?"

"The last day of December, your highness."

"God be merciful to my soul! I shall not live to the New Year. Long ago it was foretold me that every fifth year death is near me."

"God is kind, your highness."

"God is with Sapyeha," said the prince, gloomily.

All at once he looked around and said: "Cold comes to me from it. I do not see it, but I feel that it is here."

"What is that, your highness?"

"Death!"

"In the name of the Father, Son, and Holy Ghost!"

A moment of silence followed; nothing was heard but the whispered "Our Father," repeated by Pani Yakimovich.

"Tell me," said the prince, with a broken voice, "do you believe that outside of your faith no one can be saved?"

"Even in the moment of death it is possible to renounce errors," said Kharlamp.

The sound of shots had become at that moment more frequent. The thunder of cannon began to shake the window-panes, which answered each report with a plaintive sound.

The prince listened a certain time calmly, then rose slightly on the pillow; his eyes began slowly to widen, his pupils to glitter. He sat up; for a moment he held his head with his hand, then cried suddenly, as if in bewilderment, —

"Boguslav! Boguslav! Boguslav!"

Kharlamp ran out of the room like a madman.

The whole castle trembled and quivered from the thunder of cannon.

All at once there was heard the cry of several thousand voices; then something was torn with a ghastly smashing of walls, so that brands and coals from the chimney were scattered on the floor. At the same time Kharlamp rushed into the chamber.

"Sapyeha's men have blown up the gate!" cried he. "The Swedes have fled to the tower! The enemy is here! Your highness —"

Further words died on his lips. Radzivill was sitting on the sofa with eyes starting out; with open lips he was gulping the air, his teeth bared like those of a dog when he snarls; he tore with his hands the sofa on which he was sitting, and gazing with terror into the depth of the chamber, cried, or rather gave out hoarse rattles between one breath and another, —

"It was Radzeyovski — Not I — Save me! — What do you want? Take the crown! — It was Radzeyovski — Save me, people! Jesus! Jesus! Mary!"

These were the last words of Radzivill.

Then a terrible coughing seized him; his eyes came out in still more ghastly fashion from their sockets; he stretched himself out, fell on his back, and remained motionless.

"He is dead!" said the doctor.

"He cried Mary, though a Calvinist, you have heard!" said Pani Yakimovich.

"Throw wood on the fire!" said Kharlamp to the terrified pages.

He drew near to the corpse, closed the eyelids; then he took from his own armor a gilded image of the Mother of God which he wore on a chain, and placing the hands of Radzivill together on his breast, he put the image between the dead fingers.

The light of the fire was reflected from the golden ground of the image, and that reflection fell upon the face of the voevoda and made it cheerful so that never had it seemed so calm.

Kharlamp sat at the side of the body, and resting his elbows on his knees, hid his face in his hands.

The silence was broken only by the sound of shots.

All at once something terrible took place. First of all was a flash of awful brightness; the whole world seemed turned into fire, and at the same time there was given forth such a sound as if the earth had fallen from under the castle. The walls tottered; the ceilings cracked with a terrible noise; all the windows tumbled in on the floor, and the panes were broken into hundreds of fragments. Through the empty openings of the windows that moment clouds of snow drifted in, and the whirlwind began to howl gloomily in the corners of the chamber.

All the people present fell to the floor on their faces, speechless from terror.

Kharlamp rose first and looked directly on the corpse of

the voevoda; the corpse was lying in calmness, but the gilded image had slipped a little in the hands.

Kharlamp recovered his breath. At first he felt certain that that was an army of Satans who had broken into the chamber for the body of the prince.

"The word has become flesh!" said he. "The Swedes must have blown up the tower and themselves."

But from without there came no sound. Evidently the troops of Sapyeha were standing in dumb wonder, or perhaps in fear that the whole castle was mined, and that there would be explosion after explosion.

"Put wood on the fire!" said Kharlamp to the pages.

Again the room was gleaming with a bright, quivering light. Round about a deathlike stillness continued; but the fire hissed, the whirlwind howled, and the snow rolled each moment more densely through the window openings.

At last confused voices were heard, then the clatter of spurs and the tramp of many feet; the door of the chamber was opened wide, and soldiers rushed in.

It was bright from the naked sabres, and more and more figures of knights in helmets, caps, and kolpaks crowded through the door. Many were bearing lanterns in their hands, and they held them to the light, advancing carefully, though it was light in the room from the fire as well.

At last there sprang forth from the crowd a little knight all in enamelled armor, and cried, —

"Where is the voevoda of Vilna?"

"Here!" said Kharlamp, pointing to the body lying on the sofa.

Volodyovski looked at him, and said, —

"He is not living!"

"He is not living, he is not living!" went from mouth to mouth.

"The traitor, the betrayer is not living!"

"So it is," said Kharlamp, gloomily. "But if you dishonor his body and bear it apart with sabres, you will do ill, for before his end he called on the Most Holy Lady, and he holds Her image in his hand."

These words made a deep impression. The shouts were hushed. Then the soldiers began to approach, to go around the sofa, and look at the dead man. Those who had lanterns turned the light of them on his eyes; and he lay there, gigantic, gloomy, on his face the majesty of a hetman and the cold dignity of death.

The soldiers came one after another, and among them the officers; therefore Stankyevich approached, the two Skshetuskis, Horotkyevich, Yakub Kmita, Oskyerko, and Pan Zagloba.

"It is true!" said Zagloba, in a low voice, as if he feared to rouse the prince. "He holds in his hands the Most Holy Lady, and the shining from Her falls on his face."

When he said this he removed his cap. That instant all the others bared their heads. A moment of silence filled with reverence followed, which was broken at last by Volodyovski.

"Ah!" said he, "he is before the judgment of God, and people have nothing to do with him." Here he turned to Kharlamp: "But you, unfortunate, why did you for his sake leave your country and king?"

"Give him this way!" called a number of voices at once.

Then Kharlamp rose, and taking off his sabre threw it with a clatter on the floor, and said, —

"Here I am, cut me to pieces! I did not leave him with you, when he was powerful as a king, and afterward it was not proper to leave him when he was in misery and no one stayed with him. I have not grown fat in his service; for three days I have had nothing in my mouth, and the legs are bending under me. But here I am, cut me to pieces! for I confess furthermore [here Kharlamp's voice trembled] that I loved him."

When he had said this he tottered and would have fallen; but Zagloba opened his arms to him, caught him, supported him, and cried, —

"By the living God! Give the man food and drink!"

That touched all to the heart; therefore they took Kharlamp by the arms and led him out of the chamber at once. Then the soldiers began to leave it one after another, making the sign of the cross with devotion.

On the road to their quarters Zagloba was meditating over something. He stopped, coughed, then pulled Volodyovski by the skirt. "Pan Michael," said he.

"Well, what?"

"My anger against Radzivill is passed; a dead man is a dead man! I forgive him from my heart for having made an attempt on my life."

"He is before the tribunal of heaven," said Volodyovski.

"That's it, that's it! H'm, if it would help him I would

even give for a Mass, since it seems to me that he has an awfully small chance up there."

" God is merciful ! "

" As to being merciful, he is merciful; still the Lord cannot look without abhorrence on heretics. And Radzivill was not only a heretic, but a traitor. There is where the trouble is ! "

Here Zagloba shook his head and began to look upward.

" I am afraid," said he, after a while, " that some of those Swedes who blew themselves up will fall on my head ; that they will not be received there in heaven is certain."

" They were good men," said Pan Michael, with recognition ; " they preferred death to surrender, there are few such soldiers in the world."

All at once Volodyovski halted : " Panna Billevich was not in the castle," said he.

" But how do you know ? "

" I asked those pages. Boguslav took her to Taurogi."

" Ei ! " said Zagloba, " that was as if to confide a kid to a wolf. But it is not your affair; your predestined is that kernel ! "

CHAPTER XVI.

Lvoff from the moment of the king's arrival was turned into a real capital of the Commonwealth. Together with the king came the greater part of the bishops from the whole country and all those lay senators who had not served the enemy. The calls already issued summoned also to arms the nobles of Rus and of the remoter adjoining provinces, they came in numbers and armed with the greater ease because the Swedes had not been in those regions. Eyes were opened and hearts rose at sight of this general militia, for it reminded one in nothing of that of Great Poland, which at Uistsie offered such weak opposition to the enemy. On the contrary, in this case marched a warlike and terrible nobility, reared from childhood on horseback and in the field, amidst continual attacks of wild Tartars, accustomed to bloodshed and burning, better masters of the sabre than of Latin. These nobles were in fresh training yet from Hmelnitski's uprising, which lasted seven years without interval, so that there was not a man among them who was not as many times in fire as he had years of life. New swarms of these were arriving continually in Lvoff : some had marched from the Byeshchadi full of precipices, others from the Pruth, the Dniester, and the Seret; some lived on the steep banks of the Dniester, some on the wide-spreading Bug; some on the Sinyuha had not been destroyed from the face of the earth by peasant incursions; some had been left on the Tartar boundaries; — all these hurried at the call of the king to the city of the Lion,[1] some to march thence against an enemy as yet unknown. The nobles came in from Volynia and from more distant provinces, such hatred was kindled in all souls by the terrible tidings that the enemy had raised sacrilegious hands on the Patroness of the Commonwealth in Chenstohova.

And the Cossacks dared not raise obstacles, for the hearts were moved in the most hardened, and besides, they were forced by the Tartars to beat with the forehead to the king,

[1] Lvoff.

and to renew for the hundredth time their oath of loyalty. A Tartar embassy, dangerous to the enemies of the king, was in Lvoff under the leadership of Suba Gazi Bey, offering, in the name of the Khan, a horde a hundred thousand strong to assist the Commonwealth; of these forty thousand from near Kamenyets could take the field at once.

Besides the Tartar embassy a legation had come from Transylvania to carry through negotiations begun with Rakotsy concerning succession to the throne. The ambassador of the emperor was present; so was the papal nuncio, who had come with the king. Every day deputations arrived from the armies of the kingdom and Lithuania, from provinces and lands, with declarations of loyalty, and a wish to defend to the death the invaded country.

The fortunes of the king increased; the Commonwealth, crushed altogether so recently, was rising before the eyes of all to the wonder of ages and nations. The souls of men were inflamed with thirst for war and retaliation, and at the same time they grew strong. And as in spring-time a warm generous rain melts the snow, so mighty hope melted doubt. Not only did they wish for victory, but they believed in it. New and favorable tidings came in continually; though often untrue, they passed from mouth to mouth. Time after time men told now of castles recovered, now of battles in which unknown regiments under leaders hitherto unknown had crushed the Swedes, now of terrible clouds of peasants sweeping along, like locusts, against the enemy. The name of Stefan Charnyetski was more and more frequent on every lip.

The details in these tidings were often untrue, but taken together they reflected as a mirror what was being done in the whole country.

But in Lvoff reigned as it were a continual holiday. When the king came the city greeted him solemnly, the clergy of the three rites, the councillors of the city, the merchants, the guilds. On the squares and streets, wherever an eye was cast, banners, white, sapphire, purple, and gilded, were waving. The Lvoff people raised proudly their golden lion on a blue field, recalling with self-praise the scarcely passed Cossack and Tartar attacks.

At every appearance of the king a shout was raised among the crowds, and crowds were never lacking.

The population doubled in recent days. Besides senators and bishops, besides nobles, flowed in throngs of peasants also, for the news had spread that the king intended to improve their condition. Therefore rustic coats and horse-blankets were mingled with the yellow coats of the towns-people. The mercantile Armenians with their swarthy faces put up booths for merchandise and arms which the assembled nobles bought willingly.

There were many Tartars also with the embassy; there were Hungarians, Wallachians, and Austrians, — a multitude of people, a multitude of troops, a multitude of different kinds of faces, many strange garments in colors brilliant and varied, troops of court servants, hence gigantic grooms, haiduks, janissaries, red Cossacks, messengers in foreign costume.

The streets were filled from morning till evening with the noise of men, now passing squadrons of a quota, now divisions of mounted nobles, the cries of command, the shining of armor and naked sabres, the neighing of horses, the rumble of cannon, and songs full of threatening and curses for the Swedes.

The bells in the churches, Polish, Russian, and Armenian, were tolling continually, announcing to all that the king was in the city, and that Lvoff, to its eternal praise, was the first of the capitals that had received the king, the exile.

They beat to him with the forehead; wherever he appeared caps flew upward, and shouts of "Vivat!" shook the air. They beat with the forehead also before the carriages of bishops, who through the windows blessed the assembled throngs; they bowed to and applauded senators, honoring in them loyalty to the king and country.

So the whole city was seething. At night they even burned on the square piles of wood, at which in spite of cold and frost those men were encamped who could not find lodgings because of the excessive multitude.

The king spent whole days in consultation with senators. Audience was given to foreign embassies, to deputations from provinces and troops; methods of filling the empty treasury with money were considered; all means were used to rouse war wherever it had not flamed up already.

Couriers were flying to the most important towns in every part of the Commonwealth, to distant Prussia, to sacred Jmud, to Tyshovtsi, to the hetmans, to Sapyeha, who after the storming of Tykotsin took his army to the south with forced marches; couriers went also to Konyetspolski, who was still with the Swedes. Where it was needful money was sent; the slothful were roused with manifestoes.

The king recognized, consecrated, and confirmed the confederation of Tyshovtsi and joined it himself; taking the direction of all affairs into his untiring hands, he labored from morning till night, esteeming the Commonwealth more than his own rest, his own health.

But this was not the limit of his efforts; for he had determined to conclude in his own name and the name of the estates a league such that no earthly power could overcome, — a· league which in future might serve to reform the Commonwealth.

The moment for this had come at last.

The secret must have escaped from the senators to the nobles, and from the nobles to the peasants, for since morning it had been said that at the hour of services something important would happen, — that the king would make some solemn vow, concerning, as was said, the condition of the peasants and a confederation with heaven. There were persons, however, who asserted that these were incredible things, without an example in history; but curiosity was excited, and everywhere something was looked for.

The day was frosty, clear; tiny flakes of snow were flying through the air, glittering like sparks. The land infantry of Lvoff and the district of Jidache, in blue half shabas, hemmed with gold, and half a Hungarian regiment were drawn out in a long line before the cathedral, holding their muskets at their feet in front of them; officers passed up and down with staffs in their hands. Between these two lines a many-colored throng flowed into the church, like a river. In front nobles and knights, after them the senate of the city, with gilded chains on their necks, and tapers in their hands. They were led by the mayor, a physician noted throughout the whole province; he was dressed in a black velvet toga, and wore a calotte. After the senate went merchants, and among them many Armenians with green and gold skull-caps on their heads, and wearing roomy Eastern gowns. These, though belonging to a special rite, went with the others to represent the estate. After the merchants came, with their banners, the guilds, such as butchers, bakers, tailors, goldsmiths, confectioners, embroiderers, linendrapers, tanners, mead-boilers, and a number of others yet; from each company representatives went with their own banner, which was borne by a man the most distinguished of all for beauty. Then came various brotherhoods and the common throng in coats, in sheepskins, in horse-blankets, in homespun; dwellers in the suburbs, peasants. Admittance was barred to no one till the church was packed closely with people of all ranks and both sexes.

At last carriages began to arrive; but they avoided the main door, for the king, the bishops, and the dignitaries had a special entrance nearer the high altar. Every moment the troops presented arms; at last the soldiers dropped their muskets to their feet, and blew on their chilled hands, throwing out clouds of steam from their breasts.

The king came with the nuncio, Vidon; then arrived the archbishop of Gnyezno and the bishop, Prince Chartoryski; next appeared the bishop of Cracow, the archbishop of Lvoff, the grand chancellor of the kingdom, many voevodas and castellans. All these vanished through the side door; and their carriages, retinues, equerries, and attendants of every description formed as it were a new army, standing at the side of the cathedral.

Mass was celebrated by the apostolic nuncio, Vidon, arrayed in purple, in a white chasuble embroidered with pearls and gold.

For the king a kneeling-stool was placed between the great altar and the pews; before the kneeling-stool was a Turkish sofa. The church arm-chairs were occupied by bishops and lay senators.

Many colored rays, passing through the windows, joined with the gleam of candles, with which the altar seemed burning, and fell upon the faces of senators in the church chairs, on the white beards, on the imposing forms, on golden chains, on violet velvet. You would have said, " A Roman senate! " such was the majesty and dignity of these old men. Here and there among gray heads was to be seen the face of a warrior senator; here and there gleamed the blond head of a youthful lord. All eyes were fixed on the altar, all were praying; the flames of the candles were glittering and quivering; the smoke from the censers was playing and curling in the bright air. The body of the church was packed with heads, and over the heads a rainbow of banners was playing, like a rainbow of flowers.

The majesty of the king, Yan Kazimir, prostrated itself, according to his custom, in the form of a cross, and humiliated itself before the majesty of God. At last the nuncio brought from the tabernacle a chalice, and bearing it before him approached the kneeling-stool, then the king raised himself with a brighter face, the voice of the nuncio was heard: "*Ecce Agnus Dei* (Behold the Lamb of God)," and the king received communion.

For a time he remained kneeling, with inclined head; at last he rose, turned his eyes toward heaven, and stretched out both hands.

There was sudden silence in the church, so that breathing was not audible. All divined that the moment had come, and that the king would make some vow; all listened with collected spirit. But he stood with outstretched arms; at last, with a voice filled with emotion, but as far reaching as a bell, he began to speak, —

"O Great Mother of Divine humanity, and Virgin! I, Yan Kazimir, king by the favor of Thy Son, King of kings and my Lord, and by Thy favor approaching Thy Most Holy feet, form this, the following pact. I to-day choose Thee my Patroness and Queen of my dominions. I commit to Thy special guardianship and protection myself, my Polish kingdom, the Grand Principality of Lithuania, Russia, Prussia, Mazovia, Jmud, Livland, and Chernigov, the armies of both nations and all common people. I beg obediently Thy aid and favor against enemies in the present affliction of my kingdom."

Here the king fell on his knees and was silent for a time. In the church a deathlike stillness continued unbroken; then rising he spoke on, —

"And constrained by Thy great benefactions, I, with the Polish people, am drawn to a new and ardent bond of service to Thee. I promise Thee in my own name and in the names of my ministers, senators, nobles, and people, to extend honor and glory to Thy Son, Jesus Christ, Our Saviour, through all regions of the Polish kingdom; to make a promise that when, with the mercy of Thy Son, I obtain victory over the Swedes, I will endeavor that an anniversary be celebrated solemnly in my kingdom to the end of the world, in memory of the favor of God, and of Thee, O Most Holy Virgin."

Here he ceased again and knelt. In the church there was a murmur; but the voice of the king stopped it quickly, and though he trembled this time with penitence and emotion, he continued still more distinctly, —

"And since, with great sorrow of heart, I confess that I endure from God just punishment, which is afflicting us all

ɪn my kingdom with various plagues for seven years, because poor, simple tillers of the soil groan in suffering,
oppressed by the soldiery, I bind myself on the conclusion
of peace to use earnest efforts, together with the estates
of the Commonwealth, to free suffering peasants from
every cruelty, in which, O Mother of Mercy, Queen, and
my Lady, since Thou hast inspired me to make this vow,
obtain for me, by grace of Thy mercy, aid from Thy Son to
accomplish what I here promise."

These words of the king were heard by the clergy, the
senators, the nobles, and the common people. A great wail
was raised in the church, which came first from hearts of
the peasants; it burst forth from them, and then became
universal. All raised their hands to heaven; weeping voices
repeated, "Amen, amen, amen!" in testimony that they
had joined their feelings and vows with the promise of the
king. Enthusiasm seized their hearts, and at that moment
made them brothers in love for the Commonwealth and its
Patroness. Indescribable joy shone on their faces like a
clear flame, and in all that church there was no one who
doubted that God would overwhelm the Swedes.

After that service the king, amid the thunder of musketry
and cannon and mighty shouts of "Victory! victory! may
he live!" went to the castle, and there he confirmed the
heavenly confederation together with that of Tyshovtsi.

CHAPTER XVII.

AFTER these solemnities various tidings flew into Lvoff like winged birds. There were older and fresh tidings more or less favorable, but all increased courage. First the confederation of Tyshovtsi grew like a conflagration; every one living joined it, nobles as well as peasants. Towns furnished wagons, firearms, and infantry; the Jews money. No one dared to oppose the manifestoes; the most indolent mounted. There came also a terrible manifesto from Wittemberg, turned against the confederation. Fire and sword were to punish those who joined it. This manifesto produced the same effect as if a man tried to quench flames with powder. The manifesto, with the knowledge assuredly of the king, and to rouse hatred more thoroughly against the Swedes, was scattered through Lvoff in great numbers, and it is not becoming to state what common people did with the copies; it suffices to say that the wind bore them terribly dishonored through the streets of the city, and the students showed, to the delight of crowds, "Wittemberg's Confusion," singing at the same time the song beginning with these words, —

> " O Wittemberg, poor man,
> Race across over the sea,
>   Like a hare !
> But when thy buttons are lost
> Thou wilt drop down thy trousers,
>   While racing away ! "

And Wittemberg, as if making the words of the song true, gave up his command in Cracow to the valiant Wirtz, and betook himself hurriedly to Elblang, where the King of Sweden was sojourning with the queen, spending his time at feasts, and rejoicing in his heart that he had become the lord of such an illustrious kingdom.

Accounts came also to Lvoff of the fall of Tykotsin, and minds were gladdened. It was strange that men had begun to speak of that event before a courier had come; only they did not say whether Radzivill had died or was in captivity.

It was asserted, however, that Sapyeha, at the head of a considerable force, had gone from Podlyasye to Lyubelsk to join the hetmans; that on the road he was beating the Swedes and growing in power every day.

At last envoys came from Sapyeha himself in a considerable number, for the voevoda had sent neither less nor more than one whole squadron to be at the disposal of the king, desiring in this way to show honor to the sovereign, to secure his person from every possible accident, and perhaps specially to increase his significance.

The squadron was brought by Volodyovski, well known to the king; so Yan Kazimir gave command that he should stand at once in his presence, and taking Pan Michael's head between his hands, he said, —

"I greet thee, famous soldier! Much water has flowed down since we lost sight of thee. I think that we saw thee last at Berestechko, all covered with blood."

Pan Michael bent to the knees of the king, and said, —

"It was later, in Warsaw, Gracious Lord; also in the castle with the present castellan of Kieff, Pan Charnyetski."

"But are you serving all the time? Had you no desire to enjoy leisure at home?"

"No; for the Commonwealth was in need, and besides, in these public commotions my property has been lost. I have no place in which to put my head, Gracious Lord; but I am not sorry for myself, thinking that the first duty of a soldier is to the king and the country."

"Ah, would there were more such! The enemy would not be so rich. God grant the time for rewards will come; but now tell me what you have done with the voevoda of Vilna?"

"The voevoda of Vilna is before the judgment of God. The soul went out of him just as we were going to the final storm."

"How was that?"

"Here is Pan Sapyeha's report," said Volodyovski.

The king took Sapyeha's letter and began to read; he had barely begun when he stopped.

"Pan Sapyeha is mistaken," said he, "when he writes that the grand baton of Lithuania is unoccupied; it is not, for I give it to him."

"There is no one more worthy," said Pan Michael, "and to your Royal Grace the whole army will be grateful till death for this deed."

The king smiled at the simple soldierly confidence, and read on. After a while he sighed, and said, —

" Radzivill might have been the first pearl in this glorious kingdom, if pride and the errors which he committed had not withered his soul. It is accomplished! Inscrutable are the decisions of God! Radzivill and Opalinski — almost in the same hour! Judge them, O Lord, not according to their sins, but according to Thy mercy."

Silence followed ; then the king again began to read.

" We are thankful to the voevoda," said he, when he had finished, " for sending a whole squadron and under the greatest cavalier, as he writes. But I am safe here; and cavaliers, especially such as you, are more needed in the field. Rest a little, and then I will send you to assist Charnyetski, for on him evidently the greatest pressure will be turned."

" We have rested enough already at Tykotsin, Gracious Lord," said the little knight, with enthusiasm; " if our horses were fed a little, we might move to-day, for with Charnyetski there will be unspeakable delights. It is a great happiness to look on the face of our gracious lord, but we are anxious to see the Swedes."

The king grew radiant. A fatherly kindness appeared on his face, and he said, looking with pleasure on the sulphurous figure of the little knight, —

" You were the first little soldier to throw the baton of a colonel at the feet of the late prince voevoda."

" Not the first, your Royal Grace ; but it was the first, and God grant the last, time for me to act against military discipline." Pan Michael stopped, and after a while added, " It was impossible to do otherwise."

" Certainly," said the king. " That was a grievous hour for those who understood military duty ; but obedience must have its limits, beyond which guilt begins. Did many officers remain with Radzivill ? "

" In Tykotsin we found only one officer, Pan Kharlamp, who did not leave the prince at once, and who did not wish afterward to desert him in misery. Compassion alone kept Kharlamp with Radzivill, for natural affection drew him to us. We were barely able to restore him to health, such hunger had there been in Tykotsin, and he took the food from his own mouth to nourish the prince. He has come here to Lvoff to implore pardon of your Royal Grace, and I too fall at your feet for him ; he is a tried and good soldier."

"Let him come hither," said the king.

"He has also something important to tell, which he heard in Kyedani from the mouth of Prince Boguslav, and which relates to the person of your Royal Grace, which is sacred to us."

"Is this about Kmita?"

"Yes, Gracious Lord."

"Did you know Kmita?"

"I knew him and fought with him; but where he is now, I know not."

"What do you think of him?"

"Gracious Lord, since he undertook such a deed there are no torments of which he is not worthy, for he is an abortion of hell."

"That story is untrue," said the king; "it is all an invention of Prince Boguslav. But putting that affair aside, what do you know of Kmita in times previous?"

"He was always a great soldier, and in military affairs incomparable. He used to steal up to Hovanski so that with a few hundred people he brought the whole force of the enemy to misery; no other man could have done that. It is a miracle that the skin was not torn from him and stretched over a drum. If at that time some one had placed Prince Radzivill himself in the hands of Hovanski, he would not have given him so much pleasure as he would had he made him a present of Kmita. Why! it went so far that Kmita ate out of Hovanski's camp-chests, slept on his rugs, rode in his sleighs and on his horse. But he was an infliction on his own people too, terribly self-willed; like Pan Lashch, he might have lined his cloak with sentences, and in Kyedani he was lost altogether."

Here Volodyovski related in detail all that had happened in Kyedani.

Yan Kazimir listened eagerly, and when at last Pan Michael told how Zagloba had freed first himself and then all his comrades from Radzivill's captivity, the king held his sides from laughter.

"*Vir incomparabilis! vir incomparabilis* (an incomparable man)!" he repeated. "But is he here with you?"

"At the command of your Royal Grace!" answered Volodyovski.

"That noble surpasses Ulysses! Bring him to me to dinner for a pleasant hour, and also the Skshetuskis; and now tell me what you know more of Kmita."

"From letters found on Roh Kovalski we learned that we were sent to Birji to die. The prince pursued us afterward and tried to surround us, but he did not take us. We escaped luckily. And that was not all, for not far from Kyedani we caught Kmita, whom I sent at once to be shot."

"Oh!" said the king, "I see that you had sharp work there in Lithuania."

"But first Pan Zagloba had him searched to find letters on his person. In fact, a letter from the hetman was found, in which we learned that had it not been for Kmita we should not have been taken to Birji, but would have been shot without delay in Kyedani."

"But you see!" said the king.

"In view of that we could not take his life. We let him go. What he did further I know not, but he did not leave Radzivill at that time. God knows what kind of man he is. It is easier to form an opinion of any one else than of such a whirlwind. He remained with Radzivill and then went somewhere. Later he warned us that the prince was marching from Kyedani. It is hard to belittle the notable service he did us, for had it not been for that warning Radzivill would have fallen on unprepared troops, and destroyed the squadrons one after the other. I know not myself, Gracious Lord, what to think, — whether that was a calumny which Prince Boguslav uttered."

"That will appear at once," said the king; and he clapped his hands. "Call hither Pan Babinich!" said he to a page who appeared on the threshold.

The page vanished, and soon the door of the king's chamber opened, and in it stood Pan Andrei. Volodyovski did not know him at once, for he had changed greatly and grown pale, as he had not recovered from the struggle in the pass. Pan Michael therefore looked at him without recognition.

"It is a wonder," said he at last; "were it not for the thinness of lips and because your Royal Grace gives another name, I should say this is Pan Kmita."

The king smiled and said, —

"This little knight has just told me of a terrible disturber of that name, but I explained as on my palm that he was deceived in his judgment, and I am sure that Pan Babinich will confirm what I say."

"Gracious Lord," answered Babinich, quickly, "one word from your grace will clear that disturber more than my greatest oath."

"And the voice is the same," said Pan Michael, with growing astonishment; "but that wound across the mouth was not there."

"Worthy sir," answered Kmita, "the head of a noble is a register on which sometimes a man's hand writes with a sabre. And here is your note; recognize it."

He bowed his head, shaven at the sides, and pointed at the long whitish scar.

"My hand!" cried Volodyovski.

"But I say that you do not know Kmita," put in the king.

"How is that, Gracious Lord?"

"For you know a great soldier, but a self-willed one, an associate in the treason of Radzivill. But here stands the Hector of Chenstohova, to whom, next to Kordetski, Yasna Gora owes most; here stands the defender of the country and my faithful servant, who covered me with his own breast and saved my life when in the pass I had fallen among the Swedes as among wolves. Such is this new Kmita. Know him and love him, for he deserves it."

Volodyovski began to move his yellow mustaches, not knowing what to say; and the king added, —

"And know that not only did he promise Prince Boguslav nothing, but he began on him the punishment for Radzivill intrigues, for he seized him and intended to give him into your hands."

"And he warned us against Prince Yanush!" cried Volodyovski. "What angel converted you?"

"Embrace each other!" said the king.

"I loved you at once!" said Kmita to Volodyovski.

Then they fell into each other's embraces, and the king looked on them and pursed out his lips with delight, time after time, as was his habit. But Kmita embraced the little knight with such feeling that he raised him as he would a cat, and not soon did he place him back on his feet.

Then the king went to the daily council, for the two hetmans of the kingdom had come to Lvoff; they were to form the army there, and lead it later to the aid of Charnyetski, and the confederate divisions marching, under various leaders, throughout the country.

The knights were alone.

"Come to my quarters," said Volodyovski; "you will find there Pan Yan, Pan Stanislav, and Zagloba, who will be glad to hear what the king has told me. There too is Kharlamp."

But Kmita approached the little knight with great disquiet on his face. "Did you find many people with Radzivill?" asked he.

"Of officers, Kharlamp alone was there."

"I do not ask about the military, but about women."

"I know what you mean," answered Pan Michael, flushing somewhat. "Prince Boguslav took Panna Billevich to
Taurogi."

Kmita's face changed at once; first it was pale as a
parchment, then purple, and again whiter than before. He
did not find words at once; but his nostrils quivered while
he was catching breath, which apparently failed in his
breast. Then he seized his temples with both hands, and
running through the room like a madman, began to repeat, —

"Woe to me, woe, woe!"

"Come! Kharlamp will tell you better, for he was present," said Volodyovski.

CHAPTER XVIII.

WHEN they had left the king's chamber the two knights walked on in silence. Volodyovski did not wish to speak; Kmita was unable to utter a word, for pain and rage were gnawing him. They broke through the crowds of people who had collected in great numbers on the streets in consequence of tidings that the first detachment of the Tartars promised by the Khan had arrived, and was to enter the city to be presented to the king. The little knight led on; Kmita hastened after him like one beside himself, with his cap pulled over his eyes and stumbling against men on the way.

When they had come to a more spacious place Pan Michael seized Kmita by the wrist and said, —

"Control yourself! Despair will do nothing."

"I am not in despair," answered Kmita, "but I want his blood."

"You may be sure to find him among the enemies of the country."

"So much the better," answered Kmita, feverishly; "but even should I find him in a church — "

"In God's name, do not commit sacrilege!" interrupted the little colonel, quickly.

"That traitor will bring me to sin."

They were silent for a time. Then Kmita asked, "Where is he now?"

"Maybe in Taurogi, and maybe not. Kharlamp will know better."

"Let us go."

"It is not far. The squadron is outside the town, but we are here; and Kharlamp is with us."

Then Kmita began to breathe heavily like a man going up a steep mountain. "I am fearfully weak yet," said he.

"You need moderation all the more, since you will have to deal with such a knight."

"I had him once, and here is what remained." Kmita pointed to the scar on his face.

"Tell me how it was, for the king barely mentioned it."

Kmita began to tell; and though he gritted his teeth, and even threw his cap on the ground, still his mind escaped from misfortune, and he calmed himself somewhat.

"I knew that you were daring," said Volodyovski; "but to carry off Radzivill from the middle of his own squadron, I did not expect that, even of you."

Meanwhile they arrived at the quarters. Pan Yan and Pan Stanislav, Zagloba, Jendzian, and Kharlamp were looking at Crimean coats made of sheepskin, which a trading Tartar had brought. Kharlamp, who knew Kmita better, recognized him at one glance of the eye, and dropping the coat exclaimed, —

"Jesus, Mary!"

"May the name of the Lord be praised!" cried Jendzian.

But before all had recovered breath after the wonder, Volodyovski said, —

"I present to you, gentlemen, the Hector of Chenstohova, the faithful servant of the king, who has shed his blood for the faith, the country, and the sovereign."

When astonishment had grown still greater, the worthy Pan Michael began to relate with enthusiasm what he had heard from the king of Kmita's services, and from Pan Andrei himself of the seizure of Prince Boguslav; at last he finished thus, —

"Not only is what Prince Boguslav told of this knight not true, but the prince has no greater enemy than Pan Kmita, and therefore he has taken Panna Billevich from Kyedani, so as to pour out on him in some way his vengeance."

"And this cavalier has saved our lives and warned the confederates against Prince Yanush," cried Zagloba. "In view of such services, previous offences are nothing. As God lives, it is well that he came to us with you, Pan Michael, and not alone; it is well also that our squadron is outside the city, for there is a terrible hatred against him among the Lauda men, and before he could have uttered a syllable they would have cut him to pieces."

"We greet you with full hearts as a brother and future comrade," said Pan Yan.

Kharlamp seized his head.

"Such men never sink," said he; "they swim out on every side, and besides bring glory to the shore."

"Did I not tell you that?" cried Zagloba. "The minute I saw him in Kyedani I thought at once, 'That is a soldier, a man of courage.' And you remember that we fell to kissing each other straightway. It is true that Radzivill was ruined through me, but also through him. God inspired me in Billeviche not to let him be shot. Worthy gentlemen, it is not becoming to give a dry reception to a cavalier like him; he may think that we are hypocrites."

When he heard this Jendzian packed off the Tartar with his coats, and bustled around with the servant to get drinks.

But Kmita was thinking only how to hear most quickly from Kharlamp about the removal of Olenka.

"Where were you then?" asked he.

"I scarcely ever left Kyedani," answered Great Nose. "Prince Boguslav came to our prince voevoda. He so dressed himself for supper that one's eyes ached in looking at him; it was clear that Panna Billevich had pleased him mightily, for he was almost purring from pleasure, like a cat rubbed on the back. It is said that a cat repeats prayers; but if Boguslav prayed he was praising the devil. Oh, but he was agreeable, and sweet and pleasant spoken."

"Let that go!" said Pan Michael, "you cause too great pain to the knight."

"On the contrary. Speak! speak!" cried Kmita.

"He said then at table," continued Kharlamp, "that it was no derogation even to a Radzivill to marry the daughter of a common noble, and that he himself would prefer such a lady to one of those princesses whom the King and Queen of France wished to give him, and whose names I cannot remember, for they sounded as when a man is calling hounds in the forest."

"Less of that!" said Zagloba.

"He said it evidently to captivate the lady; we, knowing that, began one after another to look and mutter, thinking truly that he was setting traps for the innocent."

"But she? but she?" asked Kmita, feverishly.

"She, like a maiden of high blood and lofty bearing, showed no satisfaction, did not look at him; but when Boguslav began to talk about you, she fixed her eyes on him quickly. It is terrible what happened when he said that you offered for so many ducats to seize the king and deliver him dead or alive to the Swedes. We thought the soul would go out of her; but her anger against you was so great that it overcame her woman's weakness. When he told with what disgust he had rejected your offer, she began to respect him, and look at him thankfully; afterward she did not withdraw her hand from him when he wished to escort her from the table."

Kmita covered his eyes with his hands. " Strike, strike, whoso believes in God ! " said he. Suddenly he sprang from his place. " Farewell, gentlemen ! "

" How is this ?   Whither ? " asked Zagloba, stopping the way.

" The king will give me permission ; I will go and find him," said Kmita.

" By God's wounds, wait !   You have not yet learned all, and to find him there is time.   With whom will you go ? Where will you find him ? "

Kmita perhaps might not have obeyed, but strength failed him ; he was exhausted from wounds, therefore he dropped on the bench, and resting his shoulders against the wall, closed his eyes.   Zagloba gave him a glass of wine ; he seized it with trembling hands, and spilling some on his beard and breast, drained it to the bottom.

" There is nothing lost," said Pan Yan ; " but the greatest prudence is needed, for you have an affair with a celebrated man.   Through hurried action and sudden impulse you may ruin Panna Billevich and yourself."

" Hear Kharlamp to the end," said Zagloba.

Kmita gritted his teeth.   " I am listening with patience."

" Whether the lady went willingly I know not," said Kharlamp, " for I was not present at her departure.   I know that the sword-bearer of Rossyeni protested when they urged him previously ; then they shut him up in the barracks, and finally he was allowed to go to Billeviche without hindrance.   The lady is in evil hands ; this cannot be concealed, for according to what they say of the young prince no Mussulman has such greed of the fair sex.   If any fair head strikes his eye, though she be married, he is ready to disregard even that."

" Woe ! woe ! " repeated Kmita.

" The scoundrel ! " cried Zagloba.

" But it is a wonder to me that the prince voevoda gave her to Boguslav," said Pan Yan.

" I am not a statesman, therefore I repeat only what the officers said, and namely Ganhoff, who knew all the secrets of the prince ; I heard with my own ears how some one cried out in his presence, ' Kmita will have nothing after our young prince ! ' and Ganhoff answered, ' There is more of politics in this removal than love.   Prince Boguslav,' said he, 'lets no one off; but if the lady resists he will not be able to treat her like others, in Taurogi, for a noise would be made. Yanush's princess is living there with her daughter; therefore Boguslav must be very careful, for he seeks the hand of his cousin. It will be hard for him to simulate virtue,' said he, 'but he must in Taurogi.'"

"A stone has of course fallen from your heart," cried Zagloba, "for from this it is clear that nothing threatens the lady."

"But why did they take her away?" cried Kmita.

"It is well that you turn to me," said Zagloba, "for I reason out quickly more than one thing over which another would break his head for a whole year in vain. Why did he take her away? I do not deny that she must have struck his eye; but he took her away to restrain through her all the Billeviches, who are numerous and powerful, from rising against the Radzivills."

"That may be!" said Kharlamp. "It is certain that in Taurogi he must curb himself greatly; there he cannot go to extremes."

"Where is he now?"

"The prince voevoda supposed in Tykotsin that he must be at Elblang with the King of Sweden, to whom he had to go for reinforcements. It is certain that he is not in Taurogi at present, for envoys did not find him there."

Here Kharlamp turned to Kmita. "If you wish to listen to a simple soldier I will tell you what I think : If any misadventure has happened to Panna Billevich in Taurogi, or if the prince has been able to arouse in her affection, you have no reason to go; but if not, if she is with Yanush's widow and will go with her to Courland, it will be safer there than elsewhere, and a better place could not be found for her in this whole Commonwealth, covered with the flame of war."

"If you are a man of such courage as they say, and as I myself think," added Pan Yan, "you have first to get Boguslav, and when you have him in your hands, you have all."

"Where is he now?" repeated Kmita, turning to Kharlamp.

"I have told you already," answered Great Nose, "but you are forgetful from sorrow ; I suppose that he is in Elblang, and certainly will take the field with Karl Gustav against Charnyetski."

"You will do best if you go with us to Charnyetski, for in this way you will soon meet Boguslav," said Volodyovski.

"I thank you, gentlemen, for kindly advice," cried Kmita. And he began to take hasty farewell of all, and they did not detain him, knowing that a suffering man is not good for the cup or for converse; but Pan Michael said, —

"I will attend you to the archbishop's palace, for you are so reduced that you may fall somewhere on the street."

"And I!" said Pan Yan.

"Then we will all go!" put in Zagloba.

They girded on their sabres, put on warm burkas, and went out. On the streets there were still more people than before. Every moment the knights met groups of armed nobles, soldiers, servants of magnates and nobles, Armenians, Jews, Wallachians, Russian peasants from the suburbs burned during the two attacks of Hmelnitski.

Merchants were standing before their shops; the windows of the houses were filled with heads of curious people. All were repeating that the chambul had come, and would soon march through the city to be presented to the king. Every living person wished to see that chambul, for it was a great rarity to look on Tartars marching in peace through the streets of a city. In other temper had Lvoff seen these guests hitherto; the city had seen them only beyond the walls, in the form of impenetrable clouds on the background of flaming suburbs and neighboring villages. Now they were to march in as allies against Sweden. Our knights were barely able to open a way for themselves through the throng. Every moment there were cries: "They are coming, they are coming!" People ran from street to street, and were packed in such masses that not a step forward was possible.

"Ha!" said Zagloba, "let us stop a little, Pan Michael. They will remind us of the near past, for we did not look sidewise but straight into the eyes of these bull-drivers. And I too have been in captivity among them. They say that the future Khan is as much like me as one cup is like another. But why talk of past follies?"

"They are coming, they are coming!" cried the people again.

"God has changed the hearts of the dog-brothers," continued Zagloba, "so that instead of ravaging the Russian borders they come to aid us. This is a clear miracle! For I tell you that if for every pagan whom this old hand has sent

to hell, one of my sins had been forgiven, I should be canon-
ized now, and people would have to fast on the eve of my
festival, or I should have been swept up living to heaven in
a chariot of fire."

"And do you remember," asked Volodyovski, "how it
was with them when they were returning from the Vala-
dynka from Rashkoff to Zbaraj ? "

"Of course I do, Pan Michael; but somehow you fell
into a hole, and I chased through the thick wood to the
high-road. And when we came back to find you, the
knights could not restrain their astonishment, for at each
bush lay a dead beast of a Tartar."

Pan Volodyovski remembered that at the time in question it was just the opposite ; but he said nothing, for he
was wonderfully astonished, and before he could recover
breath voices were shouting for the tenth time : "They are
coming, they are coming ! "

The shout became general ; then there was silence, and all
heads were turned in the direction from which the chambul
was to come. Now piercing music was heard in the distance, the crowds began to open from the middle of the
street toward the walls of the houses, and from the end appeared the first Tartar horsemen.

"See ! they have a band even; that is uncommon with
Tartars ! "

"They wish to make the best impression," said Pan Yan ;
"but still some chambuls after they have lived long in
camp, have their own musicians. That must be a choice
body."

Meanwhile the horsemen had come up and begun to ride
past. In front on a pied horse sat a Tartar holding two
pipes in his mouth, and as tawny as if he had been dried
and smoked. Bending his head backward and closing his
eyes, he ran his fingers over those pipes, obtaining from
them notes squeaking, sharp, and so quick that the ear could
barely catch them. After him rode two others holding
staffs furnished at the ends with brass rattles, and they
were shaking these rattles as if in frenzy ; farther back
some were making shrill sounds with brass plates, some
were beating drums, while others were playing in Cossack
fashion on teorbans ; and all, with the exception of the
pipers were singing, or rather howling, from moment to
moment, a wild song, at the same time showing their teeth
and rolling their eyes. After that chaotic music, which

went like a brawl past the dwellers in Lvoff, clattered horses four abreast; the whole party was made up of about four hundred men.

This was in fact a chosen body, as a specimen, and to do honor to the King of Poland, for his own use, and as an earnest sent by the Khan. They were led by Akbah Ulan, of the Dobrudja, therefore of the sturdiest Tartars in battle, an old and experienced warrior, greatly respected in the Uluses (Tartar villages), because of his bravery and severity. He rode between the music and the rest of the party, dressed in a shuba of rose-colored velvet, but greatly faded, and too narrow for his powerful person; it was lined with tattered marten-skin. He held in front of him a baton, like those used by Cossack colonels. His red face had become blue from the cold wind, and he swayed somewhat on his lofty saddle; from one moment to another he looked from side to side, or turned his face around to his Tartars, as if not perfectly sure that they could restrain themselves at sight of the crowds, the women, the children, the open shops, the rich goods, and that they would not rush with a shout at those wonders.

But they rode on quietly, like dogs led by chains and fearing the lash, and only from their gloomy and greedy glances might it be inferred what was passing in the souls of those barbarians. The crowds gazed on them with curiosity, though almost with hostility, so great in those parts of the Commonwealth was hatred of the Pagan. From time to time cries were heard: " Ahu! ahu!" as if at wolves. Still there were some who expected much from them.

" The Swedes have a terrible fear of the Tartars, and the soldiers tell wonders of them, from which their fear increases," said some, looking at the Tartars.

" And justly," answered others. " It is not for the cavalry of Karl to war with the Tartars, who, especially those of the Dobrudja, are equal sometimes to our cavalry. Before a Swedish horseman can look around, the Tartar will have him on a lariat."

" It is a sin to call sons of Pagans to aid us," said some voice.

" Sin or no sin, they will serve us."

" A very decent chambul ! " said Zagloba.

Really the Tartars were well dressed in white, black, and party-colored sheepskin coats, the wool on the outside;

black bows, and quivers full of arrows were shaking on
their shoulders; each had besides a sabre, which was not
always the case in large chambuls, for the poorest were not
able to obtain such a luxury, using in hand-to-hand conflict
a horse-skull fastened to a club. But these were men, as
was said, to be exhibited; therefore some of them had even
muskets in felt cases, and all were sitting on good horses,
small, it is true, rather lean and short, with long forelocks
on their faces, but of incomparable swiftness.

In the centre of the party went also four camels: the
crowd concluded that in their packs were presents from
the Khan to the king; but in that they were mistaken, for
the Khan chose to take gifts, not give them; he promised,
it is true, reinforcements, but not for nothing.

When they had passed, Zagloba said: "That aid will
cost dear. Though allies, they will ruin the country.
After the Swedes and them, there will not be one sound
roof in the Commonwealth."

"It is sure that they are terribly grievous allies," said
Pan Yan.

"I have heard on the road," said Pan Michael, "that the
king has made a treaty, that to every five hundred of the
horde is to be given one of our officers, who is to have command and the right of punishment. Otherwise these friends
would leave only heaven and earth behind them."

"But this is a small chambul; what will the king do
with it?"

"The Khan sent them to be placed at the disposal of the
king almost as a gift; and though he will make account of
them, still the king can do what he likes with them, and
undoubtedly he will send them with us to Charnyetski."

"Well, Charnyetski will be able to keep them in bounds."

"Not unless he is among them, otherwise they will plunder. It cannot be, but they will give them an officer at
once."

"And will he lead them? But what will that big
Agá do?"

"If he does not meet a fool, he will carry out orders."

"Farewell, gentlemen!" cried Kmita, on a sudden.

"Whither in such haste?"

"To fall at the king's feet, and ask him to give me command of these people."

CHAPTER XIX.

THAT same day Akbah Ulan beat with his forehead to the king, and delivered to him letters of the Khan in which the latter repeated his promise of moving with one hundred thousand of the horde against the Swedes, when forty thousand thalers were paid him in advance, and when the first grass was on the fields, without which, in a country so ruined by war, it would be difficult to maintain such a great number of horses. As to that small chambul, the Khan had sent it to his "dearest brother" as a proof of his favor, so that the Cossacks, who were still thinking of disobedience, might have an evident sign that this favor endures steadily, and let but the first sound of rebellion reach the ears of the Khan, his vengeful anger will fall on all Cossacks.

The king received Akbah Ulan affably, and presenting him with a beautiful steed, said that he would send him soon to Pan Charnyetski in the field, for he wished to convince the Swedes by facts, that the Khan was giving aid to the Commonwealth. The eyes of the Tartar glittered when he heard of service under Charnyetski; for knowing him from the time of former wars in the Ukraine, he, in common with all the Agás, admired him.

But he was less pleased with the part of the Khan's letter which asked the king to attach to the chambul an officer, who knew the country well, who would lead the party and restrain the men, and also Akbah Ulan himself from plunder and excesses. Akbah Ulan would have preferred certainly not to have such a patron over him; but since the will of the Khan and the king were explicit, he merely beat with his forehead once more, hiding carefully his vexation, and perhaps promising in his soul that not he would bow down before that patron, but the patron before him.

Barely had the Tartar gone out, and the senators withdrawn, when Kmita, who had an audience at once, fell at the feet of the king, and said, —

"Gracious Lord ! I am not worthy of the favor for which I ask, but I set as much by it as by life itself. Permit me

to take command over these Tartars and move to the field
with them at once."

" I do not refuse," answered the astonished Yan Kazimir,
" for a better leader it would be difficult to find. A cavalier
of great daring and resolve is needed to hold them in check,
or they will begin straightway to burn and murder our
people. To this only am I firmly opposed, that you go to-
morrow, before your flesh has healed from the wounds made
by Swedish rapiers."

" I feel that as soon as the wind blows around me in the
field, my weakness will pass, and strength will enter me
again; as to the Tartars, I will manage them and bend
them into soft wax."

" But why in such haste ? Whither are you going ? "

" Against the Swedes, Gracious Lord; I have nothing to
wait for here, since what I wanted I have, that is your favor
and pardon for my former offences. I will go to Charnyetski with Volodyovski, or I will attack the enemy separately, as I did once Hovanski, and I trust in God that I
shall have success."

" It must be that something else is drawing you to the
field."

" I will confess as to a father, and open my whole soul.
Prince Boguslav, not content with the calumny which he
cast on me, has taken that maiden from Kyedani and confined her in Taurogi, or worse, for he is attacking her
honesty, her virtue, her honor as a woman. Gracious Lord!
the reason is confused in my head, when I think in what
hands the poor girl is at present. By the passion of the
Lord! these wounds pain less. That maiden thinks to
this moment that I offered that damned soul, that arch-
cur to raise hands on your Royal Grace — and she holds me
the lowest of all the degenerate. I cannot endure, I am
not able to endure, till I find her, till I free her. Give me
those Tartars and I swear that I will not do my own work
alone, but I will crush so many Swedes that the court of this
castle might be paved with their skulls."

" Calm yourself," said the king.

" If I had to leave service and the defence of majesty
and the Commonwealth for my own cause, it would be a
shame for me to ask, but here one unites with the other.
The time has come to beat the Swedes, I will do nothing
else. The time has come to hunt a traitor; I will hunt
him to Livland, to Courland, and even as far as the

Northerners, or beyond the sea to Sweden, should he hide there."

" We have information that Boguslav will move very soon with Karl, from Elblang."

" Then I will go to meet them."

" With such a small chambul ?   They will cover you with a cap."

" Hovanski, with eighty thousand, was covering me, but he did not succeed."

" All the loyal army is under Charnyetski.   They will strike Charnyetski first of all."

" I will go to Charnyetski.   It is needful to give him aid the more quickly."

" You will go to Charnyetski, but to Taurogi with such a small number you cannot go.   Radzivill delivered all the castles in Jmud to the enemy, and Swedish garrisons are stationed everywhere; but Taurogi, it seems to me, is somewhere on the boundary of Prussia ? "

" On the very boundary of Electoral Prussia, but on our side, and twenty miles from Tyltsa.   Wherever I have to go, I will go, and not only will I not lose men, but crowds of daring soldiers will gather to me on the road.   And consider this, Gracious Lord, that wherever I show myself the whole neighborhood will mount against the Swedes. First, I will rouse Jmud, if no one else does it.   What place may not be reached now, when the whole country is boiling like water in a pot ?   I am accustomed to be in a boil."

" But you do not think of this, — perhaps the Tartars will not like to go so far with you."

" Only let them not like!   only let them try not to like," said Kmita, gritting his teeth at the very thought, " as there are four hundred, or whatever number there is of them, I 'll have all four hundred hanged — there will be no lack of trees ! Just let them try to rebel against me."

" Yandrek ! " cried the king, falling into good humor and pursing his lips, " as God is dear to me, I cannot find a better shepherd for those lambs !   Take them and lead them wherever it pleases thee most."

" I give thanks, Gracious Lord ! " said the knight, pressing the knees of the king.

" When do you wish to start ? " asked Yan Kazimir.

" God willing, to-morrow."

" Maybe Akbah Ulan will not be ready, because his horses are road-weary."

"Then I will have him lashed to a saddle with a lariat, and he will go on foot if he spares his horse."

"I see that you will get on with him. Still use mild measures while possible. But now, Yendrek, it is late; to-morrow I wish to see you again. Meanwhile take this ring, tell your royalist lady that you have it from the king, and tell her that the king commands her to love firmly his faithful servant and defender."

"God grant me," said the young hero, with tears in his eyes, "not to die save in defence of your Royal Grace!"

Here the king withdrew, for it was already late; and Kmita went to his own quarters to prepare for the road, and think what to begin, and whither he ought to go first.

He remembered the words of Kharlamp, that should it appear that Boguslav was not in Taurogi it would really be better to leave the maiden there, for from Taurogi being near the boundary, it was easy to take refuge in Tyltsa, under care of the elector. Moreover, though the Swedes had abandoned in his last need the voevoda of Vilna, it was reasonable to expect that they would have regard for his widow; hence, if Olenka was under her care, no evil could meet her. If they had gone to Courland, that was still better. "And to Courland I cannot go with my Tartars," said Kmita to himself, "for that is another State."

He walked then, and worked with his head. Hour followed hour, but he did not think yet of rest; and the thought of his new expedition so cheered him, that though that day he was weak in the morning, he felt now that his strength was returning, and he was ready to mount in a moment.

The servants at last had finished tying the saddle-straps and were preparing to sleep, when all at once some one began to scratch at the door of the room.

"Who is there?" asked Kmita. Then to his attendant, "Go and see!"

He went, and after he had spoken to some one outside the door, he returned.

"Some soldier wants to see your grace greatly. He says that his name is Soroka."

"By the dear God! let him in," called Kmita. And without waiting for the attendant to carry out the order, he sprang to the door. "Come in, dear Soroka! come hither!"

The soldier entered the room, and with his first movement wished to fall at the feet of his colonel, for he was a friend and a servant as faithful as he was attached; but soldierly subordination carried the day, therefore he stood erect and said, —

"At the orders of your grace!"

"Be greeted, dear comrade, be greeted!" said Kmita, with emotion. "I thought they had cut you to pieces in Chenstohova." And he pressed Soroka's head, then began to shake him, which he could do without lowering himself too much, for Soroka was descended from village nobility.

Then the old sergeant fell to embracing Kmita's knees.

"Whence do you come?" asked Kmita.

"From Chenstohova."

"And you were looking for me?"

"Yes."

"And from whom did you learn that I was alive?"

"From Kuklinovski's men. The prior, Kordetski, celebrated High Mass from delight, in thanksgiving to God. Then there was a report that Pan Babinich had conducted the king through the mountains; so I knew that that was your grace, no one else."

"And Father Kordetski is well?"

"Well; only it is unknown whether the angels will not take him alive to heaven any day, for he is a saint."

"Surely he is nothing else. Where did you discover that I came with the king to Lvoff?"

"I thought, since you conducted the king you must be near him; but I was afraid that your grace might move to the field and that I should be late."

"To-morrow I go with the Tartars."

"Then it has happened well, for I bring your grace two full belts, one which I wore and the other you carried, and besides, those precious stones which we took from the caps of boyars, and those which your grace took when we seized the treasury of Hovanski."

"Those were good times when we gathered in wealth; but there cannot be much of it now, for I left a good bit with Father Kordetski."

"I do not know how much, but the prior himself said that two good villages might be bought with it."

Then Soroka drew near the table, and began to remove the belts from his body. "And the stones are in this canteen," added he, putting the canteen near the belts.

Kmita made no reply, but shook in his hand some gold ducats without counting them, and said to the sergeant, —

"Take these!"

" I fall at the feet of your grace. Ei, if I had had on the road one such ducat ! "

" How is that ? "

" Because I am terribly weak. There are few places now where they will give one morsel of bread to a man, for all are afraid; and at last I barely dragged my feet forward from hunger."

" By the dear God! but you had all this with you ! "

" I dared not use it without leave."

" Take this ! " said Kmita, giving him another handful. Then he cried to the servants, —

" Now, scoundrels, give him to eat in less time than a man might say ' Our Father,' or I 'll take your heads ! "

They sprang one in front of another, and in little while there was an enormous dish of smoked sausage before Soroka, and a flask of vodka. The soldier fastened his eyes greedily on the food, and his lips and mustaches were quivering; but he dared not sit in presence of the colonel.

" Sit down, eat ! " commanded Kmita.

Kmita had barely spoken when a dry sausage was crunching between the powerful jaws of Soroka. The two attendants looked on him with protruding eyes.

" Be off ! " cried Kmita.

They sprang out with all breath through the door ; but the knight walked with hasty steps up and down the room, not wishing to interrupt his faithful servant. But he, as often as he poured out a glass of vodka, looked sidewise at the colonel, fearing to find a frown ; then he emptied the glass and turned toward the wall.

Kmita walked, walked ; at last he began to speak to himself. " It cannot be otherwise ! " muttered he ; " it is needful to send him. I will give orders to tell her — No use, she will not believe ! She will not read a letter, for she holds me a traitor and a dog. Let him not come in her way, but let him see and tell me what is taking place there."

Then he said on a sudden: " Soroka ! "

The soldier sprang up so quickly that he came near overturning the table, and straightened as straight as a string.

" According to order ! "

" You are an honest man, and in need you are cunning. You will go on a long road, but not on a hungry one."

" According to order ! "

" To Tyltsa, on the Prussian border. There Panna Billevich is living in the castle of Boguslav Radzivill. You will learn if the prince is there, and have an eye on everything. Do not try to see Panna Billevich; but should a meeting happen of itself, tell her, and swear that I brought the king through the mountains, and that I am near his person. She will surely not give you credit; for the prince has defamed me, saying that I wished to attempt the life of the king, — which is a lie befitting a dog."

"According to order!"

"Do not try to see her, as I have said, for she will not believe you. But if you meet by chance, tell her what you know. Look at everything, and listen! But take care of yourself, for if the prince is there and recognizes you, or if any one from his court recognizes you, you will be impaled on a stake. I would send old Kyemlich, but he is in the other world, slain in the pass; and his sons are too dull. They will go with me. Have you been in Tyltsa?"

"I have not, your grace."

"You will go to Shchuchyn, thence along the Prussian boundary to Tyltsa. Taurogi is twenty miles distant from Tyltsa and opposite, on our side. Stay in Taurogi till you have seen everything, then come to me. You will find me where I shall be. Ask for the Tartars and Pan Babinich. And now go to sleep with the Kyemliches. To-morrow for the road."

After these words, Soroka went out. Kmita did not lie down to sleep for a long time, but at last weariness overcame him; then he threw himself on the bed, and slept a stone sleep.

Next morning he rose greatly refreshed and stronger than the day before. The whole court was already on foot, and the usual activity had begun. Kmita went first to the chancellery, for his commission and safe-conduct; he visited Suba Gazi Bey, chief of the Khan's embassy in Lvoff, and had a long conversation with him.

During that conversation Pan Andrei put his hand twice in his purse; so that when he was going out Suba Gazi Bey changed caps with him, gave him a baton of green feathers and some yards of an equally green cord of silk.

Armed in this fashion, Pan Andrei returned to the king, who had just come from Mass; then the young man fell once more at the knees of the sovereign; after that he went, together with the Kyemliches and his attendants, directly to the place where Akbah Ulan was quartered with his chambul.

At sight of him the old Tartar put his hand to his forehead, his mouth, and his breast; but learning who Kmita was and why he had come, he grew severe at once; his face became gloomy, and was veiled with haughtiness.

"And the king has sent you to me as a guide," said he to Kmita, in broken Russian; "you will show me the road, though I should be able to go myself wherever it is needed, and you are young and inexperienced."

"He indicates in advance what I am to be," thought Kmita, "but I will be polite to him as long as I can." Then he said aloud: "Akbah Ulan, the king has sent me here as a chief, not as a guide. And I tell you this, that you will do better not to oppose the will of his grace."

"The Khan makes appointments over the Tartars, not the king," answered Akbah Ulan.

"Akbah Ulan," repeated Kmita, with emphasis, "the Khan has made a present of thee to the king, as he would a dog or a falcon; therefore show no disrespect to him, lest thou be tied like a dog with a rope."

"Allah!" cried the astonished Tartar.

"Hei! have a care that thou anger me not!" said Kmita.

Akbah Ulan's eyes became bloodshot. For a time he could not utter a word; the veins on his neck were swollen, his hands sought his dagger.

"I'll bite, I'll bite!" said he, with stifled voice.

But Pan Andrei, though he had promised to be polite, had had enough, for by nature he was very excitable. In one moment therefore something struck him as if a serpent had stung; he seized the Tartar by the thin beard with his whole hand, and pushing back his head as if he wished to show him something on the ceiling, he began to talk through his set teeth.

"Hear me, son of a goat! Thou wouldst like to have no one above thee, so as to burn, rob, and slaughter! Thou wouldst have me as guide! Here is thy guide! thou hast a guide!" And thrusting him to the wall, he began to pound his head against a corner of it.

He let him go at last, completely stunned, but not looking for his knife now. Kmita, following the impulse of his hot blood, discovered the best method of convincing Oriental people accustomed to slavery; for in the pounded head of the Tartar, in spite of all the rage which was stifling him, the thought gleamed at once how powerful and commanding must that knight be who could act in this manner with him, Akbah Ulan; and with his bloody lips he repeated three times, —

"Bagadyr (hero), Bagadyr, Bagadyr!"

Kmita meanwhile placed on his own head the cap of Suba Gazi, drew forth the green baton, which he had kept behind his belt of purpose till that moment, and said, —

"Look at these, slave! and these!"

"Allah!" exclaimed the astonished Ulan.

"And here!" added Kmita, taking the cord from his pocket.

But Akbah Ulan was already lying at his feet, and striking the floor with his forehead.

An hour later the Tartars were marching out in a long line over the road from Lvoff to Vyelki Ochi; and Kmita, sitting on a valiant chestnut steed which the king had given him, drove along the chambul as a shepherd dog drives sheep. Akbah Ulan looked at the young hero with wonder and fear.

The Tartars, who were judges of warriors, divined at the first glance that under that leader there would be no lack of blood and plunder, and went willingly with singing and music.

And Kmita's heart swelled within him when he looked at those forms, resembling beasts of the wilderness; for they were dressed in sheepskin and camel-skin coats with the wool outside. The wave of wild heads shook with the movements of the horses; he counted them, and was thinking how much he could undertake with that force.

"It is a peculiar body," thought he, "and it seems to me as if I were leading a pack of wolves; and with such men precisely would it be possible to run through the whole Commonwealth, and trample all Prussia. Wait awhile, Prince Boguslav!"

Here boastful thoughts began to flow into his head, for he was inclined greatly to boastfulness.

"God has given man adroitness," said he to himself; "yesterday I had only the two Kyemliches, but to-day four hundred horses are clattering behind me. Only let the dance begin; I shall have a thousand or two of such roisterers as my old comrades would not be ashamed of. Wait a while, Boguslav!"

But after a moment he added, to quiet his own conscience: "And I shall serve also the king and the country."

He fell into excellent humor. This too pleased him

greatly, that nobles, Jews, peasants, even large crowds of general militia, could not guard themselves from fear in the first moment at sight of his Tartars. And there was a fog, for the thaw had filled the air with a vapor. It happened then every little while that some one rode up near, and seeing all at once whom they had before them, cried out, —

"The word is made flesh!"

"Jesus! Mary! Joseph!"

"The Tartars! the horde!"

But the Tartars passed peacefully the equipages, loaded wagons, herds of horses and travellers. It would have been different had the leader permitted, but they dared not undertake anything of their own will, for they had seen how at starting Akbah Ulan had held the stirrup of that leader.

Now Lvoff had vanished in the distance beyond the mist. The Tartars had ceased to sing, and the chambul moved slowly amid the clouds of steam rising from the horses. All at once the tramp of a horse was heard behind. In a moment two horsemen appeared. One of them was Pan Michael, the other was the tenant of Vansosh; both, passing the chambul, pushed straight to Kmita.

"Stop! stop!" cried the little knight.

Kmita held in his horse. "Is that you?"

Pan Michael reined in his horse. "With the forehead!" said he, "letters from the king: one to you, the other to the voevoda of Vityebsk."

"I am going to Pan Charnyetski, not to Sapyeha."

"But read the letter."

Kmita broke the seal and read as follows: —

We learn through a courier just arrived from the voevoda of Vityebsk that he cannot march hither to Little Poland, and is turning back again to Podlyasye, because Prince Boguslav, who is not with the King of Sweden, has planned to fall upon Tykotsin and Pan Sapyeha. And since he must leave a great part of his troops in garrisons, we order you to go to his assistance with that Tartar chambul. And since your own wish is thus gratified, we need not urge you to hasten. The other letter you will give to the voevoda; in it we commend Pan Babinich, our faithful servant, to the good will of the voevoda, and above all to the protection of God. YAN KAZIMIR, *King.*

"By the dear God! by the dear God! This is happy news for me!" cried Kmita. "I know not how to thank the king and you for it."

"I offered myself to come," said the little knight, "out of compassion, for I saw your pain; I came so that the letters might reach you surely."

"When did the courier arrive?"

"We were with the king at dinner, — I, Pan Yan, Pan Stanislav, Kharlamp, and Zagloba. You cannot imagine what Zagloba told there about the carelessness of Sapyeha, and his own services. It is enough that the king cried from continual laughter, and both hetmans were holding their sides all the time. At last the chamber servant came with a letter, when the king burst out, 'Go to the hangman, maybe evil news will spoil my fun!' When he learned that it was from Pan Sapyeha, he began to read it. Indeed he read evil news, for that was confirmed which had long been discussed; the elector had broken all his oaths, and against his own rightful sovereign had joined the King of Sweden at last."

"Another enemy, as if there were few of them hitherto!" cried Kmita; and he folded his hands. "Great God! only let Pan Sapyeha send me for a week to Prussia, and God the Merciful grant that ten generations will remember me and my Tartars."

"Perhaps you will go there," said Pan Michael; "but first you must defeat Boguslav, for as a result of that treason of the elector is he furnished with men and permitted to go to Podlyasye."

"Then we shall meet, as to-day is to-day; as God is in heaven, so shall we meet," cried Kmita, with flashing eyes. "If you had brought me the appointment of voevoda of Vilna, it would not have given me more pleasure."

"The king too cried at once: 'There is an expedition ready for Yendrek, from which the soul will rejoice in him.' He wanted to send his servant after you, but I said I will go myself, I will take farewell of him once more."

Kmita bent on his horse, and seized the little knight in his embrace.

"A brother would not have done for me what you have done! God grant me to thank you in some way."

"Tfu! Did not I want to shoot you?"

"I deserved nothing better. Never mind! May I be slain in the first battle if in all knighthood I love a man more than I love you."

Then they began to embrace again at parting, and Volodyovski said, —

"Be careful with Boguslav, be careful, for it is no easy matter with him."

" For one of us death is written. Ei! if you who are a genius at the sabre could discover your secrets to me. But there is no time. As it is, may the angels help me; and I will see his blood, or my eyes will close forever on the light of day."

" God aid you! A lucky journey, and give angelica to those traitors of Prussians!" said Volodyovski.

" Be sure on that point. The disgusting Lutherans!"

Here Volodyovski nodded to Jendzian, who during this time was talking to Akbah Ulan, explaining the former successes of Kmita over Hovanski. And both rode back to Lvoff.

Then Kmita turned his chambul on the spot, as a driver turns his wagon, and went straight toward the north.

CHAPTER XX.

THOUGH the Tartars, and especially those of the Dobrudja, knew how to stand breast to breast against armed men in the field, their most cherished warfare was the slaughter of defenceless people, the seizing of women and peasants captive, and above all, plunder. The road was very bitter therefore to that chambul which Kmita led, for under his iron hand these wild warriors had to become lambs, keep their knives in the sheaths, and the quenched tinder and coiled ropes in their saddle-bags. They murmured at first.

Near Tarnogrod a few remained behind of purpose to let free the "red birds" in Hmyelevsk and to frolic with the women. But Kmita, who had pushed on toward Tomashov, returned at sight of the first gleam of fire, and commanded the guilty to hang the guilty. And he had gained such control of Akbah Ulan, that the old Tartar not only did not resist, but he urged the condemned to hang quickly, or the "bogadyr" would be angry. Thenceforth "the lambs" marched quietly, crowding more closely together through the villages and towns, lest suspicion might fall on them. And the execution, though Kmita carried it out so severely, did not rouse even ill will or hatred against him; such fortune had that fighter that his subordinates felt just as much love for him as they did fear.

It is true that Pan Andrei permitted no one to wrong them. The country had been terribly ravaged by the recent attack of Hmelnitski and Sheremetyeff; therefore it was as difficult to find provisions and pasture as before harvest, and besides, everything had to be in time and in plenty; in Krinitsi, where the townspeople offered resistance and would not furnish supplies, Pan Andrei ordered that some of them be beaten with sticks, and the under-starosta he stretched out with the blow of a whirlbat.

This delighted the horde immensely, and hearing with pleasure the uproar of the beaten people, they said among themselves, —

"Ei! our Babinich is a falcon; he lets no man offend his lambs."

It is enough that not only did they not grow thin, but the men and horses improved in condition. Old Ulan, whose stomach had expanded, looked with growing wonder on the young hero and clicked with his tongue.

"If Allah were to give me a son, I should like such a one. I should not die of hunger in my old age in the Ulus," repeated he.

But Kmita from time to time struck him on the stomach and said, —

"Here listen, wild boar! If the Swedes do not open your paunch, you will hide the contents of all cupboards inside it."

"Where are the Swedes? Our ropes will rot, our bows will be mildewed," answered Ulan, who was homesick for war.

They were advancing indeed through a country to which a Swedish foot had not been able to come, but farther they would pass through one in which there had been garrisons afterward driven out by confederates. They met everywhere smaller and larger bands of armed nobles, marching in various directions, and not smaller bands of peasants, who more than once stopped the road to them threateningly, and to whom it was often difficult to explain that they had to do with friends and servants of the King of Poland.

They came at last to Zamost. The Tartars were amazed at sight of this mighty fortress; but what did they think when told that not long before it had stopped the whole power of Hmelnitski?

Pan Zamoyski, the owner by inheritance, permitted them as a mark of great affection and favor to enter the town. They were admitted through a brick gate, while the other two were stone. Kmita himself did not expect to see anything similar, and he could not recover from astonishment at sight of the broad streets, built in straight lines, Italian fashion; at sight of the splendid college, and the academy, the castle, walls, the great cannon and every kind of provision. As few among magnates could be compared with the grandson of the great chancellor, so there were few fortresses that could be compared with Zamost.

But the greatest ecstasy seized the Tartars, when they saw the Armenian part of the town. Their nostrils drew in greedily the odor of morocco, a great manufacture of which was carried on by industrial immigrants from Kaffa; and their eyes laughed at sight of the dried fruits and confectionery, Eastern carpets, girdles, inlaid sabres, daggers, bows, Turkish lamps, and every kind of costly article.

The cup-bearer of the kingdom himself pleased Kmita's heart greatly. He was a genuine kinglet in that Zamost of his; a man in the strength of his years, of fine presence though lacking somewhat robustness, for he had not restrained sufficiently the ardors of nature in early years. He had always loved the fair sex, but his health had not been shaken to that degree that joyousness had vanished from his face. So far he had not married, and though the most renowned houses in the Commonwealth had opened wide their doors, he asserted that he could not find in them a sufficiently beautiful maiden. He found her somewhat later, in the person of a young French lady, who though in love with another gave him her hand without hesitation, not foreseeing that the first one, disregarded, would adorn in the future his own and her head with a kingly crown.

The lord of Zamost was not distinguished for quick wit, though he had enough for his own use. He did not strive for dignities and offices, though they came to him of themselves; and when his friends reproached him with a lack of native ambition, he answered, — "It is not true that I lack it, for I have more than those who bow down. Why should I wear out the thresholds of the court? In Zamost I am not only Yan Zamoyski, but Sobiepan Zamoyski,"[1] with which name he was very well pleased. He was glad to affect simple manners, though he had received a refined education and had passed his youth in journeys through foreign lands. He spoke of himself as a common noble, and spoke emphatically of the moderateness of his station, perhaps so that others might contradict him, and perhaps so that they might not notice his medium wit. On the whole he was an honorable man, and a better son of the Commonwealth than many others.

And as he came near Kmita's heart, so did Kmita please him; therefore he invited Pan Andrei to the chambers of the castle and entertained him, for he loved this also, that men should exalt his hospitality.

Pan Andrei came to know in the castle many noted persons; above all, Princess Griselda Vishnyevetski, sister of Pan Zamoyski and widow of the great Yeremi, — a man who

[1] Self-lord Zamoyski.

in his time was well-nigh the greatest in the Commonwealth, who nevertheless had lost his whole immense fortune in the time of the Cossack incursion, so that the princess was now living at Zamost, on the bounty of her brother Yan.

But that lady was so full of grandeur, of majesty and virtue, that her brother was the first to blow away the dust from before her; and moreover he feared her like fire. There was no case in which he did not gratify her wishes, nor an affair the most important concerning which he did not advise with her. The people of the castle said that the princess ruled Zamost, the army, the treasury, and her brother; but she did not wish to take advantage of her preponderance, being given with her whole soul to grief for her husband and to the education of her son.

That son had recently returned for a short time from the court of Vienna and was living with her. He was a youth in the springtime of life; but in vain did Kmita seek in him those marks which the son of the great Yeremi should bear in his features.

The figure of the young prince was graceful; but he had a large, full face, and protruding eyes with a timid look; he had coarse lips, moist, as with people inclined to pleasures of the table; an immense growth of hair, black as a raven's wing, fell to his shoulders. He inherited from his father only that raven hair and dark complexion.

Pan Andrei was assured by those who were more intimate with the prince that he had a noble soul, unusual understanding, and a remarkable memory, thanks to which he was able to speak almost all languages; and that a certain heaviness of body and temperament with a native greed for food were the only defects of that otherwise remarkable young man.

In fact, after he had entered into conversation with him Pan Andrei became convinced that the prince not only had an understanding mind and a striking judgment touching everything, but the gift of attracting people. Kmita loved him after the first conversation with that feeling in which compassion is the greatest element. He felt that he would give much to bring back to that orphan the brilliant future which belonged to him by right of birth.

Pan Andrei convinced himself at the first dinner that what was said of the gluttony of Michael Vishnyevetski was true. The young prince seemed to think of nothing save eating. His prominent eyes followed each dish uneasily, and when they brought him the platter he took an enormous quantity on his plate and ate ravenously, smacking his lips as only gluttons do. The marble face of the princess grew clouded with still greater sorrow at that sight. It became awkward for Kmita, so that he turned away his eyes and looked at Sobiepan.

But Zamoyski was not looking either at Prince Michael or his own guest. Kmita followed his glance, and behind the shoulders of Princess Griselda he saw a wonderful sight indeed, which he had not hitherto noticed.

It was the small pretty head of a maiden, who was as fair as milk, as red as a rose, and beautiful as an image. Short wavy locks ornamented her forehead; her quick eyes were directed to the officers sitting near Zamoyski, not omitting Sobiepan himself. At last those eyes rested on Kmita, and looked at him fixedly, as full of coquetry as if they intended to gaze into the depth of his heart.

But Kmita was not easily confused; therefore he began to look at once into those eyes with perfect insolence, and then he punched in the side Pan Shurski, lieutenant of the armored castle squadron at Zamost, who was sitting near him, and asked in an undertone, —

"But who is that tailed farthing?"

"Worthy sir," answered Shurski, aloud, "do not speak slightingly when you do not know of whom you are speaking. That is Panna Anusia Borzobogati. And you will not call her otherwise unless you wish to regret your rudeness."

"You do not know, sir, that a farthing is a kind of bird and very beautiful, therefore there is no contempt in the name," answered Kmita, laughing; "but noticing your anger you must be terribly in love."

"But who is not in love?" muttered the testy Shurski. "Pan Zamoyski himself has almost looked his eyes out, and is as if sitting on an awl."

"I see that, I see that!"

"What do you see? He, I, Grabovski, Stolangyevich, Konoyadzki, Rubetski of the dragoons, Pyechynga, — she has sunk us all. And with you it will be the same, if you stay here. With her twenty-four hours are sufficient."

"Lord brother! with me she could do nothing in twenty-four months."

"How is that?" asked Shurski, with indignation; "are you made of metal or what?"

"No! But if some one had stolen the last dollar from your pocket you would not be afraid of a thief."

"Is that it?" answered Shurski.

Kmita grew gloomy at once, for his trouble came to his mind, and he noticed no longer that the black eyes were looking still more stubbornly at him, as if asking, "What is thy name, whence dost thou come, youthful knight?"

But Shurski muttered: "Bore, bore away! She bored that way into me till she bored to my heart. Now she does not even care."

Kmita shook himself out of his seriousness.

"Why the hangman does not some one of you marry her?"

"Each one prevents every other."

"The girl will be left in the lurch," said Kmita, "though in truth there must be white seeds in that pear yet."

Shurski opened his eyes, and bending to Kmita's ear said very mysteriously, —

"They say that she is twenty-five, as I love God. She was with Princess Griselda before the incursion of the rabble?"

"Wonder of wonders, I should not give her more than sixteen or eighteen at the most."

This time the devil (the girl) guessed apparently that they were talking of her, for she covered her gleaming eyes with the lids, and only shot sidelong glances at Kmita, inquiring continually: "Who art thou, so handsome? Whence dost thou come?" And he began involuntarily to twirl his mustache.

After dinner Zamoyski, who from respect to the courtly manners of Kmita treated him as an unusual guest, took him by the arm. "Pan Babinich," said he, "you have told me that you are from Lithuania?"

"That is true, Pan Zamoyski."

"Tell me, did you know the Podbipientas?"

"As to knowing I know them not, for they are no longer in the world, at least those who had the arms Tear-Cowl. The last one fell at Zbaraj. He was the greatest knight that Lithuania had. Who of us does not know of Podbipienta?"

"I have heard also of him; but I ask for this reason: There is in attendance on my sister a lady of honorable family. She was the betrothed of this Podbipienta who was killed at Zbaraj. She is an orphan, without father or mother; and though my sister loves her greatly, still, being the natural guardian of my sister, I have in this way the maiden in guardianship."

"A pleasant guardianship!" put in Kmita.

Zamoyski smiled, winked, and smacked his tongue. "Sweetcakes! is n't she?"

But suddenly he saw that he was betraying himself, and assumed a serious air.

"Oh, you traitor!" said he, half jestingly, half seriously, "you want to hang me on a hook, and I almost let it out!"

"What?" asked Kmita, looking him quickly in the eyes.

Here Zamoyski saw clearly that in quickness of wit he was not the equal of his guest, and turned the conversation at once.

"That Podbipienta," said he, "bequeathed her some estates there in your region. I don't remember the names of them, for they are strange, — Baltupie, Syrutsiani, Myshykishki, — in a word, all that he had. Would I could remember them! Five or six estates."

"They are adjoining estates, not separate. Podbipienta was a very wealthy man, and if that lady should come to his fortune she might have her own ladies-in-waiting, and seek for a husband among senators."

"Do you tell me that? Do you know those places?"

"I know only Lyubovich and Sheputy, for they are near my land. The forest boundary alone is ten miles long, and the fields and meadows are as much more."

"Where are they?"

"In Vityebsk."

"Oh, far away! the affair is not worth the trouble, and the country is under the enemy."

"When we drive out the enemy we shall come to the property. But the Podbipientas have property in other places, — in Jmud very considerable, I know, for I have a piece of land there myself."

"I see that your substance is not a bag of chopped straw."

"It brings in nothing now. But I need nothing from others."

"Advise me how to put that maiden on her feet."

Kmita laughed.

"I prefer to talk over this matter rather than others. It would be better for her to go to Pan Sapyeha. If he would take the affair in hand, he could do a great deal as voevoda of Vityebsk and the most noted man in Lithuania. He could send notices to the tribunals that the will was made to Panna Borzobogati, so that Podbipienta's more distant relatives should not seize the property."

"That is true; but now there are no tribunals, and Sapyeha has something else in his head."

"The lady might be placed in his hands and under his guardianship. Having her before his eyes, he would give aid more speedily."

Kmita looked with astonishment at Zamoyski. "What object has he in wishing to remove her from this place?" thought he.

Zamoyski continued: "It would be difficult for her to live in camp, in the tent of the voevoda of Vityebsk; but she might stay with his daughters."

"I do not understand this," thought Kmita; "would he consent to be only her guardian?"

"But here is the difficulty: how can I send her to those parts in the present time of disturbance? Several hundred men would be needed, and I cannot strip Zamost. If I could only find some one to conduct her. Now, you might take her; you are going to Sapyeha. I would give you letters, and you would give me your word of honor to take her in safety."

"I conduct her to Sapyeha?" asked Kmita, in amazement.

"Is the office unpleasant? Even if it should come to love on the road —"

"Ah," said Kmita, "another one is managing my affections; and though the tenant pays nothing, still I do not think of making a change."

"So much the better; with all the greater satisfaction can I confide her to you."

A moment of silence followed.

"Well, will you undertake it?" asked the starosta.

"I am marching with Tartars."

"People tell me that the Tartars fear you worse than fire. Well, what? Will you undertake it?"

"H'm! why not, if thereby I can oblige your grace? But —"

"Ah, you think that the princess must give permission; she will, as God is dear to me! For she, — fancy to yourself, — she suspects me."

Here the starosta whispered in Kmita's ear; at last he said aloud, —

" She was very angry with me for that, and I put my ears aside; for to war with women, — behold you! I would rather have the Swedes outside Zamost. But she will have the best proof that I am planning no evil, when I wish to send the girl away. She will be terribly amazed, it is true; but at the first opportunity I 'll talk with her touching this matter."

When he had said this, Zamoyski turned and went away. Kmita looked at him, and muttered, —

" You are setting some snare, Pan Sobiepan; and though I do not understand the object, I see the snare quickly, for you are a terribly awkward trapper."

Zamoyski was pleased with himself, though he understood well that the work was only half done; and another remained so difficult that at thought of it despair seized him, and even terror. He had to get permission of Princess Griselda, whose severity and penetrating mind Pan Sobiepan feared from his whole soul. But having begun, he wished to bring the work to completion as early as possible; therefore next morning, after Mass, and breakfast, and after he had reviewed the hired German infantry, he went to the chambers of the princess.

He found the lady embroidering a cope for the college. Behind her was Anusia winding silk hung upon two arm-chairs; a second skein of rose color she had placed around her neck, and moving her hands quickly, she ran around the chairs in pursuit of the unwinding thread.

Zamoyski's eyes grew bright at sight of her; but he assumed quickly a serious look, and greeting the princess, began as if unwillingly, —

" That Pan Babinich who has come here with the Tartars is a Lithuanian, — a man of importance, a very elegant fellow, a born knight in appearance. Have you noticed him ? "

" You brought him to me yourself," answered the princess, indifferently; " he has an honest face."

" I asked him concerning that property left Panna Borzobogati. He says it is a fortune almost equal to that of the Radzivills."

" God grant it to Anusia; her orphanhood will be the lighter, and her old age as well," said the lady.

" But there is a danger lest distant relatives tear it apart. Babinich says that Sapyeha might occupy himself with it, if he wished. He is an honest man, and very friendly to us:

I would confide my own daughter to him. It would be enough for him to send notices to the tribunals, and proclaim the guardianship. But Babinich says it is needful that Panna Anusia should go to those places in person."

"Where, — to Pan Sapyeha ? "

"Or to his daughters, so as to be there, that the formal installation might take place."

The starosta invented at that moment "formal installation," thinking justly that the princess would accept this counterfeit money instead of true coin. She thought a moment, and asked, —

"How could she go now, when Swedes are on the road ? "

"I have news that the Swedes have left Lublin. All this side of the Vistula is free."

"And who would take Anusia to Pan Sapyeha ? "

"Suppose this same Babinich."

"With Tartars ? Lord Brother, fear God ; those are wild, chaotic people ! "

"I am not afraid," put in Anusia, curtesying.

But Princess Griselda had noted already that her brother came with some plan all prepared ; therefore she sent Anusia out of the room, and began to look at Pan Sobiepan with an inquiring gaze. But he said as if to himself, —

"These Tartars are down in the dust before Babinich ; he hangs them for any insubordination."

"I cannot permit this journey," answered the princess. "The girl is honest but giddy, and rouses enthusiasm quickly. You know that best yourself. I would never confide her to a young, unknown man."

"Unknown here he is not, for who has not heard of the Babiniches as men of high family and steady people ? [Zamoyski had never heard of the Babiniches in his life.] Besides," continued he, "you might give her some sedate woman as companion, and then decorum would be observed. Babinich I guarantee. I tell you this, too, Lady Sister, that he has in those places a betrothed with whom he is, as he tells me himself, in love ; and whoso is in love has something else in his head. The foundation of the matter is this, that another such chance may not come for a long time, — the fortune may be lost to the girl, and in ripe years she may be without a roof above her."

The princess ceased embroidering, raised her head, and fixing her penetrating eyes on her brother, asked, —

"What reason have you to send her from here?"

"What reason have I?" repeated he, dropping his glance; "what can I have? —none!"

"Yan, you have conspired with Babinich against her virtue!"

"There it is! As God is dear to me, only that was wanting! You will read the letter which I shall send to Sapyeha, and give your own. I will merely say this to you, that I shall not leave Zamost. Finally examine Babinich himself, and ask him whether he will undertake the office. The moment you suspect me I step aside."

"Why do you insist so that she shall leave Zamost?"

"For I wish her good, and it is the question of an immense fortune. Besides, I confess it concerns me much that she should leave Zamost. Your suspicions have grown disagreeable; it is not to my taste that you should be frowning at me forever and looking stern. I thought that in consenting to the departure of the young lady I should find the best argument against suspicions. God knows I have enough of this, for I am no student who steals under windows at night. I tell you more: my officers are enraged one against the other, and shaking their sabres at one another. There is neither harmony, nor order, nor service as there should be. I have enough of this. But since you are boring me with your eyes, then do as you wish; but look after Michael yourself, for that is your affair, not mine."

"Michael!" exclaimed the astonished princess.

"I say nothing against the girl. She does not disturb him more than others; but if you do not see his arrowy glances and ardent affection, then I tell you this, that Cupid has not such power to blind as a mother's love."

Princess Griselda's brows contracted, and her face grew pale.

Pan Sobiepan, seeing that he had struck home at last, slapped his knees with his hands and continued, —

"Lady Sister, thus it is, thus it is! What is the affair to me? Let Michael give her silk to unwind, let his nostrils quiver when he looks at her, let him blush, let him look at her through keyholes! What is that to me? Still, I know — she has a good fortune — her family — well, she is of nobles, and I do not raise myself above nobles. If you want it yourself, all right. Their years are not the same, but again it is not my affair."

Zamoyski rose, and bowing to his sister very politely, started to go out.

The blood rushed to her face. The proud lady did not see in the whole Commonwealth a match worthy of Vishnyevetski, and abroad, perhaps among the archduchesses of Austria; therefore these words of her brother burned her like iron red hot.

"Yan!" said she, "wait!"

"Lady Sister," said Zamoyski, "I wished first to give you proof that you suspect me unjustly; second, that you should watch some one besides me. Now you will do as you please; I have nothing more to say."

Then Pan Zamoyski bowed and went out.

CHAPTER XXI.

PAN ZAMOYSKI had not uttered pure calumny to his sister when he spoke of Michael's love for Anusia, for the young prince had fallen in love with her, as had all, not excepting the pages of the castle. But that love was not over-violent, and by no means aggressive; it was rather an agreeable intoxication of the head and mind, than an impulse of the heart, which, when it loves, impels to permanent possession of the object beloved. For such action Michael had not the energy.

Nevertheless, Princess Griselda, dreaming of a brilliant future for her son, was greatly terrified at that feeling. In the first moment the sudden consent of her brother to Anusia's departure astonished her; now she ceased thinking of that, so far had the threatening danger seized her whole soul. A conversation with her son, who grew pale and trembled, and who before he had confessed anything shed tears, confirmed her in the supposition that the danger was terrible.

Still she did not conquer her scruples of conscience at once, and it was only when Anusia, who wanted to see a new world, new people, and perhaps also turn the head of the handsome cavalier, fell at her feet with a request for permission, that the princess did not find strength sufficient to refuse.

Anusia, it is true, covered herself with tears at the thought of parting with her mistress and mother; but for the clever girl it was perfectly evident that by asking for the separation she had cleared herself from every suspicion of having with preconceived purpose turned the head of Prince Michael, or even Zamoyski himself.

Princess Griselda, from desire to know surely if there was a conspiracy between her brother and Kmita, directed the latter to come to her presence. Her brother's promise not to leave Zamost had calmed her considerably, it is true; she wished, however, to know more intimately the man who was to conduct the young lady.

The conversation with Kmita set her at rest thoroughly.
There looked from the blue eyes of the young noble
such sincerity and truth that it was impossible to doubt
him. He confessed at once that he was in love with another, and besides he had neither the wish nor the head
for folly. Finally he gave his word as a cavalier that he
would guard the lady from every misfortune, even if he
had to lay down his head.

"I will take her safely to Pan Sapyeha, for Pan Zamoyski says that the enemy has left Lublin. But I can do
no more; not because I hesitate in willing service for
your highness, since I am always willing to shed my blood
for the widow of the greatest warrior and the glory of
the whole Commonwealth, but because I have my own
grievous troubles, out of which I know not whether I
shall bring my life."

"It is a question of nothing more," answered the princess,
"than that you give her into the hands of Pan Sapyeha,
and he will not refuse my request to be her guardian."

Here she gave Kmita her hand, which he kissed with
the greatest reverence, and she said in parting, —

"Be watchful, Cavalier, be watchful, and do not place
safety in this, that the country is free of the enemy."

These last words arrested Kmita; but he had no time
to think over them, for Zamoyski soon caught him.

"Gracious Knight," said he, gayly, "you are taking the
greatest ornament of Zamost away from me."

"But at your wish," answered Kmita.

"Take good care of her. She is a toothsome dainty.
Some one may be ready to take her from you."

"Let him try! Oh, ho! I have given the word of a
cavalier to the princess, and with me my word is sacred."

"Oh, I only say this as a jest. Fear not, neither take
unusual caution."

"Still I will ask of your serene great mightiness a carriage with windows."

"I will give you two. But you are not going at once,
are you?"

"I am in a hurry. As it is, I am here too long."

"Then send your Tartars in advance to Krasnystav. I
will hurry off a courier to have oats ready for them there,
and will give you an escort of my own to that place. No
evil can happen to you here, for this is my country. I
will give you good men of the German dragoons, bold

fellows and acquainted with the road. Besides, to Krasnystav the road is as if cut out with a sickle."

"But why am I to stay here?"

"To remain longer with us; you are a dear guest. I
should be glad to detain you a year. Meanwhile I shall
send to the herds at Perespa; perhaps some horse will be
found which will not fail you in need."

Kmita looked quickly into the eyes of his host; then,
as if making a sudden decision, said, —

"I thank you, I will remain, and will send on the
Tartars."

He went straight to give them orders, and taking Akbah
Ulan to one side he said, —

"Akbah Ulan, you are to go to Krasnystav by the road,
straight as if cut with a sickle. I stay here, and a day
later will move after you with Zamoyski's escort. Listen
now to what I say! You will not go to Krasnystav, but
strike into the first forest, not far from Zamost, so that a
living soul may not know of you; and when you hear a
shot on the highroad, hurry to me, for they are preparing some trick against me in this place."

"Your will," said Akbah Ulan, placing his hand on his
forehead, his mouth, and his breast.

"I have seen through you, Pan Zamoyski," said Kmita
to himself. "In Zamost you are afraid of your sister;
therefore you wish to seize the young lady, and secrete
her somewhere in the neighborhood, and make of me the
instrument of your desires, and who knows if not to take
my life. But wait! You found a man keener than yourself; you will fall into your own trap!"

In the evening Lieutenant Shurski knocked at Kmita's
door. This officer, too, knew something, and had his suspicions; and because he loved Anusia he preferred that she
should depart, rather than fall into the power of Zamoyski.
Still he did not dare to speak openly, and perhaps because
he was not sure; but he wondered that Kmita had consented to send the Tartars on in advance; he declared that
the roads were not so safe as was said, that everywhere
armed bands were wandering, — bands swift to deeds of
violence.

Pan Andrei decided to feign that he divined nothing.
"What can happen to me?" asked he; "besides, Zamoyski
gives me his own escort."

"Bah! Germans!"

"Are they not reliable men?"

"Is it possible to depend upon those dog-brothers ever? It has happened that after conspiring on the road they went over to the enemy."

"But there are no Swedes on this side of the Vistula."

"They are in Lublin, the dogs! It is not true that they have left. I advise you honestly not to send the Tartars in advance, for it is always safer in a large company."

"It is a pity that you did not inform me before. I have one tongue in my mouth, and an order given I never withdraw."

Next morning the Tartars moved on. Kmita was to follow toward evening, so as to pass the first night at Krasnystav. Two letters to Pan Sapyeha were given him, — one from the princess, the other from her brother.

Kmita had a great desire to open the second, but he dared not; he looked at it, however, before the light, and saw that inside was blank paper. This discovery was proof to him that both the maiden and the letters were to be taken from him on the road.

Meanwhile the horses came from Perespa, and Zamoyski presented the knight with a steed beautiful beyond admiration; the steed he received with thankfulness, thinking in his soul that he would ride farther on him than Zamoyski expected. He thought also of his Tartars, who must now be in the forest, and wild laughter seized him. At times again he was indignant in soul, and promised to give the master of Zamost a lesson.

Finally the hour of dinner came, which passed in great gloom. Anusia had red eyes; the officers were in deep silence. Pan Zamoyski alone was cheerful, and gave orders to fill the goblets; Kmita emptied his, one after another. But when the hour of parting came, not many persons took leave of the travellers, for Zamoyski had sent the officers to their service. Anusia fell at the feet of the princess, and for a long time could not be removed from her; the princess herself had evident disquiet in her face. Perhaps she reproached herself in secret for permitting the departure of a faithful servant at a period when mishap might come easily. But the loud weeping of Michael, who held his fists to his eyes, crying like a school-boy, confirmed the proud lady in her conviction that it was needful to stifle the further growth of this boyish affection. Besides, she was quieted by the hope that in the family of Sapyeha the young lady would find protection, safety, and also the great fortune which was to settle her fate for the rest of her life.

"I commit her to your virtue, bravery, and honor," said the princess once more to Kmita; "and remember that you have sworn to me to conduct her to Pan Sapyeha without fail."

"I will take her as I would a glass, and in need will wind oakum around her, because I have given my word; death alone will prevent me from keeping it," answered the knight.

He gave his arm to Anusia, but she was angry and did not look at him; he had treated her rather slightingly, therefore she gave him her hand very haughtily, turning her face and head in another direction.

She was sorry to depart, and fear seized her; but it was too late then to draw back.

The moment came; they took their seats, — she in the carriage with her old servant, Panna Suvalski, he on his horse, — and they started. Twelve German horsemen surrounded the carriage and the wagon with Anusia's effects. When at last the doors in the Warsaw gate squeaked and the rattle of wheels was heard on the drop-bridge, Anusia burst into loud weeping.

Kmita bent toward the carriage. "Fear not, my lady, I will not eat you!"

"Clown!" thought Anusia.

They rode some time along the houses outside the walls, straight toward Old Zamost; then they entered fields and a pine-wood, which in those days stretched along a hilly country to the Bug on one side; on the other it extended, interrupted by villages, to Zavihost.

Night had fallen, but very calm and clear; the road was marked by a silver line; only the rolling of the carriage and the tramp of the horses broke the silence.

"My Tartars must be lurking here like wolves in a thicket," thought Kmita.

Then he bent his ear.

"What is that?" asked he of the officer who was leading the escort.

"A tramp! Some horseman is galloping after us!" answered the officer.

He had barely finished speaking when a Cossack hurried up on a foaming horse, crying, —

"Pan Babinich! Pan Babinich! A letter from Pan Zamoyski."

The retinue halted. The Cossack gave the letter to Kmita.

Kmita broke the seal, and by the light of a lantern read as follows : —

" Gracious and dearest Pan Babinich! Soon after the departure of Panna Borzobogati tidings came to us that the Swedes not only have not left Lublin, but that they intend to attack my Zamost. In view of this, further journeying and peregrination become inconvenient. Considering therefore the dangers to which a fair head might be exposed, we wish to have Panna Borzobogati in Zamost. Those same knights will bring her back; but you, who must be in haste to continue your journey, we do not wish to trouble uselessly. Announcing which will of ours to your grace, we beg you to give orders to the horseman according to our wishes."

" Still he is honest enough not to attack my life; he only wishes to make a fool of me," thought Kmita. " But we shall soon see if there is a trap here or not."

Now Anusia put her head out of the window. " What is the matter ? " asked she.

" Nothing! Pan Zamoyski commends you once more to my bravery. Nothing more."

Here he turned to the driver, —

" Forward ! "

The officer leading the horsemen reined in his horse. " Stop!" cried he to the driver. Then to Kmita, " Why move on ? "

" But why halt longer in the forest ? " asked Kmita, with the face of a stupid rogue.

" For you have received some order."

" And what is that to you ? I have received, and that is why I command to move on."

" Stop ! " repeated the officer.

" Move on ! " repeated Kmita.

" What is this ? " inquired Anusia again.

" We will not go a step farther till I see the order ! " said the officer, with decision.

" You will not see the order, for it is not sent to you."

" Since you will not obey it, I will carry it out. You move on to Krasnystav, and have a care lest we give you something for the road, but we will go home with the lady."

Kmita only wished the officer to acknowledge that he

knew the contents of the order; this proved with perfect certainty that the whole affair was a trick arranged in advance.

"Move on with God!" repeated the officer now, with a threat.

At that moment the horsemen began one after another to take out their sabres.

"Oh, such sons! not to Zamost did you wish to take the maiden, but aside somewhere, so that Pan Zamoyski might give free rein to his wishes; but you have met with a more cunning man!" When Babinich had said this, he fired upward from a pistol.

At this sound there was such an uproar in the forest, as if the shot had roused whole legions of wolves sleeping near by. The howl was heard in front, behind, from the sides. At once the tramp of horses sounded with the cracking of limbs breaking under their hoofs, and on the road were seen black groups of horsemen, who approached with unearthly howling.

"Jesus! Mary! Joseph!" cried the terrified women in the carriage.

Now the Tartars rushed up like a cloud; but Kmita restrained them with a triple cry, and turning to the astonished officer, began to boast, —

"Know whom you have met! Pan Zamoyski wished to make a fool of me, a blind instrument. To you he intrusted the functions of a pander, which you undertook, Sir Officer, for the favor of a master. Bow down to Zamoyski from Babinich, and tell him that the maiden will go safely to Pan Sapyeha."

The officer looked around with frightened glance, and saw the wild faces gazing with terrible eagerness on him and his men. It was evident that they were waiting only for a word to hurl themselves on the twelve horsemen and tear them in pieces.

"Your grace, you will do what you wish, for we cannot manage superior power," said he, with trembling voice; "but Pan Zamoyski is able to avenge himself."

Kmita laughed. "Let him avenge himself on you; for had it not come out that you knew the contents of the order, and had you not opposed the advance, I should not have been sure of the trick, and should have given you the maiden straightway. Tell the starosta to appoint a keener pander than you."

The calm tone with which Kmita said this assured the

officer somewhat, at least on this point, — that death did not threaten either him or his troopers; therefore he breathed easily, and said, —

"And must we return with nothing to Zamost ? "

"You will return with my letter, which will be written on the skin of each one of you."

"Your grace — "

"Take them ! " cried Kmita; and he seized the officer himself by the shoulder.

An uproar and struggle began around the carriage. The shouts of the Tartars deadened the cries for assistance and the screams of terror coming from the breasts of the women.

But the struggle did not last long, for a few minutes later the horsemen were lying on the road tied, one at the side of the other.

Kmita gave command to flog them with bullock-skin whips, but not beyond measure, so that they might retain strength to walk back to Zamost. The common soldiers received one hundred, and the officer a hundred and fifty lashes, in spite of the prayers and entreaties of Anusia, who not knowing what was passing around her, and thinking that she had fallen into terrible hands, began to implore with joined palms and tearful eyes for her life.

"Spare my life, knight! In what am I guilty before you ? Spare me, spare me ! "

"Be quiet, young lady ! " roared Kmita.

"In what have I offended ? "

"Maybe you are in the plot yourself ? "

"In what plot ? O God, be merciful to me, a sinner ! "

"Then you did not know that Pan Zamoyski only permitted your departure apparently, so as to separate you from the princess and carry you off on the road, to make an attempt on your honor in some empty castle ? "

"O Jesus of Nazareth ! " screamed Anusia.

And there was so much truth and sincerity in that cry that Kmita said more mildly, —

"How is that ? Then you were not in the plot ? That may be ! "

Anusia covered her face with her hands, but she could say nothing; she merely repeated, time after time, —

"Jesus, Mary! Jesus, Mary ! "

"Calm yourself," said Kmita, still more mildly. "You will go in safety to Pan Sapyeha, for Pan Zamoyski did not know with whom he had to deal. See, those men whom they are flogging were to carry you off. I give them their lives, so that they may tell Pan Zamoyski how smoothly it went with them."

"Then have you defended me from shame?"

"I have, though I did not know whether you would be glad."

Anusia, instead of making answer or contradiction, seized Pan Andrei's hand and pressed it to her pale lips; and sparks went from his feet to his head.

"Give peace, for God's sake!" cried he. "Sit in the carriage, for you will wet your feet — and be not afraid! You would not be better cared for with your mother."

"I will go now with you even to the end of the world."

"Do not say such things."

"God will reward you for defending honor."

"It is the first time that I have had the opportunity," said Kmita. And then he muttered in an undertone to himself: "So far I have defended her as much as a cat sheds tears."

Meanwhile the Tartars had ceased to beat the horsemen, and Pan Andrei gave command to drive them naked and bloody along the road toward Zamost. They went, weeping bitterly. Their horses, weapons, and clothing Kmita gave his Tartars; and then moved on quickly, for it was unsafe to loiter.

On the road the young knight could not restrain himself from looking into the carriage to gaze at the flashing eyes and wonderful face of the maiden. He asked each time if she did not need something, if the carriage was convenient, or the quick travelling did not tire her too much.

She answered, with thankfulness, that it was pleasant to her as it had never been. She had recovered from her terror completely. Her heart rose in gratitude to her defender, and she thought: "He is not so rude and surly as I held at first."

"Ai, Olenka, what do I suffer for you!" said Kmita to himself; "do you not feed me with ingratitude? Had this been in old times, u-ha!"

Then he remembered his comrades and the various deeds of violence which he had committed in company with them; then he began to drive away temptation, began to repeat for their unhappy souls, "Eternal rest."

When they had reached Krasnystav, Kmita considered it better not to wait for news from Zamost, and went on farther. But at parting he wrote and sent to Zamoyski the following letter: —

SERENE GREAT MIGHTY LORD STAROSTA,[1] and to me very Gracious Favorer and Benefactor! Whomsoever God has made great in the world, to him He deals out wit in more bountiful measure. I knew at once that you, Serene Great Mighty Lord, only wished to put me on trial, when you sent the order to give up Panna Borzobogati. I knew this all the better when the horsemen betrayed that they knew the substance of the order, though I did not show them the letter, and though you wrote to me that the idea came to you only after my departure. As on the one hand I admire all the more your penetration, so on the other, to put the careful guardian more completely at rest, I promise anew that nothing will suffice to lead me away from fulfilling the function imposed on me. But since those soldiers, evidently misunderstanding your intention, turned out to be great ruffians, and even threatened my life, I think that I should have hit upon your thought if I had commanded to hang them. Because I did not do so, I beg your forgiveness ; still I gave orders to flog them properly with bullock-skin whips, which punishment, if your Great Mighty Lordship considers it too small, you can increase according to your will. With this, hoping that I have earned the increased confidence and gratitude of your Serene Great Mighty Lordship, I subscribe myself the faithful and well-wishing servant of your Serene Great Mighty Lordship.

BABINICH.

The dragoons, when they had dragged themselves to Zamost late at night, did not dare to appear before the eyes of their master; therefore he learned of the whole matter from this letter which the Krasnystav Cossack brought next day.

After he had read Kmita's letter, Zamoyski shut himself up in his rooms for three days, admitting no attendant save the chamber servants, who brought him his food. They heard, also, how he swore in French, which he did only when he was in the greatest fury.

By degrees, however, the storm was allayed. On the fourth day and fifth Zamoyski was still very silent; he was ruminating over something and pulling at his mustache; in a week, when he was very pleasant and had drunk a little at table, he began to twirl his mustache, not to pull it, and said to Princess Griselda, —

" Lady Sister, you know that there is no lack of penetration in me; a couple of days ago I tested of purpose that noble who took Anusia, and I can assure you that he will take her faithfully to Pan Sapyeha."

About a month later, as it seems, Pan Sobiepan turned his heart in another direction; and besides he became altogether convinced that what had happened, happened with his will and knowledge.

---

[1] Zamoyski was starosta of Kaluj.

CHAPTER XXII.

THE province of Lyubelsk and the greater part of Podlyasye were almost completely in the hands of Poles, that is, of the confederates and Sapyeha's men. Since the King of Sweden remained in Prussia, where he was treating with the elector, the Swedes, not feeling very powerful in presence of the general uprising, which increased every day, dared not come out of the towns and castles, and still less to cross to the eastern side of the Vistula, where the Polish forces were greatest. In those two provinces, therefore, the Poles were laboring to form a considerable and well-ordered army, able to meet the regular soldiers of Sweden. In the provincial towns they were training infantry, and since the peasants in general had risen, there was no lack of volunteers; it was only necessary to organize in bodies and regular commands those chaotic masses of men frequently dangerous to their own country.

The district captains betook themselves to this labor. Besides, the king had issued a number of commissions to old and tried soldiers; troops were enrolled in all provinces, and since there was no lack of military people in those regions, squadrons of perfect cavalry were formed. Some went west of the Vistula, others to Charnyetski, still others to Sapyeha. Such multitudes had taken arms that Yan Kazimir's forces were already more numerous than those of the Swedes.

A country over whose weakness all Europe had recently wondered, gave now an example of power unsuspected, not only by its enemies, but by its own king, and even by those whose faithful hearts, a few months before, had been rent by pain and despair. Money was found, as well as enthusiasm and bravery; the most despairing souls were convinced that there is no position, no fall, no weakness from which there may not be a deliverance, and that where children are born consolation cannot die.

Kmita went on without hindrance, gathering on his road unquiet spirits, who joined the chambul with readiness, hoping to find most blood and plunder in company with the Tartars. These he changed easily into good and prompt soldiers, for he had the gift to make his subordinates fear and obey. He was greeted joyously on the road, and that by reason of the Tartars; for the sight of them convinced men that the Khan was indeed coming with succor to the Commonwealth. It was declared openly that forty thousand chosen Tartar cavalry were marching to strengthen Sapyeha. Wonders were told of the "modesty" of these allies, — how they committed no violence or murder on the road. They were shown as an example to the soldiers of the country.

Pan Sapyeha was quartered temporarily at Byala. His forces were composed of about ten thousand regular troops, cavalry and infantry. They were the remnants of the Lithuanian armies, increased by new men. The cavalry, especially some of the squadrons, surpassed in valor and training the Swedish horsemen; but the infantry were badly trained, and lacked firearms, powder, and cannon. Sapyeha had thought to find these in Tykotsin; but the Swedes, by blowing themselves up with the powder, destroyed at the same time all the cannons of the castle.

Besides these forces there were in the neighborhood of Byala twelve thousand general militia from all Lithuania, Mazovia, and Podlyasye; but from few of these did the voevoda promise himself service, especially since having an immense number of wagons they hindered movement and turned the army into a clumsy, unwieldy multitude.

Kmita thought of one thing in entering Byala. There were under Sapyeha so many nobles from Lithuania and so many of Radzivill's officers, his former acquaintances, that he feared they would recognize him and cut him to pieces before he could cry, "Jesus! Mary!"

His name was detested in Sapyeha's camp and in all Lithuania; for men still preserved in vivid remembrance the fact that while serving Prince Yanush, he had cut down those squadrons which, opposing the hetman, had declared for the country.

Pan Andrei had changed much, and this gave him comfort. First, he had become thin; second, he had the scar on his face from Boguslav's bullet; finally, he wore a beard, rather long, pointed in Swedish fashion, and his mustache he combed upward, so that he was more like some Erickson than a Polish noble.

"If there is not a tumult against me at once, men will

judge me differently after the first battle," thought Kmita, when entering Byala.

He arrived in the evening, announced who he was, whence he had come, that he was bearing letters from the king, and asked a special audience of the voevoda.

The voevoda received him graciously because of the warm recommendation of the king, who wrote, —

" We send to you our most faithful servant, who is called the Hector of Chenstohova, from the time of the siege of that glorious place; and he has saved our freedom and life at the risk of his own during our passage through the mountains. Have him in special care, so that no injustice come to him from the soldiers. We know his real name, and the reasons for which he serves under an assumed one; no man is to hold him in suspicion because of this change, or suspect him of intrigues."

" But is it not possible to know why you bear an assumed name ? " asked the voevoda.

" I am under sentence, and cannot make levies in my own name. The king gave me a commission, and I can make levies as Babinich."

" Why do you want levies if you have Tartars ? "

" For a greater force would not be in the way."

" And why are you under sentence ? "

" Under the command and protection of whomsoever I go, him I ought to tell all as to a father. My real name is Kmita."

The voevoda pushed back a couple of steps, —

" He who promised Boguslav to carry off our king, living or dead ? "

Kmita related with all his energy how and what had happened, — how, befogged by Prince Yanush, he had served the Radzivills; how he had learned their real purposes from the mouth of Boguslav, and then carried off the latter and thus incurred his implacable vengeance.

The voevoda believed, for he could not refuse belief, especially since the king's letter confirmed the truth of Kmita's words. Besides, his soul was so delighted in the voevoda that he would at that moment have pressed his worst enemy to his heart and forgiven his greatest offence. This delight was caused by the following passage in the king's letter : —

" Though the grand baton of Lithuania, unused now after the death of the voevoda of Vilna, can by usual procedure be given to

a successor only at the Diet, still in the present extraordinary circumstances, disregarding the usual course, We give this baton to
you, greatly cherished by us, for the good of the Commonwealth
and your memorable services, thinking justly that, God giving
peace, no voice at the coming Diet will be raised against this our
choice, and that our act will find general approval."

Pan Sapyeha, as was said then in the Commonwealth,
"had pawned his coat and sold his last silver spoon;" he
had not served his country for profit, nor for honors. But
even the most disinterested man is glad to see that his ser
vices are appreciated, that they are rewarded with gratitude,
that his virtue is recognized. Therefore Sapyeha's serious
face was uncommonly radiant.

This act of the king adorned the house of Sapyeha with
new splendor; and to this no "kinglet" of that time was
indifferent, — it were well had there been none to strive for
elevation *per nefas* (through injustice). Therefore Pan
Sapyeha was ready to do for the king what was in his
power and what was out of his power.

"Since I am hetman," said he to Kmita, "you come under
my jurisdiction and are under my guardianship. There is
a multitude here of the general militia, hence tumult is
near; therefore do not show yourself over-much till I warn
the soldiers, and remove that calumny which Boguslav cast
on you."

Kmita thanked him from his heart, and then spoke of
Anusia, whom he had brought to Byala. In answer the
hetman fell to scolding, but being in excellent humor he
scolded joyously.

"You made a fool of Sobiepan, as God is dear to me!
He sits there with his sister inside the walls of Zamost, as
with the Lord God, behind the stove, and thinks that every
one can do as he does, — raise the skirts of his coat, turn to
the fire, and warm his back. I know the Podbipientas, for
they are related to the Bjostovskis, and the Bjostovskis to
me. The fortune is a lordly one, that is not to be denied;
but though war with the Northerners has weakened it for a
time, still people are alive yet in those regions. Where
can anything be found, where any courts, any officers?
Who will take the property and put the young lady in possession? They have gone stark mad! Boguslav is sitting
on my shoulders; I have my duties in the army, but they
would have me fill my head with women."

"She is not a woman, but a cherry," said Kmita. "She

is nothing however to me. They asked me to bring her here; I have brought her. They asked me to give her to you; I give her."

The hetman then took Kmita by the ear and said: "But who knows, protector, in what form you have brought her? God preserve us, people may say that from the guardianship of Sapyeha she has suffered; and I, old man, shall have to keep my eyes open. What did you do at the stopping-places? Tell me right away, Pagan, did you not learn from your Tartars some heathen customs?"

"At the stopping-places," answered Kmita, jestingly, "I commanded my attendants to plough my skin with discipline, so as to drive out the less worthy motives, which have their seat under the skin, and which I confess were plaguing me worse than horseflies."

"Ah, you see — Is she a worthy maiden?"

"Really so; and terribly pretty."

"And the Turk was at hand?"

"But she is as honest as a nun; that I must say for her. And as to suffering I think that would come sooner from the Zamoyski guardianship than from you."

Here Kmita told what had taken place and how. Then the hetman fell to clapping him on the shoulder and laughing, —

"Well, you are a crafty fellow! Not in vain do they tell so much of Kmita. Have no fear! Pan Zamoyski is not a stubborn man, and he is my friend. His first anger will pass, and he will even laugh at it himself and reward you."

"I need no reward!" interrupted Kmita.

"It is well that you have ambition and are not looking for favor. Only serve me against Boguslav, and you will not need to think of past outlawry."

Sapyeha was astonished when he looked at the soldier's face, which a moment before was so open and joyous. Kmita at mention of Boguslav grew pale in an instant, and his face took on wrinkles like the face of a dog, when preparing to bite.

"Would that the traitor were poisoned with his own spittle, if he could only fall into my hands before his death!" said he, gloomily.

"I do not wonder at your venom. Have a care, though, that your anger does not choke your adroitness, for you have to deal with no common man. It is well that the king sent you hither. You will attack Boguslav for me, as you once did Hovanski."

"I will attack him better!" said Kmita, with the same gloom.

With this the conversation ended. Kmita went away to sleep in his quarters, for he was wearied from the road.

Meanwhile the news spread through the army that the king had sent the baton to their beloved chief. Joy burst out like a flame among thousands of men. The officers of various squadrons hurried to the quarters of the hetman. The sleeping town sprang up from its slumber. Bonfires were kindled. Standard-bearers came with their standards. Trumpets sounded and kettle-drums thundered; discharges from muskets and cannon roared. Pan Sapyeha ordered a lordly feast, and they applauded the whole night through, drinking to the health of the king, the hetman, and to the coming victory over Boguslav.

Pan Andrei, as was agreed, was not present at the feast.

The hetman at the table began a conversation about Boguslav, and not telling who that officer was who had come with the Tartars and brought the baton, he spoke in general of the perversity of Boguslav.

"Both Radzivills," said he, "were fond of intrigues, but Prince Boguslav goes beyond his dead cousin. You remember, gentlemen, Kmita, or at least you have heard of him. Now imagine to yourselves, what Boguslav reported — that Kmita offered to raise his hand on the king our lord — was not true."

"Still Kmita helped Yanush to cut down good cavaliers."

"It is true that he helped Yanush; but at last he saw what he was doing, and then not only did he leave the service, but as you know, being a man of daring, he attacked Boguslav. It was close work there for the young prince, and he barely escaped with his life from Kmita's hands."

"Kmita was a great soldier!" answered many voices.

"The prince through revenge invented against him a calumny at which the soul shudders."

"The devil could not have invented a keener!"

"Do you know that I have in my hands proofs in black and white that that was revenge for the change in Kmita?"

"To put infamy in such a way on any one's name! Only Boguslav could do that! To sink such a soldier!"

"I have heard this," continued the hetman: "Kmita, seeing that nothing remained for him to do in this region, hurried off to Chenstohova, rendered there famous services, and then defended the king with his own breast."

Hearing this, the same soldiers who would have cut Kmita to pieces with their sabres began to speak of him more and more kindly.

"Kmita will not forgive the calumny, he is not such a man ; he will fall on Boguslav."

"Boguslav has insulted all soldiers, by casting such infamy on one of them."

"Kmita was cruel and violent, but he was not a parricide."

"He will have vengeance!"

"We will be first to take vengeance for him!"

"If you, serene great mighty hetman, guarantee this with your office, it must have been so."

"It was so!" said the hetman.

And they lacked little of drinking Kmita's health. But in truth there were very violent voices against this, especially among the former officers of Radzivill. Hearing these, the hetman said, —

"And do you know, gentlemen, how this Kmita comes to my mind ? Babinich, the king's courier, resembles him much. At the first moment I was mistaken myself."

Here Sapyeha began to look around with more severity and to speak with greater seriousness, —

"Though Kmita were to come here himself, since he has changed, since he has defended a holy place with immense bravery, I should defend him with my office of hetman. I ask you therefore, gentlemen, to raise no disturbance here by reason of this newly arrived. I ask you to remember that he has come here by appointment of the king and the Khan. But especially do I recommend this to you who are captains in the general militia, for with you it is harder to preserve discipline."

Whenever Sapyeha spoke thus, Zagloba alone dared to murmur, all others would sit in obedience, and so they sat now ; but when the hetman's face grew gladsome again, all rejoiced. The goblets moving swiftly filled the measure of rejoicing, and the whole town was thundering till morning, so that the walls of houses were shaking on their foundation, and the smoke of salutes veiled them, as in time of battle.

Next morning Sapyeha sent Anusia to Grodno with Pan Kotchyts. In Grodno, from which Hovanski had long since withdrawn, the voevoda's family was living.

Poor Anusia, whose head the handsome Babinich had turned somewhat, took farewell of him very tenderly ; but he was on his guard, and only at the very parting did he say to her, —

"Were it not for one devil which sits in my heart like a thorn, I should surely have fallen in love with you to kill."

Anusia thought to herself that there is no splinter which may not be picked out with patience and a needle; but she feared somewhat this Babinich, therefore she said nothing, sighed quietly, and departed.

CHAPTER XXIII.

A WEEK after the departure of Anusia with Kotchyts, Sapyeha's camp was still at Byala. Kmita, with the Tartars, was ordered to the neighborhood of Rokitno; he was resting too, for the horses needed food and rest after the long road. Prince Michael Kazimir Radzivill, the owner of the place by inheritance, came also to Byala; he was a powerful magnate of the Nyesvyej branch of Radzivills, of whom it was said that they had inherited from the Kishkis alone seventy towns and four hundred villages. This Radzivill resembled in nothing his kinsmen of Birji. Not less ambitious perhaps than they, but differing in faith, an ardent patriot, and an adherent of the lawful king, he joined with his whole soul the confederacy of Tyshovtsi, and strengthened it as best he could. His immense possessions were, it is true, greatly ravaged by the last war, but still he stood at the head of considerable forces and brought the hetman no small aid.

Not so much, however, did the number of his soldiers weigh in the balance as the fact that Radzivill stood against Radzivill; in this way the last seeming of justice was taken from Boguslav, and his acts were covered with the open character of invasion and treason.

Therefore Sapyeha saw Prince Michael in his camp with delight. He was certain now that he would overcome Boguslav, for he surpassed him much in power; but according to his custom he weighed his plans slowly, stopped, considered, and summoned councils of officers.

Kmita also was at these councils. He so hated the name Radzivill that at first sight of Prince Michael he trembled from anger and rage; but Michael knew how to win people by his countenance alone, on which beauty was united with kindness. The great qualities of this Radzivill, the grievous times which he had recently passed while defending the country from Zolotarenko and Serebryani, his genuine love for the king, made him one of the most honorable cavaliers of his time. His very presence in the camp of Sapyeha, the rival of the house of Radzivill, testified how far the young prince knew how to sacrifice private to public affairs. Whoso knew him was forced to love him. This feeling could not be resisted even by the passionate Kmita, despite his first opposition.

Finally the prince captivated the heart of Pan Andrei by his advice.

This advice was not merely to move against Boguslav, but to move without negotiations, to dash upon him at once: "Do not let him take castles; give him neither rest nor chance to draw breath; make war upon him with his own method." In such decision the prince saw speedy and certain victory.

"It cannot be that Karl Gustav has not moved also; we must have our hands free, therefore, as soon as possible, and hasten to succor Charnyetski."

Of the same opinion was Kmita, who had been fighting three days with his old evil habit of self-will so as to restrain himself from advancing without orders.

But Sapyeha liked to act with certainty, he feared every inconsiderate step; therefore he determined to wait for surer intelligence.

And the hetman had his reasons. The reported expedition of Boguslav against Podlyasye might be only a snare, a trick of war. Perhaps it was a feigned expedition with small forces, to prevent the junction of Sapyeha with the king. That done, Boguslav would escape from before Sapyeha, receiving battle nowhere, or delaying; but meanwhile Karl Gustav with the elector would strike Charnyetski, crush him with superior forces, move against the king himself, and smother the work in its inception, — the work of defence created by the glorious example of Chenstohova. Sapyeha was not only a leader, but a statesman. He explained his reasons with power at the councils, so that even Kmita was forced in his soul to agree with him. First of all, it was incumbent to know what course to take. If Boguslav's invasion proved to be merely a trick, it was sufficient to send a number of squadrons against him, and move with all speed to Charnyetski against the chief power of the enemy. The hetman might leave boldly a few or even more squadrons, for his forces were not all around Byala. Young Pan Krishtof, or the so-called Kryshtofek Sapyeha, was posted with two light squadrons and a regiment of infantry at Yavorov; Horotkyevich was moving around Tykotsin, having under him half a dragoon regiment very well trained, and five hundred volunteers, besides a light horse squadron named for Sapyeha; and in Byalystok were land infantry.

These forces would more than suffice to stand against Boguslav, if he had only a few hundred horses.

But the clear-sighted hetman sent couriers in every direction and waited for tidings.

At last tidings came; but like thunderbolts, and all the more so that by a peculiar concurrence of circumstances all came in one evening.

They were just at council in the castle of Byala when an officer of orderlies entered and gave a letter to the hetman. Barely had the hetman cast eyes on it when he changed in the face and said, —

"My relative is cut to pieces at Yavorov by Boguslav himself; hardly has he escaped with his life."

A moment of silence followed.

"The letter is written in Bransk, in fright and confusion," said he; "therefore it contains not a word touching Boguslav's power, which must, I think, be considerable, since, as I read, two squadrons and a regiment of infantry are cut to pieces. It must be, however, that Boguslav fell on them unawares. The letter gives nothing positive."

"I am certain now," said Prince Michael, "that Boguslav wants to seize all Podlyasye, so as to make of it a separate or feudal possession in the treaties. Therefore he has surely come with as much power as he could possibly get. I have no other proofs save a knowledge of Boguslav. He cares neither for the Swedes nor the Brandenburgers, only for himself. He is an uncommon warrior, who trusts in his fortunate star. He wants to win a province, to avenge Yanush, to cover himself with glory; and to do this he must have a corresponding power, and has it, otherwise he would not march on us."

"For everything the blessing of God is indispensable," said Oskyerko; "and the blessing is with us!"

"Serene great mighty hetman," said Kmita, "information is needed. Let me loose from the leash with my Tartars, and I will bring you information."

Oskyerko, who had been admitted to the secret and knew who Babinich was, supported the proposal at once and with vigor.

"As God is good to me, that is the best idea in the world!

Such a man is needed there, and such troops. If only the horses are rested."

Here Oskyerko was stopped, for the officer of orderlies entered the room again.

"Serene great mighty hetman!" said he.

Sapyeha slapped his knees and exclaimed: "They have news! Admit them."

After a while two light-horsemen entered, tattered and muddy.

"From Horotkyevich?" asked Sapyeha.

"Yes."

"Where is he now?"

"Killed, or if not killed, we know not where he is."

The hetman rose, but sat down again and inquired calmly, —

"Where is the squadron?"

"Swept away by Prince Boguslav."

"Were many lost?"

"We were cut to pieces; maybe a few were left who were taken captive like us. Some say that the colonel escaped; but that he is wounded I saw myself. We escaped from captivity."

"Where were you attacked?"

"At Tykotsin."

"Why did you not go inside the walls, not being in force?"

"Tykotsin is taken."

The hetman covered his eyes for a moment with his hand, then he began to pass his hand over his forehead.

"Is there a large force with Boguslav?"

"Four thousand cavalry, besides infantry and cannon; the infantry very well trained. The cavalry moved forward, taking us with them; but luckily we escaped."

"Whence did you escape?"

"From Drohichyn."

Sapyeha opened wide his eyes: "You are drunk. How could Boguslav come to Drohichyn? When did he defeat you?"

"Two weeks ago."

"And is he in Drohichyn?"

"His scouting-parties are. He remained in the rear himself, for some convoy is captured which Pan Kotchyts was conducting."

"He was conducting Panna Borzobogati!" cried Kmita.

A silence followed. Boguslav's success, and so sudden, had confused the officers beyond measure. All thought in their hearts that the hetman was to blame for delay, but no one dared say so aloud.

Sapyeha, however, felt that he had done what was proper, and had acted wisely. Therefore he recovered first from the surprise, sent out the men with a wave of his hand, and said, —

"These are ordinary incidents of war, which should confuse no one. Do not think, gentlemen, that we have suffered any defeat. Those regiments are a loss surely; but the loss might have been a hundred times greater if Boguslav had enticed us to a distant province. He is coming to us. We will go out to meet him like hospitable hosts."

Here he turned to the colonels: "According to my orders all must be ready to move?"

"They are ready," said Oskyerko. "Only saddle the horses and sound the trumpet."

"Sound it to-day. We move in the morning at dawn, without fail. Pan Babinich will gallop ahead with his Tartars, and seize with all haste informants."

Kmita had barely heard this when he was outside the door, and a moment later hurrying on as his horse could gallop to Rokitno.

And Sapyeha also did not delay long.

It was still night when the trumpets gave out their prolonged sounds; then cavalry and infantry poured forth into the field; after them stretched a long train of squeaking wagons. The first gleams of day were reflected on musket-barrels and spear-points.

And they marched, regiment after regiment, squadron after squadron, in great regularity. The cavalry sang their matins, and the horses snorted sharply in the morning coolness, from which the soldiers predicted sure victory for themselves.

Their hearts were full of consolation; for the knighthood knew from experience that Sapyeha weighed everything, that he labored with his head, that he considered every undertaking from both sides, that when he began a thing he would finish it, and when he moved he would strike.

At Rokitno the lairs of the Tartars were cold; they had gone the night before, hence must have pushed far in advance. It surprised Sapyeha that along the road it was difficult to learn anything of them, though the division, numbering, with volunteers, several hundred, could not pass without being seen.

The most experienced officers wondered greatly at this march, and at Pan Babinich for being able to lead in such fashion.

" Like a wolf he goes through the willows, and like a wolf he will bite," said they; " he is as if born for the work."

But Oskyerko, who, as has been said, knew who Babinich was, said to Sapyeha, —

" It was not for nothing that Hovanski put a price on his head. God will give victory to whom he chooses; but this is sure, that war with us will soon be bitter for Boguslav."

" But it is a pity that Babinich has vanished as if he had fallen into water," answered the hetman.

Three days passed without tidings. Sapyeha's main forces had reached Drohichyn, had crossed the Bug, and found no enemy in front. The hetman began to be disturbed. According to the statements of the light horse, Boguslav's scouts had reached Drohichyn; it was evident therefore that Boguslav had determined to withdraw. But what was the meaning of this withdrawal? Had Boguslav learned that Sapyeha's forces were superior, and was he afraid to measure strength with him, or did he wish to entice the hetman far toward the north, to lighten for the King of Sweden his attack on Charnyetski and the hetmans of the kingdom? Babinich was to find an informant and let the hetman know. The reports of the light horse as to the number of Boguslav's troops might be erroneous; hence the need of precise information at the earliest.

Meanwhile five days more passed, and Babinich gave no account of himself. Spring was coming; the days were growing warmer; the snow was melting. The neighborhoods were being covered with water, under which were sleeping morasses which hindered the march in an unheard of degree. The greater part of the cannons and wagons the hetman had to leave in Drohichyn, and go farther on horseback. Hence great inconvenience and murmuring, especially among the general militia. In Bransk they came upon such mud that even the infantry could not march farther. The hetman collected on the road horses from peasants and small nobles, and seated musketeers on them. The light cavalry took others; but they had gone too far already, and the hetman understood that only one thing remained, — to advance with all speed.

Boguslav retreated unceasingly. Along the road they found continual traces of him in villages burned here and there, in corpses of men hanging on trees. The small local nobles came every little while with information to Sapyeha; but the truth was lost, as is usual in contradictory statements. One saw a single squadron, and swore that the prince had no more troops; another saw two; a third three, a fourth an army five miles long. In a word they were fables such as men tell who know nothing of armies or war.

They had seen Tartars, too, here and there; but the stories concerning them seemed most improbable, for it was said that they were seen not behind the prince's army, but in front, marching ahead. Sapyeha panted angrily when any one mentioned Babinich in his presence, and he said to Oskyerko, —

"You overrated him. In an evil hour I sent away Volodyovski, for if he were here I should have had long ago as many informants as I need; but Babinich is a whirlwind, or even worse. Who knows, he may in truth have joined Boguslav and be marching in the vanguard."

Oskyerko himself did not know what to think. Meanwhile another week passed; the army had come to Byalystok.

It was midday.

Two hours later the vanguard gave notice that some detachment was approaching.

"It may be Babinich!" cried the hetman. "I'll give him *Pater Noster!*"

It was not Babinich himself. But in the camp there rose such commotion over the arrival of this detachment that Sapyeha went out to see what was taking place.

Meanwhile officers from different squadrons flew in, crying, —

"From Babinich! Prisoners! A whole band! He seized a crowd of men!"

Indeed the hetman saw a number of tens of men on poor, ragged horses. Babinich's Tartars drove nearly three hundred men with bound hands, beating them with bullock-skin whips. The prisoners presented a terrible sight. They were rather shadows than men. With torn clothing, half naked, so poor that the bones were pushing through their skin, bloody, they marched half alive, indifferent to all things, even to the whistle of the whips which cut them, and to the wild shouts of the Tartars.

"What kind of men are they?" asked the hetman.

"Boguslav's troops!" answered one of Kmita's volunteers who had brought the prisoners together with the Tartars.

"But where did you get so many?"

"Nearly half as many more fell on the road, from exhaustion."

With this an old Tartar, a sergeant in the horde, approached, and beating with the forehead, gave a letter from Kmita to Sapyeha.

The hetman, without delay, broke the seal and began to read aloud: —

"Serene great mighty hetman! If I have sent neither news nor informants with news hitherto, it is because I went in front, and not in the rear of Prince Boguslav's army, and I wished to learn the most possible."

The hetman stopped reading.

"That is a devil!" said he. "Instead of following the prince, he went ahead of him."

"May the bullets strike him!" added Oskyerko, in an undertone.

The hetman read on.

"It was dangerous work, as Boguslav's scouts marched in a wide front; but after I had cut down two parties and spared none, I worked to the van of the army, from which movement great confusion came upon the prince, for he fell to thinking at once that he was surrounded, and as it were was crawling into a trap."

"That is the reason of this unexpected withdrawal!" cried the hetman. "A devil, a genuine devil!"

He read on with still more curiosity, —

"The prince, not understanding what had happened, began to lose his head, and sent out party after party, which we cut up notably, so that none of them returned in the same number. Marching in advance, we seized provisions, cut dams, destroyed bridges, so that Boguslav's men advanced with great trouble, neither sleeping nor eating, having rest neither day nor night. They could not stir from the camp, for the Tartars seized the unwary; and when the camp was sleeping, the Tartars howled terribly in the willows; so the en-

emy, thinking that a great army was moving on them, had to stand
under arms all night. The prince was brought to great despair, not
knowing what to begin, where to go, how to turn, — for this reason
it is needful to march on him quickly, before his fear passes. He
had six thousand troops, but has lost nearly a thousand. His horses
are dying. His cavalry is good; his infantry is passable; God, however, has granted that from day to day it decreases, and if our army
comes up it will fly apart. I seized in Byalystok the prince's carriages, some of his provision chests and things of value, with two
cannons; but I was forced to throw most of these into the river.
The traitor from continual rage has grown seriously ill, and is
barely able to sit on his horse; fever leaves him neither night nor
day. Panna Borzobogati is taken, but being ill the prince can make
no attack on her honor. These reports, with the account of Boguslav's desperation, I got from the prisoners whom my Tartars
touched up with fire, and who if they are touched again will repeat
the truth. Now I commend my obedient services to you, serene
great mighty hetman, begging for forgiveness if I have erred.
The Tartars are good fellows, and seeing a world of plunder, serve
marvellously."

"Serene great mighty lord," said Oskyerko, "now you
surely regret less that Volodyovski is away, for he could
not equal this devil incarnate. Oh, he is an ambitious piece;
he even hurled the truth into the eyes of Prince Yanush, not
caring whether it was pleasant or unpleasant for that het
man to hear it. This was his style with Hovanski, but
Hovanski had fifteen times more troops."

"If that is true, we need to advance at the greatest speed,"
said Sapyeha.

"Before the prince can collect his wits."

"Let us move on, by the dear God! Babinich will cut
the dams, and we will overtake Boguslav!"

Meanwhile the prisoners, whom the Tartars had kept in a
group in front of Sapyeha, seeing the hetman, fell to groaning and weeping, showing their misery and calling for mercy
in various tongues; for there were among them Swedes,
Germans, and the Scottish guards of Prince Boguslav.
Sapyeha took them from the Tartars, and gave command to
feed them and take their testimony without torture. Their
statements confirmed the truth of Kmita's words; therefore
the rest of Sapyeha's army advanced at great speed.

CHAPTER XXIV.

KMITA's next report came from Sokolka, and was brief:

"The prince, to mislead our troops, has feigned a march toward Shchuchyn, whither he has sent a party. He has gone himself with his main force to Yanov, and has received there a reinforcement of infantry, led by Captain Kyritz, eight hundred good men. From the place where we are the prince's fires are visible. In Yanov he intends to rest one week. The prisoners say that he is ready for battle. The fever is shaking him continually."

On receipt of this statement Sapyeha, leaving the remainder of his cannon and wagons, moved on with cavalry to Sokolka; and at last the two armies stood eye to eye. It was foreseen too that a battle was unavoidable; for on one side they could flee no longer, the others pursuing. Meanwhile, like wrestlers who after a long chase are to seize each other by the bodies, they lay opposite each other, catching breath in their panting throats, and resting.

When the hetman saw Kmita he seized him by the shoulders, and said, —

"I was angry with you for not giving an account of yourself for so long, but I see that you have accomplished more than I could hope for; and if God gives victory, not mine but yours will be the merit. You went like an angel guardian after Boguslav."

An ill-omened light gleamed in Kmita's eyes. "If I am his angel guardian, I must be present at his death."

"God will order that," said the hetman, seriously; "but if you wish the Lord to bless you, then pursue the enemy of the country, not your own."

Kmita bowed in silence; but it could not be learned whether the beautiful words of the hetman made any impression on him. His face expressed implacable hatred, and was the more threatening that the toil of pursuit after Boguslav had emaciated it still more. Formerly in that countenance was depicted only daring and insolent wildness; now it had become also stern and inexorable. You could easily see that he against whom that man had recorded ven-

geance in his soul ought to guard himself, even if he were
Radzivill.

He had, in truth, avenged himself terribly. The services
he had rendered in that campaign were immense. By push‧
ing himself in front of Boguslav he had beaten him from
the road, had made his reckoning false, had fixed in him
the conviction that he was surrounded, and had forced him
to retreat. Further he went before him night and day. He
destroyed scouting-parties ; he was without mercy for prisoners. In Syemyatiche, in Botski, in Orel and Byelsk he
had fallen in the dark night on the whole camp.

In Voishki, not far from Zabludovo, in a purely Radzivill
country, he had fallen like a blind hurricane on the quarters of the prince himself, so that Boguslav, who had just
sat down to dinner, almost fell into his hands ; and thanks
to Sakovich alone, did he take out his head alive.

At Byalystok Kmita seized the carriages and camp-chests
of Boguslav. He wearied, weakened, and inflicted hunger
on Boguslav's troops. The choice German infantry and
Swedish cavalry which the prince had brought with him
were like walking skeletons, from wandering, from surprises, from sleeplessness. The mad howling of the Tartars
and Kmita's volunteers was heard in front of them, at the
flanks, and in the rear. Scarcely had a wearied soldier
closed his eyes when he had to seize his weapons. The
farther on, the worse the condition.

The small nobility inhabiting those neighborhoods joined
with the Tartars, partly through hatred of the Radzivills of
Birji, partly through fear of Kmita; for he punished beyond
measure those who resisted. His forces increased therefore ; those of Boguslav melted.

Besides, Boguslav himself was really ill ; and though in the
heart of that man care never had its nest long, and though
the astrologers, whom he believed blindly, had foretold him
in Prussia that his person would meet no harm in that expedition, his ambition suffered harshly more than once. He,
whose name had been repeated with admiration in the Netherlands, on the Rhine, and in France, was beaten every day
in those deep forests by an unseen enemy, and overcome
without a battle.

There was, besides, in that pursuit such uncommon stubbornness and impetuosity passing the usual measure of war,
that Boguslav with his native quickness divined after a few
days that some inexorable personal enemy was following

him. He learned the name Babinich easily, for the whole neighborhood repeated it; but that name was strange to him. Not less glad would he be to know the person; and on the road in times of pursuit he arranged tens and hundreds of ambushes, — always in vain. Babinich was able to avoid traps, and inflicted defeats where they were least expected.

At last both armies came to the neighborhood of Sokolka. Boguslav found there the reinforcement under Kyritz, who, not knowing hitherto where the prince was, went to Yanov, where the fate of Boguslav's expedition was to be decided.

Kmita closed hermetically all the roads leading from Yanov to Sokolka, Korychyn, Kuznitsa, and Suhovola. The neighboring forests, willow woods, and thickets were occupied by the Tartars. Not a letter could pass; no wagon with provisions could be brought in. Boguslav himself was in a hurry for battle before his last biscuit in Yanov should be eaten.

But as a man of quick wit, trained in every intrigue, he determined to try negotiations first. He did not know yet that Sapyeha in this kind of intrigue surpassed him greatly in reasoning and quickness. From Sokolka then in Boguslav's name came Pan Sakovich, under-chamberlain and starosta of Oshmiana, the attendant and personal friend of Prince Boguslav, with a letter and authority to conclude peace.

This Pan Sakovich was a wealthy man, who reached senatorial dignity later in life, for he became voevoda of Smolensk and treasurer of the Grand Principality; he was at that time one of the most noted cavaliers in Lithuania, famed equally for bravery and beauty. Pan Sakovich was of medium stature; the hair of his head and brows was black as a raven's wing, but he had pale blue eyes which gazed with marvellous and unspeakable insolence, so that Boguslav said of him that he stunned with his eyes as with the back of an axe. He wore foreign garments which he brought from journeys made with Boguslav; he spoke nearly all languages; in battle he rushed into the greatest whirl so madly that among his enemies he was called "the doomed man." But, thanks to his uncommon strength and presence of mind, he always came out unharmed. It was said that he had strength to stop a carriage in its course by seizing the hind wheel; he could drink beyond measure, could toss off a quart of cream in vodka, and be as sober as if he had taken nothing in his mouth. With men he was morose, haughty, offensive; in Boguslav's hand he was as soft as wax. His manners were polished, and though in the king's chambers he knew how to bear himself, he had a certain wildness in his spirit which burst forth at times like a flame.

Pan Sakovich was rather a companion than a servant of Boguslav. Boguslav, who in truth had never loved any one in his life, had an unconquerable weakness for this man. By nature exceedingly sordid, he was generous to Sakovich alone. By his influence he raised him to be under-chamberlain, and had him endowed with the starostaship of Oshmiana. After every battle Boguslav's first question was: "Where is Sakovich? has he met with no harm?" The prince depended greatly on the starosta's counsels, and employed him in war and in negotiations in which the courage and impudence of Sakovich were very effective.

This time he sent him to Sapyeha. But the mission was difficult, — first, because the suspicion might easily fall on the starosta that he had come only to spy out and discover Sapyeha's strength; second, because the envoy had much to ask and nothing to offer.

Happily, Pan Sakovich did not trouble himself with anything. He entered as a victor who comes to dictate terms to the vanquished, and struck Sapyeha with his pale eyes.

Sapyeha smiled when he saw that pride, but half of his smile was compassion. Every man may impose much with daring and impudence, but on people of a certain measure; the hetman was above the measure of Sakovich.

"My master, prince in Birji and Dubinki, commander-in-chief of the armies of his princely highness the elector," said Sakovich, "has sent me with a greeting, and to ask about the health of your worthiness."

"Thank the prince, and say that you saw me well."

Sapyeha took the letter, opened it carelessly enough, read it, and said, —

"Too bad to lose time. I cannot see what the prince wants. Do you surrender, or do you wish to try your fortune?"

Sakovich feigned astonishment.

"Whether we surrender? I think that the prince proposes specially in this letter that you surrender; at least my instructions —"

"Of your instructions we will speak later, my dear Pan Sakovich. We have chased you nearly a hundred and fifty miles, as a hound does a hare. Have you ever heard of a hare proposing to a hound to surrender ? "

" We have received reinforcements."

" Von Kyritz, with eight hundred men, and so tired that they will lay down their arms before battle. I will give you Hmelnitski's saying · 'There is no time to talk ! ' "

" The elector with all his power is with us."

" That is well, — I shall not have far to seek him; for I wish to ask him by what right he sends troops into the Commonwealth, of which he is a vassal, and to which he is bound in loyalty."

" The right of the strongest."

" Maybe in Prussia such a right exists, but not with us. But if you are the stronger, take the field."

" The prince would long since have attacked you, were it not for kindred blood."

" I wonder if that is the only hindrance ! "

" The prince wonders at the animosity of the Sapyehas against the house of Radzivill, and that your worthiness for private revenge hesitates not to spill the blood of the country."

" Tfu ! " cried Kmita, listening behind the hetman's arm-chair to the conversation.

Pan Sakovich rose, went to Kmita, and struck him with his eyes. But he met his own, or better; and in the eyes of Pan Andrei the starosta found such an answer that he dropped his glance to the floor.

The hetman frowned. " Take your seat, Pan Sakovich. And do you preserve calm " (turning to Kmita). Then he said to Sakovich, —

" Conscience speaks only the truth, but mouths chew it and spit it into the world as calumny. He who with for-eign troops attacks a country, inflicts wrong on him who defends it. God hears this, and the heavenly chronicler will inscribe."

" Through hatred of the Sapyehas to the Radzivills was the prince voevoda oı Vilna consumed."

" I hate traitors, not the Radzivills ; and the best proof of this is that Prince Michael Radzivill is in my camp now. Tell me what is your wish ? "

" Your worthiness, I will tell what I have in my heart; he hates who sends secret assassins."

Pan Sapyeha was astonished in his turn.

" I send assassins against Prince Boguslav ? "

"That is the case!"

"You have gone mad!"

"The other day they caught, beyond Yanov, a murderer who once made an attack on the life of the prince. Tortures brought him to tell who sent him."

A moment of silence followed; but in that silence Pan Sapyeha heard how Kmita, standing behind him, repeated twice through his set lips, "Woe, woe!"

"God is my judge," answered the hetman, with real senatorial dignity, "that neither to you nor your prince shall I ever justify myself; for you were not made to be my judges. But do you, instead of loitering, tell directly what you have come for, and what conditions your prince offers."

"The prince, my lord, has destroyed Horotkyevich, has defeated Pan Krishtof Sapyeha, taken Tykotsin; therefore he can justly call himself victor, and ask for considerable advantages. But regretting the loss of Christian blood, he desires to return in quiet to Prussia, requiring nothing more than the freedom of leaving his garrisons in the castles. We have also taken prisoners not a few, among whom are distinguished officers, not counting Panna Anusia Borzobogati, who has been sent already to Taurogi. These may be exchanged on equal terms."

"Do not boast of your victories, for my advance guard, led by Pan Babinich here present, pressed you for a hundred and fifty miles; you retreated before it, lost twice as many prisoners as you took previously; you lost wagons, cannon, camp-chests. Your army is fatigued, dropping from hunger, has nothing to eat; you know not whither to turn. You have seen my army; I did not ask to have your eyes bound purposely, that you might know whether you are able to measure forces with us. As to that young lady, she is not under my guardianship, but that of Pan Zamoyski and Princess Griselda Vishnyevetski. The prince will reckon with them if he does her any injustice. But speak with wisdom; otherwise I shall order Pan Babinich to march at once."

Sakovich, instead of answering, turned to Kmita: "Then you are the man who made such onsets on the road? You must have learned your murderous trade under Kmita—"

"Learn on your own skin whether I practised well!"

The hetman again frowned. "You have nothing to do here," said he to Sakovich; "you may go."

"Your worthiness, give me at least a letter."

"Let it be so. Wait at Pan Oskyerko's quarters for a letter."

Hearing this, Pan Oskyerko conducted Sakovich at once to his quarters. The hetman waved his hand as a parting; then he turned to Pan Andrei. "Why did you say 'Woe,' when he spoke of that man whom they seized?" asked he, looking quickly and severely into the eyes of the knight. "Has hatred so deadened your conscience that you really sent a murderer to the prince?"

"By the Most Holy Lady whom I defended, no!" answered Kmita; "not through strange hands did I wish to reach his throat."

"Why did you say 'Woe'? Do you know that man?"

"I know him," answered Kmita, growing pale from emotion and rage. "I sent him from Lvoff to Taurogi — Prince Boguslav took Panna Billevich to Taurogi — I love that lady. We were to marry — I sent that man to get me news of her. She was in such hands — "

"Calm yourself!" said the hetman. "Have you given him any letters?"

"No; she would not read them."

"Why?"

"Boguslav told her that I offered to carry away the king."

"Great are your reasons for hating him."

"True, your worthiness, true."

"Does the prince know that man?"

"He knows him. That is the sergeant Soroka. He helped me to carry off Boguslav."

"I understand," said the hetman; "the vengeance of the prince is awaiting him."

A moment of silence followed.

"The prince is in a trap," said the hetman, after a while; "maybe he will consent to give him up."

"Let your worthiness," said Kmita, "detain Sakovich, and send me to the prince. Perhaps I may rescue Soroka."

"Is his fate such a great question for you?"

"An old soldier, an old servant; he carried me in his arms. A multitude of times he has saved my life. God would punish me were I to abandon him in such straits." And Kmita began to tremble from pity and anxiety.

But the hetman said: "It is no wonder to me that the soldiers love you, for you love them. I will do what I can. I will write to the prince that I will free for him whomso-

ever he wishes for that soldier, who besides at your command has acted as an innocent agent."

Kmita seized his head : " What does he care for prisoners ?
he will not let him go for thirty of them."

"Then he will not give him to you; he will even attempt
your life."

"He would give him for one, — for Sakovich."

"I cannot imprison Sakovich; he is an envoy."

"Detain him, and I will go with a letter to the prince.
Perhaps I shall succeed — God be with him ! I will abandon my revenge, if he will give me that soldier."

"Wait," said the hetman; "I can detain Sakovich. Besides that I will write to the prince to send me a safe-
conduct without a name."

The hetman began to write at once. An hour later a
Cossack was galloping with a letter to Yanov, and toward
evening he returned with Boguslav's answer : —

" I send according to request the safe-conduct with which every
envoy may return unharmed, though it is a wonder to me that your
worthiness should ask for a conduct while you have such a hostage
as my servant and friend Pan Sakovich, for whom I have so much
love that I would give all the officers in my army for him. It is
known also that envoys are not killed, but are usually respected
even by wild Tartars with whom your worthiness is making war
against my Christian army. Now, guaranteeing the safety of your
envoy by my personal princely word, I subscribe myself, etc."

That same evening Kmita took the safe-conduct and went
with the two Kyemliches. Pan Sakovich remained in Sokolka as a hostage.

CHAPTER XXV.

It was near midnight when Pan Andrei announced himself to the advanced pickets of the prince, but no one was sleeping in the whole camp. The battle might begin at any moment, therefore they had prepared for it carefully. Boguslav's troops had occupied Yanov itself; they commanded the road from Sokolka, which was held by artillery, managed by the elector's trained men. There were only three cannons, but abundance of powder and balls. On both sides of Yanov, among the birch groves, Boguslav gave orders to make intrenchments and to occupy them with double-barrelled guns and infantry. The cavalry occupied Yanov itself, the road behind the cannons, and the intervals between the trenches. The position was defensible enough, and with fresh men defence in it might be long and bloody; but of fresh soldiers there were only eight hundred under Kyritz; the rest were so wearied that they could barely stand on their feet. Besides, the howling of the Tartars was heard in Suhovola at midnight, and later in the rear of Boguslav's ranks; hence a certain fear was spread among the soldiers. Boguslav was forced to send in that direction all his light cavalry, which after it had gone three miles dared neither return nor advance, for fear of ambushes in the forest.

Boguslav, though fever together with violent chills was tormenting him more than ever, commanded everything in person; but since he rode with difficulty he had himself carried by four soldiers in an open litter. In this way he had examined the road as well as the birch groves, and was entering Yanov when he was informed that an envoy from Sapyeha was approaching.

They were already on the street. Boguslav was unable to recognize Kmita because of the darkness, and because Pan Andrei, through excess of caution on the part of officers in the advance guard, had his head covered with a bag in which there was an opening only for his mouth.

The prince noticed the bag when Kmita, after dismounting, stood near him; he gave command to remove it at once.

"This is Yanov," said he, "and there is no reason for secrecy." Then he turned in the darkness to Pan Andrei: "Are you from Pan Sapyeha?"

"I am."

"And what is Pan Sakovich doing there?"

"Pan Oskyerko is entertaining him."

"Why did you ask for a safe conduct when you have Sakovich? Pan Sapyeha is too careful, and let him see to it that he is not too clever."

"That is not my affair," answered Kmita.

"I see that the envoy is not over-given to speech."

"I have brought a letter, and in the quarters I will speak of my own affair."

"Is there a private question?"

"There will be a request to your highness."

"I shall be glad not to refuse it. Now I beg you to follow. Mount your horse; I should ask you to the litter, but it is too small."

They moved on. The prince in the litter and Kmita at one side on horseback. They looked in the darkness without being able to distinguish the faces of each other. After a while the prince, in spite of furs, began to shake so that his teeth chattered. At last he said, —

"It has come on me grievously; if it were — brr! — not for this, I would give other conditions."

Kmita said nothing, and only wished to pierce with his eyes the darkness, in the middle of which the head and face of the prince were outlined in indefinite gray and white features. At the sound of Boguslav's voice and at sight of his figure all the former insults, the old hatred, and the burning desire for revenge so rose in Kmita's heart that they turned almost to madness. His hand of itself sought the sword, which had been taken from him; but at his girdle he had the baton with an iron head, the ensign of his rank of colonel; the devil then began to whirl in his brain at once, and to whisper: "Cry in his ear who you are, and smash his head into bits. The night is dark, you will escape. The Kyemliches are with you. You will rub out a traitor and pay for injustice. You will rescue Olenka, Soroka — Strike! strike!"

Kmita came still nearer the litter, and with trembling hand began to draw forth the baton. "Strike!" whispered the devil; "you will serve the country."

Kmita had now drawn out the baton, and he squeezed the

handle as if wishing to crush it in his hand. "One, two, three!" whispered the devil.

But at that moment Kmita's horse, whether because he had hit the helmet of the soldier with his nose, or had shied, it is enough that he stumbled violently. Kmita pulled the reins. During this time the litter had moved on several steps. The hair stood on the head of the young man.

"O Most Holy Mother, restrain my hand!" whispered he, through his set teeth. "O Most Holy Mother, save me! I am here an envoy; I came from the hetman, and I want to murder like a night assassin. I am a noble; I am a servant of Thine. Lead me not into temptation!"

"But why are you loitering?" asked Boguslav, in a voice broken by fever.

"I am here!"

"Do you hear the cocks crowing beyond the fences? It is needful to hurry, for I am sick and want rest."

Kmita put the baton behind his belt and rode farther, near the litter. Still he could not find peace. He understood that only with cool blood and self-command could he free Soroka; therefore he stipulated with himself in advance what words to use with the prince so as to incline and convince him. He vowed to have only Soroka in view, to mention nothing else, and especially not Olenka. And he felt how in the darkness a burning blush covered his face at the thought that perhaps the prince himself would mention her, and maybe mention something that Pan Andrei would not be able to endure or listen to.

"Let him not mention her," said he to himself; "let him not allude to her, for in that is his death and mine. Let him have mercy upon himself, if he lacks shame."

Pan Andrei suffered terribly; his breath failed him, and his throat was so straitened that he feared lest he might not be able to bring forth the words when he came to speak. In this stifling oppression he began the Litany.

After a time relief came; he was quieted considerably, and that grasp as it were of an iron hand squeezing his throat was relaxed.

They had now arrived at the prince's quarters. The soldiers put down the litter; two attendants took the prince by the armpits; he turned to Kmita, and with his teeth chattering continually, said, —

"I beg you to follow. The chill will soon pass; then we can speak."

After a while they found themselves in a separate apartment in which heaps of coals were glowing in a fireplace, and in which was unendurable heat. His servants placed Prince Boguslav on a long campaign arm-chair covered with furs, and brought a light. Then the attendants withdrew. The prince threw his head back, closed his eyes, and remained in that position motionless for a time; at last he said, —

"Directly, — let me rest."

Kmita looked at him. The prince had not changed much, but the fever had pinched his face. He was painted as usual, and his cheeks touched with color; but just for that reason, when he lay there with closed eyes and head thrown back, he was somewhat like a corpse or a wax figure. Pan Andrei stood before him in the bright light. The prince began to open his lids lazily; suddenly he opened them completely, and a flame, as it were, flew over his face. But it remained only an instant; then again he closed his eyes.

"If thou art a spirit, I fear thee not," said he; "but vanish."

"I have come with a letter from the hetman," answered Kmita.

Boguslav shuddered a little, as if he wished to shake off visions; then he looked at Kmita and asked, —

"Have I been deceived in you?"

"Not at all," answered Pan Andrei, pointing with his finger to the scar.

"That is the second!" muttered the prince to himself; and he added aloud, "Where is the letter?"

"Here it is," said Kmita, giving the letter.

Boguslav began to read, and when he had finished a marvellous light flashed in his eyes.

"It is well," said he; "there is loitering enough! To-morrow the battle — and I am glad, for I shall not have a fever."

"And we, too, are glad," answered Kmita.

A moment of silence followed, during which these two inexorable enemies measured each other with a certain terrible curiosity. The prince first resumed the conversation.

"I divine that it was you who attacked me with the Tartars?"

"It was I."

"And did you not fear to come here?"

Kmita did not answer.

"Did you count on our relationship through the Kishkis? For you and I have our reckonings. I can tear you out of your skin, Sir Cavalier."

"You can, your highness."

"You came with a safe-conduct, it is true. I understand now why Pan Sapyeha asked for it. But you have attempted my life. Sakovich is detained there; but Sapyeha has no right to Sakovich, while I have a right to you, cousin."

"I have come with a prayer to your highness."

"I beg you to mention it. You can calculate that for you everything will be done. What is the prayer?"

"You have here a captive soldier, one of those men who aided me in carrying you off. I gave orders, he acted as a blind instrument. Be pleased to set that man at liberty."

Boguslav thought awhile.

"I am thinking," said he, "which is greater, — your daring as a soldier, or your insolence as a petitioner."

"I do not ask this man from you for nothing."

"And what will you give me for him?"

"Myself."

"Is it possible that he is such a precious soldier? You pay bountifully, but see that that is sufficient; for surely you would like to ransom something else from me."

Kmita came a step nearer to the prince, and grew so awfully pale that Boguslav, in spite of himself, looked at the door, and notwithstanding all his daring he changed the subject of conversation.

"Pan Sapyeha will not entertain such an agreement. I should be glad to hold you; but I have guaranteed with my word of a prince your safety."

"I will write by that soldier to the hetman that I remain of my own will."

"And he will declare that, in spite of your will, I must send you. You have given him services too great. He will not set Sakovich free, and Sakovich I prize higher than you."

"Then, your highness, free that soldier, and I will go on my word where you command."

"I may fall to-morrow; I care nothing for treaties touching the day after."

"I implore your highness for that man. I — "

"What will you do?"

"I will drop my revenge."

"You see, Pan Kmita, many a time have I gone against a bear with a spear, not because I had to do so, but from desire. I am glad when some danger threatens, for life is less dull for me. In this case I reserve your revenge as a pleasure; for you are, I must confess, of that breed of bears which seek the hunter themselves."

"Your highness," said Kmita, "for small mercies God often forgives great sins. Neither of us knows when it will come to him to stand before the judgment of Christ."

"Enough!" said the prince. "I compose psalms for myself in spite of the fever, so as to have some merit before the Lord; should I need a preacher I should summon my own. You do not know how to beg with sufficient humility, and you go in round-about ways. I will show you the method myself: strike to-morrow in the battle on Sapyeha, and after to-morrow I will let out the soldier and forgive you your sins. You betrayed Radzivill; betray now Sapyeha."

"Is this the last word of your highness? By all the saints, I implore you!"

"No! Devil take you! And you change in the face — But don't come too near, for, though I am ashamed to call attendants — look here! You are too bold!"

Boguslav pointed at a pistol-barrel peeping from under the fur with which it was covered, and looked with sparkling eyes into Kmita's eyes.

"Your highness!" cried Kmita, almost joining his hands in prayer, but with a face changed by wrath.

"You beg, but you threaten," said Boguslav; "you bend your neck, but the devil is gnashing his teeth at me from behind your collar. Pride is gleaming in your eyes, and in your mouth it sounds as in a cloud. With your forehead to the Radzivill feet when you beg, my little man! Beat with your forehead on the floor, then I will answer."

Pan Andrei's face was as pale as a piece of linen; he drew his hand over his moist forehead, his eyes, his face; and he spoke with such a broken voice, as if the fever from which the prince suffered had suddenly sprung upon him.

"If your highness will free for me that old soldier, I am ready to fall at your feet."

Satisfaction gleamed in Boguslav's eyes. He had brought down his enemy, bent his proud neck. Better food he could not give to his revenge and hatred.

Kmita stood before him with hair erect in his forelock,

trembling in his whole body. His face, resembling even in
rest the head of a hawk, recalled all the more an enraged
bird of prey. You could not tell whether at the next moment he would throw himself at the feet, or hurl himself
at the breast of the prince. But Boguslav not taking his
eyes from him, said, —

"Before witnesses! before people!" And he turned to
the door. "Hither!"

A number of attendants, Poles and foreigners, came in;
after them officers entered.

"Gracious gentlemen!" said the prince, "behold Pan
Kmita, the banneret of Orsha and envoy of Pan Sapyeha,
who has come to beg a favor of me, and he wishes to have
all you gentlemen as witnesses."

Kmita tottered like a drunken man, groaned, and fell at
Boguslav's feet. The prince stretched his feet purposely so
that the end of his riding-boot touched the forehead of the
knight.

All looked in silence, astonished at the famous name, as
well as at this, — that he who bore it was now an envoy from
Pan Sapyeha. All understood, too, that something uncommon was taking place.

The prince rose, and without saying a word passed into
the adjoining chamber, beckoning to two attendants to
follow him.

Kmita rose. His face showed no longer either anger or
rapacity, merely indifference and insensibility. He appeared unconscious of what was happening to him, and his
energy seemed broken completely.

Half an hour passed; an hour. Outside the windows was
heard the tramp of horses' feet and the measured tread of
soldiers; he sat continually as if of stone.

Suddenly the door opened. An officer entered, an old
acquaintance of Kmita's from Birji, and eight soldiers, —
four with muskets, four without firearms, — with sabres.

"Gracious Colonel, rise!" said the officer, politely.

Kmita looked on him wanderingly. "Glovbich!" said
he, recognizing the officer.

"I have an order," answered Glovbich, "to bind your
hands and conduct you beyond Yanov. The binding is for
a time, then you will go free; therefore I beg you not to
resist."

"Bind!" answered Kmita.

And he permitted them to tie him. But they did not tie

his feet. The officer led him out of the room and on foot through Yanov. Then they advanced for about an hour. On the road some horsemen joined them. Kmita heard them speaking in Polish; the Poles, who served with Boguslav, all knew the name of Kmita, and therefore were most curious to know what would happen to him. The party passed the birch grove and came to an open field, on which Pan Andrei saw a detachment of the light Polish squadron of Boguslav.

The soldiers stood in rank, forming a square; in the middle was a space in which were two foot-soldiers holding horses harnessed to draw, and some men with torches.

By the light of the torches Pan Andrei saw a freshly sharpened stake lying on the ground with the large end fastened in a great log.

A shiver passed through Kmita involuntarily. "That is for me," thought he; "Boguslav has ordered them to draw me on the stake with horses. He sacrifices Sakovich to his vengeance."

But he was mistaken; the stake was intended first for Soroka.

By the quivering flames Pan Andrei saw Soroka himself; the old soldier was sitting there at the side of the log on a stool, without a cap and with bound hands, guarded by four soldiers. A man dressed in a short shuba without sleeves was at that moment giving him in a shallow cup gorailka, which Soroka drank eagerly enough. When he had drunk, he spat; and since at that very moment Kmita was placed between two horsemen in the first rank, Soroka saw him, sprang from the stool and straightened himself as if on military parade.

For a while they looked the one at the other. Soroka's face was calm and resigned; he only moved his jaws as if chewing.

"Soroka!" groaned Kmita, at last.

"At command!" answered the soldier.

And again silence followed. What had they to say at such a moment? Then the executioner, who had given Soroka the vodka, approached him.

"Well, old man," said he, "it is time for you!"

"And you will draw me on straight?"

"Never fear."

Soroka feared not; but when he felt on his shoulder the

hand of the executioner, he began to pant quickly and loudly. At last he said, —

"More gorailka!"

"There is none!"

Suddenly one of the soldiers pushed out of the rank and gave a canteen, —

"Here is some; give it to him."

"To the rank!" commanded Glovbich.

Still the man in the short shuba held the canteen to Soroka's mouth; he drank abundantly, and after he had drunk breathed deeply.

"See!" said he, "the lot of a soldier after thirty years' service. Well, if it is time, it is time!"

Another executioner approached and they began to undress him.

A moment of silence. The torches trembled in the hands of those holding them; it became terrible for all.

Meanwhile from the ranks surrounding the square was wrested a murmur of dissatisfaction, which became louder each instant: "A soldier is not an executioner; he gives death himself, but does not wish to see torture."

"Silence!" cried Glovbich.

The murmur became a loud bustle, in which were heard single words: "Devils!" "Thunders!" "Pagan service!"

Suddenly Kmita shouted as if they had been drawing him on to the stake, —

"Stop!"

The executioner halted involuntarily. All eyes were turned to Kmita.

"Soldiers!" shouted Pan Andrei, "Prince Boguslav is a traitor to the king and the Commonwealth! You are surrounded, and to-morrow you will be cut to pieces. You are serving a traitor; you are serving against the country! But whoso leaves this service leaves the traitor; to him forgiveness of the king, forgiveness of the hetman! Choose! Death and disgrace, or a reward to-morrow! I will pay wages, and a ducat a man, — two ducats a man! Choose! It is not for you, worthy soldiers, to serve a traitor! Long life to the king! Long life to the grand hetman of Lithuania!"

The disturbance was turned into thunder; the ranks were broken. A number of voices shouted, —

"Long life to the king!"

"We have had enough of this service!"

"Destruction to traitors!"

"Stop! stop!" shouted other voices.

"To-morrow you will die in disgrace!" bellowed Kmita.

"The Tartars are in Suhovola!"

"The prince is a traitor!"

"We are fighting against the king!"

"Strike!"

"To the prince!"

"Halt!"

In the disturbance some sabre had cut the ropes tying Kmita's hands. He sprang that moment on one of the horses which were to draw Soroka on the stake, and cried from the horse, —

"Follow me to the hetman!"

"I go!" shouted Glovbich. "Long life to the king!"

"May he live!" answered fifty voices, and fifty sabres glittered at once.

"To horse, Soroka!" commanded Kmita.

There were some who wished to resist, but at sight of the naked sabres they grew silent. One, however, turned his horse and vanished from the eye in a moment. The torches went out. Darkness embraced all.

"After me!" shouted Kmita. An orderless mass of men moved from the place, and then stretched out in a long line.

When they had gone two or three furlongs they met the infantry pickets who occupied in large parties the birch grove on the left side.

"Who goes?"

"Glovbich with a party!"

"The word?"

"Trumpets!"

"Pass!"

They rode forward, not hurrying over-much; then they went on a trot.

"Soroka!" said Kmita.

"At command!" answered the voice of the sergeant at his side.

Kmita said nothing more, but stretching out his hand, put his palm on Soroka's head, as if wishing to convince himself that he was riding there. The soldier pressed Pan Andrei's hand to his lips in silence.

Then Glovbich called from the other side, —

"Your grace! I wanted long to do what I have done to-day."

" You will not regret it ! "

" I shall be thankful all my life to you."

" Tell me, Glovbich, why did the prince send you, and not a foreign regiment, to the execution ? "

" Because he wanted to disgrace you before the Poles. The foreign soldiers do not know you."

" And was nothing to happen to me ? "

" I had the order to cut your bonds ; but if you tried to defend Soroka we were to bring you for punishment to the prince."

" Then he was willing to sacrifice Sakovich," muttered Kmita.

Meanwhile Prince Boguslav in Yanov, wearied with the fever and the toil of the day, had gone to sleep. He was roused from slumber by an uproar in front of his quarters and a knocking at the door.

" Your highness, your highness ! " cried a number of voices.

" He is asleep, do not rouse him ! " answered the pages.

But the prince sat up in bed and cried, —

" A light ! "

They brought in a light, and at the same time the officer on duty entered.

" Your highness," said he, " Sapyeha's envoy has brought Glovbich's squadron to mutiny and taken it to the hetman."

Silence followed.

" Sound the kettle-drums and other drums ! " said Boguslav at last; " let the troops form in rank ! "

The officer went out; the prince remained alone.

" That is a terrible man ! " said he to himself : and he felt that a new paroxysm of fever was seizing him.

CHAPTER XXVI.

It is easy to imagine Sapyeha's amazement when Kmita not only returned safely himself, but brought with him a number of tens of horsemen and his old servant. Kmita had to tell the hetman and Oskyerko twice what had happened, and how it had happened; they listened with curiosity, clapping their hands frequently and seizing their heads.

"Learn from this," said the hetman, "that whoso carries vengeance too far, from him it often slips away like a bird through the fingers. Prince Boguslav wanted to have Poles as witnesses of your shame and suffering so as to disgrace you the more, and he carried the matter too far. But do not boast of this, for it was the ordinance of God which gave you victory, though, in my way, I will tell you one thing, — he is a devil; but you too are a devil! The prince did ill to insult you."

"I will not leave him behind in vengeance, and God grant that I shall not overdo it."

"Leave vengeance altogether, as Christ did; though with one word he might have destroyed the Jews."

Kmita said nothing, and there was no time for discussion; there was not even time for rest. He was mortally wearied, and still he had determined to go that night to his Tartars, who were posted in the forests and on the roads in the rear of Boguslav's army. But people of that period slept soundly on horseback. Pan Andrei simply gave command then to saddle a fresh horse, promising himself to slumber sweetly on the road.

When he was mounting Soroka came to him and stood straight as in service.

"Your grace!" said he.

"What have you to say, old man?"

"I have come to ask when I am to start?"

"For what place?"

"For Taurogi."

Kmita laughed: "You will not go to Taurogi, you will go with me."

"At command!" answered the sergeant, striving not to show his delight.

They rode on together. The road was long, for they had to go around by forests, so as not to fall into Boguslav's hands; but Kmita and Soroka slept a hundred fold, and came to the Tartars without any accident.

Akbah Ulan presented himself at once before Babinich, and gave him a report of his activity. Pan Andrei was satisfied. Every bridge had been burned, the dams were cut; that was not all, the water of springtime had overflowed, changing the fields, meadows, and roads in the lower places into muddy quagmires.

Boguslav had no choice but to fight, to conquer or perish; it was impossible for him to think of retreat.

"Very well," said Kmita; "he has good cavalry, but heavy. He will not have use for it in the mud of to-day."

Then he turned to Akbah Ulan. "You have grown poor," said he, striking him on the stomach with his fist; "but after the battle you will fill your paunch with the prince's ducats."

"God has created the enemy, so that men of battle might have some one to plunder," said the Tartar, with seriousness.

"But Boguslav's cavalry stands in front of you."

"There are some hundreds of good horses, and yesterday a regiment of infantry came and intrenched itself."

"But could they not be enticed to the field?"

"They will not come out."

"But turn them, leave them in the rear, and go to Yanov."

"They occupy the road."

"Then we must think of something!" Kmita began to stroke his forelock with his hand: "Have you tried to steal up to them? How far will they follow you out?"

"A furlong, two, — not farther."

"Then we must think of something!" repeated Kmita.

But that night they thought of nothing. Next morning, however, Kmita went with the Tartars toward the camp lying between Suhovol and Yanov, and discovered that Akbah Ulan had exaggerated, saying that the infantry was intrenched on that side; for they had little ditches, nothing more. It was possible to make a protracted defence from them, especially against Tartars, who did not go readily to the attack of such places; but it was impossible for men in them to think of enduring any kind of siege.

"If I had infantry," thought Kmita, "I would go into fire."

But it was difficult even to dream of bringing infantry; for, first, Sapyeha himself had not very many; second, there was no time to bring them.

Kmita approached so closely that Boguslav's infantry opened fire on him; but he did not care. He rode among the bullets and examined, looked around; and the Tartars, though less enduring of fire, had to keep pace with him. Then cavalry rushed out and undertook to flank him. He retreated about three thousand yards and turned again. But they had ridden back toward the trenches. In vain did the Tartars let off a cloud of arrows after them. Only one man fell from his horse, and that one his comrades saved, carried in.

Kmita on returning, instead of riding straight to Suhovola, rushed toward the west and came to the Kamyonka.

This swampy river had overflowed widely, for that year the springtime was wonderfully abundant in water. Kmita looked at the river, threw a number of broken branches into it so as to measure the speed of the current, and said to Ulan, —

"We will go around their flank and strike them in the rear."

"Horses cannot swim against the current."

"It goes slowly. They will swim! The water is almost standing."

"The horses will be chilled, and the men cannot endure it. It is cold yet."

"Oh, the men will swim holding to the horses' tails! That is your Tartar way."

"The men will grow stiff."

"They will get warm under fire."

"Kismet (fate)!"

Before it had grown dark in the world, Kmita had ordered them to cut bunches of willows, dry reeds, and rushes, and tie them to the sides of the horses. When the first star appeared, he sent about eight hundred horses into the water, and they began to swim. He swam himself at the head of them; but soon he saw that they were advancing so slowly that in two days they would not swim past the trenches. Then he ordered them to swim to the other bank.

That was a dangerous undertaking. The other bank was steep and swampy. The horses, though light, sank in it to their bellies. But Kmita's men pushed forward, though slowly and saving one another, while advancing a couple of furlongs.

The stars indicated midnight. Then from the south came to them echoes of distant fighting.

"The battle has begun!" shouted Kmita.

"We shall drown!" answered Akbah Ulan.

"After me!"

The Tartars knew not what to do, when on a sudden they saw that Kmita's horse issued from the mud, evidently finding firm footing.

In fact, a bench of sand had begun. On the top of it there was water to the horses' breasts, but under foot was solid ground. They went therefore more swiftly. On the left distant fires were gleaming.

"Those are the trenches!" said Kmita, quietly. "Let us avoid them, go around!"

After a while they had really passed the trenches. Then they turned to the left, and put their horses into the river again, so as to land beyond the trenches.

More than a hundred horses were swamped at the shore; but almost all the men came out. Kmita ordered those who had lost their beasts to sit behind other horsemen, and they moved toward the trenches. First he left volunteers with the order not to disturb the trenches till he should have gone around them to the rear. When he was approaching he heard shots, at first few, then more frequent.

"It is well!" said he; "Sapyeha is attacking!"

And he moved on.

In the darkness was visible only a multitude of heads jumping with the movement of the horses; sabres did not rattle, armor did not sound; the Tartars and volunteers knew how to move in silence, like wolves.

From the side of Yanov the firing became more and more vigorous; it was evident that Sapyeha was moving along the whole line.

But on the trenches toward which Kmita was advancing shouts were heard also. A number of piles of wood were burning near them, casting around a strong light. By this light Pan Andrei saw infantry firing rarely, more occupied in looking in front at the field, where cavalry was fighting with volunteers.

They saw him too from the trenches, but instead of firing they greeted the advancing body with a loud shout. The soldiers thought that Boguslav had sent them reinforcements.

But when barely a hundred yards separated the approaching body from the trenches, the infantry began to move about unquietly; an increasing number of soldiers, shading their eyes with their hands, were looking to see what kind of people were coming.

When fifty yards distant a fearful howl tore the air, and Kmita's force rushed like a storm, took in the infantry, surrounded them like a ring, and that whole mass of men began to move convulsively. You would have said that a gigantic serpent was stifling a chosen victim.

In this crowd piercing shouts were heard. "Allah!" "Herr Jesus!" "Mein Gott!"

Behind the trenches new shouts went up; for the volunteers, though in weaker numbers, recognizing that Pan Babinich was in the trenches, pressed on the cavalry with fury. Meanwhile the sky, which had been cloudy for some time, as is common in spring, poured down a heavy, unexpected rain. The blazing fires were put out, and the battle went on in the darkness.

But the battle did not last long. Attacked on a sudden, Boguslav's infantry went under the knife. The cavalry, in which were many Poles, laid down their arms. The foreigners, namely, one hundred dragoons, were cut to pieces.

When the moon came out again from behind the clouds, it lighted only crowds of Tartars finishing the wounded and taking plunder.

But neither did that last long. The piercing sound of a pipe was heard; Tartars and volunteers as one man sprang to their horses.

"After me!" cried Kmita.

And he led them like a whirlwind to Yanov.

A quarter of an hour later the ill-fated place was set on fire at four corners, and in an hour one sea of flame was spread as widely as Yanov extended. Above the conflagration pillars of fiery sparks were flying toward the ruddy sky.

Thus did Kmita let the hetman know that he had taken the rear of Boguslav's army.

He himself like an executioner, red from the blood of men, marshalled his Tartars amid the fire, so as to lead them on farther.

They were already in line and extending into column, when suddenly, on a field as bright as in day, from the fire, he saw before him a division of the elector's gigantic cavalry.

A knight led them, distinguishable from afar, for he wore silver-plate armor, and sat on a white horse.

"Boguslav!" bellowed Kmita, with an unearthly voice, and rushed forward with his whole Tartar column.

They approached one another, like two waves driven by two winds. A considerable space divided them; the horses on both sides reached their greatest speed, and went with ears down like hounds, almost sweeping the earth with their bellies. On one side large men with shining breast-plates, and sabres held erect in their right hands; on the other, a black swarm of Tartars.

At last they struck in a long line on the clear field; but then something terrible took place. The Tartar swarm fell as grain bent by a whirlwind; the gigantic men rode over it and flew farther, as if the men and the horses had the power of thunderbolts and the wings of a storm.

Some of the Tartars sprang up and began to pursue. It was possible to ride over the wild men, but impossible to kill them at once; so more and more of them hastened after the fleeing cavalry. Lariats began to whistle in the air.

But at the head of the retreating cavalry the rider on the white horse ran ever in the first rank, and among the pursuers was not Kmita.

Only in the gray of dawn did the Tartars begin to return, and almost every man had a horseman on his lariat. Soon they found Kmita, and carried him in unconsciousness to Pan Sapyeha.

The hetman himself took a seat at Kmita's bedside. About midday Pan Andrei opened his eyes.

"Where is Boguslav?" were his first words.

"Cut to pieces. God gave him fortune at first; then he came out of the birch groves and in the open field fell on the infantry of Pan Oskyerko; there he lost men and victory. I do not know whether he led away even five hundred men, for your Tartars caught a good number of them."

"But he himself?"

"Escaped!"

Kmita was silent awhile; then said, —

"I cannot measure with him yet. He struck me with a double-handed sword on the head, and knocked me down with my horse. My morion was of trusty steel, and did not let the sword through; but I fainted."

"You should hang up that morion in a church."

"I will pursue him, even to the end of the world!" said Kmita.

To this the hetman answered: "See what news I have received to-day after the battle!"

Kmita read aloud the following words, —

The King of Sweden has moved from Elblang; he is marching on Zamost, thence to Lvoff against Yan Kazimir. Come, your worthiness, with all your forces, to save king and country, for I cannot hold out alone.

CHARNYETSKI.

A moment of silence.

"Will you go with us, or will you go with the Tartars to Taurogi?"

Kmita closed his eyes. He remembered the words of Father Kordetski, and what Volodyovski had told him of Pan Yan, and said, —

"Let private affairs wait! I will meet the enemy at the side of the country!"

The hetman pressed Pan Andrei's head. "You are a brother to me!" said he; "and because I am old, receive my blessing."

CHAPTER XXVII.

At a time when all living men in the Commonwealth were mounting their horses Karl Gustav stayed continually in Prussia, busied in capturing the towns of that province and in negotiating with the elector.

After an easy and unexpected conquest, the quick soldier soon saw that the Swedish lion had swallowed more than his stomach could carry. After the return of Yan Kazimir he lost hope of retaining the Commonwealth; but while making a mental abdication of the whole, he wished at least to retain the greater part of his conquest, and above all Royal Prussia, — a province fruitful, dotted with large towns, wealthy, and adjoining his own Pomerania. But as that province was first to defend itself, so did it continue faithful to its lord and the Commonwealth. The return of Yan Kazimir, and the war begun by the confederation of Tyshovtsi might revive the courage of Prussia, confirm it in loyalty, give it will for endurance; therefore Karl Gustav determined to crush the uprising, and to wipe out Kazimir's forces so as to take from Prussians the hope of resistance.

He had to do this for the sake of the elector, who was ever ready to side with the stronger. The King of Sweden knew him thoroughly, and doubted not for a moment that if the fortune of Yan Kazimir should preponderate, the elector would be on his side again.

When, therefore, the siege of Marienburg advanced slowly, — for the more it was attacked the more stubbornly did Pan Weiher defend it, — Karl Gustav marched to the Commonwealth, so as to reach Yan Kazimir again, even in the remotest corner of the land.

And since with him deed followed decision as swiftly as thunder follows lightning, he raised his army disposed in towns; and before any one in the Commonwealth had looked around, before the news of his march had spread, he had passed Warsaw and had rushed into the greatest blaze of conflagration.

Driven by anger, revenge, and bitterness, he moved on like a storm. Behind him ten thousand horse trampled the fields, which were still covered with snow; and taking the infantry from the garrisons, he went on, like a whirl-wind, toward the far south of the Commonwealth.

On the road he burned and pursued. He was not now that recent Karl Gustav, the kindly, affable, and joyous lord, clapping his hands at Polish cavalry, winking at feasts, and praising the soldiers. Now, wherever he showed himself the blood of peasants and nobles flowed in a torrent. On the road he annihilated " parties," hanged prisoners, spared no man.

But as when, in the thick of the pine-woods, a mighty bear rushes forward with heavy body crushing branches and brush on the way, while wolves follow after, and not daring to block his path, pursue, press nearer and nearer behind, so did those " parties " pursuing the armies of Karl join in throngs denser and denser, and follow the Swedes as a shadow a man, and still more enduringly than a shadow, for they followed in the day and the night, in fair and foul weather; before him too bridges were ruined, provisions de-stroyed, so that he had to march as in a desert, without a place for his head or anything with which to give strength to his body when hungry.

Karl Gustav noted quickly how terrible his task was. The war spread around him as widely as the sea spreads around a ship lost in the waters. Prussia was on fire; on fire was Great Poland, which had first accepted his sov-ereignty, and first wished to throw off the Swedish yoke; Little Poland was on fire, and so were Russia, Lithuania, and Jmud. In the castles and large towns the Swedes main-tained themselves yet, as if on islands; but the villages, the forests, the fields, the rivers, were already in Polish hands. Not merely a single man, or small detachments, but a whole regiment might not leave the main Swedish army for two hours; for if it did the regiment vanished without tidings, and prisoners who fell into the hands of peasants died in terrible tortures.

In vain had Karl Gustav given orders to proclaim in vil-lages and towns that whoso of peasants should bring an armed noble, living or dead, would receive freedom forever and land as a reward; for peasants, as well as nobles and townsmen, marched off to the woods. Men from the moun-tains, men from deep forests, men from meadows and fields, hid in the woods, formed ambushes on the roads against the Swedes, fell upon the smaller garrisons, and cut scouting-parties to pieces. Flails, forks, and scythes, no less than the sabres of nobles, were streaming with Swedish blood.

All the more did wrath rise in the heart of Karl, that a few months before he had gathered in that country so easily; hence he could hardly understand what had happened, whence these forces, whence that resistance, whence that awful war for life or death, the end of which he saw not and could not divine.

Frequent councils were held in the Swedish camp. With the king marched his brother Adolph, prince of Bipont, who had command over the army; Robert Douglas; Henry Horn, relative of that Horn who had been slain by the scythe of a peasant at Chenstohova; Waldemar, Prince of Denmark, and that Miller who had left his military glory at the foot of Yasna Gora; Aschemberg, the ablest cavalry leader among the Swedes; Hammerskiold, who commanded the artillery; and the old robber Marshal Arwid Wittemberg, famed for rapacity, living on the last of his health, for he was eaten by the Gallic disease; Forgell, and many others, all leaders skilled in the capture of cities, and in the field yielding in genius to the king only.

These men were terrified in their hearts lest the whole army with the king should perish through toil, lack of food, and the fury of the Poles. Old Wittemberg advised the king directly against the campaign: "How will you go, O King," said he, "to the Russian regions after an enemy who destroys everything on the way, but is unseen himself? What will you do if horses lack not only hay, but even straw from the roofs of cottages, and men fall from exhaustion? Where are the armies to come to our aid, where are the castles in which to draw breath and rest our weary limbs? My fame is not equal to yours; but were I Karl Gustav, I would not expose that glory acquired by so many victories to the fickle fortune of war."

To which Karl Gustav answered: "And neither would I, were I Wittemberg."

Then he mentioned Alexander of Macedon, with whom he liked to be compared, and marched forward, pursuing Charnyetski. Charnyetski, not having forces so great nor so well trained, retreated before him, but retreated like a wolf ever ready to turn on his enemy. Sometimes he went in advance of the Swedes, sometimes at their flanks, and

sometimes in deep forests he let them go in advance; so that
while they thought themselves the pursuers, he, in fact, was
the hunter. He cut off the unwary; here and there he
hunted down a whole party, destroyed foot-regiments marching slowly, attacked provision-trains. The Swedes never
knew where he was. More than once in the darkness of
night they began to fire from muskets and cannons into
thickets, thinking that they had an enemy before them.
They were mortally wearied; they marched in cold, in hunger, in affliction, and that *vir molestissimus* (most harmful
man) hung about them continually, as a hail-cloud hangs
over a grain-field.

At last they attacked him at Golamb, not far from the
junction of the Vyepr and the Vistula. Some Polish squadrons being ready for battle charged the enemy, spreading
disorder and dismay. In front sprang Volodyovski with
his Lauda squadron, and bore down Waldemar, prince of
Denmark; but the two Kavetskis, Samuel and Yan, urged
from the hill the armored squadron against English mercenaries under Wilkinson, and devoured them in a moment,
as a pike gulps a whiting; and Pan Malavski engaged so
closely with the Prince of Bipont that men and horses
were confounded like dust which two whirlwinds sweeping
from opposite quarters bring together and turn into one
circling column. In the twinkle of an eye the Swedes
were pushed to the Vistula, seeing which Douglas hastened
to the rescue with chosen horsemen. But even these reinforcements could not check the onset; the Swedes began
to spring from the high bank to the ice, falling dead so
thickly that they lay black on the snow-field, like letters on
white paper. Waldemar, Prince of Denmark, fell; Wilkinson fell; and the Prince of Bipont, thrown from his horse,
broke his leg. But of Poles both Kavetskis fell; killed also
were Malavski, Rudavski, Rogovski, Tyminski, Hoinski, and
Porvanyetski. Volodyovski alone, though he dived among
the Swedish ranks like a seamew in water, came out without having suffered the slightest wound.

Now Karl Gustav himself came up with his main force
and with artillery. Straightway the form of the battle
changed. Charnyetski's other regiments, undisciplined and
untrained, could not take position in season; some had not
their horses in readiness, others had been in distant villages, and in spite of orders to be always ready, were taking their leisure in cottages. When the enemy pressed

suddenly on these men, they scattered quickly and began to retreat to the Vyepr. Therefore Charnyetski gave orders to sound the retreat so as to spare those regiments that had opened the battle. Some of the fleeing went beyond the Vistula; others to Konskovoli, leaving the field and the glory of the victory to Karl; for specially those who had crossed the Vyepr were long pursued by the squadrons of Zbrojek and Kalinski, who remained yet with the Swedes.

There was delight beyond measure in the Swedish camp. No great trophies fell to the king, it is true, — sacks of oats, and a few empty wagons; but it was not at that time a question of plunder for Karl. He comforted himself with this, — that victory followed his steps as before; that barely had he shown himself when he inflicted defeat on that very Charnyetski on whom the highest hopes of Yan Kazimir and the Commonwealth were founded. He could trust that the news would run through the whole country; that every mouth would repeat, "Charnyetski is crushed;" that the timid would exaggerate the proportions of the defeat, and thus weaken hearts and take courage from those who had grasped their weapons at the call of the confederation of Tyshovtsi.

So when they brought in and placed at his feet those bags of oats, and with them the bodies of Wilkinson and Prince Waldemar, he turned to his fretful generals and said, —

"Unwrinkle your foreheads, gentlemen, for this is the greatest victory which I have had for a year, and may end the whole war."

"Your Royal Grace," answered Wittemberg, who, weaker than usual, saw things in a gloomier light, "let us thank God even for this, — that we shall have a farther march in peace, though Charnyetski's troops scatter quickly and rally easily."

"Marshal," answered the king, "I do not think you a worse leader than Charnyetski; but if I had beaten you in this fashion, I think you would not be able to assemble your troops in two months."

Wittemberg only bowed in silence, and Karl spoke on: "Yes, we shall have a quiet march, for Charnyetski alone could really hamper it. If Charnyetski's troops are not before us, there is no hindrance."

The generals rejoiced at these words. Intoxicated with victory, the troops marched past the king with shouts and with songs. Charnyetski ceased to threaten them like a cloud. Charnyetski's troops were scattered; he had ceased to exist. In view of this thought their past sufferings were forgotten and their future toils were sweet. The king's words, heard by many officers, were borne through the camp; and all believed that the victory had uncommon significance, that the dragon of war was slain once more, and that only days of revenge and dominion would come.

The king gave the army some hours of repose; mean· while from Kozyenitsi came trains with provisions. The troops were disposed in Golamb, in Krovyeniki, and in Jyrzynie. The cavalry burned some deserted houses, hanged a few peasants seized with arms in their hands, and a few camp-servants mistaken for peasants ; then there was a feast in the Swedish camp, after which the soldiers slept a sound sleep, since for a long time it was the first quiet one.

Next day they woke in briskness, and the first words which came to the mouths of all were : " There is no Charnyetski ! "

One repeated this to another, as if to give mutual assurance of the good news. The march began joyously. The day was dry, cold, clear. The hair of the horses and their nostrils were covered with frost. The cold wind froze soft places on the Lyubelsk highroad, and made marching easy. The troops stretched out in a line almost five miles long, which they had never done previously. Two dragoon regiments, under command of Dubois, a Frenchman, went through Markushev and Grabov, five miles from the main force. Had they marched thus three days before they would have gone to sure death, but now fear and the glory of victory went before them.

" Charnyetski is gone," repeated the officers and soldiers to one another.

In fact, the march was made in quiet. From the forest depths came no shouts ; from thickets fell no darts, hurled by invisible hands.

Toward evening Karl Gustav arrived at Grabov, joyous and in good humor. He was just preparing for sleep when Aschemberg announced through the officer of the day that he wished greatly to see the king.

After a while he entered the royal quarters, not alone, but with a captain of dragoons. The king, who had a quick eye and a memory so enormous that he remembered nearly every soldier's name, recognized the captain at once.

" What is the news, Freed ? " asked he. " Has Dubois returned ? "

" Dubois is killed."

The king was confused ; only now did he notice that the

captain looked as if he had been taken from the grave, and his clothes were torn.

"But the dragoons?" inquired he, "those two regiments?"

"All cut to pieces. I alone was let off alive."

The dark face of the king became still darker; with his hands he placed his locks behind his ears.

"Who did this?"

"Charnyetski.'

Karl Gustav was silent, and looked with amazement at Aschemberg; but he only nodded as if wishing to repeat: "Charnyetski, Charnyetski, Charnyetski!"

"All this is incredible," said the king, after a while. "Have you seen him with your own eyes?"

"As I see your Royal Grace. He commanded me to bow to you, and to declare that now he will recross the Vistula, but will soon be on our track again. I know not whether he told the truth."

"Well," said the king, "had he many men with him?"

"I could not estimate exactly, but I saw about four thousand, and beyond the forest was cavalry of some kind. We were surrounded near Krasichyn, to which Colonel Dubois went purposely from the highroad, for he was told that there were some men there. Now, I think that Charnyetski sent an informant to lead us into ambush, since no one save me came out alive. The peasants killed the wounded. I escaped by a miracle."

"That man must have made a compact with hell," said the king, putting his hand to his forehead; "for to rally troops after such a defeat, and be on our neck again, is not human power."

"It has happened as Marshal Wittemberg foresaw," put in Aschemberg.

"You all know how to foresee," burst out the king, "but how to advise you do not know."

Aschemberg grew pale and was silent. Karl Gustav, when joyous, seemed goodness itself; but when once he frowned he roused indescribable fear in those nearest him, and birds do not hide so before an eagle as the oldest and most meritorious generals hid before him. But this time he moderated quickly, and asked Captain Freed again, —

"Has Charnyetski good troops?"

"I saw some unrivalled squadrons, such cavalry as the Poles have."

"They are the same that attacked with such fury in Golamb ; they must be old regiments. But Charnyetski himself, — was he cheerful, confident ? "

"He was as confident as if he had beaten us at Golamb. Now his heart must rise the more, for they have forgotten Golembo and boast of Krasichyn. Your Royal Grace, what Charnyetski told me to repeat I have repeated ; but when I was on the point of departing some one of the high officers appoached me, an old man, and told me that he was the person who had stretched out Gustavus Adolphus in a hand-to-hand conflict, and he poured much abuse on your Royal Grace ; others supported him. So do they boast. I left amid insults and abuse."

"Never mind," said Karl Gustav, "Charnyetski is not broken, and has rallied his army ; that is the main point. All the more speedily must we march so as to reach the Polish Darius at the earliest. You are free to go, gentlemen. Announce to the army that those regiments perished at the hands of peasants in unfrozen morasses. We advance ! "

The officers went out ; Karl Gustav remained alone. For something like an hour he was in gloomy thought. Was the victory at Golamb to bring no fruit, no change to the position, but to rouse still greater rage in that entire country ?

Karl, in presence of the army and of his generals, always showed confidence and faith in himself ; but when he was alone he began to think of that war, — how easy it had been at first, and then increased always in difficulty. More than once doubt embraced him. All the events seemed to him in some fashion marvellous. Often he could see no outcome, could not divine the end. At times it seemed to him that he was like a man who, going from the shore of the sea into the water, feels at every step that he is going deeper and deeper and soon will lose the ground under his feet.

But he believed in his star. And now he went to the window to look at the chosen star, — that one which in the Wain or Great Bear occupies the highest place and shines brightest. The sky was clear, and therefore at that moment the star shone brightly, twinkled blue and red ; but from afar, lower down on the dark blue of the sky, a lone cloud was blackening serpent-shaped, from which extended as it were arms, as it were branches, as it were the feelers of a monster of the sea, and it seemed to approach the king's star continually.

CHAPTER XXVIII.

NEXT morning the king marched farther and reached Lublin. There he received information that Sapyeha had repulsed Boguslav's invasion, and was advancing with a considerable army; he left Lublin the same day, merely strengthening the garrison of that place.

The next object of his expedition was Zamost; for if he could occupy that strong fortress he would acquire a fixed base for further war, and such a notable preponderance that he might look for a successful end with all hope. There were various opinions touching Zamost. Those Poles still remaining with Karl contended that it was the strongest fortress in the Commonwealth, and brought as proof that it had withstood all the forces of Hmelnitski.

But since Karl saw that the Poles were in no wise skilled in fortification, and considered places strong which in other lands would scarcely be held in the third rank; since he knew also that in Poland no fortress was properly mounted, — that is, there were neither walls kept as they should be, nor earthworks, nor suitable arms, — he felt well touching Zamost. He counted also on the spell of his name, on the fame of an invincible leader, and finally on treaties. With treaties, which every magnate in the Commonwealth was authorized to make, or at least permitted himself to make, Karl had so far effected more than with arms. As an adroit man, and one wishing to know with whom he had to deal, he collected carefully all information touching the owner of Zamost. He inquired about his ways, his inclinations, his wit and fancy.

Yan Sapyeha, who at that time by his treason still spotted the name, to the great affliction of Sapyeha the hetman, gave the fullest explanations to the king concerning Zamoyski. They spent whole hours in council. But Yan Sapyeha did not consider that it would be easy for the king to captivate the master of Zamost.

" He cannot be tempted with money," said Yan, " for he is terribly rich. He cares not for dignities, and never wished them, even when they sought him themselves. As

to titles, I have heard him at the court reprimand Des
Noyers, the queen's secretary, because in addressing him
he said, 'Mon prince.' 'I am not a prince,' answered he,
'but I have had archdukes as prisoners in my Zamost.'
The truth is, however, that not he had them, but his grandfather, who among our people is surnamed the Great."

"If he will open the gates of Zamost, I will offer him
something which no Polish king could offer."

It did not become Yan Sapyeha to ask what that might
be; he merely looked with curiosity at Karl Gustav. But
the king understood the look, and answered, gathering, as
was his wont, his hair behind his ears, —

"I will offer him the province of Lyubelsk as an independent principality; a crown will tempt him. No one of
you could resist such a temptation, not even the present
voevoda of Vilna."

"Endless is the bounty of your Royal Grace," replied
Sapyeha, not without a certain irony in his voice.

But Karl answered with a cynicism peculiar to himself:
"I give it, for it is not mine."

Sapyeha shook his head: "He is an unmarried man and
has no sons. A crown is dear to him who can leave it to
his posterity."

"What means do you advise me to take?"

"I think that flattery would effect most. The man is
not too quick-witted, and may be easily over-reached. It is
necessary to represent that on him alone depends the pacification of the Commonwealth; it is necessary to tell him
that he alone may save it from war, from all defeats and
future misfortunes; and that especially by opening the
gates. If the fish will swallow that little hook, we shall
be in Zamost; otherwise not."

"Cannon remain as the ultimate argument."

"H'm! To that argument there is something in Zamost
with which to give answer. There is no lack of heavy guns
there; we have none, and when thaws come it will be impossible to bring them."

"I have heard that the infantry in the fortress is good;
but there is a lack of cavalry."

"Cavalry are needed only in the open field, and besides,
since Charnyetski's army, as is shown, is not crushed,
he can throw in one or two squadrons for the use of the
fortress."

"You see nothing save difficulties."

"But I trust ever in the lucky star of your Royal Grace."

Yan Sapyeha was right in foreseeing that Charnyetski would furnish Zamost with cavalry needful for scouting and seizing informants. In fact, Zamoyski had enough of his own, and needed no assistance whatever; but Charnyetski sent the two squadrons which had suffered most at Golamb — that is, the Shemberk and Lauda — to the fortress to rest, recruit themselves and change their horses, which were fearfully cut up. Sobiepan received them hospitably, and when he learned what famous soldiers were in them he exalted these men to the skies, covered them with gifts, and seated them every day at his table.

But who shall describe the joy and emotion of Princess Griselda at sight of Pan Yan and Pan Michael, the most valiant colonels of her great husband? Both fell at her feet shedding warm tears at sight of the beloved lady; and she could not restrain her weeping. How many reminiscences of those old Lubni days were connected with them; when her husband, the glory and love of the people, full of the strength of life, ruled with power a wild region, rousing terror amid barbarism with one frown of his brow, like Jove. Such were those times not long past; but where are they now? To-day the lord is in his grave, barbarians have taken the land, and she, the widow, sits on the ashes of happiness, of greatness, living only with her sorrow and with prayer.

Still in those reminiscences sweetness was so mingled with bitterness that the thoughts of those three flew gladly to times that were gone. They spoke then of their past lives, of those places which their eyes were never to see, of the past wars, finally of the present times of defeat and God's anger.

"If our prince were alive," said Pan Yan, "there would be another career for the Commonwealth. The Cossacks would be rubbed out, the Trans-Dnieper would be with the Commonwealth, and the Swede would find his conqueror. God has ordained as He willed of purpose to punish us for sins."

"Would that God might raise up a defender in Pan Charnyetski!" said Princess Griselda.

"He will!" cried Pan Michael. "As our prince was a head above other lords, so Charnyetski is not at all like other leaders. I know the two hetmans of the kingdom, and Sapyeha of Lithuania. They are great soldiers; but there is something uncommon in Charnyetski; you would say, he is an eagle, not a man. Though kindly, still all fear him; even Pan Zagloba in his presence forgets his jokes frequently. And how he leads his troops and moves them, passes imagination. It cannot be otherwise than that a great warrior will rise in the Commonwealth."

" My husband, who knew Charnyetski as a colonel, prophesied greatness for him," said the princess.

"It was said indeed that he was to seek a wife in our court," put in Pan Michael.

" I do not remember that there was talk about that," answered the princess.

In truth she could not remember, for there had never been anything of the kind; but Pan Michael, cunning at times, invented this, wishing to turn the conversation to her ladies and learn something of Anusia; for to ask directly he considered improper, and in view of the majesty of the princess, too confidential. But the stratagem failed. The princess turned her mind again to her husband and the Cossack wars; then the little knight thought: " Anusia has not been here, perhaps, for God knows how many years." And he asked no more about her. He might have asked the officers, but his thoughts and occupations were elsewhere. Every day scouts gave notice that the Swedes were nearer; hence preparations were made for defence. Pan Yan and Pan Michael received places on the walls, as officers knowing the Swedes and warfare against them. Zagloba roused courage in the men, and told tales of the enemy to those who had no knowledge of them yet; and among warriors in the fortress there were many such, for so far the Swedes had not come to Zamost.

Zagloba saw through Pan Zamoyski at once; the latter conceived an immense love for the bulky noble, and turned to him on all questions, especially since he heard from Princess Griselda how Prince Yeremi had venerated Zagloba and called him *vir incomparabilis* (the incomparable man). Every day then at table all kept their ears open; and Zagloba discoursed of ancient and modern times, told of the wars with the Cossacks, of the treason of Radzivill, and how he himself had brought Pan Sapyeha into prominence among men.

"I advised him," said he, " to carry hempseed in his pocket, and use a little now and then. He has grown so accustomed to this that he takes a grain every little while.

puts it in his mouth, bites it, breaks it, eats it, spits out the husk. At night when he wakes he does the same. His wit is so sharp now from hempseed that his greatest intimates do not recognize him."

"How is that?" asked Zamoyski.

"There is an oil in hempseed through which the man who eats it increases in wit."

"God bless you," said one of the colonels; "but oil goes to the stomach, not to the head."

"Oh, there is a method in things!" answered Zagloba. "It is needful in this case to drink as much wine as possible; oil, being the lighter, is always on top; wine, which goes to the head of itself, carries with it every noble substance. I have this secret from Lupul the Hospodar, after whom, as is known to you, gentlemen, the Wallachians wished to create me hospodar; but the Sultan, whose wish is that the hospodar should not have posterity, placed before me conditions to which I could not agree."

"You must use a power of hempseed yourself," said Sobiepan.

"I do not need it at all, your worthiness; but from my whole heart I advise you to take it."

Hearing these bold words, some were frightened lest the starosta might take them to heart; but whether he failed to notice them or did not wish to do so, it is enough that he merely laughed and asked, —

"But would not sunflower seeds take the place of hemp?"

"They might," answered Zagloba; "but since sunflower oil is heavier, it would be necessary to drink stronger wine than that which we are drinking at present."

The starosta understood the hint, was amused, and gave immediate order to bring the best wines. Then all rejoiced in their hearts, and the rejoicing became universal. They drank and gave vivats to the health of the king, the host, and Pan Charnyetski. Zagloba fell into good humor and let no one speak. He described at great length the affair at Golamb, in which he had really fought well, for, serving in the Lauda squadron, he could not do otherwise. But because he had learned from Swedish prisoners taken from the regiments of Dubois of the death of Prince Waldemar, Zagloba took responsibility for that death on himself.

"The battle," said he, "would have gone altogether differently were it not that the day before I went to Baranov to the canon of that place, and Charnyetski, not knowing where I was, could not advise with me. Maybe the Swedes too had heard of that canon, for he has splendid mead, and they went at once to Golamb. When I returned it was too late; the king had attacked, and it was necessary to strike at once. We went straight into the fire; but what is to be done when the general militia choose to show their contempt for the enemy by turning their backs? I don't know how Charnyetski will manage at present without me."

"He will manage, have no fear on that point," said Volodyovski.

"I know why. The King of Sweden chooses to pursue me to Zamost rather than seek Charnyetski beyond the Vistula. I do not deny that Charnyetski is a good soldier; but when he begins to twist his beard and look with his wildcat glance, it seems to an officer of the lightest squadron that he is a dragoon. He pays no attention to a man's office; and this you yourselves saw when he gave orders to drag over the square with horses an honorable man, Pan Jyrski, only because he did not reach with his detachment the place to which he was ordered. With a noble, gracious gentlemen, it is necessary to act like a father, not like a dragoon. Say to him, 'Lord brother,' be kind, rouse his feelings, — he will call to mind the country and glory, will go farther for you than a dragoon who serves for a salary."

"A noble is a noble, and war is war," remarked Zamoyski.

"You have brought that out in a very masterly manner," answered Zagloba.

"Pan Charnyetski will turn the plans of Karl into folly," said Volodyovski. "I have been in more than one war, and I can speak on this point."

"First, we will make a fool of him at Zamost," said Sobiepan, pouting his lips, puffing, and showing great spirit, staring, and putting his hands on his hips. "Bah! Tfu! What do I care? When I invite a man I open the door to him. Well!"

Here Zamoyski began to puff still more mightily, to strike the table with his knees, bend forward, shake his head, look stern, flash his eyes, and speak, as was his habit, with a certain coarse carelessness.

"What do I care? He is lord in Sweden; but Zamoyski is lord for himself in Zamost. *Eques polonus sum* (I am a

Polish nobleman), nothing more. But I am in my own house; I am Zamoyski, and he is King of Sweden; but Maximilian was Austrian, was he not? Is he coming? Let him come. We shall see! Sweden is small for him, but Zamost is enough for me. I will not yield it."

"It is a delight, gracious gentlemen, to hear not only such eloquence, but such honest sentiments," cried Zagloba.

"Zamoyski is Zamoyski!" continued Pan Sobiepan, delighted with the praise. "We have not bowed down, and we will not. I will not give up Zamost, and that is the end of it."

"To the health of the host!" thundered the officers.

"Vivat! vivat!"

"Pan Zagloba," cried Zamoyski, "I will not let the King of Sweden into Zamost, and I will not let you out."

"I thank you for the favor; but, your worthiness, do not do that, for as much as you torment Karl with the first decision, so much will you delight him with the second."

"Give me your word that you will come to me after the war is over."

"I give it."

Long yet did they feast, then sleep began to overcome the knights; therefore they went to rest, especially as sleepless nights were soon to begin for them, since the Swedes were already near, and the advance guards were looked for at any hour.

"So in truth he will not give up Zamost," said Zagloba, returning to his quarters with Pan Yan and Volodyovski. "Have you seen how we have fallen in love with each other? It will be pleasant here in Zamost for me and you. The host and I have become so attached to each other that no cabinet-maker could join inlaid work better. He is a good fellow — h'm! If he were my knife and I carried him at my belt, I would whet him on a stone pretty often, for he is a trifle dull. But he is a good man, and he will not betray like those bull-drivers of Birji. Have you noticed how the magnates cling to old Zagloba? I cannot keep them off. I'm scarcely away from Sapyeha when there is another at hand. But I will tune this one as a bass-viol, and play such an aria on him for the Swedes that they will dance to death at Zamost. I will wind him up like a Dantzig clock with chimes."

Noise coming from the town interrupted further conversation. After a time an officer whom they knew passed quickly near them.

"Stop!" cried Volodyovski; "what is the matter?"

"There is a fire to be seen from the walls. Shchebjeshyn is burning! The Swedes are there!"

"Let us go on the walls," said Pan Yan.

"Go; but I will sleep, since I need my strength for to-morrow," answered Zagloba.

CHAPTER XXIX.

THAT night Volodyovski went on a scouting expedition, and about morning returned with a number of informants. These men asserted that the King of Sweden was at Shchebjeshyn in person, and would soon be at Zamost.

Zamoyski was rejoiced at the news, for he hurried around greatly, and had a genuine desire to try his walls and guns on the Swedes. He considered, and very justly, that even if he had to yield in the end he would detain the power of Sweden for whole months; and during that time Yan Kazimir would collect troops, bring the entire Tartar force to his aid, and organize in the whole country a powerful and victorious resistance.

"Since the opportunity is given me," said he, with great spirit, at the military council, "to render the country and the king notable service, I declare to you, gentlemen, that I will blow myself into the air before a Swedish foot shall stand here. They want to take Zamoyski by force. Let them take him! We shall see who is better. You, gentlemen, will, I trust, aid me most heartily."

"We are ready to perish with your grace," said the officers, in chorus.

"If they will only besiege us," said Zagloba, "I will lead the first sortie."

"I will follow, Uncle!" cried Roh Kovalski; "I will spring at the king himself!"

"Now to the walls!" commanded Zamoyski.

All went out. The walls were ornamented with soldiers as with flowers. Regiments of infantry, so splendid that they were unequalled in the whole Commonwealth, stood in readiness, one at the side of the other, with musket in hand, and eyes turned to the field. Not many foreigners served in these regiments, merely a few Prussians and French; they were mainly peasants from Zamoyski's inherited lands. Sturdy, well-grown men, who, wearing colored jackets and trained in foreign fashion, fought as well as the best Cromwellians of England. They were specially powerful when after firing it came to rush on the enemy in hand-to-hand conflict. And now, remembering their former triumphs over Hmelnitski, they were looking for the Swedes with impatience. At the cannons, which stretched out through the embrasures their long necks to the fields as if in curiosity, served mainly Flemings, the first of gunners. Outside the fortress, beyond the moat, were squadrons of light cavalry, safe themselves, for they were under cover of cannon, certain of refuge, and able at any moment to spring out whithersoever it might be needed.

Zamoyski, wearing inlaid armor and carrying a gilded baton in his hand, rode around the walls, and inquired every moment, —

"Well, what — not in sight yet?" And he muttered oaths when he received negative answers on all sides. After a while he went to another side, and again he asked, —

"Well, what — not in sight yet?"

It was difficult to see the Swedes, for there was a mist in the air; and only about ten o'clock in the forenoon did it begin to disappear. The heaven shining blue above the horizon became clear, and immediately on the western side of the walls they began to cry, —

"They are coming, they are coming, they are coming!"

Zamoyski, with three adjutants and Zagloba, entered quickly an angle of the walls from which there was a distant view, and the four men began to look through field-glasses. The mist was lying a little on the ground yet, and the Swedish hosts, marching from Vyelanchy, seemed to be wading to the knees in that mist, as if they were coming out of wide waters. The nearer regiments had become very distinct, so that the naked eye could distinguish the infantry; they seemed like clouds of dark dust rolling on toward the town. Gradually more regiments, artillery, and cavalry appeared.

The sight was beautiful. From each quadrangle of infantry rose an admirably regular quadrangle of spears; between them waved banners of various colors, but mostly blue with white crosses, and blue with golden lions. They came very near. On the walls there was silence; therefore the breath of the air brought from the advancing army the squeaking of wheels, the clatter of armor, the tramp of horses, and the dull sound of human voices. When they had come within twice the distance of a shot from a culverin, they began to dispose themselves before the fortress.

Some quadrangles of infantry broke ranks; others prepared to pitch tents and dig trenches.

"They are here!" said Zamoyski.

"They are the dog-brothers!" answered Zagloba. "They could be counted, man for man, on the fingers. Persons of my long experience, however, do not need to count, but simply to cast an eye on them. There are ten thousand cavalry, and eight thousand infantry with artillery. If I am mistaken in one common soldier or one horse, I am ready to redeem the mistake with my whole fortune."

"Is it possible to estimate in that way?"

"Ten thousand cavalry and eight thousand infantry. I have hope in God that they will go away in much smaller numbers; only let me lead one sortie."

"Do you hear? They are playing an aria."

In fact, trumpeters and drummers stepped out before the regiments, and military music began. At the sound of it the more distant regiments approached, and encompassed the town from a distance. At last from the dense throngs a few horsemen rode forth. When half-way, they put white kerchiefs on their swords, and began to wave them.

"An embassy!" cried Zagloba; "I saw how the scoundrels came to Kyedani with the same boldness, and it is known what came of that."

"Zamost is not Kyedani, and I am not the voevoda of Vilna," answered Zamoyski.

Meanwhile the horsemen were approaching the gate. After a short time an officer of the day hurried to Zamoyski with a report that Pan Yan Sapyeha desired, in the name of the King of Sweden, to see him and speak with him.

Zamoyski put his hands on his hips at once, began to step from one foot to the other, to puff, to pout, and said at last, with great animation, —

"Tell Pan Sapyeha that Zamoyski does not speak with traitors. If the King of Sweden wishes to speak with me, let him send me a Swede by race, not a Pole, — for Poles who serve the Swedes may go as embassadors to my dogs; I have the same regard for both."

"As God is dear to me, that is an answer!" cried Zagloba, with unfeigned enthusiasm.

"But devil take them!" said the starosta, roused by his own words and by praise. "Well, shall I stand on ceremony with them?"

"Permit me, your worthiness, to take him that answer," said Zagloba. And without waiting, he hastened away with the officer, went to Yan Sapyeha, and, apparently, not only repeated the starosta's words, but added something very bad from himself; for Sapyeha turned from the town as if a thunderbolt had burst in front of his horse, and rode away with his cap thrust over his ears.

From the walls and from the squadrons of the cavalry which were standing before the gate they began to hoot at the men riding off, —

"To the kennel with traitors, the betrayers! Jew servants! Huz, huz!"

Sapyeha stood before the king, pale, with compressed lips. The king too was confused, for Zamost had deceived his hopes. In spite of what had been said, he expected to find a town of such power of resistance as Cracow, Poznan, and other places, so many of which he had captured; meanwhile he found a fortress powerful, calling to mind those of Denmark and the Netherlands, which he could not even think of taking without guns of heavy calibre.

"What is the result?" asked the king, when he saw Sapyeha.

"Nothing! Zamoyski will not speak with Poles who serve your Royal Grace. He sent out his jester, who reviled me and your Royal Grace so shamefully that it is not proper to repeat what he said."

"It is all one to me with whom he wants to speak, if he will only speak. In default of other arguments, I have iron arguments; but meanwhile I will send Forgell."

Half an hour later Forgell, with a purely Swedish suite, announced himself at the gate. The drawbridge was let down slowly over the moat, and the general entered the fortress amid silence and seriousness. Neither the eyes of the envoy nor those of any man in his suite were bound; evidently Zamoyski wished him to see everything, and be able to report to the king touching everything. The master of Zamost received Forgell with as much splendor as an independent prince would have done, and arranged all, in truth, admirably, for Swedish lords had not one twelfth as much wealth as the Poles had; and Zamoyski among Poles was well-nigh the most powerful. The clever Swede began at once to treat him as if the king had sent the embassy to a monarch equal to himself; to begin with, he called him "Princeps." and continued to address him thus, though Pan Sobiepan interrupted him promptly in the beginning, —

"Not princeps, *eques polonus* (a Polish nobleman), but for that very reason the equal of princes."

"Your princely grace," said Forgell, not permitting himself to be diverted, "the Most Serene King of Sweden and Lord," here he enumerated his titles, "has not come here as an enemy in any sense; but, speaking simply, has come on a visit, and through me announces himself, having, as I believe, a well-founded hope that your princely grace will desire to open your gates to him and his army."

"It is not a custom with us," answered Zamoyski, "to refuse hospitality to any man, even should he come uninvited. There will always be a place at my table for a guest; but for such a worthy person as the Swedish monarch the first place. Inform then the Most Serene King of Sweden that I invite him, and all the more gladly since the Most Serene Carolus Gustavus is lord in Sweden, as I am in Zamost. But as your worthiness has seen, there is no lack of servants in my house; therefore his Swedish Serenity need not bring his servants with him. Should he bring them I might think that he counts me a poor man, and wishes to show me contempt."

"Well done!" whispered Zagloba, standing behind the shoulders of Pan Sobiepan.

When Zamoyski had finished his speech he began to pout his lips, to puff and repeat, —

"Ah, here it is, this is the position!"

Forgell bit his mustache, was silent awhile, and said, —

"It would be the greatest proof of distrust toward the king if your princely grace were not pleased to admit his garrison to the fortress. I am the king's confidant. I know his innermost thoughts, and besides this I have the order to announce to your worthiness, and to give assurance by word in the name of the king, that he does not think of occupying the possessions of Zamost or this fortress permanently. But since war has broken out anew in this unhappy land, since rebellion has raised its head, and Yan Kazimir, unmindful of the miseries which may fall on the Commonwealth, and seeking only his own fortune, has returned within the boundaries, and, together with pagans, comes forth against our Christian troops, the invincible king, my lord, has determined to pursue him, even to the wild steppes of the Tartars and the Turks, with the sole purpose of restoring peace to the country, the reign of justice, prosperity, and freedom to the inhabitants of this illustrious Commonwealth."

Zamoyski struck his knee with his hand without saying a word; but Zagloba whispered, —

"The Devil has dressed himself in vestments, and is ringing for Mass with his tail."

"Many benefits have accrued to this land already from the protection of the king," continued Forgell; "but thinking in his fatherly heart that he has not done enough, he has left his Prussian province again to go once more to the rescue of the Commonwealth, which depends on finishing Yan Kazimir. But that this new war should have a speedy and victorious conclusion, it is needful that the king occupy for a time this fortress. It is to be for his troops a point from which pursuit may begin against rebels. But hearing that he who is the lord of Zamost surpasses all, not only in wealth, antiquity of stock, wit, high-mindedness, but also in love for the country, the king, my master, said at once: 'He will understand me, he will be able to appreciate my intentions respecting this country, he will not deceive my confidence, he will surpass my hopes, he will be the first to put his hand to the prosperity and peace of this country.' This is the truth! So on you depends the future fate of this country. You may save it and become the father of it; therefore I have no doubt of what you will do. Whoever inherits from his ancestors such fame should not avoid an opportunity to increase that fame and make it immortal. In truth, you will do more good by opening the gates of this fortress than if you had added a whole province to the Commonwealth. The king is confident that your uncommon wisdom, together with your heart, will incline you to this; therefore he will not command, he prefers to request, he throws aside threats, he offers friendship; not as a ruler with a subject, but as powerful with powerful does he wish to deal."

Here General Forgell bowed before Zamoyski with as much respect as before an independent monarch. In the hall it grew silent. All eyes were fixed on Zamoyski. He began to twist, according to his custom, in his gilded arm-chair, to pout his lips, and exhibit stern resolve; at last he thrust out his elbows, placed his palms on his knees, and shaking his head like a restive horse, began, —

"This is what I have to say! I am greatly thankful to

his Swedish Serenity for the lofty opinion which he has of my wit and my love for the Commonwealth. Nothing is dearer to me than the friendship of such a potentate. But I think that we might love each other all the same if his Swedish Serenity remained in Stockholm and I in Zamost; that is what it is. For Stockholm belongs to his Swedish Serenity, and Zamost to me. As to love for the Commonwealth, this is what I think. The Commonwealth will not improve by the coming in of the Swedes, but by their departure. That is my argument! I believe that Zamost might help his Swedish Serenity to victory over Yan Kazimir; but your worthiness should know that I have not given oath to his Swedish Grace, but to Yan Kazimir; therefore I wish victory to Yan Kazimir, and I will not give Zamost to the King of Sweden. That is my position!'

"That policy suits me!" said Zagloba.

A joyous murmur rose in the hall; but Zamoyski slapped his knees with his hands, and the sounds were hushed.

Forgell was confused, and was silent for a time; then he began to argue anew, insisted a little, threatened, begged, flattered. Latin flowed from his mouth like a stream, till drops of sweat were on his forehead; but all was in vain, for after his best arguments, so strong that they might move walls, he heard always one answer, —

"But still I will not yield Zamost; that is my position!"

The audience continued beyond measure; at last it became awkward and difficult for Forgell, since mirth was seizing those present. More and more frequently some word fell, some sneer, — now from Zagloba, now from others, — after which smothered laughter was heard in the hall. Forgell saw finally that it was necessary to use the last means; therefore he unrolled a parchment with seals, which he held in his hand, and to which no one had turned attention hitherto, and rising said with a solemn, emphatic voice, —

"For opening the gates of the fortress his Royal Grace," here again he enumerated the titles, "gives your princely grace the province of Lubelsk in perpetual possession."

All were astonished when they heard this, and Zamoyski himself was astonished for a moment. Forgell had begun to turn a triumphant look on the people around him, when suddenly and in deep silence Zagloba, standing behind Zamoyski, said in Polish, —

"Your worthiness, offer the King of Sweden the Netherlands in exchange."

Zamoyski, without thinking long, put his hands on his hips and fired through the whole hall in Latin, —

"And I offer to his Swedish Serenity the Netherlands!"

That moment the hall resounded with one immense burst of laughter. The breasts of all were shaking, and the girdles on their bodies were shaking; some clapped their hands, others tottered as drunken men, some leaned on their neighbors, but the laughter sounded continuously. Forgell was pale; he frowned terribly, but he waited with fire in his eyes and his head raised haughtily. At last, when the paroxysm of laughter had passed, he asked in a short, broken voice, —

"Is that the final answer of your worthiness?"

Zamoyski twirled his mustache. "No!" said he, raising his head still more proudly, "for I have cannon on the walls."

The embassy was at an end.

Two hours later cannons were thundering from the trenches of the Swedes, but Zamoyski's guns answered them with equal power. All Zamost was covered with smoke, as with an immense cloud; moment after moment there were flashes in that cloud, and thunder roared unceasingly. But fire from the heavy fortress guns was preponderant. The Swedish balls fell in the moat or bounded without effect from the strong angles; toward evening the enemy were forced to draw back from the nearer trenches, for the fortress was covering them with such a rain of missiles that nothing living could endure it. The Swedish king, carried away by anger, commanded to burn all the villages and hamlets, so that the neighborhood seemed in the night one sea of fire; but Zamoyski cared not for that.

"All right!" said he, "let them burn. We have a roof over our heads, but soon it will be pouring down their backs."

And he was so satisfied with himself and rejoiced that he made a great feast that day and remained till late at the cups. A resounding orchestra played at the feast so loudly that, in spite of the thunder of artillery, it could be heard in the remotest trenches of the Swedes.

But the Swedes cannonaded continually, so constantly indeed that the firing lasted the whole night. Next day a number of guns were brought to the king, which as soon as

they were placed in the trenches began to work against the
fortress. The king did not expect, it is true, to make a
breach in the walls; he merely wished to instil into Zamoyski the conviction that he had determined to storm furiously
and mercilessly. He wished to bring terror on them; but
that was bringing terror on Poles.[1] Zamoyski paid no attention to it for a moment, and often while on the walls he
said, in time of the heaviest cannonading, —

"Why do they waste powder?"

Volodyovski and the others offered to make a sortie, but
Zamoyski would not permit it; he did not wish to waste
blood. He knew besides that it would be necessary to deliver open battle; for such a careful warrior as the king and
such a trained army would not let themselves be surprised.
Zagloba, seeing this fixed determination, insisted all the
more, and guaranteed that he would lead the sortie.

"You are too bloodthirsty!" answered Zamoyski. "It
is pleasant for us and unpleasant for the Swedes; why
should we go to them? You might fall, and I need you as
a councillor; for it was by your wit that I confounded Forgell so by mentioning the Netherlands."

Zagloba answered that he could not restrain himself
within the walls, he wanted so much to get at the Swedes;
but he was forced to obey. In default of other occupation
he spent his time on the walls among the soldiers, dealing
out to them precautions and counsel with importance, which
all heard with no little respect, holding him a greatly experienced warrior, one of the foremost in the Commonwealth;
and he was rejoiced in soul, looking at the defence and the
spirit of the knighthood.

"Pan Michael," said he to Volodyovski, "there is another
spirit in the Commonwealth and in the nobles. No one
thinks now of treason or surrender; and every one out of
good-will for the Commonwealth and the king is ready to
give his life sooner than yield a step to the enemy. You
remember how a year ago from every side was heard, 'This
one has betrayed, that one has betrayed, a third has accepted protection;' and now the Swedes need protection
more than we. If the Devil does not protect them, he will
soon take them. We have our stomachs so full here that
drummers might beat on them, but their entrails are twisted
into whips from hunger."

[1] "Strachy na Lachy" (Terror on Poles) is a Polish saying, about
equivalent to "impossible."

Zagloba was right. The Swedish army had no supplies; and for eighteen thousand men, not to mention horses, there was no place from which to get supplies. Zamoyski, before the arrival of the enemy, had brought in from all his estates for many miles around food for man and horse. In the more remote neighborhoods of the country swarmed parties of confederates and bands of armed peasants, so that foraging detachments could not go out, since just beyond the camp certain death was in waiting.

In addition to this, Pan Charnyetski had not gone to the west bank of the Vistula, but was circling about the Swedish army like a wild beast around a sheepfold. Again nightly alarms had begun, and the loss of smaller parties without tidings. Near Krasnik appeared certain Polish troops, which had cut communication with the Vistula. Finally, news came that Pavel Sapyeha, the hetman, was marching from the north with a powerful Lithuanian army; that in passing he had destroyed the garrison at Lublin, had taken Lublin, and was coming with cavalry to Zamost.

Old Wittemberg, the most experienced of the Swedish leaders, saw the whole ghastliness of the position, and laid it plainly before the king.

"I know," said he, "that the genius of your Royal Grace can do wonders; but judging things in human fashion, hunger will overcome us, and when the enemy fall upon our emaciated army not a living foot of us will escape."

"If I had this fortress," answered the king, "I could finish the war in two months."

"For such a fortress a year's siege is short."

The king in his soul recognized that the old warrior was right, but he did not acknowledge that he saw no means himself, that his genius was strained. He counted yet on some unexpected event; hence he gave orders to fire night and day.

"I will bend the spirit in them," said he; "they will be more inclined to treaties."

After some days of cannonading so furious that the light could not be seen behind the smoke, the king sent Forgell again to the fortress.

"The king, my master," said Forgell, appearing before Zamoyski, "considers that the damage which Zamost must have suffered from our cannonading will soften the lofty mind of your princely grace and incline it to negotiations."

To which Zamoyski said: " Of course there is damage !
Why should there not be ? You killed on the market square
a pig, which was struck in the belly by the fragment of a
bomb. If you cannonade another week, perhaps you'll kill
another pig."

Forgell took that answer to the king. In the evening a
new council was held in the king's quarters; next day the
Swedes began to pack their tents in wagons and draw their
cannon out of the trenches, and in the night the whole army
moved onward.

Zamost thundered after them from all its artillery, and
when they had vanished from the eye two squadrons, the
Shemberk and the Lauda, passed out through the southern
gate and followed in their track.

The Swedes marched southward. Wittemberg advised,
it is true, a return to Warsaw, and with all his power he
tried to convince the king that that was the only road of
salvation; but the Swedish Alexander had determined absolutely to pursue the Polish Darius to the remotest boundaries of the kingdom.

CHAPTER XXX.

THE spring of that year approached with wonderful roads; for while in the north of the Commonwealth snow was already thawing, the stiffened rivers were set free, and the whole country was filled with March water, in the south the icy breath of winter was still descending from the mountains to the fields, woods, and forests. In the forests lay snow-drifts, in the open country frozen roads sounded under the hoofs of horses; the days were dry, the sunsets red, the nights starry and frosty. The people living on the rich clay, on the black soil, and in the woods of Little Poland comforted themselves with the continuance of the cold, stating that the field-mice and the Swedes would perish from it. But inasmuch as the spring came late, it came as swiftly as an armored squadron advancing to the attack of an enemy. The sun shot down living fire from heaven, and at once the crust of winter burst; from the Hungarian steppes flew a strong warm wind, and began to blow on the fields and wild places. Straightway in the midst of shining ponds arable ground became dark, a green fleece shot up on the low river-lands, and the forests began to shed tears from bursting buds on their branches.

In the heavens continually fair were seen, daily, rows of cranes, wild ducks, teal, and geese. Storks flew to their places of the past year, and the roofs were swarming with swallows; the twitter of birds was heard in the villages, their noise in the woods and ponds, and in the evening the whole country was ringing with the croaking and singing of frogs, which swam with delight in the waters.

Then came great rains, which were as if they had been warmed; they fell in the daytime, they fell in the night, without interruption.

The fields were turned into lakes, the rivers overflowed, the fords became impassable; then followed the "stickiness and the impossible of muddy roads." Amid all this water, mud, and swamp the Swedish legions dragged onward continually toward the south.

But how little was that throng, advancing as it were to destruction, like that brilliant army which in its time marched under Wittemberg to Great Poland! Hunger had stamped itself on the faces of the old soldiers; they went on more like spectres than men, in suffering, in toil, in sleeplessness, knowing that at the end of the road not food was awaiting, but hunger; not sleep, but a battle; and if rest, then the rest of the dead.

Arrayed in iron these skeletons of horsemen sat on skeletons of horses. The infantry hardly drew their legs along; barely could they hold spears and muskets with trembling hands. Day followed day; they went onward continually. Wagons were broken, cannons were fastened in sloughs; they went on so slowly that sometimes they were able to advance hardly five miles in one day. Diseases fell on the soldiers, like ravens on corpses; the teeth of some were chattering from fever; others lay down on the ground simply from weakness, choosing rather to die than advance.

But the Swedish Alexander hastened toward the Polish Darius unceasingly. At the same time he was pursued himself. As in the night-time jackals follow a sick buffalo waiting to see if he will soon fall, and he knows that he will fall and he hears the howl of the hungry pack, so after the Swedes went "parties," nobles and peasants, approaching ever nearer, attacking ever more insolently, and snatching away.

At last came Charnyetski, the most terrible of all the pursuers, and followed closely. The rearguards of the Swedes as often as they looked behind saw horsemen, at one time far off on the edge of the horizon, at another a furlong away, at another twice the distance of a musket-shot, at another time, when attacking, on their very shoulders.

The enemy wanted battle; with despair did the Swedes pray to the Lord of Hosts for battle. But Charnyetski did not receive battle, he bided his time; meanwhile he preferred to punish the Swedes, or let go from his hand against them single parties as one would falcons against water birds.

And so they marched one after the other. There were times, however, when Charnyetski passed the Swedes, pushed on, and blocked the road before them, pretending to prepare for a general battle. Then the trumpet sounded joyously from one end of the Swedish camp to the other, and, oh miracle! new strength, a new spirit seemed to vivify on a sudden the wearied ranks of the Scandinavians. Sick, wet, weak, like Lazaruses, they stood in rank promptly for battle, with flaming faces, with fire in their eyes. Spears and muskets moved with as much accuracy as if iron hands held them ; the shouts of battle were heard as loudly as if they came from the healthiest bosoms, and they marched forward to strike breast against breast.

Then Charnyetski struck once, twice; but when the artillery began to thunder he withdrew his troops, leaving to the Swedes as profit, vain labor and the greater disappointment and disgust.

When, however, the artillery could not come up, and spears and sabres had to decide in the open field, he struck like a thunderbolt, knowing that in a hand-to-hand conflict the Swedish cavalry could not stand, even against volunteers.

And again Wittemberg implored the king to retreat and thus avoid ruin to himself and the army; but Karl Gustav in answer compressed his lips, fire flashed from his eyes, and he pointed to the south, where in the Russian regions he hoped to find Yan Kazimir, and also fields open to conquest, rest, provisions, pastures for horses, and rich plunder.

Meanwhile, to complete the misfortune, those Polish regiments which had served him hitherto, and which in one way or another were now alone able to meet Charnyetski, began to leave the Swedes. Pan Zbrojek resigned first; he had held to Karl hitherto not from desire of gain, but from blind attachment to the squadron, and soldierly faithfulness to Karl. He resigned in this fashion, that he engaged in conflict with a regiment of Miller's dragoons, cut down half the men, and departed. After him resigned Pan Kalinski, who rode over the Swedish infantry. Yan Sapyeha grew gloomier each day ; he was meditating something in his soul, plotting something. He had not gone hitherto himself, but his men were deserting him daily.

Karl Gustav was marching then through Narol, Tsyeshanov, and Oleshytse, to reach the San. He was upheld by the hope that Yan Kazimir would bar his road and give him battle. A victory might yet repair the fate of Sweden and bring a change of fortune. In fact, rumors were current that Yan Kazimir had set out from Lvoff with the quarter soldiers and the Tartars. But Karl's reckonings deceived him. Yan Kazimir preferred to await the junction of the armies and the arrival of the Lithuanians under Sapyeha. Delay was his best ally; for he was growing daily in strength, while Karl was becoming weaker.

"That is not the march of troops nor of an army, but a funeral procession!" said old warriors in Yan Kazimir's suite.

Many Swedish officers shared this opinion. Karl Gustav however repeated still that he was going to Lvoff; but he was deceiving himself and his army. It was not for him to go to Lvoff, but to think of his own safety. Besides, it was not certain that he would find Yan Kazimir in Lvoff; in every event the "Polish Darius" might withdraw far into Podolia, and draw after him the enemy into distant steppes where the Swedes must perish without rescue.

Douglas went to Premysl to try if that fortress would yield, and returned, not merely with nothing, but plucked. The catastrophe was coming slowly, but inevitably. All tidings brought to the Swedish camp were simply the announcement of it. Each day fresh tidings and ever more terrible.

"Sapyeha is marching; he is already in Tomashov!" was repeated one day. "Lyubomirski is marching with troops and mountaineers!" was announced the day following. And again: "The king is leading the quarter soldiers and the horde one hundred thousand strong! He has joined Sapyeha!"

Among these tidings were "tidings of disaster and death," untrue and exaggerated, but they always spread fear. The courage of the army fell. Formerly whenever Karl appeared in person before his regiments, they greeted him with shouts in which rang the hope of victory; now the regiments stood before him dull and dumb. And at the fires the soldiers, famished and wearied to death, whispered more of Charnyetski than of their own king. They saw him everywhere. And, a strange thing! when for a couple of days no party had perished, when a few nights passed without alarms or cries of "Allah!" and "Strike, kill!" their disquiet became still greater. "Charnyetski has fled; God knows what he is preparing!" repeated the soldiers.

Karl halted a few days in Yaroslav, pondering what to do. During that time the Swedes placed on flat-bottomed boats sick soldiers, of whom there were many in camp, and sent them by the river to Sandomir, the nearest fortified town still in Swedish hands. After this work had been finished, and just when the news of Yan Kazimir's march from Lvoff had come in, the King of Sweden determined to discover where Yan Kazimir was, and with that object Colonel Kanneberg with one thousand cavalry passed the San and moved to the east.

"It may be that you have in your hands the fate of the war and us all," said the king to him at parting.

And in truth much depended on that party, for in the worst case Kanneberg was to furnish the camp with provisions; and if he could learn certainly where Yan Kazimir was, the Swedish King was to move at once with all his forces against the "Polish Darius," whose army he was to scatter and whose person he was to seize if he could.

The first soldiers and the best horses were assigned, therefore, to Kanneberg. Choice was made the more carefully as the colonel could not take artillery or infantry; hence he must have with him men who with sabres could stand against Polish cavalry in the field.

March 20, the party set out. A number of officers and soldiers took farewell of them, saying: "God conduct you! God give victory! God give a fortunate return!" They marched in a long line, being one thousand in number, and went two abreast over the newly built bridge which had one square still unfinished, but was in some fashion covered with planks so that they might pass.

Good hope shone in their faces, for they were exceptionally well fed. Food had been taken from others and given to them; gorailka was poured into their flasks. When they were riding away they shouted joyfully and said to their comrades, —

"We will bring you Charnyetski himself on a rope."

Fools! They knew not that they were going as go bullocks to slaughter at the shambles!

Everything combined for their ruin. Barely had they crossed the river when the Swedish sappers removed the temporary covering of the bridge, so as to lay stronger planks over which cannon might pass. The thousand turned toward Vyelki Ochi, singing in low voices to themselves; their helmets glittered in the sun on the turn once and a second time; then they began to sink in the dense pine-wood.

They rode forward two miles and a half, — emptiness, silence around them; the forest depths seemed vacant altogether. They halted to give breath to the horses; after that they moved slowly forward. At last they reached Vyelki Ochi, in which they found not a living soul. That emptiness astonished Kanneberg.

"Evidently they have been waiting for us here," said he to Major Sweno; "but Charnyetski must be in some other place, since he has not prepared ambushes."

"Does your worthiness order a return?" asked Sweno.

"We will go on even to Lvoff itself, which is not very far. I must find an informant, and give the king sure information touching Yan Kazimir."

"But if we meet superior forces?"

"Even if we meet several thousand of those brawlers whom the Poles call general militia, we will not let ourselves be torn apart by such soldiers."

"But we may meet regular troops. We have no artillery, and against them cannons are the main thing."

"Then we will draw back in season and inform the king of the enemy, and those who try to cut off our retreat we will disperse."

"I am afraid of the night!" replied Sweno.

"We will take every precaution. We have food for men and horses for two days; we need not hurry."

When they entered the pine-wood beyond Vyelki Ochi, they acted with vastly more caution. Fifty horsemen rode in advance musket in hand, each man with his gunstock on his thigh. They looked carefully on every side; examined the thickets, the undergrowth; frequently they halted, listened; sometimes they went from the road to one side to examine the depths of the forest, but neither on the roads nor at the sides was there a man.

But one hour later, after they had passed a rather sudden turn, two troopers riding in advance saw a man on horseback about four hundred yards ahead.

The day was clear and the sun shone brightly; hence the man could be seen as something on the hand. He was a soldier, not large, dressed very decently in foreign fashion. He seemed especially small because he sat on a large cream-colored steed, evidently of high breed.

The horseman was riding at leisure, as if not seeing that troops were rolling on after him. The spring floods had dug deep ditches in the road, in which muddy water was sweeping along. The horseman spurred his steed in front of the ditches, and the beast sprang across with the nimbleness of a deer, and again went on at a trot, throwing his head and snorting vivaciously from time to time.

The two troopers reined in their horses and began to look around for the sergeant. He clattered up in a moment, looked, and said: " That is some hound from the Polish kennel."

" Shall I shout at him ? "

" Shout not; there may be more of them. Go to the colonel."

Meanwhile the rest of the advance guard rode up, and all halted ; the small horseman halted too, and turned the face of his steed to the Swedes as if wishing to block the road to them. For a certain time they looked at him and he at them.

"There is another! a second! a third! a fourth! a whole party ! " were the sudden cries in the Swedish ranks.

In fact, horsemen began to pour out from both sides of the road; at first singly, then by twos, by threes. All took their places in line with him who had appeared first.

But the second Swedish guard with Sweno, and then the whole detachment with Kanneberg, came up. Kanneberg and Sweno rode to the front at once.

" I know those men ! " cried Sweno, when he had barely seen them ; " their squadron was the first to strike on Prince Waldemar at Golamb ; those are Charnyetski's men. He must be here himself ! "

These words produced an impression; deep silence followed in the ranks, only the horses shook their bridle-bits.

" I sniff some ambush," continued Sweno. "There are too few of them to meet us, but there must be others hidden in the woods."

He turned here to Kanneberg : " Your worthiness, let us return."

" You give good counsel," answered the colonel, frowning. " It was not worth while to set out if we must return at sight of a few ragged fellows. Why did we not return at sight of one ? Forward ! "

The first Swedish rank moved at that moment with the greatest regularity ; after it the second, the third, the fourth. The distance between the two detachments was becoming less.

" Cock your muskets ! " commanded Kanneberg.

The Swedish muskets moved like one; their iron necks were stretched toward the Polish horsemen.

But before the muskets thundered, the Polish horsemen turned their horses and began to flee in a disorderly group.

" Forward ! " cried Kanneberg.

The division moved forward on a gallop, so that the ground trembled under the heavy hoofs of the horses.

The forest was filled with the shouts of pursuers and pursued. After half an hour of chasing, either because the Swedish horses were better, or those of the Poles were wearied by some journey, the distance between the two bodies was decreasing.

But at once something wonderful happened. The Polish band, at first disorderly, did not scatter more and more as the flight continued, but on the contrary, they fled in ever better order, in ranks growing more even, as if the very speed of the horses brought the riders into line.

Sweno saw this, urged on his horse, reached Kanneberg, and called out, —

" Your worthiness, that is an uncommon party ; those are regular soldiers, fleeing designedly and leading us to an ambush."

" Will there be devils in the ambush, or men ? " asked Kanneberg.

The road rose somewhat and became ever wider, the forest thinner, and at the end of the road was to be seen an unoccupied field, or rather a great open space, surrounded on all sides by a dense, deep gray pine-wood.

The Polish horsemen increased their pace in turn, and it transpired that hitherto they had gone slowly of purpose ; for now in a short time they pushed forward so rapidly that the Swedish leader knew that he could never overtake them. But when he had come to the middle of the open plain and saw that the enemy were almost touching the other end of it, he began to restrain his men and slacken speed.

But, oh marvel! the Poles, instead of sinking in the opposite forest, wheeled around at the very edge of the half-circle and returned on a gallop toward the Swedes, putting themselves at once in such splendid battle order that they roused wonder even in their opponents.

" It is true ! " cried Kanneberg, " those are regular soldiers. They turned as if on parade. What do they want for the hundredth time ? "

" They are attacking us ! " cried Sweno.

In fact, the squadron was moving forward at a trot. The little knight on the cream-colored steed shouted something to his men, pushed forward, again reined in his horse, gave signs with his sabre; evidently he was the leader.

"They are attacking really!" said Kanneberg, with astonishment.

And now the horses, with ears dropped back, were coming at the greatest speed, stretched out so that their bellies almost touched the ground. Their riders bent forward to their shoulders, and were hidden behind the horse manes. The Swedes standing in the first rank saw only hundreds of distended horse-nostrils and burning eyes. A whirlwind does not move as that squadron tore on.

"God with us! Sweden! Fire!" commanded Kanneberg, raising his sword.

All the muskets thundered; but at that very moment the Polish squadron fell into the smoke with such impetus that it hurled to the right and the left the first Swedish ranks, and drove itself into the density of men and horses, as a wedge is driven into a cleft log. A terrible whirl was made, breast-plate struck breast-plate, sabre struck rapier; and the rattle, the whining of horses, the groan of dying men roused every echo, so that the whole pine-wood began to give back the sounds of the battle, as the steep cliffs of mountains give back the thunder.

The Swedes were confused for a time, especially since a considerable number of them fell from the first blow; but soon recovering, they went powerfully against the enemy. Their flanks came together; and since the Polish squadron was pushing ahead anyhow, for it wished to pass through with a thrust, it was soon surrounded. The Swedish centre yielded before the squadron, but the flanks pressed on it with the greater power, unable to break it; for it defended itself with rage and with all that incomparable adroitness which made the Polish cavalry so terrible in hand-to-hand conflict. Sabres toiled then against rapiers, bodies fell thickly; but the victory was just turning to the Swedish side when suddenly from under the dark wall of the pine-wood rolled out another squadron, and moved forward at once with a shout.

The whole right wing of the Swedes, under the lead of Sweno, faced the new enemy in which the trained Swedish soldiers recognized hussars. They were led by a man on a valiant dapple gray; he wore a burka, and a wild-cat skin cap with a heron feather. He was perfectly visible to the eye, for he was riding at one side some yards from the soldiers.

"Charnyetski! Charnyetski!" was the cry in the Swedish ranks.

Sweno looked in despair at the sky, then pressed his horse with his knees and rushed forward with his men.

But Charnyetski led his hussars a few yards farther, and when they were moving with the swiftest rush, he turned back alone.

With that a third squadron issued from the forest, he galloped to that and led it forward; a fourth came out, he led that on; pointing to each with his baton, where it must strike. You would have said that he was a man leading harvesters to his field and distributing work among them.

At last, when the fifth squadron had come forth from the forest, he put himself at the head of that, and with it rushed to the fight.

But the hussars had already forced the right wing to the rear, and after a while had broken it completely; the three other squadrons, racing around the Swedes in Tartar fashion and raising an uproar, had thrown them into disorder; then they fell to cutting them with steel, to thrusting them with lances, scattering, trampling, and finally pursuing them amid shrieks and slaughter.

Kanneberg saw that he had fallen into an ambush, and had led his detachment as it were under the knife. For him there was no thought of victory now; but he wished to save as many men as possible, hence he ordered to sound the retreat. The Swedes, therefore, turned with all speed to that same road by which they had come to Vyelki Ochi; but Charnyetski's men so followed them that the breaths of the Polish horses warmed the shoulders of the Swedes.

In these conditions and in view of the terror which had seized the Swedish cavalry, that return could not take place in order; and soon Kanneberg's brilliant division was turned into a crowd fleeing in disorder and slaughtered almost without resistance.

The longer the pursuit lasted, the more irregular it became; for the Poles did not pursue in order, each of them drove his horse according to the breath in the beast's nostrils, and attacked and slew whom he wished.

Both sides were mingled and confused in one mass. Some Polish soldiers passed the last Swedish ranks; and it happened that when a Pole stood in his stirrups to strike with more power the man fleeing in front of him, he fell himself thrust with a rapier from behind. The road to

Vyelki Ochi was strewn with Swedish corpses; but the end of the chase was not there. Both sides rushed with the same force along the road through the next forest; there however the Swedish horses, wearied first, began to go more slowly, and the slaughter became still more bloody.

Some of the Swedes sprang from their beasts and vanished in the forest; but only a few did so, for the Swedes knew from experience that peasants were watching in the forest, and they preferred to die from sabres rather than from terrible tortures, of which the infuriated people were not sparing. Some asked quarter, but for the most part in vain; for each Pole chose to slay an enemy, and chase on rather than take him prisoner, guard him, and leave further pursuit.

They cut then without mercy, so that no one might return with news of the defeat. Volodyovski was in the van of pursuit with the Lauda squadron. He was that horseman who had appeared first to the Swedes as a decoy; he had struck first, and now, sitting on a horse which was as if impelled by a whirlwind, he enjoyed himself with his whole soul, wishing to be sated with blood, and avenge the defeat of Golamb. Every little while he overtook a horseman, and when he had overtaken him he quenched him as quickly as he would a candle; sometimes he came on the shoulders of two, three, or four, but soon, only in a moment, that same number of horses ran riderless before him. More than one hapless Swede caught his own rapier by the point, and turning the hilt to the knight for quarter implored with voice and with eyes. Volodyovski did not stop, but thrusting his sabre into the man where the neck joins the breast, he gave him a light, small push, and the man dropped his hands, gave forth one and a second word with pale lips, then sank in the darkness of death.

Volodyovski, not looking around, rushed on and pushed new victims to the earth.

The valiant Sweno took note of this terrible harvester, and summoning a few of the best horsemen he determined with the sacrifice of his own life to restrain even a little of the pursuit in order to save others. They turned therefore their horses, and pointing their rapiers waited with the points toward the pursuers. Volodyovski, seeing this, hesitated not a moment, spurred on his horse, and fell into the midst of them.

And before any one could have winked, two helmets had

fallen. More than ten rapiers were directed at once to the single breast of Volodyovski; but at that instant rushed in Pan Yan and Pan Stanislav, Yuzva Butrym, Zagloba and Roh Kovalski, of whom Zagloba related, that even when going to the attack he had his eyes closed in sleep, and woke only when his breast struck the breast of an enemy.

Volodyovski put himself under the saddle so quickly that the rapiers passed through empty air. He learned this method from the Tartars of Bailgorod; but being small and at the same time adroit beyond human belief, he brought it to such perfection that he vanished from the eye when he wished, either behind the shoulder or under the belly of the horse. So he vanished this time, and before the astonished Swedes could understand what had become of him he was erect on the saddle again, terrible as a wild-cat which springs down from lofty branches among frightened dogs.

Meanwhile his comrades gave him aid, and bore around death and confusion. One of the Swedes held a pistol to the very breast of Zagloba. Roh Kovalski, having that enemy on his left side, was unable to strike him with a sabre; but he balled his fist, struck the Swede's head in passing, and that man dropped under the horse as if a thunderbolt had met him, and Zagloba, giving forth a shout of delight, slashed in the temple Sweno himself, who dropped his hands and fell with his forehead to the horse's shoulder. At sight of this the other Swedes scattered. Volodyovski, Yuzva Footless, Pan Yan, and Pan Stanislav followed and cut them down before they had gone a hundred yards.

And the pursuit lasted longer. The Swedish horses had less and less breath in their bodies, and ran more and more slowly. At last from a thousand of the best horsemen, which had gone out under Kanneberg, there remained barely a hundred and some tens; the rest had fallen in a long belt over the forest road. And this last group was decreasing, for Polish hands ceased not to toil over them.

At last they came out of the forest. The towers of Yaroslav were outlined clearly in the azure sky. Now hope entered the hearts of the fleeing, for they knew that in Yaroslav was the king with all his forces, and at any moment he might come to their aid. They had forgotten that immediately after their passage the top had been taken from the last square of the bridge, so as to put stronger planks for the passage of cannon.

Whether Charnyetski knew of this through his spies, or wished to show himself of purpose to the Swedish king and cut down before his eyes the last of those unfortunate men, it is enough that not only did he not restrain the pursuit, but he sprang forward himself with the Shemberk squadron, slashed, cut with his own hand, pursuing the crowd in such fashion as if he wished with that same speed to strike Yaroslav.

At last they ran to within a furlong of the bridge; shouts from the field came to the Swedish camp. A multitude of soldiers and officers ran out from the town to see what was taking place beyond the river; they had barely looked when they saw and recognized the horsemen who had gone out of camp in the morning.

"Kanneberg's detachment! Kanneberg's detachment!" cried thousands of voices.

"Almost cut to pieces! Scarcely a hundred men are running!"

At that moment the king himself galloped up; with him Wittemberg, Forgell, Miller, and other generals.

The king grew pale. "Kanneberg!" said he.

"By Christ and his wounds! the bridge is not finished," cried Wittemberg; "the enemy will cut them down to the last man."

The king looked at the river, which had risen with spring waters, roaring with its yellow waves; to give aid by swimming was not to be thought of.

The few men still left were coming nearer.

Now there was a new cry: "The king's train and the guard are coming! They too will perish!"

In fact, it had happened that a part of the king's provision-chests with a hundred men of the infantry guard had come out at that moment by another road from adjoining forests. When they saw what had happened, the men of the escort, in the conviction that the bridge was ready, hastened with all speed toward the town.

But they were seen from the field by the Poles. Immediately about three hundred horsemen rushed toward them at full speed; in front of all, with sabre above his head and fire in his eyes, flew the tenant of Vansosh, Jendzian. Not many proofs had he given hitherto of his bravery; but at sight of the wagons in which there might be rich plunder, daring so rose in his heart that he went some tens of yards in advance of the others. The infantry at the wagons, seeing that they could not escape, formed themselves into a quadrangle, and a hundred muskets were directed at once at the breast of Jendzian. A roar shook the air, a line of smoke flew along the wall of the quadrangle; but before the smoke had cleared away the rider had urged on his horse so that the forefeet of the beast were above the heads of the men, and the lord tenant fell into the midst of them like a thunderbolt.

An avalanche of horsemen rushed after him. And as when wolves overcome a horse, and he, lying yet on his back, defends himself desperately with his hoofs, and they cover him completely and tear from him lumps of living flesh, so those wagons and the infantry were covered completely with a whirling mass of horses and riders. But terrible shouts rose from that whirl, and reached the ears of the Swedes standing on the other bank.

Meanwhile still nearer the bank the Poles were finishing the remnant of Kanneberg's cavalry. The whole Swedish army had come out like one man to the lofty bank of the San. Infantry, cavalry, artillery were mingled together; and all looked as if in an ancient circus in Rome at the spectacle; but they looked with set lips, with despair in their hearts, with terror and a feeling of helplessness. At moments from the breasts of those unwilling spectators was wrested a terrible cry. At moments a general weeping was heard; then again silence, and only the panting of the excited soldiers was audible. For that thousand men whom Kanneberg had led out were the front and the pride of the whole Swedish army; they were veterans, covered with glory in God knows how many lands, and God knows how many battles. But now they are running, like a lost flock of sheep, over the broad fields in front of the Swedish army, dying like sheep under the knife of the butcher. For that was no longer a battle, but a hunt. The terrible Polish horsemen circled about, like a storm, over the field of struggle, crying in various voices and running ahead of the Swedes. Sometimes a number less than ten, sometimes a group more than ten fell on one man. Sometimes one met one, sometimes the hunted Swede bowed down on the saddle as if to lighten the blow for the enemy, sometimes he withstood the brunt; but oftener he perished, for with edged weapons the Swedish soldiers were not equal to Polish nobles trained in all kinds of fencing.

But among the Poles the little knight was the most terrible of all, sitting on his cream-colored steed, which was as nimble and as swift as a falcon. The whole army noted him; for whomsoever he pursued he killed, whoever met him perished it was unknown how and when, with such small and insignificant movements of his sword did he hurl the sturdiest horsemen to the earth. At last he saw Kanneberg himself, whom more than ten men were chasing; the little knight shouted at them, stopped the pursuit by command, and attacked the Swede himself.

The Swedes on the other bank held the breath in their breasts. The king had pushed to the edge of the river and looked with throbbing heart, moved at once with alarm and hope; for Kanneberg, as a great lord and a relative of the king, was trained from childhood in every species of sword exercise by Italian masters; in fighting with edged weapons he had not his equal in the Swedish army. All eyes therefore were fixed on him now, barely did they dare to breathe; but he, seeing that the pursuit of the crowd had ceased, and wishing after the loss of his troops to save his own glory in the eyes of the king, said to his gloomy soul, —

"Woe to me if having first lost my men, I do not seal with my own blood the shame, or if I do not purchase my life by having overturned this terrible man. In another event, though the hand of God might bear me to that bank, I should not dare to look in the eyes of any Swede." When he had said this he turned his horse and rushed toward the yellow knight.

Since those Poles who had cut him off from the river had withdrawn, Kanneberg had the hope that if he should finish his opponent, he might spring into the water, and then what would be would be; if he could not swim the stormy stream, its current would bear him far with the horse, and his brothers would provide him some rescue.

He sprang therefore like a thunderbolt at the little knight, and the little knight at him. The Swede wished during the rush to thrust the rapier up to the hilt under the arm of his opponent; but he learned in an instant that though a master himself he must meet a master as well, for his sword merely slipped along the edge of the Polish sabre, only quivered somehow wonderfully in his hand, as if his arm had suddenly grown numb; barely was he able to defend himself from the blow which the knight then gave him; luckily at that moment their horses bore them away in opposite directions.

Both wheeled in a circle and returned simultaneously;

but they rode now more slowly against each other, wishing to have more time for the meeting and even to cross weapons repeatedly. Kanneberg withdrew into himself so that he became like a bird which presents to view only a powerful beak from the midst of upraised feathers. He knew one infallible thrust in which a certain Florentine had trained him, — infallible because deceitful and almost impossible to be warded off, — consisting in this: that the point of the sword was directed apparently at the breast, but by avoiding obstacles at the side it passed through the throat till the hilt reached the back of the neck. This thrust he determined to make now.

And, sure of himself, he approached, restraining his horse more and more; but Volodyovski rode toward him with short springs. For a moment he thought to disappear suddenly under the horse like a Tartar, but since he had to meet with only one man, and that before the eyes of both armies, though he understood that some unexpected thrust was waiting for him, he was ashamed to defend himself in Tartar and not in knightly fashion.

"He wishes to take me as a heron does a falcon with a thrust," thought Pan Michael to himself; "but I will use that windmill which I invented in Lubni."

And this idea seemed to him best for the moment; therefore it surrounded him like a glittering shield of light, and he struck his steed with his spurs and rushed on Kanneberg.

Kanneberg drew himself in still more, and almost grew to the horse; in the twinkle of an eye the rapier caught the sabre, and quickly he stuck out his head like a snake and made a ghastly thrust.

But in that instant a terrible whirling began to sound, the rapier turned in the hands of the Swede; the point struck empty space, but the curved end of the sabre fell with the speed of lightning on the face of Kanneberg, cut through a part of his nose, his mouth and beard, struck his shoulder-blade, shattered that, and stopped only at the sword-belt which crossed his shoulder.

The rapier dropped from the hands of the unfortunate man, and night embraced his head; but before he fell from his horse, Volodyovski dropped his own weapon and seized him by the shoulder.

The Swedes from the other bank roared with one outburst, but Zagloba sprang to the little knight.

"Pan Michael, I knew it would be so, but I was ready to avenge you!"

"He was a master," answered Volodyovski. "You take the horse, for he is a good one."

"Ha! if it were not for the river we could rush over and frolic with those fellows. I would be the first — "

The whistle of balls interrupted further words of Zagloba; therefore he did not finish the expression of his thoughts, but cried, —

"Let us go, Pan Michael; those traitors are ready to fire."

"Their bullets have no force, for the range is too great."

Meanwhile other Polish horsemen came up congratulating Volodyovski and looking at him with admiration; but he only moved his mustaches, for he was a cause of gladness to himself as well as to them.

But on the other bank among the Swedes, it was seething as in a beehive. Artillerists on that side drew out their cannons in haste; and in the nearer Polish ranks trumpets were sounded for withdrawal. At this sound each man sprang to his squadron, and in a moment all were in order. They withdrew then to the forest, and halted again, as if offering a place to the enemy and inviting them across the river. At last, in front of the ranks of men and horses, rode out on his dapple gray the man wearing a burka and a cap with a heron's feather, and bearing a gilded baton in his hand.

He was perfectly visible, for the reddish rays of the setting sun fell on him, and besides he rode before the regiments as if reviewing them. All the Swedes knew him at once, and began to shout, —

"Charnyetski! Charnyetski!"

He said something to the colonels. It was seen how he stopped longer with the knight who had slain Kanneberg, and placed his hand on his shoulder; then he raised his baton, and the squadrons began to turn slowly one after another to the pine-woods.

Just then the sun went down. In Yaroslav the bells sounded in the church; then all the regiments began to sing in one voice as they were riding away, "The Angel of the Lord announced to the Most Holy Virgin Mary;" and with that song they vanished from the eyes of the Swedes.

CHAPTER XXXI.

THAT evening the Swedes lay down to sleep without putting food into their mouths, and without hope that they would have anything to strengthen themselves with on the morrow. They were not able to sleep from the torment of hunger. Before the second cock-crow the suffering soldiers began to slip out of the camp singly and in crowds to plunder villages adjoining Yaroslav. They went like night-thieves to Radzymno, to Kanchuya, to Tychyno, where they hoped to find food of some kind. Their confidence was increased by the fact that Charnyetski was on the other side of the river; but even had he been able to cross, they preferred death to hunger. There was evidently a great relaxation in the camp, for despite the strictest orders of the king about fifteen hundred men went out in this way.

They fell to ravaging the neighborhood, burning, plundering, killing; but scarcely a man of them was to return. Charnyetski was on the other side of the San, it is true, but on the left bank were various " parties " of nobles and peasants; of these the strongest, that of Stjalkovski, formed of daring nobles of the mountains, had come that very night to Prohnik, as if led by the evil fate of the Swedes. When he saw the fire and heard the shots, Stjalkovski went straight to the uproar and fell upon the plunderers. They defended themselves fiercely behind fences; but Stjalkovski broke them up, cut them to pieces, spared no man. In other villages other parties did work of the same kind. Fugitives were followed to the very camp, and the pursuers spread alarm and confusion, shouting in Tartar, in Wallachian, in Hungarian, and in Polish; so that the Swedes thought that some powerful auxiliary of the Poles was attacking them, maybe the Khan with the whole horde.

Confusion began, and — a thing without example hitherto — panic, which the officers put down with the greatest effort. The king, who remained on horseback till daylight, saw what was taking place; he understood what might come of that, and called a council of war at once in the morning.

That gloomy council did not last long, for there were not two roads to choose from. Courage had fallen in the army, the soldiers had nothing to eat, the enemy had grown in power.

The Swedish Alexander, who had promised the whole world to pursue the Polish Darius even to the steppes of the Tartars, was forced to think no longer of pursuit, but of his own safety.

"We can return by the San to Sandomir, thence by the Vistula to Warsaw and to Prussia," said Wittemberg; "in that way we shall escape destruction."

Douglas seized his own head: "So many victories, so many toils, such a great country conquered, and we must return."

To which Wittemberg said: "Has your worthiness any advice?"

"I have not," answered Douglas.

The king, who had said nothing hitherto, rose, as a sign that the session was ended, and said,

"I command the retreat!"

Not a word further was heard from his mouth that day.

Drums began to rattle, and trumpets to sound. News that the retreat was ordered ran in a moment from one end of the camp to the other. It was received with shouts of delight. Fortresses and castles were still in the hands of the Swedes; and in them rest, food, and safety were waiting.

The generals and soldiers betook themselves so zealously to preparing for retreat that that zeal, as Douglas remarked, bordered on disgrace.

The king sent Douglas with the vanguard to repair the difficult crossings and clear the forests. Soon after him moved the whole army in order of battle; the front was covered by artillery, the rear by wagons, at the flanks marched infantry. Military supplies and tents sailed down the river on boats.

All these precautions were not superfluous; barely had the march begun, when the rearguard of the Swedes saw Polish cavalry behind, and thenceforth they lost it almost never from sight. Charnyetski assembled his own squadrons, collected all the "parties" of that region, sent to Yan Kazimir for reinforcements, and pursued. The first stopping-place, Pjevorsk, was at the same time the first place of alarm. The Polish divisions pushed up so closely that

several thousand infantry with artillery had to turn against
them. For a time the king himself thought that Charnyetski was really attacking; but according to his wont he only
sent detachment after detachment. These attacked with an
uproar and retreated immediately. All the night passed in
these encounters, — a troublesome and sleepless night for
the Swedes.

The whole march, all the following nights and days
were to be like this one.

Meanwhile Yan Kazimir sent two squadrons of very well
trained cavalry, and with them a letter stating that the hetmans would soon march with cavalry, and that he himself
with the rest of the infantry and with the horde would
hasten after them. In fact, he was detained only by
negotiations with the Khan, with Rakotsy, and with the
court of Vienna. Charnyetski was rejoiced beyond measure by this news; and when the day after the Swedes advanced in the wedge between the Vistula and the San, he
said to Colonel Polyanovski, —

"The net is spread, the fish are going in."

"And we will do like that fisherman," said Zagloba, "who
played on the flute to the fish so that they might dance, and
when they would not, he pulled them on shore; then they
began to jump around, and he fell to striking them with a
stick, crying: 'Oh, such daughters! you ought to have
danced when I begged you to do so.'"

"They will dance," answered Charnyetski; "only let the
marshal, Pan Lyubomirski, come with his army, which
numbers five thousand."

"He may come any time," remarked Volodyovski.

"Some nobles from the foot-hills arrived to-day," said Zagloba; "they say that he is marching in haste; but whether
he will join us instead of fighting on his own account is
another thing."

"How is that?" asked Charnyetski, glancing quickly at
Zagloba.

"He is a man of uncommon ambition and envious of glory.
I have known him many years; I was his confidant and
made his acquaintance when he was still a lad, at the court
of Pan Krakovski. He was learning fencing at that time
from Frenchmen and Italians. He fell into terrible anger
one day when I told him that they were fools, not one of
whom could stand before me. We had a duel, and I laid
out seven of them one following the other. After that

Lyubomirski learned from me, not only fencing, but the military art. By nature his wit is a little dull; but whatever he knows he knows from me."

"Are you then such a master of the sword?" asked Polyanovski.

"As a specimen of my teaching, take Pan Volodyovski; he is my second pupil. From that man I have real comfort."

"True, it was you who killed Sweno."

"Sweno? If some one of you, gentlemen, had done that deed, he would have had something to talk about all his life, and besides would invite his neighbors often to dinner to repeat the story at wine; but I do not mind it, for if I wished to take in all I have done, I could pave the road from this place to Sandomir with such Swenos. Could I not? Tell me, any of you who know me."

"Uncle could do it," said Roh Kovalski.

Charnyetski did not hear the continuation of this dialogue, for he had fallen to thinking deeply over Zagloba's words. He too knew of Lyubomirski's ambition, and doubted not that the marshal would either impose his own will on him, or would act on his own account, even though that should bring harm to the Commonwealth. Therefore his stern face became gloomy, and he began to twist his beard.

"Oho!" whispered Zagloba to Pan Yan, "Charnyetski is chewing something bitter, for his face is like the face of an eagle; he will snap up somebody soon."

Then Charnyetski said: "Some one of you, gentlemen, should go with a letter from me to Lyubomirski."

"I am known to him, and I will go," said Pan Yan.

"That is well," answered Charnyetski; "the more noted the messenger, the better."

Zagloba turned to Volodyovski and whispered: "He is speaking now through the nose; that is a sign of great change."

In fact, Charnyetski had a silver palate, for a musket-ball had carried away his own years before at Busha. Therefore whenever he was roused, angry, and unquiet, he always began to speak with a sharp and clinking voice. Suddenly he turned to Zagloba: "And perhaps you would go with Pan Skshetuski?"

"Willingly," answered Zagloba. "If I cannot do anything, no man can. Besides, to a man of such great birth it will be more proper to send two."

Charnyetski compressed his lips, twisted his beard, and repeated as if to himself: "Great birth, great birth —"

"No one can deprive Lyubomirski of that," remarked Zagloba.

Charnyetski frowned.

"The Commonwealth alone is great, and in comparison with it no family is great, all of them are small; and I would the earth swallowed those who make mention of their greatness."

All were silent, for he had spoken with much vehemence; and only after some time did Zagloba say, —

"In comparison with the whole Commonwealth, certainly."

"I did not grow up out of salt, nor out of the soil, but out of that which pains me," said Charnyetski; "and the Cossacks who shot this lip through pained me, and now the Swedes pain me; and either I shall cut away this sore with the sabre, or die of it myself, so help me God!"

"And we will help you with our blood!" said Polyanovski.

Charnyetski ruminated some time yet over the bitterness which rose in his heart, over the thought that the marshal's ambition might hinder him in saving the country; at last he grew calm and said, —

"Now it is necessary to write a letter. I ask you, gentlemen, to come with me."

Pan Yan and Zagloba followed him, and half an hour later they were on horseback and riding back toward Radymno; for there was news that the marshal had halted there with his army.

"Yan," said Zagloba, feeling of the bag in which he carried Charnyetski's letter, "do me a favor; let me be the only one to talk to the marshal."

"But, father, have you really known him, and taught him fencing?"

"Hei! that came out of itself, so that the breath should not grow hot in my mouth, and my tongue become soft, which might easily happen from too long silence. I neither knew him nor taught him. Just as if I had nothing better to do than be a bear-keeper, and teach the marshal how to walk on hind legs! But that is all one; I have learned him through and through from what people tell of him, and I shall be able to bend him as a cook bends pastry. Only one thing I beg of you: do not say that we have a letter from Charnyetski, and make no mention of it till I give the letter myself."

"How is that? Should I not do the work for which I

was sent? In my life such a thing has not happened, and it will not happen! Even if Charnyetski should forgive me, I would not do that for ready treasure."

"Then I will draw my sabre and hamstring your horse so that you cannot follow me. Have you ever seen anything miscarry that I invented with my own head? Tell me, have you ever come into evil plight yourself with Zagloba's stratagems? Did Pan Michael come out badly, or your Helena, or any of you, when I freed you all from Radzivill's hands? I tell you that more harm than good may come of that letter; for Charnyetski wrote it in such agitation that he broke three pens. Finally, you can speak of it when my plans fail. I promise to give it then, but not before."

"If I can only deliver the letter, it is all one when."

"I ask for no more. Now on, for there is a terrible road before us."

They urged the horses, and went at a gallop. But they did not need to ride long, for the marshal's vanguard had not only passed Radymno, but Yaroslav; and Lyubomirski himself was at Yaroslav, and occupied the former quarters of the King of Sweden.

They found him at dinner, with the most important officers. But when the envoys were announced, Lyubomirski gave orders to receive them at once; for he knew the names, since they were mentioned at that time in the whole Commonwealth.

All eyes were turned on the envoys as they entered; the officers looked with especial admiration and curiosity at Pan Yan. When the marshal had greeted them courteously, he asked at once, —

"Have I that famous knight before me who brought the letters from besieged Zbaraj to the king?"

"I crept through," said Pan Yan.

"God grant me as many such officers as possible! I envy Pan Charnyetski nothing so much; as to the rest, I know that even my small services will not perish from the memory of men."

"And I am Zagloba," said the old knight, pushing himself forward.

Here he passed his eye around the assembly; and the marshal, as he wished to attract every one to himself, exclaimed, —

"Who does not know of the man who slew Burlai, the leader of the barbarians; of the man who raised Radzivill's army in rebellion — "

"And I led Sapyeha's army, who, if the truth is told, chose me, not him for leader," added Zagloba.

"And why did you wish, being able to have such a high office, to leave it and serve under Pan Charnyetski?"

Here Zagloba's eye gleamed at Skshetuski, and he said: "Serene great mighty marshal, from your worthiness I as well as the whole country take example how to resign ambition and self-interest for the good of the Commonwealth."

Lyubomirski blushed from satisfaction, and Zagloba, putting his hands on his hips, continued, —

"Pan Charnyetski has sent us to bow to your worthiness in his name and that of the whole army, and at the same time to inform you of the considerable victory which God has permitted us to gain over Kanneberg."

"I have heard of it already," said the marshal, dryly enough, in whom envy had now begun to move, "but gladly do I hear it again from an eyewitness."

Zagloba began at once to relate, but with certain changes, for the forces of Kanneberg grew in his mouth to two thousand men. He did not forget either to mention Sweno or himself, and how before the eyes of the king the remnant of the cavalry were cut to pieces near the river; how the wagons and three hundred men of the guards fell into the hands of the fortunate conquerors; in a word, the victory increased in his narrative to the dimensions of an unspeakable misfortune for the Swedes.

All listened with attention, and so did the marshal; but he grew gloomier and gloomier, his face was chilled as if by ice, and at last he said, —

"I do not deny that Charnyetski is a celebrated warrior, but still he cannot devour all the Swedes himself; something will remain for others to gulp."

"Serene great mighty lord," answered Zagloba, "it is not Pan Charnyetski who gained the victory."

"But who?"

"But Lyubomirski!"

A moment of universal astonishment followed. The marshal opened his mouth, began to wink, and looked at Zagloba with such an astonished gaze, as if he wished to ask: "Is there not a stave lacking in your barrel?"

Zagloba did not let himself be beaten from the track, but pouting his lips with great importance (he borrowed this gesture from Zamoyski), said, —

"I heard Charnyetski say before the whole army: 'It is

not our sabres that slay them; 't is the name of Lyubomirski that cuts them down. Since they have heard that he is right here marching on, their courage has so gone out of them that they see in every one of our soldiers the army of the marshal, and they put their heads under the knife like sheep.'"

If all the rays of the sun had fallen at once on the face of the marshal, that face could not have been more radiant.

"How is that?" asked he; "did Charnyetski himself say that?"

"He did, and many other things; but I do not know that 't is proper for me to repeat them, for he told them only to intimates."

"Tell! Every word of Pan Charnyetski deserves to be repeated a hundred times. He is an uncommon man, and I said so long ago."

Zagloba looked at the marshal, half closing his one eye, and muttered: "You have swallowed the hook; I'll land you this minute."

"What do you say?" asked the marshal.

"I say that the army cheered your worthiness in such fashion that they could not have cheered the king better; and in Pjevorsk, where we fought all night with the Swedes, wherever a squadron sprang out the men cried: 'Lyubomirski! Lyubomirski!' and that had a better effect than 'Allah!' and 'Slay, kill!' There is a witness here too, — Pan Skshetuski, no common soldier, and a man who has never told a lie in his life."

The marshal looked involuntarily at Pan Yan, who blushed to his ears, and muttered something through his nose. Meanwhile the officers of the marshal began to praise the envoys aloud, —

"See, Pan Charnyetski has acted courteously, sending such polished cavaliers; both are famous knights, and honey simply flows from the mouth of one of them."

"I have always understood that Pan Charnyetski was a well-wisher of mine, but now there is nothing that I would not do for him," cried the marshal, whose eyes were veiled with a mist from delight.

At this Zagloba broke into enthusiasm: "Serene great mighty lord, who would not render homage to you, who would not honor you, the model of all civic virtues, who recall Aristides in justice, the Scipios in bravery! I have read many books in my time, have seen much, have meditated much, and my soul has been rent from pain; for what have I seen in this Commonwealth ? The Opalinskis, the Radzeyovskis, the Radzivills, who by their personal pride, setting their own ambition above all things, were ready at every moment to desert the country for their own private gain. I thought further, this Commonwealth is lost through the viciousness of its own sons. But who has comforted me, who has consoled me in my suffering ? Pan Charnyetski, for he said : 'The Commonwealth has not perished, since Lyubomirski has risen up in it. These others,' said he, 'think of themselves alone; he is only looking, only seeking how to make an offering of his own interests on the common altar. These are pushing themselves forward; he is pushing himself back, for he wants to illustrate by his example. Now,' said he, ' he is marching with a powerful conquering army, and I have heard,' said he, ' that he wishes to give me the command over it, in order to teach others how they should sacrifice their ambition, though even just, for the country. Go, then,' said he, ' to Pan Lyubomirski, declare to him that I do not want the sacrifice, I do not desire it, since he is a better leader than I am ; since, moreover, not only as leader, but — God grant our Kazimir a long life ! — as king are we ready to choose him, and — we will choose him ! ' "

Here Zagloba was somewhat frightened lest he had passed the measure, and really after the exclamation, "We will choose him !" followed silence ; but before the magnate heaven opened ; he grew somewhat pale at first, then red, then pale again, and laboring heavily with his breast, said, after the silence of a moment, —

"The Commonwealth is and will ever remain in control of its own will, for on that ancient foundation do our liberties rest. But I am only a servant of its servants, and God is my witness that I do not raise my eyes to those heights at which a citizen should not gaze. As to command over the army, Pan Charnyetski must accept it. I demand it especially for this, to give an example to those who, having continually the greatness of their family in mind, are unwilling to recognize any authority whenever it is necessary to forget the greatness of their family for the good of the country. Therefore, though perhaps I am not such a bad leader, still I, Lyubomirski, enter willingly under the command of Charnyetski, praying to God only to send us victory over the enemy !"

"Roman ! Father of the country !" exclaimed Zagloba, seizing the marshal's hand and pressing it to his lips.

But at the same moment the old rogue turned his eye on Pan Yan, and began to wink time after time.

Thundering shouts were heard from the officers. The throng in the quarters increased with each moment.

" Wine ! " cried the marshal.

And when they brought in goblets he raised at once a toast to the king, then to Charnyetski, whom he called his leader, and finally to the envoys. Zagloba did not remain behind with the toasts, and he so caught the hearts of all that the marshal himself conducted them to the threshold, and the knights to the gates of Yaroslav.

At last Pan Yan and Zagloba were alone; then Zagloba stopped the road in front of Pan Yan, reined in his horse, and putting his hands on his hips, said, —

" Well, Yan, what do you think ? "

" God knows," answered Pan Yan, " that if I had not seen it with my own eyes and heard it with my own ears, I would not believe, even if an angel had told me."

" Ha ! do you know ? I will swear to you that Charnyetski himself at the most asked and begged Lyubomirski to go in company with him. And do you know what he would have done ? Lyubomirski would have gone alone; for if Charnyetski has adjured in the letter by the love of country, or if he mentioned private interests, and I am sure that he has, the marshal would have been offended at once, and would have said : ' Does he want to be my preceptor, and teach me how to serve the country ? ' I know those men ! Happily old Zagloba took the matter in hand, and hardly had he opened his mouth when Lyubomirski not only wanted to go with Charnyetski, but to go under his command. Charnyetski is killing himself with anxiety, but I will comfort him. Well, Yan, does Zagloba know how to manage the magnates ? "

" I tell you that I am not able to let the breath go from my lips from astonishment."

" I know them ! Show one of them a crown and a corner of the ermine robe, and you may rub him against the grain like a hound pup, and besides, he will bend up to you and present his back himself. No cat will so lick his chops, even if you hold before him a dinner of pure cheese. The eyes of the most honest of them will be bursting out from desire ; and if a scoundrel happens, such as the voevoda of Vilna, he is ready to betray the country. Oh, the vanity of man ! Lord Jesus ! if Thou hadst given me as many thousands of ducats as Thou hast created candidates for this crown, I should be a candidate myself. For if any of them imagines that I hold myself inferior to him, then may his stomach burst from his own pride. Zagloba is as good as Lyubomirski; in fortune alone is the difference. This is true, Yan. Do you think that I really kissed him on the hand? I kissed my own thumb, and shoved his hand up to my nose. Certain it is that since he is alive no one has so fooled him. I have spread him like butter on toast for Charnyetski. God grant our king as long a life as possible; but in case of election, I would rather give a vote to myself than to Lyubomirski. Roh Kovalski would give me another, and Pan Michael would strike down my opponents. As God lives! I would make you grand hetman of the kingdom straightway, and Pan Michael, after Sapyeha, grand hetman of Lithuania, — but Jendzian, treasurer. He would punish the Jews with taxes! But enough; the main thing is that I have caught Lyubomirski on a hook and put the line in Charnyetski's hand. For whomsoever the flour, it will be ground on the Swedes; and whose is the merit? What do you think? Should the chroniclers inscribe it to some one else? But I have no luck. It will be well even if Charnyetski does not break out on the old man for not having given the letter. Such is human gratitude. This is not my first, not my first — others are sitting in starostaships, and are grown around with fat, like badgers; but do you, old man, shake your poor stomach on a horse as before."

Here Zagloba waved his hand. "Human gratitude may go to the hangman! And whether in this or that position you must die, still it is pleasant to serve the country. The best reward is good company. As soon as a man is on horseback, then, with such comrades as you and Michael, he is ready to ride to the end of the world, — such is our Polish nature. If a German, a Frenchman, an Englishman, or a dark Spaniard is on horseback, he is ready at once to gallop into your eyes; but a Pole, having inborn patience, will endure much, and will permit even a Swedish fellow to pluck him; but when the limit is passed and the Pole whacks him in the snout, such a Swede will cover himself three times with his legs. For there is metal yet in the Poles, and while the metal lasts the Commonwealth will last. Beat that into yourself, Yan."

And so spoke Zagloba for a long time, for he was very glad; and whenever he was very glad he was talkative beyond usual measure, and full of wise sentences.

CHAPTER XXXII.

CHARNYETSKI, in truth, did not even dare to think that the marshal of the kingdom would put himself under his command. He wished merely joint action, and he feared that even that would not be attained because of the great ambition of Lyubomirski; for the proud magnate had mentioned more than once to his officers that he wished to attack the Swedes independently, for thus he could effect something; but if he and Charnyetski won a victory together, the whole glory would flow to Charnyetski.

Such was the case, in fact. Charnyetski understood the marshal's reasons, and was troubled. He was reading now, for the tenth time, the copy of the letter which he had sent from Pjevorsk, wishing to see if he had written anything to offend so irritable a man as Lyubomirski.

He regretted certain phrases; finally he began to regret, on the whole, that he had sent the letter. Therefore he was sitting gloomy in his quarters, and every little while he approached the window and looked out on the road to see if the envoys were not returning. The officers saw him through the window, and divined what was passing in his mind, for evident trouble was on his forehead.

"But look," said Polyanovski to Pan Michael, "there will be nothing pleasant, for the castellan's face has become spotted, and that is a bad sign."

Charnyetski's face bore numerous traces of small-pox, and in moments of great emotion or disquiet it was covered with white and dark spots. As he had sharp features, a very high forehead and cloudy, Jupiter brows, a bent nose, and a glance cutting straight through, when in addition those spots appeared, he became terrible. The Cossacks in their time called him the spotted dog; but in truth, he was more like a spotted eagle, and when he led men to the attack and his burka spread out like great wings, the likeness struck both his own men and the enemy.

He roused fear in these and those. During the Cossack wars leaders of powerful bands lost their heads when forced to act against Charnyetski. Hmelnitski himself feared him, but especially the counsels which he gave the king.

They brought upon the Cossacks the terrible defeat of Bere-stechko. But his fame increased chiefly after Berestechko, when, together with the Tartars, he passed over the steppes like a flame, crushed the uprisen crowds, took towns and trenches by storm, rushing with the speed of a whirlwind from one end of the Ukraine to the other.

With this same raging endurance was he plucking the Swedes now. "Charnyetski does not knock out my men, he steals them away," said Karl Gustav. But Charnyetski was tired of stealing away; he thought that the time had come to strike. But he lacked artillery and infantry alto-gether, without which nothing decisive could be done, nothing important effected; hence his eagerness for a junction with Lyubomirski, who had a small number of cannon, it is true, but brought with him infantry composed of mountaineers. These, though not over-much trained as yet, had still been under fire more than once, and might, for want of better, be used against the incomparable infantry legions of Karl Gustav.

Charnyetski, therefore, was as if in a fever. Not being able to endure in the house, he went outside, and seeing Volodyovski and Polyanovski, he asked, —

"Are the envoys not in sight?"

"It is clear that they are glad to see them," answered Volodyovski.

"They are glad to see them, but not glad to read my letter, or the marshal would have sent his answer."

"Pan Castellan," said Polyanovski, whom Charnyetski trusted greatly, "why be careworn? If the marshal comes, well; if not, we will attack as of old. As it is, blood is flow-ing from the Swedish pot; and we know that when a pot once begins to leak, everything will run out of it."

"There is a leak in the Commonwealth too," said Charny-etski. "If the Swedes escape this time, they will be rein-forced, succor will come to them from Prussia, our chance will be lost." Then he struck his side with his hand in sign of impatience. Just then was heard the tread of horses and the bass voice of Zagloba singing, —

> " Kaska to the bakehouse went her way,
> And Stah said to her, ' Take me in, let me in,
>   My love.
> For the snow is falling, and the wind is blowing;
> Where shall I, poor fellow, put my head
>   Till morning ? ' "

"It is a good sign! They are returning joyously," cried Polyanovski.

That moment the envoys, seeing Charnyetski, sprang from their saddles, gave their horses to an attendant, and went quickly to the entrance. Zagloba threw his cap suddenly into the air, and imitating the voice of the marshal so excellently that whoever was not looking on might be deceived, cried, —

"Vivat Pan Charnyetski, our leader!"

The castellan frowned, and asked quickly : "Is there a letter for me ? "

"There is not," answered Zagloba; "there is something better. The marshal with his army passes voluntarily under command of your worthiness."

Charnyetski pierced him with a look, then turned to Pan Yan, as if wishing to say: "Speak you, for this one has been drinking ! "

Zagloba was in fact a little drunk; but Skshetuski confirmed his words, hence astonishment was reflected on the face of the castellan.

"Come with me," said he to the two. "I beg you also," said he to Polyanovski and Pan Michael.

All entered his room. They had not sat down yet when Charnyetski asked : " What did he say to my letter ? "

" He said nothing," answered Zagloba, "and why he did not will appear at the end of my story; but now *incipiam* (I will begin)."

Here he told all as it had happened, — how he had brought the marshal to such a favorable decision. Charnyetski looked at him with growing astonishment, Polyanovski seized his own head, Pan Michael's mustaches were quivering.

"I have not known you hitherto, as God is dear to me!" cried Charnyetski, at last. "I cannot believe my own ears."

"They have long since called me Ulysses," said Zagloba, modestly.

"Where is my letter ? "

" Here it is."

" I must forgive you for not delivering it. He is a finished rogue ! A vice-chancellor might learn from him how to make treaties. As God lives, if I were king, I would send you to Tsargrad."

"If he were there, a hundred thousand Turks would be here now ! " cried Pan Michael.

To which Zagloba said: "Not one, but two hundred thousand, as true as I live."

"And did the marshal hesitate at nothing?" asked Charnyetski.

"He? He swallowed all that I put to his lips, just as a fat gander gulps pellets; his eyes were covered with mist. I thought that from delight he would burst, as a Swedish bomb bursts. With flattery that man might be taken to hell."

"If it can only be ground out on the Swedes, if it can only be ground out, and I have hope that it will be," said Charnyetski, delighted. "You are a man adroit as a fox; but do not make too much sport of the marshal, for another would not have done what he has to-day. Much depends on him. We shall march to Sandomir itself over the estates of the Lyubomirskis, and the marshal can raise with one word the whole region, command peasants to injure crossings, burn bridges, hide provisions in the forests. You have rendered a service which I shall not forget till death; but I must thank the marshal, for as I believe he has not done this from mere vanity."

Then he clapped his hands and cried: "A horse for me at once! Let us forge the iron while it is hot!" Then he turned to the colonels: "Come, all of you gentlemen, with me, so that the suite may be the most imposing."

"And must I go too?" asked Zagloba.

"You have built the bridge between me and the marshal, it is proper that you be the first to pass over. Besides, I think that they will see you gladly. Come, come, lord brother, or I shall say that you wished to leave a half-finished work."

"Hard to refuse. I must draw my belt tighter, however, lest I shake into nothing. Not much strength is left me, unless I fortify it with something."

"But with what?"

"Much has been told me of the castellan's mead which I have not tasted as yet, and I should like to know if it is better than the marshal's."

"We will drink a stirrup cup now, but after our return we shall not limit the cups in advance. You will find a couple of decanters of it in your own quarters."

Then the castellan commanded to bring goblets; they drank enough for brightness and good humor, mounted and rode away.

The marshal received Charnyetski with open arms, entertained him with food and drink, did not let him go till morning; but in the morning the two armies were joined, and marched farther under command of Charnyetski.

Near Syenyava the Poles attacked the Swedes again with such effect that they cut the rearguard to pieces and brought disorder into the main army. Only at daybreak did the artillery disperse them. At Lejaysk, Charnyetski attacked with still greater vigor. Considerable detachments of the Swedes were mired in soft places, caused by rains and inundations, and those fell into the hands of the Poles. The roads became of the worst for the Swedes. Exhausted, hungry, and tortured by desire of sleep, the regiments barely marched. More and more soldiers stopped on the way. Some were found so terribly reduced that they no longer wished to eat or drink, they only begged for death. Others lay down and died on hillocks; some lost presence of mind, and looked with the greatest indifference on the approaching pursuers. Foreigners, who were counted frequently in the ranks of the Swedes, began to disappear from the camp and go over to Charnyetski. Only the unbroken spirit of Karl Gustav held the remnant of its dying strength in the whole army.

For not only did an enemy follow the army; various "parties" under unknown leaders and bands of peasants crossed its road continually. Those bodies, unformed and not very numerous, could not, it is true, strike it with offensive warfare, but they wearied it mortally. And wishing to instil into the Swedes the conviction that Tartars had already come with assistance, all the Polish troops gave forth the Tartar shout; therefore " Allah ! Allah ! " was heard night and day without a moment's cessation. The Swedish soldiers could not draw breath, could not put aside their armor for an instant. More than once a few men alarmed the whole camp. Horses fell by tens, and were eaten immediately; for the transport of provisions had become impossible. From time to time the Polish horsemen found Swedish corpses terribly disfigured; here they recognized at once the hands of peasants. The greater part of the villages in the triangle between the San and the Vistula belonged to the marshal and his relatives; therefore all the peasants in those parts rose up as one man, for the marshal, unsparing of his own fortune, had announced that whoever took up arms would be freed from subjection. Scarcely had this news gone the round of the region when the peasants put their scythes on staffs and began to bring Swedish heads into camp: they brought them in every day till Lyubomirski was forced to prohibit that custom as unchristian. Then they brought in gloves and boots. The Swedes, driven to desperation, flayed those who fell into their hands; and the war became more and more dreadful. Some of the Polish troops adhered yet to the Swedes, but they adhered only through fear. On the road to Lejaysk many of them deserted; those who remained made such tumults in the camp daily that Karl Gustav gave orders to shoot a number of officers. This was the signal for a general withdrawal, which was effected sabre in hand. Few, if any, Poles remained; but Charnyetski, gaining new strength, attacked with still greater vigor.

The marshal gave most effectual assistance. During this period, which by the way was short, the nobler sides of Lyubomirski's nature gained, perhaps, the upper hand over his pride and self-love; therefore he omitted no toil, he spared neither his health nor his person, he led squadrons frequently, gave the enemy no rest; and as he was a good soldier he rendered good services. These, added to his later ones, would have secured him a glorious memory in the nation, were it not for that shameless rebellion which toward the end of his career he raised in order to hinder the reform of the Commonwealth.

But at this time he did everything to win glory, and he covered himself with it as with a robe. Pan Vitovski, the castellan of Sandomir, an old and experienced soldier, vied with him. Vitovski wished to equal Charnyetski himself; but he could not, for God had denied him greatness.

All three crushed the Swedes more and more, and with such effect that the infantry and cavalry regiments, to whom it came to form the rearguard on the retreat, marched with so much fear that a panic arose among them from the slightest cause. Then Karl Gustav decided to march always with the rearguard, so as to give courage by his presence.

But in the very beginning he almost paid for this position with his life. It happened that having with him a detachment of the life-guards, — the largest of all the regiments, for the soldiers in it were selected from the whole Scandinavian people, — the king stopped for refreshment at the village of Rudnik. When he had dined with the parish priest he de-

cided to sleep a little, since he had not closed his eyes the
night preceding. The life-guards surrounded the house, to
watch over the safety of the king. Meanwhile the priest's
horse-boy stole away from the village, and coming up to a
mare in the field, sprang upon her colt and raced off to
Charnyetski.

Charnyetski was ten miles distant at this time; but his
vanguard, composed of the regiment of Prince Dymitri
Vishnyevetski, was marching under Shandarovski, the lieutenant, about two miles behind the Swedes. Shandarovski
was just talking to Roh Kovalski, who had ridden up that
moment with orders from Charnyetski, when suddenly both
saw the lad flying toward them at all horse speed.

"What devil is that racing up so," asked Shandarovski, "and besides on a colt?"

"Some village lad," said Kovalski.

Meanwhile the boy had ridden to the front of the rank,
and only stopped when the colt, frightened at horses and
men, stood on his hind legs and dug his hoofs into the
earth. The youth sprang off, and holding the colt by the
mane, bowed to the knights.

"Well, what have you to say?" asked the lieutenant,
approaching him.

"The Swedes are with us at the priest's house; they say
that the king himself is among them!" said the youth, with
sparkling eyes.

"Many of them?"

"Not more than two hundred horses."

Shandarovski's eyes now flashed in their turn; but he
was afraid of an ambush, therefore he looked threateningly
at the boy and asked, —

"Who sent you?"

"Who was to send me? I jumped myself on the colt, I
came near falling, and lost my cap. It is well that the
Swedish carrion did not see me!"

Truth was beating out of the sunburned face of the youth;
he had evidently a great animosity against the Swedes,
— he was panting, his cheeks were burning, he stood
before the officers holding the mane of the colt with one
hand, his hair disordered, the shirt open on his bosom.

"Where is the rest of the Swedish army?" asked the
lieutenant.

"At daybreak so many passed that we could not count
them; those went farther, only cavalry remained. But

there is one sleeping at the priest's, and they say that he is the king."

"Boy," answered Shandarovski, "if you are lying, your head will fall; but if you speak the truth, ask what you please."

"As true as I live! I want nothing unless the great mighty lord officer would command to give me a sabre."

"Give him some blade," cried Shandarovski to his attendants, completely convinced now.

The other officers fell to inquiring of the boy where the house was, where the village, what the Swedes were doing.

"The dogs! they are watching. If you go straight they will see you; but I will take you behind the alder grove."

Orders were given at once, and the squadron moved on, first at a trot and then at a gallop. The youth rode before the first rank bareback on his colt without a bridle. He urged the colt with his heels, and every little while looked with sparkling eyes on the naked sabre.

When the village was in sight, he turned out of the willows and led by a somewhat muddy road to the alder grove, in which it was still muddier; therefore they slackened the speed of the horses.

"Watch!" said the boy; "they are about ten rods on the right from the end of the alder grove."

They advanced now very slowly, for the road was difficult and heavy; the cavalry horses sank frequently to their knees. At last the alder grove began to grow thinner, and they came to the edge of the open space.

Not more than three hundred yards distant, they saw a broad square rising somewhat, and in it the priest's house surrounded by poplars, among which were to be seen the tops of straw beehives. On the square were two hundred horsemen in rimmed helmets and breastplates.

The great horsemen sat on enormous lean horses, and were in readiness, — some with rapiers at their shoulders, others with muskets on their thighs; but they were looking in another direction toward the main road, from which alone they expected the enemy. A splendid blue standard with a golden lion was waving above their heads.

Farther on, around the house stood guards by twos. One was turned toward the alder grove; but because the sun shone brightly and struck his eyes, and in the alders, which were already covered with thick leaves, it was almost dark, he could not see the Polish horsemen.

In Shandarovski, a fiery horseman, the blood began to boil like water in a pot; but he restrained himself and waited till the ranks should be in order. Meanwhile Roh Kovalski put his heavy hand on the shoulder of the youth, —

"Listen, horsefly!" said he; "have you seen the king?"

"I saw him, great mighty lord!" whispered the lad.

"How did he look? How can he be known?"

"He is terribly black in the face, and wears red ribbons at his side."

"Did you see his horse?"

"The horse is black, with a white face."

"Look out, and show him to me."

"I will. But shall we go quickly?"

"Shut your mouth!"

Here they were silent; and Roh began to pray to the Most Holy Lady to permit him to meet Karl, and to direct his hand at the meeting.

The silence continued still a moment, then the horse under Shandarovski himself snorted. At that the horseman on guard looked, quivered as if something had been thrown at his saddle, and fired his pistol.

"Allah! Allah! Kill, slay! Uha-u, slay!" was heard in the alder grove; and the squadron, coming out of the shadow like lightning, rushed at the Swedes.

They struck into the smoke before all could turn front to them, and a terrible hewing began; only sabres and rapiers were used, for no man had time to fire. In the twinkle of an eye the Poles pushed the Swedes to the fence, which fell with a rattle under the pressure of the horses' rumps, and the Poles began to slash them so madly that they were crowded and confused. Twice they tried to close, and twice torn asunder they formed two separate bodies which in a twinkle divided into smaller groups; at last they were scattered as peas thrown by a peasant through the air with a shovel.

All at once were heard despairing voices: "The king, the king! Save the king!"

But Karl Gustav, at the first moment of the encounter, with pistols in hand and a sword in his teeth, rushed out. The trooper who held the horse at the door gave him the beast that moment; the king sprang on, and turning the corner, rushed between the poplars and the beehives to escape by the rear from the circle of battle.

Reaching the fence he spurred his horse, sprang over,

and fell into the group of his men who were defending
themselves against the right wing of the Poles, who had
just surrounded the house and were fighting with the Swedes
behind the garden.

"To the road!" cried Karl Gustav. And overturning
with the hilt of his sword the Polish horseman who was
raising his sabre above him, with one spring he came out
of the whirl of the fight; the Swedes broke the Polish
rank and sprang after him with all their force, as a herd of
deer hunted by dogs rush whither they are led by their
leader.

The Polish horsemen turned their horses after them, and
the chase began. Both came out on the highroad from
Rudnik to Boyanovka. They were seen from the front
yard where the main battle was raging, and just then it
was that the voices were heard crying, —

"The king, the king! Save the king!"

But the Swedes in the front yard were so pressed by Shandarovski that they could not think even of saving themselves; the king raced on then with a party of not more
than twelve men, while after him were chasing nearly
thirty, and at the head of them all Roh Kovalski.

The lad who was to point out the king was involved
somewhere in the general battle, but Roh himself recognized Karl Gustav by the knot of red ribbons. Then he
thought that his opportunity had come; he bent in the saddle, pressed his horse with the spurs, and rushed on like
a whirlwind.

The pursued, straining the last strength from their horses,
stretched along over the broad road. But the swifter and
lighter Polish horses began soon to gain on them. Roh
came up very quickly with the hindmost Swede; he rose
in his stirrups for a better blow, and cut terribly; with one
awful stroke he took off the arm and the shoulder, and
rushed on like the wind, fastening his eyes again on the
king.

The next horseman was black before his eyes; he hurled
him down. He split the head and the helmet of the third,
and tore farther, having the king, and the king only, in his
eye. Now the horses of the Swedes began to pant and fall;
a crowd of Polish horsemen overtook them and cut down
the riders in a twinkle.

Roh had already passed horses and men, so as not to lose
time; the distance between him and Karl Gustav began to

decrease. There were only two men between him and the king.

Now an arrow, sent from a bow by some one of the Poles, sang near the ear of Pan Roh, and sank in the loins of the rider rushing before him. The man trembled to the right and the left; at last he bent backward, bellowed with an unearthly voice, and fell from the saddle.

Between Roh and the king there was now only one man. But that one, wishing evidently to save the king, instead of fleeing turned his horse. Kovalski came up, and a cannon-ball does not sweep a man from the saddle as he hurled him to the ground; then, giving a fearful shout, he rushed forward like a furious stag.

The king might perhaps have met him, and would have perished inevitably; but others were flying on behind Roh, and arrows began to whistle; any moment one of them might wound his horse. The king, therefore, pressed his heels more closely, bent his head to the mane, and shot through the space in front of him like a sparrow pursued by a hawk.

But Roh began not only to prick his own horse with the spurs, but to beat him with the side of the sabre; and so they sped on one after the other. Trees, stones, willows, flashed before their eyes; the wind whistled in their ears. The king's hat fell from his head; at last he threw down his purse, thinking that the pitiless rider might be tempted by it and leave the pursuit; but Kovalski did not look at the purse, and rolled his horse on with more and more power till the beast was groaning from effort.

Roh had evidently forgotten himself altogether; for racing onward he began to shout in a voice in which besides threats there was also a prayer, —

"Stop, for God's mercy!"

Then the king's horse stumbled so violently that if the king had not held the bridle with all his power the beast would have fallen. Roh bellowed like an aurochs; the distance dividing him from Karl Gustav had decreased notably.

After a while the steed stumbled a second time, and again before the king brought him to his feet Roh had approached a number of yards.

Then he straightened himself in the saddle as if for a blow. He was terrible; his eyes were bursting out, his teeth were gleaming from under his reddish mustaches.

One more stumble of the horse, another moment, and the fate of the Commonwealth, of all Sweden, of the entire war would have been decided. But the king's horse began to run again; and the king, turning, showed the barrels of two pistols, and twice did he fire.

One of the bullets shattered the knee of Kovalski's horse; he reared, then fell on his forefeet, and dug the earth with his nose.

The king might have rushed that moment on his pursuer and thrust him through with his rapier; but at the distance of two hundred yards other Polish horsemen were flying forward; so he bent down again in his saddle, and shot on like an arrow propelled from the bow of a Tartar.

Kovalski freed himself from his horse. He looked for a while unconsciously at the fleeing man, then staggered like one drunk, sat on the road, and began to roar like a bear.

But the king was each instant farther, farther, farther! He began to diminish, to melt, and then vanished in the dark belt of pine scrub.

Meanwhile, with shouting and roaring, came on Kovalski's companions. There were fifteen of them whose horses held out. One brought the king's purse, another his hat, on which black ostrich feathers were fastened with diamonds. These two began to cry out, —

"These are yours, comrade! they belong to you of right."

Others asked: "Do you know whom you were chasing? That was Karl himself."

"As God is true! In his life he has never fled before any man as before you. You have covered yourself with immense glory!"

"And how many men did you put down before you came up with the king?"

"You lacked only little of freeing the Commonwealth in one flash, with your sabre."

"Take the purse!"

"Take the hat!"

"The horse was good, but you can buy ten such with these treasures."

Roh gazed at his comrades with dazed eyes; at last he sprang up and shouted, —

"I am Kovalski, and this is Pani Kovalski! Go to all the devils!"

"His mind is disturbed!" cried they.

"Give me a horse! I'll catch him yet," shouted Roh.

But they took him by the arms, and though he struggled they brought him back to Rudnik, pacifying and comforting him along the road.

"You gave him Peter!" cried they. "See what has come to this victor, this conqueror of so many towns and villages!"

"Ha, ha! He has found out Polish cavaliers!"

"He will grow tired of the Commonwealth. He has come to close quarters."

"Vivat, Roh Kovalski!"

"Vivat, vivat, the most manful cavalier, the pride of the whole army!"

And they fell to drinking out of their canteens. They gave Roh one, and he emptied the bottle at a draught.

During the pursuit of the king along the Boyanovka road the Swedes defended themselves in front of the priest's house with bravery worthy of their renowned regiment. Though attacked suddenly and scattered very quickly, they rallied as quickly around their blue standard, for the reason that they were surrounded by a dense crowd. Not one of them asked for quarter, but standing horse to horse, shoulder to shoulder, they thrust so fiercely with their rapiers that for a time victory seemed to incline to their side. It was necessary either to break them again, which became impossible since a line of Polish horsemen surrounded them completely, or to cut them to pieces. Shandarovski recognized the second plan as the better; therefore encircling the Swedes with a still closer ring, he sprang on them like a wounded falcon on a flock of long-billed cranes. A savage slaughter and press began. Sabres rattled against rapiers, rapiers were broken on the hilts of sabres. Sometimes a horse rose, like a dolphin above the sea waves, and in a moment fell in the whirl of men and horses. Shouts ceased; there were heard only the cry of horses, the sharp clash of steel, gasping from the panting breasts of the knights; uncommon fury had mastered the hearts of Poles and Swedes. They fought with fragments of sabres and rapiers; they closed with one another like hawks, caught one another by the hair, by mustaches, gnawed with their teeth; those who had fallen from their horses and were yet able to stand stabbed with their knives horses in the belly and men in the legs; in the smoke, in the steam from horses, in the terrible frenzy of

battle, men were turned into giants and gave the blows of
giants; arms became clubs, sabres lightning. Steel helmets
were broken at a blow, like earthen pots; heads were cleft;
arms holding sabres were swept away. They hewed
without rest; they hewed without mercy, without pity.
From under the whirl of men and horses blood began to
flow along the yard in streams.

The great blue standard was waving yet above the Swedish circle, but the circle diminished with each moment. As
when harvesters attack grain from two sides, and the sickles
begin to glitter, the standing grain disappears and the men
see one another more nearly each moment, thus did the
Polish ring become ever narrower, and those fighting on
one side could see the bent sabres fighting on the opposite
side.

Pan Shandarovski was wild as a hurricane, and ate into
the Swedes as a famished wolf buries his jaws in the flesh
of a freshly killed horse; but one horseman surpassed him
in fury, and that was the youth who had first let them know
that the Swedes were in Rudnik, and now had sprung in
with the whole squadron on the enemy. The priest's colt,
three years old, which till that time had walked quietly over
the land, shut in by the horses, could not break out of the
throng; you would have said he had gone mad, like his
master. With ears thrown back, with eyes bursting out
of his head, with erect mane, he pushed forward, bit, and
kicked; but the lad struck with his sabre as with a flail; he
struck at random, to the right, to the left, straight ahead;
his yellow forelock was covered with blood, the points of
rapiers had been thrust into his shoulders and legs, his
face was cut; but these wounds only roused him. He fought
with madness, like a man who has despaired of life and
wishes only to avenge his own death.

But now the Swedish body had decreased like a pile of
snow on which men are throwing hot water from every
side. At last around the king's standard less than twenty
men remained. The Polish swarm had covered them completely, and they were dying gloomily, with set teeth; no
hand was stretched forth, no man asked for mercy. Now
in the crowd were heard voices: "Seize the standard!
The standard!"

When he heard this, the lad pricked his colt and rushed
on like a flame. When every Swede had two or three
Polish horsemen against him, the lad slashed the standard-

bearer in the mouth; he opened his arms, and fell on the horse's mane. The blue standard fell with him.

The nearest Swede, shouting terribly, grasped after the staff at once; but the boy caught the standard itself, and pulling, tore it off in a twinkle, wound it in a bundle, and holding it with both hands to his breast, began to shout to the sky, —

"I have it, I won't give it! I have it, I won't give it!"

The last remaining Swedes rushed at him with rage; one thrust the flag through, and cut his shoulder.

Then a number of men stretched their bloody hands to the lad, and cried: "Give the standard, give the standard!"

Shandarovski sprang to his aid, and commanded: "Let him alone! He took it before my eyes; let him give it to Charnyetski himself."

"Charnyetski is coming!" cried a number of voices.

In fact, from a distance trumpets were heard; and on the road from the side of the field appeared a whole squadron, galloping to the priest's house. It was the Lauda squadron; and at the head of it rode Charnyetski himself. When the men had ridden up, seeing that all was over, they halted; and Shandarovski's soldiers began to hurry toward them.

Shandarovski himself hastened with a report to the castellan; but he was so exhausted that at first he could not catch breath, for he trembled as in a fever, and the voice broke in his throat every moment.

"The king himself was here: I don't know — whether he has escaped!"

"He has, he has!" answered those who had seen the pursuit.

"The standard is taken! There are many killed!"

Charnyetski, without saying a word, hurried to the scene of the struggle, where a cruel and woful sight presented itself. More than two hundred bodies of Swedes and Poles were lying like a pavement, one at the side of the other, and often one above the other. Sometimes one held another by the hair; some had died biting or tearing one another with their nails; and some again were closed as in a brotherly embrace, or they lay one with his head on the breast of his enemy. Many faces were so trampled that there remained nothing human in them; those not crushed by hoofs had their eyes open full of terror, the fierceness of

battle, and rage. Blood spattered on the softened earth
under the feet of Charnyetski's horse, which were soon
red above the fetlocks; the odor of blood and the sweat
of horses irritated the nostrils and stopped breath in the
breast.

The castellan looked on those corpses of men as the agri-
culturist looks on bound sheaves of wheat which are to fill
out his stacks. Satisfaction was reflected on his face. He
rode around the priest's house in silence, looked at the bodies
lying on the other side, beyond the garden; then returned
slowly to the chief scene.

"I see genuine work here, and I am satisfied with you,
gentlemen."

They hurled up their caps with bloody hands.

"Vivat Charnyetski!"

"God grant another speedy meeting. Vivat! vivat!"

And the castellan said: "You will go to the rear for rest.
But who took the standard?"

"Give the lad this way!" cried Shandarovski; "where
is he?"

The soldiers sprang for him, and found him sitting at the
wall of the stable near the colt, which had fallen from
wounds and was just breathing out his last breath. At the
first glance it did not seem that the lad would last long, but
he held the standard with both hands to his breast.

They bore him away at once, and brought him before
Charnyetski. The youth stood there barefoot, with disordered hair, with naked breast, his shirt and his jacket in
shreds, smeared with Swedish blood and his own, tottering,
bewildered, but with unquenched fire in his eyes.

Charnyetski was astounded at sight of him. "How is
this?" asked he. "Did he take the royal standard?"

"With his own hand and his own blood," answered Shandarovski. "He was the first also to let us know of the
Swedes; and afterward, in the thickest of the whirl, he did
so much that he surpassed me and us all."

"It is truth, genuine truth, as if some one had written
it!" cried others.

"What is thy name?" asked Charnyetski of the lad.

"Mihalko."

"Whose art thou?"

"The priest's."

"Thou hast been the priest's, but thou wilt be thy own!"
said Charnyetski.

Mihalko heard not the last words, for from his wounds and the loss of blood he tottered and fell, striking the castellan's stirrup with his head.

"Take him and give him every care. I am the guaranty that at the first Diet he will be the equal of you all in rank, as to-day he is the equal in spirit."

"He deserves it! he deserves it!" cried the nobles.

Then they took Mihalko on a stretcher, and bore him to the priest's house.

Charnyetski listened to the further report, which not Shandarovski gave, but those who had seen the pursuit of the king by Roh Kovalski. He was wonderfully delighted with that narrative, so that he caught his head, and struck his thighs with his hands; for he understood that after such an adventure the spirit must fall considerably in Karl Gustav.

Zagloba was not less delighted, and putting his hands on his hips, said proudly to the knights, —

"Ha! he is a robber, is n't he? If he had reached Karl, the devil himself could not have saved the king! He is my blood, as God is dear to me, my blood!"

In course of time Zagloba believed that he was Roh Kovalski's uncle.

Charnyetski gave orders to find the young knight; but they could not find him, for Roh, from shame and mortification, had crept into a barn, and burying himself in the straw, had fallen asleep so soundly that he came up with the squadron only two days later. But he still suffered greatly, and dared not show himself before the eyes of his uncle. His uncle, however, sought him out, and began to comfort him, —

"Be not troubled, Roh!" said he. "As it is, you have covered yourself with great glory; I have myself heard the castellan praise you: 'To the eye a fool,' said he, 'so that he looks as though he could not count three, and I see that he is a fiery cavalier who has raised the reputation of the whole army.'"

"The Lord Jesus has not blessed me," said Roh; "for I got drunk the day before, and forgot my prayers."

"Don't try to penetrate the judgments of God, lest you add blasphemy to other deeds. Whatever you can take on your shoulders take, but take nothing on your mind; if you do, you will fail."

"But I was so near that the sweat from his horse was

flying to me. I should have cut him to the saddle! Uncle thinks that I have no reason whatever!"

"Every creature," said Zagloba, "has its reason. You are a sprightly lad, Roh, and you will give me comfort yet more than once. God grant your sons to have the same reason in their fists that you have!"

"I do not want that! I am Kovalski, and this is Pani Kovalski."

CHAPTER XXXIII.

AFTER the affair at Rudnik the king advanced farther toward the point of the wedge between the San and the Vistula, and did not cease as before to march with the rearguard; for he was not only a famous leader, but a knight of unrivalled daring. Charnyetski, Vitovski, and Lyubomirski followed, and urged him on as a wild beast is urged to a trap. Detached parties made an uproar night and day around the Swedes. The retreating troops had less and less provisions; they were more and more wearied and drooping in courage, looking forward to certain destruction.

At last the Swedes enclosed themselves in the very corner where the two rivers meet, and rested. On one side the Vistula defended them, on the other the San, both overflowed, as usual in springtime; the third side of the triangle the king fortified with strong intrenchments, in which cannons were mounted.

That was a position not to be taken, but it was possible to die there from hunger. But even in that regard the Swedes gained better courage, for they hoped that the commandants would send them provisions by water from Cracow and other river fortresses. For instance, right there at hand was Sandomir, in which Colonel Schinkler had collected considerable supplies. He sent these in at once; therefore the Swedes ate, drank, slept; and when they woke they sang Lutheran psalms, praising God that he had saved them from such dire distress.

But Charnyetski was preparing new blows for them.

Sandomir in Swedish hands could always come to the aid of the main army. Charnyetski planned, therefore, to take the town with the castle at a blow, and cut off the Swedes.

"We will prepare a cruel spectacle for them," said he, at a council of war. "They will look on from the opposite bank when we strike the town, and they will not be able to give aid across the Vistula; and when we have Sandomir we will not let provisions come from Wirtz in Cracow."

Lyubomirski, Vitovski, and others tried to dissuade Charnyetski from that undertaking. "It would be well," said they, "to take such a considerable town, and we might injure the Swedes greatly; but how are we to take it? We have no infantry, siege guns we have not; it would be hard for cavalry to attack walls."

"But do our peasants," asked Charnyetski, "fight badly as infantry? If I had two thousand such as Mihalko, I would take not only Sandomir, but Warsaw."

And without listening to further counsel he crossed the Vistula. Barely had his summons gone through the neighborhood when a couple of thousand men hurried to him, one with a scythe, another with a musket, the third with carabine; and they marched against Sandomir.

They fell upon the place rather suddenly, and in the streets a fierce conflict set in. The Swedes defended themselves furiously from the windows and the roofs, but they could not withstand the onrush. They were crushed like worms in the houses, and pushed entirely out of the town. Schinkler took refuge, with the remnant of his forces, in the castle; but the Poles followed him with the same impetuosity. A storm against the gates and the walls began. Schinkler saw that he could not hold out, even in the castle; so he collected what he could of men, articles and supplies of provisions, and putting them on boats, crossed to the king, who looked from the other bank on the defeat of his men without being able to succor them.

The castle fell into the hands of the Poles; but the cunning Swede ·hen departing put under the walls in the cellars kegs of powder with lighted matches.

When he appeared before the king he told him of this at once, so as to rejoice his heart.

"The castle," said he, "will fly into the air with all the men. Charnyetski may perish."

"If that is true, I want myself to see how the pious Poles will fly to heaven," said the king; and he remained on the spot with all the generals.

In spite of the commands of Charnyetski, who foresaw deceit, the volunteers and the peasants ran around through the whole castle to seek hidden Swedes and treasure. The trumpets sounded an alarm for every man to take refuge in the town; but the searchers in the castle did not hear the trumpets, or would not heed them.

All at once the ground trembled under their feet, an awful thunder and a roar tore the air, a gigantic pillar of fire rose to the sky, hurling upward earth, walls, roofs, the whole castle, and more than five hundred bodies of those who had not been able to withdraw.

Karl Gustav held his sides from delight, and his favor-seeking courtiers began at once to repeat his words: "The Poles are going to heaven, to heaven!"

But that joy was premature; for none the less did Sandomir remain in Polish hands, and could no longer furnish food for the main army enclosed between the rivers.

Charnyetski disposed his camp opposite the Swedes, on the other side of the Vistula, and guarded the passage.

Sapyeha, grand hetman of Lithuania and voevoda of Vilna, came from the other side and took his position on the San.

The Swedes were invested completely; they were caught as it were in a vise.

"The trap is closed!" said the soldiers to one another in the Polish camps.

For every man, even the least acquainted with military art, understood that inevitable destruction was hanging over the invaders, unless reinforcements should come in time and rescue them from trouble.

The Swedes too understood this. Every morning officers and soldiers, coming to the shore of the Vistula, looked with despair in their eyes and their hearts at the legions of Charnyetski's terrible cavalry standing black on the other side.

Then they went to the San; there again the troops of Sapyeha were watching day and night, ready to receive them with sabre and musket.

To cross either the San or the Vistula while both armies stood near was not to be thought of. The Swedes might return to Yaroslav by the same road over which they had come, but they knew that in that case not one of them would ever see Sweden.

For the Swedes grievous days and still more grievous nights now began, for these days and nights were uproarious and quarrelsome. Again provisions were at an end.

Meanwhile Charnyetski, leaving command of the army to Lyubomirski and taking the Lauda squadron as guard, crossed the Vistula above the mouth of the San. to visit

Sapyeha and take counsel with him touching the future of the war.

This time the mediation of Zagloba was not needed to make the two leaders agree; for both loved the country more than each one himself, both were ready to sacrifice to it private interests, self-love, and ambition.

The Lithuanian hetman did not envy Charnyetski, nor did Charnyetski envy the hetman, but each did homage to the other; so the meeting between them was of such character that tears stood in the eyes of the oldest soldiers.

"The Commonwealth is growing, the dear country is rejoicing, when such sons of heroes take one another by the shoulders," said Zagloba to Pan Michael and Pan Yan. "Charnyetski is a terrible soldier and a true soul, but put Sapyeha to a wound and it will heal. Would there were more such men! The skin would fly off the Swedes, could they see this love of the greatest patriots. How did they conquer us, if not through the rancor and envy of magnates? Have they overcome us with force? This is how I understand! The soul jumps in a man's body at sight of such a meeting. I will guarantee, too, that it will not be dry; for Sapyeha loves a feast wonderfully, and with such a friend he will willingly let himself out."

"God is merciful! the evil will pass," said Pan Yan.

"Be careful that you do not blaspheme," said Zagloba; "every evil must pass, for should it last forever it would prove that the Devil governs the world, and not the Lord Jesus, who has mercy inexhaustible."

Their further conversation was interrupted by the sight of Babinich, whose lofty form they saw from a distance over the wave of other heads.

Pan Michael and Zagloba began to beckon to him, but he was so much occupied in looking at Charnyetski that he did not notice them at first.

"See," said Zagloba, "how thin the man has grown!"

"It must be that he has not done much against Boguslav," said Volodyovski; "otherwise he would be more joyful."

"It is sure that he has not, for Boguslav is before Marienburg with Steinbock, acting against the fortress."

"There is hope in God that he will do nothing."

"Even if he should take Marienburg," said Zagloba, "we will capture Karl Gustav right away; we shall see if they will not give the fortress for the king."

"See! Babinich is coming to us!" interrupted Pan Yan.

He had indeed seen them, and was pushing the crowd to both sides; he motioned with his cap, smiling at them from a distance. They greeted one another as good friends and acquaintances.

"What is to be heard? What have you done with the prince?" asked Zagloba.

"Evil, evil! But there is no time to tell of it. We shall sit down to table at once. You will remain here for the night; come to me after the feast to pass the night among my Tartars. I have a comfortable cabin; we will talk at the cups till morning."

"The moment a man says a wise thing it is not I who will oppose," said Zagloba. "But tell us why you have grown so thin?"

"That hell-dweller overthrew me and my horse like an earthen pot, so that from that time I am spitting fresh blood and cannot recover. There is hope in the mercy of our Lord Christ that I shall let the blood out of him yet. But let us go now, for Sapyeha and Charnyetski are beginning to make declarations and to be ceremonious about precedence, — a sign that the tables are ready. We wait for you here with great pleasure, for you have shed Swedish pig-blood in plenty."

"Let others speak of what I have done," said Zagloba; "it does not become me."

Meanwhile whole throngs moved on, and all went to the square between the tents on which were placed tables. Sapyeha in honor of Charnyetski entertained like a king. The table at which Charnyetski was seated was covered with Swedish flags. Mead and wine flowed from vats, so that toward the end both leaders became somewhat joyous. There was no lack of gladsomeness, of jests, of toasts, of noise; though the weather was marvellous, and the sun warm beyond wonder. Finally the cool of the evening separated the feasters.

Then Kmita took his guests to the Tartars. They sat down in his tent on trunks packed closely with every kind of booty, and began to speak of Kmita's expedition.

"Boguslav is now before Marienburg," said Pan Andrei, "though some say that he is at the elector's, with whom he is to march to the relief of the king."

"So much the better; then we shall meet! You young fellows do not know how to manage him; let us see what the old man will do. He has met with various persons, but not yet with Zagloba. I say that we shall meet, though Prince Yanush in his will advised him to keep far from Zagloba."

"The elector is a cunning man," said Pan Yan; "and if he sees that it is going ill with Karl, he will drop all his promises and his oath."

"But I tell you that he will not," said Zagloba. "No one is so venomous against us as the Prussian. When your servant who had to work under your feet and brush your clothes becomes your master by change of fortune, he will be sterner to you, the kinder you were to him."

"But why is that?" asked Pan Michael.

"His previous condition of service will remain in his mind, and he will avenge himself on you for it, though you have been to him kindness itself."

"What of that?" asked Pan Michael. "It often happens that a dog bites his master in the hand. Better let Babinich tell about his expedition."

"We are listening," said Pan Yan.

Kmita, after he had been silent awhile, drew breath and began to tell of the last campaign of Sapyeha against Boguslav, and the defeat of the latter at Yanov; finally how Prince Boguslav had broken the Tartars, overturned him with his horse, and escaped alive.

"But," interrupted Volodyovski, "you said that you would follow him with your Tartars, even to the Baltic."

"And you told me also in your time," replied Kmita, "how Pan Yan here present, when Bogun carried off his beloved maiden, forgot her and revenge because the country was in need. A man becomes like those with whom he keeps company; I have joined you, gentlemen, and I wish to follow your example."

"May the Mother of God reward you, as she has Pan Yan!" said Zagloba. "Still I would rather your maiden were in the wilderness than in Boguslav's hands."

"That is nothing!" exclaimed Pan Michael; "you will find her!"

"I have to find not only her person, but her regard and love."

"One will come after the other," said Pan Michael, "even if you had to take her person by force, as at that time — you remember?"

"I shall not do such a deed again."

Here Pan Andrei sighed deeply, and after a while he said, "Not only have I not found her, but Boguslav has taken another from me."

"A pure Turk! as God is dear to me!" cried Zagloba.

And Pan Yan inquired: "What other?"

"Oh, it is a long story, a long story," said Kmita. "There was a maiden in Zamost, wonderfully fair, who pleased Pan Zamoyski. He, fearing Princess Vishnyevetski, his sister, did not dare to be over-bold before her; he planned, therefore, to send the maiden away with me, as if to Sapyeha, to find an inheritance in Lithuania, but in reality to take her from me about two miles from Zamost, and put her in some wilderness where no one could stand in his way. But I sounded his intention. You want, thought I to myself, to make a pander of me; wait! I flogged his men, and the lady in all maidenly honor I brought to Sapyeha. Well, I say to you that the girl is as beautiful as a goldfinch, but honest. I am now another man, and my comrades, the Lord light their souls! are long ago dust in the earth."

"What sort of maiden was she?" asked Zagloba.

"From a respectable house, a lady-in-waiting on Princess Griselda. She was once engaged to a Lithuanian, Podbipienta, whom you, gentlemen, knew."

"Anusia Borzobogati!" shouted Volodyovski, springing from his place.

Zagloba jumped up too from a pile of felt. "Pan Michael, restrain yourself!"

But Volodyovski sprang like a cat toward Kmita. "Is it you, traitor, who let Boguslav carry her off?"

"Be not unjust to me," said Kmita. "I took her safely to the hetman, having as much care for her as for my own sister. Boguslav seized her, not from me, but from another officer with whom Pan Sapyeha sent her to his own family; his name was Glovbich or something, I do not remember well."

"Where is he now?"

"He is no longer living, he was slain; so at least Sapyeha's officers said. I was attacking Boguslav separately, with the Tartars; therefore I know nothing accurately save what I have told you. But noticing your changed face, I see that a similar thing has met us; the same man has wronged us, and since that is the case let us join against him to avenge the wrong and take vengeance in company. He is a great lord and a great knight, and still I think it

will be narrow for him in the whole Commonwealth, if he
has two such enemies."

"Here is my hand!" said Volodyovski. "Henceforth
we are friends for life and death. Whoever meets him
first will pay him for both. God grant me to meet him
first, for that I will let his blood out is as sure as that there
is Amen in 'Our Father.'"

Here Pan Michael began to move his mustaches terribly
and to feel of his sabre. Zagloba was frightened, for he
knew that with Pan Michael there was no joking.

"I should not care to be Prince Boguslav now," said he,
"even if some one should add Livonia to my title. It is
enough to have such a wildcat as Kmita against one, but
what will he do with Pan Michael? And that is not all;
I will conclude an alliance with you. My head, your
sabres! I do not know as there is a potentate in Christen-
dom who could stand against such an alliance. Besides,
the Lord God will sooner or later take away his luck, for it
cannot be that for a traitor and a heretic there is no punishment; as it is, Kmita has given it to him terribly."

"I do not deny that more than one confusion has met
him from me," said Pan Andrei. And giving orders to
fill the goblets, he told how he had freed Soroka from captivity. But he did not tell how he had cast himself first
at the feet of Radzivill, for at the very thought of that his
blood boiled.

Pan Michael was rejoiced while hearing the narrative,
and said at the end, —

"May God aid you, Yendrek! With such a daring man
one could go to hell. The only trouble is that we shall not
always campaign together, for service is service. They may
send me to one end of the Commonwealth and you to the
other. It is not known which will meet him first."

Kmita was silent a moment.

"In justice I should reach him — if only I do not come
out again with confusion, for I am ashamed to acknowledge
that I cannot meet that hell-dweller hand to hand."

"Then I will teach you all my secrets," said Pan Michael.

"Or I!" said Zagloba.

"Pardon me, your grace, I prefer to learn from Michael,"
said Kmita.

"Though he is such a knight, still I and Pani Kovalski
are not afraid of him, if only I had a good sleep," put in
Roh.

"Be quiet, Roh!" answered Zagloba; "may God not punish you through his hand for boasting."

"Oh, tfu! nothing will happen to me from him."

Poor Kovalski was an unlucky prophet, but it was steaming terribly from his forelock, and he was ready to challenge the whole world to single combat. Others too drank heavily to one another, and to the destruction of Boguslav and the Swedes.

"I have heard," said Kmita, "that as soon as we rub out the Swedes here and take the king, we shall march straight to Warsaw. Then surely there will be an end of the war. After that will come the elector's turn."

"Oh, that's it! that's it!" said Zagloba.

"I heard Sapyeha say that once, and he, as a great man, calculates better than others; he said: 'There will be a truce with the Swedes; with the Northerners there is one already, but with the elector we should not make any conditions. Pan Charnyetski,' he says, 'will go with Lyubomirski to Brandenburg, and I with the treasurer of Lithuania to Electoral Prussia; and if after that we do not join Prussia to the Commonwealth, it is because in our chancellery we have no such head as Pan Zagloba, who in autograph letters threatened the elector.'"

"Did Sapyeha say that?" asked Zagloba, flushing from pleasure.

"All heard him. And I was terribly glad, for that same rod will flog Boguslav; and if not earlier, we will surely reach him at that time."

"If we can finish with these Swedes first," said Zagloba. "Devil take them! Let them give up Livland and a million, I will let them off alive."

"The Cossack caught the Tartar, and the Tartar is holding him by the head!" said Pan Yan, laughing. "Karl is still in Poland; Cracow, Warsaw, Poznan, and all the most noted towns are in his hands, and father wants him to ransom himself. Hei, we shall have to work much at him yet before we can think of the elector."

"And there is Steinbock's army, and the garrisons, and Wirtz," put in Pan Stanislav.

"But why do we sit here with folded hands?" asked Roh Kovalski, on a sudden, with staring eyes; "cannot we beat the Swedes?"

"You are foolish, Roh," said Zagloba.

"Uncle always says one thing; but as I am alive, I saw

a boat at the shore. We might go and carry off even the sentry. It is so dark that you might strike a man on the snout and he would n't know who did it; before they could see we should return and exhibit the courage of cavaliers to both commanders. If you do not wish to go, I will go myself."

"The dead calf moved his tail, wonder of wonders!" said Zagloba, angrily.

But Kmita's nostrils began to quiver at once. "Not a bad idea! not a bad idea!" said he.

"Good for camp-followers, but not for him who regards dignity. Have respect for yourselves! You are colonels, but you wish to amuse yourselves with wandering thieves!"

"True, it is not very becoming," added Volodyovski. "We would better go to sleep."

All agreed with that idea; therefore they kneeled down to their prayers and repeated them aloud; after that they stretched themselves on the felt cloth, and were soon sleeping the sleep of the just.

But an hour later all sprang to their feet, for beyond the river the roaring of guns was heard; while shouts and tumult rose in Sapyeha's whole camp.

"Jesus! Mary!" exclaimed Zagloba. "The Swedes are coming!"

"What are you talking about?" asked Volodyovski, seizing his sabre.

"Roh, come here!" cried Zagloba, for in cases of surprise he was glad to have his sister's son near him.

But Roh was not in the tent.

They ran out on the square. Crowds were already before the tents, and all were making their way toward the river, for on the other side was to be seen flashing of fire, and an increasing roar was heard.

"What has happened, what has happened?" was asked of the numerous guards disposed along the bank.

But the guards had seen nothing. One of the soldiers said that he had heard as it were the plash of a wave, but as fog was hanging over the water he could see nothing; he did not wish therefore to raise the camp for a mere sound.

When Zagloba heard this he caught himself by the head in desperation, —

"Roh has gone to the Swedes! He said that he wished to carry off a sentry."

" For God's sake, that may be ! " cried Kmita.

" They will shoot the lad, as God is in heaven ! " continued Zagloba, in despair. " Worthy gentlemen, is there no help ? Lord God, that boy was of the purest gold ; there is not another such in the two armies ! What shot that idea into his stupid head ? Oh, Mother of God, save him in trouble ! "

" Maybe he will return ; the fog is dense. They will not see him."

" I will wait for him here even till morning. O Mother of God, Mother of God ! "

Meanwhile shots on the opposite bank lessened, lights went out gradually, and after an hour dull silence set in. Zagloba walked along the bank of the river like a hen with ducklings, and tore out the remnant of hair in his forelock ; but he waited in vain, he despaired in vain. The morning whitened the river, the sun rose, but Roh came not.

CHAPTER XXXIV.

ZAGLOBA in unbroken despair betook himself to Charnyetski, with a request that he would send to the Swedes
to see what had happened to Kovalski. Is he alive yet,
is he groaning in captivity, or has he paid with his life for
his daring ?

Charnyetski agreed to this willingly, for he loved Zagloba. Then comforting him in his suffering, he said, —

"I think your sister's son must be alive, otherwise the
water would have brought him ashore."

"God grant that he is!" answered Zagloba; "still it
would be hard for the water to raise him, for not only had
he a heavy hand, but his wit was like lead, as is shown by
his action."

"You speak justly," answered Charnyetski. "If he is
alive I ought to give orders to drag him with a horse over
the square, for disregard of discipline. He might alarm
the Swedish army, but he has alarmed both armies; besides, he was not free to touch the Swedes without command and my order. Is this a general militia or what
the devil, that every man has a right to act on his own
account ? "

"He has offended, I agree; I will punish him myself, if
only the Lord will bring him back."

"But I forgive him in remembrance of the Rudnik
affair. I have many prisoners to exchange, and more distinguished officers than Kovalski. Do you go to the Swedes
and negotiate about exchange; I will give two or three for
him if need be, for I do not wish to make your heart bleed.
Come to me for a letter to the king, and go quickly."

Zagloba sprang with rejoicing to Kmita's tent, and told
his comrades what had happened. Pan Andrei and Volodyovski exclaimed at once that they too would go with
him, for both were curious to see the Swedes; besides
Kmita might be very useful, since he spoke German almost as fluently as Polish.

Preparations did not delay them long. Charnyetski,
without waiting for the return of Zagloba, sent the letter

by a messenger; then they provided a piece of white cloth fixed to a pole, took a trumpeter, sat in a boat, and moved on.

At first they went in silence, nothing save the plash of oars was to be heard; at last Zagloba was somewhat alarmed and said, —

"Let the trumpeter announce us immediately, for those scoundrels are ready to fire in spite of the white flag."

"What do you say?" answered Volodyovski; "even barbarians respect envoys, and this is a civilized people."

"Let the trumpeter sound, I say. The first soldier who happens along will fire, make a hole in the boat, and we shall get into the water; the water is cold, and I have no wish to get wet through their courtesy."

"There, a sentry is visible!" said Kmita.

The trumpeter sounded. The boat shot forward quickly; on the other shore a hurried movement began, and soon a mounted officer rode up, wearing a yellow leather cap. When he had approached the edge of the water he shaded his eyes with his hand and began to look against the light. A few yards from the shore Kmita removed his cap in greeting; the officer bowed to him with equal politeness.

"A letter from Pan Charnyetski to the Most Serene King of Sweden!" cried Pan Andrei, showing the letter.

The guard standing on the shore presented arms. Pan Zagloba was completely reassured; presently he fixed his countenance in dignity befitting his position as an envoy, and said in Latin, —

"The past night a certain cavalier was seized on this shore; I have come to ask for him."

"I cannot speak Latin," answered the officer.

"Ignoramus!" muttered Zagloba.

The officer turned then to Pan Andrei, —

"The king is in the farther end of the camp. Be pleased, gentlemen, to stay here; I will go and announce you." And he turned his horse.

The envoys looked around. The camp was very spacious, for it embraced the whole triangle formed by the San and the Vistula. At the summit of the triangle lay Panyev, at the base Tarnobjeg on one side, and Rozvadov on the other. Apparently it was impossible to take in the whole extent at a glance; still, as far as the eye could reach, were to be seen trenches, embankments, earthworks, and fascines at which were cannons and men. In the very centre of the place, in Gojytsi, were the quarters of the king; there also the main forces of the army.

"If hunger does not drive them out of this place, we can do nothing with them," said Kmita. "The whole region is fortified. There is pasture for horses."

"But there are not fish for so many mouths," said Zagloba. "Lutherans do not like fasting food. Not long since they had all Poland, now they have this wedge; let them sit here in safety, or go back to Yaroslav."

"Very skilful men made these trenches," added Volodyovski, looking with the eye of a specialist on the work. "We have more swordsmen, but fewer learned officers; and in military art we are behind others."

"Why is that?" asked Zagloba.

"Why? It does not beseem me as a soldier who has served all his life in the cavalry, to say this, but everywhere infantry and cannon are the main thing; hence those campaigns and military manœuvres, marches, and countermarches. A man in a foreign army must devour a multitude of books and turn over a multitude of Roman authors before he becomes a distinguished officer; but there is nothing of that with us. Cavalry rushes into the smoke in a body, and shaves with its sabres; and if it does not shave off in a minute, then they shave it off."

"You speak soundly, Pan Michael; but what nation has won so many famous victories?"

"Yes, because others in old times warred in the same way, and not having the same impetus they were bound to lose; but now they have become wiser, and see what they are doing."

"Wait for the end. Place for me now the wisest Swedish or German engineer, and against him I will put Roh, who has never turned over books, and let us see."

"If you could put him," interrupted Kmita.

"True, true! I am terribly sorry for him. Pan Andrei, jabber a little in that dog's language of those breeches fellows, and ask what has happened to Roh."

"You do not know regular soldiers. Here no man will open his lips to you without an order; they are stingy of speech."

"I know that they are surly scoundrels. While if to our nobles, and especially to the general militia, an envoy comes, immediately talk, talk, they will drink gorailka with him, and will enter into political discussion with him; and see how these fellows stand there like posts and bulge out their eyes at us! I wish they would smother to the last man!"

In fact, more and more foot-soldiers gathered around the envoys, looking at them curiously. The envoys were dressed so carefully in elegant and even rich garments, that they made an imposing appearance. Zagloba arrested most attention, for he bore himself with almost senatorial dignity; Volodyovski was less considered, by reason of his stature.

Meanwhile the officer who received them first on the bank returned with another of higher rank, and with soldiers leading horses. The superior officer bowed to the envoys and said in Polish, —

"His Royal Grace asks you, gentlemen, to his quarters; and since they are not very near we have brought horses."

"Are you a Pole?" asked Zagloba.

"No, I am a Cheh, — Sadovski, in the Swedish service."

Kmita approached him at once. "Do you know me?"

Sadovski looked at him quickly. "Of course! At Chenstohova you blew up the largest siege gun, and Miller gave you to Kuklinovski. I greet you, greet you heartily as a famous knight."

"And what is going on with Kuklinovski?" asked Kmita.

"But do you not know?"

"I know that I paid him with that with which he wanted to treat me, but I left him alive."

"He died."

"I thought he would freeze to death," said Pan Andrei, waving his hand.

"Worthy Colonel," put in Zagloba, "have you not a certain Roh Kovalski?"

Sadovski laughed: "Of course."

"Praise be to God and the Most Holy Lady! The lad is alive and I shall get him. Praise be to God!"

"I do not know whether the king will be willing to yield him up," said Sadovski.

"But why not?"

"Because he has pleased him greatly. He recognized him at once as the same man who had pushed after him with such vigor at Rudnik. We held our sides listening to the narrative of the prisoner. The king asked: 'Why did you pick me out?' and he answered, 'I made a vow.' Then the king asked again, 'But will you do so again?' 'Of course!' answered the prisoner. The king began to laugh. 'Put away your vow,' said he, 'and I will give you your life and freedom.' 'Impossible!' 'Why?' 'For my uncle would proclaim me a fool.' 'And are you so sure that you could manage me in a hand-to-hand fight?' 'Oh, I could manage five men like you,' said he. Then the king asked again: 'And do you dare to raise your hand against majesty?' 'Yes,' said he, 'for you have a vile faith.' They interpreted every word to the king, and he was more and more pleased, and continued to repeat: 'This man has pleased me.' Then wishing to see whether in truth he had such strength, he gave orders to choose twelve of the strongest men in camp and bring them to wrestle in turn with the prisoner. But he is a muscular fellow! When I came away he had stretched out ten one after another, and not a man of them could rise again. We shall arrive just at the end of the amusement."

"I recognize Roh, my blood!" said Zagloba. "We will give for him even three famous officers!"

"You will find the king in good humor," said Sadovski, "which is a rare thing nowadays."

"Oh, I believe that!" answered the little knight.

Meanwhile Sadovski turned to Kmita, and asked how he had not only freed himself from Kuklinovski, but put an end to him. Kmita told him in detail. Sadovski, while listening, seized his own head with amazement; at last he pressed Kmita's hand again, and said, —

"Believe me, I am sincerely glad; for though I serve the Swedes, every true soldier's heart rejoices when a real cavalier puts down a ruffian. I must acknowledge to you that when a daring man is found among you, one must look with a lantern through the universe to find his equal."

"You are a courteous officer," said Zagloba.

"And a famous soldier, we know that," added Volodyovski.

"I learned courtesy and the soldier's art from you," answered Sadovski, touching his cap.

Thus they conversed, vying with one another in courtesy, till they reached Gojytsi, where the king's quarters were. The whole village was occupied by soldiers of various arms. Our envoys looked with curiosity at the groups scattered among the fences. Some, wishing to sleep away their hunger, were dozing around cottages, for the day was very clear and warm; some were playing dice on drums, drinking beer; some were hanging their clothes on the fences; others were sitting in front of the cottages singing Scandinavian songs, rubbing with brick-dust their breastplates and helmets, from which bright gleams went forth. In places they were cleaning horses, or leading them out; in a word, camp life was moving and seething under the bright sky.   There were men, it is true, who bore signs of terrible toil and hunger, but the sun covered their leanness with gold; besides, days of rest were beginning for those incomparable warriors, therefore they took courage at once, and assumed a military bearing.   Volodyovski admired them in spirit, especially the infantry regiments, famous through the whole world for endurance and bravery.   Sadovski gave explanations as they passed, saying, —

"This is the Smaland regiment of the royal guard.   This is the infantry of Delekarlia, the very best."

"In God's name, what little monsters are these ? " cried Zagloba on a sudden, pointing to a group of small men with olive complexions and black hair hanging on both sides of their heads.

"Those are Laplanders, who belong to the remotest Hyperboreans."

"Are they good in battle ?   It seems to me that I might take three in each hand and strike with their heads till I was tired."

"You could surely do so.   They are useless in battle.   The Swedes bring them for camp servants, and partly as a curiosity.   But they are the most skilful of wizards; each of them has at least one devil in his service, and some have five."

"How do they get such friendship with evil spirits ? " asked Kmita, making the sign of the cross.

"Because they wander in night, which with them lasts half a year or more ; and you know that it is easier to hold converse with the Devil at night."

"But have they souls ? "

"It is unknown; but I think that they are more in the nature of animals."

Kmita turned his horse, caught one of the Laplanders by the shoulders, raised him up like a cat, and examined him curiously; then he put him on his feet, and said, —

"If the king would give me one such, I would give orders to have him dried and hung up in the church in Orsha, where, among other curiosities, are ostrich eggs."

"In Lubni, at the parish church, there were jaws of a whale or even of a giant," said Volodyovski.

"Let us go on, for something evil will fall on us here," said Zagloba.

"Let us go," repeated Sadovski. "To tell the truth, I ought to have had bags put on your heads, as is the custom; but we have nothing here to hide, and that you have looked on the trenches is all the better for us."

They spurred on their horses, and after a while were before the castle at Gojytsi. In front of the gate they sprang from their saddles, and advanced on foot; for the king was before the house.

They saw a large number of generals and very celebrated officers. Old Wittemberg was there, Douglas, Löwenhaupt, Miller, Erickson, and many others. All were sitting on the balcony, a little behind the king, whose chair was pushed forward; and they looked on the amusement which Karl Gustav was giving himself with the prisoner. Roh had just stretched out the twelfth cavalier, and was in a coat torn by the wrestlers, panting and sweating greatly. When he saw his uncle in company with Kmita and Volodyovski, he thought at once that they too were prisoners. He stared at them, opened his mouth, and advanced a couple of steps; but Zagloba gave him a sign with his hand to stand quietly, and the envoy stood himself with his comrades before the face of the king.

Sadovski presented the envoys; they bowed low, as custom and etiquette demanded, then Zagloba delivered Charnyetski's letter.

The king took the letter, and began to read; meanwhile the Polish envoys looked at him with curiosity, for they had never seen him before. He was a man in the flower of his age, as dark in complexion as though born an Italian or a Spaniard. His long hair, black as a raven's wing, fell behind his ears to his shoulders. In brightness and color his eyes brought to mind Yeremi Vishnyevetski; his brows were greatly elevated, as if he were in continual astonishment. In the place where the brows approached, his forehead was raised in a large protuberance, which made him resemble a lion; a deep wrinkle above his nose, which did not leave him even when he was laughing, gave his face a threatening and wrathful expression. His lower lip protruded like that of Yan Kazimir, but his face was heavier and his chin larger; he wore mustaches in the form of cords, brushed out somewhat at the ends. In general, his face indicated an uncommon man, one of those who when they walk over the earth press blood out of it. There was in him grandeur, the pride of a monarch, the strength of a lion, and the quickness of genius; but though a kindly smile never left his mouth, there was lacking that kindness of heart which illuminates a face from within with a mild light, as a lamp placed in the middle of an alabaster urn lights it. He sat in the arm-chair, with crossed legs, the powerful calves of which were indicated clearly from under the black stockings, and blinking as was his wont, he read with a smile the letter from Charnyetski. Raising his lids, he looked at Pan Michael, and said, —

"I knew you at once; you slew Kanneberg."

All eyes were turned immediately on Volodyovski, who, moving his mustaches, bowed and answered, —

"At the service of your Royal Grace."

"What is your office?" asked the king.

"Colonel of the Lauda squadron."

"Where did you serve before?"

"With the voevoda of Vilna."

"And did you leave him with the others? You betrayed him and me."

"I was bound to my own king, not to your Royal Grace."

The king said nothing; all foreheads were frowning, eyes began to bore into Pan Michael; but he stood calmly, merely moving his mustaches time after time.

All at once the king said, —

"It is pleasant for me to know such a famous cavalier. Kanneberg passed among us as incomparable in hand-to-hand conflict. You must be the first sabre in the kingdom?"

"*In universo* (In the universe)!" said Zagloba.

"Not the last," answered Volodyovski.

"I greet you, gentlemen, heartily. For Pan Charnyetski I have a real esteem as for a great soldier, though he broke his word to me, for he ought to be sitting quietly till now in Syevej."

"Your Royal Grace," said Kmita, "Pan Charnyetski was not the first to break his word, but General Miller, who seized Wolf's regiment of royal infantry."

Miller advanced a step, looked in the face of Kmita, and began to whisper something to the king, who, blinking all the time, listened attentively; looking at Pan Andrei, he said at last, —

"I see that Pan Charnyetski has sent me chosen cavaliers. I know from of old that there is no lack of daring men among you; but there is a lack of faith in keeping promises and oaths."

"Holy are the words of your Royal Grace," answered Zagloba.

"How do you understand that ?"

"If it were not for this vice of our people, your Royal Grace would not be here."

The king was silent awhile ; the generals again frowned at the boldness of the envoys.

"Yan Kazimir himself freed you from the oath," said Karl, "for he left you and took refuge abroad."

"From the oath we can be freed only by the Vicar of Christ, who resides in Rome ; and he has not freed us."

"A truce to that!" said the king. "I have acquired the kingdom by this," here he struck his sword, "and by this I will hold it. I do not need your suffrages nor your oaths. You want war, you will have it. I think that Pan Charnyetski remembers Golembo yet."

"He forgot it on the road from Yaroslav," answered Zagloba.

The king, instead of being angry, smiled : "I'll remind him of it."

"God rules the world."

"Tell him to visit me ; I shall be glad to receive him. But he must hurry, for as soon as my horses are in condition I shall march farther."

"Then we shall receive your Royal Grace," said Zagloba, bowing and placing his hand slightly on his sabre.

"I see," said the king, "that Pan Charnyetski has sent in the embassy not only the best sabres, but the best mouth. In a moment you parry every thrust. It is lucky that the war is not of words, for I should find an opponent worthy of my power. But I will come to the question. Pan Charnyetski asks me to liberate this prisoner, offering two officers of distinction in return. I do not set such a low price on my soldiers as you think, and I have no wish to redeem them too cheaply; that would be against my own and their ambition. But since I can refuse Pan Charnyetski nothing, I will make him a present of this cavalier."

"Gracious Lord," answered Zagloba, "Pan Charnyetski did not wish to show contempt for Swedish officers, but compassion for me ; for this is my sister's son, and I, at the service of your Royal Grace, am Pan Charnyetski's adviser."

"In truth," said the king, "I ought not to let the prisoner go, for he has made a vow against me, unless he will give up his vow in view of this favor."

Here he turned to Roh, who was standing in front of the porch, and beckoned: "But come nearer, you strong fellow!"

Roh approached a couple of steps, and stood erect.

"Sadovski," said the king, "ask him if he will let me go in case I free him."

Sadovski repeated the king's question.

"Impossible!" cried Roh.

The king understood without an interpreter, and began to clap his hands and blink.

"Well, well! How can I set such a man free? He has twisted the necks of twelve horsemen, and promises me as the thirteenth. Good, good! the cavalier has pleased me. Is he Pan Charnyetski's adviser too? If he is, I will let him go all the more quickly."

"Keep your mouth shut!" muttered Zagloba to Roh.

"A truce to amusement!" said the king, suddenly. "Take him, and have still one more proof of my clemency. I can forgive, as the lord of this kingdom, since such is my will and favor; but I will not enter into terms with rebels."

Here the king frowned, and the smile left his face: "Whoso raises his hand against me is a rebel, for I am his lawful king. Only from kindness to you have I not punished hitherto as was proper. I have been waiting for you to come to your minds; but the hour will strike when kindness will be exhausted and the day of punishment will rise. Through your self-will and instability the country is flaming with fire; through your disloyalty blood is flowing. But I tell you the last days are passing; you do not wish to hear admonitions, you do not wish to obey laws, you will obey the sword and the gallows!"

Lightnings flashed in Karl's eyes. Zagloba looked on him awhile with amazement, unable to understand whence that storm had come after fair weather; finally he too began to grow angry,-therefore he bowed and said only, —

"We thank your Royal Grace."

Then he went off, and after him Kmita, Volodyovski, and Roh Kovalski.

"Gracious, gracious!" said Zagloba, "and before you can look around he bellows in your ear like a bear. Beautiful end to an embassy! Others give honor with a cup at parting, but he with the gallows! Let him hang dogs, not nobles! O my God! how grievously we have sinned against our king, who was a father, is a father, and will be a father, for there is a Yagyellon heart in him. And such a king traitors deserted, and went to make friendship with scarecrows from beyond the sea. We are served rightly, for we were not worthy of anything better. Gibbets! gibbets! He is fenced in, and we have squeezed him like curds in a bag, so that whey is coming out, and still he threatens with sword and gibbet. Wait awhile! The Cossack caught a Tartar, and the Tartar has him by the head. It will be closer for you yet. — Roh, I wanted to give you a slap on the face or fifty blows on a carpet, but I forgive you now since you acted so like a cavalier and promised to hunt him still farther. Let me kiss you, for I am delighted with you."

"Uncle is still glad!" said Roh.

"The gibbet and the sword! And he told that to my eyes," said Zagloba again, after a while. "You have protection! The wolf protects in the same fashion a sheep for his own eating. And when does he say that? Now, when there is goose skin on his own back. Let him take his Laplanders for counsellors, and with them seek Satan's aid. But the Most Holy Lady will help us, as she did Pan Bobola in Sandomir when powder threw him and his horse across the Vistula, and he was not hurt. He looked around to see where he was, and arrived in time to dine with the priest. With such help we will pull them all by the necks like lobsters out of a wicker trap."

CHAPTER XXXV.

ALMOST twenty days passed. The king remained continually at the junction of the rivers, and sent couriers to fortresses and commands in every direction toward Cracow and Warsaw, with orders for all to hasten to him with assistance. They sent him also provisions by the Vistula in as great quantities as possible, but insufficient. After ten days the Swedes began to eat horse-flesh; despair seized the king and the generals at thought of what would happen when the cavalry should lose their horses, and when there would be no beasts to draw cannon. From every side too there came unpleasant news. The whole country was blazing with war, as if some one had poured pitch over it and set fire. Inferior commands and garrisons could not hasten to give aid, for they were not able to leave the towns and villages. Lithuania, held hitherto by the iron hand of Pontus de la Gardie, rose as one man. Great Poland, which had yielded first of all, was the first to throw off the yoke, and shone before the whole Commonwealth as an example of endurance, resolve, and enthusiasm. Parties of nobles and peasants rushed not only on the garrisons in villages, but even attacked towns. In vain did the Swedes take terrible vengeance on the country, in vain did they cut off the hands of prisoners, in vain did they send up villages in smoke, cut settlements to pieces, raise gibbets, bring instruments of torture from Germany to torture insurgents. Whoso had to suffer, suffered; whoso had to die, died; but if he was a noble, he died with a sabre; if a peasant, with a scythe in his hand. And Swedish blood was flowing throughout all Great Poland; the peasants were living in the forests, even women rushed to arms; punishments merely roused vengeance and increased rage. Kulesha, Jegotski, and the voevoda of Podlyasye moved through the country like flames, and besides their parties all the pine-woods were filled with other parties. The fields lay untilled, fierce hunger increased in the land; but it twisted most the entrails of the Swedes, for they were confined in towns behind closed gates, and could not go to the open country. At last breath was failing in their bosoms.

In Mazovia the condition was the same. There the Bark-shoe people dwelling in forest gloom came out of their wildernesses, blocked the roads, seized provisions and couriers. In Podlyasye a numerous small nobility marched in thousands either to Sapyeha or to Lithuania. Lyubelsk was in the hands of the confederates. From the distant Russias came Tartars, and with them the Cossacks constrained to obedience.

Therefore all were certain that if not in a week in a month, if not in a month in two, that river fork in which Karl Gustav had halted with the main army of the Swedes would be turned into one great tomb to the glory of the nation; a great lesson for those who would attack the Commonwealth.

The end of the war was foreseen already; there were some who said that one way of salvation alone remained to Karl, — to ransom himself and give Swedish Livland to the Commonwealth.

But suddenly the fortune of Karl and the Swedes was bettered. Marienburg, besieged hitherto in vain, surrendered, March 20, to Steinbock. His powerful and valiant army had then no occupation, and could hasten to the rescue of the king.

From another direction the Markgraf of Baden, having finished levies, was marching also to the river fork with ready forces, and soldiers yet unwearied.

Both pushed forward, breaking up the smaller bands of insurgents, destroying, burning, slaying. Along the road they gathered in Swedish garrisons, took the smaller commands, and increased in power, as a river increases the more it takes streams to its bosom.

Tidings of the fall of Marienburg, of the army of Steinbock, and the march of the Markgraf of Baden came very quickly to the fork of the river, and grieved Polish hearts. Steinbock was still far away; but the markgraf, advancing by forced marches, might soon come up and change the whole position at Sandomir.

The Polish leaders then held a council in which Charny-etski, Sapyeha, Michael Radzivill, Vitovski, and Lyubo-mirski, who had grown tired of being on the Vistula, took part. At this council it was decided that Sapyeha with the Lithuanian army was to remain to watch Karl, and pre-

vent his escape, Charnyetski was to move against the
Markgraf of Baden and meet him as quickly as possible; if
God gave him victory, he would return to besiege Karl
Gustav.

Corresponding orders were given at once. Next morning the trumpets sounded to horse so quietly that they
were barely heard; Charnyetski wished to depart unknown
to the Swedes. At his recent camp-ground a number of
unoccupied parties of nobles and peasants took position
at once. They kindled fires and made an uproar, so that
the enemy might think that no one had left the place; but
Charnyetski's squadrons moved out one after another.
First marched the Lauda squadron, which by right should
have remained with Sapyeha; but since Charnyetski had
fallen greatly in love with this squadron, the hetman was
loath to take it from him. After the Lauda went the Vansovich squadron, chosen men led by an old soldier half of
whose life had been passed in shedding blood; then followed the squadron of Prince Dymitri Vishnyevetski, under
the same Shandarovski who at Rudnik had covered himself with immeasurable glory; then two regiments of
Vitovski's dragoons, two regiments of the starosta of
Yavorov; the famed Stapkovski led one; then Charnyetski's own regiment, the king's regiment under Polyanovski, and Lyubomirski's whole force. No infantry was
taken, because of haste; nor wagons, for the army went
on horseback.

All were drawn up together at Zavada in good strength
and great willingness. Then Charnyetski himself went
out in front, and after he had arranged them for the march,
he withdrew his horse somewhat and let them pass so as
to review well the whole force. The horse under him
sniffed, threw up his head and nodded, as if wishing to
greet the passing regiments; and the heart swelled in the
castellan himself. A beautiful view was before him. As
far as the eye reached a river of horses, a river of stern
faces of soldiers, welling up and down with the movement
of the horses; above them still a third river of sabres and
lances, glittering and gleaming in the morning sun. A
tremendous power went forth from them, and Charnyetski
felt the power in himself; for that was not some kind of
collection of volunteers, but men forged on the anvil of
battle, trained, exercised, and in conflict so "venomous"
that no cavalry on earth of equal numbers could withstand

them. Therefore Charnyetski felt with certainty, without doubt, that he would bear asunder with sabres and hoofs the army of the Markgraf of Baden; and that victory, felt in advance, made his face so radiant that it gleamed on the regiments.

"With God to victory!" cried he at last.

"With God! We will conquer!" answered mighty voices.

And that shout flew through all the squadrons like deep thunder through clouds. Charnyetski spurred his horse to come up with the Lauda squadron, marching in the van.

The army moved forward.

They advanced not like men, but like a flock of ravening birds which having wind of a battle from afar, fly to outstrip the tempest. Never, even among Tartars in the steppes, had any man heard of such a march. The soldiers slept in the saddles; they ate and drank without dismounting; they fed the horses from their hands. Rivers, forests, villages, were left behind them. Scarcely had peasants hurried out from their cottages to look at the army when the army had vanished behind clouds of dust in the distance. They marched day and night, resting only just enough to escape killing the horses.

At Kozyenitsi they came upon eight Swedish squadrons under Torneskiold. The Lauda men, marching in the van, first saw the enemy, and without even drawing breath sprang at them straightway and into the fire. Next advanced Shandarovski, then Vansovich, and then Stapkovski.

The Swedes, thinking that they had to deal with some mere common parties, met them in the open field, and two hours later there was not a living man left to go to the markgraf and tell him that Charnyetski was coming. Those eight squadrons were simply swept asunder on sabres, without leaving a witness of defeat. Then the Poles moved straight on to Magnushev, for spies informed them that the markgraf was at Varka with his whole army.

Volodyovski was sent in the night with a party to learn how the army was disposed, and what its power was.

Zagloba complained greatly of that expedition, for even the famed Vishnyevetski had never made such marches as this; therefore the old man complained, but he chose to go with Pan Michael rather than remain with the army.

"It was a golden time at Sandomir," said he, stretching himself in the saddle; "a man ate, drank, and looked at the besieged Swedes in the distance; but now there is not time even to put a canteen to your mouth. I know the military arts of the ancients, of the great Pompey and Cæsar; but Charnyetski has invented a new style. It is contrary to every rule to shake the stomach so many days and nights. The imagination begins to rebel in me from hunger, and it seems to me continually that the stars are buckwheat pudding and the moon cheese. To the dogs with such warfare! As God is dear to me, I want to gnaw my own horses' ears off from hunger."

"To-morrow, God grant, we shall rest after finishing the Swedes."

"I would rather have the Swedes than this tediousness! O Lord! O Lord! when wilt Thou give peace to this Commonwealth, and to Zagloba a warm place at the stove and heated beer, even without cream? Batter along, old man, on your nag, batter along, till you batter your body to death. Has any one there snuff? Maybe I could sneeze out this sleepiness through my nostrils. The moon is shining through my mouth, looking into my stomach, but I cannot tell what the moon is looking for there; it will find nothing. I repeat, to the dogs with such warfare!"

"If Uncle thinks that the moon is cheese, then eat it, Uncle," said Roh Kovalski.

"If I should eat you I might say that I had eaten beef; but I am afraid that after such a roast I should lose the rest of my wit."

"If I am an ox and Uncle is my uncle, then what is Uncle?"

"But, you fool, do you think that Althea gave birth to a firebrand because she sat by the stove?"

"How does that touch me?"

"In this way. If you are an ox, then ask about your father first, not about your uncle; for a bull carried off Europa, but her brother, who was uncle to her children, was a man for all that. Do you understand?"

"To tell the truth, I do not; but as to eating I could eat something myself."

"Eat the devil and let me sleep! What is it, Pan Michael? Why have we halted?"

"Varka is in sight," answered Volodyovski. "See, the church tower is gleaming in the moonlight."

"But have we passed Magnushev?"

"Magnushev is behind on the right. It is a wonder to

me that there is no Swedish party on this side of the river.
Let us go to those thickets and stop; perhaps God may send
us some informant."

Pan Michael led his detachment to the thicket, and disposed it about a hundred yards from the road on each side,
ordering the men to remain silent, and hold the bridles
closely so the horses might not neigh.

"Wait," said he. "Let us hear what is being done on
the other side of the river, and perhaps we may see something."

They stood there waiting; but for a long time nothing
was to be heard. The wearied soldiers began to nod in the
saddles. Zagloba dropped on the horse's neck and fell
asleep; even the horses were slumbering. An hour passed.
The accurate ear of Volodyovski heard something like the
tread of a horse on a firm road.

"Hold! silence!" said he to the soldiers.

He pushed out himself to the edge of the thicket, and
looked along the road. Th road was gleaming in the
moonlight like a silver ribbon; there was nothing visible
on it, still the sound ᶠ horses came nearer.

"They are coming surely!" said Volodyovski.

All held their horses more closely, each one restraining
his breath. Meanwhil on the road appeared a Swedish
party of thirty horsemen. They rode slowly and carelessly
enough, not in line, but in a straggling row. Some of the
soldiers were talking, others were singing in a low voice;
for the night, warm as in May, ᵃ ted on the ardent souls
of the soldiers. Without ᵤuspicion they passed near Pan
Michael, who was standing so hard by the edge of the
thicket that he could catch the odor of horses and the
smoke of pipes which the soldiers had lighted.

At last they vanished at the turn of the road. Volodyovski waited till the tramp had died in the distance; then
only did he go to his men and say to Pan Yan and Pan
Stanislav, —

"Let us drive them now, like geese, to the camp of the
castellan. Not a man must escape, lest he give warning."

"If Charnyetski does not let us eat then and sleep," said
Zagloba, "I will resign his service and return to Sapyo.
With Sapyo, when there is a battle, there is a battle; but
when there is a respite, there is a feast. If you had four
lips, he would give each one of them enough to do. He is
the leader for me! And in truth tell me by what devil are

we not serving with Sapyo, since this regiment belongs to him by right?"

"Father, do not blaspheme against the greatest warrior in the Commonwealth," said Pan Yan.

"It is not I that blaspheme, but my entrails, on which hunger is playing, as on a fiddle — "

"The Swedes will dance to the music," interrupted Volodyovski. "Now, gentlemen, let us advance quickly! I should like to come up with them exactly at that inn in the forest which we passed in coming hither."

And he led on the squadron quickly, but not too quickly. They rode into a dense forest in which darkness enclosed them. The inn was less than two miles distant. When Volodyovski had drawn near, he went again at a walk, so as not to alarm the Swedes too soon. When not more than a cannon-shot away, the noise of men was heard.

"They are there and making an uproar!" said Pan Michael.

The Swedes had, in fact, stopped at the inn, looking for some living person to give information. But the place was empty. Some of the soldiers were shaking up the main building; others were looking in the cow-house, in the shed, or raising the thatch on the roof. One half of the men remained on the square holding the horses of those who were searching.

Pan Michael's division approached within a hundred yards, and began to surround the inn with a Tartar crescent. Those of the Swedes standing in front heard perfectly, and at last saw men and horses; since, however, it was dark in the forest they could not see what kind of troops were coming; but they were not alarmed in the least, not admitting that others than Swedes could come from that point. At last the movement of the crescent astonished and disturbed them. They called at once to those who were in the buildings.

Suddenly a shout of "Allah!" was heard, and the sound of shots. In one moment dark crowds of soldiers appeared as if they had grown out of the earth. Now came confusion, a flash of sabres, oaths, smothered shouts; but the whole affair did not last longer than the time needed to say the Lord's Prayer twice.

There remained on the ground before the inn five bodies of men and horses; Volodyovski moved on, taking with him twenty-five prisoners.

They advanced at a gallop, urging the Swedish horses with the sides of their sabres, and arrived at Magnushev at daybreak. In Charnyetski's camp no one was sleeping; all were ready. The castellan himself came out leaning on his staff, thin and pale from watching.

"How is it?" asked he of Pan Michael. "Have you many informants?"

"Twenty-five prisoners."

"Did many escape?"

"All are taken."

"Only send you, soldier, even to hell! Well done! Take them at once to the torture, I will examine them."

Then the castellan turned, and when departing said, —

"But be in readiness, for perhaps we may move on the enemy without delay."

"How is that?" asked Zagloba.

"Be quiet!" said Volodyovski.

The prisoners, without being burned, told in a moment what they knew of the forces of the markgraf, — how many cannons he had, what infantry and cavalry. Charnyetski grew somewhat thoughtful; for he learned that it was really a newly levied army, but formed of the oldest soldiers, who had taken part in God knows how many wars. There were also many Germans among them, and a considerable division of French; the whole force exceeded that of the Poles by several hundred. But it appeared from the statements of the prisoners that the markgraf did not even admit that Charnyetski was near, and believed that the Poles were besieging Karl Gustav with all their forces at Sandomir.

The castellan had barely heard this when he sprang up and cried to his attendant: "Vitovski, give command to sound the trumpet to horse!"

Half an hour later the army moved and marched in the fresh spring morning through forests and fields covered with dew. At last Varka — or rather its ruins, for the place had been burned almost to the ground six years before — appeared on the horizon.

Charnyetski's troops were marching over an open flat; therefore they could not be concealed from the eyes of the Swedes. In fact they were seen; but the markgraf thought that they were various "parties" which had combined in a body with the intent of alarming the camp.

Only when squadron after squadron, advancing at a trot, appeared from beyond the forest, did a feverish activity rise in the Swedish camp. Charnyetski's men saw smaller divisions of horsemen and single officers hurrying between the regiments. The bright-colored Swedish infantry began to pour into the middle of the plain; the regiments formed one after another before the eyes of the Poles and were numerous, resembling a flock of many-colored birds. Over their heads were raised toward the sun quadrangles of strong spears with which the infantry shielded themselves against attacks of cavalry. Finally, were seen crowds of Swedish armored cavalry advancing at a trot along the wings; the artillery was drawn up and brought to the front in haste. All the preparations, all the movements were as visible as something on the palm of the hand, for the sun had risen clearly, splendidly, and lighted up the whole country.

The Pilitsa separated the two armies.

On the Swedish bank trumpets and kettle-drums were heard, and the shouts of soldiers coming with all speed into line. Charnyetski ordered also to sound the crooked trumpets, and advanced with his squadrons toward the river.

Then he rushed with all the breath of his horse to the Vansovich squadron, which was nearest the Pilitsa.

"Old soldier!" cried he to Vansovich, "advance for me to the bridge, there dismount and to muskets! Let all their force be turned on you! Lead on!"

Vansovich merely flushed a little from desire, and waved his baton. The men shouted and shot after him like a cloud of dust driven by wind.

When they came within three hundred yards of the bridge, they slackened the speed of their horses; then two thirds of them sprang from the saddles and advanced on a run to the bridge.

But the Swedes came from the other side; and soon muskets began to play, at first slowly, then every moment more briskly, as if a thousand flails were beating irregularly on a barn-floor. Smoke stretched over the river. Shouts of encouragement were thundering from one and the other command. The minds of both armies were bent to the bridge, which was wooden, narrow, difficult to take, but easy to defend. Still over this bridge alone was it possible to cross to the Swedes.

A quarter of an hour later Charnyetski pushed forward Lyubomirski's dragoons to the aid of Vansovich.

But the Swedes now attacked the opposite front with

artillery. They drew up new pieces one after another, and bombs began to fly with a howl over the heads of Vansovich's men and the dragoons, to fall in the meadow and dig into the earth, scattering mud and turf on those fighting.

The markgraf, standing near the forest in the rear of the army, watched the battle through a field-glass. From time to time he removed the glass from his eyes, looked at his staff, shrugged his shoulders and said with astonishment : " They have gone mad ; they want absolutely to force the bridge. A few guns and two or three regiments might defend it against a whole army."

Vansovich advanced still more stubbornly with his men; hence the defence grew still more resolute. The bridge became the central point of the battle, toward which the whole Swedish line was approaching and concentrating. An hour later the entire Swedish order of battle was changed, and they stood with flank to their former position. The bridge was simply covered with a rain of fire and iron. Vansovich's men were falling thickly; meanwhile orders came more and more urgent to advance absolutely.

" Charnyetski is murdering those men ! " cried Lyubomirski on a sudden.

Vitovski, as an experienced soldier, saw that evil was happening, and his whole body quivered with impatience; at last he could endure no longer. Spurring his horse till the beast groaned piteously, he rushed to Charnyetski, who during all this time, it was unknown why, was pushing men toward the river.

" Your grace," cried Vitovski, " blood is flowing for nothing ; we cannot carry that bridge ! "

" I do not want to carry it ! " answered Charnyetski.

" Then what does your grace want ? What must we do ? "

" To the river with the squadrons ! to the river ! And you to your place ! "

Here Charnyetski's eyes flashed such lightnings that Vitovski withdrew without saying a word.

Meanwhile the squadrons had come within twenty paces of the bank, and stood in a long line parallel with the bed of the river. None of the officers or the soldiers had the slightest suspicion of what they were doing.

In a flash Charnyetski appeared like a thunderbolt before the front of the squadrons. There was fire in his face, lightning in his eyes. A sharp wind had raised the burka on his shoulders so that it was like strong wings; his horse sprang and reared, casting fire from his nostrils. The castellan dropped his sword on its pendant, took the cap from his head, and with hair erect shouted to his division, —

"Gentlemen! the enemy defends himself with this water, and jeers at us! He has sailed through the sea to crush our fatherland, and he thinks that we in defence of it cannot swim through this river!"

Here he hurled his cap to the earth, and seizing his sabre pointed with it to the swollen waters. Enthusiasm bore him away, for he stood in the saddle and shouted more mightily still, —

"To whom God, faith, fatherland, are all, follow me!"

And pressing the horse with the spurs so that the steed sprang as it were into space, he rushed into the river. The wave plashed around him; man and horse were hidden under water, but they rose in the twinkle of an eye.

"After my master!" cried Mihalko, the same who had covered himself with glory at Rudnik; and he sprang into the water.

"After me!" shouted Volodyovski, with a shrill but thin voice; and he sprang in before he had finished shouting.

"O Jesus! O Mary!" bellowed Zagloba, raising his horse for the leap.

With that an avalanche of men and horses dashed into the river, so that it struck both banks with wild impetus. After the Lauda squadron went Vishnyevetski's, then Vitovski's, then Stapkovski's, after that all the others. Such a frenzy seized the men that the squadrons crowded one another in emulation; the shouts of command were mingled with the roar of the soldiers; the river overflowed the banks and foamed itself into milk in a moment. The current bore the regiments down somewhat; but the horses, pricked with spurs, swam like a countless herd of dolphins, snorting and groaning. They filled the river to such a degree that the mass of heads of horses and riders formed as it were a bridge on which a man might have passed with dry foot to the other bank.

Charnyetski swam over first; but before the water had dropped from him the Lauda squadron had followed him to land; then he waved his baton, and cried to Volodyovski, —

"On a gallop! Strike!"

And to the Vishnyevetski squadron under Shandarovski,— "With them!"

And so he sent the squadrons one after another, till he had sent all. He stood at the head of the last himself, and shouting, "In the name of God! with luck!" followed the others.

Two regiments of Swedish cavalry posted in reserve saw what was happening; but such amazement had seized the colonels that before they could move from their tracks the Lauda men, urging their horses to the highest speed, and sweeping with irresistible force, struck the first regiment, scattered that, as a whirlwind scatters leaves, hurled it against the second, brought that to disorder; then Shandarovski came up, and a terrible slaughter began, but of short duration; after a while the Swedish ranks were broken, and a disordered throng plunged forward toward the main army.

Charnyetski's squadron pursued them with a fearful outcry, slashing, thrusting, strewing the field with corpses.

At last it was clear why Charnyetski had commanded Vansovich to carry the bridge, though he had no thought of crossing it. The chief attention of the whole army had been concentrated on that point; therefore no one defended, or had time to defend, the river itself. Besides nearly all the artillery and the entire front of the Swedish army was turned toward the bridge; and now when three thousand cavalry were rushing with all impetus against the flank of that army, it was needful to change the order of battle, to form a new front, to defend themselves even well or ill against the shock. Now rose a terrible haste and confusion; infantry and cavalry regiments turned with all speed to face the enemy, straining themselves in their hurry, knocking one against another, not understanding commands in the uproar, acting independently. In vain did the officers make superhuman efforts; in vain did the markgraf move straightway the regiments of cavalry posted at the forest; before they came to any kind of order, before the infantry could put the butt ends of their lances in the ground to hold the points to the enemy, the Lauda squadron fell, like the spirit of death, into the very midst of their ranks; after it a second, a third, a fourth, a fifth, and a sixth squadron. Then began the day of judgment! The smoke of musketry fire covered, as if with a cloud, the whole scene of conflict; and in that cloud screams, seething, unearthly voices of despair, shouts of triumph, the sharp clang of steel, as if in an infernal forge, the rattling of muskets; at times a flag shone and fell in the smoke; then the gilded point of a regimental banner, and again you saw nothing; but a roar was heard more and more terrible, as if the earth had broken on a sudden under the river, and its waters were tumbling down into fathomless abysses.

Now on the flank other sounds were heard. This was Vansovich, who had crossed the bridge and was marching on the new flank of the enemy. After this the battle did not last long.

From out that cloud large groups of men began to push, and run toward the forest in disorder, wild, without caps, without helmets, without armor. Soon after them burst out a whole flood of people in the most dreadful disorder. Artillery, infantry, cavalry mingled together fled toward the forest at random, in alarm and terror. Some soldiers cried in sky-piercing voices; others fled in silence, covering their heads with their hands. Some in their haste threw away their clothing; others stopped those running ahead, fell down themselves, trampled one another; and right there behind them, on their shoulders and heads, rushed a line of Polish cavaliers. Every moment you saw whole ranks of them spurring their horses and rushing into the densest throngs of men. No one defended himself longer; all went under the sword. Body fell upon body. The Poles hewed without rest, without mercy, on the whole plain ; along the bank of the river toward the forest, as far as the eye could reach you saw merely pursued and pursuing; only here and there scattered groups of infantry offered an irregular, despairing resistance; the cannons were silent. The battle ceased to be a battle ; it had turned into a slaughter.

All that part of the army which fled toward the forest was cut to pieces; only a few squadrons of Swedish troopers entered it. After them the light squadrons of Poles sprang in among the trees.

But in the forest peasants were waiting for that unslain remnant, — the peasants who at the sound of the battle had rushed together from all the surrounding villages.

The most terrible pursuit, however, continued on the road to Warsaw, along which the main forces of the Swedes were fleeing. The young Markgraf Adolph struggled twice to cover the retreat; but beaten twice, he fell into captivity himself. His auxiliary division of French infantry, composed of four hundred men, threw away their arms; three thousand chosen soldiers, musketeers and cavalry, fled as far as Mnishev. The musketeers were cut down in Mnishev; the cavalry were pursued toward Chersk, until they were scattered completely through the forest, reeds, and brush; there the peasants hunted them out one by one on the morrow.

Before the sun had set, the army of Friederich, Markgraf of Baden, had ceased to exist.

On the first scene of battle there remained only the standard-bearers with their standards, for all the troops had followed the enemy. And the sun was well inclined to its setting when the first bodies of cavalry began to appear from the side of the forest and Mnishev. They returned with singing and uproar, hurling their caps in the air, firing from pistols. Almost all led with them crowds of bound prisoners. These walked at the sides of the horses they were without caps, without helmets, with heads drooping on their breasts, torn, bloody, stumbling every moment against the bodies of fallen comrades. The field of battle presented a terrible sight. In places, where the struggle had been fiercest, there lay simply piles of bodies half a spear-length in height. Some of the infantry still held in their stiffened hands long spears. The whole ground was covered with spears. In places they were sticking still in the earth; here and there pieces of them formed as it were fences and pickets. But on all sides was presented mostly a dreadful and pitiful mingling of bodies, of men mashed with hoofs, broken muskets, drums, trumpets, caps, belts, tin boxes which the infantry carried; hands and feet sticking out in such disorder from the piles of bodies that it was difficult to tell to what body they belonged. In those places specially where the infantry defended itself whole breastworks of corpses were lying.

Somewhat farther on, near the river, stood the artillery, now cold, some pieces overturned by the onrush of men, others as it were ready to be fired. At the sides of them lay the cannoneers now held in eternal sleep. Many bodies were hanging across the guns and embracing them with their arms, as if those soldiers wished still to defend them after death. The brass, spotted with blood and brains, glittered with ill omen in the beams of the setting sun. The golden rays were reflected in stiffened blood, which here and there formed little lakes. Its nauseating odor was mingled over the whole field with the smell of powder, the exhalation from bodies, and the sweat of horses.

Before the setting of the sun Charnyetski returned with the king's regiment, and stood in the middle of the field. The troops greeted him with a thundering shout. Whenever a detachment came up it cheered without end. He stood in the rays of the sun, wearied beyond measure, but all radiant, with bare head, his sword hanging on his belt, and he answered to every cheer, —

"Not to me, gentlemen, not to me, but to the name of God!"

At his side were Vitovski and Lyubomirski, the latter as bright as the sun itself, for he was in gilded plate armor, his face splashed with blood; for he had worked terribly and labored with his own hand as a simple soldier, but discontented and gloomy, for even his own regiments shouted, —

"Vivat Charnyetski, *dux et victor* (commander and conqueror)!"

Envy began then to dive into the soul of the marshal.

Meanwhile new divisions rolled in from every side of the field; each time an officer came up and threw a banner, captured from the enemy, at Charnyetski's feet. At sight of this rose new shouts, new cheers, hurling of caps into the air, and the firing of pistols.

The sun was sinking lower and lower.

Then in the one church that remained after the fire in Varka they sounded the Angelus; that moment all uncovered their heads. Father Pyekarski, the company priest, began to intone: "The Angel of the Lord announced unto the Most Holy Virgin Mary!" and a thousand iron breasts answered at once, with deep voices: "And she conceived of the Holy Ghost!"

All eyes were raised to the heavens, which were red with the evening twilight; and from that bloody battle-field began to rise a pious hymn to the light playing in the sky before night.

Just as they had ceased to sing, the Lauda squadron began to come up at a trot; it had chased the enemy farthest. The soldiers threw more banners at Charnyetski's feet. He rejoiced in heart, and seeing Volodyovski, urged his horse toward him and asked, —

"Have many of them escaped?"

Pan Michael shook his head as a sign that not many had

escaped, but he was so near being breathless that he was unable to utter one word; he merely gasped with open mouth, time after time, so that his breast was heaving. At last he pointed to his lips, as a sign that he could not speak. Charnyetski understood him and pressed his head.

"He has toiled!" said he; "God grant us more such."

Zagloba hurried to catch his breath, and said, with chattering teeth and broken voice, —

"For God's sake! The cold wind is blowing on me, and I am all in a sweat. Paralysis will strike me. Pull the clothes off some fat Swede and give them to me, for everything on me is wet, — wet, and it is wet in this place. I know not what is water, what is my own sweat, and what is Swedish blood. If I have ever expected in my life to cut down so many of those scoundrels, I am not fit to be the crupper of a saddle. The greatest victory of this war! But I will not spring into water a second time. Eat not, drink not, sleep not, and then a bath! I have had enough in my old years. My hand is benumbed; paralysis has struck me already; gorailka, for the dear God!"

Charnyetski, hearing this, and seeing the old man really covered completely with the blood of the enemy, took pity on his age and gave him his own canteen.

Zagloba raised it to his mouth, and after a while returned it empty; then he said, —

"I have gulped so much water in the Pilitsa, that we shall soon see how fish will hatch in my stomach; but that gorailka is better than water."

"Dress in other clothes, even Swedish," said Charnyetski.

"I'll find a big Swede for Uncle!" said Roh.

"Why should I have bloody clothes from a corpse?" said Zagloba; "take off everything to the shirt from that general whom I captured."

"Have you taken a general?" asked Charnyetski, with animation.

"Whom have I not taken, whom have I not slain?" answered Zagloba.

Now Volodyovski recovered speech: "We have taken the younger markgraf, Adolph; Count Falckenstein, General Wegier, General Poter Benzij, not counting inferior officers."

"But the Markgraf Friederich?" asked Charnyetski.

"If he has not fallen here, he has escaped to the forest; but if he has escaped, the peasants will kill him."

Volodyovski was mistaken in his previsions. The Markgraf Friederich with Counts Schlippenbach and Ehrenhain, wandering through the forest, made their way in the night to Chersk; after sitting there in the ruined castle three days and nights in hunger and cold, they wandered by night to Warsaw. That did not save them from captivity afterward; this time, however, they escaped.

It was night when Charnyetski came to Varka from the field. That was perhaps the gladdest night of his life, for such a great disaster the Swedes had not suffered since the beginning of the war. All the artillery, all the flags, all the officers, except the chief, were captured. The army was cut to pieces, driven to the four winds; the remnants of it were forced to fall victims to bands of peasants. But besides, it was shown that those Swedes who held themselves invincible could not stand before regular Polish squadrons in the open field. Charnyetski understood at last what a mighty result this victory would work in the whole Commonwealth, — how it would raise courage, how it would rouse enthusiasm; he saw already the whole Commonwealth, in no distant future, free from oppression, triumphant. Perhaps, too, he saw with the eyes of his mind the gilded baton of the grand hetman on the sky.

He was permitted to dream of this, for he had advanced toward it as a true soldier, as a defender of his country, and he was of those who grow not from salt nor from the soil, but from that which pains them.

Meanwhile he could hardly embrace with his whole soul the joy which flowed in upon him; therefore he turned to Lyubomirski, riding at his side, and said, —

"Now to Sandomir! to Sandomir with all speed! Since the army knows now how to swim rivers, neither the San nor the Vistula will frighten us!"

Lyubomirski said not a word; but Zagloba, riding a little apart in Swedish uniform, permitted himself to say aloud, —

"Go where you like, but without me, for I am not a weathercock to turn night and day without food or sleep."

Charnyetski was so rejoiced that he was not only not angry, but he answered in jest, —

"You are more like the belfry than the weathercock, since, as I see, you have sparrows in your head. But as to eating and rest it belongs to all."

To which Zagloba said, but in an undertone. "Whoso has a beak on his face has a sparrow on his mind."

CHAPTER XXXVI.

AFTER that victory Charnyetski permitted at last the army to take breath and feed the wearied horses; then he was to return to Sandomir by forced marches, and bend the King of Sweden to his fall.

Meanwhile Kharlamp came to the camp one evening with news from Sapyeha. Charnyetski was at Chersk, whither he had gone to review the general militia assembled at that town. Kharlamp, not finding the chief, betook himself at once to Pan Michael, so as to rest at his quarters after the long journey.

His friends greeted him joyously; but he, at the very beginning, showed them a gloomy face and said, —

" I have heard of your victory. Fortune smiled here, but bore down on us in Sandomir. Karl Gustav is no longer in the sack, for he got out, and, besides, with great confusion to the Lithuanian troops."

" Can that be ? " cried Pan Michael, seizing his head.

Pan Yan, Pan Stanislav, and Zagloba were as if fixed to the earth.

" How was it ? Tell, by the living God, for I cannot stay in my skin ! "

." Breath fails me yet," said Kharlamp; " I have ridden day and night, I am terribly tired. Charnyetski will come, then I will tell all from the beginning. Let me now draw breath a little."

" Then Karl has gone out of the sack. I foresaw that, did I not ? Do you not remember that I prophesied it ? Let Kovalski testify."

" Uncle foretold it," said Roh.

" And whither has Karl gone ? " asked Pan Michael.

" The infantry sailed down in boats; but he, with cavalry, has gone along the Vistula to Warsaw."

" Was there a battle ? "

" There was and there was not. In brief, give me peace, for I cannot talk."

" But tell me one thing. Is Sapyeha crushed altogether ? "

"How crushed! He is pursuing the king; but of course Sapyeha will never come up with anybody."

"He is as good at pursuit as a German at fasting," said Zagloba.

"Praise be to God for even this, that the army is intact!" put in Volodyovski.

"The Lithuanians have got into trouble!" said Zagloba. "Ah, it is a bad case! Again we must watch a hole in the Commonwealth together."

"Say nothing against the Lithuanian army," said Kharlamp. "Karl Gustav is a great warrior, and it is no wonder to lose against him. And did not you, from Poland, lose at Uistsie, at Volbor, at Suleyov, and in ten other places? Charnyetski himself lost at Golembo. Why should not Sapyeha lose, especially when you left him alone like an orphan?"

"But why did we go to a dance at Varka?" asked Zagloba, with indignation.

"I know that it was not a dance, but a battle, and God gave you the victory. But who knows, perhaps it had been better not to go; for among us they say that the troops of both nations (Lithuanian and Poland) may be beaten separately, but together the cavalry of hell itself could not manage them."

"That may be," said Volodyovski; "but what the leaders have decided is not for us to discuss. This did not happen, either, without your fault."

"Sapyo must have blundered; I know him!" said Zagloba.

"I cannot deny that," muttered Kharlamp.

They were silent awhile, but from time to time looked at one another gloomily, for to them it seemed that the fortune of the Commonwealth was beginning to sink, and yet such a short time before they were full of hope and confidence.

"Charnyetski is coming!" said Volodyovski; and he went out of the room.

The castellan was really returning; Volodyovski went to meet him, and began to call from a distance, —

"The King of Sweden has broken through the Lithuanian army, and escaped from the sack. There is an officer here with letters from the voevoda of Vilna."

"Bring him here!" cried Charnyetski. "Where is he?"

"With me; I will present him at once."

Charnyetski took the news so much to heart that he would not wait, but sprang at once from his saddle and entered Volodyovski's quarters.

All rose when they saw him enter; he barely nodded and said, —

"I ask for the letter!"

Kharlamp gave him a sealed letter. The castellan went to the window, for it was dark in the cottage, and began to read with frowning brow and anxious face. From instant to instant anger gleamed on his countenance.

"The castellan has changed," whispered Zagloba to Pan Yan; "see how his beak has grown red. He will begin to lisp right away, he always does when in anger."

Charnyetski finished the letter. For a time he twisted his beard with his whole hand; at last he called out with a jingling, indistinct voice, —

"Come this way, officer!"

"At command of your worthiness!"

"Tell me the truth," said Charnyetski, with emphasis, "for this narrative is so artfully put together that I am unable to get at the affair. But—tell me the truth, do not color it—is the army dispersed?"

"Not dispersed at all, your grace."

"How many days are needed to assemble it?"

Here Zagloba whispered to Pan Yan: "He wants to come at him from the left hand as it were."

But Kharlamp answered without hesitation, —

"Since the army is not dispersed, it does not need to be assembled. It is true that when I was leaving, about five hundred horse of the general militia could not be found, were not among the fallen; but that is a common thing, and the army does not suffer from that; the hetman has even moved after the king in good order."

"You have lost no cannon?"

"Yes, we lost four, which the Swedes, not being able to take with them, spiked."

"I see that you tell the truth; tell me then how everything happened."

"*Incipiam* (I will begin)," said Kharlamp. "When we were left alone, the enemy saw that there was no army on the Vistula, nothing but parties and irregular detachments. We thought—or, properly speaking, Pan Sapyeha thought—that the king would attack those, and he sent reinforcements, but not considerable, so as not to weaken himself. Meanwhile there was a movement and a noise among the Swedes, as in a beehive. Toward evening they began to come out in crowds to the San. We were at the voevoda's quarters. Pan Kmita, who is called Babinich now, a soldier of the first degree, came up and reported this. But Pan Sapyeha was just sitting down to a feast, to which a multitude of noble women from Krasnik and Yanov had assembled — for the voevoda is fond of the fair sex —"

"And he loves feasting!" interrupted Charnyetski.

"I am not with him; there is no one to incline him to temperance," put in Zagloba.

"Maybe you will be with him sooner than you think; then you can both begin to be temperate," retorted Charnyetski. Then he turned to Kharlamp: "Speak on!"

"Babinich reported, and the voevoda answered: 'They are only pretending to attack; they will undertake nothing! First,' said he, 'they will try to cross the Vistula; but I have an eye on them, and I will attack myself. At present,' said he, 'we will not spoil our pleasure, so that we may have a joyous time! We will eat and drink.' The music began to tear away, and the voevoda invited those present to the dance."

"I'll give him dancing!" interrupted Zagloba.

"Silence, if you please!" said Charnyetski.

"Again men rush in from the bank saying that there is a terrible uproar. 'That's nothing!' the voevoda whispered to the page; 'do not interrupt me!' We danced till daylight, we slept till midday. At midday we see that the intrenchments are bristling, forty-eight pound guns on them; and the Swedes fire from time to time. When a ball falls it is the size of a bucket; it is nothing for such a one to fill the eyes with dust."

"Give no embellishments!" interrupted Charnyetski; "you are not with the hetman."

Kharlamp was greatly confused, and continued: "At midday the voevoda himself went out. The Swedes under cover of these trenches began to build a bridge. They worked till evening, to our great astonishment; for we thought that as to building they would build, but as to crossing they would not be able to do that. Next day they built on. The voevoda put the troops in order, for he expected a battle."

"All this time the bridge was a pretext, and they crossed lower down over another bridge, and turned your flank?" interrupted Charnyetski.

Kharlamp stared and opened his mouth, he was silent in amazement; but at last said, —

"Then your worthiness has had an account already?"

"No need of that!" said Zagloba; "our grandfather guesses everything concerning war on the wing, as if he had seen it in fact."

"Speak on!" said Charnyetski.

"Evening came. The troops were in readiness, but with the first star there was a feast again. This time the Swedes passed over the second bridge lower down, and attacked us at once. The squadron of Pan Koshyts, a good soldier, was at the edge. He rushed on them. The general militia which was next to him sprang to his aid; but when the Swedes spat at them from the guns, they took to their heels. Pan Koshyts was killed, and his men terribly cut up. Now the general militia, rushing back in a crowd on the camp, put everything in disorder. All the squadrons that were ready advanced; but we effected nothing, lost cannon besides. If the king had had more cannon and infantry, our defeat would have been severe; but fortunately the greater number of the infantry regiments with the cannon had sailed away in boats during the night. Of this no one of us knew."

"Sapyo has blundered! I knew it beforehand!" cried Zagloba.

"We got the correspondence of the king," added Kharlamp, "which the Swedes dropped. The soldiers read in it that the king is to go to Prussia to return with the elector's forces, for, he writes, that with Swedish troops alone he cannot succeed."

"I know of that," said Charnyetski. "Pan Sapyeha sent me that letter." Then he muttered quietly, as if speaking to himself: "We must follow him to Prussia."

"That is what I have been saying this long time," put in Zagloba.

Charnyetski looked at him for a while in thoughtfulness. "It is unfortunate," said he, aloud; "for if I had returned to Sandomir the hetman and I should not have let a foot of them out alive. Well! it has passed and will not return. The war will be longer; but death is fated to this invasion and to these invaders."

"It cannot be otherwise!" cried the knights in chorus; and great consolation entered their hearts, though a short time before they had doubted.

Meanwhile Zagloba whispered something in Jendzian's ear; he vanished through the door, and soon returned with a decanter. Seeing this, Volodyovski inclined to the knee of the castellan.

"It would be an uncommon favor for a simple soldier," he began.

"I will drink with you willingly," said Charnyetski; "and do you know why? — because we must part."

"How is that?" cried the astonished Pan Michael.

"Sapyeha writes that the Lauda squadron belongs to the Lithuanian army, and that he sent it only to assist the forces of the kingdom; that now he will need it himself, especially the officers, of whom he has a great lack. My Volodyovski, you know how much I love you; it is hard for me to part with you, but here is the order. It is true Pan Sapyeha as a courteous man leaves the order in my power and discretion. I might not show it to you. — Well, it is as pleasant to me as if the hetman had broken my best sabre. I give you the order precisely because it is left to my discretion, and do your duty. To your health, my dear soldier!"

Volodyovski bowed again to the castellan's knees; but he was so distressed that he could not utter a word, and when Charnyetski embraced him tears ran in a stream over his yellow mustaches.

"I would rather die!" cried he, pitifully. "I have grown accustomed to toil under you, revered leader, and there I know not how it will be."

"Pan Michael, do not mind the order," cried Zagloba, with emotion. "I will write to Sapyo myself, and rub his ears for him fittingly."

But Pan Michael first of all was a soldier; therefore he flew into a passion, —

"But the old volunteer is ever sitting in you. You would better be silent when you know not the question. Service!"

"That is it," said Charnyetski.

CHAPTER XXXVII.

ZAGLOBA when he stood before the hetman did not answer his joyous greeting, but put his hands behind his back, pouted his lips, and looked on him like a just but stern judge. Sapyeha was pleased when he saw that mien, for he expected some pleasantry and said, —

"How are you, old rogue? Why twist your nose as if you had found some unvirtuous odor?"

"In the whole camp of Sapyeha it smells of hashed meat and cabbage."

"Why? Tell me."

"Because the Swedes have cut up a great many cabbage-heads!"

"There you are! You are already criticising us. It is a pity they did not cut you up too."

"I was with a leader under whom we are the cutters, not the cut."

"The hangman take you! if they had even clipped your tongue!"

"Then I should have nothing to proclaim Sapyeha's victory with."

"Ah, lord brother, spare me! The majority already forget my service to the country, and belittle me altogether. I know too that there are many who make a great outcry against my person; still, had it not been for that rabble of a general militia, affairs might have gone differently. They say that I have neglected the enemy for night feasting; but the whole Commonwealth has not been able to resist that enemy."

Zagloba was somewhat moved at the words of the hetman, and answered, —

"Such is the custom with us, always to put the blame on the leader. I am not the man to speak evil of feasting, for the longer the day, the more needful the feast. Pan Charnyetski is a great warrior; still, according to my head, he has this defect, — that he gives his troops for breakfast, for dinner, and for supper nothing but Swedes' flesh. He is a

better leader than cook; but he acts ill, for from such food
war may soon become disgusting to the best cavaliers."

"Was Charnyetski very much enraged at me?"

"No, not very. In the beginning he showed a great
change; but when he discovered that the army was unbroken, he said at once: 'The will of God, not the might
of men! That is nothing! any general may lose a battle.
If we had Sapyehas only in the land, we should have a
country in which every man would be an Aristides.'"

"For Pan Charnyetski I would not spare my blood!"
answered Sapyeha. "Every other would have lowered me,
so as to exalt himself and his own glory, especially after a
fresh victory; but he is not that kind of man."

"I will say nothing against him but this, — that I am too
old for such service as he expects of soldiers, and especially
for those baths which he gives the army."

"Then are you glad to return to me?"

"Glad and not glad, for I hear of feasting for an hour,
but somehow I don't see it."

"We will sit down to the table this minute. But what
is Charnyetski undertaking now?"

"He is going to Great Poland to help those poor people;
from there he will march against Steinbock and to Prussia,
hoping to get cannon and infantry from Dantzig."

"The citizens of Dantzig are worthy people, and give a
shining example to the whole Commonwealth. We shall
meet Charnyetski at Warsaw, for I shall march there, but
will stop a little first around Lublin."

"Then have the Swedes besieged Lublin again?"

"Unhappy place! I know not how many times it has
been in the hands of the enemy. There is a deputation
here now from Lubelsk, and they will appear with a petition asking me to save them. But as I have letters
to despatch to the king and the hetmans, they must wait
awhile."

"I will go gladly to Lublin, for there the fair heads are
comely beyond measure, and sprightly. When a woman of
that place is cutting bread, and puts the loaf against herself, the crust on the lifeless bread blushes from delight."

"Oh, Turk!"

"Your worthiness, as a man advanced in years, cannot
understand this; but I, like May, must let my blood out
yet."

"But you are older than I."

"Only in experience, not in years. I have been able *conservare juventutem meam* (to preserve my youth), and more than one man has envied me that power. Permit me, your worthiness, to receive the Lubelsk deputation. I will promise to aid them at once; let the poor men comfort themselves before we comfort the poor women."

"That is well," said the hetman; "then I will write the letters." And he went out.

Immediately after were admitted the deputies from Lubelsk, whom Zagloba received with uncommon dignity and seriousness. He promised assistance on condition that they would furnish the army with provisions, especially with every kind of drink. When the conditions were settled, he invited them in the name of the voevoda to supper. They were glad, for the army marched that night toward Lublin. The hetman himself was active beyond measure, for it was a question with him of effacing the memory of the Sandomir defeat by some military success.

The siege began, but advanced rather slowly. During this time Kmita was learning from Volodyovski to work with the sabre, and made uncommon progress. Pan Michael, knowing that his art was to be used against Boguslav's neck, held back no secret. Often too they had better practice; for, approaching the castle, they challenged to single combat the Swedes, many of whom they slew. Soon Kmita had made such advance that he could meet Pan Yan on equal terms; no one in the whole army of Sapyeha could stand before him. Then such a desire to try Boguslav seized his soul that he was barely able to remain at Lublin, especially since the spring brought back to him strength and health. His wounds had healed, he ceased to spit blood, life played in him as of old, and fire gleamed in his eyes. At first the Lauda men looked at him frowningly; but they dared not attack, for Volodyovski held them with iron hand; and later, when they considered his acts and his deeds, they were reconciled completely, and his most inveterate enemy, Yuzva Butrym, said, —

"Kmita is dead; Babinich is living, let him live."

The Lubelsk garrison surrendered at last, to the great delight of the army; then Sapyeha moved his squadrons toward Warsaw. On the road they received tidings that Yan Kazimir himself, with the hetmans and a fresh army, was advancing to aid them. News came too from Charnyetski, who was marching to the capital from Great Poland.

The war, scattered through the whole country, was gather-ing at Warsaw, as a cloud scattered in the sky gathers and thickens to give birth to a storm with thunders and lightnings.

Sapyeha marched through Jelehi, Garvolin, and Minsk to the Syedlets highway, to join the general militia of Pod-lyasye. Pan Yan took command of this multitude; for though living in Lubelsk, he was near the boundary of Podlyasye, and was known to all the nobles, and greatly esteemed by them as one of the most famous knights in the Commonwealth. In fact, he soon changed that nobility, gal-lant by nature, into a squadron second in no way to regular troops.

Meanwhile they moved from Minsk forward to Warsaw very hastily, so as to stop at Praga one day. Fair weather favored the march. From time to time May showers sped past, cooling the ground and settling the dust; but on the whole the weather was marvellously fair, — not too hot, not too cold. The eye saw far through the transparent air. From Minsk they went mounted; the wagons and cannon were to follow next day. An immense eagerness reigned in the regiments; the dense forests on both sides of the whole road were ringing with echoes of military songs, the horses nodded as a good omen. The squadrons regularly and in order flowed on, one after the other, like a river shining and mighty; for Sapyeha led twelve thousand men, besides the general militia. The captains leading the regiments were gleaming in their polished cuirasses; the red flags waved like gigantic flowers above the heads of the knights.

The sun was well toward its setting when the first squadron, that of Lauda, marching in advance, beheld the towers of the capital. At sight of this, a joyful shout tore from the breasts of the soldiers.

"Warsaw! Warsaw!"

That shout flew like thunder through all the squadrons, and for some time was to be heard over two miles of road the word, "Warsaw! Warsaw!"

Many of Sapyeha's knights had never been in the capital; many of them had never seen it; therefore the sight made an uncommon impression on them. Involuntarily all reined in their horses; some removed their caps, others made the sign of the cross; tears streamed from the eyes of others, and they stood in silent emotion. All at once Sapyeha came out from the rear ranks on a white horse, and began to fly along the squadrons.

"Gentlemen!" cried he, in a piercing voice, "we are here first! To us luck, to us honor! We will drive the Swedes out of the capital!"

"We'll drive them! We'll drive them! We'll drive them!"

And there rose a sound and a thunder. Some shouted continually, "We'll drive them!" Others cried, "Strike, whoso has manhood!" Others, "Against them, the dog-brothers!" The rattle of sabres was mingled with the shouts of the knights. Eyes flashed lightning, and from under fierce mustaches teeth were gleaming. Sapyeha himself was sputtering like a pine torch. All at once he raised his baton, and cried, —

"Follow me!"

Near Praga the voevoda restrained the squadron and commanded a slow march. The capital rose more and more clearly out of the bluish distance. Towers were outlined in a long line on the azure of the sky. The red many-storied roofs of the Old City were gleaming in the evening light. The Lithuanians had never seen anything more imposing in their lives than those white lofty walls pierced with multitudes of narrow windows; those walls standing like lofty swamp-reeds over the water. The houses seemed to grow some out of others, high and still higher; but above that dense and close mass of walls with windows and roofs, pointed towers pierced the sky. Those of the soldiers who had been in the capital previously, either at an election or on private affairs, explained to the others what each pile meant and what name it bore. Zagloba especially, as a person of experience, told all to the Lauda men, and they listened to him eagerly, wondering at his words and the city itself.

"Look at that tower in the very centre of Warsaw! That is the citadel of the king. Oh that I could live as many years as I have eaten dinners at the king's table! I would twist Methuselah into a ram's horn. The king had no nearer confidant than me; I could choose among starosta-ships as among nuts, and give them away as easily as hob-nails. I have given promotion to multitudes of men, and when I came in senators used to bow to me to the girdle, in Cossack fashion. I fought duels also in presence of the king,

for he loved to see me at work; the marshal of the palace
had to close his eyes."

"That is a tremendous building!" said Roh Kovalski;
"and to think that these dogs have it all in hand!"

"And they plunder terribly," added Zagloba. "I hear
that they even take columns out of the walls and send them
to Sweden; these columns are of marble and other valuable
stones. I shall not recognize the dear corners; various
writers justly describe this castle as the eighth wonder of
the world. The King of France has a respectable palace,
but it is a fool in comparison with this one."

"And that other tower over there near it, on the right?"

"That is St. Yan. There is a gallery from the castle
to it. I had a vision in that church, for I remained behind
once after vespers; I heard a voice from the arches, crying,
'Zagloba, there will be war with such a son the Swedish
king, and great calamities will follow.' I was running with
all my breath to the king to tell him what I had heard, when
the primate caught me by the neck with his crosier. 'Don't
tell follies,' said he; 'you were drunk!' That other church
just at the side belongs to the Jesuit college; the third tower
at a distance is the law courts; the fourth at the right is the
marshals, and that green roof is the Dominicans. I could
not name them all, even if I could wield my tongue as well
as I do my sabre."

"It must be that there is not another such city in the
world," said one of the soldiers.

"That is why all nations envy us!" answered Zagloba.

"And that wonderful pile on the left of the castle?"

"Behind the Bernardines?"

"Yes."

"That is the Radzeyovski Palace, formerly the Kazanovski. It is considered the ninth wonder of the world; but
there is a plague on it, for in those walls began the misfortune of the Commonwealth."

"How is that?" asked a number of voices.

"When the vice-chancellor Radzeyovski began to dispute and quarrel with his wife, the king took her part.
You know, gentlemen, what people said of this; and it is
true that the vice-chancellor thought that his wife was in
love with the king, and the king with her; then afterward,
through hatred, he fled to the Swedes, and war began. To
tell the truth, I was in the country at the moment, and did
not see the end of the affair, I got it from hearsay; but I

know this, that she made sweet eyes, not at the king, but at some one else."

"At whom?"

Zagloba began to twirl his mustaches: "At him to whom all are hurrying like ants to honey; but it does not beseem me to mention his name, for I have always hated boastfulness. Besides, the man has grown old, and from sweeping out the enemy of the country, I am worn as a broom; but once there was no greater beauty and lovemaker than I. Let Roh Kovalski—"

Here Zagloba saw that by no means could Roh remember those times; therefore he waved his hand, and said, —

"But what does he know of this affair?"

Then he pointed out the palaces of Ossolinski and Konyetspolski, palaces which were in size almost equal to the Radzeyovski; finally the splendid villa Regia; and then the sun went down, and the darkness of night began to fill the air.

The thunder of guns was heard on the walls of Warsaw, and trumpets were sounded a considerable time and prolonged, in sign that the enemy was approaching.

Sapyeha also announced his coming by firing from muskets, to give courage to the inhabitants; and that night he began to transport his army across the Vistula. First the Lauda squadron passed; second the squadron of Pan Kotvich; then Kmita's Tartars; then Vankovich's squadron; after that, eight thousand men. In this way the Swedes, with their accumulated plunder, were surrounded and deprived of communication; but nothing remained to Sapyeha except to wait till Charnyetski from one side, and from the other Yan Kazimir with the hetmans of the kingdom, marched up, and meanwhile to see that no reinforcements stole through to the city.

The first news came from Charnyetski, but not overfavorable, for he reported that his troops and horses were so exhausted that at that moment he could not take part in the siege. From the time of the battle of Varka, they were under fire day after day; and from the first months of the year they had fought twenty-one great battles with the Swedes, not counting the engagements of scouting-parties and the attacks on smaller detachments. He had not obtained infantry in Pomerania, and had not been able to advance to Dantzig; he promised, at most, to hold in check with the rest of his forces that Swedish army which under the brother of the king, Radzivill, and Douglas, was stationed at Narev, and apparently was preparing to come to the aid of the besieged.

The Swedes prepared for defence with the bravery and skill peculiar to them. They burned Praga before the arrival of Sapyeha; they had begun already to throw bombs into all the suburbs, such as the Cracow and the Novy-Sviat, and on the other side against the church of St. Yerzy and the Virgin Mary. Then houses, great buildings, and churches flamed up. In the daytime smoke rolled over the city like clouds, thick and dark. At night those clouds became red, and bundles of sparks burst forth from them toward the sky. Outside the walls, crowds of people were wandering, without roofs over their heads, without bread; women surrounded Sapyeha's camp, and cried for charity; people were seen as thin as pincers from hunger; children were dying for want of food, in the arms of emaciated mothers; the suburbs were turned into a vale of tears and misery.

Sapyeha, having neither infantry nor cannon, waited and waited for the coming of the king. Meanwhile he aided the poor, sending them in groups to the less injured neighborhoods, in which they might survive in some way. He was troubled not a little when he foresaw the difficulties of the siege, for the skilled engineers of Sweden had turned Warsaw into a strong fortress. Behind the walls were three thousand trained soldiers, led by able and experienced generals; on the whole, the Swedes passed as masters in besieging and defending great fortresses. To solace this trouble, Sapyeha arranged daily feasts, during which the goblets circled freely; for that worthy citizen and uncommon warrior had this failing, — he loved company and the clatter of glasses above all things, and therefore neglected frequently service for pleasure.

His diligence in the daytime he balanced by negligence at night. Till sunset he worked faithfully, sent out scouts, despatched letters, inspected pickets himself, examined the informants brought in; but with the first star even fiddles were heard in his quarters. And when once he felt joyous he permitted everything, sent for officers even though on guard or appointed to scouting expeditions, and was angry if any one failed to appear, since for him there was no feast without a throng. In the morning Zagloba reproached him seriously, but in the night the servants bore Zagloba himself without consciousness to Volodyovski's quarters.

"Sapyeha would make a saint fall." he explained next day

to his friends; "and what must happen to me, who have been always fond of sport? Besides, he has some kind of special passion to force goblets on me, and I, not wishing to seem rude, yield to his pressing; this I do to avoid offending the host. But I have made a vow that at the coming Advent I shall have my back well covered with discipline (stripes), for I understand myself that this yielding cannot remain without penance; but now I have to keep on good terms with him, out of fear that I might fall into worse company and indulge myself altogether."

There were officers who without the eye of the hetman accomplished their service; but some neglected it terribly in the evenings, as ordinary soldiers do when they feel no iron hand above them.

The enemy was not slow to take advantage of this. Two days before the coming of the king and the hetmans, Sapyeha arranged his most splendid feast, for he was rejoiced that all the troops were coming, and that the siege would begin in earnest. All the best known officers were invited; the hetman, ever in search of an opportunity, announced that that feast would be in honor of the king. To Kmita, Zagloba, Pan Yan, Pan Stanislav, and Kharlamp were sent special orders to come without fail, for the hetman wished to honor them particularly for their great services. Pan Andrei had just mounted his horse to go with a party, so that the orderly found the Tartars outside the gate.

"You cannot show the hetman disrespect, and return rudeness for kindness," said the officer.

Kmita dismounted and went to ask advice of his comrades.

"This is dreadfully awkward for me," said he. "I have heard that a considerable body of cavalry has appeared near Babitsi. The hetman himself commanded me to learn absolutely who they are, and now he asks me to the feast. What must I do?"

"The hetman has sent an order to let Akbah Ulan go with the scouting-party," answered the officer.

"An order is an order!" said Zagloba, "and whoso is a soldier must obey. Be careful not to give an evil example; and besides it would not be well for you to incur the ill-will of the hetman."

"Say that I will come," said Kmita to the orderly.

The officer went out. The Tartars rode off under Akbah Ulan; and Kmita began to dress a little, and while dressing said to his comrades, —

"To-day there is a feast in honor of his Royal Grace; to-morrow there will be one in honor of the hetmans of the kingdom, and so on to the end of the siege."

"Only let the king come and this will be at an end," answered Volodyovski; "for though our gracious lord is fond of amusing himself in every trouble, still service must go on more diligently, since every man, and among others Pan Sapyeha, will endeavor to show his zeal."

"We have had too much of this, too much! There is no question on that point," said Pan Yan. "Is it not a wonder to you that such a laborious leader, such a virtuous man, such a worthy citizen, has this weakness?"

"Just let night come and straightway he is another person, and from a grand hetman turns into a reveller."

"But do you know why these banquets are not to my taste?" asked Kmita. "It was the custom of Yanush Radzivill to have them almost every evening. Imagine that, as if by some wonder, whenever there was a banquet, either some misfortune happened, some evil tidings came, or some new treason of the hetman was published. I do not know whether it was blind chance or an ordinance of God; but it is enough that evil never came except in time of a banquet. I tell you that at last it went so far that whenever they were setting the table the skin began to creep on us."

"True, as God is dear to me!" added Kharlamp. "But it came from this, that the prince hetman chose that time to announce his intrigues with the enemy of the country."

"Well," said Zagloba, "at least we have nothing to fear from the honest Sapyeha. If he will ever be a traitor, I am of as much value as my boot-heel."

"There is nothing to be said on that point. He is as honest as bread without a raw spot," put in Pan Michael.

"And what he neglects in the evening he repairs in the day-time," added Kharlamp.

"Then we will go," said Zagloba, "for to tell the truth I feel a void in my stomach."

They went out, mounted their horses, and rode off; for Sapyeha was on the other side of the city and rather far away. When they arrived at the hetman's quarters they found in the yard a multitude of horses, and a crowd of grooms, for whom a keg of beer had been set out, and who, as is usual, drinking without measure, had begun to quarrel; they grew quiet, however, at sight of the approaching

knights, especially when Zagloba fell to striking with the
side of his sabre those who were in his way, and to crying
with a stentorian voice: "To your horses, rascals, to your
horses! You are not the persons invited to the banquet."

Sapyeha received the officers as usual, with open arms;
and since he had been drinking a little with his guests, he
began at once to tease Zagloba.

"With the forehead, Lord Commander!" said he.

"With the forehead, Lord Kiper," answered Zagloba.

"If you call me that," said Sapyeha, "I will give you
wine which is working yet."

"Very good, if it will make a tippler of a hetman!"

Some of the guests, hearing this, were alarmed; but
Zagloba, when he saw the hetman in good humor, permitted
himself everything, and Sapyeha had such a weakness for
Zagloba that he not only was not angry, but he held his
sides, and called those present to witness what he endured
from that noble.

Then began a noisy and joyous banquet. Sapyeha drank
to each guest separately, raised toasts to the king, the
hetmans, the armies of both peoples (Poland and Lithuania),
Pan Charnyetski, the whole Commonwealth. Pleasure
increased, and with it noise and talk. From toasts it came
to songs. The room was filled with steam from the heads
of the guests, and the odor of mead and wines. From outside the windows came in no less of an uproar, and even
the noise of steel. The servants had begun to fight with
sabres. Some nobles rushed out to restore order, but they
increased the confusion.

Suddenly there rose a shout so great that the banqueters
in the hall became silent.

"What is that?" asked one of the colonels. "The
grooms cannot make such an uproar as that."

"Silence, gentlemen!" said the hetman, disturbed.

"Those are not ordinary shouts!"

All at once the windows shook from the thunder of
cannon and discharges of musketry.

"A sortie!" cried Volodyovski; "the enemy is advancing!"

"To horse! To sabres!"

All sprang to their feet. There was a throng at the door;
then a crowd of officers rushed to the yard, calling to their
grooms for horses.

But in the disturbance it was not easy for each one to

find his own. Meanwhile from beyond the yard alarmed voices began to shout in the darkness, —

"The enemy is advancing! Pan Kotvich is under fire!"

All rushed with what breath was in their horses to their squadrons, jumping over fences and breaking their necks in the darkness. An alarm began in the whole camp. Not all the squadrons had horses at hand, and those who had not began the uproar first of all. Throngs of soldiers on foot and on horseback struck against one another, not being able to come to order, not knowing who was a friend and who an enemy, shouting and roaring in the middle of the dark night. Some cried that the King of Sweden was advancing with his whole army.

The Swedish sortie had really struck with a mighty impetus on Kotvich's men. Fortunately, being sick, he was not at the banquet, and therefore could offer some kind of immediate resistance; still it was not a long one, for he was attacked by superior numbers and covered with musketry fire, hence was forced to retreat. Oskyerko came first to his assistance with his dragoons. They answered musketry fire with musketry fire. But neither could Oskyerko's dragoons withstand the pressure, and in a moment they began to withdraw more and more hastily, leaving the ground covered with corpses. Twice did Oskyerko endeavor to bring them to order, and twice was he beaten back, so that the soldiers could only cover their retreat by firing in groups. At last they scattered completely; but the Swedes pressed on like an irrepressible torrent toward the hetman's quarters. More and more regiments issued from the city to the field; after the infantry came cavalry; they brought out even field-guns. It looked like a general battle, and it seemed as though the enemy sought one.

Volodyovski, rushing from the hetman's quarters, met his own squadron, which was always in readiness, half way, going toward the sound of the alarm and the shots. It was led by Roh Kovalski, who, like Kotvich, was not at the banquet; but Roh was not there because he had not been invited. Volodyovski gave orders to set fire with all speed to a couple of sheds, so as to light up the field, and he hurried to the battle. On the road he was joined by Kmita with his terrible volunteers, and that half of the Tartars which had not gone on the scouting expedition. Both came just in time to save Kotvich and Oskyerko from utter disaster.

The sheds had now blazed up so well that everything could be seen as at noontide. In this light the Lauda men, aided by Kmita, struck the infantry regiments, and passing through their fire took them on sabres. The Swedish cavalry sprang to assist their own men, and closed mightily with the Lauda squadron. For a certain time they struggled exactly like two wrestlers who seizing each other by the bodies use their last strength, — now this one bends the other, and now the other bends this; but men fell so frequently in their ranks that at last the Swedes began to be confused. Kmita with his fighters rushed into the thick of the struggle. Volodyovski as usual cleared an opening; near him the two gigantic Skshetuskis fought, and Kharlamp with Roh Kovalski; the Lauda men emulated Kmita's fighters, — some shouting terribly, others, as the Butryms, rolling on in a body and in silence.

New regiments rushed forward to the aid of the broken Swedes; but Vankovich, whose quarters were near Volodyovski's and Kmita's, was a little later than they and supported them. At last the hetman led all the troops to the engagement, and began to advance in order. A fierce battle sprang up along the whole line from Mokotov to the Vistula.

Then Akbah Ulan, who had gone with the scouts, appeared on a foaming horse before the hetman.

"Effendi!" cried he; "a chambul of cavalry is marching from Babitsi to the city, and convoying wagons; they wish to enter the gates."

Sapyeha understood in one moment what that sortie in the direction of Mokotov meant. The enemy wished to draw away troops on the meadow road, so that that auxiliary cavalry and a provision train might enter the gates.

"Run to Volodyovski!" cried the hetman to Akbah Ulan; "let the Lauda squadron, Kmita, and Vankovich stop the road. I will send them reinforcements at once."

Akbah Ulan put spurs to his horse; after him flew one, and a second, and a third orderly. All rushed to Volodyovski and repeated the order of the hetman.

Volodyovski turned his squadron immediately; Kmita and the Tartars caught up with him; going across the field, they shot on together, and Vankovich after them.

But they arrived too late. Nearly two hundred wagons had entered the gate; a splendid detachment of cavalry following them was almost within radius of the fortress

Only the rearguard, composed of about one hundred men, had not come yet under cover of the artillery. But these too were going with all speed. The officer, riding behind, urged them on.

Kmita, seeing them by the light of the burning shed, gave forth such a piercing and terrible shout, that the horses at his side were frightened; he recognized Boguslav's cavalry, that same which had ridden over him and his Tartars at Yanov.

Mindful of nothing, he rushed like a madman toward them, passed his own men, and fell first blindly among their ranks. Fortunately the two Kyemliches, Kosma and Damian, sitting on the foremost horses, rode with him. At that moment Volodyovski struck the flank like lightning, and with this one blow cut off the rearguard from the main body.

Cannon began to thunder from the walls; but the main division, sacrificing their comrades, rushed in with all speed after the wagons. Then the Lauda men and Kmita's forces surrounded the rearguard as with a ring, and a merciless slaughter began.

But it was of short duration. Boguslav's men, seeing that there was no rescue on any side, sprang from their horses in a moment, threw down their weapons, and shouted with sky-piercing voices, heard in the throng and the uproar, that they surrendered.

Neither the volunteers nor the Tartars regarded their shouts, but hewed on. At this moment was heard the threatening and shrill voice of Volodyovski, who wanted informants, —

"Stop! stop! take them alive!"

"Take them alive!" cried Kmita.

The biting of steel ceased. The Tartars were commanded to bind the enemy, and with the skill peculiar to them they did this in a twinkle; then the squadrons pushed back hastily from the cannon-fire. The colonels marched toward the sheds, — the Lauda men in advance, Vankovich in the rear, and Kmita, with the prisoners, in the centre, all in perfect readiness to repulse attack should it come. Some of the Tartars led prisoners on leashes; others of them led captured horses. Kmita, when he came near the sheds, looked carefully into the faces of the prisoners to see if Boguslav was among them; for though one of them had sworn under a sword-point that the prince was not in the detachment, still Kmita thought that perhaps they were hiding him purposely. Then some voice from under the stirrup of a Tartar cried to him, —

"Pan Kmita! Colonel! Rescue an acquaintance! Give command to free me from the rope on parole."

"Hassling!" cried Kmita.

Hassling was a Scot, formerly an officer in the cavalry of the voevoda of Vilna, whom Kmita knew in Kyedani, and in his time loved much.

"Let the prisoner go free!" cried he to the Tartar, "and down from the horse yourself!"

The Tartar sprang from the saddle as if the wind had carried him off, for he knew the danger of loitering when the "bagadyr" commanded.

Hassling, groaning, climbed into the Tartar's lofty saddle. Kmita then caught him above the palm, and pressing his hand as if he wished to crush it, began to ask insistently, —

"Whence do you come? Tell me quickly, whence do you come? For God's sake, tell quickly!"

"From Taurogi," answered the officer.

Kmita pressed him still more.

"But — Panna Billevich — is she there?"

"She is."

Pan Andrei spoke with still greater difficulty, for he pressed his teeth still more closely.

"And — what has the prince done with her?"

"He has not succeeded in doing anything."

Silence followed; after a while Kmita removed his lynx-skin cap, drew his hand over his forehead and said, —

"I was struck in the battle; blood is leaving me, and I have grown weak."

CHAPTER XXXVIII.

THE sortie had attained its object only in part; though Boguslav's division had entered the city, the sortie itself had not done great things. It is true that Pan Kotvich's squadron and Oskyerko's dragoons had suffered seriously; but the Swedes too had strewn the field with many corpses, and one regiment of infantry, which Volodyovski and Vankovich had struck, was almost destroyed. The Lithuanians boasted that they had inflicted greater loss on the enemy than they had endured themselves. Pan Sapyeha alone suffered internally, because a new "confusion" had met him from which his fame might be seriously affected. The colonels attached to the hetman comforted him as well as they could; and to tell the truth this lesson was useful, for henceforward he had no more such wild banquets, and if there was some pleasure the greatest watchfulness was observed during the time of its continuance. The Swedes were caught the day after. Supposing that the hetman would not expect a repetition of the sortie so soon, they came outside the walls again; but driven from their ground and leaving a number of dead, they returned.

Meanwhile they were examining Hassling in the hetman's quarters; this made Pan Andrei so impatient that he almost sprang out of his skin, for he wished to have the Scot to himself at the earliest, and talk with him touching Taurogi. He prowled about the quarters all day, went in every little while, listened to the statements, and sprang up whenever Boguslav's name was mentioned in the question.

But in the evening he received an order to go on a scouting expedition. He said nothing, only set his teeth; for he had changed greatly already, and had learned to defer private affairs for public service. But he pushed the Tartars terribly during the expedition, burst out in anger at the least cause, and struck with his baton till the bones cracked. They said one to another that the "bagadyr" was mad, and marched silently, as silently as cowards, looking only to the eyes of the leader and guessing his thoughts on the wing.

On returning he found Hassling in his quarters, but so ill that he could not speak, for his capture had affected him so cruelly that after the additional torture of a whole day's inquisition he had a fever, and did not understand what was said to him. Kmita therefore was forced to be satisfied with what Zagloba told of Hassling's statements; but they touched only public, not private affairs. Of Boguslav the young officer said only this, — that after his return from the expedition to Podlyasye and the defeat at Yanov he had become terribly ill from rage and melancholy; he fell into a fever, but as soon as he had recovered somewhat, he moved with his troops to Pomerania, whither Steinbock and the elector invited him most earnestly.

"But where is he now?" asked Kmita.

"According to what Hassling tells me, and he has no reason to lie, he is with the king's brother, at the fortified camp on the Narev and the Bug, where Boguslav is commanding a whole cavalry division," answered Zagloba.

"Ha! and they think to come here with succor to the besieged. We shall meet, as God is in heaven, even if I had to go to him in disguise."

"Do not grow angry for nothing! To Warsaw they would be glad to come with succor, but they cannot, for Charnyetski has placed himself in their way. Having neither infantry nor cannon, he cannot attack their camp, and they are afraid to go out against him, for they know that their soldiers could not withstand his in the field, and they know too that if they went out, they could not shield themselves with the river. If the king himself were there he would give battle, for under his command the soldiers fight better, being confident that he is a great warrior; but neither Douglas, nor the king's brother, nor Prince Boguslav, though all three are daring men, would venture against Charnyetski."

"But where is the king?"

"He has gone to Prussia. The king does not believe that we are before Warsaw already, and that we shall capture Wittemberg. But whether he believes or not, he had to go for two reasons, — first, because he must win over the elector, even at the price of all Great Poland; second, because the army, which he led out of the sack, is of no use until it has rested. Toil, watching, and continual alarms have so gnawed it that the soldiers are not able to hold muskets in their hands; and still they are the choicest regiments in the whole army, which through all the German and Danish regions have won famous victories."

Further conversation was interrupted by the coming of Volodyovski.

"How is Hassling?" asked he on the threshold.

"He is sick and imagines every folly," answered Kmita.

"And you, my dear Michael, what do you want of Hassling?" asked Zagloba.

"Just as if you do not know!"

"I could not know that it is a question with you of that cherry-tree which Prince Boguslav has planted in his garden. He is a diligent gardener; he does not need to wait a year for fruit."

"I wish you were killed for such jokes!" cried the little knight.

"Look at him, tell him the most innocent thing, and immediately his mustaches are quivering like the horns of a mad grasshopper. In what am I to blame? Seek vengeance on Boguslav, not on me."

"God grant me to seek and to find!"

"Just now Babinich has said the same! Before long I see that he will raise the whole army against the prince; but Boguslav is taking good care of himself, and without my stratagems you will not be able to succeed."

Here both young men sprang to their feet and asked, —

"Have you any stratagems?"

"But do you think it is as easy to take a stratagem out of the head as a sabre out of the sheath? If Boguslav were here, surely I should find more than one; but at that distance, not only a stratagem, but a cannon will not strike. Pan Andrei, give orders to bring me a goblet of mead, for it is hot here to-day."

"I'll give you a keg of it if you will invent something."

"First, why do you stand over this Hassling like an executioner? He is not the only man captured; you can ask others."

"I have already tortured others, but they are common soldiers; they know nothing, but he, as an officer, was at the court," answered Kmita.

"That is a reason!" answered Zagloba. "I must talk with him too; from what he tells me of the person and ways of Prince Boguslav, stratagems may be important. Now the main thing is to finish the siege soon, for afterward we shall move surely against that army on the Narev. But

somehow our gracious lord and the hetmans are a long time
invisible."

"How so ?" asked Volodyovski. "I have returned this
minute from the hetman, who has just received news that
the king will take up position here this evening with the
auxiliary divisions, and the hetmans with cavalry will come
to-morrow. They are advancing from Sokal itself, resting
but little, making forced marches. Besides, it has been
known for two days that they are almost in sight."

"Are they bringing many troops ?"

"Nearly five times as many as Sapyeha has, infantry
Russian and Hungarian, very excellent; six thousand
Tartars under Suba Gazi, but probably it is impossible
to let them out for even a day, for they are very self-
willed and plunder all around."

"Better give them to Pan Andrei to lead," said Zagloba.

"Yes," said Kmita, "I should lead them straightway
from Warsaw, for they are of no use in a siege; I should take
them to the Bug and the Narev."

"They are of use," replied Volodyovski, "for none can
see better than they that provisions do not enter the
fortress."

"Well, it will be warm for Wittemberg. Wait, old
criminal !" cried Zagloba. "You have warred well, I will
not deny that, but you have robbed and plundered still
better ; you had two mouths, — one for false oaths, the other
for breaking promises, — but this time you will not beg off
with both of them. The Gallic disease will dry up your
skin, and doctors will tear it from you; but we will flay
you better, Zagloba's head for that !"

"Nonsense ! he will surrender on conditions to the king,
who will not do anything to him," answered Pan Michael ;
"and we shall have to give him military honors besides."

"He will yield on conditions, will he ? Indeed !" cried
Zagloba. "We shall see !"

Here he began to pound the table with such force that
Roh Kovalski, who was coming in at the moment, was
frightened and stood as if fixed to the threshold.

"May I serve as a waiting-lad to Jews," shouted the old
man, "if I let free out of Warsaw that blasphemer of the
faith, that robber of churches, that oppressor of widows,
that executioner of men and women, that hangman's assistant, that ruffian, that blood-spiller and money-grabber, that
purse-gnawer, that flayer ! All right ! The king will let

him out on conditions; but I, as I am a Catholic, as I am Zagloba, as I wish for happiness during life and desire God at death, will make such a tumult against him as no man has ever heard of in this Commonwealth before! Don't wave your hand, Pan Michael! I'll make a tumult! I repeat it, I'll make a tumult!"

"Uncle will make a tumult!" thundered Roh Kovalski.

Just then Akbah Ulan thrust in his beast-like face at the door.

"Effendi!" said he to Kmita, "the armies of the king are visible beyond the Vistula."

All sprang to their feet and rushed forth.

The king had come indeed. First arrived the Tartar squadrons, under Suba Gazi, but not in such numbers as was expected; after them came the troops of the kingdom, many and well armed, and above all full of ardor. Before evening the whole army had passed the bridge freshly built by Oskyerko. Sapyeha was waiting for the king with squadrons drawn out as if ready for battle, standing one by the side of the other, like an immense wall, the end of which it was difficult to reach with the eye. The captains stood before the regiments; near them the standard-bearers, each with lowered ensign; the trumpets, kettle-drums, crooked trumpets, and drums made a noise indescribable. The squadrons of the kingdom, in proportion as they passed, stood just opposite the Lithuanians in line; between one and the other army was an interval of a hundred paces.

Sapyeha with baton in hand went on foot to that open space; after him the chief civil and military dignitaries. On the other side, from the armies of the kingdom approached the king on a splendid Frisian horse, given him by Lyubomirski; he was arrayed as if for battle, in light armor of blue and gold, from under which was to be seen a black velvet kaftan, with a lace collar coming out on the breastplate, but instead of a helmet he wore the ordinary Swedish hat, with black feathers; but he wore military gloves, and long yellow boots coming far above his knees.

After him rode the papal nuncio, the archbishop of Lvoff, the bishop of Kamenyets, the priest Tsyetsishovski, the voevoda of Cracow, the voevoda of Rus, Baron Lisola, Count Pöttingen, Pan Kamenyetski, the ambassador of Moscow, Pan Grodzitski, general of artillery, Tyzenhauz, and many others. Sapyeha advanced as marshal of the kingdom to hold the king's stirrup; but the king sprang lightly from the saddle, hurried to Sapyeha and without saying a word, seized him in his embrace.

And Yan Kazimir held him a long time, in view of both armies; silent all the while, but tears flowed down his cheeks in a stream, for he pressed to his bosom the truest servant of the king and the country, — a man who, though he did not equal others in genius, though he even erred at times, still soared in honesty above all the lords of that Commonwealth, never wavered in loyalty, sacrificed without a moment's thought his whole fortune, and from the beginning of the war exposed his breast for his king and the country.

The Lithuanians, who had whispered previously among themselves that perhaps reprimands would meet Pan Sapyeha because he had let Karl Gustav escape from near Sandomir and for the recent carelessness at Warsaw, or at least a cool reception, seeing this heartiness of the king, raised in honor of the kindly monarch a tremendous heaven-echoing shout. The armies of the kingdom answered it immediately with one thunder-roll, and for some time above the noise of the music, the rattle of drums, the roar of musketry, were heard only these shouts, —

" Vivat Yoannes Casimirus ! "

" Long life to the armies of the crown ! "

" Long life to the Lithuanians ! "

So they greeted one another at Warsaw. The walls trembled, and behind the walls the Swedes.

" I shall bellow, as God is dear to me ! " cried Zagloba, with emotion; " I cannot restrain myself. See our king, our father ! — gracious gentlemen, I am blubbering, — our father, our king ! the other day a wanderer deserted by all; now here — now here are a hundred thousand sabres at call ! O merciful God ! I cannot keep from tears; yesterday a wanderer, to-day the Emperor of Germany has not such good soldiers — "

Here the sluices were opened in the eyes of Zagloba, and he began to sob time after time; then he turned suddenly to Roh, —

" Be silent ! what are you whimpering about ? "

" And is Uncle not whimpering ? " answered Roh.

" True, as God is dear to me ! — I was ashamed, gracious gentlemen, of this Commonwealth. But now I would not change with any nation ! A hundred thousand sabres, — let others show the like. God has brought them to their minds; God has given this, God has given it ! "

Zagloba had not made a great mistake, for really there were nearly seventy thousand men at Warsaw, not counting Charnyetski's division, which had not arrived yet, and not counting the armed camp attendants who rendered service when necessary, and who straggled after every camp in countless multitudes.

After the greeting and a hurried review of the troops, the king thanked Sapyeha's men, amid universal enthusiasm, for their faithful services, and went to Uyazdov. The troops occupied the positions assigned them. Some squadrons remained in Praga; others disposed themselves around the city. A gigantic train of wagons continued to cross the Vistula till the following midday.

Next morning the suburbs of the city were as white with tents as if they had been covered with snow. Countless herds of horses were neighing on the adjoining meadows. After the army followed a crowd of Armenians, Jews, Tartars; another city, more extensive and tumultuous than that which was besieged, grew up on the plain.

The Swedes, amazed during the first days at the power of the King of Poland, made no sorties, so that Pan Grodzitski, general of artillery, could ride around the city quietly and form his plan of siege.

On the following day the camp attendants began to raise intrenchments here and there, according to Grodzitski's plan; they placed on them at once the smaller cannon, for the larger ones were to appear only a couple of weeks later.

Yan Kazimir sent a message to old Wittemberg summoning him to surrender the city and lay down his arms, giving favorable conditions, which, when known, roused discontent in the army. That discontent was spread mainly by Zagloba, who had a special hatred of the Swedish commander.

Wittemberg, as was easy to foresee, rejected the conditions and resolved on a defence to continue till the last drop of blood was shed, and to bury himself in the ruins of the city rather than yield it to the king. The size of the besieging army did not frighten him a whit, for he knew that an excessive number was rather a hindrance than help in a siege. He was informed also in good season that in the camp of Yan Kazimir there was not one siege gun, while the Swedes had more than enough of them, not taking into consideration their inexhaustible supply of ammunition.

It was in fact to be foreseen that they would defend themselves with frenzy, for Warsaw had served them hitherto as a storehouse for booty. All the immense treasures looted in castles, in churches, in cities, in the whole Commonwealth, came to the capital, whence they were despatched in parties to Prussia, and farther to Sweden. But at the present time, when the whole country had risen, and castles defended by the smaller Swedish garrisons did not insure safety, booty was brought to Warsaw all the more. The Swedish soldier was more ready to sacrifice his life than his booty. A poor people who had seized the treasures of a wealthy land had acquired the taste of them to such a degree that the world had never seen more grasping robbers. The king himself had grown famous for greed; the generals followed his example, and Wittemberg surpassed them all. When it was a question of gain, neither the honor of a knight nor consideration for the dignity of rank restrained officers. They seized, they extorted, they skinned everything that could be taken. In Warsaw itself colonels of high office and noble birth were not ashamed to sell spirits and tobacco to their own soldiers, so as to cram their purses with the pay of the army.

This too might rouse the Swedes to fury in defence, that their foremost men were at that time in Warsaw. First was Wittemberg himself, next in command to Karl Gustav. He was the first who had entered the Commonwealth and brought it to decline at Uistsie. In return for that service a triumph was prepared for him in Sweden as for a conqueror. In the city was Oxenstiern, the chancellor, a statesman renowned throughout the world, respected for honesty even by his enemies. He was called the Minerva of the king. To his counsel Karl was indebted for all his victories in negotiation. In the capital was also Wrangel, the younger Horn, Erickson, the second Lowenhaupt, and many Swedish ladies of high birth, who had followed their husbands to the country as to a new Swedish colony.

The Swedes had something to defend. Yan Kazimir understood, therefore, that the siege, especially through the lack of heavy guns on his side, would be long and bloody. The hetmans understood this also, but the army would not think of it. Barely had Grodzitski raised the intrenchments in some fashion, barely had he pushed forward somewhat to the walls, when deputations went from all the squadrons to ask the king to permit volunteers to storm the walls. The king had to explain to them a long time that fortresses were not taken with sabres, before he could restrain their ardor.

Meanwhile the works were pushed forward as rapidly as possible. The troops, not being able to storm, took eager part with the camp servants in raising these works; men from the foremost regiments, nay, even officers brought earth in wheelbarrows, carried fascines, labored. More than once the Swedes tried to hinder, and not a day passed without sorties; but barely were the Swedish musketeers outside the gate, when the Poles, working at the intrenchments, throwing aside wheelbarrows, bundles of twigs, spades and pickaxes, ran with sabres into the smoke so furiously that the Swedes had to hide in the fortress with all haste. In these engagements bodies fell thickly; the fosses and the open space as far as the intrenchments were full of graves, in which were placed sometimes small bundles of the weapons of the dead. At last even time failed for burial, so that bodies lay on the ground spreading a terrible odor around the city and the besiegers.

In spite of the greatest difficulty citizens stole forth to the king's camp every day, reporting what happened in the city, and imploring on their knees to hasten the storm. The Swedes, they said, had a plenty of provisions as yet, but the people were dying of hunger on the streets; they lived in want, in oppression under the terrible hand of the garrison. Every day echoes brought to the Polish camp sounds of musket-shots in the city, and fugitives brought intelligence that the Swedes were shooting citizens suspected of good-will to Yan Kazimir. The hair stood on end at the stories of the fugitives. They said that the whole population, sick women, newly born infants, old men, all lived at night on the streets, for the Swedes had driven them from their houses, and made passages from wall to wall, so that the garrison, in case Yan Kazimir's troops should enter, might withdraw and defend themselves. Rains fell on the people in their camping-places; on clear days the sun burned them, at night the cold pinched them. Citizens were not allowed to kindle fires; they had no means of preparing warm food. Various diseases spread more and more, and carried away hundreds of victims.

Yan Kazimir's heart was ready to burst when he heard these narratives. He sent therefore courier after courier to hasten the coming of the heavy guns. Days and weeks passed; but it was impossible to undertake anything more important than the repulse of sorties. Still the besiegers were strengthened by the thought that the garrison must fail of provisions at last, since the roads were blocked in such fashion that a mouse could not reach the fortress. The besieged lost hope of assistance; the troops under Douglas, which were posted nearest, were not only unable to come to the rescue, but had to think of their own skin; for Yan Kazimir, having even too many men, was able to harass them.

At last the Poles, even before the coming of the heavy guns, opened on the fortress with the smaller ones. Pan Grodzitski from the side of the Vistula, raised in front of himself, like a mole, earth defences, pushed to within six yards of the moat, and vomited a continual fire on the unfortunate city. The magnificent Kazanovski Palace was ruined; and the Poles did not regret it, for the building belonged to the traitor Radzeyovski. The shattered walls were barely standing, shining with their empty windows; day and night balls were dropping on the splendid terraces and in the gardens, smashing the beautiful fountains, bridges, arbors, and marble statues, terrifying the peacocks which with pitiful screams gave notice of their unhappy condition.

Pan Grodzitski hurled fire on the Bernardine bell-tower, for he had decided to begin the assault on that side.

Meanwhile the camp servants begged permission to attack the city, for they wished greatly to reach the Swedish treasures earliest. The king refused at first, but finally consented. A number of prominent officers undertook to lead them, and among others Kmita, who was imbittered by delay, and not only that, but in general he knew not what to do with himself; for Hassling, having fallen into a grievous fever, lay without consciousness for some weeks and could speak of nothing.

Men therefore were summoned to the storm. Grodzitski opposed this to the last moment, insisting that until a breach was made the city could not be taken, even though the regular infantry were to go to the assault. But as the king had given permission, Grodzitski was forced to yield.

June 15, about six thousand camp servants assembled; ladders, bundles of brush, and bags of sand were prepared Toward evening a throng, barefoot and armed for the greater

part only with sabres, began to approach the city where the
trenches and earth defences came nearest the moat. When
it had become perfectly dark, the men rushed, at a given signal, toward the moat with a terrible uproar, and began to
fill it. The watchful Swedes received them with a murderous fire from muskets and cannons, and a furious battle
sprang up along the whole eastern side of the city. Under
cover of darkness the Poles filled the moat in a twinkle and
reached the walls in an orderless mass. Kmita, with two
thousand men, fell upon an earth fort, which the Poles
called "the mole-hill," and which stood near the Cracow
gate. In spite of a desperate defence he captured this place
at a blow; the garrison was cut to pieces with sabres, not
a man was spared. Pan Andrei gave command to turn the
guns on the gate and some of them to the farther walls, so
as to aid and cover somewhat those crowds who were
striving to scale the walls.

These men, however, were not so fortunate. They put the
ladders in position, and ascended them so furiously that the
best trained infantry could not have done better; but
the Swedes, safe behind battlements, fired into their very
faces, and hurled stones and blocks prepared for the purpose; under the weight of these the ladders were broken
into pieces, and at last the infantry pushed down the
assaulters with long spears, against which sabres had no
effect.

More than five hundred of the best camp servants were
lying at the foot of the wall; the rest passed the moat under
an incessant fire, and took refuge again in the Polish
intrenchments.

The storm was repulsed, but the little fort remained in
the hands of the Poles. In vain did the Swedes roll at it
all night from their heaviest guns; Kmita answered them
in like manner from those cannon which he had captured.
Only in the morning, when light came, were his guns dismounted to the last one. Wittemberg, for whom that intrenchment was as his head, sent infantry at once with the
order not to dare return without retaking what had been
lost; but Grodzitski sent reinforcements to Kmita, by the
aid of which he not only repulsed the infantry, but fell upon
and drove them to the Cracow gate.

Grodzitski was so delighted that he ran in person to the
king with the report.

"Gracious Lord," said he, "I was opposed to yesterday's

work, but now I see that it was not lost. While that intrenchment was in the enemy's hands I could do nothing against the gate; but now only let the heavy guns come, and in one night I will make a breach."

The king, who was grieved that so many good men had fallen, was rejoiced at Grodzitski's words, and asked at once, —

"But who has command in that intrenchment?"

"Pan Babinich," answered a number of voices.

The king clapped his hands. "He must be first everywhere! Worthy General, I know him. He is a terribly stubborn cavalier, and will not let himself be smoked out."

"It would be a mistake beyond forgiveness, Gracious Lord, if we should permit that. I have already sent him infantry and small cannon; for that they will try to smoke him out is certain. It is a question of Warsaw! That cavalier is worth his weight in gold."

"He is worth more; for this is not his first, and not his tenth achievement," said the king.

Then Yan Kazimir gave orders to bring quickly a horse and a field-glass, and he rode out to look at the earthwork. But it was not to be seen from behind the smoke, for a number of forty-eight-pounders were blowing on it with ceaseless fire; they hurled long balls, bombs, and grape-shot. Still the intrenchment was so near the gate that musketballs almost reached it; the bomb-shells could be seen perfectly when they flew up like cloudlets, and, describing a closely bent bow, fell into that cloud of smoke, bursting with terrible explosion. Many fell beyond the intrenchment, and they prevented the approach of reinforcements.

"In the name of the Father, Son, and Holy Ghost!" said the king. "Tyzenhauz, look! A pile of torn earth is all that remains. Tyzenhauz, do you know who is there?"

"Gracious King, Babinich is there. If he comes out living, he will be able to say that he was in hell during life."

"We must send him fresh men. Worthy General —"

"The orders are already given, but it is difficult for them to go, since bombs pass over and fall very thickly on this side of the fort."

"Turn all the guns on the walls so as to make a diversion," said the king.

Grodzitski put spurs to his horse and galloped to the

trenches. After a while cannonading was heard on the whole line, and somewhat later it was seen that a fresh division of Mazovian infantry went out of the nearest trenches, and on a run to the mole-hill.

The king stood there, looking continually. At last he cried: "Babinich should be relieved in the command. And who, gentlemen, will volunteer to take his place?"

Neither Pan Yan, Pan Stanislav, nor Volodyovski was near the king, therefore a moment of silence followed.

"I!" said suddenly Pan Topor Grylevski, an officer of the light squadron of the primate.

"I!" said Tyzenhauz.

"I! I! I!" called at once a number of voices.

"Let the man go who offered himself first," said the king.

Pan Topor Grylevski made the sign of the cross, raised the canteen to his mouth, then galloped away.

The king remained looking at the cloud of smoke with which the mole-hill was covered, and the smoke rose above it like a bridge up to the very wall. Since the fort was near the Vistula, the walls of the city towered above it, and therefore the fire was terrible.

Meanwhile the thunder of cannon decreased somewhat, though the balls did not cease to describe arcs, and a rattle of musketry was given out as if thousands of men were beating threshing-floors with flails.

"It is evident that they are going to the attack again," said Tyzenhauz. "If there were less smoke, we should see the infantry."

"Let us approach a little," said the king, urging his horse.

After him others moved on, and riding along the bank of the Vistula from Uyazdov they approached almost to the Solets itself; and since the gardens of the palaces and the cloisters coming down to the Vistula had been cleared by the Swedes in the winter for fuel, trees did not cover the view, they could see even without field-glasses that the Swedes were really moving again to the storm.

"I would rather lose that position," said the king all at once, "than that Babinich should die."

"God will defend him!" said the priest Tsyetsishovski.

"And Pan Grodzitski will not fail to send him reinforcements," added Tyzenhauz.

Further conversation was interrupted by some horseman

who was approaching from the direction of the city at all speed. Tyzenhauz, having such sight that he saw better with the naked eye than others through field-glasses, caught his head at sight of him, and said, —

"Grylevski is returning! It must be that Kmita has fallen, and the fort is captured."

The king shaded his eyes with his hands. Grylevski rushed up, reined in his horse, and, panting for breath, exclaimed, —

"Gracious Lord!"

"What has happened? Is he killed?" asked the king.

"Pan Babinich says that he is well, and does not wish any one to take his place; he begs only to send him food, for he has had nothing to eat since morning."

"Is he alive then?" cried the king.

"He says that he is comfortable there!" repeated Grylevski.

But others, catching breath from wonder, began to cry : "That is courage! He is a soldier!"

"But it was necessary to stay there and relieve him absolutely," said the king to Grylevski. "Is it not a shame to come back? Were you afraid, or what? It would have been better not to go."

"Gracious Lord," answered Grylevski, "whoso calls me a coward, him I will correct on any field, but before majesty I must justify myself. I was in the ant-hill itself, but Babinich flew into my face because of my errand: 'Go,' said he, 'to the hangman! I am at work here, I am almost creeping out of my skin, and I have no time to talk, but I will not share either my glory or command with any man. I am well here and I will stay here, but I'll give orders to take you outside the trench! I wish you were killed!' said he. 'We want to eat, and they send us a commandant instead of food!' What had I to do, Gracious Lord? I do not wonder at his temper, for their hands are dropping from toil."

"And how is it?" asked the king; "is he holding the place?"

"Desperately. What would he not hold? I forgot to tell besides that he shouted to me when I was going: 'I'll stay here a week and will not surrender, if I have something to eat!'"

"Is it possible to hold out there?"

"There, Gracious Lord. is the genuine day of judgment!

Bomb is falling after bomb; pieces of shells are whistling, like devils, around the ear; the earth is dug out into ditches; it is impossible to speak from smoke. The balls hurl around sand and earth, so that every moment a man must shake himself to avoid being buried. Many have fallen, but those who are living lie in furrows in the intrenchments, and have made defences before their heads of stakes strengthened with earth. The Swedes constructed the place carefully, and now it serves against them. While I was there, infantry came from Grodzitski, and now there is fighting again."

"Since we cannot attack the walls until a breach is made," said the king, "we will strike the palace on the Cracow suburbs to-day; that will be the best diversion."

"The palace is wonderfully strengthened, almost changed into a fortress," remarked Tyzenhauz.

"But they will not hurry from the city to give aid, for all their fury will be turned on Babinich," said the king. "So will it be, as I am here alive, so will it be! I will order the storm at once; but first I will bless Babinich."

Then the king took from the priest a golden crucifix in which were splinters of the true cross, and raising it on high he began to bless the distant mound, covered with fire and smoke, saying, —

"O God of Abraham, Isaac, and Jacob, have mercy on Thy people, and give salvation to the dying! Amen! amen! amen!"

CHAPTER XXXIX.

A BLOODY storm followed from the side of the Novy Svyat
against the Cracow suburbs, not over-successful, but in so far
effective that it turned the attention of the Swedes from the
intrenchment defended by Kmita, and permitted the garrison
enclosed in it to rest somewhat. The Poles pushed forward
however, to the Kazimirovski Palace, but they could not
hold that point.

On the other side they stormed up to the Danillovich
Palace and to Dantzig House, equally without result. A
number of hundreds of people fell again. The king, however, had this consolation: he saw that even the general
militia rushed to the walls with the greatest daring and devotion, and that after those attempts, more or less unsuc-
cessful, their courage not only had not fallen, but on the
contrary assurance of victory was growing strong in the
army.

The most fortunate event of the day was the arrival
of Pan Yan Zamoyski and Pan Charnyetski. The first
brought very excellent infantry and guns from Zamost, so
heavy that the Swedes had nothing like them in Warsaw.
The second, in agreement with Sapyeha, having besieged
Douglas, and with some Lithuanian troops and the general
militia of Podlyasye, under command of Pan Yan, had
come to Warsaw to take part in the general storm. It was
hoped by Charnyetski as well as others that this would be
the last storm.

Zamoyski's heavy guns were placed in the position taken
by Kmita; they began work immediately against the walls
and the gate, and forced the Swedish howitzers to silence
at once. General Grodzitski himself occupied the "mole-
hill," and Kmita returned to his Tartars.

But he had not reached his quarters when he was summoned to Uyazdov. The king in presence of the whole
staff applauded the young knight; neither Charnyetski, Sapyeha, Lyubomirski, nor the hetmans spared praises on him.
He stood there in torn garments covered with earth, his face
entirely discolored with powder smoke; without sleep,

soiled, but joyous because he had held the place, had won so much praise, and gained immeasurable glory in both armies. Among other cavaliers Pan Michael and Pan Yan congratulated him.

"You do not know indeed, Pan Andrei," said the little knight, "what great weight you have with the king. I was at the council of war yesterday, for Pan Charnyetski took me with him. They talked of the storm, and then of the news which had just come in from Lithuania, the war there, and the cruelties which Pontus de la Gardie and the Swedes permit. They were considering at the council how to strengthen resistance. Sapyeha said it was best to send thither a couple of squadrons and a man who could be there what Charnyetski was at the beginning of the war in Poland. To which the king answered: 'There is only one such man, Babinich.' The others confirmed this at once."

"I would go most willingly to Lithuania, and especially to Jmud," answered Kmita. "I resolved to ask of the king myself permission to go, but I am waiting till Warsaw is taken."

"There will be a general storm to-morrow," said Zagloba.

"I know, but how is Kettling?"

"Who is that? Hassling?"

"All one, for he has two names, as is the custom among the English, the Scots, and many other nations."

"True," answered Zagloba, "and a Spaniard every day of the week has a new name for himself. Your servant told me that Hassling, or Kettling, is well; he has begun to talk, walks, the fever has left him, he calls for food every hour."

"Have you been with him?" asked Kmita of Pan Michael.

"I have not, for I have had no time. Who has a head for anything but the storm?"

"Then let us go now."

"Go to sleep first," said Zagloba.

"True! true! I am barely standing on my feet."

So when he came to his own quarters Pan Andrei followed Zagloba's advice, especially as he found Hassling asleep. But Zagloba and Volodyovski came to see him in the evening; they sat down in the broad summer-house which the Tartars had made for their "bagadyr." The Kyemliches poured out for them mead a hundred years old, which the king had sent to Kmita; and they drank it willingly, for the air was hot outside. Hassling, pale and emaciated, seemed to draw life and strength from the precious liquid. Zagloba clicked with his tongue, and wiped perspiration from his forehead.

"Hei! how the great guns are thundering!" said the young Scot, listening. "To-morrow you will go to the storm — it is well! — for the healthy — God give you blessing! I am of foreign blood, and serve him whom it was my duty to serve, but you have my best wishes. Ah, what mead this is! Life enters me."

Thus speaking, he threw back his golden hair and raised his blue eyes toward heaven; he had a wonderful face, half childlike as yet. Zagloba looked at him with a certain emotion.

"You speak Polish as well as any of us," said he. "Become a Pole, love this our country, and you will do an honorable deed, and mead will not be lacking to you. It is not difficult for a soldier to receive naturalization with us."

"All the more easy since I am a noble," answered Hassling. "My name is Hassling-Kettling of Elgin. My family come from England, though settled in Scotland."

"Those countries beyond the sea are far away, and somehow it is more decent for a man to live here," said Zagloba.

"It is pleasant for me here."

"But unpleasant for us," said Kmita, who from the beginning was twisting impatiently on the bench, "for we are anxious to hear what is going on in Taurogi; but you are talking genealogies."

"Ask me; I will answer."

"Have you seen Panna Billevich often?"

Over the pale face of Hassling blushes passed. "Every day!" said he.

Kmita looked at him quickly. "Were you such a confidant? Why do you blush? Every day, — how every day?"

"For she knew that I wished her well, and I rendered her some services. That will appear from the further narrative, but now it is necessary to commence at the beginning. You, gentlemen, know, perhaps, that I was not at Kyedani when Prince Boguslav came and took that lady to Taurogi? Therefore I will not repeat why that happened, for different people gave different accounts. I will only say that they had scarcely arrived when all saw at once that the prince was terribly in love —"

"God punish him!" cried Kmita.

"Amusements followed, such as had not been before,—

tilting at the ring and tournaments. Any one would have
thought it a time of the greatest peace; but letters were coming in every day, as well as envoys from the elector and from
Prince Yanush. We knew that Prince Yanush was pushed
by Sapyeha and the confederates; he implored for rescue
by the mercy of God, for destruction was threatening him.
We did nothing. On the elector's boundary troops were
standing ready, captains were coming with letters; but we
did not go with assistance, for the prince had no success
with the lady."

"Is that why Boguslav did not give aid to his cousin?"
asked Zagloba.

"It is. Patterson said the same, and all the persons
nearest the prince. Some complained of this; others were
glad that the Radzivills were falling. Sakovich conducted
all public business for the prince, answered letters, and held
council with the envoys; but the prince was laboring on one
idea only, to contrive some kind of amusement, either a cavalcade or hunt. He, a miser, scattered money on every side.
He gave orders to fell forests for whole miles, so that the
lady might have a better view from her windows; in a word,
he really scattered flowers under her feet, and received her
in such fashion that had she been Queen of Sweden he could
have invented nothing better. Many pitied her and said,
'All this is for her ruin; as to marrying, the prince will not
marry, and if he can only catch her heart he will deceive
her.' But it appeared that she was not a lady to be conducted whither virtue does not go. Oh!"

"Well, what?" cried Kmita, springing up. "I know that
better than others!"

"How did Panna Billevich receive these royal homages?"
asked Pan Michael.

"At first with affable face, though it was evident that
she was bearing some sorrow in her heart. She was present at the hunts, at the masquerades, cavalcades, and tournaments, thinking indeed that these were usual court
amusements with the prince. It happened on a time that
the prince, straining his imagination over various spectacles,
wished to show the lady the counterfeit of war; he had a
settlement burned near Taurogi, infantry defended it, the
prince stormed the place. Evidently he gained a great victory, after which, being sated with praise, he fell at the
lady's feet and begged for a return of his love. It is not
known what he proposed to her, but from that time their

friendship was at an end. She began to hold night and day to the sleeve of her uncle, the sword-bearer of Rossyeni; but the prince —"

"Began to threaten her, did he?" cried Kmita.

"What, threaten! He dressed himself as a Greek shepherd, as Philemon; special couriers were flying to Königsberg for patterns of shepherd's garments, for ribbons and wigs. He feigned despair, he walked under her windows, and played on a lute. And here I tell you, gentlemen, what I really think. He was a savage executioner of the virtue of ladies, and it may be boldly said of him, as is said in our country of such people, his sighs filled out the sails of more than one lady; but this time he fell in love in earnest, — which is no wonder, for the lady reminds one more of a goddess than a dweller in this earthly vale."

Here Hassling blushed again, but Pan Andrei did not see it; for seizing his sides with satisfaction and pride, he looked with a triumphant glance at Zagloba and Volodyovski.

"We know her, a perfect Diana; she needs only the moon in her hair!" said the little knight.

"What, Diana! Diana's dogs would howl at Diana if they could see Panna Billevich."

"Therefore I said it is 'no wonder,'" answered Hassling.

"Well! But for that 'no wonder' I would burn him with a slow fire; for that 'no wonder' I would have him shod with hob-nails —"

"Give us peace!" interrupted Zagloba. "Get him first, then play pranks; but now let this cavalier speak."

"More than once I was on watch before the room in which he slept," continued Hassling. "I know how he turned on his bed, sighed, talked to himself, and hissed, as if from pain; evidently desires were burning him. He changed terribly, dried up. It may be, too, that the illness under which he afterward fell was diving into him. Meanwhile news flew through the whole court that the prince had become so distracted that he wanted to marry. This came to Yanush's princess, who with her daughter was living at Taurogi. Then began anger and disputes; for, as you know, Boguslav, according to agreement, is to marry Yanush's daughter when she comes of age. But he forgot everything, so pierced was his heart. Yanush's princess, falling into a rage, went with her daughter to Courland. That same evening he made a proposal to **Panna** Billevich."

"Did he make proposals?" cried Zagloba, Kmita, and Pan Michael, with astonishment.

"He did. First to the sword-bearer of Rossyeni, who was no less astonished than you, and would not believe his own ears; but convinced at last he was barely able to control himself from delight, for it was no small splendor for the house of Billevich to be united with the Radzivills. It is true, as Patterson said, that there is some connection already, but it is old and forgotten."

"Tell on!" said Kmita, trembling from impatience.

"Both went to the lady with all ostentation, as is the custom on such occasions. The whole court was trembling. Evil tidings came from Prince Yanush. Sakovich alone read them, but no one paid attention to them, nor even to Sakovich, for he had fallen out of favor because he had proposed the marriage. But among us some said that it was no novelty for the Radzivills to marry ordinary noble women ; that in the Commonwealth all nobles were equal, and that the house of Billevich went back to Roman times. And this was said by those who wished to gain for themselves the favor of the coming princess. Others asserted that this was a stratagem of the prince to come to great intimacy with the lady, which happens not infrequently between persons betrothed."

"That was it! Nothing else," said Zagloba.

"And so I think," said Hassling; "but listen further. When we were deliberating in the court among ourselves in this fashion, the report went out like a thunderbolt that the lady had cut all doubt as with a sabre, for she refused him directly."

"God bless her!" cried Kmita.

"She refused him directly," continued Hassling. "It was enough to look at the prince to know that. He, to whom princesses yielded, could not endure resistance, and almost went mad. It was dangerous to appear before him. We all saw that it would not remain long thus, and that the prince would use force sooner or later. In fact, the sword-bearer of Rossyeni was carried off the next day to Tyltsa, beyond the elector's boundary. That day the lady implored the officer keeping guard before her door to give her a loaded **pistol**. The officer did not refuse that, for being a **noble**

and man of honor he felt compassion for the lady and homage for her beauty and resolution."

"Who was that officer?" asked Kmita.

"I," answered Hassling, dryly.

Pan Andrei seized him by the shoulders, so that
the young Scot, being weak, called out from pain.

"That is nothing!" cried Kmita. "You are not a
prisoner; you are my brother, my friend! Tell me what
you wish! In God's name, tell me what you wish!"

"To rest awhile," answered Hassling, breathing heavily;
and he was silent. He merely pressed the hands which
Pan Michael and Zagloba gave him. At last, seeing that
all were burning with curiosity, he continued, —

"I forewarned her too of what all knew, that the prince's
physician was preparing some intoxicating drug. Meanwhile fears turned out to be groundless, for God interfered
in the affair. He touched the prince with his finger, threw
him on a bed of sickness, and kept him there a month. It
is a marvel, gentlemen, but it happened as if he had been
cut from his feet, as with a scythe, that same day, when he
intended to attack the virtue of this lady. The hand of
God, I say, nothing else! He thought that himself, and
was afraid; may be too that during his sickness the desire
left him, may be he was waiting to regain his strength;
it is enough, that when he came to himself he left her in
peace, and even permitted the sword-bearer to come from
Tyltsa. It is true, also, that the sickness which confined him
to his bed left him, but not the fever, which is, I believe,
crushing him to this day. It is true, also, that soon after
he left the bed he had to go on the expedition to Tykotsin,
where defeat met him. He returned with a still greater
fever; then the elector sent for him. But meanwhile a change
took place at Taurogi, of which it is wonderful and laugh-
able to tell; it is enough that the prince cannot count on the
loyalty of any officer or any attendant, unless on very old
ones, who neither hear nor see perfectly, and therefore guard
nothing well."

"What happened?" asked Zagloba.

"During the Tykotsin campaign, before the defeat at
Yanov, they captured a certain Panna Anusia Borzobogati,
and sent her to Taurogi."

"There, Grandmother, you have cakes!" exclaimed
Zagloba.

Pan Michael began to blink and move his mustaches; at

last he said : " Say nothing bad of her, or when you recover
you will have to meet me."

"Even if I wished I could say nothing bad of that lady.
But if she is your betrothed, I say that you take poor
care of her ; and if she is a relative, you know her too well
to deny what I say. It is enough that in one week she made
all in the company, old and young, in love with her, and
only by using her eyes with the addition of some tricks of
witchcraft, of which I can give no account."

"She ! I should know her in hell by this," muttered
Zagloba.

"It is a wonderful thing !" said Hassling. "Panna Billevich is equal to her in beauty, but has such dignity and un-
approachableness that a man while admiring and doing
homage to her does not dare to raise his eyes, much less to
conceive any hope. You know yourselves, gentlemen, that
there are different kinds of ladies : some are like ancient ves-
tals ; others, you have barely seen them and you wish — "

"Worthy sir !" said Pan Michael, threateningly.

"Don't make a fool of yourself, Michael, for he tells the
truth," said Zagloba. "You go around like a young cock-
erel and show the whites of your eyes ; but that she is a
coquette we all know, and you have said so more than a
hundred times."

"Let us leave this matter," said Hassling. "I wished
simply to explain to you, gentlemen, why only a few were
in love with Panna Billevich, those who could really appreciate her unrivalled perfection [here he blushed again],
and with Panna Borzobogati nearly all. As God is dear to
me, I had to laugh, for it was just as if some plague had
come upon hearts. Disputes and duels increased in the
twinkle of an eye. And about what ? For what ? You
must know that there was no one who could boast of the
love of the lady ; each one believed blindly in this alone,
that earlier or later he would have some success — "

"He has painted her, as it were !" muttered Pan
Michael.

"But these two young ladies became wonderfully fond
of each other," continued Hassling ; "one would not move
a step without the other, and Panna Borzobogati manages in
Taurogi as it pleases her."

"How is that ?" asked the little knight.

"For she rules everybody. Sakovich did not go on a
campaign this time, because he is in love ; and Sakovich is

absolute master in all the possessions of Prince Boguslav.
And Panna Anusia governs through him."

"Is he so much in love with her?" asked Pan Michael.

"He is, and has the greatest confidence in himself, for
he is a very rich man."

"And his name is Sakovich?"

"You wish, I see, to remember him well."

"Certainly!" answered Pan Michael, as it were, carelessly,
but at the same time he moved his mustaches so ominously
that a shudder went through Zagloba.

"I only wish to add," continued Hassling, "that if Panna
Borzobogati should command Sakovich to betray the prince
and lighten her escape and that of her friend, I think he
would do it without hesitation; but so far as I know she
wishes to do that without his knowledge, maybe to spite
him, who knows? It is enough that an officer, a relative
of mine, but not a Catholic, assured me that the departure
of the sword-bearer with the ladies is arranged; officers
are involved in the conspiracy, and it is to take place
soon."

Here Hassling began to breathe heavily, for he was weary
and was using the last of his strength.

"And this is the most important thing that I had to tell
you," added he, hurriedly.

Volodyovski and Kmita seized their heads.

"Whither are they going to flee?"

"To the forests and through the forests to Byalovyej."

Further conversation was interrupted by the entrance of
Sapyeha's orderly, who delivered to Pan Michael and Kmita
a quarter of a sheet of paper folded in four. Volodyovski
had barely unfolded his when he said, —

"The order to occupy positions for to-morrow's work."

"Do you hear how the cannons are roaring?" asked
Zagloba.

"Well, to-morrow! to-morrow!"

"Uf! hot!" said Zagloba, "a bad day for a storm, —
may the devil take such heat! Mother of God! But more
than one will grow cold in spite of the heat; but not those —
not those who commend themselves to Thee, our Patroness — But the cannons are thundering! I am too old for
storms; the open field is something else."

Another officer appeared in the door.

"Is his grace Pan Zagloba here?" asked he.

"I am here."

"By the command of our Gracious King, you are to be near his person to-morrow."

"Ha ! he wishes to keep me from the storm, for he knows that the old man will move first, only let the trumpets sound. He is a kind lord, mindful ; I should not like to annoy him ; but whether I shall restrain myself I know not, for when the desire presses me I think of nothing, and roll straight into the smoke. Such is my nature ! A kind lord ! Do you hear how the trumpets are sounding for every one to take his place ? Well, to-morrow, to-morrow. Saint Peter will have work ; he must have his books ready. In hell too they have put fresh pitch in the kettles, a bath for the Swedes. Uf! uf! to-morrow ! "

CHAPTER XL.

JULY 1, between Povanski and the settlement afterward called Marymont, was celebrated a great field Mass, which ten thousand men of the quarter-soldiers heard with attentive mind. The king made a vow that in case of victory he would build a church to the Most Holy Lady. Dignitaries, the hetmans, the knights made vows, and even simple soldiers, following the example, each according to his means, for this was to be the day of the final storm.

After the Mass each of the leaders moved to his own command. Sapyeha took his position opposite the Church of the Holy Ghost, which at that time was outside the walls; but because it was the key to the walls, it was greatly strengthened by the Swedes, and occupied in fitting manner by the troops. Charnyetski was to capture Dantzig House, for the rear wall of that building formed a part of the city wall, and by passing through the building it was possible to reach the city. Pyotr Opalinski, the voevoda of Podlyasye, with men from Great Poland and Mazovia, was to attack from the Cracow suburbs and the Vistula. The quarter-regiments were to attack the gates of New City. There were so many men that they almost exceeded the approaches to the walls; the entire plain, all the neighboring suburban villages and the meadows were overflowed with a sea of soldiers. Beyond the men were white tents, after the tents wagons far away; the eye was lost in the blue distance before it could reach the end of that swarm.

Those legions were standing in perfect readiness, with weapons point forward, and one foot in advance for the run; they were ready at any moment to rush to the breaches made by the guns of heavy calibre, and especially by Zamoyski's great guns. The guns did not cease to play for a moment; the storm was deferred only because they were waiting for the final answer of Wittemberg to the letter which the grand chancellor Korytsinski had sent him. When about midday the officer returned with a refusal, the ominous trumpets rang out around the city, and the storm began.

The armies of the kingdom under the hetmans, Charnyetski's men, the regiments of the king, the infantry regiments of Zamoyski, the Lithuanians of Sapyeha, and the
legions of the general militia rushed toward the walls like a
swollen river. But from behind the walls bloomed out against
them rolls of white smoke and darts of flame; heavy cannon, arquebuses, double-barrelled guns, muskets thundered
simultaneously; the earth was shaken in its foundations.
The balls broke into that throng of men, ploughed long
furrows in it; but the men ran on and tore up to the fortress,
regarding neither fire nor death. Clouds of powder smoke
hid the sun.

Each attacked furiously what was nearest him, — the hetmans the gates of New City; Charnyetski, Dantzig House;
Sapyeha with the Lithuanians, the Church of the Holy
Ghost; the Mazovians and men of Great Poland, the Cracow
suburbs.

The heaviest work fell to the last-mentioned men, for the
palaces and houses along the Cracow suburbs were turned
into fortresses. But that day such fury of battle had seized
the Mazovians that nothing could stand before their onset.
They took by storm house after house, palace after palace;
they fought in windows, in doors, in passages.

After the capture of one house, before the blood was dry
on their hands and faces, they rushed to another; again a
hand-to-hand battle, and again they rushed farther. The
private regiments vied with the general militia, and the
general militia with the infantry. They had been commanded before advancing to the storm to carry at their
breasts bundles of unripe grain to ward off the bullets, but
in the ardor and frenzy of battle they hurled aside every
defence, and ran forward with bare bosoms. In the
midst of a bloody struggle the chapel of the Tsar Shuiski
and the lordly palace of the Konyetspolskis were captured.
The Swedes were destroyed to the last man in the smaller
buildings, in the stables of the magnates, in the gardens descending to the Vistula. Near the Kazanovski Palace the
Swedish infantry tried to make a stand in the street, and
reinforced from the walls of the palace, from the church
and the bell-tower of the Bernardines, which was turned
into a strong fortress, they received the attack with a cutting fire.

But the hail of bullets did not stop the attack for a moment; and the nobles, with the cry of "Mazovians victo-

rious!" rushed with sabres into the centre of the quadrangle; after them came the land infantry, servants armed with poles, pickaxes, and scythes. The quadrangle was broken in a twinkle, and hewing began. The Swedes and Poles were so mingled together that they formed one gigantic mass, which squirmed, twisted, and rolled in its own blood between the Kazanovski Palace, the house of Radzeyovski, and the Cracow gate.

But new legions of warriors breathing blood came on continually, like a foaming river, from the direction of the Cracow gate. The Swedish infantry was cut to pieces at last, and then began that famous storm of the Kazanovski Palace and the Bernardines' Church which in great part decided the fate of the day.

Zagloba commanded, for he was mistaken the day before in thinking that the king called him to his person only to be present; for, on the contrary, he confided to him, as to a famous and experienced warrior, command over the camp servants, who with the quarter-soldiers and the general militia were to go as volunteers to storm from that side. Zagloba was willing, it is true, to go with these men in the rear, and content himself with occupying the palaces already captured; but when in the very beginning all vying with one another were mingled completely, the human current bore him on with the others. So he went; for although he had from nature great circumspection as a gift, and preferred, where it was possible, not to expose his life to danger, he had for so many years become accustomed to battles in spite of himself, had been present in so many dreadful slaughters, that when the inevitable came he fought with others, and even better than others, for he fought with desperation and rage in a manful heart.

So at this time he found himself at the gate of the Kazanovski Palace, or rather in the hell which was raging dreadfully in front of that gate; that is, amid a whirlpool, heat, crushing, a storm of bullets, fire, smoke, groans and shouts of men. Thousands of scythes, picks, and axes were driven against the gate; a thousand arms pressed and pushed it furiously. Some men fell as if struck by lightning; others pushed themselves into their places, trampled their bodies, and forced themselves forward, as if seeking death of purpose. No one had seen or remembered a more stubborn defence, but also not a more resolute attack. From the highest stories bullets were rained and pitch poured down on the gate; but those who were under fire, even had they wished, could not withdraw, so powerfully were they pressed from behind. You saw single men, wet from perspiration, black from smoke, with set teeth, with wild eyes, hurling at the gate beams of such size that at an ordinary time three strong men would not have been able to lift them. So their strength was trebled by frenzy. All the windows were stormed simultaneously, ladders were placed at the upper stories, lattices were hewn from the walls. But still from those lattices and windows, from openings cut in the walls, were sticking out musket-barrels, which did not cease to smoke for a moment. But at last such smoke ascended, such dust rose, that on that bright sunny day the assailants could scarcely recognize one another. In spite of that they did not desist from the struggle, but climbed ladders the more fiercely, attacked the gate the more wildly, because the sounds from the Church of the Bernardines announced that there other parties were storming with similar energy.

Now Zagloba cried with a voice so piercing that it was heard amid the uproar and shots: "A box with powder under the gate!"

It was brought to him in a twinkle; he gave command at once to cut just beneath the bolt an opening of such size that the box alone would find place in it. When the box was fitted in, Zagloba himself set fire to the sulphur thread, then commanded, —

"Aside! Close to the wall!"

Those standing near rushed to both sides, toward those who had placed the ladders at the farther windows. A moment of expectation followed.

A mighty report shook the air, and new bundles of smoke rose toward the sky. Zagloba sprang forward with his men; they saw that the explosion had not rent the gate to small pieces, but had torn the hinges from the right side, wrested away a couple of strong beams, already partly cut, turned the handle, and pulled off one half of the lower part, so that a passage was open through which large men might enter easily.

Sharpened stakes, axes, and scythes began to beat violently on the weakened door; a hundred arms pushed it with utmost effort, a sharp crash was heard, and all one half fell, uncovering the depth of the dark antechamber.

In that darkness gleamed discharges of musketry; but the human river rushed forward with an irresistible torrent, — the palace was captured.

At the same time they broke in through the windows, and
a terrible battle with cold weapons began in the interior of
the palace. Chamber was taken after chamber, corridor
after corridor, story after story. The walls had been so
shattered and weakened beforehand that the ceiling in many
rooms fell with a crash, covering with their ruins Poles and
Swedes. But the Mazovians advanced like a conflagration;
they penetrated every place, overturning with their long
knives, cutting and thrusting. No man of the Swedes asked
for quarter, but neither was it given. In some corridors
and passages the piles of bodies so blocked the way that
the Swedes made barricades of them; the Poles pulled them
out by the feet, by the hair, and hurled them through the
windows. Blood flowed in streams through the passages.
Groups of Swedes defended themselves yet here and there,
and repelled with weakening hands the furious blows of the
stormers. Blood had covered their faces, darkness was
covering their eyes, more than one sank on his knees, and
still fought; pressed on every side, suffocated by the throng
of opponents, the Scandinavians died in silence, in accord
with their fame, as beseemed warriors. The statues of divin-
ities and ancient heroes, bespattered with blood, looked
with lifeless eyes on that death.

Roh Kovalski raged specially in the upper stories; but
Zagloba rushed with his men to the terraces, and when he
had cut to pieces the infantry defending themselves there,
he hurried from the terraces to those wonderful gardens
which were famed throughout Europe. The trees were already cut down, the rare plants destroyed by Polish balls,
the fountains broken, the earth ploughed up by bombshells, —
in a word, everywhere a desert and destruction, though the
Swedes had not raised their robber hands against this place,
out of regard for the person of Radzeyovski. A savage
struggle set in there, too; but it lasted only a short time,
for the Swedes gave but feeble resistance, and were cut to
pieces under the personal command of Zagloba. The soldiers dispersed now through the garden, and the whole palace was plundered.

Zagloba betook himself to a corner of the garden, to a
place where the walls formed a strong "angle," and
where the sun did not come, for the knight wished to rest
somewhat; and he rubbed the sweat from his heated forehead. All at once he espied some strange monsters, looking
at him with hostility through an iron grating.

The cage was fixed in a corner of the wall, so that balls falling from the outside could not reach it. The door of the cage was wide open; but those meagre and ugly creatures did not think of taking advantage of this. Evidently terrified by the uproar, the whistling of bullets, and the fierce slaughter at which they had looked a moment before, they crowded into a corner of the cage, and hidden in the straw, gave note of their terror only by muttering.

"Are those monkeys or devils?" said Zagloba to himself.

Suddenly anger seized him, courage swelled in his breast, and raising his sabre he fell upon the cage.

A terrible panic was the answer to the first blow of his sabre. The monkeys, which the Swedish soldiers had treated kindly and fed from their own slender rations, fell into such a fright that madness simply seized them; and since Zagloba stopped their exit, they began to rush through the cage with unnatural springs, hanging to the sides, to the top, screaming and biting. At last one in frenzy sprang on Zagloba's shoulder, and seizing him by the head, fastened to it with all his power; another hung to his right shoulder, a third caught him in front by the neck, the fourth hung to his long split sleeves which were tied together behind; and Zagloba, stifled, sweating, struggled in vain, in vain struck blindly toward the rear. Breath soon failed him, his eyes were standing out of his head, and he began to cry with despairing voice, —

"Gracious gentlemen! save me!"

The cry brought a number of men, who, unable to understand what was happening, rushed to his aid with blood-streaming sabres; but they halted at once in astonishment, they looked at one another, and as if under the influence of some spell they burst out in one great laugh. More soldiers ran up, a crowd was formed; but laughter was communicated to all as an epidemic. They staggered as if drunk, they held their sides; their faces, besmeared with the gore of men, were twisting spasmodically, and the more Zagloba struggled the more did they laugh. Now Roh Kovalski ran down from an upper story, scattered the crowd, and freed his uncle from the Simian embraces.

"You rascals!" cried the panting Zagloba, "I would you were slain! You are laughing to see a Catholic in oppression from these African monsters. I would you were slain! Were it not for me you would be butting your heads to this moment against the gate, for you deserve nothing better. I wish you were dead, because you are not worth these monkeys."

"I wish you were dead yourself, king of the monkeys!" cried the man standing nearest.

"*Simiarum destructor* (destroyer of monkeys)!" cried another.

"Victor!" cried the third.

"What, victor! he is *victus* (conquered)!"

Here Roh Kovalski came again to the aid of his uncle, and struck the nearest man in the breast with his fist; the man dropped to the earth that instant with blood coming from his mouth. Others retreated before the anger of Kovalski, some drew their sabres; but further disputes were interrupted by the uproar and shots coming from the Bernardines' Church. Evidently the storm continued there yet in full force, and judging from the feverish musketry-fire, the Swedes were not thinking of surrender.

"With succor! to the church! to the church!" cried Zagloba.

He sprang himself to the top of the palace; there, from the right wing, was to be seen the church, which seemed to be in flames. Crowds of stormers were circling around it convulsively, not being able to enter and perishing for nothing in a cross fire; for bullets were rained on them from the Cracow gate as thickly as sand.

"Cannon to the windows!" shouted Zagloba.

There were guns enough, large and small, in the Kazanovski Palace, therefore they were drawn to the windows; from fragments of costly furniture and pedestals of statues, platforms were constructed; and in the course of half an hour a number of guns were looking out through the empty openings of the windows toward the church.

"Roh!" said Zagloba, with uncommon irritation, "I must do something considerable, or my glory is lost through those monkeys, — would that the plague had stifled them! The whole army will ridicule me; and though there is no lack of words in my mouth, still I cannot meet the whole world. I must wipe away this confusion, or wide as this Commonwealth is they will herald me through it as king of the monkeys!"

"Uncle must wipe away this confusion!" repeated Roh, with a thundering voice.

"And the first means will be that, as I have captured the

Kazanovski Palace, — for let any one say that it was not I who did it — "

"Let any one say that it was not Uncle who did it!" repeated Roh.

"I will capture that church, so help me the Lord God, amen!" concluded Zagloba.

Then he turned to his attendants who were there at the guns, —

"Fire!"

Fear seized the Swedes, who were defending themselves with despair in the church, when the whole side wall began on a sudden to tremble. Bricks, rubbish, lime, fell on those who were sitting in the windows, at the port-holes, on the fragments of the inside cornices, at the pigeon-holes, through which they were firing at the besiegers. A terrible dust rose in the house of God, and mixed with the smoke began to stifle the wearied men. One man could not see another in the darkness. Cries of "I am suffocating, I am suffocating!" still increased the terror. The noise of balls falling through the windows, of leaden lattice falling to the floor, the heat, the exhalations from bodies, turned the retreat of God into a hell upon earth. The frightened soldiers stood aside from entrances, windows, and port-holes. The panic is changed into frenzy. Again terrified voices call: "I am suffocating! Air! Water!" Hundreds of voices begin to roar, —

"A white flag! a white flag!"

Erskine, who is commanding, seizes the flag with his own hand to display it outside. At that moment the entrance bursts, a line of stormers rush in like an avalanche of Satans, and a slaughter follows. There is sudden silence in the church; there is heard only the beast-like panting of the strugglers, the bite of steel on bones, and on the stone floor groans, the patter of blood; and at times some voice in which there is nothing human cries, "Quarter! Quarter!" After an hour's fighting the bell on the tower begins to thunder, and thunders, thunders, — to the victory of the Mazovians, to the funeral of the Swedes.

The Kazanovski Palace, the cloister, and the bell-tower are captured.

Pyotr Opalinski himself, the voevoda of Podlyasye, appeared in the blood-stained throng before the palace on his horse.

"Who came to our aid from the palace?" cried he, wishing to outcry the sound and the roar of men.

" He who captured the palace ! " said a powerful man, appearing before the voevoda, — " I ! "

" What is your name ? "

" Zagloba."

"Vivat Zagloba!" bellowed thousands of throats.

But the terrible Zagloba pointed with his stained sabre toward the gate, —

"We have not done enough yet. Turn the cannon toward the wall and against the gate. Advance! follow me!"

The mad throng rush in the direction of the gate. Meanwhile, oh wonder! the fire of the Swedes instead of increasing is growing weak. At the same moment some voice unexpected and piercing cries from the top of the bell-tower, —

" Charnyetski is in the city ! I see our squadrons !"

The Swedish fire was weakening more and more.

" Halt ! halt ! " commanded the voevoda.

But the throng did not hear him and rushed at random. That moment a white flag appeared on the Cracow gate.

In truth, Charnyetski, having forced his way through Dantzig House, rushed like a hurricane into the precincts of the fortress ; when the Danillovich Palace was taken, and when a moment later the Lithuanian colors glittered on the walls near the Church of the Holy Ghost, Wittemberg saw that further resistance was vain. The Swedes might defend themselves yet in the lofty houses of Old and New City ; but the inhabitants had already taken arms, and the defence would end in a terrible slaughter of the Swedes without hope of victory.

The trumpeters began then to sound on the walls and to wave white flags. Seeing this, the Polish commanders withheld the storm. General Löwenhaupt, attended by a number of colonels, went out through the gate of New City, and rushed with all breath to the king.

Yan Kazimir had the city in his hands now ; but the kind king wished to stop the flow of Christian blood, therefore he settled on the conditions offered to Wittemberg at first. The city was to be surrendered, with all the booty collected in it. Each Swede was permitted to take with him only what he had brought from Sweden. The garrison with all the generals and with arms in hand were to march out of the city, taking their sick and wounded and the Swedish ladies, of whom a number of tens were in Warsaw. To the Poles who were serving with the Swedes, amnesty was given, with the idea

that surely none were serving of their own will. Boguslav
Radzivill alone was excepted. To this Wittemberg agreed
the more readily since the prince was at that moment with
Douglas on the Bug.

The conditions were signed at once. All the bells in the
churches announced to the city and the world that the
capital had passed again into the hands of its rightful
monarch. An hour later a multitude of the poorest people
came out from behind the walls, seeking charity and bread
in the Polish camp; for all in the city except the Swedes
were in want of food. The king commanded to give what
was possible, and went himself to look at the departure of
the Swedish garrison.

He was surrounded by church and lay dignitaries, by a
suite so splendid that it dazzled the people. Nearly all
the troops — that is, the troops of the kingdom under the
hetmans, Charnyetski's division, the Lithuanians under
Sapyeha, and an immense crowd of general militia, together
with the camp servants — assembled around his Majesty;
or all were curious to see those Swedes with whom a few
hours before they had fought so terribly and bloodily.
Polish commissioners were posted at all the gates, from
the moment of signing the conditions; these commissioners
were intrusted with the duty of seeing that the Swedes
bore off no booty. A special commission was occupied with
receiving the booty in the city itself.

In the van came the cavalry, which was not numerous,
especially since Boguslav's men were excluded from the
right of departure; next came the field artillery with light
guns; the heavy pieces were given to the Poles. The men
marched at the sides of the guns with lighted matches.
Before them waved their unfurled flags, which as a mark
of honor were lowered before the Polish king, recently a
wanderer. The artillerists marched proudly, looking straight
into the eyes of the Polish knights, as if they wished to say,
" We shall meet again ! " And the Poles wondered at their
haughty bearing and courage unbent by misfortune. Then
appeared the wagons with officers and wounded. In the
first one lay Benedikt Oxenstiern the chancellor, before
whom Yan Kazimir had commanded the infantry to present
arms, wishing to show that he knew how to respect virtue
even in an enemy.

Then to the sound of drums, and with waving flags,
marched the quadrangle of unrivalled Swedish infantry, re-

sembling, according to the expression of Suba Gazi, moving castles. After them advanced a brilliant party of cavalry, armored from foot to head, and with a blue banner on which a golden lion was embroidered. These surrounded the chief of staff. At sight of them a murmur passed through the crowd, —

"Wittemberg is coming! Wittemberg is coming!"

In fact, the field-marshal himself was approaching; and with him the younger Wrangel, Horn, Erskine, Löwenhaupt, Forgell. The eyes of the Polish knights were turned with eagerness toward them, and especially toward the face of Wittemberg. But his face did not indicate such a terrible warrior as he was in reality. It was an aged face, pale, emaciated by disease. He had sharp features, and above his mouth a thin, small mustache turned up at the ends. The pressed lips and long, pointed nose gave him the appearance of an old and grasping miser. Dressed in black velvet and with a black hat on his head, he looked more like a learned astrologer or a physician; and only the gold chain on his neck, the diamond star on his breast, and a field-marshal's baton in his hand showed his high office of leader.

Advancing, he cast his eyes unquietly on the king, on the king's staff, on the squadrons standing in rank; then his eyes took in the immense throngs of the general militia, and an ironical smile came out on his pale lips.

But in those throngs a murmur was rising ever greater, and the word "Wittemberg! Wittemberg!" was in every mouth.

After a while the murmur changed into deep grumbling, but threatening, like the grumbling of the sea before a storm. From instant to instant it was silent; and then far away in the distance, in the last ranks, was heard some voice in peroration. This voice was answered by others; greater numbers answered them; they were heard ever louder and spread more widely, like ominous echoes. You would swear that a storm was coming from a distance, and that it would burst with all power.

The officers were anxious and began to look at the king with disquiet.

"What is that? What does that mean?" asked Yan Kazimir.

Then the grumbling passed into a roar as terrible as if thunders had begun to wrestle with one another in the sky. The immense throng of general militia moved violently, precisely like standing grain when a hurricane is sweeping around it with giant wing. All at once some tens of thousands of sabres were glittering in the sun.

"What is that? What does that mean?" asked the king, repeatedly.

No one could answer him. Then Volodyovski, standing near Sapyeha, exclaimed: "That is Pan Zagloba!"

Volodyovski had guessed aright. The moment the conditions of surrender were published and had come to the ears of Zagloba, the old noble fell into such a terrible rage that speech was taken from him for a while. When he came to himself his first act was to spring among the ranks of the general militia and fire up the minds of the nobles. They heard him willingly; for it seemed to all that for so much bravery, for such toil, for so much bloodshed under the walls of Warsaw, they ought to have a better vengeance against the enemy. Therefore great circles of chaotic and stormy men surrounded Zagloba, who threw live coals by the handful on the powder, and with his speech fanned into greater proportions the fire which all the more easily seized their heads, that they were already smoking from the usual libations consequent on victory.

"Gracious gentlemen!" said he, "behold these old hands have toiled fifty years for the country; fifty years have they been shedding the blood of the enemy at every wall of the Commonwealth; and to-day — I have witnesses — they captured the Kazanovski Palace and the Bernardines' Church! And when, gracious gentlemen, did the Swedes lose heart, when did they agree to capitulate? It was when we turned our guns from the Bernardines to the Old City. We have not spared our blood, brothers; it has been shed bountifully, and no one has been spared but the enemy. But we, brothers, have left our lands without masters, our servants without lords, our wives without husbands, our children without fathers, — oh, my dear children, what is happening to you now? — and we have come here with our naked breasts against cannon. And what is our reward for so doing? This is it: Wittemberg goes forth free, and besides, they give him honor for the road. The executioner of our country departs, the blasphemer of religion departs; the raging enemy of the Most Holy Lady, the burner of our houses, the thief of our last bit of clothing, the murderer of our wives and children, — oh, my children, where are you now ? — the disgracer of the clergy and virgins consecrated to God! Woe to thee, O country! Shame to you, nobles! A new agony is awaiting you. Oh, our holy faith! Woe to you, suffering churches! weeping to thee and complaint, O Chenstohova! for Wittemberg is departing in freedom, and will return soon to press out tears and blood, to finish killing those whom he has not yet killed, to burn that which he has not yet burned, to put shame on that which he has not yet put to shame! Weep, O Poland and Lithuania! Weep, ranks of people, as I weep, — an old soldier who, descending to the grave, must look on your agony! Woe to thee, Ilion, the city of aged Priam! Woe! woe! woe!"

So spoke Zagloba; and thousands listened to him, and wrath raised the hair on the heads of the nobles; but he moved on farther. Again he complained, tore his clothing, and laid bare his breast. He entered also into the army, which gave a willing ear to his complaints; for, in truth, there was a terrible animosity in all hearts against Wittemberg. The tumult would have burst out at once; but Zagloba himself restrained it, lest, if it burst too early, Wittemberg might save himself somehow; but if it broke out when he was leaving the city and would show himself to the general militia, they would bear him apart on their sabres before any one could see what was done.

And his reckoning was justified. At sight of the tyrant frenzy seized the brains of the chaotic and half-drunken nobles, and a terrible storm burst forth in the twinkle of an eye. Forty thousand sabres were flashing in the sun, forty thousand throats began to bellow, —

"Death to Wittemberg! Give him here! Make mince-meat of him! make mince-meat of him!"

To the throngs of nobles were joined throngs more chaotic still and made brutal by the recent shedding of blood, the camp servants; even the more disciplined regular squadrons began to murmur fiercely against the oppressor, and the storm began to fly with rage against the Swedish staff.

At the first moment all lost their heads, though all understood what the matter was. "What is to be done?" cried voices near the king. "Oh, merciful Jesus!" "Rescue! defend! It is a shame not to observe the conditions!"

Enraged crowds rush in among the squadrons, press upon them; the squadrons are confused, cannot keep their places. Around them are sabres, sabres, and sabres; under the sabres are inflamed faces, threatening eyes, howling mouths; uproar, noise, wild cries grow with amazing rapid· ity. In front are rushing camp servants, camp followers, and every kind of army rabble, more like beasts or devils than men.

Wittemberg understood what was happening. His face grew pale as a sheet; sweat, abundant and cold, covered his forehead in a moment; and, oh wonder! that field-marshal who hitherto was ready to threaten the whole world, that conqueror of so many armies, that captor of so many cities, that old soldier was then so terribly frightened at the howling mass that presence of mind left him utterly. He trembled in his whole body, he dropped his hands and groaned, spittle began to flow from his mouth to the golden chain, and the field-marshal's baton dropped from his hand. Meanwhile the terrible throng was coming nearer and nearer; ghastly forms were surrounding already the hapless generals; a moment more, they would bear them apart on sabres, so that not a fragment of them would remain.

Other Swedish generals drew their sabres, wishing to die weapon in hand, as beseemed knights; but the aged oppressor grew weak altogether, and half closed his eyes.

At this moment Volodyovski, with his men, sprang to the rescue of the staff. Going wedge-form on a gallop, he split the mob as a ship moving with all sails bears apart the towering waves of the sea. The cry of the trampled rabble was mingled with the shouts of the Lauda squadron; but the horsemen reached the staff first, and surrounded it in the twinkle of an eye with a wall of horses, a wall of their own breasts and sabres.

"To the king!" cried the little knight.

They moved on. The throng surrounded them from every side, ran along the flanks and the rear, brandished sabres and clubs, howled more and more terribly; but the Lauda men pushed forward, thrusting out their sabres from moment to moment at the sides, as a strong stag thrusts with his antlers when surrounded by wolves.

Then Voynillovich sprang to the aid of Volodyovski; after him Vilchkovski with a regiment of the king, then Prince Polubinski; and all together, defending themselves unceasingly, conducted the staff to the presence of Yan Kazimir.

The tumult increased instead of diminishing. It seemed, after a time, that the excited rabble would try to seize the Swedish generals without regard to the king. Wittemberg recovered; but fear did not leave him in the least. He sprang from his horse then; and as a hare pressed by dogs or wolves takes refuge under a wagon in motion, so did he, in spite of his gout, throw himself at the feet of Yan Kazimir.

Then he dropped on his knees, and seizing the king's stirrup, began to cry: " Save me, Gracious Lord, save me ! I have your royal word; the agreement is signed. Save me, save me ! Have mercy on us ! Do not let them murder me !"

The king, at sight of such abasement and such shame, turned away his eyes with aversion and said, —

" Field-marshal, pray be calm."

But he had a troubled face himself, for he knew not what to do. Around them were gathering crowds ever greater, and approaching with more persistence. It is true that the squadrons stood as if for battle, and Zamoyski's infantry had formed a terrible quadrangle round about; but what was to be the end of it all ?

The king looked at Charnyetski; but Charnyetski only twisted his beard with rage, his soul was storming with such anger against the disobedience of the general militia. Then the chancellor, Korytsinski, said, —

" Gracious Lord, we must keep the agreement."

" We must !" replied the king.

Wittemberg, who was looking carefully into their eyes, breathed more freely.

" Gracious Lord," said he, " I believe in your words as in God."

To which Pototski, the old hetman of the kingdom, cried, —

" And why have you broken so many oaths, so many agreements, so many terms of surrender ? With what any man wars, from that will he perish. Why did you seize, in spite of the terms of capitulation, the king's regiment commanded by Wolf ? "

" Miller did that, not I," answered Wittemberg.

The hetman looked at him with disdain; then turned to the king, —

" Gracious Lord, I do not say this to incite your Royal Grace to break agreements also, for let perfidy be on their side alone."

"What is to be done?" asked the king.

"If we send them to Prussia, fifty thousand nobles will follow and cut them to pieces before they reach Pultusk, unless we give them the whole regular army as a guard, and we cannot do that. Hear, your Royal Grace, how the militia are howling! In truth, there is a well-founded animosity against Wittemberg. It is needful first to safeguard his person, and then to send all away when the fire has cooled down."

"There is no other way!" said Korytsinski.

"But where are they to be kept? We cannot keep them here; for here, devil take it! civil war would break out," said the voevoda of Rus.

Now Sobiepan Zamoyski appeared, and pouting his lips greatly, said with his customary spirit, —

"Well, Gracious Lord, give them to me at Zamost; let them sit there till calm comes. I will defend Wittemberg there from the nobles. Let them try to get him from me!"

"But on the road will your worthiness defend the field-marshal?" asked the chancellor.

"I can depend on my servants yet. Or have I not infantry and cannon? Let any one take him from Zamoyski! We shall see."

Here he put his hands on his hips, struck his thighs, and bent from one side of the saddle to the other.

"There is no other way," said the chancellor.

"I see no other," added Lantskoronski.

"Then take them," said the king to Zamoyski.

But Wittemberg, seeing that his life was threatened no longer, considered it proper to protest.

"We did not expect this!" said he.

"Well, we do not detain you; the road is open," said Pototski, pointing to the distance with his hand.

Wittemberg was silent.

Meanwhile the chancellor sent a number of officers to declare to the nobles that Wittemberg would not depart in freedom, but would be sent to Zamost. The tumult, it is true, was not allayed at once; still the news had a soothing effect. Before night fell attention was turned in another direction. The troops began to enter the city, and the sight of the recovered capital filled all minds with the delight of triumph.

The king rejoiced; still the thought that he was unable to observe the conditions of the agreement troubled him not a little, as well as the endless disobedience of the general militia.

Charnyetski was chewing his anger. " With such troops one can never be sure of to-morrow," said he to the king. " Sometimes they fight badly, sometimes heroically, all from impulse ; and at any outbreak rebellion is ready."

" God grant them not to disperse," said the king, "for they are needed yet, and they think that they have finished everything."

"The man who caused that outbreak should be torn asunder with horses, without regard to the services which he has rendered," continued Charnyetski.

The strictest orders were given to search for Zagloba, for it was a secret to no man that he had raised the storm ; but Zagloba had as it were dropped into water. They searched for him in the tents, in the tabor, even among the Tartars, all in vain. Tyzenhauz even said that the king, always kind and gracious, wished from his whole soul that they might not find him, and even undertook a nine days' devotion to that effect.

But a week later, after some dinner when the heart of the monarch was big with joy, the following words were heard from the mouth of Yan Kazimir, —

"Announce that Pan Zagloba is not to hide himself longer, for we are longing for his jests."

When Charnyetski was horrified at this, the king said, —

" Whoso in this Commonwealth should have justice without mercy in his heart would be forced to carry an axe in his bosom, and not a heart. Faults come easier here than anywhere, but in no land does repentance follow so quickly."

Saying this, the king had Babinich more in mind than Zagloba ; and he was thinking of Babinich because the young man had bowed down to the king's feet the day before with a petition that he would not hinder him from going to Lithuania. He said that he wished to freshen the war there, and attack the Swedes, as he had once attacked Hovanski. And as the king intended to send there a soldier experienced in partisan warfare, he permitted Babinich to go, gave him the means, blessed him, and whispered some wish in his ear, after which the young knight fell his whole length at his feet.

Then, without loitering, Kmita moved briskly toward the

east. Suoa Gazi, captured by a considerable present, permitted him to take five hundred fresh Dobrudja Tartars; fifteen hundred other good men marched with him, — a force with which it was possible to begin something. And the young man's head was fired with a desire for battle and warlike achievements The hope of glory smiled on him; he heard already how all Lithuania was repeating his name with pride and wonder. He heard especially how one beloved mouth repeated it, and his soul gave him wings.

And there was another reason why he rode forward so briskly. Wherever he appeared he was the first to announce the glad tidings: "The Swede is defeated, and Warsaw is taken!" Wherever his horse's hoofs sounded, the whole neighborhood rang with these words; the people along the roads greeted him with weeping; they rang bells in the church-towers and sang *Te Deum Laudamus!* When he rode through the forest the dark pines, when through the fields the golden grain, rocked by the wind, seemed to repeat and sound joyously, —

"The Swede is defeated! Warsaw is taken! Warsaw is taken!"

CHAPTER XLI.

THOUGH Kettling was near the person of Prince Boguslav, he did not know all, and could not tell of all that was done in Taurogi, for he was blinded himself by love for Panna Billevich.

Boguslav had also another confidant, Pan Sakovich, the starosta of Oshmiana; and he alone knew how deeply the prince was involved by love for his charming captive, and what means he was using to gain her heart and her person.

That love was merely a fierce desire, for Boguslav's heart was not capable of other feelings; but the desire was so violent that that experienced cavalier lost his head. And often in the evening, when alone with the starosta, he seized his own hair and cried, —

"I am burning, Sakovich, I am burning!"

Sakovich found means at once.

"Whoso wishes to take honey must drug the bees," said he. "And has your physician few of such intoxicating herbs? Give him the word to-day, and to-morrow the affair will be over."

But the prince did not like such a method, and that for various reasons. First, on a time, old Heraclius Billevich, the grandfather of Olenka, appeared to him in a dream, and standing at his pillow, looked with threatening eyes till the first crowing of the cocks. Boguslav remembered the dream; for that knight, without fear, was superstitious, dreaded charms, dream warnings, and supernatural apparitions so much that a shiver passed through him at thought of the terror and the shape in which that phantom might come a second time should he follow Sakovich's counsel. The starosta of Oshmiana himself, who did not believe greatly in God, but who, like the prince, dreaded dreams and enchantments, staggered somewhat in giving advice.

The second reason of Boguslav's delay was that the "Wallachian woman" was living with her step-daughter in Taurogi. They called Princess Radzivill, the wife of Yanush, "the Wallachian woman." That lady, coming from a country in which her sex have rather free manners, was not, in truth, over-stern; nay, maybe she understood too well the amusements of courtiers and ladies-in-waiting; still she could not endure that at her side a man, the coming husband of her step-daughter, should do a deed calling to heaven for vengeance.

But even later, when through the persuasions of Sakovich, and with the consent of the prince voevoda of Vilna, "the Wallachian woman" went with Yanush's daughter to Courland, Boguslav did not dare to do the deed. He feared the terrible outcry which would rise throughout all Lithuania. The Billeviches were wealthy people; they would not fail to crush him with a prosecution. The law punished such deeds with loss of property, honor, and life.

The Radzivills, it is true, were powerful, and might trample on law; but when victory in war was inclining to the side of Yan Kazimir, the young prince might fall into serious difficulties, in which he would lack power, friends, and henchmen. And just then it was hard to foresee how the war would end. Forces were coming every day to Yan Kazimir; the power of Karl Gustav was decreasing absolutely by the loss of men and the exhaustion of money.

Prince Boguslav, an impulsive but calculating man, reckoned with the position. His desires tormented him with fire, his reason advised restraint, superstitious fear bridled the outbursts of his blood. At the same time disease fell upon him; great and urgent questions rose, involving frequently the fate of the whole war; and all these causes rent the soul of the prince till he was mortally wearied.

Still, it is unknown how the struggle might have ended had it not been for Boguslav's self-love. He was a man of immense self-esteem. He counted himself an unequalled statesman, a great leader, a great knight, and an invincible captor of the hearts of women. Was he to use force or intoxicating drugs, — he who carried around with him a bound casket filled with love-letters from various foreign ladies of celebrity? Were his wealth, his titles, his power almost royal, his great name, his beauty and courtliness not equal to the conquest of one timid noble woman?

Besides, how much greater the triumph, how much

greater the delight, when the resistance of the maiden
drops, when she herself willingly, and with a heart beating like that of a seized bird, with burning face and eyes
veiled with mist, falls into those arms which are stretched
toward her!

A quiver passed through Boguslav at thought of that
moment, and he desired it as greatly as he did Olenka herself. He hoped always that that moment would come. He
writhed, he was impatient, he deceived himself. At one
time it seemed to him nearer, at another farther; and then
he cried that he was burning. But he did not cease to
work.

To begin with, he surrounded the maiden with minute
care, so that she must be thankful to him and think that he
is kind; for he understood that the feeling of gratitude and
friendship is that mild and warm flame which only needs to
be fanned and it will turn into a great fire. Their frequent
intercourse was to bring this about the more surely; hence
Boguslav showed no insistence, not wishing to chill confidence or frighten it away.

At the same time every look, every touch of the hand,
every word was calculated; nothing passed in vain, everything was the drop wearing the stone. All that he did for
Olenka might be interpreted as the hospitality of a host,
that innocent friendly attraction which one person feels for
another; but still it was done to create love. The boundary
was purposely blurred and indefinite, so that to pass it
would become easy in time; and thus the maiden might the
more lightly wander into those labyrinths where each form
might mean something or nothing. That play did not
agree, it is true, with the native impulsiveness of Boguslav.
Still he restrained himself, for he judged that that alone
would lead to the object; and at the same time he found
in it such satisfaction as the spider finds when weaving
his web, the traitorous bird-catcher when spreading his
net, or the hunter tracking patiently and with endurance
the wild beast. His own penetration, subtlety, and quickness, developed by life at the French court, amused the
prince.

He entertained Panna Aleksandra as if she were a sovereign princess; but in such a way that again it was not
easy for her to divine whether this was done exclusively
for her, or whether it flowed from his innate and acquired
politeness toward the fair sex in general. It is true

that he made her the chief person in all the entertainments, plays, cavalcades, and hunting expeditions; but
this came somewhat from the nature of things. After
the departure of Yanush's princess to Courland, she was
really first among the ladies at Taurogi. A multitude of
noble ladies from all Jmud had taken refuge in Taurogi, as
in a place lying near the boundary, so as to be protected by
the Swedes under the guardianship of the prince; but they
recognized Panna Billevich as first among all, since she
was the daughter of the most noted family. And while the
whole Commonwealth was swimming in blood, there was
no end to entertainments. You would have said that the
king's court with all the courtiers and ladies had gone to the
country for leisure and entertainment.

Boguslav ruled as an absolute monarch in Taurogi and in
all adjoining Electoral Prussia, in which he was frequently a
guest; therefore everything was at his orders. Towns furnished money and troops on his notes; the Prussian nobles
came gladly, in carriages and on horseback, to his feasts,
hunts, and tournaments. Boguslav even renewed, in honor
of his lady, the conflicts of knights within barriers, which
were already in disuse.

On a certain occasion he took active part in them; dressed
in silver armor, and girded with a silver sash which Panna
Billevich had to bind on him, he hurled from their horses
four of the first knights of Prussia, Kettling the fifth, and
Sakovich the sixth, though the last had such gigantic
strength that he stopped carriages in their course by seizing
a hind wheel. And what enthusiasm rose in the crowd of
spectators when afterward the silver-clad knight, kneeling
before his lady, took from her hand the crown of victory!
Shouts rang like the thunder of cannon, handkerchiefs were
waving, flags were lowered; but he raised his visor and
looked into her blushing face with his beautiful eyes,
pressing at the same time her hand to his lips.

Another time when in the enclosure a raging bear was
fighting with dogs and had torn them all one after another,
the prince, dressed only in light Spanish costume, sprang in
with his spear, and pierced not only the savage beast, but
also a soldier, who, seeing the moment of danger had sprung
to his aid.

Panna Aleksandra, the grand-daughter of an old soldier,
reared in traditions of blood, war, and reverence for knightly
superiority, could not restrain at sight of these deeds

her wonder, and even homage; for she had been taught from childhood to esteem bravery as almost the highest quality of man.

Meanwhile the prince gave daily proofs of daring almost beyond human, and always in honor of her. The assembled guests in their praises and enthusiasm for the prince, which were so great that even a deity might be satisfied with them, were forced involuntarily to connect in their conversations the name of Panna Billevich with the name of Boguslav. He was silent, but with his eyes he told her what he did not dare to utter with his lips. The spell surrounded her perfectly.

Everything was so combined as to bring them together, to connect them, and at the same time to separate them from the throng of other people. It was difficult for any one to mention him without mentioning her. Into the thoughts of Olenka herself Boguslav was thrust with an irresistible force. Every moment of the day was so arranged as to lend power to the spell.

In the evening, after amusements, the chambers were lighted by many colored lamps casting mysterious rays, as if from the land of splendid dreams transferred to reality; intoxicating eastern odors filled the air; the low sounds of invisible harps, lutes, and other instruments fondled the hearing; and in the midst of these odors, lights, sounds, he moved in the glory of universal homage, like an enchanted king's son in a myth-tale, beautiful, knightly, sun-bright from jewels, and as deeply in love as a shepherd.

What maiden could resist these spells, what virtue would not grow faint amid such allurements? But to avoid the prince there was no possibility for one living with him under the same roof and enjoying his hospitality, which, though given perforce, was still dispensed with sincerity and in real lordly fashion. Besides, Olenka had gone without unwillingness to Taurogi, for she wished to be far from hideous Kyedani, as she preferred to Yanush, an open traitor, the knightly Boguslav, who feigned love for the deserted king and the country. Hence in the beginning of her visit at Taurogi she was full of friendly feeling for the young prince; and seeing soon how far he was striving for her friendship, she used her influence more than once to do good to people.

During the third month of her stay a certain artillery officer, a friend of Kettling, was condemned by the prince to be shot; Panna Billevich, hearing of this from the young Scot, interceded for him.

"A divinity may command, not implore," said Boguslav to her; and tearing the sentence of death he threw it at her feet. "Ordain, command! I will burn Taurogi, if at that price I can call forth on your face even a smile. I ask no other reward save this, that you be joyous and forget that which once pained you."

She could not be joyous, having pain in her heart, pity and an unutterable contempt for the man whom she had loved with first love, and who at that time was in her eyes a worse criminal than a parricide. That Kmita, promising to sell the king for gold, as Judas sold Christ, became fouler and more repulsive in her eyes, till in the course of time he was turned into a human monster, a grief and reproach to her. She could not forgive herself for having loved him, and at the same time she could not forget him while she hated.

In view of these feelings it was indeed difficult for her even to feign gladness; but still she had to be thankful to the prince even for this, that he would not put his hand to Kmita's crime, and for all that he had done for her. It was a wonder to her that the prince, such a knight and so full of noble feeling, did not hasten to the rescue of the country, since he had not consented to the intrigues of Yanush; but she judged that such a statesman knew what he was doing, and was forced by a policy which she, with her simple maiden's mind, could not sound. Boguslav told her also, explaining his frequent journeys to Prussian Tyltsa, which was near by, that his strength was failing him from overwork; that he was conducting negotiations between Yan Kazimir, Karl Gustav, and the elector, and that he hoped to bring the country out of difficulty.

"Not for rewards, not for offices, do I do this," said he to her. "I will sacrifice my cousin Yanush, who was to me a father, for I know not whether I shall be able to implore his life for him from the animosity of Queen Ludvika; but I will do what my conscience and love for the dear mother, my country, demands."

When he spoke thus with sadness on his delicate face, with eyes turned to the ceiling, he seemed to her as lofty as those heroes of antiquity of which Heraclius Billevich had told her, and of whom he himself had read in Cornelius Nepos. And the heart swelled within her with admiration and homage. By degrees it went so far that when thoughts of the hated Andrei Kmita had tortured her too much, she thought of Boguslav to cure and strengthen herself. Kmita became for her a terrible and gloomy darkness; Boguslav, light in which every troubled soul would gladly bathe itself. The sword-bearer and Panna Kulvyets, whom they had brought also from Vodokty, pushed Olenka still more along that incline by singing hymns of praise from morning till night in honor of Boguslav. The sword-bearer and the aunt wearied the prince, it is true, so that he had been thinking how to get rid of them politely; but he won them to himself, especially the sword-bearer, who though at first displeased and even enraged, still could not fight against the friendship and favors of Boguslav.

If Boguslav had been merely a noble of noted stock, but not Radzivill, nor a prince, not a magnate invested with almost the majesty of a monarch, perhaps Panna Billevich might have loved him for life and death, in spite of the will of the old colonel, which left her a choice only between the cloister and Kmita. But she was a stern lady for her own self, and a very just soul; therefore she did not even admit to her head a dream of anything save gratitude and admiration so far as the prince was concerned.

Her family was not so great that she could become the wife of Radzivill, and was too great for her to become his mistress; she looked on him, therefore, as she would on the king, were she at the king's court. In vain did Boguslav endeavor to give her other thoughts; in vain did he, forgetting himself in love, partly from calculation, partly from enthusiasm, repeat what he had said the first evening in Kyedani, — that the Radzivills had married ordinary noble women more than once; these thoughts did not cling to her, as water does not cling to the breast of a swan; and she remained as she had been, thankful, friendly, homage-giving, seeking consolation in the thought of a hero, but undisturbed in heart.

He could not catch her through her feelings, though often it seemed to him that he was near his object. But he saw himself with shame and internal anger that he was not so daring with her as he had been with the first ladies in Paris, Brussels, and Amsterdam. Perhaps this was because he was really in love, and perhaps because in that lady, in her face, in her dark brows and stern eyes, there was that which enforced respect. Kmita was the one and only man who in

his time did not submit to that influence and paid no regard,
prepared boldly to kiss those proud eyes and stern lips; but
Kmita was her betrothed.

All other cavaliers, beginning with Pan Volodyovski and
ending with the very vulgar Prussian nobles in Taurogi and
the prince himself, were less confident with her than with
other ladies in the same condition. Impulsiveness carried
away the prince; but when once in a carriage he pressed
against her feet, whispering at the same time, "Fear not!"
she answered that she did fear to regret the confidence
reposed in him, Boguslav was confused, and returned to
his former method of conquering her heart by degrees.

But his patience was becoming exhausted. Gradually he
began to forget the terrible dream, he began to think more
frequently of what Sakovich had counselled, and that the
Billeviches would all perish in the war; his desires tormented him more powerfully, when a certain event changed
completely the course of affairs in Taurogi.

One day news came like a thunderbolt that Tykotsin was
taken by Pan Sapyeha, and that Prince Yanush had lost his
life in the ruins of the castle.

Everything began to seethe in Taurogi. Boguslav himself
sprang up and went off that same day to Königsberg, where
he was to see the ministers of the King of Sweden and the
elector.

His stay there exceeded his original plan. Meanwhile
bodies of Prussian and even of Swedish troops were assembling at Taurogi. Men began to speak of an expedition against Sapyeha. The naked truth was coming to the
surface more and more clearly, that Boguslav was a partisan
of the Swedes, as well as his cousin Yanush.

It happened that at the same time the sword-bearer of
Rossyeni received news of the burning of his native Billeviche by the troops of Löwenhaupt, who, after defeating the
insurgents in Jmud, at Shavli, ravaged the whole country
with fire and sword.

The old noble sprang up and set out, wishing to see
the damage with his own eyes; and Prince Boguslav did
not detain him, but sent him off willingly, adding at
parting, —

"Now you will understand why I brought you to
Taurogi; for, speaking plainly, you owe your life to
me."

Olenka remained alone with Panna Kulvyets. They

shut themselves up in their own chambers at once, and received no one but a few women. When these women brought tidings that the prince was preparing an expedition against the Poles, Olenka would not believe them at first; but wishing to be certain, she gave orders to summon Kettling, for she knew that from her the young Scot would hide nothing.

He appeared before her at once, happy that he was called, that for a time he could speak with her who had taken possession of his soul.

"Cavalier," said Panna Billevich, "so many reports are circulating about Taurogi that we are wandering as in a forest. Some say that the prince voevoda died a natural death; others that he was borne apart on sabres. What was the cause of his death?"

Kettling hesitated for a while. It was evident that he was struggling with innate indecision. At last he blushed greatly, and said, —

"You are the cause of the fall and the death of Prince Yanush."

"I?" asked Panna Billevich, with amazement.

"You; for our prince chose to remain in Taurogi rather than go to relieve his cousin. He forgot everything near you, my lady."

Now she blushed in her turn like a purple rose, and a moment of silence followed.

The Scot stood, hat in hand, with downcast eyes, his head bent, in a posture full of homage and respect. At last he raised his head, shook his bright curls, and said, —

"My lady, if these words have offended you, let me kneel down and beg forgiveness."

"Do not," said she, quickly, seeing that the young knight was bending his knees already. "I know that what you have said was said with a clean heart; for I have long noticed that you wish me well."

The officer raised his blue eyes, and putting his hand on his heart, with a voice as low as the whisper of a breeze and as sad as a sigh, replied, —

"Oh, my lady! my lady!"

At this moment he was frightened lest he had said too much, and again he bent his head toward his bosom, and took the posture of a courtier who is listening to the commands of a queen.

"I am here among strangers, without a guardian," said Olenka; "and though I shall be able to watch over myself alone, and God will preserve me from harm, still I need the aid of men also. Do you wish to be my brother? Do you wish to warn me in need, so that I may know what to do, and avoid every snare?"

As she said this, she extended her hand; but he kneeled, in spite of her prohibition, and kissed the tips of her fingers.

"Tell me," said she, "what is happening around me."

"The prince loves you," said Kettling. "Have you not seen that?"

She covered her face with her hands. "I saw and I did not see. At times it seemed to me that he was only very kind."

"Kind!" repeated Kettling, like an echo.

"But when it came into my head that I, unfortunate woman, might rouse in him unhappy wishes, I quieted myself with this, that no danger threatened me from him. I was thankful to him for what he had done, though God sees that I did not look for new kindnesses, since I feared those he had already shown me."

Kettling breathed more freely.

"May I speak boldly?" asked he.

"Speak."

"The prince has only two confidants, — Pan Sakovich and Patterson; but Patterson is very friendly to me, for we come from the same country, and he carried me in his arms. What I know, I know from him. The prince loves you; desires are burning in him as pitch in a pine torch. All things done here — all these feasts, hunts, tournaments, through which, thanks to the prince's hand, blood is flowing from my mouth yet — were arranged for you. The prince loves you, my lady, to distraction, but with an impure fire; for he wishes to disgrace, not to marry you. For though he could not find a worthier, even if he were king of the whole world, not merely a prince, still he thinks of another, — the princess, Yanush's daughter, and her fortune are predestined to him. I learned this from Patterson; and the great God, whose gospel I take here to witness, knows that I speak the pure truth. Do not believe the prince, do not trust his kindness, do not feel safe in his moderation. Watch, guard yourself; for they are plotting treason against you here at every step. The breath is stopping in my breast from what

Patterson has told me. There is not a criminal in the world equal to Sakovich, — I cannot speak of him, I cannot. Were it not for the oath which I have taken to guard the prince, this hand and this sword would free you from continual danger. But I would slay Sakovich first. This is true. Him first, before all men, — even before those who in my own country shed my father's blood, took my fortune, made me a wanderer and a hireling."

Here Kettling trembled from emotion. For a while he merely pressed the hilt of his sword with his hand, not being able to utter a word; then he recovered, and in one breath told what methods Sakovich had suggested to the prince.

Panna Aleksandra, to his great surprise, bore herself calmly enough while looking at the threatening precipice before her; only her face grew pale and became still more serious. Unbending resolution was reflected in her stern look.

"I shall be able to save myself," said she, "so help me God and the holy cross!"

"The prince has not consented hitherto to follow Sakovich's counsel," added Kettling. "But when he sees that the road he has chosen leads to nothing — " and he began to tell the reasons which restrained Boguslav.

The lady listened with frowning brow, but not with superfluous attention, for she had already begun to ponder on means to wrest herself free of this terrible guardianship. But there was not a place in the whole country unsprinkled with blood, and plans of flight did not seem to her clear; hence she preferred not to speak of them.

"Cavalier," said she at last, "answer me one question. Is Prince Boguslav on the side of the King of Sweden or the King of Poland?"

"It is a secret to none of us," answered the young officer, "that the prince wishes the division of this Commonwealth, so as to make of Lithuania an independent principality for himself."

Here Kettling was silent, and you would have thought that his mind was following involuntarily the thoughts of Olenka; for after a while he added, —

"The elector and the Swedes are at the service of the prince; and since they will occupy the Commonwealth, there is no place in which to hide from him."

Olenka made no answer.

The young man waited awhile longer, to learn if she would ask him other questions; but when she was silent, occupied with her own thoughts, he felt that it was not proper for him to interrupt her; therefore he bent double in a parting bow, sweeping the floor with the feathers in his cap.

"I thank you, cavalier," said Olenka, extending her hand to him.

The officer, without turning, withdrew toward the door. All at once there appeared on her face a slight flush. She hesitated a moment, and then said, —

"One word, cavalier."

"Every word is for me a favor."

"Did you know Pan Andrei Kmita?"

"I made his acquaintance, my lady, in Kyedani. I saw him the last time in Pilvishki, when we were marching hither from Podlyasye."

"Is what the prince says true, that Pan Kmita offered to do violence to the person of the King of Poland?"

"I know not, my lady. It is known to me that they took counsel together in Pilvishki; then the prince went with Pan Kmita to the forest, and it was so long before he returned that Patterson was alarmed and sent troops to meet him. I led those troops. We met the prince. I saw that he was greatly changed, as if strong emotion had passed through his soul. He was talking to himself, which never happens to him. I heard how he said: 'The devil would have undertaken that —' I know nothing more. But later, when the prince mentioned what Kmita offered, I thought, 'If this was it, it must be true.'"

Panna Billevich pressed her lips together.

"I thank you," said she. And after a while she was alone.

The thought of flight mastered her thoroughly. She determined at any price to tear herself from those infamous places, and from the power of that treacherous prince. But where was she to find refuge? The villages and towns were in Swedish hands, the cloisters were ruined, the castles levelled with the earth; the whole country was swarming with soldiers, and with worse than soldiers, — with fugitives from the army, robbers, all kinds of ruffians. What

fate could be waiting for a maiden cast as a prey to that
storm ? Who would go with her ? Her aunt Kulvyets, her
uncle, and a few of his servants. Whose power would protect her ? Kettling would go, perhaps ; maybe a handful of
faithful soldiers and friends might even be found who would
accompany him. But as Kettling had fallen in love with her
beyond question, then how was she to incur a debt of gratitude to him, which she would have to pay afterward with a
great price ? Finally, what right had she to close the career
of that young man, scarcely more than a youth, and expose
it to pursuit, to persecution, to ruin, if she could not offer
him anything in return save friendship ? Therefore, she
asked herself, what was she to do, whither was she to flee,
since here and there destruction threatened her, here and
there disgrace ?

In such a struggle of soul she began to pray ardently;
and more especially did she repeat one prayer with earn-
estness to which the old colonel had constant recourse in
evil times, beginning with the words, —

> " God saved Thee with Thy Infant
> From the malice of Herod ;
> In Egypt he straightened the road
> For Thy safe passage — "

At this moment a great whirlwind rose, and the trees in
the garden began to make a tremendous noise. All at once
the praying lady remembered the wilderness on the borders
of which she had grown up from infancy ; and the thought
that in the wilderness she would find the only safe refuge
flew through her head like lightning.

Then Olenka breathed deeply, for she had found at last
what she had been seeking. To Zyelonka, to Rogovsk !
There the enemy would not go, the ruffian would not seek
booty. There a man of the place, if he forgot himself,
might go astray and wander till death ; what must it be to
a stranger not knowing the road ? There the Domasheviches, the Smoky Stakyans ; and if they are gone, if they
have followed Pan Volodyovski, it is possible to go by those
forests far beyond and seek quiet in other wildernesses.

The remembrance of Pan Volodyovski rejoiced Olenka.
Oh, if she had such a protector ! He was a genuine soldier ; his was a sabre under which she might take refuge
from Kmita and the Radzivills themselves. Now it oc-
curred to her that he was the man who had advised, when

he caught Kmita in Billeviche, to seek safety in the Bya-lovyej wilderness.

And he spoke wisely! Rogovsk and Zyelonka are too near the Radzivills, and near Byalovyej stands that Sapyeha who rubbed from the face of the earth the most terrible Radzivill.

To Byalovyej then, to Byalovyej, even to-day, to-morrow! Only let her uncle come, she would not delay.

The dark depths of Byalovyej will protect her, and after-ward, when the storm passes, the cloister. There only can be real peace and forgetfulness of all men, of all pain, sorrow, and contempt.

CHAPTER XLII.

THE sword-bearer of Rossyeni returned a few days later. In spite of the safe-conduct of Boguslav, he went only to Rossyeni; to Billeviche itself he had no reason to go, for it was no longer in the world. The house, the buildings, the village, everything was burned to the ground in the last battle, which Father Strashevich, a Jesuit, had fought at the head of his own detachment against the Swedish captain Rossa. The inhabitants were in the forests or in armed parties. Instead of rich villages there remained only land and water.

The roads were filled with "ravagers," — that is, fugitives from various armies, who, going in considerable groups, were busied with robbery, so that even small parties of soldiers were not safe from them. The sword-bearer then had not even been able to convince himself whether the barrels filled with plate and money and buried in the garden were safe, and he returned to Taurogi,very angry and peevish, with a terrible animosity in his heart against the destroyers.

He had barely put foot out of his carriage, when Olenka hurried him to her own room, and recounted all that Hassling-Kettling had told her.

The old soldier shivered at the recital, since, not having children of his own, he loved the maiden as his daughter. For a while he did nothing but grasp his sword-hilt, repeating, "Strike, who has courage!" At last he caught himself by the head, and began to say, —

"*Mea culpa, mea maxima culpa* (It is my fault, my greatest fault); for at times it came into my head, and this and that man whispered that that hell-dweller was melting from love of you, and I said nothing, was even proud, thinking: 'Well, he will marry! We are relatives of the Gosyevskis, of the Tyzenhauzes; why should we not be relatives of the Radzivills?' For pride, God is punishing me. The traitor prepared a respectable relationship. That's the kind of relative he wanted to be. I would he were killed! But wait! this hand and this sabre will moulder first."

"We must think of escape," said Olenka.

"Well, give your plans of escape."

The sword-bearer, having finished panting, listened carefully; at last he said, —

"Better collect my subjects and form a party! I will attack the Swedes as Kmita did Hovanski. You will be safer in the forest and in the field than in the court of a traitor and a heretic."

"That is well," answered the lady.

"Not only will I not oppose," said the sword-bearer, "but I will say the sooner the better. And I lack neither subjects nor scythes. They burned my residence, never mind that! I will assemble peasants from other villages. All the Billeviches in the field will join us. We will show you relationship, young man, — we will show what it is to attack the Billevich honor. You are a Radzivill! What of that? There are no hetmans in the Billevich family, but there are also no traitors! We shall see whom all Jmud will follow! We will put you in Byalovyej and return ourselves," said he, turning to Olenka. "It cannot be otherwise! He must give satisfaction for that affair, for it is an injustice to the whole estate of nobles. Infamous is he who does not declare for us! God will help us, our brethren will help us, citizens will help us, and then fire and sword! The Billeviches will meet the Radzivills! Infamous he who is not with us! infamous he who will not flash his sword in the eyes of the traitor! The king is with us; so is the Diet, so is the whole Commonwealth."

Here the sword-bearer, red as blood and with bristling forelock, fell to pounding the table with his fist.

"This war is more urgent than the Swedish, for in us the whole order of knighthood, all laws, the whole Commonwealth is injured and shaken in its deepest foundations. Infamous is he who does not understand this! The land will perish unless we measure out vengeance and punishment on the traitor!"

And the old blood played more and more violently, till Olenka was forced to pacify her uncle. He sat calmly, then, though he thought that not only the country, but the whole world was perishing when the Billeviches were touched; in this he saw the most terrible precipice for the Commonwealth, and began to roar like a lion.

But the lady, who had great influence over him, was able at last to pacify her uncle, explaining that for their safety and for the success of their flight it was specially needful

to preserve the profoundest secrecy, and not to show the
prince that they were thinking of anything.

He promised sacredly to act according to her directions;
then they took counsel about the flight itself. The affair
was not over-difficult, for it seemed that they were not
watched at all. The sword-bearer decided to send in advance a youth, with letters to his overseers to assemble
peasants at once from all the villages belonging to him and
the other Billeviches, and to arm them.

Six confidential servants were to go to Billeviche, as it
were, for the barrels of money and silver, but really to halt
in the Girlakol forests, and wait there with horses, bags,
and provisions. They decided to depart from Taurogi in
sleighs and accompanied by two servants, as if going merely
to the neighboring Gavna; afterward they would mount
horses and hurry on with all speed. To Gavna they used to
go often to visit the Kuchuk-Olbrotovskis, where sometimes
they passed the night; they hoped therefore that their journey would not attract the attention of any one, and that no
pursuit would follow, unless two or three days later, at
which time they would be in the midst of armed bands and
in the depth of impenetrable forests. The absence of Prince
Boguslav strengthened them in this hope.

Meanwhile the sword-bearer was greatly busied with
preparations. A messenger with letters went out on the
following morning. The day after that, Pan Tomash talked
in detail with Patterson of his buried money, which, as he
said, exceeded a hundred thousand, and of the need of bringing it to safe Taurogi. Patterson believed easily; for Billevich was a noble and passed as a very rich man, which he was
in reality.

"Let them bring it as soon as possible," said the Scot;
"if you need them, I will give you soldiers."

"The fewer people who see what I am bringing the better. My servants are faithful, and I will order them to
cover the barrels with hemp, which is brought often from
our villages to Prussia, or with staves which no one will
covet."

"Better with staves," said Patterson; "for people could
feel with a sabre or a spear through the hemp that there
was something else in the wagon. But you would better give the coin to the prince on his recognition. I know,
too, that he needs money, for his revenues do not come
regularly."

"I should like so to serve the prince that he would never need anything," answered the old man.

The conversation ended there, and all seemed to combine most favorably, for the servants started at once, while the sword-bearer and Olenka were to go next morning. But in the evening Boguslav returned most unexpectedly at the head of two regiments of Prussian cavalry. His affairs seemed to advance not too favorably, for he was angry and fretful.

That evening he summoned a council of war, which was composed of the representatives of the elector, Count Seydevitz, Patterson, Sakovich, and Kyritz, a colonel of cavalry. They sat till three in the morning; and the object of their deliberation was the campaign to Podlyasye against Sapyeha.

"The elector and the King of Sweden have reinforced me in proportion to their strength," said the prince. "One of two things will happen,—either I shall find Sapyeha in Podlyasye, and in that event I must rub him out; or I shall not find him, and I shall occupy Podlyasye without resistance. For all this, however, money is needed; and money neither the elector nor the King of Sweden has given me, for they have n't it themselves."

"Where is money to be found if not with your highness?" asked Seydevitz. "Through the whole world men speak of the inexhaustible wealth of the Radzivills."

"Pan Seydevitz," answered Boguslav, "if I received all the income from my inherited estates, I should surely have more money than five of your German princes taken together. But there is war in the country; revenues do not come in, or are intercepted by rebels. Ready money might be obtained for notes from the Prussian towns; but you know best what is happening in them, and that purses are opened only for Yan Kazimir."

"But Königsberg?"

"I took what I could get, but that was little."

"I think myself fortunate to be able to serve you with good counsel," said Patterson.

"I would rather you served me with ready money."

"My counsel means ready money. Not longer ago than yesterday Pan Billevich told me that he had a good sum hidden in the garden of Billeviche, and that he wishes to bring it here for safety, and give it to your highness for a note."

"Well, you have really fallen from heaven to me, and this noble as well!" cried Boguslav. "But has he much money?"

"More than a hundred thousand, besides silver and valuables, which are worth perhaps an equal amount."

"The silver and valuables he will not wish to turn into money, but they can be pawned. I am thankful to you, Patterson, for this comes to me in time. I must talk to Billevich in the morning."

"Then I will forewarn him, for he is preparing to go to-morrow with the lady to Gavna to the Kuchuk-Olbrotovskis."

"Tell him not to go till he sees me."

"He has sent the servants already; I am only alarmed for their safety."

"A whole regiment can be sent after them; but we will talk later. This is timely for me, timely! And it will be amusing if I rend Podlyasye from the Commonwealth with the money of this royalist and patriot."

Then the prince dismissed the council, for he had to put himself yet in the hands of his chamber attendants, whose task it was every night before he went to rest to preserve his uncommon beauty with baths, ointments, and various inventions known only in foreign lands. This lasted usually an hour, and sometimes two; besides, the prince was road-weary and the hour late.

Early in the morning Patterson detained Billevich and Olenka with the announcement that the prince wished to see them. It was necessary to defer their journey; but this did not disturb them over-much, for Patterson told what the question was.

An hour later the prince appeared. In spite of the fact that Pan Tomash and Olenka had promised each other most faithfully to receive him in former fashion, they could not do so, though they tried with every effort.

Olenka's countenance changed, and blood came to the face of the sword-bearer at sight of Prince Boguslav; for a time both stood confused, excited, striving in vain to regain their usual calmness.

The prince, on the contrary, was perfectly at ease. He had grown a little meagre about the eyes, and his face was less colored than common; but that paleness of his was set off wonderfully by the pearl-colored morning dress, inter-woven with silver. He saw in a moment that they received

him somewhat differently, and were less glad than usual to
see him.   But he thought at once that those two royalists
had learned of his relations with the Swedes; hence the coolness of the reception.   Therefore he began at once to throw
sand in their eyes, and, after the compliments of greeting,
said, —

"Lord Sword-bearer, my benefactor, you have heard,
without doubt, what misfortunes have met me."

"Does your highness wish to speak of the death of Prince
Yanush?" asked the sword-bearer.

"Not of his death alone.   That was a cruel blow; still, I
yielded to the will of God, Who, as I hope, has rewarded
my cousin for all the wrongs done him; but He has sent a
new burden to me, for I must be leader in a civil war; and
that for every citizen who loves his country is a bitter
portion."

The sword-bearer said nothing; he merely looked a little
askance at Olenka.   But the prince continued, —

"By my labor and toil, and God alone knows at what outlay, I had brought peace to the verge of realization.   It was
almost a question of merely signing the treaties.   The Swedes
were to leave Poland, asking no remuneration save the consent of the king and the estates that after the death of Yan
Kazimir Karl Gustav would be chosen to the throne of Poland.   A warrior so great and mighty would be the salvation
of the Commonwealth.   And what is more important, he
was to furnish at once reinforcements for the war in the
Ukraine and against Moscow.   We should have extended
our boundaries; but this was not convenient for Pan Sapyeha,
for then he could not crush the Radzivills.   All agreed to
this treaty. He alone opposes it with armed hand.   The
country is nothing to him, if he can only carry out his personal designs.   It has come to this, that arms must be used
against him.   This function has been confided to me,
according to the secret treaty between Yan Kazimir and
Karl Gustav.   This is the whole affair!   I have never
shunned any service, therefore I must accept this; though
many will judge me unjustly, and think that I begin a
brother-killing war from pure revenge only."

"Whoso knows your highness," said the sword-bearer,
"as well as we do will not be deceived by appearances, and
will always be able to understand the real intentions of your
highness."

Here the sword-bearer was so delighted with his own

cunning and courtesy, and he muttered so expressively at Olenka, that she was alarmed lest the prince should notice those signs.

And he did notice them. "They do not believe me," thought he. And though he showed no wrath on his face, Billevich had pricked him to the soul. He was convinced with perfect sincerity that it was an offence not to believe a Radzivill, even when he saw fit to lie.

"Patterson has told me," continued he, after a while, "that you wish to give me ready money for my paper. I agree to this willingly; for I acknowledge that ready money is useful to me at the moment. When peace comes, you can do as you like, — either take a certain sum, or I will give you a couple of villages as security, so that the transaction will be profitable for you. — Pardon," said the prince, turning to Olenka, "that in view of such material questions we are not speaking of sighs or ideals. This conversation is out of place; but the times are such that it is impossible to give their proper course to homage and admiration."

Olenka dropped her eyes, and seizing her robe with the tips of her fingers, made a proper courtesy, not wishing to give an answer. Meanwhile the sword-bearer formed in his mind a project of unheard-of unfitness, but which he considered uncommonly clever.

"I will flee with Olenka and will not give the money," thought he.

"It will be agreeable to me to accommodate your highness. Patterson has not told of all, for there is about half a pot of gold ducats buried apart, so as not to lose all the money in case of accident. Besides, there are barrels belonging to other Billeviches; but these during my absence were buried under the direction of this young lady, and she alone is able to calculate the place, for the man who buried them is dead."

Boguslav looked at him quickly. "How is that? Patterson said that you have already sent men; and since they have gone, they must know where the money is."

"But of the other money no one knows, except her."

"Still it must be buried in some definite place, which can be described easily in words or indicated on paper."

"Words are wind; and as to pictures, the servants know nothing of them. We will both go; that is the thing."

"For God's sake! you must know your own gardens. Therefore go alone. Why should Panna Aleksandra go?"

"I will not go alone!" said Billevich, with decision.

Boguslav looked at him inquiringly a second time; then he seated himself more comfortably, and began to strike his boots with a cane which he held in his hand.

"Is that final?" asked he. "Well! In such an event I will give a couple of regiments of cavalry to take you there and bring you back."

"We need no regiments. We will go and return ourselves. This is our country. Nothing threatens us here."

"As a host, sensitive to the good of his guests, I cannot permit that Panna Aleksandra should go without armed force. Choose, then. Either go alone, or let both go with an escort."

Billevich saw that he had fallen into his own trap; and that brought him to such anger that, forgetting all precautions, he cried, —

"Then let your highness choose. Either we shall both go unattended, or I will not give the money!"

Panna Aleksandra looked on him imploringly; but he had already grown red and begun to pant. Still, he was a man cautious by nature, even timid, loving to settle every affair in good feeling; but when once the measure was exceeded in dealing with him, when he was too much excited against any one, or when it was a question of the Billevich honor, he hurled himself with a species of desperate daring at the eyes of even the most powerful enemy. So that now he put his hand to his left side, and shaking his sabre, began to cry with all his might, —

"Is this captivity? Do they wish to oppress a free citizen, and trample on cardinal rights?"

Boguslav, with shoulders leaning against the arms of the chair, looked at him attentively; but his look became colder each moment, and he struck the cane against his boots more and more quickly. Had the sword-bearer known the prince better, he would have known that he was bringing down terrible danger on his own head.

Relations with Boguslav were simply dreadful. It was never known when the courteous cavalier, the diplomat accustomed to self-control, would be overborne by the wild and unrestrained magnate who trampled every resistance with the cruelty of an Eastern despot. A brilliant education and refinement, acquired at the first courts of

Europe; reflection and studied elegance, which he had gained in intercourse with men, — were like wonderful and strong flowers under which was secreted a tiger.

But the sword-bearer did not know this, and in his angry blindness shouted on, —

"Your highness, dissemble no further, for you are known! And have a care, for neither the King of Sweden nor the elector, both of whom you are serving against your own country, nor your princely position, will save you before the law; and the sabres of nobles will teach you manners, young man!"

Boguslav rose; in one instant he crushed the cane in his iron hands, and throwing the pieces at the feet of the sword-bearer, said with a terrible, suppressed voice, —

"That is what your rights are for me! That your tribunals! That your privileges!"

"Outrageous violence!" cried Billevich.

"Silence, paltry noble!" cried the prince. "I will crush you into dust!" And he advanced to seize the astonished man and hurl him against the wall.

Now Panna Aleksandra stood between them. "What do you think to do?" inquired she.

The prince restrained himself. But she stood with nostrils distended, with flaming face, with fire in her eyes like an angry Minerva. Her breast heaved under her bodice like a wave of the sea, and she was marvellous in that anger, so that Boguslav was lost in gazing at her; all his desires crept into his face, like serpents from the dens of his soul.

After a time his anger passed, presence of mind returned; he looked awhile yet at Olenka. At last his face grew mild; he bent his head toward his breast, and said, —

"Pardon, angelic lady! I have a soul full of gnawing and pain, therefore I do not command myself." Then he left the room.

Olenka began to wring her hands; and Billevich, coming to himself, seized his forelock, and cried, —

"I have spoiled everything; I am the cause of your ruin!"

The prince did not show himself the whole day. He even dined in his own room with Sakovich. Stirred to the bottom of his soul, he could not think so clearly as usual. Some kind of ague was wasting him. It was the herald of a grievous fever which was to seize him soon with such force that during its attacks he was benumbed altogether, so that his attendants had to rub him most actively. But at this time he ascribed his strange state to the power of love, and thought that he must either satisfy it or die. When he had told Sakovich the whole conversation with the sword-bearer, he said, —

"My hands and feet are burning, ants are walking along my back, in my mouth are bitterness and fire; but, by all the horned devils, what is this? Never has this attacked me before!"

"Your highness is as full of scruples as a baked capon of buckwheat grits. The prince is a capon, the prince is a capon. Ha, ha!"

"You are a fool!"

"Very well."

"I don't need your ideas."

"Worthy prince, take a lute and go under the windows of the maiden. Billevich may show you his fist. Tfu! to the deuce! is that the kind of bold man that Boguslav Radzivill is?"

"You are an idiot!"

"Very well. I see that your highness is beginning to speak with yourself and tell the truth to your own face. Boldly, boldly! Pay no heed to rank."

"You see, Sakovich, that my Castor is growing familiar with me; as it is, I kick him often in the ribs, but a greater accident may meet you."

Sakovich sprang up as if red with anger, like Billevich a little while before; and since he had an uncommon gift of mimicry, he began to cry in a voice so much like that of Billevich that any one not seeing who was talking, might have been deceived.

"What! is this captivity? Do they wish to oppress a free citizen, to trample on cardinal rights?"

"Give us peace! give us peace!" said the prince, fretfully. "She defended that old fool with her person, but here there is one to defend you."

"If she defended him, she should have been taken in pawn!"

"There must be some witchcraft in this place! Either she must have given me something, or the constellations are such that I am simply leaving my mind. If you could have seen her when she was defending that mangy old uncle of hers! But you are a fool! It is growing cloudy in my head. See how my hands are burning! To love such a woman, to gain her — with such a woman to — "

"To have posterity!" added Sakovich.

"That's so, that's so! — as if you knew that must be; otherwise I shall burst as a bomb. For God's sake! what is happening to me? Must I marry, or what, by all the devils of earth and hell?"

Sakovich grew serious. "Your princely highness, you must not think of that!"

"I am thinking of just that, precisely because I wish it. I will do that, though a regiment of Sakoviches repeated a whole day to me, 'Your princely highness must not think of that!'"

"Oh, I see this is no joke."

"I am sick, enchanted."

"Why do you not follow my advice at last?"

"I must follow it, — may the plague take all the dreams, all the Billeviches, all Lithuania with the tribunals, and Yan Kazimir to boot! I shall not succeed otherwise; I see that I shall not! I have had enough of this, have I not? A great question! And I, the fool, was considering both sides hitherto; was afraid of dreams, of Billeviches, of lawsuits, of the rabble of nobles, the fortune of Yan Kazimir. Tell me that I am a fool! Do you hear? I command you to tell me that I am a fool!"

"But I will not obey, for now you are really Radzivill, and not a Calvinist minister. But in truth you must be ill, for I have never seen you so changed."

"True! In the most difficult positions I merely waved my hand and whistled, but now I feel as if some one were thrusting spurs into my sides."

"This is strange, for if that maiden has given you something designedly, she has not done so to run away afterward; but still, from what you say, it seems that they wish to flee in secret."

"Ryff told me that this is the influence of Saturn, on which burning exhalations rise during this particular month."

"Worthy prince, rather take Jove as a model, for he was happy without marriage. All will be well; only do not think of marriage, unless of a counterfeit one."

All at once the starosta of Oshmiana struck his forehead.

"But wait, your highness! I have heard of such a case in Prussia."

" Is the Devil whispering something into your ear ? Tell
me ! "

But Sakovich was silent for a long time; at last his face
brightened, and he said, —

" Thank the fortune that gave you Sakovich as friend."

" What news, what news ? "

" Nothing. I will be your highness's best man " (here Sakovich bowed), — " no small honor for such a poor fellow ! "

" Don't play the jester; speak quickly ! "

" There is in Tyltsa one Plaska, or something like that,
who in his time was a priest in Nyevorani, but who falling
away from the faith became a Lutheran, got married, took
refuge under the elector, and now is dealing in dried fish with
people of this region. Bishop Parchevski tried to lure him
back to Jmud, where in good certainty there was a fire waiting for him; but the elector would not yield up a fellow-
believer."

" How does that concern me ? Do not loiter."

" How does that concern your highness ? In this way it
must concern you; for he will sew you and her together with
stitches on the outside, you understand ? And because he
is a fool of a workman, and does not belong to the guild, it
will be easy to rip the work after him. Do you see ? The
guild does not recognize this sewing as valid; but still there
will be no violence, no outcry ; you can twist the neck of
the workman afterward, and you will complain that you
were deceived, do you understand ? But before that time
crescite et multiplicamini. I 'll be the first to give you my
blessing."

" I understand, and I don't understand," said the prince.
" The devil I understand there perfectly. Sakovich, you
must have been born, like a witch, with teeth in your mouth.
The hangman is waiting for you; it cannot be otherwise,
O Starosta ! But while I live a hair will not fall from your
head; a fitting reward will not miss you. I then — "

" Your highness will make a formal proposal to Panna
Billevich, to her and to her uncle. If they refuse, if they
do not consent, then give command to tear the skin from
me, make sandal strings out of it, and go on a pilgrimage
of penance to — to Rome. It is possible to resist a Radzivill
if he wishes simply to be a lover; but if he wishes to marry,
he need not try to please any noble. You must only tell
Billevich and the lady that out of regard for the elector and
the King of Sweden, who want you to marry the Princess

of Bipont, your marriage must remain secret till peace is declared. Besides, you will write the marriage contract as you like. Both churches will be forced to declare it invalid. Well, what do you think?"

Boguslav was silent for a while, but on his face red fever-spots appeared under the paint; then he cried, —

"There is no time in three days. I must move against Sapyeha."

"That is just the position! Were there more time, it would be impossible to justify the pretext. Is not this true? Only through lack of time can you explain that the first priest at hand officiates, as happens in sudden emergencies, and marries on a bolting-cloth. They will think too, 'It is sudden, for it must be sudden!' She is a knightly maiden; you can take her with you to the field. Dear bride-groom, if Sapyeha conquers, even then you will have half the victories of the campaign."

"That is well, that is well!" said the prince.

But at that moment the first paroxysm seized him so that his jaws closed and he could not say another word. He grew rigid, and then began to quiver and flounder like a fish out of water. But before the terrified Sakovich could bring the physician, the paroxysm had passed.

CHAPTER XLIII.

AFTER his conversation with Sakovich, Prince Boguslav
betook himself on the afternoon of the morrow directly to
Billevich.

"My benefactor," said he, to begin with, "I was grievously
to blame the last time we met, for I fell into anger in my
own house.   It is my fault, and all the more so that I gave
this affront to a man of a family friendly to the Radzivills.
But I come to implore forgiveness.   Let a sincere confession
be satisfaction to you, and my atonement.   You know the
Radzivills of old; you know that we are not in haste to beg
pardon; still, since I was to blame before age and dignity, I
come without considering who I am, with a penitent head.
And you, old friend of our house, will not refuse me your
hand, I am certain."

Then he extended his hand; and Billevich, in whose soul
the first outburst had passed, did not dare to refuse his own,
though he gave it with hesitation.

"Your highness, return to us our freedom; that will be
the best satisfaction."

"You are free, and may go, even to-day."

"I thank your highness," said the astonished Billevich.

"I interpose only one condition, which you, God grant,
will not reject."

"What is that ?" asked Billevich, with fear.

"That you listen patiently to what I am going to say."

"If that is all, I will listen even till evening."

"Do not give me your answer at once, but think an hour
or two."

"God sees that if I receive my freedom I wish peace."

"You will receive your freedom; but I do not know
whether you will use it, or whether you will be urgent to
leave my threshold.   I should be glad were you to consider
my house and all Taurogi as your own; but listen to me
now.   Do you know, my benefactor, why I was opposed to
the departure of Panna Billevich ?   This is why, — because I
divined that you wished to flee simply ; and I have fallen in
love with your niece, so that to see her I should be ready to
swim a Hellespont each day, like Leander."

Billevich grew red again in a moment. "Does your highness dare to say that to me?"

"To you especially, my benefactor."

"Worthy prince, seek your fortune with court ladies, but touch not noble maidens. You may imprison her, you may confine her in a vault, but you may not disgrace her."

"I may not disgrace her," said the prince; "but I may bow down to the old man Billevich, and say to him, 'Listen, father, give me your niece as wife, for I cannot live without her.'"

The sword-bearer was so amazed that he could not utter a word; for a time he merely moved his mustaches, and his eyes were staring; then he began to rub his hands and look, now on the prince, now around the room; at last he said, —

"Is this in a dream, or is it real?"

"Do not hasten! To convince you still better, I will repeat with all the titles: I, Boguslav, Prince Radzivill, Marshal of the Grand Principality of Lithuania, ask you, Tomash Billevich, sword-bearer of Rossyeni, for the hand of your niece, Panna Aleksandra, chief-hunter's daughter."

"Is this true? In God's name! have you considered the matter?"

"I have considered; now do you consider, my benefactor, whether the cavalier is worthy of the lady."

"My breath is stopped from wonder."

"Now see if I had any evil intentions."

"And would your highness not consider our small station?"

"Are the Billeviches so cheap? Do you value your shield of nobility and the antiquity of your family thus? Does a Billevich say this?"

"I know, gracious prince, that the origin of our family is to be sought in ancient Rome; but —"

"But," interrupted the prince, "you have neither hetmans nor chancellors. That is nothing! You are soldiers, like my uncle in Brandenburg. Since a noble in our Commonwealth may be elected king, there are no thresholds too lofty for his feet. My sword-bearer and, God grant, my uncle, I was born of a Brandenburg princess; my father's mother was an Ostrogski; but my grandfather of mighty memory, Kryshtof I., he whom they called Thunder, grand hetman, chancellor, and voevoda of Vilna, was married the first time to Panna Sobek; but for this reason the coronet did not fall from his head, for Panna Sobek was a noble woman, as honorably born as others. When my late father married the daughter of the elector, they wondered why he did not remember his own dignity, though he allied himself with a reigning house. Such is the devilish pride of you nobles! But acknowledge, my benefactor, you do not think a Sobek better than a Billevich, do you?"

Speaking thus, the prince began to tap the old man on the shoulder with great familiarity. The noble melted like wax, and answered, —

"God reward your highness for honorable intentions! A weight has fallen from my heart! But now, if it were not for difference of faith!"

"A Catholic priest will perform the ceremony. I do not want another myself."

"I shall be thankful for this all my life, since here it is a question of the blessing of God, which certainly the Lord Jesus would withdraw if some vile —"

Here the old man bit his tongue, for he saw that he was saying something disagreeable to the prince. But Boguslav did not notice it; he smiled graciously and said, —

"And as to posterity, I shall not be stubborn; for there is nothing that I would not do for that beauty of yours."

Billevich's face grew bright as if a ray of the sun had fallen on it: "Indeed, God has not been sparing of beauty to her, it is true. Oh! there will be a shout all over Jmud. And what will the Sitsinskis say when the Billeviches increase so? They would not leave the old colonel at rest, though he was a man of Roman mould, respected by the whole Commonwealth."

"We will drive them out of Jmud, worthy Sword-bearer."

"O great God, merciful God! undiscoverable are Thy judgments; but if in them it lies that the Sitsinskis are to burst from envy, then let Thy will be done!"

"Amen!" added Boguslav.

"Your highness, do not take it ill that I do not clothe myself in dignity, as befits a person of whom a man asks a maiden, and that I show too evident rejoicing. But we have been here in vexation, not knowing what was awaiting us and interpreting everything for the worst. It came to this that we thought evil of your highness, until it turns out that our fears and judgments were not just, and that we may return to our previous homage. I say this as if some one had taken a burden from my shoulders."

"And did Panna Aleksandra judge me thus?"

"She? Even Cicero could not have described properly her

previous admiration for your highness. I think that only
virtue and a certain inborn timidity stood in the way of
love. But when she hears of the sincere intentions of your
highness, then I am sure she will at once give the reins to
her heart."

"Cicero could not have said that better!" said Boguslav.

"With happiness comes eloquence. But since your highness has been pleased to listen to everything I have said,
then I will be sincere to the last."

"Be sincere, Pan Billevich."

"Though this maiden is young, she is a woman with a man's
cast of mind altogether; it is wonderful what a character
she has. Where more than one man of experience would
hesitate, she hesitates not a moment. What is evil she puts
on the left, what is good on the right, and goes herself to
the right as if it were sweet. When she has once chosen
the road, even though there were cannon before her, that
is nothing to her! She would not go aside for the cannon.
She is like her grandfather and me. Her father was a born
soldier, but mild; her mother, from the house of Voynillovich, was also strong-willed."

"I am glad to hear this, Pan Billevich."

"Your highness will not believe how incensed she is
against the Swedes, and all enemies of the Commonwealth.
If she held any one guilty of treason, she would feel an utter
detestation of him, though he were an angel and not a human
being. Your highness,— forgive an old man who might be
your father in years, if not in dignity,— leave the Swedes;
they are worse for the country than Tartars! Move your
troops against such sons, and not only I, but she, will follow
you to the field. Pardon me, your highness, pardon me.
Now I have said what I had on my mind."

Boguslav mastered himself after a moment's silence, and
said: "My benefactor, you might have supposed yesterday, but you may not suppose to-day that I wish merely
to throw sand in your eyes, when I say that I am on the
side of the king and the country. Here under oath to you
as a relative I repeat that what I stated touching peace and
its conditions was the pure truth. I, too, should prefer to
march to the field, for my nature draws me thither; but because I saw that salvation was not in the field, I was forced
through simple devotion to seize another method. And I can
say that I have accomplished an unheard of thing; for after
a lost war to conclude a peace of such kind that the con-

quering power serves the conquered, — of this Mazarin, the
most cunning of men, need not be ashamed. Not Panna
Aleksandra alone, but I equally with her, bear hatred to the
enemy. But what is to be done ? How save this country ?
Not even Hercules against many can conquer. Therefore
I thought thus, 'Instead of destroying, which would be
easier and more amusing, it is needful to save.' And since
I had practised in affairs of this kind with great statesmen,
since I am a relative of the elector, and since, by reason of
my cousin Yanush, I am well considered by the Swedes, I
began negotiations ; and what their course was and what
the benefit to the Commonwealth was, that you know, — an
end of the war, freedom from oppression for your Catholic
faith, for churches, for clergy, for the estate of nobles, and
for the common people ; the assistance of the Swedes in the
war against Moscow and the Cossacks ; and, God grant, an
extension of boundary. And this all on one condition, —
that Karl Gustav be king after Yan Kazimir. Whoso has
done more for his country in these times, let him stand before my eyes."

"True, a blind man could see that ; but it will be very
sad for the nobles that a free election will cease."

"And which is more important, — an election or the
country ?"

"They are the same, your highness ; for an election is
the main basis of the Commonwealth. And what is the
country, if not a collection of laws, privileges, and liberties
serving the nobles ? A king can be found even in a foreign
land."

Anger and disgust flew like lightning over Boguslav's
face.

"Karl Gustav," said he, "will sign the *pacta conventa*, as
his predecessors have signed it ; and after his death we will
elect whom we choose, even that Radzivill who will be born
of your niece."

The sword-bearer stood for a while as if dazzled by the
thought ; at last he raised his hand and cried with great
enthusiasm, —

"*Consentior* (I agree) !"

"I think, too, that you would agree, even if the throne
should become hereditary in our family. Such are you
all ! But that is a later question. Now it is necessary
that the stipulations come to reality. You understand, my
uncle ?"

"As true as life, it is necessary!" repeated Billevich, with deep conviction.

"They must for this reason,— that I am a mediator agreeable to his Swedish Majesty, and do you know for what reasons? Karl Gustav has one sister married to De la Gardie, and another, Princess Bipont, still unmarried; and he wishes to give her to me, so as to be allied to our house and have a party in Lithuania. Hence his favor toward me, to which my uncle, the elector, inclines him."

"How is that?" asked the disquieted sword-bearer.

"I would give all the princesses of Bipont [1] for your dove, together with the principalities, not only of the two, but of all the bridges in the world. But I may not anger the Swedish beast, therefore I give willing ear to their discussions; but only let them sign the treaty, then we shall see."

"Would they be ready then not to sign if they should discover that you were married?"

"Worthy sword-bearer," said the prince, with seriousness, "you have cond mned me of crookedness toward the country; but I, as a tru citizen, ask you, have I a right to sacrifice public affairs o my private interests?"

Pan Tomash list ned. "What will happen then?"

"Think to yourself what must happen."

"As God is true, I see already that the marriage must be deferred; and the proverb says: 'What is deferred, escapes.'"

"I will not change my heart, for I have fallen in love for life. You must know that for faithfulness I could put to shame the most enduring Penelope."

Billevich was alarmed still more; for he had an entirely opposite opinion touching the prince's constancy, confirmed as it was by Boguslav's general reputation. But the prince added, as if for a finishing stroke, —

"You are right, that no one is sure of his to-morrow. I may fall ill; nay, some kind of sickness is coming on me even now, for yesterday I grew so rigid that Sakovich barely saved me. I may fall in a campaign against Sapyeha; and what delays, what troubles and vexations there will be, could not be written on an ox-hide."

"By the wounds of God, give advice, your highness."

"What advice can I give?" asked the prince. "Though I should be glad myself to have the latch fall as soon as possible."

[1] "Two-bridged" or "of two bridges," from *bis* and *pons*.

"Well, let it fall. Marry, and then what will be, will be."
Boguslav sprang to his feet.

"By the holy Gospel! With your wit you should be chancellor of Lithuania. Another man would not have thought
out in three days what has come to your mind in a twinkle.
That is it! marry, and remain quiet. There is sense in that!
As it is, I shall march in two days against Sapyeha, for
I must. During that time secret passages to the lady's
chamber can be made; and then to the road! That is the
head of a statesman! We will let two or three confidants
into the secret, and take them as witnesses, so that the marriage may be formal. I will write a contract, secure the
jointure, to which I will add a bequest; and let there be
silence for the time. My benefactor, I thank you; from my
heart, I thank you. Come to my arms, and then go to my
beauty. I will wait for her answer, as if on coals. Meanwhile I will send Sakovich for the priest. Be well, father,
and, God grant soon, the grandfather of a Radzivill."

When he had said this, he let the astonished noble go from
his embrace, and rushed out of the room.

"For God's sake!" said the sword-bearer, recovering himself. "I gave such wise advice that Solomon himself would
not be ashamed of it, and I should prefer to do without it.
A secret is a secret; but break your head, crush your
forehead against a wall, it cannot be otherwise. A blind
man can see that! Would that the frost might oppress and
kill those Swedes to the last! If it were not for those
negotiations, the marriage would take place with ceremony, and all Jmud would come to the wedding. But
here a husband must walk to his wife on felt, so as not
to make noise. Tfu, to the deuce! The Sitsinskis will
not burst so soon. Yet, praise be to God! that bursting
will not miss them."

When he had said this, he went to Olenka. Meanwhile the prince was taking further counsel with Sakovich.

"The old man danced on two paws like a bear," said the
prince; "but he tormented the life out of me. Uf! but I
squeezed him so that I thought that the boots and straw
would fly off his feet. And when I called him 'Uncle,' his
eyes stuck out, as if a keg of cabbage hash were choking him.
Tfu! tfu! wait! I will make you uncle; but I have scores
upon scores of such uncles throughout the whole world. Sakovich, I see how she is waiting for me in her room; and she
will receive me with her eyes closed and her hands crossed.

Wait, I will kiss those eyes for you— Sakovich, you will receive for life the estate of Prudy, beyond Oshmiana. When can Plaska be here ? "

"Before evening. I thank your highness for Prudy."

"That is nothing! Before evening? That means any moment. If the ceremony could be performed to-day, even before midnight! Have you the contract ready ? "

"I have. I was liberal in the name of your highness. I assigned Birji as the jointure of the lady. The sword-bearer will howl like a dog when it is taken from him afterward."

"He will sit in a dungeon, then he will be quiet."

"Even that will not be needed. As soon as the marriage is invalid, all will be invalid. But did I not tell you that they would agree ? "

"He did not make the least difficulty. I am curious to know what she will say. I care nothing about him ! "

"Oh, they have fallen each into the arms of the other, are weeping from emotion, are blessing your highness, and are carried away by your kindness and beauty."

"I don't know that they are by my beauty; for in some way I look wretched. I am all the time out of health, and I am afraid that yesterday's numbness will come again."

"No ; you will take something warm."

The prince was already before the mirror.

"It is blue under my eyes. And that fool, Fouret, dark-ened my eyebrows crooked. See if they are not crooked! I 'll give orders to thumbscrew him, and make a monkey my body-servant. Why does the old man not come? I should like to go to the lady now, for she will permit me to kiss her before the marriage. How quickly it grows dark to-day! If Plaska flinches, we must put pincers into the fire."

"Plaska will not flinch. He is a scoundrel from under a dark star."

"And he will perform the marriage in scoundrel fashion ? "

"A scoundrel will perform the marriage for a scoundrel in scoundrel fashion."

The prince fell into good humor, and said, —

"When there is a pander for best man, there cannot be another kind of marriage."

For a while they were silent ; then both began to laugh

But their laughter sounded with marvellous ill-omen through the dark room.   Night fell deeper and deeper.

The prince began to walk through the room, striking audibly with his hammer-staff, on which he leaned heavily, for his feet did not serve him well after the last numbness.

Now the servants brought in candelabra with candles, and went out; but the rush of air bent the flames of the candles, so that for a long time they did not burn straight upward, melting meanwhile much wax.

"See how the candles are burning!" said the prince. "What do you prophesy from that?"

"That one virtue will melt to-day like wax."

"It is wonderful how long that talk lasts."

"Maybe the spirit of old Billevich is flying over the flames."

"You are a fool!" answered Boguslav, abruptly.   "You have chosen a time to talk of spirits!"

Silence followed.

"They say in England," said the prince, "that when there is a spirit in the room every light burns blue; but see, now they are burning yellow, as usual."

"Trash!" answered Sakovich.   "There are people in Moscow — "

"But be still!" interrupted Boguslav.   "The sword-bearer is coming.   No! that is the wind moving the shutters. The devils have brought that old maid of an aunt, Kulvyets-Hippocentaurus!   Has any one ever heard of the like? And she looks like a chimera."

"If you wish, your highness, I'll marry her; then she will not be in the way,   Plaska will solder us while you are waiting."

"Well, I will give her a maple spade as a marriage present, and you a lantern, so as to have something to light her way."

"I will not be your uncle — Bogus."

"Remember Castor," answered the prince.

"Do not stroke Castor, my Pollux, against the grain, for he can bite."

Further conversation was interrupted by the sword-bearer and Panna Kulvyets. The prince stepped up to him quickly, leaning on his hammer.   Sakovich rose.

"Well, what?   May I go to Olenka?" asked the prince.

The sword-bearer spread out his arms and dropped his head on his breast.

"Your highness, my niece says that Colonel Billevich's will forbids her to decide her own fate ; and even if it did not forbid, she would not marry your highness, not having the heart to do so."

"Sakovich, do you hear?" said Boguslav, with a terrible voice.

"I too knew of that will," continued the sword-bearer, "but at the first moment I did not think it an invincible impediment."

"I jeer at the wills of you nobles," said the prince; "I spit on your wills! Do you understand?"

"But we do not jeer at them," said the aroused Pan Tomash; "and according to the will the maiden is free to enter the cloister or marry Kmita."

"Whom, you sorry fellow? Kmita? I'll show you Kmita! I'll teach you!"

"Whom do you call sorry fellow, — a Billevich?"

And the sword-bearer caught at his side in the greatest fury ; but Boguslav, in one moment, struck him on the breast with his hammer, so that Billevich groaned and fell to the floor. The prince then kicked him aside, to open a way to the door, and rushed from the room without a hat.

"Jesus! Mary! Joseph!" cried Panna Kulvyets.

But Sakovich, seizing her by the shoulder, put a dagger to her breast, and said, —

"Quiet, my little jewel, quiet, dearest dove, or I will cut thy sweet throat, like that of a lame hen. Sit here quietly, and go not upstairs to thy niece's wedding."

But in Panna Kulvyets there was knightly blood too; therefore she had barely heard the words of Sakovich, when straightway her terror passed into despair and frenzy.

"Ruffian! bandit! pagan!" cried she; "slay me, for I will shout to the whole Commonwealth. The brother killed, the niece disgraced, I do not wish to live! Strike, slay, robber! People, come see!"

Sakovich stifled further words by putting his powerful hand over her mouth.

"Quiet, crooked distaff, dried rue!" said he; "I will not cut thy throat, for why should I give the Devil that which is his anyhow? But lest thou scream like a peacock before roosting, I will tie up thy pretty mouth with thy kerchief, and take a lute and play to thee of 'sighs.' It cannot be but thou wilt love me."

So saying, the starosta of Oshmiana, with the dexterity of a genuine pickpocket, encircled the head of Panna Kulvyets with her handkerchief, tied her hands in the twinkle of an eye, and threw her on the sofa; then he sat by her, and stretching himself out comfortably, asked her as calmly as though he had begun an ordinary conversation, —

"Well, what do you think? I suppose Bogus will get on as easily as I have."

With that he sprang to his feet, for the door opened, and in it appeared Panna Aleksandra. Her face was as white as chalk, her hair was somewhat dishevelled, her brows were frowning, and threat was in her eyes. Seeing her uncle on the floor, she knelt near him and passed her hand over his head and breast.

The sword-bearer drew a deep breath, opened his eyes, half raised himself, and began to look around in the room, as if roused from sleep; then resting his hand on the floor, he tried to rise, which he did after a while with the help of the lady ; then he came with tottering step to a chair, into which he threw himself. Only now did Olenka see Panna Kulvyets lying on the sofa.

"Have you murdered her?" asked she of Sakovich.

"God preserve me!" answered the starosta of Oshmiana.

"I command you to unbind her!"

There was such power in that voice that Sakovich said not a word, as if the command had come from Princess Radzivill herself, and began to unbind the unconscious Panna Kulvyets.

"And now," said the lady, "go to your master, who is lying up there."

"What has happened?" cried Sakovich, coming to himself. "You will answer for him!"

"Not to thee, serving-man! Be off!"

Sakovich sprang out of the chamber as if possessed.

CHAPTER XLIV.

SAKOVICH did not leave Boguslav's bedside for two days, the second paroxysm being worse than the first. The prince's jaws closed so firmly that attendants had to open them with a knife to pour medicine into his mouth. He regained consciousness immediately after; but he trembled, quivered, floundered in the bed, and stretched himself like a wild beast mortally wounded. When that had passed, a wonderful weakness came; he gazed all night at the ceiling without saying a word. Next day, after he had taken drugs, he fell into a sound sleep, and about midday woke covered with abundant perspiration.

"How does your highness feel?" asked Sakovich.

"I am better. Have any letters come?"

"Letters from the elector and Steinbock are lying on the table; but the reading must be put off till later, for you have not strength enough yet."

"Give them at once! — do you hear?"

Sakovich brought the letters, and Boguslav read them twice; then he thought awhile and said, —

"We will move for Podlyasye to-morrow."

"You will be in bed to-morrow, as you are to-day."

"I will be on horseback as well as you. Be silent, no interference!"

The starosta ceased, and for a while silence continued, broken only by the tick-tick of the Dantzig clock.

"The advice was stupid, the idea was stupid, and I too was stupid to listen."

"I knew that if it did not succeed the blame would fall on me," answered Sakovich.

"For you blundered."

"The counsel was clever; but if there is some devil at their service who gives warning of everything, I am not to blame."

The prince rose in the bed. "Do you think that they employ a devil?" asked he, looking quickly at Sakovich.

"But does not your highness know the Papists?"

"I know, I know! And it has often come into my head

that there might be enchantment. Since yesterday I am certain. You have struck my idea; therefore I asked if you really think so. But which of them could enter into company with unclean power? Not she, for she is too virtuous; not the sword-bearer, for he is too stupid."

"But suppose the aunt?"

"That may be."

"To make certain I bound her yesterday, and put a dagger to her throat; and imagine, — I look to-day, the dagger is as if melted in fire."

"Show it."

"I threw it into the river, though there was a good turquoise in the hilt. I preferred not to touch it again."

"Then I'll tell you what happened to me yesterday. I ran into her room as if mad. What I said I do not remember; but I know this, — that she cried, 'I'll throw myself into the fire first.' You know what an enormous chimney there is there; she sprang right into it, I after her. I dragged her out on the floor. Her clothes were already on fire. I had to quench the fire and hold her at the same time. Meanwhile dizziness seized me, my jaws became fixed, — you would have said that some one had torn the veins in my neck; then it seemed to me that the sparks flying near us were turned into bees, were buzzing like bees. And this is as true as that you see me here."

"And what came later?"

"I remember nothing, but such terror as if I were flying into an immense well, into some depth without bottom. What terror! I tell you what terror! Even now the hair is standing on my head. And not terror alone, but — how can I explain it? — an emptiness, a measureless weariness and torment beyond understanding. Luckily the powers of heaven were with me, or I should not be speaking with you this day."

"Your highness had a paroxysm. Sickness itself often brings visions before the eye; but for safety's sake we may have a hole cut in the river ice, and let the old maid float down."

"Oh, devil take her! We will march to-morrow in any event, and afterward spring will come; there will soon be other stars, and the nights will be short, weakening every unclean power."

"If we must march to-morrow, then you would better let the girl go."

"Even if I wished not, I must. All desire has fallen away from me."

"Never mind them; let them go to the devil!"

"Impossible!"

"Why?"

"The old man has confessed that he has a tremendous lot of money buried in Billeviche. If I let them alone, they will dig up the money and go to the forests. I prefer to keep them here, and take the money in requisition. There is war now, and this is permissible. Besides, he offered it himself. We shall give orders to dig up the whole garden, foot by foot; we must find the money. While Billevich is sitting here, at least, he will not make a noise and shout over all Lithuania that he is plundered. Rage seizes me when I think how much I have spent on those amusements and tournaments, — and all for nothing, for nothing!"

"Rage against that maiden seized me long ago. And I tell your highness that when she came yesterday and said to me, as to the last camp follower, 'Be off, serving-man! go up, for thy master is lying there!' I came near twisting her head like a starling; for I thought that she had stabbed you with a knife or shot you from a pistol."

"You know that I do not like to have any one manage in my house like a gray goose. It is well that you did not do as you say, for I should have given orders to nip you with those pincers which were heated for Plaska. Keep away from her!"

"I sent Plaska back. He was terribly astonished, not knowing why he was brought nor why he was sent home. He wanted something for his fatigue, 'because this,' said he, 'is loss in my trade;' but I told him, 'You bear home a sound skin as reward.' Do we really march to-morrow for Podlyasye?"

"As God is in heaven. Are the troops sent off according to my orders?"

"The cavalry has gone already to Kyedani, whence it is to march to Kovno and wait there. Our Polish squadrons are here yet; I did not like to send them in advance. The men seem reliable; still they might meet the confederates. Glovbich will go with us; also the Cossacks under Vrotynski. Karlström marches with the Swedes in the vanguard. He has orders to exterminate rebels, and especially peasants on the way."

"That is well."

"Kyritz with infantry is to march slowly, so that we may have some one to fall back upon in difficulty. If we are to advance like a thunderbolt, — and our entire calculation lies in swiftness, — I do not know whether the Prussian and Swedish cavalry will be useful. It is a pity that the Polish squadrons are not reliable; for between us, there is nothing superior to Polish cavalry."

"Has the artillery gone?"

"It has."

"And Patterson too?"

"No, Patterson is here; he is nursing Kettling, of whom he is very fond, and who wounded himself rather badly with his own sword. If I did not know Kettling to be a daring officer, I should think that he had cut himself of purpose to avoid the campaign."

"It will be needful to leave about a hundred men here, also in Rossyeni and in Kyedani. The Swedish garrisons are small, and De la Gardie, as it is, is asking men every day from Löwenhaupt. Besides, when we march out, the rebels, forgetting the defeat of Shavli, will raise their heads."

"They are growing strong as it is. I have heard again that the Swedes are cut down in Telshi."

"By nobles or peasants?"

"By peasants under the leadership of a priest; but there are parties of nobles, particularly near Lauda."

"The Lauda men have gone out under Volodyovski."

"There is a multitude of youths and old men at home. These have taken arms, for they are warriors by blood."

"The rebellion can do nothing without money."

"But we shall get a supply of that in Billeviche."

"A man must be a genius like your highness to find means in everything."

"There is more esteem in this country," said Boguslav, with a bitter smile, "for the man who can please the queen and the nobles. Neither genius nor virtue has value. It is lucky that I am also a prince of the Empire, and therefore they will not tie me by the legs to a pine-tree. If I could only have the revenues regularly from my estates, I should not care for the Commonwealth."

"But will they not confiscate these estates?"

"We will first confiscate Podlyasye, if not all Lithuania. Now summon Patterson."

Sakovich went out, and returned soon with Patterson. At Boguslav's bedside a council was held, at which it was determined to move before daylight next morning and go to Podlyasye by forced marches. The prince felt so much better in the evening that he feasted with the officers and amused himself with jests till late, listening with pleasure to the neighing of horses and the clatter of arms in the squadrons preparing to march. At times he breathed deeply, and stretched himself in the chair.

"I see that this campaign will bring back my health," said he to the officers, "for amid all these negotiations and amusements I have neglected the field notably. But I hope in God that the confederates and our ex-cardinal (the king) in Poland will feel my hand."

To this Patterson made bold to answer: "It is lucky that Delilah did not clip Samson's hair."

Boguslav looked at him for a while with a strange expression, from which the Scot was growing confused; but after a time the countenance of the prince grew bright with a threatening smile, and he said, —

"If Sapyeha is my pillar, I will shake him so that the whole Commonwealth will fall on his head."

The conversation was carried on in German; therefore all the foreign officers understood it perfectly, and answered in chorus, —

"Amen!"

The column, with Boguslav at the head of it, marched before daybreak next morning. The Prussian nobles whom the brilliant court attracted, began at the same time to return to their homes. After them marched to Tyltsa those who in Taurogi had sought refuge from the terrors of war, and to whom now Tyltsa seemed safer. Only Billevich, Olenka, and Panna Kulvyets remained, not counting Kettling and the old officer Braun, who held command over the slender garrison.

Billevich, after that blow of the hammer, lay for some days bleeding from the mouth at intervals; but since no bone was broken, he recovered by degrees and began to think of flight.

Meanwhile an official came from Billeviche with a letter from Boguslav himself. The sword-bearer did not wish at first to read the letter, but soon changed his mind, following in this the advice of Olenka, who thought it better to know all the plans of the enemy.

Very gracious Pan Billevich!—*Concordia res parvæ crescunt; discordia maximæ dillabuntur* (By concord small things grow great; by discord the greatest are ruined)! The fates brought it about that we did not part in such harmony as my love for you and your charming niece demands, in which God knows I am not to blame, for you know yourself that you fed me with ingratitude in return for my sincere intentions. But for friendship's sake what is done in anger should not be remembered; I think, therefore, that you will excuse my deeds of impulse, because of the injustice which I experienced at your hands. I, too, forgive you from my heart, as Christian charity enjoins, and I wish to return to a good understanding. To give you a proof that no offence has remained in my heart, I have not thought it proper to refuse the service which you have asked of me, and I accept your money.

Here Billevich stopped reading, struck the table with his fist, and cried, —

"He will see me in dreams rather than receive one coin from my caskets!"

"Read on!" said Olenka.

Billevich raised the letter again to his eyes.

"Not wishing to trouble you and expose your health to hazard in the present stormy times while getting this money, we have ordered ourselves to get it and count it."

At this point Billevich's voice failed, and the letter fell from his hands to the floor. For a while it seemed that speech was taken from the noble, for he only caught after his hair and pulled it with all his power.

"Strike, whoso believes in God!" cried he at last.

"One injustice the more, the punishment of God nearer; for the measure will soon be filled." said Olenka.

CHAPTER XLV.

THE despair of the sword-bearer was so great that Olenka had to comfort him, and give assurance that the money was not to be looked on as lost, for the letter itself would serve as a note; and Radzivill, the master of so many estates in Lithuania and Russia, had something from which to recover.

But since it was difficult to foresee what might still meet them, especially if Boguslav returned to Taurogi victorious, they began to think of flight the more eagerly.

Olenka advised to defer everything till Kettling's recovery; for Braun was a gloomy and surly old soldier, carrying out commands blindly, and it was impossible to influence him.

As to Kettling, the lady knew well that he had wounded himself to remain in Taurogi; hence her deep faith that he would do everything to aid her. It is true that conscience disturbed her incessantly with the question whether for self-safety she had the right to sacrifice the career, and perhaps the life, of another; but the terrors hanging over her in Taurogi were so dreadful that they surpassed a hundred-fold the dangers to which Kettling could be exposed.

Kettling, as an excellent officer, might find service, and a more noble service, elsewhere, and with it powerful protectors, such as the king, Pan Sapyeha, or Pan Charnyetski; and he would, besides, serve a just cause, and would find a career grateful to that country which had received him as an exile. Death threatened him only in case he fell into Boguslav's hands; but Boguslav did not command yet the whole Commonwealth.

Olenka ceased to hesitate; and when the health of the young officer had improved, she sent for him.

Kettling stood before her, pale, emaciated, without a drop of blood in his face, but always full of respect, homage, and submission. At sight of him tears came to Olenka's eyes; for he was the only friendly soul in Taurogi, and at the same time so thin and suffering that when Olenka asked how his health was, he answered. —

"Alas, my lady, health is returning, and it would be so pleasant to die."

"You should leave this service," said she, looking at him with sympathy; "for such an honorable man needs assurance that he is serving a just cause and a worthy master."

"Alas!" repeated the officer.

"When will your service end?"

"In half a year."

Olenka was silent awhile; then she raised her wonderful eyes, which at that moment had ceased to be stern, and said, —

"Listen to me. I will speak to you as to a brother, as to a sincere confidant. You can, and you should resign."

When she had said this, she confessed to him everything, — both their plans of escape, and that she relied on his assistance. She represented to him that he could find service everywhere, and a service as good as was his spirit, and honorable as knightly honor could obtain. At last she finished with the following words: —

"I shall be grateful to you till death. I wish to take refuge under the guardianship of God, and to make a vow to the Lord in a cloister. But wherever you may be, far or near, in war or in peace, I shall pray for you. I will implore God to give peace and happiness to my brother and benefactor; for I can give him nothing save gratitude and prayer."

Here her voice trembled; and the officer listened to her words, growing pale as a kerchief. At last he knelt, put both hands to his forehead, and said, in a voice like a groan, —

"I cannot, my lady; I cannot!"

"Do you refuse me?" asked Olenka, with amazement.

"O great, merciful God!" said he. "From childhood no lie has risen on my lips, no unjust deed has ever stained me. While still a youth, I defended with this weak hand my king and country. Why, Lord, dost Thou punish me so grievously, and send on me suffering for which, as Thou seest, strength fails me?" Here he turned to Olenka: "My lady, you do not know what an order is for a soldier. In obedience is not only his duty, but his honor and reputation. An oath binds me, my lady, — and more than an oath, the word of a knight, — that I shall not throw up my service before the time, and that I will fulfil what belongs to it blindly. I am a soldier and a

noble; and, so help me God, never in my life will I follow
the example of those who betray honor and service. And
I will not break my word, even at your command, at your
prayer, though I say this in suffering and pain. If, having
an order not to let any one out of Taurogi, I were on guard at
the gate, and if you yourself wished to pass against the order,
you would pass only over my corpse. You did not know me,
my lady; and you were mistaken in me. But have pity on
me; understand that I cannot aid you to escape. I ought
not to hear of such a thing. The order is express, for Braun
and the five remaining officers of us here have received it.
My God, my God! if I had foreseen such an order, I should
have preferred to go on the campaign. I shall not convince
you; you will not believe me. And still God sees — let God
judge me after death whether it is true — that I would give
my life without hesitation. But my honor — I cannot, I
cannot!"

Then Kettling wrung his hands, was silent from exhaustion, and began to breathe quickly.

Olenka had not recovered yet from her amazement.
She had not time to pause, or estimate properly that spirit,
exceptional in its nobleness. She felt only that the last
plank of salvation was slipping from her hands, the only
means of escape from hated captivity was failing her. But
still she tried to resist.

"I am," said she, after a while, "the granddaughter and
the daughter of a soldier. My grandfather and father
also valued honor above life; but, precisely for that reason, they would not let themselves be used blindly for
every service."

Kettling drew, with trembling hand, from his coat a
letter, gave it to Olenka, and said, —

"Judge, my lady, if this command does not concern
service."

Olenka cast her eyes over the letter, and read as
follows : —

" Since it has come to our knowledge that Billevich, the sword-
bearer of Rossyeni, intends to leave our residence in secret, with
plans hostile to us, — namely, to excite his acquaintances, connections, relatives, and clients to rebellion against his Swedish Majesty
and us, — we recommend to the officers remaining in garrison at
Taurogi to guard Billevich and his niece as hostages and prisoners
of war, and not to permit their flight under pain of loss of honor
and court-martial," etc.

"The order came from the first stopping-place after the departure of the prince," said Kettling; "therefore it is in writing."

"The will of God be done!" said Olenka, after a while. "It is accomplished!"

Kettling felt that he ought to go; still he did not stir. His pale lips moved from moment to moment, as if he wished to say something and could not get the voice.

He was oppressed by the desire to fall at her feet and implore forgiveness; but on the other hand he felt that she had enough of her own misfortune, and he found a certain wild delight in this, — that he was suffering and would suffer without complaint.

At last he bowed and went out in silence; but in the corridor he tore the bandages from his fresh wound, and fell fainting to the floor. When an hour later the palace guard found him lying near the staircase and took him to the barracks, he became seriously ill and did not leave his bed for a fortnight.

Olenka, after the departure of Kettling, remained some time as if dazed. Death had seemed to her more likely to come than that refusal; and therefore, at first, in spite of all her firm temper of spirit, strength, energy failed her; she felt weak, like an ordinary woman, and though she repeated unconsciously, "Let the will of God be done!" sorrow for the disappointment rose above her resignation, copious and bitter tears flowed from her eyes.

At that moment her uncle entered, and looking at his niece, divined at once that she had evil news to impart; hence he asked quickly, —

"For God's sake, what is it?"

"Kettling refuses!"

"All here are ruffians, scoundrels, arch-curs! How is this? And he will not help?"

"Not only will he not help," answered she, complaining like a little child, "but he says that he will prevent, even should it come to him to die."

"Why? by the Lord's wounds, why?"

"For such is our fate! Kettling is not a traitor; but such is our fate, for we are the most unhappy of all people."

"May the thunderbolts crush all those heretics!" cried Billevich. "They attack virtue, plunder, steal, imprison. Would that all might perish! It is not for honest people to live in such times!"

Here he began to walk with hurried step through the

chamber, threatening with his fists; at last he said, gritting his teeth, —

"The voevoda of Vilna was better; I prefer a thousand times even Kmita to these perfumed ruffians without honor and conscience."

When Olenka said nothing, but began to cry still more, Billevich grew mild, and after a while said, —

"Do not weep. Kmita came to my mind only because that he at least would have been able to wrest us out of this Babylonian captivity. He would have given it to all the Brauns, Kettlings, Pattersons, to Boguslav himself! But they are all the same type of traitors. Weep not! You can do nothing with weeping; here it is necessary to counsel. Kettling will not help, — may he be twisted! We will do without him. You have as it were a man's courage in you, but in difficulty you are only able to sob. What does Kettling say?"

"He says that the prince has given orders to guard us as prisoners of war, fearing, Uncle, that you would collect a party and go to the confederates."

Billevich put his hands on his hips: "Ha, ha, ha! he is afraid, the scoundrel! And he is right, for I will do so, as God is in heaven."

"Having a command relating to service, Kettling must carry it out on his honor."

"Well! we shall get on without the assistance of heretics."

Olenka wiped her eyes. "And does my uncle think it is possible?"

"I think it is necessary; and if it is necessary it is possible, though we had to let ourselves down by ropes from these windows."

"It was wrong for me to shed tears: let us make plans as quickly as we can."

Her tears were dry, her brows contracted again from thought and her former endurance and energy.

It appeared, in fact, that Billevich could find no help, and that the imagination of the lady was much richer in means. But it was difficult for her, since it was clear that they were guarded carefully.

They determined, therefore, not to try before the first news came from Boguslav. In this they placed all their hope, trusting that the punishment of God would come on the traitor and the dishonorable man. Besides, he might fall, he might be confined to his bed, he might be killed by Sapyeha, and then without fail there would rise in all Taurogi a panic, and the gate would not be guarded so carefully.

"I know Sapyeha," said Billevich, comforting himself and Olenka; "he is a slow warrior, but accurate and wonderfully stubborn. An example of this, his loyalty to the king and country. He pledged and sold everything, and thus has gained a power before which Boguslav is as nothing. One is a dignified senator, the other a fop; one a true Catholic, the other a heretic; one is cleverness itself, the other a water-burner. With whom may victory and the blessing of God be? This Radzivill might well yield to Sapyeha's day. Just as if there are not punishment and justice in this world! We will wait for news, and pray for Sapyeha's success."

Then they began to wait; but a month passed — long, wearisome for afflicted hearts — before the first courier came; and he was sent not to Taurogi, but to Steinbock in Royal Prussia.

Kettling, who from the time of the last conversation dared not appear before Olenka's eyes, sent her at once a card with the following announcement: —

"Prince Boguslav has defeated Pan Kryshtof Sapyeha near Bransk; some squadrons of cavalry and infantry are cut to pieces. He is marching on Tykotsin, where Horotkyevich is stationed."

For Olenka this was simply a thunderbolt. The greatness of a leader and the bravery of a knight meant for her the same thing. Since she had seen Boguslav, at Taurogi, over-coming the most valiant knights with ease, she imagined him to herself, especially after that news, as an evil but invincible power, against which no one could stand.

The hope that Boguslav might be defeated died in her completely. In vain did her uncle quiet her and comfort her with this, — that the prince had not yet met Sapyeha; in vain did he guarantee to her that the very dignity of hetman with which the king had invested him recently, must give positive preponderance over Boguslav; she did not believe this, she dared not.

"Who can conquer Boguslav; who can meet him?" asked she, continually.

Further news seemed to confirm her fears.

A few days later Kettling sent another card with infor-mation touching the defeat of Horotkyevich and the capture of Tykotsin. "All Podlyasye," writes he, "is in the hands of the prince, who, without waiting for Sapyeha, is moving against him with forced marches."

"And Sapyeha will be routed!" thought the maiden.

Meanwhile news from other directions flew to them, like a swallow heralding spring-time. To that seashore of the Commonwealth this news came late; but because of its lateness it was decked in all the rainbow gleams of wonderful legend from the first ages of Christianity, when saints proclaiming truth and justice still travelled over the earth.

"Chenstohova! Chenstohova!" was repeated by every mouth.

Ice thawed from hearts which bloomed like flowers in the earth warmed by the sun of spring. "Chenstohova has defended itself. Men had seen the Queen of Poland Herself (the Virgin Mary) shielding the walls with Her heavenly mantle; the bombs of the robbers at Her holy feet, crouching like house-dogs; the hands of the Swedes were withered, their muskets grew fast to their faces, till they retreated in terror and shame."

Men, strangers to one another, when they heard these tidings fell the one into the embraces of the other, weeping from delight. Others complained that the tidings came too late.

"But we were here in weeping," said they, "we were in pain, we lived in torment so long, when we should have been rejoicing."

Then it began to roar through the whole Commonwealth, and terrible thunders were heard from the Euxine to the Baltic, so that the waves of both seas were trembling; then faithful people, pious people rose up like a storm in defence of their queen. Consolation entered all hearts, all eyes were flashing with fire; what hitherto had seemed terrible and invincible grew small in their eyes.

"Who will finish him?" said Billevich. "Who will be his equal? Now do you know who? The Most Holy Lady."

The old man and his niece lay for whole days in the form of a cross, thanking God for his mercy on the Commonwealth, and doubting their own rescue no longer.

But for a long period there was silence concerning Boguslav, as if he with all his forces had fallen into water. The officers remaining in Taurogi began to be disquieted and to think of their uncertain future. They would have preferred defeat to that deep silence. But no news could come, for just then the terrible Babinich was rushing with his Tartars in front of the prince and stopping all couriers.

CHAPTER XLVI.

But a certain day Panna Anusia Borzobogati arrived at Taurogi with a convoy of some tens of soldiers.

Braum received her very politely, for he had to do so, since he was thus commanded by a letter from Sakovich, signed by Boguslav himself, enjoining him to have every regard for this lady-in-waiting of Princess Griselda Vishnyevetski. The young lady herself was full of vivacity; from the first moment she began to pierce Braun with her eyes, so that the sullen German moved about as if some one were touching him with fire; she began also to command other officers, — in a word, to manage in Taurogi as in her own house. In the evening of the same day she made the acquaintance of Olenka, who received her with distrust, it is true, but politely, in the hope that she would get news from her.

In fact, Anusia had news in plenty. Her conversation began with Chenstohova, since the prisoners in Taurogi were most eager for that news. The sword-bearer listened with special diligence; he held his hands behind his ears so as to lose no word, merely interrupting Anusia's narrative from time to time with the exclamation, —

"Praise be to God on high!"

"It is a wonder to me," said Anusia, at last, "that news of these miracles of the Most Holy Lady have only just reached you, for that is an old story. I was still in Zamost, and Pan Babinich had not come for me — ai! how many weeks was it before that? Then they began to beat the Swedes everywhere, in Great Poland and with us; but most of all Pan Charnyetski, before whose very name they fly."

"Oh, Charnyetski!" cried the sword-bearer, rubbing his hands; "he will give them pepper! I heard of him even from the Ukraine, as of a great warrior."

Anusia merely shook her dress, and exclaimed to herself with aversion, as if it were a question of the smallest matter: "Oh, it is all over with the Swedes!"

Old Pan Tomash could not restrain himself. Seizing her

small hand, he buried the little thing entirely in his enormous mustaches and kissed it eagerly; at last he cried, —

"Oh, my beauty! honey flows from your mouth, as
God is dear to me! It cannot be but an angel has come to
Taurogi."

Anusia began at once to twist the ends of her tresses, tied
with rosy ribbons, and cutting with her eyes from under her
brows, said, —

"Oh, it is far from me to the angels! But the hetmans
of the kingdom have begun to beat the Swedes, and all the
quarter soldiers with them, and the knights; and they have
formed a confederation in Tyshovtsi. The king has joined
it, and they have given out manifestoes; even the peasants
are beating the Swedes, and the Most Holy Lady gives Her
blessing."

She spoke as if a bird were warbling, but from that warbling Billevich's heart grew soft, though some of the news
was already known to him. He bellowed at last like an
aurochs from delight; tears, too, began to flow over the face
of Olenka, silent and many.

Seeing this, Anusia, having a good heart from nature,
sprang to her at once, and putting her arms around her
neck, began to say quickly, —

"Do not cry; I am sorry for you, and cannot see you
shed tears. Why do you weep?"

There was so much sincerity in her voice that Olenka's
distrust vanished at once; but the poor girl wept still
more.

"You are so beautiful," said Anusia, comforting her.
"Why do you cry?"

"From joy," answered Olenka, "but also from suffering;
for we are here in grievous captivity, knowing neither the
day nor the hour."

"How is that? Are you not with Prince Boguslav?"

"That traitor! that heretic!" roared Billevich.

"The same has happened to me," said Anusia; "but I do
not cry for that reason. I do not deny that the prince is a
traitor and a heretic; but he is a courteous cavalier, and re-
spects our sex."

"God grant that in hell they will respect him in the same
fashion! Young lady, you know him not, for he has not attacked you as he has this maiden. He is an arch-ruffian,
and that Sakovich is another. God give Sapyeha to defeat
them both!"

"As to defeating, he will defeat them. Prince Boguslav is terribly sick, and he has not a great force. It is true that he advanced quickly, scattered some squadrons, and took Tykotsin and me; but it is not for him to measure with the forces of Pan Sapyeha. You may trust me, for I saw both armies. With Pan Sapyeha are the greatest cavaliers, who will be able to manage Prince Boguslav."

"Well, do you see! have I not told you?" asked the old man, turning to Olenka.

"I know Prince Boguslav from of old," continued Anusia, "for he is a relative of the Vishnyevetskis and Zamoyski; he came once to us at Lubni, when Prince Yeremi himself was campaigning against the Tartars in the Wilderness. He remembered that I was at home there and nearest the princess. I was such a little thing then, not as I am to-day. My God! who could think at that time that he would be a traitor? But grieve not; for either he will fail to return, or we shall escape from this place in some way."

"We have tried that already," said Olenka.

"And you did not succeed?"

"How could we?" asked Billevich. "We told the secret to an officer whom we thought ready to aid us; but it turned out that he was ready to hinder, not to help. Seniority over all here is with Braun, — the Devil himself could not win that man."

Anusia dropped her eyes.

"Maybe I can. If Pan Sapyeha would only come, so that we might have some one with whom to take refuge."

"God give him at the earliest," answered Pan Tomash, "for among his men we have many relatives, acquaintances, and friends. Among them, too, are former officers of the great Yeremi, — Volodyovski, Skshetuski, Zagloba, — I know them."

"But they are not with Sapyeha. Oh, if they were, especially Volodyovski, for Shshetuski is married, I should not be here, for Pan Volodyovski would not let himself be picked up as Pan Kotchyts did."

"He is a great cavalier," said Billevich.

"The glory of the whole Commonwealth," added Olenka.

"Have they not fallen, since you did not see them?"

"Oh, no!" answered Anusia, "for the loss of such knights would be spoken of; but nothing was said. You do not know them, they will never yield; only a bullet will kill them, for no man can stand before Skshetuski, Zagloba, or Pan Michael."

Though Pan Michael is small, I remember what Prince Yeremi said of him, — that if the fate of the whole Commonwealth depended on a battle between one man and another, he would choose Pan Michael for the battle. He was the man who conquered Bogun. Oh, no, Pan Michael will help himself always."

Billevich, satisfied that he had some one with whom to talk, began to walk with long strides through the room, asking, —

"Well, well! Then do you know Pan Volodyovski so intimately?"

"Yes; for we lived in the same place so many years."

"Indeed! Then certainly not without love?"

"I 'm not to blame for that," answered Anusia, taking a timid posture; "but before this time surely Pan Michael is married."

"And he is just not married."

"Even if he were, it is all one to me."

"God grant you to meet! But I am troubled because you say that they are not with the hetman, for with such soldiers victory would be easier."

"There is some one there who is worth them all."

"Who is he?"

"Pan Babinich from Vityebsk. Have you heard of him?"

"Not a word; which is a wonder to me."

Anusia began to relate the history of her departure from Zamost, and everything that happened on the road. Babinich grew in her narrative to such a mighty hero that the sword-bearer was at a loss to know who he was.

"I know all Lithuania," said he. "There are houses, it is true, with similar names, such as Babonaubek, Babill, Babinovski, Babinski, and Babiski. Babinich I have not heard, and I think it must be an assumed name; for many who are in parties take such names, so that their property and relatives may not suffer from the enemy. Hm! Babinich! He is some fiery cavalier, since he was able to settle Zamoyski in that fashion."

"Oh, how fiery!" cried Anusia.

The old man fell into good humor. "How is that?" asked he, stopping before Anusia and putting his hands on his hips.

"If I tell you, you 'll suppose God knows what."

"God preserve me, I will suppose nothing."

"Barely had we come out of Zamost when Pan Babinich

told me that some one else had occupied his heart, and though he received no rent, still he did not think of changing the tenant."

"And do you believe that?"

"Of course I believe it," answered Anusia, with great vivacity; "he must be in love to his ears, since after so long a time — since — since — "

"Oh, there is some 'since he would not,'" said the old man, laughing.

"But I say that," repeated Anusia, stamping her foot, "since —   Well, we shall soon hear of him."

"God grant it!"

"And I will tell you why. As often as Pan Babinich mentioned Prince Boguslav, his face grew white, and his teeth squeaked like doors."

"He will be our friend!" said the sword-bearer.

"Certainly! And we will flee to him, if he shows himself."

"If I could escape from this place, I would have my own party, and you would see that war is no novelty to me either, and that this old hand is good for something yet."

"Go under command of Pan Babinich."

"You have a great wish to go under his command."

They chatted yet for a long time in this fashion, and always more joyously; so that Olenka, forgetting her grief, became notably more cheerful, and Anusia began at last to laugh loudly at the sword-bearer. She was well rested; for at the last halting-place in Rossyeni she had slept soundly; she left them then only late in the evening.

"She is gold, not a maiden!" said Billevich, after she had gone.

"A sincere sort of heart, and I think we shall soon come to confidence," answered Olenka.

"But you looked at her frowningly at first."

"For I thought that she was some one sent here. Do I know anything surely? I fear every one in Taurogi."

"She sent? Perhaps by good spirits! But she is as full of tricks as a weasel. If I were younger I don't know to what it might come; even as it is, a man is still desirous."

Olenka was delighted, and placing her hands on her knees, she put her head on one side, mimicking Anusia, and looking askance at her uncle.

"So, dear uncle ! you wish to bake an aunt for me out of that flour ? "

"Oh, be quiet, be quiet!" said the sword-bearer.

But he laughed and began to twist his mustache with his whole hand; after a time he added, —

"Still she roused such a staid woman as you; I am certain that great friendship will spring up between you."

In truth, Pan Tomash was not deceived, for in no long time a very lively friendship was formed between the maidens; and it grew more and more, perhaps just for this reason, — that the two were complete opposites. One had dignity in her spirit, depths of feeling, invincible will, and reason; the other, with a good heart and purity of thought, was a tufted lark. One, with her calm face, bright tresses, and an unspeakable repose and charm in her slender form, was like an ancient Psyche ; the other, a real brunette, reminded one rather of an *ignis fatuus*, which in the night hours entices people into pathless places and laughs at their vexation. The officers in Taurogi, who looked at both every day, were seized with the desire to kiss Olenka's feet, but Anusia's lips.

Kettling, having the soul of a Scottish mountaineer, hence full of melancholy, revered and adored Olenka; but from the first glance he could not endure Anusia, who paid him in kind, making up for her losses on Braun and others, not excepting the sword-bearer of Rossyeni himself.

Olenka soon won great influence over her friend, who with perfect sincerity of heart said to Pan Tomash, —

"She can say more in two words than I in a whole day."

But the dignified lady could not cure her vain friend of one defect, coquetry; for let Anusia only hear the rattle of spurs in the corridor, immediately she would pretend that she had forgotten something, that she wanted to see if there were tidings from Sapyeha; would rush into the corridor, fly like a whirlwind, and coming up against an officer, cry out, —

"Oh, how you frightened me !"

Then a conversation would begin, intermingled with twisting of her skirts, glancing from under her brows, and various artful looks, through the aid of which the hardest heart may be conquered.

This coquetry Olenka took ill of her, all the more that

Anusia after a few days confessed to a secret love for Babinich. They discussed this among themselves more than once.

"Others beg like minstrels," said Anusia; "but this dragon chose to look at his Tartars rather than at me, and he never spoke otherwise than in command, — 'Come out, my lady! eat, my lady! drink, my lady!' And if he had been rude at the same time, but he was not; if he had not been painstaking, but he was! In Krasnystav I said to myself, 'Do not look at me — wait!' And in Lanchna I was so overcome that it was terrible. I tell you that when I looked into his blue eyes, and when he laughed, gladness seized me, such a prisoner was I."

Olenka dropped her head, for blue eyes came to her memory too; and that one spoke in the same way, and he had command ever on his lips, activity ever in his face, but neither conscience nor the fear of God.

Anusia, following her own thoughts, continued, —

"When he flew over the field on his horse, with his baton, I thought, That is an eagle or some hetman. The Tartars feared him more than fire. When he came, there had to be obedience; and when there was a battle, fires were striking him from desire of blood. I saw many worthy cavaliers in Lubni, but one such that fear seized me in his presence I have never seen."

"If the Lord God has predestined him to you, you will get him; but that he did not love you, I cannot believe."

"As to love, he loves me a little, but the other more. He told me himself more than once, 'It is lucky that I am not able to forget or cease loving, for it would be better to confide a kid to a wolf than such a maiden as you are to me.'"

"What did you say to that?"

"I said, 'How do you know that I would return your love?' And he answered, 'I should not have asked you.' Now, what are you to do with such a man? That other woman is foolish not to love him, and she must have callousness in her heart. I asked what her name is, but he would not tell me. 'Better,' said he, 'not to touch that, for it is a sore; and another sore,' said he, 'is the Radzivills,— the traitors!' And then he made such a terrible face that I would have hidden in a mouse-hole. I simply feared him. But what is the use in talking? He is not for me!"

"Ask Saint Michael for him; I know from Aunt Kulvyets that he is the best aid in such cases. Only be careful not to offend the saint by duping more men."

"I never will, except so much, — the least little bit."

Here Anusia showed on her finger how much; and she indicated at most about half the length of the nail, so as not to anger Saint Michael.

"I do not act so from waywardness," explained she to Billevich, who also had begun to take her frivolity to heart; "but I must, for if these officers do not help us we shall never escape."

"Braun will not let us out."

"Braun is overcome!" replied Anusia, with a thin voice, dropping her eyes.

"But Fitz-Gregory?"

"He is overcome too!" with a voice still thinner.

"And Ottenhagen?"

"Overcome!"

"And Von Irhen?"

"Overcome!"

"May the forest surround you! I see that Kettling is the only man whom you could not manage."

"I cannot endure him! But some one else will manage him. Besides, we can go without his permission."

"And you think that when we wish to flee they will not hinder?"

"They will go with us!" said Anusia, stretching her neck and blinking.

"For God's sake! then why do we stay here? I should like to be far away this day."

But from the consultation which followed at once, it appeared needful to await the decision of Boguslav's fate and Pan Sapyeha's arrival in the neighborhood of Jmud. Otherwise they would be threatened by terrible destruction from even their own people. The society of foreign officers not only would not be a defence, but would add to their danger; for the peasants were so terribly envenomed against foreigners that they murdered without mercy every one who did not wear a Polish dress. Even Polish dignitaries wearing foreign costume, not to speak of Austrian and French diplomats, could not travel save under the protection of powerful bodies of troops.

"You will believe me, for I have passed through the whole country," said Anusia. "In the first village, in the first forest, ravagers would kill us without asking who we are. It is impossible to flee except to an army."

"But I shall have my own party."

"Before you could collect it, before you could reach a village where you are known, you would lose your life. News from Prince Boguslav must come soon. I have ordered Braun to inform me at once."

But Braun reported nothing for a long time.

Kettling, however, began to visit Olenka; for she, meeting him on a certain day, extended her hand to him. The young officer prophesied evil from this profound silence. According to him the prince, out of regard for the elector and the Swedes, would not hold silence touching the least victory, and would rather exaggerate by description than weaken by silence the significance of real successes.

"I do not suppose that he is cut to pieces," said the young officer; "but he is surely in such a difficult position that it is hard to find a way out."

"All tidings arrive here so late," said Olenka, "and the best proof is that we learned first from Panna Borzobogati, the particulars of the miraculous defence of Chenstohova."

" I, my lady, knew of that long ago, but, as a foreigner, not knowing the value which that place has for Poles, I did not mention it. That in a great war some small castle defends itself for a time, and repulses a number of storms, happens always, and importance is not attached to it usually."

"But still for me that would have been the most welcome news!"

"I see in truth that I did ill; for from what has happened since the defence, as I hear now, I know that to be an important event, which may influence the whole war. Still, returning to the campaign of the prince in Podlyasye, it is different. Chenstohova is far away, Podlyasye is nearer. And when the prince succeeded at first, you remember how quickly news came. Believe me, my lady, I am a young man, but from the fourteenth year of my life I am a soldier, and experience tells me that this silence is prophetic of evil."

"Rather good," said the lady.

"Let it be good!" answered Kettling. "In half a year my service will be ended. In half a year my oath will cease."

A few days after this conversation news came at last. It was brought by Pan Byes of the shield Kornie; called, at

Boguslav's court, Cornutus.[1] He was a Polish noble, but altogether foreignized; for serving in foreign armies almost from years of boyhood, he had wellnigh forgotten Polish, or at least spoke it like a German. He had also a foreignized soul, hence was greatly attached to Prince Boguslav. He was going on an important mission to Königsberg, and stopped in Taurogi merely to rest.

Braun and Kettling brought him at once to Olenka and Anusia, who at that time lived and slept together.

Braun stood like a soldier before Anusia ; then turned to Byes and said, —

"This lady is a relative of Pan Zamoyski, therefore of the prince our lord, who has commanded to show her every attention; and she wishes to hear news from the mouth of an eyewitness."

Pan Byes in his turn stood erect, as if on service, and awaited the questions.

Anusia did not deny relationship with Boguslav, for the homage of the military pleased her ; therefore she motioned to Pan Byes to sit down. When he had taken his place she asked, —

"Where is the prince at present ? "

"The prince is retreating on Sokolka, God grant successfully," said the officer.

"Tell the pure truth : how is it with him ? "

"I will tell the pure truth and hide nothing, thinking that your worthiness will find strength in your soul to hear news less favorable."

"I will!" said Anusia, striking one heel against the other under her robe, with satisfaction that she was called "worthiness," and that the news was "less favorable."

"At first everything went well with us," said Byes. "We rubbed out on the road several bands of peasants; we scattered the forces of the younger Sapyeha, and cut up two squadrons of cavalry with a regiment of good infantry, sparing no one. Then we defeated Pan Horotkyevich, so that he barely escaped, and some say that he was killed. After that we occupied the ruins of Tykotsin."

"We know all this. Tell us quickly the unfavorable news," interrupted Anusia, on a sudden.

"Be pleased, my lady, to listen calmly. We came to Drohichyn, and there the map was unfolded. We had news that Sapyeha was still far away; meanwhile two of

---

[1] Byes means "devil;" so Byes Cornutus is "horned devil."

our scouting parties were as if they had sunk through the earth. Not a witness returned from the slaughter. Then it appeared that some troops were marching in front of us. A great confusion rose out of that. The prince began to think that all preceding information was false, and that Sapyeha had not only advanced, but had cut off the road. Then we began to retreat, for in that way it was possible to catch the enemy and force him to a general battle, which the prince wished absolutely. But the enemy did not give the field; he attacked and attacked without ceasing. From that everything began to melt in our hands; we had rest neither day nor night. The roads were ruined before us, the dams cut, provisions intercepted. Reports were soon circulated that Charnyetski himself was crushing us. The soldiers did not eat, did not sleep; their courage fell. Men perished in the camp itself, as if the ground were swallowing them. In Byalystok the enemy seized a whole party again, camp-chests, the prince's carriages and guns. I have never seen anything like it. It was not seen in former wars, either. The prince was changed. He wanted nothing but a general battle, and he had to fight ten small ones every day, and lose them. Order became relaxed. And how can our confusion and alarm be described when we learned that Sapyeha himself had not come up yet, and that in front of us was merely a strong party which had caused so many disasters? In this party were Tartar troops."

Further words of the officer were interrupted by a scream from Anusia, who, throwing herself suddenly on Olenka's neck, cried, —

"Pan Babinich!"

The officer was surprised when he heard the name; but he judged that terror and hatred had wrested this cry from the breast of the worthy lady; so only after a while did he continue his narrative: —

"To whomsover God has given greatness, he has given also strength to bear grievous misfortunes; be pleased, therefore, my lady, to calm yourself. Such indeed is the name of this hell-dweller who has undermined the success of the whole expedition, and become the cause of other immense evils. His name, which your worthiness has divined with such wonderful quickness, is repeated now with fear and rage by every mouth in our camp."

"I saw that Babinich at Zamost," said Anusia, hastily; "and could I have guessed — "

Here she was silent, and no one knew what would have happened in such an event. The officer, after a moment's silence, continued, —

"Thaws and heat set in, despite, it may be said, the regular order of nature; for we had news that in the south of the Commonwealth there was still severe winter; but we were wading in spring mud, which fastened our heavy cavalry to the earth. But he, having light troops, advanced with more ease. We lost wagons and cannon at every step, and were forced at last to go on horseback. The inhabitants round about, in their blind venom, favored the attackers. What God gives will happen; but I left the whole camp in a desperate condition, as well as the prince himself, whom a malignant fever does not leave, and who loses his power for whole days. A general battle will come quickly; but how it will end, God knows. If He favors, we may hope for wonders."

"Where did you leave the prince?"

"A day's journey from Sokolka. The prince intends to intrench himself at Suhovola or Yanov and receive battle. Sapyeha is two days distant. When I came away, we had a little more freedom; for from a captured informant we learned that Babinich himself had gone to the main camp; without him the Tartars dare not attack, satisfying themselves with annoying scouting parties. The prince, who is an incomparable leader, places all his hopes on a general battle, but, of course, when he is well; if the fever seizes him, he must think of something else, the best proof of which is that he has sent me to Prussia."

"Why do you go?"

"Either the prince will win the battle or lose it. If he loses it, all Electoral Prussia will be defenceless, and it may happen easily that Sapyeha will pass the boundaries, force the elector to a decision, — I say this, for it is no secret, I go to forewarn them to have some defence prepared for those provinces; for the unbidden guests may come in too great numbers. That is the affair of the elector and the Swedes, with whom the prince is in alliance, and from whom he has the right to expect rescue."

The officer finished.

Anusia heaped a multitude of other questions on him, preserving with difficulty dignity sufficient. When he went out, she gave way to herself completely. She fell to striking her skirts with her hands, turning on her heels like a top, kissing Olenka on the eyes, pulling Billevich by the sleeves, and crying, —

"Well, now, what did I say? Who has crushed Prince Boguslav? Maybe Pan Sapyeha? A fig for Sapyeha! Who will crush the Swedes in the same style? Who will exterminate traitors? Who is the greatest cavalier, who is the greatest knight? Pan Andrei, Pan Andrei!"

"What Andrei?" asked Olenka, growing pale suddenly.

"Have I not told you that his name is Andrei? He told me that himself. Pan Babinich! Long life to Babinich! Volodyovski could not have done better! — What is the matter, Olenka?"

Panna Billevich shook herself as if wishing to throw off a burden of grievous thoughts. "Nothing! I was thinking that traitors themselves bear that name. For there was one who offered to sell the king, dead or alive, to the Swedes or to Boguslav; and he had the same name, — Andrei."

"May God condemn him!" roared Billevich. "Why mention traitors at night? Let us be glad when we have reason."

"Only let Pan Babinich come here!" added Anusia. "That's what is needed! I will fool Braun still more. I will, I will, of purpose to raise the whole garrison, and go over with men and horses to Pan Babinich."

"Do that, do that!" cried Billevich, delighted.

"And afterward — a fig for all those Germans! Maybe he will forget that good-for-nothing woman, and give me his lo—"

Then again her thin voice piped; she covered her face with her hands. All at once an angry thought must have come to her, for she clapped her hands, and said, —

"If not, I will marry Volodyovski!"

CHAPTER XLVII.

Two weeks later it was boiling in all Taurogi. On a certain evening disorderly parties of Boguslav's troops came in, — thirty or forty horsemen in a body, reduced, torn, more like spectres than men, — and brought news of the defeat of Boguslav at Yanov. Everything had been lost, — arms, horses, cannon, the camp. Six thousand choice men went out on that expedition with the prince; barely four hundred returned, — these the prince himself led out of the ruin.

Of the Poles no living soul came back save Sakovich; for all who had not fallen in battle, all whom the terrible Babinich had not destroyed in his attacks, went over to Sapyeha. Many foreign officers chose of their own will to stand at the chariot of the conqueror. In one word, no Radzivill had ever yet returned from an expedition more crushed, ruined, and beaten.

And as formerly court adulation knew no bounds in exalting Boguslav as a leader, so now all mouths sounded loudly an unceasing complaint against the incompetent management of the war. Among the remaining soldiers there was endless indignation, which in the last days of the retreat brought complete disorder, and rose to that degree that the prince considered it wiser to remain somewhat in the rear.

The prince and Sakovich halted in Rossyeni. Kettling, hearing of this from soldiers, went immediately with the news to Olenka.

"The main thing," said she, when the news came, "is whether Sapyeha and that Babinich are pursuing the prince, and whether they intend to bring the war to this region."

"I could learn nothing from the statements of the soldiers," answered Kettling, "for fear exaggerates every danger. Some say even that Babinich is here; but since the prince and Sakovich have remained behind, I infer that the pursuit cannot be rapid."

"Still it must come, for it is difficult to think otherwise. Who after victory would not pursue the defeated enemy?"

"That will be shown. I wished to speak of something else. The prince by reason of illness and defeat must be irritated, therefore inclined to deeds of violence. Do not separate now from your aunt and Panna Borzobogatı. Do not consent to the journey of your uncle to Tyltsa, as the last time, before the campaign."

Olenka said nothing. Her uncle had, in fact, not been sent to Tyltsa; he had merely been ill for some days after the hammer-stroke given by Prince Boguslav. Sakovich, to hide the prince's deed from the people, spread the report that the old man had gone to Tyltsa. Olenka preferred to be silent on this before Kettling, for the proud maiden was ashamed to confess that any man living had struck a Billevich.

"I thank you for the warning," said she, after a moment's silence.

"I considered it my duty."

But her heart swelled with bitterness; for not long before Kettling might have enabled her to avoid this new danger. If he had consented to the flight, she would have been far away, free of Boguslav forever.

"It is really fortunate for me," said she, "that this warning does not touch your honor, that the prince has not issued an order for you not to warn me."

Kettling understood the reproach, and uttered a speech which Olenka did not expect of him: —

"As to what touches my military service, to guard which my honor commands, I will accomplish that or forfeit my life. Other choice I have not, and do not wish to have. Outside my service I am free to provide against lawlessness. Therefore, as a private man, I leave with you this pistol, and I say, Defend yourself, for danger is near; in case of need, kill! Then my oath will be at an end, and I will hasten to save you."

He bowed and turned toward the door, but Olenka detained him.

"Cavalier, free yourself from that service! Defend a good cause; defend the injured, for you are worthy to do so; you are honorable. It is a pity that you should be lost on a traitor!"

"I should have freed myself long since, and resigned,"

said Kettling, "had I not thought that by remaining I might serve you. Now it is too late. If the prince had returned victorious, I should not have hesitated a moment; but when he is coming back conquered, — when, perhaps, the enemy is pursuing him, — it would be cowardice to ask for dismissal before the end of the term itself will free me. You will see sufficiently how people of small heart desert in crowds a defeated man. This pistol will send a ball even through armor with ease."

Kettling went out, leaving on the table the weapon, which Olenka secreted at once. Fortunately the previsions of the young officer and her own fear proved groundless.

The prince arrived in the evening with Sakovich and Patterson, but so crushed and ill that he was barely able to hold himself on his feet. Besides, he did not know well whether Sapyeha was advancing or had sent Babinich in pursuit with the light squadrons. Boguslav had overthrown, it is true, the latter in his attack, together with his horse; but he dared not hope that he had killed him, since it seemed to him that the double-handed sword had turned in the blow on Babinich's helmet. Besides, he had fired before from a pistol straight into his face, and that had not taken effect.

The prince's heart was aching at the thought of what such a Babinich would do with his estates should he reach them with his Tartars, — and he had nothing with which to defend them; and not only his estates, but his own person. Among his hirelings there were not many like Kettling, and it was just to suppose that at the first news of the coming of Sapyeha's troops they would desert him to a man.

The prince did not purpose to remain in Taurogi longer than two or three days, for he had to hasten to Royal Prussia to the elector and Steinbock, who might furnish him with new forces, and employ him either in capturing Prussian towns, or send him to aid the king himself, who intended an expedition to the heart of the Commonwealth.

In Taurogi he had to leave some one of the officers to bring order into the remnant of the army, ward off patriot peasants and nobles, defend the property of the two Radzivills, and continue the understanding with Löwenhaupt, commander-in-chief of the Swedes in Jmud.

With this object, after he had come to Taurogi, and after a night's rest, the prince summoned to council Sakovich, the only man whom he could trust, and to whom alone he could open his heart.

That first "good day" in Taurogi was wonderful, when the two friends saw each other after the ill-starred campaign. For some time they gazed on each other without a word. The prince broke the silence first, —

"Well, the devils! they carried the day."

"They carried the day!" repeated Sakovich.

"It must have been so with such weather. If I had had more light squadrons, or if some devil had not brought that Babinich, — twice the same man! The gallow's bird changed his name. Do not tell any one of him, so as not to increase his glory."

"I will not tell. But will not the officers trumpet it, for you presented him before your boots as Banneret of Orsha?"

"The German officers know nothing of Polish names. It is all one to them, — Kmita or Babinich. But by the horns of Lucifer, if I could get him! I had him; and the scoundrel brought my men into rebellion, besides leading off Glovbich's troops. He must be some bastard of our blood; it cannot be otherwise! I had him, and he escaped, — that gnaws me more than the whole lost campaign."

"You had him, Prince, but at the price of my head."

"I tell you sincerely that I would let them flay you, if I might make a drum out of Kmita's skin!"

"Thank you, Bogus; I could not expect less from your friendship."

The prince laughed: "But you would have squirmed on Sapyeha's gridiron. All your scoundrelism would have been fried out of you. I should have been glad to see that!"

"I should be glad to see you in the hands of Kmita, your dear relative. You have a different face, but in form you are like each other, and you have feet of the same size; you are sighing for the same maiden, only she without experience divines that he is stronger, and that he is a better soldier."

"I could manage two such as you, and I rode over his breast. If I had had two minutes' time, I should be able to give you my word now that my cousin is not living. You have always been rather dull, hence I took a fancy to you; but in these recent days your wit has left you completely."

"You have always had your wit in your heels, and therefore you swept away in such fashion before Sapyeha that I have lost all fancy for you, and am ready myself to go to Sapyeha."

"On a rope?"

"On that with which they will bind Radzivill."

"Enough!"

"At the service of your highness!"

"It would be well to shoot some of the noisiest of those horsemen, and introduce order."

"I commanded this morning to hang six of them. They are cold now, and are dancing stubbornly on the ropes, for the wind is fierce."

"You have done well. But listen! Do you wish to remain in the garrison at Taurogi, for I must leave some one here?"

"I do, and I ask for that office. No one can manage better. The soldiers fear me more than others, for they know that with me there is no trifling. With respect to Löwenhaupt, it is necessary that some one be here more important than Patterson."

"Can you manage the rebels?"

"I assure your highness that the pine-trees of Jmud will bear weightier fruit than the cones of last year. I will form about two regiments of infantry out of the peasants, and train them in my fashion. I will have my eyes on the estates; and if the rebels attack one of them, I will throw suspicion immediately on some rich noble and squeeze him like cheese in a bag. At first I shall need merely money to pay wages and equip the infantry."

"I will leave what I can."

"From the dowry money?"

"How is that?"

"That means from the Billevich money which you took out of the dowry for yourself in advance."

"If you could only twist the neck of old Billevich in some polite way, it would be well; for it could be done easily, and he has my letter."

"I will try. But the point is in this, — has he not sent the note somewhere, or has the maiden not sewed it into her shift? Would you not like to discover?"

"It will come to that; but now I must go, and besides that cursed fever has taken all my strength."

"Your highness, envy me for staying in Taurogi."

"You have a strange kind of wish; but if you meanwhile — I should have you torn apart with hooks. Why do you insist on this office?"

"For I want to marry."

"Whom ? " asked the prince, sitting up in bed.

"Panna Borzobogati."

"That is a good idea, an excellent idea!" said Boguslav. "I have heard of some will."

"There is a will from Pan Longin Podbipienta. Your highness knows what a powerful family that is, and the estates of Pan Longin are in a number of districts. It is true that the Moscow troops have occupied some; there will be lawsuits, fights, disputes, and attacks without number; but I will help myself, and will not yield one point to any man. Besides, the girl has pleased me greatly; she is pretty and enticing. I noticed in a moment when we captured her that she feigned terror, and shot at me with her eyes at the same time. Only let me stay here as commandant, and from idleness alone the love-making will begin."

"One thing I tell you. I will not forbid you to marry; but listen well, — no excesses, you understand ? That maiden is from the Vishnyevetskis; she is a confidant of Princess Griselda herself; and because of my esteem for the princess, I do not wish to offend her, nor do I wish to offend Pan Zamoyski."

"There is no need of warning," answered Sakovich; "for since I wish to marry regularly, I must make regular approaches."

"I wish you might get a refusal."

"I know a man who got a refusal, though he is a prince; but I think that that will not come to me. That eye-cutting gives me great consolation."

"Don't tell that man who got a refusal not to give you horns! I will give an addition to your shield, or you will receive a surname, Sakovich Rogaty.[1] She is Borzobogaty, and he is Bardzorogaty. You will be a chosen pair. But marry, yes, marry, and let me know of the wedding. I will be your best man."

Fierce anger appeared on Sakovich's face, terrible without that. His eyes were covered for a moment as if by smoke; but he soon recovered, and turning the prince's words into a jest, he said, —

"Poor man! you are not able to go downstairs alone, and you make threats. You have your Panna Billevich

---

[1] Rogaty means "horned." Borzobogaty means "quickly rich." Bardzorogaty means "greatly horned."

here; go your way, skeleton! go your way! You'll nurse Babinich's children yet!"

"God break your tongue, such a son! You are making sport of the sickness which came within a hair of killing me. I would you were enchanted as I was."

"What enchantments are there here? At times, when I see how everything goes in the natural world, I think enchantment is stupid."

"You are stupid yourself! Be silent! do not summon the Devil. You disgust me more and more."

"Would that I were not the last Pole who has remained faithful to your highness! For my loyalty you feed me with ingratitude. I will return to my dens at home, and sit quietly awaiting the end of the war."

"Oh, give us peace! You know that I love you."

"It is grievous for me to see that. The Devil thrust this love for your highness on me. If there is enchantment in anything, it is in that."

The starosta told the truth; for he loved Boguslav really. The prince knew this, and therefore paid him, if not with strong attachment, with gratitude, which vain people ever have for those who do them homage. Therefore Boguslav agreed willingly to Sakovich's plans touching Anusia, and determined to aid him in person. In view of this, about midday, when he felt better, he had himself dressed and went to Anusia.

"I have come because of old acquaintance," said he, " to inquire after your health and ask if the visit to Taurogi has pleased you."

"In captivity one must be pleased with all things," answered Anusia, sighing.

The prince laughed. "You are not in captivity. You were taken together with Sapyeha's soldiers, that is true; and I gave orders to send you here, but only for safety. Not a hair will fall from your head. Be convinced that there are few people whom I respect as I do Princess Griselda, to whose heart you are near; and the Vishnyevetskis and Zamoyskis are connections of mine. You will find here every freedom and every care. I come to you as a well-wishing friend, and I say if you wish to go I will give you an escort, though I have few soldiers myself. I advise you to stay. You, as I have heard, were sent here to seek property willed to you. Be assured that this is not the time to think of such business; and even in time of peace the aid of Sapyeha would not avail in these regions, for he could act only in Vityebsk; here he can do nothing. I shall not touch that affair personally, but through an agent. You need a friendly man, and adroit, esteemed, and feared. If such a man were to take up this matter, surely he would not let people thrust straw instead of grain into his hand."

"Where shall I, an orphan, find such a protector?" asked Anusia.

"Precisely in Taurogi."

"Your highness would be pleased yourself —"

Here Anusia put her hands together, and looked so prettily into Boguslav's eyes that if the prince had not been wearied and broken, he would surely have begun to think less sincerely of Sakovich's cause; but since he had no gallantry in his head at that moment, he said quickly, —

"Could I do it myself, I should not intrust such a pleasant office to any man; but I am going away, for I must go. I leave in my place, as commandant of Taurogi, the starosta of Oshmiana, Pan Sakovich, a great cavalier, a famous soldier, and a man so adroit that there is not another such in all Lithuania. So I repeat: Stay in Taurogi, for you have no place to go to, since every point is full of ravagers and ruffians, while rebels infest all the roads. Sakovich will protect you here; Sakovich will defend you. Sakovich will see what can be done to obtain those estates; and once he undertakes the affair, I guarantee that no man on earth could bring it to a favorable issue sooner. He is my friend, therefore I know him, and I will say only this: if I had taken those estates from you, and afterward learned that Sakovich was coming to oppose me, I would give them up of my own will, for it is dangerous to struggle with him."

"If Pan Sakovich would be ready to come to the aid of an orphan —"

"Only be not unjust to him, and he will do anything for you, for your beauty has touched his heart deeply. He is going around sighing now —"

"How could I touch the heart of any man?"

"She is a rascal, the maiden!" thought the prince. But he added aloud: "Let Sakovich explain how that happened. Only do him no wrong; for he is a worthy man and of a noted family, therefore I do not wish that disdain should be shown such a person."

CHAPTER XLVIII.

NEXT morning the prince received a summons from the elector to go with all speed to Königsberg to take command of the newly levied troops which were to march to Marienburg or Dantzig. The letter contained also news of the daring campaign of Karl Gustav through the whole length of the Commonwealth to Russian regions. The elector foresaw a disastrous end to the campaign; but just for that reason he desired to be at the head of as many troops as possible, that he might in case of need be indispensable to one side or the other, sell himself dearly, and decide the fate of the war. For those reasons he enjoined on the young prince all possible haste, so greatly was he concerned about avoiding delay; but after the first courier he sent a second, who arrived twelve hours later.

The prince, therefore, had not a moment to lose, and not time enough to rest, for the fever returned with its previous violence. Still he had to go. So when he had delegated his authority to Sakovich, he said, —

"Perhaps we shall have to transport Billevich and the maiden to Königsberg. There it will be easier in quiet to handle a hostile man firmly; but the girl I will take to the camp, for I have had enough of these ceremonies."

"It is well, and the cavalry may be increased," answered Sakovich at parting.

An hour later the prince was no longer in Taurogi. Sakovich remained, an unlimited despot, recognizing no power above himself but that of Anusia. And he began to blow away the dust from before her feet, as on a time the prince had before the feet of Olenka. Restraining his wild nature, he was courteous, anticipating her wishes, divining her thoughts, and at the same time he held himself at a distance, with all the respect which a polished cavalier should have toward a lady for whose hand and heart he is striving.

It must be confessed that this reigning in Taurogi pleased Anusia; it was grateful to her to think that when evening came, in the lower halls, in the corridors, in the barracks, in the garden still covered with winter frost, the sighs of old and young officers were heard; that the astrologer was sighing while looking at the stars from his tower; that even old Billevich interrupted his evening rosary with sighs.

While the best of maidens, she was still glad that those swift affections went not to Olenka, but to her. She was glad also with respect to Babinich; for she felt her power, and it came to her head that if no man had resisted her anywhere, she must have burned on his heart also permanent marks with her eyes.

"He will forget that woman, it cannot be otherwise, for she feeds him with ingratitude; and when he forgets her he knows where to seek me, — and he will seek me, the robber!"

Then she threatened him in her soul: "Wait! I will pay you before I console you."

Meanwhile, though not in real truth caring much for Sakovich, she saw him with pleasure. It is true that he justified himself in her eyes from reproaches of treason in the same way in which Boguslav had explained himself to the sword-bearer. He said, therefore, that peace was already concluded with the Swedes; that the Commonwealth might recover and flourish, had not Pan Sapyeha ruined everything for his own private ends.

Anusia, not knowing over-much of these matters, let the words pass her ears; but she was struck by something else in Sakovich's narrative.

"The Billeviches," said he, "scream in heaven-piercing voices of injustice and captivity; but nothing has happened to them here, and nothing will happen. The prince has not let them go from Taurogi, it is true; but that is for their good, for three furlongs beyond the gate they would perish from ravagers or forest bandits. He has not let them go also, because he loves Panna Billevich, and that also is true. But who will not justify him? Who would act otherwise, who had a feeling heart and a breast burdened with sighs? If he had had less honorable intentions, being such a powerful man, he might have given rein to himself; but he wanted to marry her, he wanted to elevate that stubborn lady to his princely estate, to cover her with happiness, place the coronet of the Radzivills on her head; and these thankless people are hurling invectives at him, thus trying to diminish his honor and fame."

Anusia, not believing this greatly, asked Olenka that same

day if the prince wished to marry her. Olenka could not deny; and because they had become intimate, she explained her reasons for refusal. They seemed just and sufficient to Anusia; but still she thought to herself that it was not so grievous for the Billeviches in Taurogi, and that the prince and Sakovich were not such criminals as Pan Tomash had proclaimed.

Then, also, came news that Sapyeha and Babinich were not only not approaching Taurogi, but had gone with forced marches against the King of Sweden, far away toward Lvoff. Anusia fell into a rage at first, and then began to understand that if the hetman and Babinich had gone, there was no reason to flee from Taurogi, for they might lose their lives, or in the most favorable event change a quiet existence into a captivity full of dangers.

For this reason it came to disputes between her on one side, and Olenka and Billevich on the other; but even they were forced to admit that the departure of Sapyeha rendered their flight very difficult, if not quite impossible, especially since the country was growing more and more excited, and no inhabitant could be certain of the morrow. Finally, even should they not accept Anusia's reason, flight without her aid was impossible, in view of the watchfulness of Sakovich and the other officers. Kettling alone was devoted to them, but he would not let himself be involved in any plot against his service; besides, he was absent often, for Sakovich was glad to employ him against armed bands of confederates and ravagers, since he was an experienced soldier and a good officer, therefore he sent him frequently from Taurogi.

But it was pleasanter and pleasanter for Anusia. Sakovich made a declaration to her a month after the departure of the prince; but, the deceiver! she answered cunningly that she did not know him, that men spoke variously concerning him, that she had not time yet to love, that without permission of Princess Griselda she could not marry, and finally, that she wished to subject him to a year's trial.

The starosta gnawed his anger, gave orders that day to give three thousand stripes to a cavalry soldier for a trifling offence, — after this the poor soldier was buried; but the starosta had to agree to Anusia's conditions. She told the lordling that if he would serve still more faithfully, diligently, and obediently, in a year he would receive whatever love she had.

In this way she played with the bear; and she so succeeded

in mastering him that he stifled even his growling. He merely said, —

"With the exception of treason to the prince, ask anything of me, even ask me to walk on my knees."

If Anusia had seen what terrible results of Sakovich's impatience were falling on the whole neighborhood, she would not have teased him so greatly. Soldiers and residents in Taurogi trembled before him, for he punished grievously and altogether without cause, punished beyond every measure. Prisoners died in chains from hunger, or were burned with hot iron.

More than once it seemed that the wild starosta wished to cool in the blood of men his spirit, at once raging and burning with love, for he started up suddenly and went on an expedition. Victory followed him nearly everywhere. He cut to pieces parties of rebels, and ordered, as an example, that the right hands be cut from captured peasants, who were then sent home free.

The terror of his name girded Taurogi as with a wall; even the most considerable bodies of patriots did not dare to go beyond Rossyeni. Peace was established in all parts, and he formed new regiments of German vagrants and the local peasants with the money extorted from neighboring citizens and nobles, and increased in power so as to furnish men to the prince in case of urgent necessity.

A more loyal and terrible servant Boguslav could not have found.

But Sakovich gazed more and more tenderly at Anusia with his terrible, pale-blue eyes, and played to her on a lute. Life, therefore, in Taurogi passed for Anusia joyously and with amusement; for Olenka it was sore and monotonous. From one there went gleams of gladness, like that light which issues at night from the firefly; the face of the other grew paler and paler, more serious, sterner; her dark brows were contracted more resolutely on her white forehead, so that finally they called her a nun. And she had something in her of the nun; she began to accept the thought that she would become one, — that God himself would through suffering and disappointment lead her to peace behind the grating. She was no longer that maiden with beautiful bloom on her face and happiness in her eyes; not that Olenka who on a time while riding in a sleigh with her betrothed, Andrei Kmita, cried, "Hei! hei!" to the pine woods and forests.

Spring appeared in the world. A wind strong and warm

shook the waters of the Baltic, now liberated from ice; later on, trees bloomed, flowers shot out from their harsh leafy enclosures; then the sun grew hot, and the poor girl was waiting in vain for the end of Taurogi captivity, — for Anusia did not wish to flee, and in the country it was ever more terrible.

Fire and sword were raging as though the pity of God were never to be manifest. Nay more, whoso had not seized the sabre or the lance in winter, seized it in spring; snow did not betray his tracks, the pine wood gave better concealment, and warmth made war the easier.

News flew swallow-like to Taurogi, — sometimes terrible, sometimes comforting; and to these and to those the maiden devoted her prayers, and shed tears of sorrow or joy.

Previous mention had been made of a terrible uprising of the whole people. As many as the trees in the forests of the Commonwealth, as many as the ears of grain waving on its fields, as many as the stars shining on it at night between the Carpathians and the Baltic, were the warriors who rose up against the Swedes. These men, being nobles, were born to the sword and to war by God's will and nature's order; those who cut furrows with the plough, sowed land with grain; those who were occupied with trade and handicraft in towns; those who lived in the wilderness, from bee-keeping, from pitch-making, who lived with the axe or by hunting; those who lived on the rivers and labored at fishing; those who were nomads in the steppes with their cattle, — all seized their weapons to drive out the invader.

The Swede was now drowning in that multitude as in a swollen river.

To the wonder of the whole world, the Commonwealth, powerless but a short time before, found more sabres in its defence than the Emperor of Germany or the King of France could have.

Then came news of Karl Gustav, — how he was marching ever deeper into the Commonwealth, his feet in blood, his head in smoke and flames, his lips blaspheming. It was hoped any moment to hear of his death and the destruction of all the Swedish armies.

The name of Charnyetski was heard with increasing force from boundary to boundary, transfixing the enemy with terror, pouring consolation into the hearts of the Poles.

"He routed them at Kozyenitsi!" was said one day.
"He routed them at Yaroslav!" was repeated a few weeks
later; a distant echo repeated: "He has beaten them at
Sandomir!" The only wonder was where so many Swedes
could still come from after so many defeats.

Finally a new flock of swallows flew in, and with them
the report of the imprisonment of the king and the whole
Swedish army in the fork of the rivers. It seemed that
the end was right there. Sakovich stopped his expeditions; he merely wrote letters at night and sent them in
various directions.

Billevich seemed bewildered. He rushed in every evening with news to Olenka. Sometimes he gnawed his
hands, when he remembered that he had to sit in Taurogi.
The old soldier soul was yearning for the field. At last he
began to shut himself up in his room, and to ponder over
something for hours at a time. Once he seized Olenka in
his arms, burst out into great weeping, and said, —

"You are a dear girl, my only daughter, but the country
is dearer." And next day he vanished, as if he had fallen
through the earth. Olenka found merely a letter, and in
it the following words: —

"God bless thee, beloved child! I understood well that they
are guarding thee and not me, and that it would be easier for me
to escape alone. Let God judge me, thou poor orphan, if I did
this from hardness of heart and lack of fatherly love for thee.
But the torment surpassed my endurance. I swear, by Christ's
wounds, that I could endure no longer. For when I thought that
the best Polish blood was flowing in a river *pro patria et libertate*
(for the country and liberty), and in that river there was not one
drop of my blood, it seemed to me that the angels of heaven were
condemning me. If I had not been born in our sacred Jmud,
where love of country and bravery are cherished, if I had not been
born a noble, a Billevich, I should have remained with thee and
guarded thee. But thou, if a man, wouldst have done as I have;
therefore thou 'lt forgive me for leaving thee alone, like Daniel in
the lions' den, whom God in His mercy preserved; so I think that
the protection of our Most Holy Lady the Queen will be better
over thee than mine."

Olenka covered the letter with tears; but she loved her
uncle still more because of this act, for her heart rose with
pride. Meanwhile no small uproar was made in Taurogi.
Sakovich himself rushed to the maiden in great fury, and
without removing his cap asked, —

"Where is your uncle?"

"Where all, except traitors, are, — in the field!"

"Did you know of this?" cried he.

But she, instead of being abashed, advanced some steps and measuring him with her eyes, said with inexpressible contempt, —

"I knew — and what?"

"Ah, if it were not for the prince! You will answer to the prince!"

"Neither to the prince nor to his serving-lad. And now I beg you — " And she pointed to the door.

Sakovich gnashed his teeth and went out.

That same day news of the victory at Varka was ringing through Taurogi, and such fear fell on all partisans of the Swedes that Sakovich himself dared not punish the priests who sang publicly in the neighboring churches *Te Deum.*

A great burden fell from his heart, when a few weeks later a letter came from Boguslav, who was before Marienburg, with information that the king had escaped from the river sack. But the other news was very disagreeable. The prince asked reinforcements, and directed to leave in Taurogi no more troops than were absolutely needed for defence.

All the cavalry ready marched the next day, and with it Kettling, Oettingen, Fitz-Gregory, — in a word, all the best officers, except Braun, who was indispensable to Sakovich.

Taurogi was still more deserted than after the prince's departure. Anusia grew weary, and annoyed Savokich all the more. The starosta thought of removing to Prussia; for parties, made bold by the departure of the troops, began again to push beyond Rossyeni. The Billeviches themselves had collected about five hundred horse, small nobles and peasants. They had inflicted a sensible defeat on Bützov, who had marched against them, and they ravaged without mercy all villages belonging to Radzivill.

Men rallied to them willingly; for no family, not even the Hleboviches, enjoyed such general honor and respect. Sakovich was sorry to leave Taurogi at the mercy of the enemy; he knew that in Prussia it would be difficult for him to get money and reinforcements, that he managed here as he liked, there his power must decrease; still he lost hope more and more of being able to maintain himself.

Bützov, defeated, took refuge under him; and the tidings which he brought of the power and growth of the rebellion made Sakovich decide at last on the Prussian journey.

As a positive man, and one loving to bring into speedy effect that which he had planned, he finished his preparations in ten days, issued orders, and was ready to march.

Suddenly he met with an unlooked for resistance, and from a side from which he had least expected it, — from Anusia Borzobogati.

Anusia did not think of going to Prussia. She was comfortable in Taurogi. The advances of confederate "parties" did not alarm her in the least; and if the Billeviches had attacked Taurogi itself, she would have been glad. She understood also that in a strange place, among Germans, she would be at Sakovich's mercy completely, and that she might the more easily be brought there to obligation, for which she had no desire; therefore she resolved to insist on remaining. Olenka, to whom she explained her reasons, not only confirmed the justness of them, but implored with all her power, with tears in her eyes, to oppose the journey.

"Here," said she, "salvation may come, — if not to-day, to-morrow; there we should both be lost utterly."

"But see, you almost abused me because I wanted to conquer the starosta, though I knew of nothing; as I love Princess Griselda, it only came somehow of itself. But now would he regard my resistance were he not in love? What do you think?"

"True, Anusia, true," responded Olenka.

"Do not trouble yourself, my most beautiful flower! We shall not stir a foot out of Taurogi; besides, I shall annoy Sakovich terribly."

"God grant you success!"

"Why should I not have it? I shall succeed, first, because he cares for me, and second, as I think he cares for my property. It is easy for him to get angry with me; he can even wound me with his sabre; but then all would be lost."

And it turned out that she was right. Sakovich came to her joyful and confident; but she greeted him with disdainful mien.

"Is it possible," asked she, "that you wish to flee to Prussia from dread of the Billeviches?"

"Not before the Billeviches," answered he, frowning;

"not from fear; but I go there from prudence, so as to act against those robbers with fresh forces."

"Then a pleasant journey to you."

"How is that? Do you think that I will go without you, my dearest hope?"

"Whoso is a coward may find hope in flight, not in me."

Sakovich was pale from anger. He would have punished her; but seeing before whom he was standing, he restrained himself, softened his fierce face with a smile, and said, as if jesting, —

"Oh, I shall not ask. I will seat you in a carriage and take you along."

"Will you?" asked she. "Then I see that I am held here in captivity against the will of the prince. Know then, sir, that if you do that, I shall not speak another word to you all my life, so help me the Lord God! for I was reared in Lubni, and I have the greatest contempt for cowards. Would that I had not fallen into such hands! Would that Pan Babinich had carried me off for good into Lithuania, for he was not afraid of any man!"

"For God's sake!" cried Sakovich. "Tell me at least why you are unwilling to go to Prussia."

But Anusia feigned weeping and despair.

"Tartars as it were have taken me into captivity, though I was reared by Princess Griselda, and no one had a right to me. They seize me, imprison me, take me beyond the sea by force, will condemn me to exile. It is soon to be seen how they will tear me with pincers! O my God! my God!"

"Have the fear of that God on whom you are calling!" cried the starosta. "Who will tear you with pincers?"

"Oh, save me, all ye saints!" cried Anusia, sobbing.

Sakovich knew not what to do; he was choking with rage. At times he thought that he would go mad, or that Anusia had gone mad. At last he threw himself at her feet and said that he would stay in Taurogi. Then she began to entreat him to go away, if he was afraid; with which she brought him to final despair, so that, springing up and going out, he said, —

"Well! we shall remain in Taurogi, and whether I fear the Billeviches will soon be seen."

And collecting that very day the remnant of Bützov's defeated troops and his own, he marched, but not to Prussia, only to Rossyeni, against the Billeviches, who were encamped in the forests of Girlakol. They did not expect an attack, for news of the intended withdrawal of the troops from Taurogi had been repeated in the neighborhood for several days. The starosta struck them while off their guard, cut them to pieces, and trampled them. The sword-bearer himself, under whose leadership the party was, escaped from the defeat; but two Billeviches of another line fell, and with them a third part of the soldiers; the rest fled to the four points of the world. The starosta brought a number of tens of prisoners to Taurogi, and gave orders to slay every one, before Anusia could intercede in their defence.

There was no further talk of leaving Taurogi; and the starosta had no need of doing so, for after this victory parties did not go beyond the Dubisha.

Sakovich put on airs and boasted beyond measure, saying that if Löwenhaupt would send him a thousand good horse he would rub out the rebellion in all Jmud. But Löwenhaupt was not in those parts then. Anusia gave a poor reception to this boasting.

"Oh, success against the sword-bearer was easy," said she; "but if he before whom both you and the prince fled had been there, of a certainty you would have left me and fled to Prussia beyond the sea."

These words pricked the starosta to the quick.

"First of all, do not imagine to yourself that Prussia is beyond the sea, for beyond the sea is Sweden; and second, before whom did the prince and I flee?"

"Before Pan Babinich!" answered she, courtesying with great ceremony.

"Would that I might meet him at a sword's length!"

"Then you would surely lie a sword's depth in the ground; but do not call the wolf from the forest."

Sakovich, in fact, did not call that wolf with sincerity; for though he was a man of incomparable daring, he felt a certain, almost superstitious, dread of Babinich, — so ghastly were the memories that remained to him after the recent campaign. He did not know, besides, how soon he would hear that terrible name.

But before that name rang through all Jmud, there came in time other news, — for some the most joyful of joyful, but for Sakovich most terrible, — which all mouths repeated in three words throughout the whole Commonwealth, —

"Warsaw is taken!"

It seemed that the earth was opening under the feet of

traitors; that the whole Swedish heaven was falling on their heads, together with all the deities which had shone in it hitherto like suns. Ears would not believe that the chancellor Oxenstiern was in captivity; that in captivity were Erskine, Löwenhaupt, Wrangel; in captivity the great Wittemberg himself, who had stained the whole Commonwealth with blood, who had conquered one half of it before the coming of Karl Gustav; that the king, Yan Kazimir, was triumphing, and after the victory would pass judgment on the guilty.

And this news flew as if on wings; roared like a bomb through the Commonwealth; went through villages, for peasant repeated it to peasant; went through the fields, for the wheat rustled it; went through the forest, for pine-tree told it to pine-tree; the eagles screamed it in the air; and all living men still the more seized their weapons.

In a moment the defeat of Girlakol was forgotten around Taurogi. The recently terrible Sakovich grew small in everything, even in his own eyes. Parties began again to attack bodies of Swedes; the Billeviches, recovering after their last defeat, passed the Dubisha again, at the head of their own men and the remainder of the Lauda nobles.

Sakovich knew not himself what to begin, whither to turn, from what side to look for salvation. For a long time he had no news from Prince Boguslav, and he racked his head in vain. Where was he, with what troops could he be? And at times a mortal terror seized him: had not the prince too fallen into captivity? He called to mind the prince's saying that he would turn his tabor toward Warsaw, and that if they would make him commandant over the garrison in the capital, he would prefer to be there, for he could look more easily on every side.

There were not wanting also people who asserted that the prince must have fallen into the hands of Yan Kazimir.

"If the prince were not in Warsaw," said they, "why should our gracious lord the king exclude him alone from amnesty, which he extended in advance to all Poles in the garrison? He must be already in the power of the king; and since it is known that Prince Yanush's head was destined for the block, it is certain that Prince Boguslav's will fall."

In consequence of these thoughts Sakovich came to the same conviction, and wrestled with despair, — first, because he loved the prince; second, because he saw that if this powerful protector were dead, the wildest beast would more easily find a place to hide its head in the Commonwealth than he, the right hand of the traitor.

All that seemed left to him was to flee to Prussia without regard to Anusia's opposition, and seek there bread, service.

"But what would happen?" asked the starosta of himself more than once, "if the elector, fearing the anger of Yan Kazimir, should give up all fugitives?"

There was no issue but to seek safety beyond the sea, in Sweden itself.

Fortunately, after a week of this torment and doubt, a courier came from Prince Boguslav with a long autograph letter.

"Warsaw is taken from the Swedes," wrote the prince. "My tabor and effects are lost. It is too late for me to recede, for the king's advisers are so envenomed against me that I was excepted from amnesty. Babinich harassed my troops at the very gates of Warsaw. Kettling is in captivity. The King of Sweden, the elector, and I, with Steinbock and all forces, are marching to the capital, where there will be a general battle soon. Karl Gustav swears that he will win it, though the skill of Yan Kazimir in leading armies confounds him not a little. Who could have foreseen in that ex-Jesuit such a strategist? But I recognized him as early as Berestechko, for there everything was done with his head and Vishnyevetski's. We have hope in this, — that the general militia, of which there are several tens of thousands with Yan Kazimir, will disperse to their homes, or that their first ardor will cool and they will not fight as at first. God grant some panic in that rabble; then Karl Gustav can give them a general defeat, though what will come later is unknown, and the generals themselves tell one another in secret that the rebellion is a hydra on which new heads are growing every moment. First of all, 'Warsaw must be taken a second time.' When I heard this from the mouth of Karl, I asked, 'What next?' He said nothing. Here our strength is crumbling, theirs is increasing. We have nothing with which to begin a new war. And courage is not the same; no Poles will join the Swedes as at first. My uncle the elector is silent as usual; but I see well that if we lose a battle, he will begin to-morrow to beat the Swedes, so as to buy himself into Yan Kazimir's favor. It is bitter to bow down, but we must. God grant that I be accepted, and come out whole without losing my property. I trust only in God; but it is hard to escape fear, and we must foresee evil. Therefore what property you can sell or mortgage for ready money, sell and mortgage; even enter into relations with confederates in secret. Go yourself with the whole tabor to Birji, as from there to Courland is nearer. I should advise you to go to Prussia; but soon it will not be safe from fire and sword in Prussia, for immediately after the taking of Warsaw Babinich was ordered to march through Prussia to Lithuania, to excite the rebellion and burn and slay on the road. And you know that he will carry out that order. We tried to catch him at the Bug; and Steinbock himself sent a considerable force against him, of which not one man returned to give news of the disaster. Do not try to measure yourself with Babinich, for you will not be able, but hasten to Birji.

" The fever has left me entirely; here there are high and dry plains, not such swamps as in Jmud. I commit you to God, etc."

The starosta was as much grieved at the news as he was rejoiced that the prince was alive and in health; for if the prince foresaw that the winning of a general battle could not much better the shattered fortune of Sweden, what could be hoped for in future? Perhaps the prince might save himself from ruin under the robe of the crafty elector, and he, Sakovich, under the prince; but what could be done in the mean while? Go to Prussia?

Pan Sakovich did not need the advice of the prince to restrain him from meeting Babinich. Power and desire to do that were both lacking. Birji remained, but too late for that also. On the road was a Billevich party; then a second party, — nobles, peasants, people of the prince, and God knows what others, — who at a mere report would assemble and sweep him away as a whirlwind sweeps withered leaves ; and even if they did not assemble, even if he could anticipate them by a swift and bold march, it would be needful to fight on the road with others; at every village, at every swamp, in every field and forest, a new battle. What forces should he have to take even thirty horses to Birji ? Was he to remain in Taurogi ? That was bad, for meanwhile the terrible Babinich would come at the head of a powerful Tartar legion; all the parties would fly to him ; they would cover Taurogi as with a flood, and wreak a vengeance such as man had not heard of till that day.

For the first time in his life the hitherto insolent starosta felt that he lacked counsel in his head, strength in undertaking, and decision in danger ; and the next day he summoned to counsel Bützov, Braun, and some of the most important officers.

It was decided to remain in Taurogi and await tidings from Warsaw.

But Braun from that council went straight to another, to one with Anusia.

Long, long did they deliberate together. At last Braun came out with face greatly moved; but Anusia rushed like a storm to Olenka, —

"Olenka, the time has come!" cried she, on the threshold. "We must flee!"

"When?" asked the valiant girl, growing a little pale, but rising at once in sign of immediate readiness.

"To-morrow, to-morrow! Braun has the command, and Sakovich will sleep in the town, for Pan Dzyeshuk has invited him to a banquet. Pan Dzyeshuk was long ago prepared, and he will put something in Sakovich's wine. Braun says that he will go himself and take fifty horse. Oh, Olenka, how happy I am! how happy!"

Here Anusia threw herself on Panna Billevich's neck, and began to press her with such an outburst of joy that she asked, —

"What is the matter, Anusia? You might have brought Braun to this long ago."

"I might, I might. I have told you nothing yet! O my God! my God! Have you heard of nothing? Pan Babinich is marching hither! Sakovich and all of them are dying of fear! Pan Babinich is marching, burning, and slaying. He has destroyed one party, has beaten Steinbock himself, and is advancing with forced marches, so as to hurry. And to whom can he hurry hither? Tell me, am I not a fool?"

Here tears glistened in Anusia's eyes. Olenka placed her hands together as if in prayer, and raising her eyes said, —

"To whomsoever he is hastening, may God straighten his paths, bless him, and guard him!"

CHAPTER XLIX.

KMITA, wishing to pass from Warsaw to Royal Prussia and Lithuania, had really no easy task in the very beginning, for not farther from Warsaw than Serotsk was a great Swedish force. Karl Gustav in his time had commanded it to take position there purposely to hinder the siege of the capital. But since Warsaw was captured, that army had nothing better to do than stop the divisions which Yan Kazimir might send to Lithuania or Prussia. At the head of the Swedish force were two Polish traitors, Radzeyovski and Radzivill, with Douglas, a skilful warrior, trained as no other of the Swedish generals in sudden warfare; with them were two thousand chosen infantry and cavalry, with artillery of equal number. When the leaders heard of Kmita's expedition, since it was necessary for them in every event to approach Lithuania to save Tykotsin, besieged anew by Mazovians and men of Podlyasye, they spread widely their nets for Pan Andrei in the triangle on the Bug, between Serotsk on one side and Zlotorya on the other, and Ostrolenko at the point.

Kmita had to pass through that triangle, for he was hurrying, and there lay his nearest road. He noticed in good season that he was in a net, but because he was accustomed to that method of warfare he was not disconcerted. He counted on this, — that the net was too greatly extended, and therefore the meshes in it were so widely stretched that he would be able to pass through them. What is more, though they hunted him diligently, not only did he double back, not only did he escape, but he hunted them. First, he passed the Bug behind Serotsk, pushed along the bank of the river to Vyshkov in Branshchyk; he cut to pieces three hundred horse sent on a reconnoissance, so that, as the prince had written, not a man returned to give account of the disaster. Douglas himself pushed him into Dlugosyodle; but Kmita, dispersing the cavalry, turned back, and instead of fleeing with all his might, went straight to the eyes of the enemy as far as the Narev, which he crossed by

swimming. Douglas stood on the bank waiting for boats;
but before they were brought Kmita returned in the dark
through the river, and striking the vanguard of the Swedes
brought panic and disorder to Douglas's whole division.

The old general was amazed at this movement; but next
day his amazement was greater, when he learned that Kmita
had gone around the whole army, and doubling back to the
spot from which they had started him like a wild beast, had
seized at Branshchyk Swedish wagons following the army,
together with booty and money, cutting down at the same
time fifty men of the infantry convoy.

Sometimes the Swedes saw Kmita's Tartars for whole
days with the naked eye on the edge of the horizon, but
could not reach them. Still Pan Andrei carried off something every moment. The Swedish soldiers were wearied,
and the Polish squadrons which held yet with Radzeyovski,
though formed of dissenters, served unwillingly. But the
population served Kmita with enthusiasm. He knew every
movement of the smallest scouting-party, of each wagon
which went forward or remained in the rear. Sometimes
it seemed that he was playing with the Swedes, but that was
tiger-play. He spared no prisoners; he ordered the Tartars
to hang them, for the Swedes did the same. At times you
would say that irrepressible fury had come upon him, for he
hurled himself with blind insolence on superior forces.

" An insane man leads that division ! " said Douglas.

" Or a mad dog ! " said Radzeyovski.

Boguslav thought he was one and the other, but under-
neath both a consummate soldier. The prince related boastingly to the generals that he had hurled that cavalier twice
to the earth, with his own hand.

In fact, Babinich attacked Boguslav most furiously. He
sought him evidently ; the pursued became himself the
pursuer.

Douglas divined that there must be some personal hatred
in the matter.

The prince did not deny this, though he gave no explanations. He paid Babinich with the same coin; for following
the example of Hovanski, he put a price on his head ; and
when that availed nothing, he thought to take advantage of
Kmita's hatred and through it bring him into a trap.

" It is a shame for us to bother so long with this robber,"
said he to Douglas and Radzeyovski; " he is prowling around
us like a wolf around a sheepfold. I will go against him

with a small division as a decoy; and when he strikes me I
will detain him till you come up; then we will not let the
craw-fish out of the net."

Douglas, whom this chase had long since annoyed, made
only small opposition, asserting that he could not and should
not expose the life of such a great dignitary and relative of
kings to the chance of being seized by one marauder. But
when Boguslav insisted, he agreed.

It was determined that the prince should go with a detachment of five hundred troopers, that each man should have
behind him a foot soldier with a musket. This stratagem
was to lead Babinich into error.

"He will not restrain himself when he hears of only five
hundred horsemen, and he will attack undoubtedly," said
the prince. "When the infantry spit in his eyes, his Tartars will scatter like sand; he will fall himself, or we shall
take him alive."

This plan was carried out quickly and with great accuracy.
First, news was sent out, two days in advance, that a party
of five hundred horse was to march under Prince Boguslav.
The generals calculated with certainty that the local inhabitants would inform Babinich of this. In fact, they
did inform him.

The prince marched in the deep and dark night toward
Vansosh and Yelonka, passed the river at Cherevino, and
leaving his cavalry in the open field, stationed his infantry
in the neighboring groves, whence they might issue unexpectedly. Meanwhile Douglas was to push along by the bank
of the Narev, feigning to march on Ostrolenko. Radzeyovski
was in advance, with the lighter cavalry from Ksyenjopole.

Neither of the three leaders knew well where Babinich
was at that moment, for it was impossible to learn anything
from the peasants, and the cavalry were not able to seize
Tartars. But Douglas supposed that Babinich's main forces
were in Snyadovo, and he wished to surround them, so that if
Babinich should move on Boguslav, he would intercept him
on the side of the Lithuanian boundary and cut off his retreat.

Everything seemed to favor the Swedish plans. Kmita
was really in Snyadovo; and barely had the news of Boguslav's approach reached him, when he fell at once into the
forest, so as to come out unexpectedly near Cherevino.

Douglas, turning aside from the Narev, struck in a few
days upon the traces of the Tartar march, and advanced by
the same road, therefore from the rear after Babinich. Heat

tormented the horses greatly, as well as the men encased in iron armor; but the general advanced without regard to those hindrances, absolutely certain that he would come upon Babinich's army unexpectedly and in time of battle.

Finally, after two days' march he came so near Cherevino that the smoke of the cottages was visible. Then he halted, and occupying all the passages and narrow pathways, waited.

Some officers wished to advance as a forlorn hope and strike at once; but Douglas restrained them, saying, —

"Babinich, after attacking the prince, when he sees that he has to do not with cavalry alone, but also with infantry, will be obliged to retreat; and as he can retreat only by the old road, he will fall as it were into our open arms."

In fact, it seemed that all they had to do was to listen, and soon Tartar howling would be heard, and the first discharges of musketry.

Meanwhile one day passed, and in the forests of Cherevino it was as silent as if a soldier's foot had never been in it.

Douglas grew impatient, and toward night sent forward a small party to the field, enjoining on them the utmost caution.

The party returned in the depth of the night, without having seen or done anything. At daylight Douglas himself advanced with his whole force. After a march of some hours he reached a place filled with traces of the presence of soldiers. His men found remnants of biscuits, broken glass, bits of clothing, and a belt with cartridges such as the Swedish infantry use; it became certain that Boguslav's infantry had stopped in that place, but they were not visible anywhere. Farther on in the damp forest Douglas's vanguard found many tracks of heavy cavalry horses, but on the edge tracks of Tartar ponies; still farther on lay the carcass of a horse, from which the wolves had recently torn out the entrails. About a furlong beyond they found a Tartar arrow without the point, but with the shaft entire. Evidently Boguslav was retreating, and Babinich was following him.

Douglas understood that something unusual must have happened. But what was it? To this there was no answer. Douglas fell to pondering. Suddenly his meditation was interrupted by an officer from the vanguard.

"Your worthiness!" said the officer, "through the thicket about a furlong away are some men in a crowd. They do not move, as if they were on watch. I have brought the guard to a halt, so as to report to you."

"Cavalry or infantry?" asked Douglas.

"Infantry. There are four or five of them in a group; it was not possible to count them accurately, for the branches hide them. But they seem yellow, like our musketeers."

Douglas pressed his horse with his knees, pushed forward quickly to the vanguard, and advanced with it. Through the thickets, now thinner, were to be seen in the remoter deep forest a group of soldiers perfectly motionless, standing under a tree.

"They are ours, they are ours!" said Douglas. "The prince must be in the neighborhood."

"It is a wonder to me," said the officer; "they are on watch, and none of them calls, though we march noisily."

Here the thickets ended, and the forest was clean of undergrowth. The men approached and saw four persons standing in a group, one at the side of the other, as if they were looking at something on the ground. From the head of each one rose a dark strip directly upward.

"Your worthiness!" said the officer at once, "these men are hanging."

"That is true!" answered Douglas.

They sprang forward, and stood for a while near the corpses. Four foot-soldiers were hanging together by ropes, like a bunch of thrushes, their feet barely an inch above the ground, for they were on the lower branches.

Douglas looked at them indifferently enough; then said as if to himself, "Now we know that the prince and Babinich have passed this way."

Then he fell to thinking again, for he did not know well whether to continue on by the forest path or go out on the Ostrolenko highway.

Half an hour later they found two other corpses. Evidently they were marauders or sick men whom Babinich's Tartars had seized while pursuing the prince.

"But why did the prince retreat?"

Douglas knew him too well — that is, both his daring and his military experience — to admit even for a moment that the prince had not sufficient reasons. Therefore something must have intervened.

Only next day was the affair explained. Pan Byes Kornie had come from Prince Boguslav, with a party of thirty horse, to report that Yan Kazimir had sent beyond the Bug against Douglas the full hetman Pan Gosyevski, with six thousand Lithuanians and Tartar horse.

"We learned this," said Pan Byes, "before Babinich came up; for he advanced very carefully and attacked frequently, therefore annoyingly. Gosyevski is twenty or twenty-five miles distant. When the prince received the tidings, he was forced to retreat in haste, so as to join Radzeyovski, who might be cut to pieces easily. But by marching quickly we made the junction. The prince sent out at once parties of a few tens of men in every direction, with a report to your worthiness. Many of them will fall into Tartar or peasant hands, but in such a war it cannot be otherwise."

"Where are the prince and Radzeyovski?"

"Ten miles from here, at the river."

"Did the prince bring back all his forces?"

"He was forced to leave the infantry, which is coming through the thickest forest, so as to escape the Tartars."

"Such cavalry as the Tartar is made to go through the densest forests. I do not expect to see that infantry again. But no one is to blame, and the prince acted like an experienced leader."

"The prince threw out one party the most considerable to Ostrolenko, to lead Gosyevski into error. He will go to Ostrolenko at once, thinking that our whole force is there."

"That is well!" said Douglas, comforted. "We will manage Gosyevski."

And he marched without delay to join Boguslav and Radzeyovski. They met that same day, to the great delight, especially, of Radzeyovski, who feared captivity more than death, for he knew that as a traitor and the originator of all the misfortunes of the Commonwealth he would have to give a terrible answer. But now, after the junction with Douglas, the Swedish army had more than four thousand men ; therefore it was able to offer an effective resistance to the forces of the full hetman. He had, it is true, six thousand cavalry ; but Tartars — except those of Babinich, who were trained — could not be used in offensive battle, and Pan Gosyevski himself, though a skilled and learned warrior, was not able, like Charnyetski, to inspire men with an enthusiasm which nothing could resist.

But Douglas was at a loss to understand why Yan Kazimir should send the full hetman beyond the Bug. The Swedish king with the elector was marching on Warsaw ; a general battle must therefore follow, sooner or later. And though Yan Kazimir was at the head of a force superior in numbers to the Swedes and the Brandenburgers, still six thousand men formed too great a force for the King of Poland to set aside voluntarily.

It is true that Gosyevski had saved Babinich from

trouble, but still the king did not need to send out a whole division to the rescue of Babinich. Hence there was in this expedition some secret object, which the Swedish general, despite all his penetration, could not divine.

In the letter of the King of Sweden sent a week later great alarm was evident, and as it were astonishment caused by that expedition, but a few words explained the reasons of this. According to the opinion of Karl Gustav, the hetman was not sent to attack Douglas's army, nor to go to Lithuania to aid the uprising there, for in Lithuania the Swedes, as it was, were not able to do anything but to threaten Royal Prussia, namely, the eastern part of it, which was completely stripped of troops.

" The calculation is," wrote the king, " to make the elector waver in faithfulness to the treaty of Marienburg and to us; which may easily happen, since the elector is ready to enter into alliance with Christ against the Devil and at the same time with the Devil against Christ, so as to win something from both."

The letter ended by enjoining on Douglas to strive with all his forces not to let the hetman go to Prussia, " who if he cannot reach there in the course of a few weeks, will be forced beyond doubt to return to Warsaw."

Douglas saw that the task given him did not surpass his powers at all. Not so long before he had met with a certain success in opposing Charnyetski himself; therefore Gosyevski was not terrible. The Swedish general did not hope, it is true, to crush Gosyevski's division, but he felt certain that he would be able to stop him and curb all his movements.

In fact, from that moment began very skilful approaches of the two armies, which, avoiding on both sides a general battle, endeavored each to flank the other. Both leaders emulated each other; but the experienced Douglas was in so far superior that he did not let Gosyevski advance beyond Ostrolenko. But Babinich, saved from Boguslav's attack, did not hasten to join the Lithuanian division, for he occupied himself with great zeal on that infantry which Boguslav in his hurried march to Radzeyovski was forced to leave behind. Babinich's Tartars, guided by local woodmen, pursued night and day, finishing every moment the incautious or those who dropped into the rear. Lack of provisions forced the Swedes at last to separate into small detachments which could find food more easily; this was all that Babinich was waiting for.

He divided his forces into three commands, under lead of

Akbah Ulan, Soroka, and himself, and in a few days he destroyed the greater part of that infantry. It was an untiring hunt after men in forest thickets, in willows, in reeds, —
a hunt full of noise, uproar, shouting, shooting, and death.

Widely did it spread the glory of Babinich's name among
the Mazovians. Bands collected and joined Gosyevski at
Ostrolenko itself, when the full hetman, whose march was
only a demonstration, received a command from the king to
march back to Warsaw. For a short period only could Babinich rejoice with his acquaintances; namely, with Zagloba
and Volodyovski, who at the head of the Lauda squadron
attended the hetman. But they greeted one another very
cordially, for great friendship and intimacy existed already
between them. The young colonels were sharply annoyed
that they could not act now against Boguslav; but Zagloba
consoled them by pouring frequently into their glasses,
and saying, —

"That is nothing! My head has been working since May
over stratagems, and I have never racked it over anything in
vain. I have a number ready, — very excellent stratagems;
but there is no time to apply them, unless at Warsaw, whither
we are all marching."

"I must go to Prussia," said Babinich, "and cannot be
at Warsaw."

"Can you reach Prussia?" asked Volodyovski.

"As God is in heaven, I shall spring through; and I
promise you sacredly to make not the worst cabbage-hash,
for I shall say to my Tartars, 'Riot, my soul!' They would
be glad even here to draw the knife across people's throats;
but I have told them that pay for every violence is the rope.
But in Prussia I will give way even to my own will. Why
should I not spring through? You were not able; but
that is another thing, for it is easier to stop a large force
than such a party as mine, with which it is easy to hide.
More than once was I sitting in the rushes, and Douglas's
men passed right there, knowing nothing of me. Douglas
too will surely follow you, and leave the field free to me."

"But, as we hear, you have wearied him out too," said
Pan Michael, with satisfaction.

"Ah, the scoundrel!" added Zagloba. "He had to change
his shirt every day, he sweated so. You never stole up to
Hovanski better than to him, and I must acknowledge that
I could not have done better myself, though, in his time,
Konyetspolski said that Zagloba in partisan warfare was
unsurpassed."

"It seems to me," said Pan Michael to Kmita, "that if Douglas returns he will leave Boguslav here to attack you."

"God grant it! I have the same hope," answered Kmita, quickly. "Were I to seek him, and he me, we should find each other. He will not pass through me a third time; and if he does, then I shall not rise again. I remember your secrets well; and all the Lubni thrusts I have in memory like 'Our Father.' Every day, too, I try them with Soroka, so as to train my hand."

"What are stratagems good for?" exclaimed Pan Michael; "the sabre is the main thing."

This maxim touched Zagloba somewhat; therefore he said at once: "Every windmill thinks that the main thing is to whirl its wings. Do you know why, Michael? Because it has chaff under its roof; that is, in its head. Military art rests on stratagems; if not, Roh Kovalski might be grand hetman and you full hetman."

"And what is Pan Kovalski doing?" asked Kmita.

"Pan Kovalski has now an iron helmet on his head, and justly, for cabbage is best out of a pot. He has grown rich on plunder in Warsaw, has come into good repute, and gone to the hussars, to Prince Polubinski, and all so as to be able to put a spear into Karl Gustav. He comes every day to our tent, and stares to see if the neck of the decanter is sticking out of the straw. I cannot break that lad of drinking. Good example goes for nothing; but I prophesied to him that this desertion of the Lauda squadron would turn out evil. The rogue! the thankless fellow! in return for all the benefits which I have shown him, such a son for a lance!"

"But did you rear him?"

"My dear sir, do not make me a bear-trainer! To Sapyeha, who asked me the same question, I answered that he and Roh had the same preceptor, but not me; for I in youthful years was a cooper, and knew how to set staves very well."[1]

"To begin with, you would not dare to tell that to Sapyeha," said Volodyovski; "and secondly, though you grumble at Kovalski, you love him as the apple of your eye."

"I prefer him to you, Pan Michael; for I could never endure May-bugs, nor soapy little fellows who at the sight of the first woman who comes along play antics like German dogs."

[1] This means that if Zagloba had been preceptor to the hetman or Kovalski, they would have had better wit. "Having a stave loose or lacking in his barrel," means, in Polish, that a man's mind is not right.

"Or like those monkeys in the Kazanovski Palace, with which you were carrying on war."

"Oh, laugh, laugh! You can take Warsaw without me next time."

"Was it you, then, who took Warsaw?"

"But who captured the Cracow Gate? Who invented captivity for the generals? They are sitting now on bread and water in Zamost; and when Wittemberg looks at Wrangel, he says, 'Zagloba put us here!' and both fall to weeping. If Sapyeha were not ill, and if he were present, he would tell you who first drew the Swedish claw from the skin of Warsaw."

"For God's sake!" said Kmita, "do this for me, — send news of that battle for which they are preparing at Warsaw. I shall be counting the days and nights on my fingers till I know something certain."

Zagloba put his finger to his forehead. "Listen to my forecast," said he, "for what I tell you will be accomplished as surely as that this glass is standing before me — Is it not standing before me?"

"It is, it is! Speak on."

"We shall either lose this general battle, or we shall win it —"

"Every man knows that!" put in Volodyovski.

"You might be silent, Michael, and learn something. Supposing that we lose this battle, do you know what will happen? You see you do not know, for you are moving those little awls under your nose like a rabbit. Well, I will tell you that nothing will happen —"

Kmita, who was very quick, sprang up, struck his glass on the table, and said, —

"You are beating around the bush!"

"I say nothing will happen!" repeated Zagloba. "You are young, therefore you do not know. As affairs now stand, our king, our dear country, our armies may lose fifty battles one after another, and the war will go on in the old fashion, — the nobles will assemble, and with them the lower ranks. But if they do not succeed one time, they will another, until the enemy's force has melted away. But when the Swedes lose one great battle, the Devil will take them without salvation, and with them the elector to boot."

Here Zagloba grew animated, emptied his glass, struck it on the table, and continued, —

"Listen, — for you will not hear this from every mouth, for

not every one knows how to take a general view of things.
Many a man is thinking, 'What is waiting for us now?
how many battles, how many defeats,' — which, in warring
with Karl, are not unlikely, — 'how many tears, how much
bloodshed, how many grievous paroxysms?' And many a
one will doubt and blaspheme against the mercy of God
and the Most Holy Mother. But I tell you this: do you
know what is waiting for those vandal enemies? — destruction; do you know what is waiting for us? — victory!
If they beat us one hundred times, very well; but we
will beat them the hundred and first time, and that will
be the end."

When he had said this, Zagloba closed his eyes for a moment, but soon opened them. He looked ahead with gleaming vision, and suddenly shouted with the whole force of
his breast: "Victory! victory!"

Kmita was flushed from delight: "In God's name, he is
right, he speaks justly. It cannot be otherwise! Such an
end has to come!"

"It must be acknowledged that you are not lacking here,"
said Volodyovski, putting his finger on his forehead. "The
Commonwealth may be occupied; but to stay in it is impossible, so at last the Swedes will have to go out."

"Well, is that it? I am not lacking!" said Zagloba,
rejoiced at the praise. "If that is true, then I will prophesy
further. God is with the just!" Here he turned to Kmita.
"You will finish the traitor Radzivill; you will go to Taurogi,
recover the maiden, marry her, rear posterity. May I have
the pip on my tongue if this will not happen as I say! But
for God's sake, don't smother me!"

Zagloba was rightfully cautious, for Kmita seized him in
his arms, raised him, and began to hug him so that the old
man's eyes were bursting out. He had barely come to his
feet and recovered breath, when Pan Michael, greatly delighted, seized him by the hand, —

"It is my turn! Tell what awaits me."

"God bless you, Michael! your pretty tufted lark will
hatch out a whole brood, — never fear. Uf!"

"Vivat!" cried Volodyovski.

"But first, we will make an end of the Swedes," added
Zagloba.

"We will, we will!" cried the young colonels, shaking
their sabres.

"Vivat! victory!"

CHAPTER L.

A WEEK later Kmita crossed the boundaries of Electoral Prussia at Raygrod. It came to him easily enough; for before the departure of the full hetman he disappeared in the woods so secretly that Douglas felt sure that his party too had marched with the whole Tartar-Lithuanian division to Warsaw, and he left merely small garrisons in the castles for the defence of those parts.

Douglas, with Radzeyovski and Radzivill, followed Gosyevski.

Kmita heard of this before passing the boundary, and grieved greatly that he could not meet his mortal enemy eye to eye, and lest punishment might come to Boguslav from other hands, — namely, from Volodyovski, who also had made a vow against him.

Hence, not being able to wreak vengeance on the person of the traitor for the wrongs done the Commonwealth and himself, he wreaked it in terrible fashion on the lands of the elector.

That very night in which the Tartars had passed the boundary pillar, the heavens grew red from flames. An uproar was heard, with the weeping of people trampled by the foot of war. Whoso was able to beg for mercy in the Polish tongue was spared at command of the leader; but German settlements, colonies, villages, and hamlets were turned into a river of fire, and the terrified inhabitants went under the knife.

And not so swiftly does oil spread over the sea when the sailor pours it to pacify the waves, as that chambul of Tartars and volunteers spread over quiet and hitherto safe regions. It seemed that every Tartar was able to double and treble himself, to be at the same time in a number of places, to burn, to slay. They spared not even grain in the field, nor trees in the gardens.

Kmita had held his Tartars so long in the leash that at last, when he let them free like a flock of birds of prey, they grew almost wild in the midst of slaughter and destruction. One surpassed the other; and since they could not take captives, they swam from morning till evening in blood.

Kmita himself, having in his heart no little fierceness, gave it full freedom, and though he did not steep his own hands in the blood of defenceless people, he looked with pleasure on the flow of blood. In his soul he was at rest, and conscience reproached him with nothing; for this was not Polish blood, and besides it was the blood of heretics; therefore he judged that he was doing a work pleasing to God, and especially to the saints of the Lord.

The elector, a vassal, therefore a servant of the Commonwealth and living from its bounties, was the first to raise his sacrilegious hand against it; therefore punishment was his due, and Kmita was purely an instrument of God's vengeance.

For this reason, when in the evening he was repeating his Litany in peace by the blaze of burning German settlements, and when the screams of the murdered interrupted the tally of his prayers, he began again from the beginning, so as not to burden his soul with the sin of inattention to the service of God.

But he did not cherish in his heart savage feelings alone; for, besides piety, various other feelings moved it, connected by memory with distant years. Therefore those times came frequently to his mind when he attacked Hovanski with such glory, and his former comrades stood as if alive before his eyes, — Kokosinski; the gigantic Kulvyets-Hippocentaurus; the spotted Ranitski, with senatorial blood in his veins; Uhlik, playing on the flageolet; Rekuts, on whom human blood was not weighing; and Zend, imitating birds and every kind of beast.

They all, save perhaps Rekuts alone, were burning in hell; and behold, if they were living now, they might wallow in blood without bringing sin on their souls, and with profit to the Commonwealth.

Here Pan Andrei sighed at the thought of how destructive a thing license is, since in the morning of youth it stops the road for the ages of ages to beautiful deeds.

But he sighed more than all for Olenka. The deeper he entered the Prussian country, the more fiercely did the wounds of his heart burn him, as if those fires which he kindled roused at the same time his old love. Almost every day then he said in his heart to the maiden, —

"Dearest dove, you may have forgotten me, or if you remember, disgust fills your heart; but I, at a distance or near, in the night or the day-time, in labor for the country and toils, am thinking ever of you, and my soul flies to you over pine-woods and waters, like a tired bird, to drop down at your feet. Only to the country and to you would I give all my blood; but woe is me, if in your heart you proclaim me an outlaw forever.

Thus meditating, he went ever farther to the north along the boundary belt. He burned and slew, sparing no one. Sadness throttled him terribly. He would like to be in Taurogi on the morrow; but the road was still long and difficult, for at last they began to ring all the bells in the province of Prussia.

Every one living seized arms to resist the dreadful destroyers; garrisons were brought in from towns the remotest, regiments were formed of even village youths, and soon they were able to place twenty men against every Tartar.

Kmita rushed at these commands like a thunderbolt, beat them, hanged men, escaped, hid, and again sailed out on a wave of fire; but still he could not advance so swiftly as at first. More than once it was necessary to attack in Tartar fashion, and hide for whole weeks in thickets or reeds at the banks of a lake. The inhabitants rushed forth more and more numerously, as if against a wolf; and he bit too like a wolf, — with one snap of his jaws he gave death, and not only defended himself, but did not desist from attack.

Loving genuine work, he did not leave a given district, in spite of pursuit, until he had annihilated it for miles around with fire and sword. His name reached, it is unknown by what means, the mouths of the people, and bearing terror and fright, thundered on to the shores of the Baltic.

Babinich might, it is true, return within the boundaries of the Commonwealth, and in spite of Swedish detachments, move quickly to Taurogi; but he did not wish to do so, for he desired to serve not only himself but the country.

Now came news which gave courage for defence and revenge to the people in Prussia, but pierced the heart of Babinich with savage sorrow. News came like a thunderclap of a great battle at Warsaw, which the King of Poland had lost. "Karl Gustav and the elector have beaten all the troops of Yan Kazimir," people repeated to one and another with delight throughout Prussia. "Warsaw is recaptured!"

" This is the greatest victory of the war, and now comes the end of the Commonwealth ! " All men whom the Tartars seized and put on the coals to obtain information, repeated the same; there was also exaggerated news, as is common in time of war and uncertainty. According to this news the Poles were cut to pieces, the hetmans had fallen, and Yan Kazimir was captured.

Was all at an end, then ? Was that rising and triumphing Commonwealth naught but an empty illusion ? So much power, so many troops, so many great men and famous warriors; the hetmans, the king, Charnyetski with his invincible division, the marshal of the kingdom, other lords with their attendants, — had all perished, had all rolled away like smoke ? And are there no other defenders of this hapless country, save detached parties of insurgents who certainly at news of the disaster will pass away like a fog ?

Kmita tore the hair from his head and wrung his hands; he seized the wet earth, pressed palms-full of it to his burning head.

" I shall fall too," said he ; " but first this land will swim in blood."

And he began to fight like a man in despair. He did not hide longer, he did not attack in the forest and reeds, he sought death; he rushed like a madman on forces three times greater than his own, and cut them to pieces with sabres and hoofs. In his Tartars all traces of human feeling died out, and they were turned into a herd of wild beasts. A predatory people, but not over-much fitted for fighting in the open field, without losing their genius for surprises and ambush, they, by continual exercise, by continual conflict, had trained themselves so that breast to breast they could hold the field against the first cavalry, and scatter quadrangles even of the Swedish guard. In their struggles with the armed mob of Prussia, a hundred of those Tartars scattered with ease two and even three hundred sturdy men armed with spears and muskets.

Kmita weaned them from weighting themselves with plunder; they took only money and gold, which they sewed up in their saddles, so that when one of them fell the survivors fought with rage for his horse and his saddle. Growing rich in this manner, they lost none of their swiftness, well-nigh superhuman. Recognizing that under no leader on earth could they find such rich harvests, they grew attached to Babinich, as hounds to the hunter, and with real Mohammedan honesty placed after battle in the hands of Soroka and the Kyemliches the lion's share of the plunder which belonged to the "bagadyr."

"Allah!" said Akbah Ulan, "few of them will see Bagche-Serai, but all who go back will be murzas."

Babinich, who from of old knew how to live upon war, collected great riches; but death, which he sought more than gold, he found not.

A month passed again in battles and labors surpassing belief. The Tartar horses, though fed with barley and Prussian wheat, needed absolutely even a couple of days' rest; therefore the young colonel, wishing also to gain news and fill the gaps in his ranks with fresh volunteers, withdrew, near Dospada, to the Commonwealth.

News soon came, and so joyful that Kmita almost lost his wits. It turned out to be true that the equally valiant and unfortunate Yan Kazimir had lost a great three-days' battle at Warsaw, but for what reason?

The general militia in an immense majority had gone home, and the part which remained did not fight with such spirit as at the taking of Warsaw, and on the third day of the battle a panic set in. But for the first two days the victory was inclining to the side of Poland. The regular troops, not in sudden partisan warfare, but in a great battle with the most highly trained soldiers of Europe, exhibited such skill and endurance that amazement seized the Swedish and Brandenburg generals themselves.

Yan Kazimir had won immortal glory. It was said that he had shown himself a leader equal to Karl Gustav, and that if all his commands had been carried out the enemy would have lost the general battle, and the war would have been ended.

Kmita received these tidings from eye-witnesses, for he had stumbled upon nobles who, serving in the general militia, had taken part in the battle. One of them told him of the brilliant attack of the hussars, during which Karl himself, who, despite the entreaties of his generals, would not withdraw, came near perishing. All showed the falsehood of the report that the army had been routed or the hetmans had fallen. On the contrary, the whole force, except the general militia, remained intact, and withdrew in good order along the country.

From the bridge of Warsaw which was giving way cannon had fallen; but they were pulled through the Vistula in a breath. The army swore by everything that under such a leader as Yan Kazimir they would, in the coming battle, conquer Karl Gustav, the elector, and whomsoever it might be necessary to conquer. As to the recent battle it was only a trial, though unfavorable, but full of solace for the future.

Kmita was at a loss to know how the first news could have been so terrible. They explained to him that Karl Gustav had sent out exaggerated reports purposely; in fact, he did not know well what to do. The Swedish officers whom Pan Andrei seized a week later confirmed this opinion.

He learned also from them that beyond others the elector lived in fear, and was thinking more and more of his own safety; for a multitude of his men had fallen at Warsaw, and disease had seized those remaining so terribly that it was destroying them more quickly than battles. At the same time the men of Great Poland, eager to make good Uistsie and all wrongs, had attacked the monarchy of Brandenburg itself, burning and slaying, leaving nothing behind them but land and water. According to the officers, the hour was near in which the elector would abandon the Swedes, and join the more powerful.

"It is needful to touch him with fire somewhat," thought Kmita, "so that he may do this the more quickly."

And since his horses were rested already, and he had made good the losses among his men, he passed the boundary again at Dospada, and rushed on the German settlements like a spirit of destruction.

Various "parties" followed his example. He found a weaker defence; hence he accomplished more. News came ever more joyful, more gladdening, so that it was difficult to believe it.

First of all, it was said that Karl Gustav, who, after the Warsaw battle, had pushed on to Radom, was retreating at breakneck speed to Royal Prussia. What had happened? Why was he retreating? There was no answer to this for a time, till at last the name of Charnyetski thundered again through the Commonwealth. He was victorious at Lipets, victorious at Stjemeshno; at Rava itself he had cut to pieces the rearguard of the retreating Karl; then, learning that two thousand cavalry were returning from Cracow, he attacked that body, and did not let one man escape to announce the defeat. Colonel Forgell, brother of the general, thirteen captains, and twenty-four lieutenants went into captivity. Others gave the numbers as twice greater; some insisted in their enthusiasm that Yan Kazimir had not suffered a defeat, but had won a victory at Warsaw, and that his march along the country was only a stratagem for the destruction of the enemy.

Kmita himself began to think the same; for being a soldier from youthful years, he understood war, but had never heard of a victory after which the victor was in a worse condition than before. The Swedes were evidently in a worse condition, and just after the battle at Warsaw.

Pan Andrei called to mind at that moment the words of Zagloba, when at their last meeting he said that victories would not improve the Swedish cause, but that one defeat might destroy it.

"That is a chancellor's head," pondered Kmita, "which reads in the future as in a book."

Here he remembered the further predictions, — how he, Kmita or Babinich, would go to Taurogi, find his Olenka, persuade her, marry her, and have descendants to the glory of the Commonwealth. When he remembered this, fire entered his veins; he wished not to lose a moment, but to leave Prussians and slaughter for a time, and fly to Taurogi.

On the eve of his starting there came to him a noble of Lauda, of Volodyovski's squadron, with a letter from the little knight.

"We are going with Sapyeha and Prince Michael Radzivill against Boguslav and Waldeck," wrote Pan Michael. "Join us, since a field for just vengeance will be found, and it is proper to pay the Prussians for harm done the Commonwealth."

Pan Andrei could not believe his own eyes, and for some time he suspected the noble of being sent by some Prussian or Swedish commandant of purpose to lead him with the chambul into ambush. Had Gosyevski come a second time to Prussia? It was impossible not to believe. The handwriting was Volodyovski's, the arms Volodyovski's, and Pan Andrei remembered the noble too. Then he inquired where Gosyevski was, and to what point he intended to go.

The noble was rather dull. It was not for him to know whither the hetman was marching; he knew only that he was two days distant, and that the Lauda squadron was with him. Charnyetski had borrowed it for a while, but had sent it back long ago, and now it was marching under lead of the hetman. "They say," concluded the noble, "that we must go to Prussia, and the soldiers are greatly delighted. But our work is to obey and to strike."

Kmita, when he had heard the narrative, did not hesitate long. He turned his chambul, went with forced marches to the hetman, and after two days fell late at night into the arms of Volodyovski, who, pressing him, said at once, —

"Count Waldeck and Prince Boguslav are in Prostki, making intrenchments to secure themselves with a fortified camp. We shall march on them."

"To-day?" asked Kmita.

"To-morrow before daybreak, — that is, in two or three hours."

Here they embraced each other again.

"Something tells me that God will give him into our hands!" exclaimed Kmita, with emotion.

"And I think so too."

"I have made a vow to fast till death on the day in which I meet him."

"The protection of God will not fail you," said Volodyovski. "I shall not be envious, either, if this lot falls to you, for your wrong is greater. Yendrek, let me look at you! You have grown perfectly black from the weather; but you have acquitted yourself. The whole division looks with the greatest esteem on your labor. Nothing behind you but ruins and corpses! You are a born soldier; and it would go hard with Zagloba himself, were he here, to invent in self-praise deeds better than those you have done."

"But where is Zagloba?"

"He remained with Sapyeha; for he fell into weeping and despair after Kovalski."

"Then has Kovalski fallen?"

Volodyovski pressed his lips. "Do you know who killed him?"

"Whence should I know? Tell me!"

"Prince Boguslav!"

Kmita turned in his place, as if thrust with a point, and began to draw in air with a hiss; at last he gritted his teeth, and casting himself on the bench, rested his head on his palms in silence.

Volodyovski clapped his hands, and ordered the attendant to bring drink; then he sat near Kmita, filled a cup for him, and began, —

"Roh Kovalski died such a cavalier's death that God

grant any man of us to die no worse. It is enough to inform
you that Karl Gustav himself after the battle celebrated his
funeral, and a whole regiment of the guards fired a salute
over his coffin."

"If only not at those hands, at those hellish hands!"
exclaimed Kmita.

"Yes, at the hands of Boguslav; we know that from
hussars who with their own eyes saw the sad end."

"Were you not there then?"

"In battle places are not chosen, but a man stands where
he is ordered. If I had been there, either I should not be
here now, or Boguslav would not be making trenches at
Prostki."

"Tell me how it all happened. It will only increase the
anger."

Pan Michael drank, wiped his yellow mustaches, and
began: —

"Of a certainty you are not lacking in narratives of the
Warsaw battle, for every one is speaking of it; therefore I
shall not dwell on it too long. Our gracious lord — God give
him health and long years! for under another king the
country would have perished amid disasters — has shown
himself a famous leader. Had there been such obedience
as there was command, had we been worthy of the king,
the chroniclers would have to describe a new Polish victory
at Warsaw equal to those at Grünwald and Berestechko.
Speaking briefly, on the first day we beat the Swedes; on
the second, fortune inclined now to one, now to the other,
but still we were uppermost. At that time the Lithuanian
hussars, in which Kovalski served under Prince Polubinski,
a great soldier, went to the attack. When they were passing I saw them I see you this moment, for I was with the
Lauda men on a height near the intrenchments. They were
twelve hundred strong, — men and horses such as the world
had not seen. They passed twenty rods distant from our
flank; and I tell you that the earth trembled under them.
We saw the Brandenburg infantry planting their pikes in
the ground in a hurry, to meet the first onrush. Then
began firing from muskets, till the smoke covered them entirely. We looked. The hussars had given rein to their
horses. O God, what a sweep! They fell into the smoke, —
disappeared! My soldiers began to shout, 'They will break
them, they will break them!' For a while the hussars were
invisible; then something thundered, and there was a sound
as if in a thousand forges men were beating anvils with

hammers. We look. Jesus! Mary! The elector's men are lying like stones on a street, like wheat through which a tempest has passed; and the hussars far away beyond, their streamers glittering. They are bearing down on the Swedes! They struck cavalry; the cavalry were down like a pavement! They struck a second regiment; they left that like a pavement! There was a roar, cannon were thundering; we saw them when the wind bore the smoke aside. They were smashing Swedish infantry. Everything was fleeing, rolling, opening; they went on as if over a highway. They had passed almost through the whole army, when they struck a regiment of the horse-guard, in which was Karl Gustav himself; and like a whirlwind they scattered the horse-guard."

Here Pan Michael stopped, for Kmita had closed his eyes with his fists and was exclaiming, —

"O Mother of God! To see such a thing once and then die!"

"Such an attack my eyes will never see again," continued the little knight. "We too were commanded to spring forward. I saw no more, but what I tell I heard from the mouth of a Swedish officer who was at the side of Karl and saw with his own eyes the end. That Forgell who fell into our hands afterward at Rava, rushed up to Karl. 'O King,' cried he, 'save Sweden! save yourself! Aside, aside! Nothing can stop them!' But Karl answered: 'No use to yield; we must meet them or perish.' Other generals rush up, implore, entreat, in vain. The king moved forward; they strike. The Swedes are broken more quickly than you can count ten. One fell, another was trampled, others were scattered like peas. The king defended himself single-handed. Kovalski rode up and knew Karl Gustav, for he had seen him twice before. A horseman shielded the king; but those who were present said that lightning does not kill more quickly than Kovalski cut him in two. Then the king rushed at Pan Roh.

Volodyovski again interrupted his narrative and breathed deeply; but Kmita cried at once, —

"Oh, finish, or the soul will go out of me!"

"They rushed at each other so that the breasts of the horses struck. They raged. 'I look,' said the officer; 'the king with his horse is on the ground.' He freed himself, touched the trigger of his pistol, missed. The king's hat had fallen. Roh then made for the head of Karl Gustav, — had his sword raised; the Swedes were weak from terror, for there was no time to save Karl, when Boguslav rose as if from under the earth, fired into the very ear of Kovalski, broke his head and his helmet."

" O my God ! he had not time to bring down the sword ? " screamed Pan Andrei, tearing his hair.

" God did not grant him that grace," said Pan Michael. " Zagloba and I talked of what had happened. The man had served with the Radzivills from years of youth; he considered them his masters, and at sight of Radzivill it must be that he was confused. Perhaps the thought had never come to his head to raise a hand on Radzivill. It happens that way ! Well, he paid with his life. Zagloba is a wonderful man, for he is not Roh's uncle at all, and not his relative; still another man would not have been in such despair for a son. And, to tell the truth, there was no reason, for one might envy Kovalski such a glorious death; a noble and a soldier is born to give his life, if not on the present day then on the morrow; men will write of Kovalski, and posterity will celebrate his name."

Pan Michael was silent; after a while he made the sign of the cross and said, —

" Eternal rest give him, O Lord, and may light shine on him forever ! "

" For the ages of ages ! " said Kmita.

Both whispered prayers for a certain time, maybe asking for themselves a similar death, if only not at the hands of Prince Boguslav. At last Pan Michael said, —

" Father Pyekarski assured us that Roh went straight to heaven."

" Of course he did, and our prayers are not needed for him."

" Prayers are always needed; for they are inscribed to the credit of others, and maybe to our own."

" My hope is in the mercy of God," said Kmita, sighing. " I trust that for what I have done in Prussia, even a couple of years will be taken from me in purgatory."

" Everything there is reckoned. What a man works out here with his sabre, the heavenly secretary records."

" I too served with Radzivill," said Kmita, " but I shall not be confused at sight of Boguslav. My God, my God ! Prostki is not far away ! Remember, O Lord, that he is Thy enemy too, for he is a heretic who more than once has blasphemed Thy true faith."

" And is an enemy of the country," added Pan Michael.

'We have hope that his end is approaching. Zagloba, speaking in grief and in tears and as if inspired, foretold the same after that attack of the hussars. He cursed Boguslav so that the hair stood on the head of every man listening. Prince Michael Radzivill, who is marching with us against him, saw also in a dream two golden trumpets, which the Radzivills have on their shield, gnawed by a bear, and he said at once next day, 'Misfortune will meet me or some other Radzivill.'"

"By a bear?" asked Kmita, growing pale.

"By a bear."

Pan Andrei's face became clear as if a gleam of the morning dawn had fallen on it; he raised his eyes, stretched his hands toward heaven and said with a solemn voice, —

"I have a bear on my shield. Praise to Thee, O Lord on high! Praise to Thee, Most Holy Mother! O Lord, O Lord! I am not worthy of this grace."

When he heard this Pan Michael was greatly moved, for he recognized at once that that was an omen from heaven.

"Yendrek!" cried he, "to make sure, press the feet of Christ before the battle; and I will implore him against Sakovich."

"Prostki! Prostki!" repeated Kmita, as in a fever. "When do we move?"

"Before day, and soon it will begin to dawn."

Kmita approached the broken window of the cottage and cried: "The stars are paling already. *Ave, Maria.*"

Then came the distant crowing of a cock, and with it low trumpeting. A few "Our Fathers" later, movement began in the whole village. The clatter of steel was heard, and the snorting of horses. Dark masses of cavalry assembled on the highway.

The air began to be filled with light; a pale gleam was silvering the points of the spears, twinkling on the naked sabres, bringing out of the shade mustached threatening faces, helmets, kolpaks, Tartar sheepskin caps, fur cloaks, quivers. At last the advance with Kmita in the vanguard was moving toward Prostki; the troops stretched in a long line over the road, and marched quickly.

The horses in the first ranks fell to snorting greatly, after them others, as a good portent for the soldiers.

White mists hid the meadows yet, and the fields.

Round about was silence; only land-rails were playing in the grass, wet with dew.

CHAPTER LI.

SEPTEMBER 6, the Polish troops arrived at Vansosh and disposed themselves for rest, so that before battle horses and men might gain strength. Pan Gosyevski, the hetman, decided to halt there four or five days; but events interfered with his reckoning.

Babinich, as a man knowing the boundary well, was sent on a reconnoissance; he was given two light Lithuanian squadrons and a fresh chambul of Tartars, for his own Tartars were over-much wearied.

Gosyevski enjoined on him earnestly, before starting, to obtain an informant and not to return empty-handed. But Babinich merely laughed, thinking to himself that he needed no urging, and that he would bring prisoners, even if he had to find them in the intrenchments of Prostki.

In fact, he returned in forty-eight hours, bringing a number of Prussians and Swedes, and among them an officer of note, Von Rössel, captain in a Prussian regiment under Boguslav.

The party was received in the camp with great applause. There was no need of torturing the captain, for Babinich had already done that on the road by putting the sword-point to his throat. From his statements it transpired that not only the Prussian regiments of Count Waldeck were in Prostki, but also six Swedish regiments under command of Major-General Israel; of these, four were of cavalry under Peters, Frytjotson, Tauben, and Ammerstein, with two of infantry under the brothers Engel. Of Prussian regiments, which were very well equipped, besides that of Count Waldeck himself, there were four, — those of the Prince of Wismar, Bruntsl, Konnaberg, General Wahlrat, — with four squadrons of Boguslav's command, two being of Prussian nobles, and two of his own men.

Supreme command was held by Count Waldeck; in reality, however, he obeyed in everything Prince Boguslav, to whose influence the Swedish general Israel also yielded.

But the most important intelligence given by Rössel was this, — that two thousand chosen infantry of Pomerania were hastening from Elko to reinforce Prostki; but Count Waldeck, fearing lest these men might be taken by the horde, wished to leave the fortified camp, join the Pomeranians, and then make intrenchments a second time. Boguslav, according to Rössel, was so far rather strongly opposed to leaving Prostki, and only during the last days began to incline toward this action. Gosyevski on hearing this news was greatly rejoiced, for he was certain that victory would not miss him. The enemy might defend themselves for a long time in the intrenchments, but neither the Swedish nor the Prussian cavalry could resist the Poles in the open field.

Prince Boguslav seemed to understand this fact as well as Gosyevski, and for this special reason he did not much approve Waldeck's plans. But he was too vain not to yield before even the reproach of excessive caution. Besides, he was not distinguished for patience. It might be reckoned almost with certainty that he would grow weary of waiting in trenches, and would seek fame and victory in the open field. Gosyevski had simply to hasten his advance on the enemy at the moment when they were leaving the intrenchments.

So thought he; so thought other colonels, such as Hassan Bey, who led the horde; Voynillovich, who led the king's regiment; Korsak, a light-horse colonel; Volodyovski, Kotvich, and Babinich. All agreed on one point, — that it was necessary to give up further rest, and march in the night; that is, in a few hours. Meanwhile Korsak sent his banneret, Byeganski, to Prostki to inform the advancing army every hour of what was taking place in the camp. Volodyovski and Babinich took Rössel to their quarters to learn something more of Boguslav. The captain was greatly alarmed at first, for he felt still at his throat Kmita's sabre-point, but wine soon loosened his tongue. Since he had served once in the Commonwealth in a foreign command, he had learned Polish; therefore he was able to answer the questions of the little knight, who did not know German.

"Have you been long in the service of Prince Boguslav?" asked Volodyovski.

"I do not serve in his army," answered Rössel, "but in the elector's regiment, which was put under his command."

"Then do you know Pan Sakovich?"

"I have seen him in Königsberg."

"Is he with the prince?"

"He is not; he remained in Taurogi."

Volodyovski sighed and moved his mustaches. "I have no luck, as usual," said he.

"Be not grieved, Michael," said Babinich. "You will find him; if not, I shall."

Then he turned to Rössel: "You are an old soldier; you have seen both armies, and you know our cavalry of old: what do you think, — on whose side will be victory?"

"If they meet you outside the trenches, on yours; but you cannot take the trenches without infantry and cannon, especially since everything is done there with Radzivill's head."

"Then do you consider him such a great leader?"

"Not only is that my opinion, but it is the general opinion in both armies. They say that at Warsaw the Most Serene King of Sweden followed his advice, and therefore won a great battle. The prince, as a Pole, has a better knowledge of your method of warfare and can manage more quickly. I saw myself that the King of Sweden after the third day of battle embraced him in front of the army and kissed him. It is true that he owed his life to him; for had it not been for the shot of the prince — But it is a terror to think of it! He is besides an incomparable knight, whom no man can meet with any weapon."

"H'm!" said Volodyovski, "maybe there is such a man."

When he had said this, his mustaches trembled threateningly. Rössel looked at him, and grew suddenly red. For a time it seemed that either he would burst a blood-vessel or break into laughter; but at last he remembered that he was in captivity, and controlled himself quickly. But Kmita with his steel eyes looked at him steadily and said, —

"That will be shown to-morrow."

"But is Boguslav in good health?" asked Volodyovski; "for the fever shook him a long time, and must have weakened him."

"He is, and has been this long time, as healthy as a fish, and takes no medicine. The doctor at first wanted to give him many preservatives, but immediately after the first came a paroxysm. Prince Boguslav gave orders to toss that doctor up from sheets; and that helped him, for the doctor himself got a fever from fright."

"To toss him up from sheets?" asked Volodyovski.

"I saw it myself," answered Rössel. "Two sheets were placed one above the other, and the doctor put in the centre of them. Four strong soldiers took the sheets by the corners, and threw up the poor doctor. I tell you, gentlemen, that he went nearly ten ells into the air, and he had hardly come down when they hurled him up again. General Israel, Count Waldeck, and the prince were holding their sides from laughter. Many of the officers too were looking at the spectacle, till the doctor fainted. Then the prince was free of his fever, as if some hand had removed it."

Though Pan Michael and Babinich hated Boguslav, still they could not restrain themselves from laughter when they heard of this joke. Babinich struck his knees and cried, —

"Ah, the scoundrel! how he helped himself!"

"I must tell Zagloba of this medicine," said Pan Michael.

"It cured him of the fever," said Rössel; "but what is that, when the prince does not restrain sufficiently the impulses of his blood, and therefore will not live to ripe age?"

"I think so too," muttered Babinich. "Such as he do not live long."

"Does he give way to himself in the camp?" asked Pan Michael.

"Of course," answered Rössel. "Count Waldeck laughed, saying that his princely grace takes with him waiting-maids. I saw myself two handsome maidens; his attendants told me that they were there to iron his lace — but God knows."

Babinich, when he heard this, grew red and pale; then he sprang up, and seizing Rössel by the arm began to shake him violently.

"Are they Poles or Germans?"

"Not Poles," said the terrified Rössel. "One is a Prussian noblewoman; the other is a Swede, who formerly served the wife of General Israel."

Babinich looked at Pan Michael and drew a deep breath; the little knight was relieved too, and began to move his mustaches.

"Gentlemen, permit me to rest," said Rössel. "I am dreadfully tired, for the Tartar led me ten miles with a lariat."

Kmita clapped his hands for Soroka, and committed the prisoner to him; then he turned with quick step to Pan Michael.

"Enough of this!" said he. "I would rather perish a hundred times than live in this ceaseless alarm and uncertainty. When Rössel mentioned those women just now, I thought that some one was going at my temple with a club."

"It is time to finish!" said Volodyovski, shaking his sabre.

At that moment trumpets sounded at the hetman's quarters; soon trumpets answered in all the Lithuanian squadrons, and pipes in the chambuls.

The troops began to assemble, and an hour later were on the march.

Before they had gone five miles a messenger hurried up from Byeganski of Korsak's squadron, with intelligence for the hetman that a number of troopers had been seized from a considerable body occupied in collecting on that side of the river all the wagons and horses of the peasants. Interrogated on the spot, they acknowledged that the tabor of the whole army was to leave Prostki about eight o'clock in the morning, and that commands were issued already.

"Let us praise God and urge on our horses," said Gosyevski. "Before evening that army will be no longer in existence."

He sent the horde neck and head to push with utmost endeavor between Waldeck's troops and the Pomeranian infantry hastening to aid them. After the horde went Lithuanians; being mainly of the light squadrons, they came right after the horde.

Kmita was in the front rank of the Tartars, and urged on his men till the horses were steaming. On the road he bowed down on the saddle, struck his forehead on the neck of his horse, and prayed with all the powers of his soul,—

"Grant me, O Christ, to take vengeance, not for my own wrongs, but for the insults wrought on the country! I am a sinner; I am not worthy of Thy grace; but have mercy on me! Permit me to shed the blood of heretics, and for Thy praise I will fast and scourge myself every week on this day till the end of my life."

Then to the Most Holy Lady of Chenstohova, whom he had served with his blood, and to his own patron besides, did he commit himself; and strong with such protection, he felt straightway that an immense hope was entering his soul, that an uncommon power was penetrating his limbs, — a power before which everything must fall in the dust. It seemed to him that wings were growing from his shoulders; joy embraced him like a whirlwind, and he flew in front of his Tartars, so that sparks were scattered from under the hoofs of his steed. Thousands of wild warriors bent forward to the necks of their ponies, and shot along after him.

A river of pointed caps rose and fell with the rush of the horses; bows rattled behind the men's shoulders; in front went the sound from the tramp of iron hoofs; from behind flew the roar of the oncoming squadrons, like the deep roar of a great swollen river.

And thus they flew on in the rich starry night which covered the roads and the fields. They were like a mighty flock of ravening birds which had smelled blood in the distance. Fields, oak-groves, meadows, sped past, till at last the waning moon became pale and inclined in the west. Then they reined in their beasts, and halted for final refreshment. It was not farther now than two miles from Prostki.

The Tartars fed their horses with barley from their hands, so that the beasts might gain strength before battle; but Kmita sat on a fresh pony and rode farther to look at the camp of the enemy.

After half an hour's ride he found in the willows the light-horse party which Korsak had sent to reconnoitre.

"Well," asked Kmita, "what is to be heard?"

"They are not sleeping, they are bustling like bees in a hive," answered the banneret. "They would have started already, but have not wagons sufficient."

"Can the camp be seen from some point near at hand?"

"It can from that height which is covered with bushes. The camp lies over there in the valley of the river. Does your grace wish to see it?"

"Lead on."

The banneret put spurs to his horse, and they rode to the height. Day was already in the sky, and the air was filled with a golden light; but along the river on the opposite low bank there lay still a dense fog. Hidden in the bushes, they looked at that fog growing thinner and thinner.

At last about two furlongs distant a square earthwork was laid bare. Kmita's glance was fixed on it with eagerness; but at the first moment he saw only the misty outlines of tents and wagons standing in the centre along the intrenchments. The blaze of fires was not visible; he saw only smoke rising in lofty curls to the sky in sign of fine weather. But as the fog vanished Pan Andrei could distinguish through his field-glass blue Swedish and yellow Prussian banners planted on the intrenchments; then masses of soldiers, cannon, and horses.

Around there was silence, broken only by the rustle of bushes moved by the breeze, and the glad morning twitter of birds; but from the camp came a deep sound.

Evidently no one was sleeping, and they were preparing to march, for in the centre of the intrenchment was an unusual stir. Whole regiments were moving from place to place; some went out in front of the intrenchments; around the wagons there was a tremendous bustle. Cannon also were drawn from the trenches.

"It cannot be but they are preparing to march," said Kmita.

"All the prisoners said: 'They wish to make a junction with the infantry; and besides they do not think that the hetman can come up before evening; and even if he were to come up, they prefer a battle in the open field to yielding that infantry to the knife.'"

"About two hours will pass before they move, and at the end of two hours the hetman will be here."

"Praise be to God!" said the banneret.

"Send to tell our men not to feed too long."

"According to order."

"But have they not sent away parties to this side of the river?"

"To this side they have not sent one. But they have sent some to their infantry, marching from Elko."

"It is well!" said Kmita.

And he descended the height, and commanding the party to hide longer in the rushes, moved back himself with all the breath in his horse to the squadron.

Gosyevski was just mounting when Babinich arrived. The young knight told quickly what he had seen and what the position was; the hetman listened with great satisfaction, and urged forward the squadrons without delay.

Babinich's party went in advance; after it the Lithuanian squadrons; then that of Voynillovich, that of Lauda, the hetman's own, and others. The horde remained behind; for

Hassan Bey begged for that with insistence, fearing that
his men might not withstand the first onset of the heavy
cavalry. He had also another reckoning.

He wished, when the Lithuanians struck the enemy's
front, to seize the camp with his Tartars; in the camp he
expected to find very rich plunder. The hetman permitted
this, thinking justly that the Tartars would strike weakly
on the cavalry, but would fall like madmen on the tabor
and might raise a panic, especially since the Prussian horses
were less accustomed to their terrible howling.

In two hours, as Kmita had predicted, they halted in
front of that elevation from which the scouting-party had
looked into the intrenchments, and which now concealed the
march of all the troops. The banneret, seeing the troops
approaching, sprang forward like lightning with intelligence that the enemy, having withdrawn the pickets from
this side of the river, had already moved, and that the rear
of the tabor was just leaving the intrenchments.

When he heard this, Gosyevski drew his baton from the
holsters of the saddle, and said, —

"They cannot return now, for the wagons block the way.
In the name of the Father, Son, and Holy Ghost! There is
no reason to hide longer!"

He beckoned to the bunchuk-bearer; and he, raising the
horse-tail standard aloft, waved it on every side. At this
sign all the horse-tail standards began to wave, trumpets
thundered, Tartar pipes squeaked, six thousand sabres were
gleaming in the air, and six thousand throats shouted, —

"Jesus! Mary!"

"Allah uh Allah!"

Then squadron after squadron rose in a trot from behind
the height. In Waldeck's camp they had not expected
guests so soon, for a feverish movement set in. The drums
rattled uninterruptedly; the regiments turned with front to
the river.

It was possible to see with the naked eye generals and
colonels flying between the regiments; they hurried to
the centre with the cannon, so as to bring them forward to
the river.

After a while both armies were not farther than a thousand yards from each other. They were divided only by
a broad meadow, in the centre of which a river flowed.
Another moment, and the first streak of white smoke
bloomed out from the Prussian side toward the Poles.

The battle had begun.

The hetman himself sprang toward Kmita's troops, —

"Advance, Babinich! advance in God's name against that line!" And he pointed with his baton to the gleaming regiment of cavalry.

"Follow me!" commanded Pan Andrei. And pressing his horse with spurs, he moved at a gallop toward the river.

More swiftly than an arrow from a bow did they shoot forward. The horses had gained their highest speed, and were running with ears dropped back, and bodies stretched out like the bodies of hounds. The riders bent forward to the manes of their horses, and howling, lashed onward the beasts, which now did not seem to touch earth; they rushed with that impetus into the river. The water did not restrain them, for they came upon a broad ford, level and sandy; they reached the other bank, and sprang on in a body.

Seeing this, the regiment of armored cavalry moved toward them, first at a walk, then at a trot, and did not go faster; but when Kmita's front had come within twenty yards, the command " Fire!" was heard, and a thousand arms with pistols were stretched forward.

A line of smoke ran from one end of the rank to the other; then the two bodies struck each other with a crash. The horses reared at the first blow; over the heads of the combatants glittered sabres through the whole length of the line. A serpent as it were of lightning flew from end to end. The ominous clang of blades against helmets and breastplates was heard to the other side of the river. It seemed as if hammers were ringing in forges on plates of steel. The line bent in one moment into a crescent; for since the centre of the German cavalry yielded, pushed back by the first onset, the wings, against which less force was directed, kept their places. But the armored soldiers did not let the centre be broken, and a terrible slaughter began. On one side enormous men covered with armor resisted with the whole weight of horses; on the other the gray host of Tartars pushed with the force of accumulated impetus, cutting and thrusting with an inconceivable rapidity which only uncommon activity and ceaseless practice can give. As when a host of woodcutters rush at a forest of pine-trees there is heard only the sound of axes, and time after time some lofty tree falls to the ground with a fearful crash, so every moment some one of the cavalry bent his shining head and rolled under his horse. The sabres of Kmita's men glittered in their eyes, cut around their faces, eyes, hands. In vain does a sturdy soldier raise his heavy sword; before he can bring it down, he feels a cold point entering his body; then the sword drops from his hand, and he falls with bloody face on the neck of his horse. When a swarm of wasps attack in an orchard him who is shaking down fruit, vainly does the man ward them off with his hands, try to free himself, dodge aside; they reach his face skilfully, reach his neck, and each one drives into him a sharp sting. So did Kmita's raging men, trained in so many battles, rush forward, hew, cut, thrust, spread terror and death more and more stubbornly, surpassing their opponents as much as a skilful craftsman surpasses the sturdiest apprentice who is wanting in practice. Therefore the German cavalry began to fall more quickly; and the centre, against which Kmita himself was fighting, became so thin that it might break at any moment. Commands of officers, summoning soldiers to shattered places, were lost in the uproar and wild shouting; the line did not come together quickly enough, and Kmita pressed with increasing power. Wearing chain-mail, a gift from Sapyeha, he fought as a simple soldier, having with him the young Kyemliches and Soroka. Their office was to guard their master; and every moment some one of them turned to the right or the left, giving a terrible blow; but Kmita rushed on his chestnut horse to the thickest of the fight, and having all the secrets of Pan Michael, and gigantic strength, he quenched men's lives quickly. Sometimes he struck with his whole sabre; sometimes he barely reached with the point; sometimes he described a small circle merely, but quick as lightning, and a horseman flew head downward under his beast, as if a thunderbolt had hurled him from the saddle. Others withdrew before the terrible man.

At last Pan Andrei slashed the standard-bearer in the temple; he gave forth a sound like that which a cock gives if his throat is cut, and dropped the standard from his hand. At that moment the centre broke, and the disordered wings forming two chaotic bodies fled swiftly to the farther lines of the Prussian army.

Kmita looked through the broken centre into the depth of the field, and saw at once a regiment of red dragoons flying like wind to the aid of the broken cavalry.

" That is nothing ! " thought he ; " Volodyovski will cross the ford in a moment to aid me."

At that instant was heard the thunder of cannon so loud that the earth trembled in its foundations; musketry rattled from the intrenchment to those ranks of the Poles who had pushed forward most. The whole field was covered with smoke, and in that smoke Kmita's volunteers and Tartars closed with the dragoons.

But from the side of the river no one came with assistance.

The enemy had let Kmita pass the ford purposely, and then covered the ford with such a dreadful shower from cannons and muskets that no living foot could pass through it.

The troops of Pan Korsak tried first, and turned back in disorder; next the squadron of Voynillovich went to the middle of the ford, and turned back, — slowly, it is true, for that was the king's regiment, one of the most valiant in the army, but with a loss of twelve noted nobles and nineteen soldiers.

The water in the ford which was the only passage through the river was plashing under the blows of balls as under a dense pouring rain. Cannon-balls flew to the other bank, casting around clouds of sand.

Gosyevski himself rode up on a gallop, and when he had seen this, he knew that it was impossible for one living man to reach the opposite bank.

And still that might decide the fate of the battle. Then the forehead of the hetman frowned sternly. For a while he looked through his glass along the whole line of the enemy's troops, and cried to the orderly, —

" Rush to Hassan Bey ; let the horde pass the deep bank as it can, and strike the tabor. What they find in the wagons will be theirs ! There are no cannon there; it will be only hand to hand."

The horseman sprang forward with what breath was in his horse; but the hetman advanced to where under willows on the meadow stood the Lauda squadron, and halted before it.

Volodyovski was at the head of the squadron, gloomy and silent; but he looked in the eyes of the hetman, and his mustaches quivered.

" What do you think ? " asked the hetman; " will the Tartars cross ?

"The Tartars will cross, but Kmita will perish!" answered the little knight.

"As God lives!" cried the hetman, suddenly; "this Kmita, if he had a head on his shoulders, might win the battle, not perish!"

Volodyovski said nothing; still he thought: "It was necessary either not to send any regiment across the river, or to send five."

The hetman looked awhile yet through his glass at the distant confusion which Kmita was making beyond the river; but the little knight, not being able to endure any longer, drew near him, and holding his sabre-point upward, said, —

"Your worthiness, if there were an order, I would try the ford again."

"Stop!" said Gosyevski, rather sharply; "it is enough that those will perish."

"They are perishing already," replied Volodyovski.

And in truth the uproar was becoming more definite and greater every moment. Evidently Kmita was retreating to the river.

"As God lives, I wanted that!" cried the hetman, suddenly; and he sprang like a thunderbolt to Voynillovich's squadron.

In fact, Kmita was retreating. After they had met the red dragoons, his men fought with their last strength; but the breath was already failing in their breasts, their wearied hands were drooping, and bodies were falling faster and faster; only hope that aid might come any moment from beyond the river kept courage in them yet.

Half an hour more passed, and the cry of "Strike!" was heard no longer; but to the aid of the red dragoons sprang Boguslav's regiment of heavy cavalry.

"Death is coming!" thought Kmita, seeing them approaching from the flank.

But he was a soldier who never had a doubt, for a moment, not only of his life, but of victory. Long and hazardous practice had given him also great knowledge of war; therefore lightning at dusk does not flash and then die out so quickly as the following thought flashed to the head of Pan Andrei: Evidently the Poles could not cross the ford to the enemy; and since they could not, he would lead the enemy to them.

Boguslav's regiment was coming on at full sweep, and not more than a hundred yards distant; in a moment they could strike and scatter his Tartars. Pan Andrei raised the pipe to his mouth, and whistled so shrilly that the nearest dragoon horses rose on their haunches.

That instant other pipes of the Tartar leaders repeated the whistle; and not so swiftly does the whirlwind twist the sand as that chambul turned its horses in flight.

The remnant of the mailed cavalry, the red dragoons, and Boguslav's regiment sprang after them with all speed.

The shouts of the officers — "Naprzod (Forward)!" and "Gott mit uns (God with us)!" — rang like a storm, and a marvellous sight was seen then. Over the broad meadow rushed the disordered and confused chambul of Tartars, straight to the ford, which was rained on with bullets and balls; and they tore onward, as if carried with wings. Every Tartar lay on the horse, flattened himself, hid himself in the mane and the neck, in such fashion that had it not been for the cloud of arrows flying back toward the cavalry, it might be said that the horses were rushing on riderless; after them, with roaring, shouting, and trampling, followed gigantic men, with upraised swords gleaming in their right hands.

The ford was nearer and nearer; there was half a furlong left yet, and evidently the Tartar horses were using their last strength, for the distance between them and the cavalry was quickly decreasing.

A few moments later the front ranks of the pursuers began to cut with their swords the Tartars closing the rear. The ford was right there; it seemed that in a few springs the horses would be in it.

Suddenly something wonderful happened.

Behold, when the chambul had run to the ford, a shrill whistle of pipes was heard again on the wings, and the whole body, instead of rushing into the river to seek safety on the other bank, opened in two, and with the speed of swallows sprang to the right and left, with and against the flow of the river.

But the heavy regiments, rushing right on their shoulders with the highest horse-speed, raced into the ford with the same force, and only when in the water did the horsemen begin to hold in their furious beasts.

The cannon, which up to that moment had been showering a rain of iron on the gravel, were silent in a second; the gunners had to spare their own army.

But Gosyevski was waiting for precisely that instant as for salvation.

The cavalry were hardly in the water when the terrible royal squadron of Voynillovich rushed at it like a hurricane; then the Lauda, the Korsak, the two squadrons of the hetman, and the volunteer squadron; after that, the armored squadron of Prince Michael Radzivill.

A terrible shout, "Kill, slay!" thundered in the air; and before the Prussian regiments could halt, concentrate, use their swords, the Voynillovich squadron had scattered them as a whirl of air scatters leaves; they crushed the red dragoons, pushed back Boguslav's regiment, cut it in two, and drove it over the field toward the main army of Prussia.

In one moment the river was red with blood. The cannon began to play again; but too late, for eight squadrons of Lithuanian cavalry were sweeping with thunder and roar over the meadow, and the whole battle was transferred to the other side of the river.

The hetman was flying with one of his own squadrons, his face radiant with joy, and with fire in his eyes; for once he had the cavalry beyond the river, he was certain of victory.

The squadrons, emulating one another in slashing and thrusting, drove before them the remnant of the dragoons and the cavalry, which fell in a dense body; for the heavy horses were not able to flee swiftly, and merely covered the pursuers against missiles from the front.

Meanwhile Waldeck, Boguslav, Radzivill, and Israel sent forward all their cavalry to restrain the onset, and hastened themselves to put the infantry in line. Regiment after regiment ran out of the tabor, and took their places on the plain. They thrust the butts of their heavy spears into the earth, with the heads pointing forward, inclined like a fence to the enemy.

In the next rank musketeers stretched forward the barrels of their muskets. Between the quadrangles of regiments they placed cannon in hot haste. Neither Boguslav nor Waldeck nor Israel flattered themselves that their cavalry could restrain that of the Poles very long, and their whole hope was in the artillery and the infantry. Meanwhile in front of the infantry the mounted regiments struck breast against breast. But that happened which the Prussian leaders foresaw.

The pressure of the Lithuanian cavalry was so terrible that their opponents could not restrain them for one moment,

and the first hussar regiments split them as a wedge splits
wood, and went without breaking a lance through the dense
mass, as a ship driven by strong wind goes through waves.
The streamers were visible nearer and nearer; at times the
heads of the hussar horses rose above the throng of the
Prussians.

"On your guard!" cried the officers, standing in the
quadrangle of infantry.

At this word the Prussian soldiers braced themselves more
firmly on their feet, and strained their arms holding the
spears; and all hearts were beating violently, for the terrible hussars had come wholly in sight, and were bearing down
straightway against them.

"Fire!" was the word of command.

Muskets rattled in the second and third ranks of the quadrangle. Smoke covered the men. A moment later the roar
of the coming squadron was nearer. They are right there!
All at once, amid the smoke, the first rank of infantry see
there above them, almost over their heads, thousands of
horses' hoofs, wide nostrils, inflamed eyes; a crash of broken
spears is heard; a fearful shout rends the air; Polish voices
shouting, "Slay!" and German voices, "Gott erbarme Dich
meiner (God have mercy on me)!"

That regiment is broken, crushed; but in the spaces between other regiments cannon begin to play. Other squadrons come up. Each one strikes after a moment on a forest
of lances; but perhaps not every one will break the forest
which it strikes, for none has such terrible force as Voynillovich's squadron. Shouting increases on the whole field of
battle. Nothing can be seen; but from the mass of combatants groups of yellow infantry escape in disorder, fleeing
from some regiment which evidently was also beaten.

Horsemen in gray colors pursue, cut, and trample these
men, and shout, —

"Lauda! Lauda!"

That was Volodyovski, who with his squadron had fought
against a second quadrangle.

But others were "sticking" yet; victory might still
incline to the Prussians, especially as at the tabor stood
two regiments intact, which, since the tabor was safe, might
be summoned at any moment.

Waldeck had in truth lost his head. Israel was not present, for he had been sent with the cavalry; but Boguslav
was watching and managing everything. He led the whole

battle, and seeing the increase of great peril, sent Pan Byes for those regiments.

Byes urged on his horse, and half an hour later returned bareheaded, with terror and despair in his face.

"The horde is in the tabor!" shouted he, hurrying up to Boguslav.

At that moment unearthly howling was heard on the right wing; this howling came nearer and nearer.

Suddenly appeared crowds of Swedish horsemen approaching in terrible panic; after them were fleeing weaponless, bareheaded infantry; after the infantry, in confusion and disorder, came wagons drawn by wild and terrified horses. All this mass was rushing at random from the tabor toward the infantry in the meadow. In a moment they fell on the infantry, put them into disorder, scattered them, especially when in front they were pressed by Lithuanian cavalry.

"Hassan Bey has reached the tabor!" cried Gosyevski, with ecstasy; and he let out his last two squadrons like falcons from their rest.

At the same moment that these two squadrons strike the infantry in front, their own wagons rush against them on the flank. The last quadrangles burst as if under the stroke of a hammer. Of the whole brilliant Swedish-Prussian army there is formed one gigantic mass, in which the cavalry are mingled with the infantry. Men are overturning, trampling, and suffocating one another; they throw off their clothing, cast away their arms. The cavalry press them, cut them, crush them, mash them. It is no longer a battle lost; it is a ruin, one of the most ghastly of the war.

Boguslav, seeing that all was lost, resolved to save at least himself and some of the cavalry. With superhuman exertion he collected a few hundred horsemen, and was fleeing along the left wing in the direction of the river's course.

He had already escaped from the main whirl, when Prince Michael Radzivill, leading his own hussars, struck him on the flank and scattered his whole detachment at a blow. After this Boguslav's men fled singly or in small groups. They could be saved only by the speed of their horses.

In fact, the hussars did not pursue, but struck on the main body of infantry, which all the other squadrons were cutting to pieces. The broken detachment fled over the field like a scattered herd of deer.

Boguslav, on Kmita's black steed, is rushing like the wind, striving in vain by cries to gather around him even a few tens of men. No one obeys him; each man flees on his own account, glad that he has escaped from the disaster, and that he has no enemy in front of him.

But rejoicing was vain. They had not gone a thousand yards when howling was heard in front, and a gray host of Tartars sprang forth from the river, near which they had been lurking till then.

This was Kmita with his men. Leaving the field, after he had brought the enemy to the ford, he turned so as to cut off retreat to the fugitives.

The Tartars, seeing the cavalry scattered, scattered themselves in a moment to catch them more easily, and a murderous pursuit began. Two or three Tartars cut off one trooper, and he rarely defended himself; more frequently he seized his rapier by the point, and extended the hilt to the Tartars, calling for mercy. But the Tartars, knowing that they could not lead these prisoners home, took only officers who could give ransom; the common soldiers received a knife in the throat, and died, unable to say even " God ! " Those who fled to the last were stabbed in the back and shoulders; those under whom the horses did not fall were caught with lariats.

Kmita rushed for a time over the field, hurling down horsemen and seeking Boguslav with his eyes; at last he beheld him, and knew him at once by the horse, by the blue ribbon, and the hat with black ostrich feathers.

A cloud of white steam surrounded the prince; for just the moment before two Nogais had attacked him. One he killed with a pistol-shot, and the other he thrust through with a rapier; then seeing a larger party rushing from one side, and Kmita from the other, he pressed his horse with spurs, and shot on like a hunted deer followed by hounds.

More than fifty men rushed in a body after him; but not all the horses ran equally, so that soon the fifty formed a long serpent, the head of which was Boguslav and the neck Kmita.

The prince bent forward in his saddle; the black horse appeared not to touch the earth with his feet, but was black over the green grass, like a swallow sweeping close to the ground; the chestnut stretched his neck like a crane, put back his ears, and seemed as if trying to spring from his skin. Single willows, clumps of them, groups of alder, shot past; the Tartars were behind, a furlong, two, three furlongs, but they ran and ran. Kmita threw his pistols from the holsters to lighten the horse's burden; with eyes fastened on Boguslav, with fixed lips, he almost lay on the neck of the horse, pricked his foaming sides with spurs, till soon the foam falling to the earth became rose-colored.

But the distance between him and the prince not only did not decrease a single inch, but began to increase.

"Woe!" thought Pan Andrei, "no horse on earth can overtake that one."

And when after a few springs the distance increased still more, he straightened himself in the saddle, let the sword drop on its pendant, and putting his hands around his mouth, shouted in a trumpet-like voice: "Flee, traitor, flee before Kmita! I will get you, if not to-day, to-morrow."

These words had barely sounded in the air, when on a sudden the prince, who heard them, looked around, and seeing that Kmita alone was pursuing, instead of fleeing farther described a circle, and with rapier in hand rushed upon him.

Pan Andrei gave forth a terrible cry of joy, and without lessening speed raised his sabre for a blow.

"Corpse! corpse!" shouted the prince; and wishing to strike the more surely, he restrained his horse.

Kmita, when he had come up, held in his own beast till his hoofs sank in the earth, and rapier met sabre.

They closed in such fashion that the two horses formed almost one body. A terrible sound of steel was heard, quick as thought; no eye could catch the lightning-like movement of rapier and sabre, nor distinguish the prince from Kmita. At times Boguslav's hat appeared black, at times Kmita's steel morion gleamed. The horses whirled around each other. The swords clinked more and more terribly.

Boguslav, after a few strokes, ceased to despise his opponent. All the terrible thrusts which he had learned from French masters were parried. Sweat was now flowing freely from his face with the rouge and white; he felt weariness in his right arm already. Wonder seized him, then impatience, then rage; therefore he determined to finish, and he thrust so terribly that the hat fell from his head.

Kmita warded with such force that the prince's rapier flew to the side of the horse; and before Boguslav could defend himself again, Kmita cut him with the very end of the sabre in the forehead.

"Christ!" cried the prince in German, rolling to the earth.

He fell on his back.

Pan Andrei was as if stunned for the moment, but re-covered quickly. He dropped his sabre on its pendant, made the sign of the cross, sprang from his horse, and seizing the hilt, again approached the prince.

He was terrible; for pale as a sheet from emotion, his lips were pressed, and inexorable hatred was in his face.

Behold his mortal enemy, and such a powerful one, lying now at his feet in blood, still alive and conscious, but conquered, and not with foreign weapons nor with foreign aid.

Boguslav looked at him with widely opened eyes, watch-ing carefully every move of the victor; and when Kmita stood there above him, he cried quickly, —

"Do not kill me! Ransom!"

Kmita, instead of answering, stood with his foot on Bogus-lav's breast, and pressed with all his power; then he placed the point of his sabre on the prince's throat so that the skin yielded under the point, — he only needed to move his hand, to press more firmly. But he did not kill him at once. He wished to sate himself yet with the sight, and make the death of his enemy more grievous. He transfixed Bogus-lav's eyes with his own eyes, and stood above him, as a lion stands above an overthrown buffalo.

The prince, from whose forehead blood was flowing more and more copiously, so that the whole upper part of his head was as if in a pool, spoke again, but now with a greatly stifled voice, for the foot of Pan Andrei was crushing his breast, —

"The maiden — listen — "

Barely had Pan Andrei heard these words when he took his foot from Boguslav's breast, and raised his sword.

"Speak!" said he.

But Boguslav only breathed deeply for a time; at last, with a voice now stronger, he said, —

"The maiden will die, if you kill me. The orders are given."

"What have you done with her?" asked Kmita.

"Spare me, and I will give her to you. I swear on the Gospel."

Pan Andrei struck his forehead with his fist. It was to be seen for a time that he was struggling with himself and with his thoughts; then he said, —

"Hear me, traitor! I would give a hundred such degenerate ruffians for one hair of hers. But I do not believe you, you oath-breaker!"

"On the Gospel!" repeated the prince. "I will give you a safe-conduct and an order in writing."

"Let it be so. I will give you your life, but I will not let you out of my hands. You will give me the letter; but meanwhile I will give you to the Tartars, with whom you will be in captivity."

"Agreed," answered Boguslav.

"Remember," said Pan Andrei, "your princely rank did not preserve you from my hand, nor your army, nor your fencing. And be assured that as many times as you cross my path, or do not keep word, nothing will save you, — even though you were made Emperor of Germany. Recognize me! Once I had you in my hands, now you are lying under my feet!"

"Consciousness is leaving me," said the prince. "Pan Kmita, there must be water near by. Give me to drink, and wash my wound."

"Die, parricide!" answered Kmita.

But the prince, secure of life, recovered all his self-command, and said, —

"You are foolish, Pan Kmita. If I die, she too —" Here his lips grew pale.

Kmita ran to see if there was not some ditch near at hand, or even some pool. The prince fainted, but for a short time; he revived, happily for himself, when the first Tartar, Selim, son of Gazi Aga, the banneret among Kmita's Tartars, was coming up, and seeing the enemy weltering in blood, determined to pin him to the earth with the spear-point of the banner. The prince in that terrible moment still had strength sufficient to seize the point, which, being loosely fastened, fell from the staff.

The sound of that short struggle brought back Pan Andrei.

"Stop! son of a dog!" cried he, running from a distance.

The Tartar, at the sound of the familiar voice, pushed up to his horse with fear. Kmita commanded him to go for water, and remained himself with the prince; for from afar were to be seen approaching at a gallop the Kyemliches, Soroka, and the whole chambul, who, after they had caught all the horsemen, came to seek their leader.

Seeing Pan Andrei, the faithful Nogais threw up their caps with loud shouts.

Akbah Ulan sprang from his horse and began to bow to him, touching with his hand his forehead, his mouth, and his breast. Others smacking their lips, in Tartar fashion, looked with greediness into the eyes of the conquered; some rushed to seize the two horses, the chestnut and the black, which were running at a distance each with flying mane.

"Akbah Ulan," said Kmita, "this is the leader of the army which we conquered this morning, Prince Boguslav Radzivill. I give him to you; and do you keep him, for dead or alive they will pay you for him liberally. Now take care of him; put on him a lariat, and lead him to camp."

"Allah! Allah! We thank the leader! We thank the conqueror!" cried all the Tartars in one voice; and again was heard the smacking of a thousand lips.

Kmita mounted and went with a part of the Tartars to the field of battle. From a distance he saw the standard-bearers with their standards, but of the squadrons there were only a few men present; the rest had gone in pursuit of the enemy. Crowds of camp servants were busy on the battle-field, plundering the corpses and fighting here and there with the Tartars, who were plundering also. The latter looked specially terrible, with knives in their hands, and with arms stained to the elbows. You would have said that a flock of crows had dropped from the clouds to the battle-plain. Their wild laughter and shouts were heard over the whole meadow.

Some holding in their lips knives still steaming drew with both hands dead men by the feet; others in sport threw at one another severed heads. Some were filling bags; others, as in a bazaar, were holding up bloody garments, praising their value, or examining the weapons which they had taken.

Kmita passed over the field where he had first met the cavalry. Bodies of men and horses, cut with swords, lay scattered there; but where squadrons had cut infantry, there were whole piles of corpses, and pools of stiffened blood plashed under foot like muddy water in a swamp.

It was difficult to advance through the fragments of

broken lances, muskets, corpses, overturned wagons, and troops of Tartars pushing around.

Gosyevski was still on the intrenchment of the fortified camp, and with him were Prince Michael Radzivill, Voynillovich, Volodyovski, Korsak, and a number of men. From this height they took in with their eyes the field far away to its uttermost edges, and were able to estimate the whole extent of the victory and the enemy's defeat.

Kmita, on beholding these gentlemen, hastened his pace; and Gosyevski, since he was not only a fortunate warrior but an honorable man without a shadow of envy in his heart, had barely seen Pan Andrei, when he cried, —

"Here comes the real victor! He is the cause of winning the day. I first declare this in public. Gracious gentlemen, thank Pan Babinich; for had it not been for him we could not have crossed the river."

"Vivat Babinich!" cried a number of voices. "Vivat, vivat!"

"Where did you learn war, O soldier," cried the hetman, with enthusiasm, "that you know what to do in a moment?"

Kmita did not answer, for he was too tired. He merely bowed on every side, and passed his hand over his face soiled with sweat and with powder-smoke. His eyes gleamed with an uncommon light, and still the vivats sounded incessantly. Division after division returned from the field on foaming horses; and those who came joined their voices from full breasts in honor of Babinich. Caps flew into the air; whoso had a pistol still loaded gave fire.

Suddenly Kmita stood in the saddle, and raising both hands high, shouted, —

"Vivat Yan Kazimir, our lord and gracious father!"

Here there was such a shout as if a new battle had begun. Unspeakable enthusiasm seized all. Prince Michael ungirded his sabre, which had a hilt set with diamonds, and gave it to Kmita. The hetman threw his own costly cloak on the shoulders of the hero, who again raised his hands, —

"Vivat our hetman, victorious leader!"

"May he increase and flourish!" answered all, in a chorus.

Then they brought together the captured banners, and thrust them into the embankment at the feet of the leaders. The enemy had not taken one of theirs. There were Prussian, Prussian of the general militia, nobles',

Swedish, and Boguslav flags ; the whole rainbow of them was waving at the embankment.

"One of the greatest victories of this war!" cried the hetman. "Israel and Waldeck are in captivity, the colonels have fallen or are in captivity, the army is cut to pieces." Here he turned to Kmita : "Pan Babinich, you were on that side, you must have met Boguslav; what has happened to him?"

Here Pan Michael looked diligently into Kmita's eyes, but Kmita said quickly, —

"God has punished Boguslav with this hand."

Then he stretched forth his right hand ; but at that moment the little knight threw himself into his arms.

"Yendrek," cried he, "I am not envious ! May God bless you!"

"You formed my hand!" answered Pan Andrei, with effusion.

But a further expression of brotherly feeling was stopped by Pan Michael Radzivill.

"Is my cousin killed?" asked he, quickly.

"Not killed," answered Kmita, "for I granted him life; but he is wounded and captive, and over there my Nogais are bringing him."

At these words astonishment was depicted on Volodyovski's face, and the eyes of the knight were turned to the plain, on which appeared a party of some tens of Tartars approaching slowly ; at last, when they had passed a group of broken wagons, they came within some tens of yards of the intrenchment.

The hetman and the officers saw that the Tartar riding in advance was leading a prisoner; all recognized Boguslav, but in what a change of fortune!

He, one of the most powerful lords in the Commonwealth ; he, who even yesterday was dreaming of independent rule ; he, a prince of the German Empire, — was walking now with a lariat around his neck, at the side of a Tartar horse, without a hat, with bloody head bound in a filthy rag ! But such was the venom in the hearts of the knights against this magnate that his terrible humiliation did not excite the pity of any, and nearly all mouths shouted at the same moment, —

"Death to the traitor ! Bear him apart on sabres ! Death, death ! "

Prince Michael covered his eyes with his hand, for still

that was a Radzivill led with such humiliation. Suddenly he grew red and shouted, —

"Gracious gentlemen! that is my cousin, that is my blood, and I have spared neither life nor property for the country. He is my enemy who will raise a hand against that ill-fated man."

The knights were silent at once.

Prince Michael was universally beloved for his bravery, liberality, and devotion to the country. Even when all Lithuania fell into the hands of the Northerners, he alone defended himself in Nyesvyej, and in the time of the Swedish wars he contemned the persuasions of Prince Yanush, and was one of the first to join the confederacy of Tyshovtsi. His voice therefore found hearing at once. Finally, it may be that no one wished to oppose so powerful a man; it is enough that the sabres were placed at once in the scabbards, and even some officers, clients of the Radzivills, exclaimed, —

"Take him from the Tartars! Let the Commonwealth judge him, but let not honorable blood be insulted by Pagans."

"Take him from the Tartars!" repeated the prince; "we will find surety, and he will pay the ransom himself. Pan Voynillovich, move your men and let them take him by force, if it is impossible otherwise."

"I offer myself as a surety to the Tartars," said Pan Gnoinski.

Then Volodyovski pushed up to Kmita and said: "Yendrek, what have you done? He will go safely out of this trouble!"

Kmita sprang forward like a wounded wild-cat.

"With the permission of your highness," cried he. "This is my prisoner! I granted him life, but under conditions to which he swore by his heretical gospel; and may I fall dead here if he will go out of the hands into which I gave him before he fulfils everything!"

When he had said this, he struck his horse, blocked the road, and his inborn impulsiveness had almost carried him away; for his face began to writhe, he distended his nostrils, and his eyes began to cast lightning.

Meanwhile Voynillovich pressed him with his horse. "Aside, Pan Babinich!" cried he.

"Aside, Pan Voynillovich!" roared Kmita, and struck with the hilt of his sabre Voynillovich's horse with such force that the steed tottered on his legs as if struck by a ball and dug the ground with his nostrils. Then there rose a fierce shout among the knights, so that Gosyevski pushed forward and cried, —

"Silence, gentlemen! Gracious prince, in virtue of my authority as hetman, I declare that Pan Babinich has a right to the prisoner, and that whoso wishes to free him from Tartar hands must give guarantee to his conqueror."

Prince Michael mastered his indignation, calmed himself, and said, directing his speech to Pan Andrei, —

"Say what you wish."

"That he observe the conditions with me before he leaves captivity."

"But he will keep them when he is free."

"Impossible! I do not believe him."

"Then I swear for him, by the Most Holy Mother, whom I recognize, and on the word of a knight, that all will be observed to you. In the opposite case you may make demand on my honor and property."

"That is sufficient for me!" said Kmita. "Let Pan Gnoinski go as hostage, for otherwise the Tartars will make resistance. I will give way on your word."

"I thank you, Cavalier!" answered Prince Michael. "Do not fear, either, that he will receive his freedom at once, for I will give him to the hetman by right, and he will remain a prisoner until the king pronounces sentence."

"That will be so!" answered the hetman; and ordering Voynillovich to sit on a fresh horse, for that one was hardly able to stand, he sent him with Pan Gnoinski for the prince.

But the affair did not pass easily yet; for Hassan Bey made a terrible resistance, and only the sight of Pan Gnoinski and the promise of a ransom of a hundred thousand thalers could pacify him.

In the evening Prince Boguslav found himself in the tents of Gosyevski. He was cared for with attention; two physicians did not leave him for a moment, and both guaranteed his life, for the wound, since it had been given with the very end of the sabre, was not too serious.

Volodyovski could not forgive Kmita for having granted the prince his life, and from sorrow avoided him all day. It was only in the evening that Pan Andrei himself went to Pan Michael's tent.

"Fear the wounds of God!" cried the little knight, at sight of him; "I should have expected this of any other than of you, to let that traitor go alive!"

"Listen to me, Michael, before you condemn me," said Kmita, gloomily. "I had him under my foot and held my sabre point at his throat, and then do you know what the traitor said ? That there were commands given to kill Olenka in Taurogi if he should be slain. What had I, unfortunate man, to do ? I purchased her life with his life. What had I to do ? By the cross of Christ, what had I to do ? "

Here Pan Andrei began to pull his hair, to stamp, from bewilderment; and Volodyovski thought for a while, then said, —

"I understand your despair; but still — you see, you have let go a traitor who may bring grievous suffering to the country. There is no denying, Yendrek, that you have rendered wonderful service to-day; but at last you sacrificed the public good to your own private ends."

"And what would you have done if you were told that there was a knife at the throat of Panna Anusia ? "

Pan Michael's mustaches quivered fiercely. "I do not offer myself as an example. H'm! what would I have done ? But Pan Yan, who has a Roman soul, would not have let him live; and besides, I am certain that God would not have let innocent blood flow for the reason he mentioned."

"Let me do penance. Punish me, O God, not according to my heavy sin, but according to Thy mercy; for to sign a sentence against that dove — " Here Kmita closed his eyes. "Angels forefend! Never, never ! "

"It is passed," said Volodyovski.

Here Pan Andrei took a paper out of his bosom. "See, Michael, what I obtained. This is a command to Sakovich, to all the officers of Radzivill, and to the Swedish commandants. We forced him to write it, though he could barely move his hand. Prince Michael himself saw to that. This is freedom for her, safety for her. I will lie in the form of a cross every day for a year, I will have myself scourged, I will build a church, but I will not sacrifice her life. I have not a Roman soul. Well, I am not a Cato like Pan Yan, true! But I will not sacrifice her; no, by a hundred thunders, I will not, even if at last I am roasted in hell on a spit — "

Kmita did not finish, for Pan Michael sprang up to him and stopped his mouth with his hand, crying in a terrified voice, —

"Do not blaspheme, for you will draw the vengeance of God on her. Beat your breast, quickly, quickly! "

And Pan Andrei began to beat his breast: "Mea culpa! mea culpa! mea maxima culpa!" At last the poor soldier burst into loud weeping, for he did not know himself what to do.

Pan Michael let him have his cry out; then he pacified him, and asked, —

"And what will you undertake now?"

"I will go with my men whither I am sent, as far as Birji. Only let the men and horses draw breath first. On the road I will shed as much heretical blood as I can, to the glory of God."

"And you will have your merit. Do not lose heart, Yendrek. God is merciful!"

"I will go directly ahead. All Prussia is open at present; only here and there shall I light upon small garrisons."

Pan Michael sighed: "Oh, I would go with you as gladly as to paradise. But I must keep my command. You are fortunate to lead volunteers. Yendrek, listen, brother! and when you find both, take care of that one, so that no evil befall her. God knows, she may be predestined to me."

When he had said this, the little knight cast himself into the arms of Pan Andrei.

CHAPTER LII.

OLENKA and Anusia, having freed themselves from Tau-rogi, under the protection of Braun, came successfully to the sword-bearer's party, which at that time was near Olsha, therefore not very far from Taurogi.

The old noble when he saw them both in good health would not believe his eyes at first; then he fell to weep-ing from delight, and finally came to such military enthusi-asm that for him danger existed no longer. Let not only Boguslav appear, but the King of Sweden himself with all his power, Pan Billevich was ready to defend his maidens against every enemy.

"I will fall," said he, "before a hair shall drop from your heads. I am no longer the man whom you knew in Taurogi, and I think that the Swedes will long remember Girlakole, Yasvoynya, and those beatings which I gave them at Ros-syeni itself. It is true that the traitor Sakovich attacked us unawares and routed us, but you see several hundred sabres on service."

Pan Billevich did not exaggerate greatly, for in truth it was difficult to recognize in him the former prisoner of Taurogi fallen in courage. He had another mind now; his energy had revived in the field, on his horse; he found himself in his element, and being a good soldier, he had really handled the Swedes several times roughly. And since he had great authority in the neighborhood, the nobles and common people flocked to him willingly, and even from some remote districts a Billevich brought him now between ten and twenty horsemen, now some tens of horsemen.

Pan Tomash's party was composed of three hundred peas-ant infantry and about five hundred horsemen. It was rare that any man in the infantry had a gun; the greater number were armed with scythes and forks. The cavalry was a col-lection of the wealthier nobles, who betook themselves to the forest with their attendants, and of the poorer nobles from villages. Their arms were better than those of the infantry, but greatly varied. Hop-poles served as lances for many; some carried rich family weapons, but frequently of a past age; the horses, of various breeds and quality, were not fitted for one rank.

With such troops the sword-bearer could block the road to Swedish patrols, he might cut off even detachments of cavalry, he might clear forests and villages of plunderers, whose numerous bands, composed of Swedish fugitives, Prussian and local ruffians, were busied with robbery; but he could not attack any town.

The Swedes had grown wiser. Immediately after the outbreak of the rebellion those who were scattered in quarters in the villages were cut down throughout Jmud and Lithuania; but now those who had survived remained mostly in fortified towns, which they left only for short expeditions. Therefore the fields, forests, hamlets, and smaller towns were in Polish hands; but the larger towns were held by Swedes, and there was no power to dislodge them.

The sword-bearer's party was one of the best; others could effect still less than he. On the boundary of Livonia the insurgents had grown so bold, it is true, that they besieged Birji twice, and at the second attack it was forced to surrender; but that temporary preponderance came from this, — that Pontus de la Gardie had assembled to the defence of Riga against the forces of the Tsar all the troops from the neighboring districts of Livonia.

His brilliant victories, rarely equalled in history, caused the belief, however, that war in that quarter would soon be at an end, and that he would bring to Jmud new Swedish troops intoxicated with triumphs. Still there was safety enough in the forests at that time; and numerous parties of insurgents capable of undertaking little alone might still be certain that the enemy would not seek them in deep wildernesses.

Therefore Pan Billevich rejected the thought of hiding in Byalovyej; for the road to it was very long, and on the way were many considerable places with large garrisons.

"The Lord God has given a dry autumn," said he to the maidens, "therefore it is easier to live *sub Jove* (in the open air). I will have a regular tent made for you; I will find a woman to wait on you, and you will stay in the camp. In these times there is no safer refuge than the forest. My Billeviche is burned to the ground; country houses are infested by ravagers and sometimes even by Swedish parties.

Where could you incline your heads more safely than with me, who have several hundred sabres at my command? Rains will come later, then some cabin will be found for you in the forest."

This idea pleased Panna Anusia greatly; for in the party were many young Billeviches, polite cavaliers, and besides it was said continually that Pan Babinich was marching in that direction.

Anusia hoped that when he came he would drive out the Swedes in a twinkle, and then — then would be what God would give. Olenka judged also that it was safest with the party; but she wished to retreat far from Taurogi, fearing the pursuit of Sakovich.

"Let us go to Vodokty," said she; "there we shall be among our own people. Although it is burned, Mitruny and all the neighboring villages are there. It is impossible that the whole country is turned into a desert. Lauda will defend us in case of danger."

"But all the Lauda men have gone with Volodyovski," said Yur Billevich, in opposition.

"The old men and the youths have remained, and even the women there are able to defend in case of need. Besides, forests are greater there than here; the Domasheviches, the hunters, or the Smoky Gostyeviches will take us to Rogovsk, where no enemy will find us."

"And when I have secured the camp and you, I will attack the Swedes, and cut to pieces those who dare to touch the rim of the wilderness," said Pan Billevich. "This is an excellent idea! We have nothing to do here; it is possible to render greater service."

Who knows whether the sword-bearer did not seize that idea of Olenka so quickly because he too in his soul was somewhat afraid of Sakovich, who, brought to despair, might be terrible?

The advice, however, was wise in itself; therefore it pleased all immediately. The sword-bearer sent out infantry that very day under command of Yur Billevich, so as to push forward by the forest in the direction of Krakinov; but he went forward himself with the cavalry two days later, obtaining in advance reliable intelligence as to whether there had not gone out from Kyedani or Rossyeni, between which he had to march, some considerable bodies of Swedish troops.

Pan Billevich marched slowly and carefully. The ladies

travelled in peasants' wagons, and sometimes on ponies
which the sword-bearer had provided.

Anusia, who had received as a gift from Yur Billevich a
light sabre, hung it bravely at her side, and in a cap, placed
jauntily on her head, brought up the squadron like some
captain. The march amused her, the sabres glittering in
the sun, and the fires disposed around at night. Young
officers and soldiers were greatly pleased with the lady,
and she shot her eyes around in every direction on the
march; she let her tresses fall so as to braid them three
times daily over the banks of bright brooks, which for her
took the place of a mirror. She said often that she wished
to see a battle, so as to give an example of bravery; but in
very truth she did not want a battle at all. She wanted
only to subdue the hearts of all the young warriors; in fact,
she did subdue an unreckoned number of them.

Olenka too revived again, as it were, after leaving Taurogi.
There the uncertainty of her future and continual fear were
killing her; now in the depths of the forest she felt safer.
The wholesome air brought back her strength. The sight
of soldiers, of weapons, the movement and bustle of camp
life, acted like balsam on her wearied soul. And the march
of troops acted agreeably on her also; possible dangers did
not alarm her in the least, for knightly blood was in her
veins. Appearing less frequently before the soldiers, not
permitting herself to gallop on a pony in front of the ranks,
she attracted fewer glances, but general respect surrounded
her. The mustached faces of the soldiers were laughing at
sight of Anusia; heads were uncovered when Olenka drew
near the fires. That was changed later to homage. But it
did not pass without this, — that some heart beat for her in
a youthful breast; but eyes did not dare to gaze at her so
directly as at that brunette of the Ukraine.

They advanced through forests and thickets, often sending scouts ahead; and only on the seventh day did they
arrive late at night in Lyubich, which, lying on the border
of the Lauda region, formed as it were the entrance to it.
The horses were so tired that in spite of Olenka's opposition it was impossible to go farther; Billevich therefore
forebade the lady to find fault, and disposed his party for
the halt. He himself with the young ladies occupied the
house, for the night was foggy and very cold. By a marvellous chance the house had not been burned. The enemy
had spared it probably through the command of Prince

Yanush Radzivill, because it was Kmita's; and though the prince learned later of Pan Andrei's secession, he forgot or had not time to give a new order. The insurgents considered the estate as belonging to the Billeviches; the ravagers did not dare to plunder near Lauda. Therefore nothing had changed in it. Olenka went under that roof with a terrible feeling of bitterness and pain. She knew every corner there, but almost with each one was bound up some memory of Kmita's betrayal. Before her is the dining-hall ornamented with the portraits of the Billeviches and with skulls of wild beasts of the forest; the skulls cracked with bullets are still on the nails; the portraits slashed with sabres are gazing from the walls, as if wishing to say, "Behold, O maiden! behold, our granddaughter! it was he who slashed with sacrilegious hand the pictures of our earthly forms, now resting long in their graves."

Olenka felt that she could not close an eye in that branded house. It seemed to her that in the dark corners of the rooms were prowling around yet the ghosts of those terrible comrades breathing fire from their nostrils. And how quickly that man, so loved by her, had passed from violence to transgression, from transgression to crimes, from the slashing of portraits to profligacy, to the burning of Upita and Volmontovichi, to carrying her off from Vodokty; further to the service of Radzivill, to treason, crowned with the promise of raising his hand against the king, against the father of the whole Commonwealth!

The night went on swiftly, but sleep did not seize the lids of unhappy Olenka. All the wounds of her soul were reopened and began to burn painfully. Shame again was scorching her cheeks; her eyes dropped no tears in that time, but immeasurable grief surrounded her heart, because it could not find place within that poor heart. Grief for what? For what might have been had he been other, — if with his bad habits, wildness, and violence, he had even had an honest heart; if finally he had even a measure in his crimes, if there existed some boundary over which he was incapable of passing? And her heart would have forgiven so much.

Anusia saw the suffering of her companion, and understood the cause; for the old sword-bearer had detailed the whole history to her previously. Since she had a kind heart, she came up to Panna Billevich, and throwing her arms around her neck, said, —

"Olenka, you are writhing from pain in this house."

Olenka at first did not wish to speak; then her whole body trembled like an aspen leaf, and at last a terrible, despairing cry burst from her bosom. Seizing Anusia's hand convulsively, she rested her bright head on that maiden's shoulder; sobbing now tore her as a whirlwind tears a thicket.

Anusia had to wait long before it passed; at last she whispered when Olenka was pacified somewhat, "Let us pray for him."

Olenka covered her eyes with both hands. "I — cannot," said she, with an effort.

After a while, gathering back feverishly the hair which had fallen on her forehead, she began to speak with a gasping voice, —

"You see — I cannot — You are happy; your Babinich is honorable, famous, before God and the country. You are happy; I am not free even to pray — Here, everywhere, is the blood of people, and here are burned ruins. If at least he had not betrayed the country, if he had not undertaken to sell the king! I had forgiven everything before, in Kyedani; for I thought — for I loved him with my whole heart. But now I cannot — O merciful God! I cannot! I could wish not to live myself, and that he were not living."

"It is permitted to pray for every soul," said Anusia; "for God is more merciful than men, and knows reasons which often men do not know."

When she had said this, Anusia knelt down to pray, and Olenka threw herself on the floor in the form of a cross, and lay thus till daybreak.

Next morning the news thundered through the neighborhood that Pan Billevich was in Lauda. At that news all who were living came forth with greeting. Therefore out of the neighboring forests issued decrepit old men, and women with small children. For two years no one had sowed any seed, no one had ploughed any land. The villages were partly burned and were deserted. The people lived in the forests. Men in the vigor of life had gone with Volodyovski or to various parties; only youths watched and guarded the remnant of cattle, and guarded well, but under cover of the wilderness.

They greeted the sword-bearer then as a savior, with a great cry of joy; for to those simple people it seemed that

if the sword-bearer had come and the "lady" was returning to the ancient nest, then there must be an end to war
and disasters. In fact, they began at once to return to the
villages, and to drive out the half-wild cattle from the
deepest forest inclosures.

The Swedes, it is true, were not far away, defended by
intrenchments in Ponyevyej; but in presence of Billevich's
forces and other neighboring parties which might be summoned in case of need, less attention was paid to them.

Pan Tomash even intended to attack Ponyevyej, so as to
clear out the whole district; but he was waiting for more
men to rally to his banner, and waiting especially till guns
were brought to his infantry. These guns the Domasheviches had secreted in considerable number in the forest;
meanwhile he examined the neighborhood, passing from
village to village.

But that was a gloomy review at Vodokty. The mansion
was burned, and half the village; Mitruny in like manner;
Volmontovichi of the Butryms, which Kmita had burned
in his time, and which had been rebuilt after the fire, by
a marvellous chance was untouched; but Drojeykani and
Mozgi of the Domasheviches was burned to the ground;
Patsuneli was half consumed, and Morezi altogether. Goshchuni experienced the harshest fate; for half the people
were cut to pieces, and all the men to boys of a few years
had their hands cut off by command of Colonel Rossa.

So terribly had war trampled those neighborhoods! such
were the results of the treason of Yanush Radzivill!

But before Billevich had finished his review and stationed his infantry, fresh tidings came, at once joyful and
terrible, which rang with thousand-fold echo from cottage
to cottage.

Yurek Billevich, who had gone with a few tens of horses
on a reconnoissance to Ponyevyej and had seized some
Swedes, was the first to learn of the battle at Prostki.
Then every report brought more details, so wondrous that
they resembled a fable.

Pan Gosyevski, it was said, had routed Count Waldeck,
Israel, and Prince Boguslav. The army was cut to pieces,
the leaders in captivity. All Prussia was blazing in one
conflagration.

A few weeks later the mouths of men began to repeat one
terrible name, — the name of Babinich.

Babinich, said they, was the main cause of the victory at

Prostki. Babinich cut down with his own hand and captured Prince Boguslav. The next news was: "Babinich is burning Electoral Prussia, is advancing like death toward Jmud, slaying, leaving behind only earth and sky."

Then came the end: "Babinich has burned Taurogi. Sakovich has fled before him, and is hiding in forests." The last event had happened too near to remain long in doubt. In fact, the news was verified perfectly.

Anusia during the whole time that news was arriving lived as if dazed; she laughed and wept in turn, stamped her feet when no one believed, and repeated to every one, whether that one would listen or not, —

"I know Pan Babinich. He brought me from Zamost to Pan Sapyeha. He is the greatest warrior in the world. I do not know whether Pan Charnyetski is his equal. He is the man who serving under Sapyeha crushed Boguslav utterly in the first campaign. He — I am sure that it is no other — conquered him at Prostki. Yes, he can finish Sakovich and ten like Sakovich ; and he will sweep out the Swedes in a month from all Jmud."

In fact, her assurances began to be justified speedily. There was not the least doubt that the terrible warrior called Babinich had moved forward from Taurogi toward the northern country.

At Koltyni he defeated Colonel Baldon and cut his troops to pieces ; at Varni he scattered the Swedish infantry, which retreated before him at Telshi ; at Telshi he won a greater victory over two colonels, Norman and Hudenskiöld, in which the latter fell, and Norman with the survivors did not halt till he reached Zagori, on the very boundary of Jmud.

From Telshi Babinich marched to Kurshani, driving before him smaller divisions of Swedes, who took refuge in haste with the more important garrisons.

From Taurogi and Polangi to Birji and Vilkomir the name of the victor was ringing. They told of the cruelties which he permitted himself against the Swedes. It was said that his forces, composed at first of a small chambul of Tartars and little squads of volunteers, increased day after day ; for all who were living rushed to him, all parties joined him, but he bound them in bonds of iron and led them against the enemy.

Minds were so far occupied by his victories that tidings of the defeat which Pan Gosyevski had sustained from Steinbock at Filipovo passed almost without an echo.

Babinich was nearer, and with Babinich they were more occupied.

Anusia implored Billevich daily to advance and join the great warrior. Olenka supported her; all the officers and nobles urged, excited by curiosity alone.

But to join the warrior was not easy. First, Babinich was in another district; second, he often disappeared, and was not heard of for weeks, and then appeared again with news of a new victory; third, all the Swedish soldiers and garrisons, protecting themselves from him, had stopped the road with large forces; finally, beyond Rossyeni a considerable body of troops had appeared under Sakovich, of whom tidings were brought saying that he was destroying everything before him, and torturing people terribly while questioning them concerning Billevich's party.

The sword-bearer not only could not march to Babinich, but he feared that it would soon be too narrow for him near Lauda. Not knowing himself what to begin, he confided to Yurek Billevich that he intended to withdraw to the forest of Rogovsk on the east. Yurek immediately gave this information to Anusia, and she went straight to the sword-bearer.

"Dearest uncle," said she, for she always called him uncle when she wanted to gain something from him, "I hear that we have to flee. Is it not a shame for so celebrated a warrior to flee at the mere report of an enemy?"

"Your ladyship must thrust your three coppers into everything," said the anxious sword-bearer. "This is not your affair."

"Very well, then, retreat, but I will stay here."

"So that Sakovich will catch you, — you'll see!"

"Sakovich will not catch me, for Pan Babinich will defend me."

"Especially when he knows where you are. I have said already that we are unable to go to him."

"But he can come to us. I am his acquaintance; if I could only send a letter to him, I am certain he would come here, after he had beaten Sakovich. He loved me a little, and he would come to rescue me."

"But who will undertake to carry a letter?"

"It can be sent through the first peasant that comes."

"It will do no harm, it will do no harm; in no case will it do harm. Olenka has quick wit, but neither are you without it. Even if we had to retreat to the woods this moment before superior force, it would still be well to have Babinich come to these parts, for we can then join him more easily. Try! Messengers will be found, and trusty men."

The delighted Anusia began to try so well that that same day she found two messengers, — and not peasants; for one was Yurek Billevich, the other Braun. Each was to take a letter of the same contents as that which the other carried, so that if one failed the other might deliver the missive to Babinich. With the letter itself Anusia had more trouble; but at last she wrote it in the following words: —

" In the last extremity I write to you. If you remember me, though I doubt if you do, come to rescue me. By the kindness which you showed me on the road from Zamost, I dare to hope that you will not leave me in misfortune. I am in the party of Pan Billevich, the sword-bearer of Rossyeni, who gave me refuge because I brought his relative, Panna Billevich, out of captivity in Taurogi. And him and us both the enemy, namely, the Swedes, have surrounded on every side, and a certain Pan Sakovich, before whose sinful importunities I had to flee and seek safety in the camp. I know that you did not love me, though God sees that I did you no harm. I wished you well, and I shall wish you well from my whole heart. But though you do not love, rescue a poor orphan from the savage hand of the enemy. God will reward you for it a hundred fold, and I will pray for you, whom to-day I call only my good protector, but hereafter my savior."

When the messengers were leaving the camp, Anusia, considering to what dangers they were exposed, was alarmed, and at last wished to stop them. Even with tears in her eyes she began to implore the sword-bearer not to permit them to go; for peasants might carry the letters, and it would be easier for the peasants to deliver them.

But Braun and Yurek Billevich were so stubborn that no remonstrance could avail. One wished to surpass the other in readiness to serve, but neither foresaw what was awaiting him. A week later Braun fell into the hands of Sakovich, who gave command to flay him; but poor Yurek was shot beyond Ponyevyej while fleeing before a Swedish party.

Both letters fell into the hands of the enemy.

CHAPTER LIII.

SAKOVICH, after he had seized and flayed Braun, arranged at once a joint attack on the Billevich party with Hamilton, the commandant of Ponyevyej, an Englishman in the Swedish service.

Babinich had just disappeared somewhere in the forest, and for a number of days no report of him had come. But Sakovich would not have regarded him, even had he been in the neighborhood. He had, it is true, in spite of all his daring, a certain instinctive dread of Babinich; but this time he was ready to perish himself, if he could accomplish his vengeance. From the time of Anusia's flight rage had not ceased for a moment to tear his soul. Deceived calculations, and wounded love especially, brought him to frenzy; and besides the heart was suffering in him. At first he wished to marry Anusia only for the property willed her by her first betrothed, Pan Podbipienta; but later he fell in love with her blindly, and to the death, as only such a man can fall in love. And it went so far that he who feared no one on earth save Boguslav, he before whose glance alone people grew pale, gazed like a dog into the eyes of that maiden, yielded to her, endured her caprices, carried out all her wishes, strove to divine her thoughts.

She used and abused her influence, deluding him with words, with a look; used him as a slave, and finally betrayed him.

Sakovich was of those men who consider that only as good and virtuous which is good for them, and as evil and criminal that which brings them harm. In his eyes, therefore, Anusia had committed the most terrible crime, and there was no punishment sufficiently great for her. If the mishap had met another, the starosta would have laughed and jeered at the man; but when it touched his own person, he roared as a wounded wild beast, and thought only of vengeance. He wished to get the guilty woman into his hands, dead or alive. He would have preferred her alive, for then he could exercise a cavalier's vengeance before her death; but if the maiden had to fall in time of attack, he cared little, if only she did not come into possession of another.

Wishing to act with certainty, he sent a bribed man to the sword-bearer with a letter as if from Babinich, in which he announced, in the name of the latter, that he would be in Volmontovichi in the course of a week.

Billevich believed easily, trusting therefore in the invincible power of Babinich; and he made no secret of the arrangement. He not only took up his headquarters for good in Volmontovichi, but by the announcement of the news he attracted almost all the population of Lauda. What remained of it assembled from the forests, — first, because the end of autumn had come, and there were heavy frosts; and second, through pure curiosity alone to see the great warrior.

Meanwhile, from the direction of Ponyevyej marched toward Volmontovichi Hamilton's Swedes, and from the direction of Kyedani was stealing forward in wolf-fashion Sakovich.

But Sakovich had no suspicion that on his tracks was advancing in wolf-fashion also a third man, who without invitation had the habit of coming where people expected him least.

Kmita knew not that Olenka was with the Billevich party. In Taurogi, which he ruined with fire and sword, he learned that she had gone with Anusia; but he supposed that they had gone to Byalovyej, where Pan Yan's wife was in hiding as well as many other noble women. He might the more easily suppose this, since he knew that Billevich had long intended to take his niece to those impassable forests.

It tortured Pan Andrei immensely that he had not found her in Taurogi, but at the same time he was glad that she had escaped from the hands of Sakovich, and would find safe refuge till the end of the war.

Not being able to go for her at once to the wilderness, he determined to attack and destroy the enemy in Jmud, until he had crushed them completely. And fortune went with him. For a month and a half victory followed victory; armed men rushed to him in such numbers that soon his chambul was barely one fourth of his force. Finally, he drove the enemy out of all western Jmud; but hearing of Sakovich, and having old scores to settle with the starosta, he set out for his own former district, and followed him. In this way both were now drawing near Volmontovichi.

Billevich, who at first had taken a position not far from the village, had been living there a week, and the thought did not even come to his head that he would soon have such terrible guests. One evening the youthful Butryms, herding horses beyond Volmontovichi, informed him that troops had issued from the forest, and were advancing from the south. Billevich was too old and experienced a soldier not to take precautions. Some of his infantry, partly furnished with fire-arms by the Domasheviches, he placed in the houses recently rebuilt, and some he stationed at the gate; with the cavalry he took possession himself of a broad pasture somewhat in the rear, beyond the fences, and which touched with one side the river. He did this mainly to gain the praise of Babinich, who must understand skilful dispositions; the place he had chosen was really a strong one.

After Kmita had burned Volmontovichi, in vengeance for the slaughter of his comrades, the village was rebuilt by degrees; but as later on the Swedish war had stopped work on it, a multitude of beams, planks, and boards were lying on the principal street. Whole piles of them rose up near the gate; and infantry, even slightly trained, might make a protracted defence from behind them.

In every case the infantry protected the cavalry from the first onset. Billevich was so eager to exhibit his military skill to Babinich, that he sent forward a small party to reconnoitre.

What was his amazement, and at the first moment alarm, when from a distance and beyond the grove there came to him the sound of musketry; then his party appeared on the road, but coming at a gallop, with a crowd of enemies at its shoulders.

The sword-bearer sprang at once to the infantry to give final orders; but from the grove rushed forth dense groups of the enemy, and advanced locust-like toward Volmontovichi, with arms glittering in the setting sun.

The grove was near. When they had approached somewhat, the cavalry pushed forward at once on a gallop, wishing to pass the gate at a blow; but the sudden fire of the infantry stopped them on the spot. The first ranks fell back, and even in considerable disorder; only a few brought their horses' breasts to the defences.

The sword-bearer recovered meanwhile, and galloping to

the cavalry ordered all who had pistols or guns to advance to the aid of the infantry.

Evidently the enemy were equally provided with muskets; for after the first onset they began a very violent, though irregular fire.

From both sides it thundered now more quickly, now more slowly; the balls whistling came up to the cavalry, struck on the houses, fence, piles of timber; the smoke rose over Volmontovichi, the smell of powder filled the street.

Anusia had what she wanted, — a battle. Both ladies mounted ponies at the first moment, by command of Billevich, so that at a given signal they might retreat with the party should the enemy's forces turn out too great. They were stationed therefore in the rear ranks of the cavalry.

But though Anusia had a small sabre at her side and a lynx-skin cap on her head, her soul fled at once into her arms. She who knew so well how to take counsel in peace with officers, had not one pinch of energy when she had to stand eye to eye with the sons of Bellona in the field. The whistle and knocking of balls terrified her; the uproar, the racing of orderlies, the rattle of muskets, and the groans of the wounded took away her presence of mind, and the smell of powder stopped the breath in her breast. She grew faint and weak, her face became pale as a kerchief, and she squirmed and whimpered like a little child, till young Pan Olesha from Kyemnar had to hold her by the arms. He held her firmly, more firmly than was needed; and he was ready to hold her in that way to the end of the world.

The soldiers around her began to laugh. "A knight in petticoats!" called voices. "Better set hens and pluck feathers!" Others cried: "Pan Olesha, that shield has come to your arm; but Cupid will shoot you all the more easily through it!" And good-humor seized the soldiers.

But others preferred to look at Olenka, who bore herself differently. At first, when bullets flew past at some distance she grew pale too, not being able to forbear inclining her head and closing her eyes; but later knightly blood began to act in her, then with face flushed like a rose she reared her head and looked forward with fearless eye. Her distended nostrils drew in as it were with pleasure the smell of powder. Since the smoke grew thicker and thicker at the gate and decreased the view greatly, the daring lady, seeing that the officers were advancing, went with them, to

follow more accurately the course of battle, not even thinking of what she was doing.

In the throng of cavalry there rose a murmur of praise.

"Oh, that is blood! that is the wife for a soldier; she is
the right kind of volunteer!"

"Vivat Panna Billevich!"

"Let us hasten, gracious gentlemen, for it is worth
while before such eyes."

"The Amazons did not meet muskets better!" cried one
of the younger men, forgetting in his enthusiasm that the
Amazons lived before the invention of powder.

"It is time to finish. The infantry have borne themselves well, and the enemy are seriously shattered!"

In fact, the enemy could do nothing with their cavalry.
Every moment they urged on their horses, attacked the
gate, but after a salvo drew back in disorder. And as a
wave which has fallen upon the flat shore leaves behind
mussels, stones, and dead fish, so after each attack a number of bodies of horses and men were left on the road
before the gate.

At last the onsets ceased. Only volunteers came up, firing in the direction of the village with pistols and guns
rather thickly, so as to occupy the attention of Billevich's
men. But the sword-bearer, coming out along the gutter
of the house, saw a movement in the rear ranks of the
enemy toward the fields and thickets extending along the
left side of Volmontovichi.

"They will try from that side!" cried he; and sent immediately a part of the cavalry between the houses so as
to give resistance to the enemy from the gardens.

In half an hour a new battle was begun on the left wing
of the party and also with fire-arms. The fenced gardens
rendered difficult a hand-to-hand struggle, and equally difficult for both sides.

The enemy, however, being extended over a longer line,
were less exposed to bullets.

The battle was becoming more stubborn and more active, and the enemy did not cease to attack the gate.

Billevich was growing uneasy. On the right flank he
had a field behind him still free, ending with a stream not
very wide, but deep and swampy, through which a passage,
especially if in haste, might be difficult. In one place only
was there a trodden road to a flat shore along which villagers drove cattle to the forest.

The sword-bearer began to look around oftener toward that side. All at once among willows which could be seen through, for they had lost their leaves, he saw in the evening light glittering weapons and a dark cloud of soldiers.

"Babinich is coming!" thought he.

But at that moment Pan Hjanstovski, who led the cavalry, rushed up to him.

"Swedish infantry are visible from the river!" cried he, in terror.

"Some treason!" cried Pan Tomash. "By Christ's wounds, gallop with your cavalry against that infantry; otherwise it will attack us on the flank."

"There is a great force!" answered Hjanstovski.

"Oppose it even for an hour, and we will escape in the rear to the forests."

The officer galloped away, and was soon rushing over the field at the head of two hundred men; seeing which the enemy's infantry began to form in the willows to receive the Poles. The squadron urged the horses, and in the willow-bushes a musketry fire was soon rattling.

Billevich had doubts, not only of victory, but of saving his own infantry. He might withdraw to the rear with a part of the cavalry with the ladies, and seek safety in the forest; but such a withdrawal would be a great defeat, for it meant leaving to the enemy's sword most of the party and the remnant of the population of Lauda, which had collected in Volmontovichi to see Billevich. Volmontovichi itself would be levelled to the ground.

There remained still the lone hope that Hjanstovski would break the infantry. Meanwhile it was growing dark in the sky; but in the village the light increased every moment, for the chips, splinters, and shavings, lying in a heap at the first house near the gate, had caught fire. The house itself caught fire from them, and a red conflagration was rising.

By the light of the burning Billevich saw Hjanstovski's cavalry returning in disorder and panic; after it the Swedish infantry were rushing from the willows, advancing to the attack on a run.

He understood then that he must retreat by the only road open. He rushed to the rest of the cavalry, waved his sword and cried, —

"To the rear, gentlemen, and in order, in order!"

Suddenly shots were heard in the rear also, mingled with shouts of soldiery.

Billevich saw then that he was surrounded, that he had fallen as it were into a trap from which there was neither issue nor rescue. It remained for him only to perish with honor; therefore he sprang out before the line of cavalry, and cried, —

"Let us fall one upon the other! Let us not spare our blood for the faith and the country!"

Meanwhile the fire of the infantry defending the gate and the left side of the village had grown weak, and the increasing shout of the enemy announced their near victory.

But what mean those hoarse trumpet sounds in the ranks of Sakovich's party, and the rattle of drums in the ranks of the Swedes?

Outcries shriller and shriller are heard, in some way wonderful, confused, as if not triumph but terror rings through them.

The fire at the gate stops in a moment, as if some one had cut it off with a knife. Groups of Sakovich's cavalry are flying at break-neck speed from the left flank to the main road. On the right flank the infantry halt, and then, instead of advancing, begin to withdraw to the willows.

"What is this?" cried Billevich.

Meanwhile the answer comes from that grove out of which Sakovich had issued; and now emerge from it men, horses, squadrons, horsetail standards, sabres, and march — no, they fly like a storm, and not like a storm, — like a tempest! In the bloody gleams of the fire they are as visible as a thing on the hand. They are hastening in thousands! The earth seems to flee from beneath them, and they speed on in dense column; one would say that some monster had issued from the oak-grove, and is sweeping across the fields to the village to swallow it. The air flies before them, driven by the impetus; with them go terror and ruin. They are almost there! Now the attack! Like a whirlwind they scatter Sakovich's men.

"O God! O great God!" cries Billevich, in bewilderment; "these are ours! That must be Babinich!"

"Babinich!" roared every throat after him.

"Babinich! Babinich!" called terrified voices in Sakovich's party.

And all the enemy's cavalry wheel to the right, to escape toward the infantry. The fence is broken with a sharp crash, under the pressure of horses' breasts. The pasture is filled with the fleeing; but the new-comers, on their

shoulders already, cut, slash, — cut without resting, cut
without pity.   The whistling of sabres, cries, groans, are
heard.   Pursuers and pursued fall upon the infantry, over-
turn, break, and scatter them.   At last the whole mass
rolls on toward the river, disappears in the brush, clam-
bers out on the opposite bank.   Men are visible yet; the
chasing continues, with cutting and cutting.   They recede.
Their sabres flash once again; then they vanish in bushes,
in space, and in darkness.

Billevich's infantry began to withdraw from the gate and
the houses, which needed no further defence.   The cavalry
stood for a time in such wonder that deep silence reigned
in the ranks; and only when the flaming house had fallen
with a crash was some voice heard on a sudden, —

"In the name of the Father, Son, and Holy Ghost, the
storm has gone by!"

"Not a foot will come out alive from that hunt!" said
another voice.

"Gracious gentlemen!" cried the sword-bearer, suddenly,
"shall we not spring at those who came at us in the rear?
They are retreating, but we will come up."

"Kill, slay!" answered a chorus of voices.

All the cavalry wheeled around and urged their horses
after the last division of the enemy.   In Volmontovichi
remained only old men, women, children, and "the lady"
with her friend.

They quenched the fire in a twinkle; joy inconceivable
seized all hearts.   Women with weeping and sobbing raised
their hands heavenward, and turning to the point where
Babinich had rushed away, cried, —

"God bless thee, invincible warrior! savior who rescued
us, with our children and houses, from ruin!"

The ancient, decrepit Butryms repeated in chorus, —

"God bless thee, God guide thee!   Without thee this
would have been the end of Volmontovichi."

Ah, had they known in that crowd that the very same
hand that had now saved the village from fire and the people from steel had two years before brought fire and the
sword to that Volmontovichi!

After the fire was quenched, all began to collect in
Billevich's wounded; the youths in a rage ran through
the battle-field, and killed, with poles from wagon-racks,
the wounded left by the Swedes and Sakovich's ravagers.

Olenka took command of the nursing.   Ever keeping her

presence of mind, full of energy and power, she did not cease her labor till every wounded man was resting in a cottage, with dressed wounds. Then all the people followed her example in repeating at the cross a litany for the dead. Through the whole night no one closed an eye in Volmontovichi; all were waiting for the return of the sword-bearer and Babinich, hurrying around at the same time to prepare for the victors a fitting reception. Oxen and sheep, herded in the forests, went under the knife; and fires were roaring till morning.

Anusia alone could take no part in anything; for at first fear deprived her of power, and later her joy was so great that it had the seeming of madness. Olenka had to care for her; she was laughing and weeping in turn, and again she threw herself in the arms of her friend, repeating without system or order, —

"Well, what? Who saved Billevich and the party and all Volmontovichi? Before whom did Sakovich flee; who overwhelmed him, and the Swedes with him? Pan Babinich! Well, now! I knew he would come, for I wrote to him. But he did not forget! I knew, I knew he would come. It was I who brought him! Olenka, Olenka! I am happy. Have I not told you that no one could conquer him? Charnyetski is not his equal. O my God, my God! Is it true that he will return? Will it be to-day? If he was not going to return, he would not have come, is it not true? Do you hear, Olenka? Horses are neighing in the distance!"

But in the distance nothing was neighing. Only toward morning a tramp was heard, shouting, singing, and Billevich came back. The cavalry on foaming horses filled the whole village. There was no end to the songs, to the shouts, to the stories.

The sword-bearer, covered with blood, panting, but joyful, related till sunrise how he had broken a body of the enemy's cavalry, how he had followed them ten miles, and cut them almost to pieces.

Billevich, as well as the troops and all the Lauda people, were convinced that Babinich might return at any moment. The forenoon came; then the sun went to the other half of the sky, and was descending; but Babinich came not.

Anusia toward evening had sunburned spots on her face. "If he cared only for the Swedes, and not for me!" thought she, in her soul; "still, he got the letter, for he came to the rescue!"

Poor woman! she knew not that the souls of Yurek Bil-

levich and Braun were long since in the other world, and
that Babinich had received no letter; for if he had received
the letter he would have returned like a lightning-flash to
Volmontovichi, — but not for thee, Anusia.

Another day passed. Billevich did not lose hope yet, and
did not leave the village. Anusia held stubborn silence.

"He has belittled me terribly! But it is good for me, for
my giddiness and my sins!" said she to herself.

On the third day Billevich sent some men on a reconnoissance. They returned four days later with information
that Babinich had taken Ponyevyej, and spared not a Swede.
Then he marched on, it was unknown whither, for tidings of
him had ceased.

"I shall not find him till he comes up again," said
Billevich.

Anusia became a nettle; whoever of the nobles or younger
officers touched her drew back quickly. But the fifth day
she said to Olenka, —

"Pan Volodyovski is just as good a soldier, but less rude."

"And maybe," answered Olenka, meditatively, "maybe
Pan Babinich has retained his constancy for that other woman, of whom he spoke to you on the road from Zamost."

"Well, all one to me!" said Anusia.

But she told not the truth; for it was not all one to her
yet, by any means.

CHAPTER LIV.

Sakovich's forces were cut up to such a degree that he was barely able himself to take refuge in the forests near Ponyevyej with four other men. Then he wandered through the forests disguised as a peasant for a whole month, not daring to put his head out into the open light.

But Babinich rushed upon Ponyevyej, cut down the infantry posted there as a garrison, and pursued Hamilton, who was unable to flee to Livonia because of the considerable Polish forces assembled in Shavli, and farther on, near Birji, turned toward the east in hope of being able to break through to Vilkomir. He had doubts about saving his own regiment, but did not wish to fall into the hands of Babinich; for the report was spread everywhere that that stern warrior, not to burden himself, gave orders to slay every prisoner.

The ill-fated Englishman therefore fled like a deer hunted by wolves, and Babinich hunted him all the more venomously. Hence he did not return to Volmontovichi, and he did not even inquire what party it was that he had saved.

The first hoar-frosts had begun to cover the earth in the morning; escape became more difficult thereby, for the tracks of hoofs remained on the earth. In the forest there was no pasture, in the field the horses suffered stern hunger. The foreign cavalry did not dare to remain longer in villages, lest the stubborn enemy might reach them any moment.

At last their misery surpassed all bounds; they lived only on leaves, bark, and those of their own horses which fell from fatigue. After a week they began to implore their colonel to turn, face Babinich, and give him battle, for they chose to die by the sword rather than by hunger. Hamilton yielded, and drew up for battle in Andronishki. The Swedish forces were inferior to that degree that the Englishman could not even think of victory, especially against such an opponent. But he was himself greatly wearied, and wanted to die. The battle, begun at Andro-

nishki, ended near Troüpi, where fell the last of the
Swedes.

Hamilton died the death of a hero, defending himself at
a cross by the roadside against a number of Tartars, who
wished at first to take him alive, but infuriated by his
resistance bore him apart on their sabres at last.

But Babinich's squadrons were so wearied too that they
had neither the strength nor the wish to advance even to
the neighboring Troüpi; but wherever one of them stood
during battle there it prepared at once for the night's
rest, kindling fires in the midst of the enemy's corpses.
After they had eaten, all fell asleep with the sleep of
stones. Even the Tartars themselves deferred till next
morning the plunder of corpses.

Kmita, who was concerned mainly about the horses, did
not oppose that rest. But next morning he rose rather
early, so as to count his own loss after the stubborn conflict and divide the spoils justly. Immediately after eating
he stood on the eminence, at that same cross under which
Hamilton had died; the Polish and Tartar officers came to
him in their turn, with the loss of their men notched on
staffs, and made reports. He listened as a country proprie-
tor listens in summer to his overseers, and rejoices in his
heart at the plentiful harvest.

Then Akbah Ulan came up, more like a fright than a
human being, for his nose had been broken at Volmontovichi by the hilt of a sabre; he bowed, gave Kmita a bloody
paper, and said, —

"Effendi, some papers were found on the Swedish leader,
which I give according to order."

Kmita had indeed given a rigorous order that all papers
discovered on corpses should be brought to him straightway after battle, for often he was able to learn from them
the plans of the enemy, and act accordingly.

But at this time he was not so urgent; therefore he
nodded and put the paper in his bosom. But Akbah Ulan
he sent to the chambul with the order to move at once to
Troüpi, where they were to have a longer rest.

The squadrons then passed before him, one after the
other. In advance marched the chambul, which now did
not number five hundred completely; the rest had been
lost in continual battles; but each Tartar had so many
Swedish riks thalers, Prussian thalers and ducats sewed
up in his saddle, in his coat, and in his cap, that he was

worth his own weight. They were in no wise like common Tartars, for whoso of them was weaker had perished from hardship; there remained only men beyond praise, broad-shouldered, of iron endurance, and venomous as hornets. Continual practice had so trained them that in hand-to-hand conflict they could meet even the regular cavalry of Poland; on the heavy cavalry or dragoons of Prussia, when equal in number, they rushed like wolves upon sheep. In battle they defended with terrible fierceness the bodies of their comrades, so as to divide afterward their booty. They passed now before Kmita with great animation, sounding their trumpets, blowing their pipes, and shaking their horse-tail standard; they went in such order that regular troops could not have marched better.

Next came the dragoons, formed with great pains by Pan Andrei from volunteers of every description, armed with rapiers and muskets. They were led by the old sergeant, Soroka, now raised to the dignity of officer, and even to that of captain. The regiment, dressed in one fashion in captured uniforms taken from Prussian dragoons, was composed chiefly of men of low station; but Kmita loved specially that kind of people, for they obeyed blindly and endured every toil without uttering a murmur.

In the two following squadrons of volunteers only smaller and higher nobles served. They were stormy spirits and restive, who under another leader would have been turned into a herd of robbers, but in Kmita's iron hands they had become like regular squadrons, and gladly called themselves "light horsemen." These were less steady under fire than the dragoons, but were more terrible in their first fury, and were more skilful in hand-to-hand conflict, for they knew every point of fencing.

After these marched, finally, about a thousand fresh volunteers, — good men, but over whom it was needful to work yet to make them like regular troops.

Each of these squadrons in passing raised a shout, saluting meanwhile Pan Andrei with their sabres. And he was more and more rejoiced. That was a considerable and not a poor force. He had accomplished much with it, had shed much of the enemy's blood, and God knows how much he might do yet. His former offences were great, but his recent services were not slight. He had risen from his fall, from his sin; and had gone to repent, not in the church, but in the field. — not in ashes, but in blood. He had defended the Most Holy Lady, the country, and the king; and now he felt that it was easier in his soul and more joyous. Nay, the heart of the young man swelled with pride, for not every one would have been able to make head as he had.

For how many fiery nobles are there, how many cavaliers in that Commonwealth! and why does no one of them stand at the head of such forces, — not even Volodyovski, nor Pan Yan? Besides, who defended Chenstohova, who defended the king in the pass, who slashed down Boguslav, who first brought fire and sword into Electoral Prussia? And behold even now in Jmud there is hardly an enemy.

Here Pan Andrei felt what the falcon feels, when, stretching his wings, he rises higher and higher. The passing squadrons greeted him with a thundering shout, and he raised his head and asked himself, "Whither shall I fly?" And his face flushed, for in that moment it seemed to him that within himself he bore a hetman. But that baton, if it comes to him, will come from the field, from wounds, from service, from praise. No traitor will flash it before his eyes as in his time Prince Yanush had done, but a thankful country will place it in his hand, with the will of the king. But it is not for him to think when it will come, but to fight, and to fight to-morrow as he fought yesterday!

Here the excited imagination of the cavalier returned to reality. Whither should he march from Troüpi, in what new place strike the Swedes?

Then he remembered the letter given him by Akbah Ulan and found on the body of Hamilton. He put his hand in his bosom, took it out and looked, and astonishment at once was reflected on his face; for on the letter was written plainly, in a woman's hand: "To his Grace Pan Babinich, Colonel of Tartar forces and volunteers."

"For me!" said Pan Andrei.

The seal was broken; therefore he opened the letter quickly, struck the paper with the back of his hand, and began to read. But he had not finished when his hands began to quiver, his face changed, and he cried, —

"Praised be the name of the Lord! O merciful God, the reward comes to me from Thy hand!"

Here he seized the foot of the cross with both hands, and began to beat his yellow hair against the wood. In another manner he was not able to thank God at that moment; he found no other words for prayer, because delight like a whirlwind had seized him and borne him far, far away to the sky.

That letter was from Anusia. The Swedes had found it on the body of Yurek Billevich, and now it had come to Kmita's hands through a second corpse. Through Pan Andrei's head thousands of thoughts were flying with the speed of Tartar arrows.

Therefore Olenka was not in the wilderness, but in Billevich's party; and he had just saved her, and with her that Volmontovichi which on a time he had sent up in smoke in avenging his comrades. Evidently the hand of God had directed his steps, so that with one blow he had made good all wrongs done Olenka and Lauda. Behold, his offences are washed away! Can she refuse now to forgive him, or can that grave brotherhood of Lauda? Can they refuse to bless him? And what will she say, that beloved maiden who holds him a traitor, when she learns that that Babinich who brought down Radzivill, who waded to his girdle in German and Swedish blood, who crushed the enemy out of Jmud, destroyed them, drove them to Prussia and Livonia, was he, — was Kmita; no longer, however, the disorderly, the outlaw, the traitor, but the defender of the faith, of the king, of the country?

Immediately after he had crossed the boundary of Jmud, Pan Andrei wished to proclaim to the four sides of the world who that far-famed Babinich was; and if he did not do so, it was only because he feared that at the very sound of his real name all would turn from him, all would suspect him, would refuse him aid and confidence. Two years had barely passed, since bewildered by Radzivill he had cut down those squadrons which were not willing to rise with Radzivill against king and country. Barely two years before, he had been the right hand of the traitor.

Now all was changed. Now, after so many victories, in such glory, he had a right to come to the maiden and say, "I am Kmita, but your savior." He had a right to shout to all Jmud, "I am Kmita, but thy savior!"

Besides, Volmontovichi was not distant. Kmita had followed Hamilton a week; but Kmita would be at the feet of Olenka in less time than a week. Here Pan Andrei stood up, pale with emotion, with flaming eyes, with gleaming face, and cried to his attendant, —

"My horse quickly! Be alive, be alive!"

The attendant brought the black steed, and sprang down to hold the stirrup; but when he had reached the ground he said, —

"Your grace, some strange men are approaching from Troüpi with Pan Soroka, and they are coming at a trot."

"I do not care for them!" answered Pan Andrei.

Now both horsemen approached to within some yards; then one of them with Soroka pushed forward on a gallop, arrived, and removing his panther-skin cap, uncovered a head red as fire.

"I see that I am standing before Pan Babinich!" said he; "I am glad that I have found you."

"With whom have I the honor to speak?" asked Kmita, impatiently.

"I am Vyershul, once captain of the Tartar squadron with Prince Yeremi Vishnyevetski. I come to my native place to make levies for a new war; and besides I bring you a letter from the grand hetman, Sapyeha."

"For a new war?" asked Kmita, frowning. "What do you say?"

"This letter will explain better than I," replied Vyershul, giving the letter of the hetman.

Kmita opened the letter feverishly. It read as follows: —

MY VERY DEAR PAN BABINICH, — A new deluge is on the country. A league of Sweden with Rakotsy has been concluded, and a division of the Commonwealth agreed upon. Eighty thousand Hungarians, Transylvanians, Wallachians, and Cossacks may cross the southern boundary at any moment. And since in these last straits it is necessary for us to exert all our forces so as to leave even a glorious name after our people for coming ages, I send to your grace this order, according to which you are to turn straight to the south without losing a moment of time, and come to us by forced marches. You will find us in Brest, whence we will send you farther without delay. This time *periculum in mora* (there is danger in delay). Prince Boguslav is freed from captivity; but Pan Gosyevski is to have an eye on Prussia and Jmud. Enjoining haste on you once more, I trust that love for the perishing country will be your best spur.

When Kmita had finished reading, he dropped the letter to the earth, and began to pass his hands over his moistened face; at last he looked wanderingly on Vyershul, and inquired in a low, stifled voice, —

"Why is Pan Gosyevski to remain in Jmud, and why must I go to the south?"

Vyershul shrugged his shoulders: "Ask the hetman in Brest for his reason; I answer nothing."

All at once terrible anger seized Pan Andrei by the throat. His eyes flashed, his face was blue, and he cried with a shrieking voice: "I will not go from here! Do you understand?"

"Is that true?" asked Vyershul. "My office was to deliver the order; the rest is your affair. With the forehead, with the forehead! I wished to beg your company for a couple of hours, but after what I have heard I prefer to look for another."

Then he wheeled his horse and rode off.

Pan Andrei sat again under the cross, and began to look around on the sky, as if wishing to take note of the weather. The attendant drew back some distance with the horses, and stillness set in all around.

The morning was clear, pale, half autumnal, half wintry. The wind was not blowing, but from the birch bushes growing at the foot of the crucifix the last leaves were dropping noiselessly, yellow and shrivelled from frost. Countless flocks of crows and jackdaws were flying over the forest; some were letting themselves down with mighty cawing right there near the crucifix, for the field and the road were covered with corpses of Swedes still unburied. Pan Andrei looked at those dark birds, blinking his eyes; you would say that he wanted to count them. Then he closed his lids and sat long without motion; at last he shuddered, frowned; presence of mind came back to his face, and he began to speak thus to himself, —

"It cannot be otherwise! I will go in two weeks, but not now. Let happen what may. It was not I who brought Rakotsy. I cannot! What is too much is too much! Have I hammered and pounded but little, passed sleepless nights in the saddle, shed my own blood and that of other men? What reward for this? If I had not received the first letter, I should have gone; but both have come in one hour, as if for the greater pain, the greater sorrow. Let the world perish, I will not go! The country will not be lost in two weeks; and besides the anger of God is evidently on it, and it is not in the might of man to oppose that. O God! the Hyperboreans [Northern Russians], the Swedes, the Prussians, the Hungarians, the Transylvanians, the Wallachians, the Cossacks, and all of them at once! Who can resist? O Lord, in what has this unfortunate land offended, in what this pious king, that Thou hast turned from them Thy face, and givest neither mercy nor rescue, and sendest new lashes? Is the bloodshed yet too little, the tears too few? People here have forgotten to rejoice, — so the wind does not blow here, it groans; so the rains do not fall, they weep, — and Thou art lashing and lashing! Mercy, O Lord! Salvation, O Father! We have sinned, but still repentance has come. We have yielded our fortunes, we have mounted our horses, we are fighting and fighting. We have abandoned violence, we have abjured private ends. Why not pardon us? Why not comfort us?"

Here conscience seized him by the hair suddenly, and shook him till he screamed; for at the same time it seemed to him that he heard some strange voice from the whole dome of heaven, saying, —

"Have you abandoned private ends? But, unfortunate, what are you doing at this moment? You are exalting your services; and when the first moment of trial comes, you rise like a wild horse, and shout, 'I will not go!' The mother is perishing; new swords are piercing her breast, and you turn away from her. You do not wish to support her with your arm; you are running after your own fortune, and crying, 'I will not go!' She is stretching forth bleeding hands; she is just falling, just fainting, just dying, and with her last voice cries, 'Rescue me, children!' But you answer, 'I will not go!' Woe to you! Woe to such people, woe to the Commonwealth!"

Here terror raised the hair on Pan Andrei's head, and his whole body began to tremble as if fever had seized it; and that moment he fell with his face to the earth, and began not to cry, but to scream in terror, —

"O Jesus, do not punish! Jesus, have mercy! Thy will be done! I will go, I will go!"

Then he lay some time without speaking, and sobbed; and when he rose at last, he had a face full of resignation and perfectly calm; and thus he prayed further, —

"Wonder not, O Lord, that I grieve, for I was on the eve of my happiness; but let it be as Thou hast ordained. I understand now that Thou didst wish to try me, and therefore didst place me as it were on the parting of the roads. Let Thy will be done. Once more I will not look behind. To Thee, O Lord, I offer this my terrible sorrow, this my yearning, this my grievous suffering. Let it all be accounted to me in punishment because I spared Prince Boguslav, at which the country wept. Thou seest now, O Lord, that that was my last work for self-interest. There will be no other. O merciful Father! But now I will kiss once more this beloved earth; yes, I will press Thy bleeding feet again, and I go, O Christ! I go —"

And he went.

In the heavenly register in which are written the evil and good deeds of men, his sins were at that moment all blotted out, for he was completely corrected.

CHAPTER LV.

It is written in no book how many battles the armies, the nobles, and the people of the Commonwealth fought with the enemy. They fought in forests, in fields, in villages, in hamlets, in towns; they fought in Prussia, in Mazovia, in Great Poland, in Little Poland, in Russia, in Lithuania, in Jmud; they fought without resting, in the day or the night.

Every clod of earth was drenched in blood. The names of knights, their glorious deeds, their great devotion, perished from the memory; for the chronicler did not write them down, and the lute did not celebrate them. But under the force of these exertions the power of the enemy bent at last. And as when a lordly lion, pierced the moment before with missiles, rises suddenly, and shaking his kingly mane, roars mightily, pale terror pierces straightway the hunters, and their feet turn to flight; so that Commonwealth rose ever more terrible, filled with anger of Jove, ready to meet the whole world. Into the bones of the aggressors there entered weakness and fear; not of plunder were they thinking then, but of this only, — to bear away home from the jaws of the lion sound heads.

New leagues, new legions of Hungarians, Transylvanians, Wallachians, and Cossacks were of no avail. The storm passed once more, it is true, between Brest, Warsaw, and Cracow; but it was broken against Polish breasts, and soon was scattered like empty vapor.

The King of Sweden, being the first to despair of his cause, went home to the Danish war; the traitorous elector, humble before the strong, insolent to the weak, beat with his forehead before the Commonwealth, and fell upon the Swedes; the robber legions of Rakotsy's "slaughterers" fled with all power to their Transylvanian reed-fields, which Pan Lyubomirski ruined with fire and sword.

But it was easier for them to break into the Commonwealth than to escape without punishment; therefore when they were attacked at the passage, the Counts of Transylvania, kneeling before Pototski, Lyubomirski, and Charnyetski, begged for mercy in the dust.

"We will surrender our weapons, we will give millions!" cried they; "only let us go!"

And receiving the ransom, the hetmans took pity on that army of unfortunate men; but the horde trampled them under hoofs at the very thresholds of their homes.

Peace began to return gradually to the plains of Poland. The king was still taking Prussian fortresses; Charnyetski was to take the Polish sword to Denmark, for the Commonwealth did not wish to limit itself to driving out the enemy.

Villages and towns were rebuilt on burned ruins; the people returned from the forests; ploughs appeared in the fields.

In the autumn of 1657, immediately after the Hungarian war, it was quiet in the greater part of the provinces and districts; it was quiet especially in Jmud.

Those of the Lauda men who in their time had gone with Volodyovski, were still somewhere far off in the field; but their return was expected.

Meanwhile in Morezi, in Volmontovichi, in Drojeykani, Mozgi, Goshchuni, and Patsuneli, women, boys, and girls, with old men, were sowing the winter grain, building with joint efforts houses in those "neighborhoods" through which fire had passed, so that the warriors on their return might find at least roofs over their heads, and not be forced to die of hunger.

Olenka had been living for some time at Vodokty, with Anusia and the sword-bearer. Pan Tomash did not hasten to his Billeviche, — first, because it was burned, and second, because it was pleasanter for him with the maidens than alone. Meanwhile, with the aid of Olenka, he managed Vodokty.

The lady wished to manage Vodokty in the best manner, for it was to be with Mitruny her dowry for the cloister; in other words, it was to become the property of the Benedictine nuns, with whom on the very day of the coming New Year poor Olenka intended to begin her novitiate.

For after she had considered everything that had met her, — those changes of fortune, disappointments, and sufferings, — she came to the conviction that thus, and not otherwise, must be the will of God. It seemed to her that some all-powerful hand was urging her to the cell, that some voice was saying to her, —

"In that place is the best pacification, and the end of all earthly anxiety."

She had determined therefore to follow that voice. Feeling, however, in the depth of her conscience that her soul had not been able yet to tear itself from the earth with completeness, she desired first to prepare it with ardent piety, with good works and labor. Frequently also in those efforts echoes from the world hindered her.

For example, people began to buzz around that that famous Babinich was Kmita. Some contradicted excitedly; others repeated the statement with stubbornness.

Olenka believed not. All Kmita's deeds, Kmita and his service with Yanush Radzivill, were too vividly present in her memory to let her suppose for one instant that he was the crusher of Boguslav, and such a trusty worker for the king, such an ardent patriot. Still her peace was disturbed, and sorrow with pain rose up afresh in her bosom.

This might be remedied by a hurried entrance to the cloister; but the cloisters were scattered. The nuns who had not perished from the violence of soldiers during war-time were only beginning to assemble.

Universal misery reigned in the land, and whoso wished to take refuge behind the walls of a convent had not only to bring bread for personal use, but also to feed the whole convent.

Olenka wished to come with bread to the cloister, — to become not merely a sister, but a nourisher of nuns.

The sword-bearer, knowing that his labor was to go to the glory of God, labored earnestly.

He went around the fields and the buildings, carrying out the labors of the autumn which with the coming spring were to bear fruit. Sometimes he was accompanied by Anusia, who, unable to endure the affront which Babinich had put upon her, threatened also to enter the cloister, and said she was merely waiting for Volodyovski to bring back the Lauda men, for she wished to bid adieu to her old friend. But more frequently the sword-bearer went with Olenka only on these circuits, for land management was irksome to Anusia.

A certain time both rode out on ponies to Mitruny, where they were rebuilding barns and cow-houses burned in time of war.

On the road they were to visit the church; for that was the anniversary of the battle of Volmontovichi, in which they were saved from the last straits by the coming of Babinich. The whole day had passed for them in various occupations, so that only toward evening could they start from Mitruny. In going there they went by the church-road, but in returning they had to pass through Lyubich and Volmontovichi. Panna Aleksandra had barely looked at the first smoke of Lyubich when she turned aside her eyes and began to repeat prayers to drive away painful thoughts; but the sword-bearer rode on in silence, and only looked around. At last, when they had passed the gate, he said, —

"That is land for a senator! Lyubich is worth two like Mitruny."

Olenka continued to say her prayers.

But in Pan Tomash was roused the old landlord by nature, and perhaps also he was given somewhat to lawsuits; for after a while he said again, as if to himself, —

"And yet it is ours by right, — old Billevich property, our sweat, our toil. That unfortunate man must have perished long since, for he has not announced himself; and if he had, the right is with us." Here he turned to Olenka: "What do you think?"

"That is a cursed place," answered she. "Let happen with it what may!"

"But you see the right is with us. The place was cursed in bad hands, but it will be blessed in good ones. The right is with us."

"Never! I do not wish to know anything of it. My grandfather willed it without restriction; let Kmita's relatives take it."

Then she urged on the pony. Billevich put spurs also to his beast, and they did not slacken speed till they were in the open field. Meanwhile night had fallen; but there was perfect light, for an enormous red moon had risen from behind the forest of Volmontovichi and lighted up the whole region with a golden shining.

"Well! God has given a beautiful night," said the sword-bearer, looking at the circle of the moon.

"How Volmontovichi gleams from a distance!" said Olenka.

"For the wood in the houses has not become black."

Their further conversation was interrupted by the squeaking of a wagon, which they could not see at first, for the road was undulating; soon, however, they saw a pair of horses, and following behind them a pair at a pole, and at the end of the pole a wagon surrounded by a number of horsemen.

"What kind of people can these be?" asked the sword bearer; and he held in his horse. Olenka stopped at his side.

"Halt!" cried Billevich. "Whom are you carrying there?"

One of the horsemen turned to them and said, —

"We are bringing Pan Kmita, who was shot by the Hungarians at Magyerovo."

"The word has become flesh!" said Billevich.

The whole world went around suddenly in Olenka's eyes; the heart died within her, breath failed her breast. Certain voices were calling in her soul: "Jesus! Mary! that is he!" Then consciousness of where she was or what was happening left her entirely.

But she did not drop from the horse to the ground, for she seized convulsively with her hand the wagon-rack; and when she came to herself her eyes fell on the motionless form of a man lying in the wagon. True, that was he, — Pan Andrei Kmita, the banneret of Orsha; and he was lying on his back in the wagon. His head was bound in a cloth, but by the ruddy light of the moon his pale and calm face was perfectly visible. His eyes were deeply sunk and closed; life did not discover itself by the least movement.

"With God!" said Billevich, removing his cap.

"Stop!" cried Olenka. And she asked with a low but quick voice, as in a fever: "Is he alive or dead?"

"He is alive, but death is over him."

Here the sword-bearer, looking at Kmita's face, said: "You will not take him to Lyubich?"

"He gave orders to take him to Lyubich without fail, for he wants to die there."

"With God! hasten forward."

"We beat with the forehead!"

The wagon moved on; and Olenka with Billevich galloped in the opposite direction with what breath was in their horses. They flew through Volmontovichi like two night phantoms, and came to Vodokty without speaking a word on the road; only when dismounting, Olenka turned to her uncle, —

"It is necessary to send a priest to him," said she, with a panting voice; "let some one go this moment to Upita."

The sword-bearer went quickly to carry out her wish; she rushed into her room, and threw herself on her knees before the image of the Most Holy Lady.

A couple of hours after, in the late evening, a bell was

heard beyond the gate at Vodokty. That was the priest passing on his way with the Lord Jesus to Lyubich.

Panna Aleksandra was on her knees continually. Her lips were repeating the litany for the dying. And when she had finished she struck the floor three times with her head, repeating: " Reckon to him, O God, that he dies at the hands of the enemy; forgive him, have mercy on him ! "

In this way the whole night passed for her. The priest remained in Lyubich till morning, and on his way home **called** at Vodokty. Olenka ran out to meet him.

" Is it all over ? " asked she; and could say no more, for breath failed her.

" He is alive yet," answered the priest.

During each of the following days a number of messengers flew from Vodokty to Lyubich, and each returned with the answer that the banneret was "alive yet." At last one brought the intelligence, which he had heard from the barber brought from Kyedani, that he was not only alive, but would recover ; for the wounds were healing successfully, and strength was coming back to the knight.

Panna Aleksandra sent bountiful offerings to Upita for a thanksgiving Mass; but from that day messengers ceased to visit Lyubich, and a wonderful thing took place in the maiden's heart. Together with peace, the former pity for Kmita began to rise. His offences came to her mind again every moment, so grievous that they were not to be forgiven. Death alone could cover them with oblivion. If he returned to health, they weighed on him anew. But still everything that could be brought to his defence Olenka repeated to herself daily.

So much had she suffered in these days, so many conflicts were there in her soul, that she began to fail in health. This disturbed Pan Tomash greatly; hence on a certain evening when they were alone, he said, —

" Olenka, tell me sincerely, what do you think of the banneret of Orsha ? "

" It is known to God that I do not wish to think of him."

" For see, you have grown thin — H'm ! Maybe that you still — I insist on nothing, but I should be glad to know what is going on in your mind. Do you not think that the will of your grandfather should be accomplished ? "

" Never ! " answered Olenka. " My grandfather left me this door open, and I will knock at it on the New Year. Thus will his will be accomplished."

"Neither do I believe at all," answered Billevich, "what some buzz around here, — that Babinich and Kmita are one; but still at Magyerovo he was with the country, fought against the enemy, and shed his blood. The reform is late, but still it is a reform."

"Even Prince Boguslav is serving the king and the country now," answered the lady, with sorrow. "Let God forgive both, and especially him who shed his blood; but people will always have the right to say that in the moment of greatest misfortune, in the moment of disaster and fall, he rose against the country, and returned to it only when the enemy's foot was tottering, and when his personal profit commanded him to hold to the victor. That is their sin! Now there are no traitors, for there is no profit from treason! But what is the merit? Is it not a new proof that such men are always ready to serve the stronger? Would to God it were otherwise, but Magyerovo cannot redeem such transgression."

"It is true! I cannot deny it," answered Billevich. "It is a bitter truth, but still true. All the former traitors have gone over in a chambul to the king."

"On the banneret of Orsha," continued the lady, "there rests a still more grievous reproach than on Boguslav, for Pan Kmita offered to raise his hand against the king, at which act the prince himself was terrified. Can a chance shot remove that? I would let this hand be cut off had that not happened; but it has, and it will never drop away. It seems clear that God has left him life of purpose for penance. My uncle, my uncle! we should be tempting our souls if we tried to beat into ourselves that he is innocent. And what good would come of this? Will conscience let itself be tempted? Let the will of God be done. What is broken cannot be bound again, and should not. I am happy that the banneret is alive, I confess; for it is evident that God has not yet turned from him His favor altogether. But that is sufficient for me. I shall be happy when I hear that he has effaced his fault; but I wish for nothing more, I desire nothing more, even if my soul had to suffer yet. May God assist him!"

Olenka was not able to speak longer, for a great and pitiful weeping overpowered her; but that was her last weeping. She had told all that she carried in her heart, and from that time forth peace began to return to her anew.

CHAPTER LVI.

THE horned, daring soul in truth was unwilling to go out of its bodily enclosure, and did not go out. In a month after his return to Lyubich Pan Andrei's wounds began to heal; but still earlier he regained consciousness, and looking around the room, he saw at once where he was. Then he called the faithful Soroka.

"Soroka," said he, "the mercy of God is upon me. I feel that I shall not die."

"According to order!" answered the old soldier, brushing away a tear with his fist.

And Kmita continued as if to himself: "The penance is over, — I see that clearly. The mercy of God is upon me!"

Then he was silent for a moment; only his lips were moving in prayer.

"Soroka!" said he again, after a time.

"At the service of your grace!"

"Who are in Vodokty?"

"The lady and the sword-bearer of Rossyeni."

"Praised be the name of the Lord! Did any one come here to inquire about me?"

"They sent from Vodokty until we told them that you would be well."

"And did they stop then?"

"Then they stopped."

"They know nothing yet, but they shall know from me," said Kmita. "Did you tell no one that I fought as Babinich?"

"There was no order," answered the soldier.

"And the Lauda men with Pan Volodyovski have not come home yet?"

"Not yet; but they may come any day."

With this the conversation of the first day was at an end. Two weeks later Kmita had risen and was walking on crutches; the following week he insisted on going to church.

"We will go to Upita," said he to Soroka; "for it is needful to begin with God, and after Mass we will go to Vodokty."

Soroka did not dare to oppose; therefore he merely ordered straw to be placed in the wagon. Pan Andrei arrayed himself in holiday costume, and they drove away.

They arrived at an hour when there were few people
yet in the church. Pan Andrei, leaning on Soroka's arm,
went to the high altar itself, and knelt in the collator's
seat; his face was very thin, emaciated, and besides he
wore a long beard which had grown during the war and
his sickness. Whoever looked at him thought that he
was some passing personage who had come in to Mass;
for there was movement everywhere, the country was full
of passing nobles who were going from the field to their
own estates.

The church filled slowly with people and with neighboring nobles; then owners of inherited land from a distance
began to arrive, for in many places churches had been
burned, and it was necessary to come to Mass as far as
Upita.

Kmita, sunk in prayer, saw no one. He was roused first
from his pious meditation by the squeaking of footstools
under the tread of persons entering the pew. Then he
raised his head, looked, and saw right there above him the
sweet, sad face of Olenka.

She also saw him, and recognized him that moment; for
she drew back suddenly, as if frightened. First a flush, and
then a deathly pallor came out on her face; but with the
greatest exercise of will she overcame her emotion, and
knelt there near him; the third place was occupied by the
sword-bearer.

And Kmita and she bowed their heads, and rested their
faces on their hands; they knelt there in silence side by
side, and their hearts beat so that both heard them perfectly. At last Pan Andrei spoke, —

" May Jesus Christ be praised ! "

" For the ages of ages," answered Olenka, in an undertone.
And they said no more.

Now the priest came out to preach. Kmita listened to
him; but in spite of his efforts he could not distinguish the
words, he could not understand the preacher. Here she is,
the desired one, for whom he had yearned during years, who
had not left his mind nor his heart; she was here now at his
side. He felt her near; and he dared not turn his eyes to
her, for he was in the church, but closing his lids, he caught
her breathing with his ear.

"Olenka! Olenka is near me!" said he to himself, "see, God has commanded us to meet in the church after absence." Then his thoughts and his heart repeated without ceasing: "Olenka, Olenka, Olenka!"

And at moments a weeping joy caught him by the throat, and again he was carried away by such an enthusiasm of thankful prayer that he lost consciousness of what was happening to him.

She knelt continually, with her face hidden in her hands.

The priest had finished the sermon, and descended from the pulpit.

All at once a clatter of arms was heard in front of the church, and a tramp of horses' hoofs. Some one cried before the threshold of the church, "Lauda returning!" and suddenly in the sanctuary itself were heard murmurs, then a bustle, then a still louder calling, —

"Lauda! Lauda!"

The crowd began to sway; all heads were turned at once toward the door.

With that there was a throng in the door, and a body of armed men appeared in the church. At the head of them marched with a clatter of spurs Volodyovski and Zagloba. The crowd opened before them; they passed through the whole church, knelt before the altar, prayed a short time, and then entered the vestry.

The Lauda men halted half-way, not greeting any one, out of respect for the place.

Ah, what a sight! Grim faces, swarthy from winds, grown thin from toils of war, cut with sabres of Swedes, Germans, Hungarians, and Wallachians! The whole history of the war and the glory of God-fearing Lauda was written on them with swords. There were the gloomy Butryms, the Stakyans, the Domasheviches, the Gostsyeviches, a few of all; but hardly one fourth returned of those who on a time had left Lauda.

Many women are seeking in vain for their husbands, many old men are searching in vain for their sons; therefore the weeping increases, for those too who find their own are weeping from joy. The whole church is filled with sobbing. From time to time some one cries out a beloved name, and is silent; and they stand in glory, leaning on their sabres, but over their deep scars tears too are falling on their mustaches.

Now a bell, rung at the door of the vestry, quieted the

weeping and the murmur. All knelt; the priest came to finish Mass, and after him Volodyovski and Zagloba.

But the priest was so moved that when he turned to the people, saying, "*Dominus vobiscum!*" his voice trembled. When he came to the Gospel, and all the sabres were drawn at once from the scabbards, as a sign that Lauda was ever ready to defend the faith, and in the church it was bright from steel, the priest had barely strength to finish the Gospel.

Then amid universal emotion the concluding prayer was sung, and Mass was ended; but the priest, when he had placed the sacrament in the tabernacle, turned, after the last Gospel, to the people, in sign that he wished to say something.

There was silence, therefore, and the priest with cordial words greeted first the returning soldiers; then he gave notice that he would read a letter from the king, brought by the colonel of the Lauda squadron.

The silence grew deeper, and after a while the voice from the altar was heard through the whole church, —

" We, Yan Kazimir, King of Poland, Grand Duke of Lithuania, Mazovia, Prussia, etc., etc., etc. In the name of the Father, Son, and Holy Ghost, Amen!

" Since wicked people must receive punishment in this temporal life for their crimes against king and country before they stand in presence of the heavenly tribunal, it is equally just that virtue receive a reward, which should add the lustre of glory to virtue itself, and give posterity the desire to follow its examples.

" Therefore we make it known to the whole order of knighthood, namely, to men of arms and civilians having office, together with all the inhabitants of the Grand Principality of Lithuania and our Starostaship of Jmud, that whatever accusations have rested on Pan Andrei Kmita, the banneret of Orsha, who is greatly beloved by us, are to vanish from the memory of men, in view of the following services and merit, and are to detract in no wise from the honor and glory of the said banneret of Orsha."

Here the priest ceased to read, and looked toward the bench on which Pan Andrei was sitting. Kmita rose for a moment, and sitting down again, rested his haggard head on the railing and closed his lids, as if in a faint.

But all eyes were turned to him; all lips began to whisper, —

"Pan Kmita! Kmita! There, near the Billeviches."

But the priest beckoned, and began to read on amid deep silence. —

"Which banneret of Orsha, though in the beginning of this unfortunate Swedish invasion he declared himself on the side of the prince voevoda, did it not from any selfishness, but from the purest good-will to the country, brought to this error by Prince Yanush Radzivill, who persuaded him that no road of safety remained to the Commonwealth save that which the prince himself took.

"But when he visited Prince Boguslav, who, thinking him a traitor, discovered to him clearly all the hostile intrigues against the country, the said banneret of Orsha not only did not promise to raise his hand against our person, but with armed force carried away Prince Boguslav himself, so as to avenge us and the suffering country."

"O God, be merciful to me, a sinner!" cried the voice of a woman right there near Pan Andrei; and in the church there broke out anew a murmur of amazement.

The priest read on, —

"He was shot by Boguslav, but had barely recovered when he went to Chenstohova, and there defended with his own breast that most sacred Retreat, giving an example of endurance and valor to all; there, in danger of his life and health, he blew up with powder the greatest siege-gun. Seized after that daring deed, he was condemned to death by cruel enemies, and tortured with living fire."

With this the weeping of women was heard here and there through the church. Olenka was trembling as in a paroxysm of fever.

"But rescued by the power of the Queen of the Angels from those terrible straits, he came to us in Silesia, and on our return to this dear country, when the treacherous enemy prepared an ambush for us, the said banneret of Orsha rushed himself, with his three attendants, on the whole power of the enemy, to save our person. There, cut down and thrust through with rapiers, swimming in his own blood, he was borne from the field as if lifeless — "

Olenka placed both her hands on her temples, and raising her head, began to catch the air into her parted lips. From her bosom came out the groan, —

"O God! O God! O God!"

And again the voice of the priest sounded, also more and more moved: —

"And when with our endeavors he returned to health, he did not rest, but continued the war, standing forth with immeasurable praise in every necessity, held up as a model to knighthood by the hetmans of both people, till the fortunate capture of Warsaw, after which he was sent to Prussia under the assumed name of Babinich — "

When that name was heard in the church, the noise of the people changed as it were into the roar of a river.

"Then he is Babinich? Then he is that crusher of the Swedes, the savior of Volmontovichi, the victor in so many battles, — that is Kmita?"

The murmur increased still more; throngs began to push toward the altar to see him more closely.

"God bless him! God bless him!" said hundreds of voices.

The priest turned to the seat and blessed Pan Andrei, who, leaning continually against the railing, was more like a dead than a living man, for the soul had gone out of him with happiness and had risen toward the sky.

The priest read on, —

"He visited the enemy's country with fire and sword, was the main cause of the victory at Prostki; with his own hand he over-threw and captured Prince Boguslav. Called late to our starosta-ship of Jmud, what immense service he rendered there, how many towns and villages he saved from the hands of the enemy, must be known to the inhabitants of that starostaship better than to others."

"It is known, it is known, it is known!" was thundered through the whole church.

"Silence!" said the priest, raising the king's letter.

"Therefore we, considering all his services to us and the country, so many that a son could not have done more for his father and his mother, have determined to publish them in this our letter, so that so great a cavalier, so great a defender of the faith, of king and Commonwealth, should no longer be pursued by the ill-will of men, but go clothed with the praise and universal love proper to the virtuous. Before then the next Diet, confirming these our wishes, shall remove from him every stain, and before we shall reward him with the starostaship of Upita, which is vacant, we ask earnestly of the inhabitants dear to us of our starostaship of Jmud to re-tain in their hearts and thoughts these our words, which justice itself, the foundation of States, has commanded us to put into their memory."

Here the priest concluded, and turning to the altar began to pray; but Pan Andrei felt on a sudden that a soft hand was seizing his hand. He looked. It was Olenka; and before he had time to come to himself, to withdraw his hand, she had raised it and pressed it to her lips in pres-ence of all, before the altar and the people.

"Olenka!" cried the astonished Kmita.

But she had arisen, and covering her face with a veil, said to old Billevich, —

"Uncle, let us go, let us go from here quickly!"

And they went out through the door of the vestry.

Pan Andrei tried to rise to follow her, but he could not. His strength left him entirely.

But a quarter of an hour later he was in front of the church, supported on one side by Pan Volodyovski, on the other by Zagloba.

The throng of people, small nobles and common men, crowded around. Women, some barely able to tear away from the breast of a husband returned from the war, led by curiosity special to the sex, ran to look at that Kmita, once terrible, now the savior of Lauda and the coming starosta. The throng became greater every instant, till the Lauda men had at last to surround him and protect him from the crush.

"Pan Andrei!" cried Zagloba, "see, we have brought you a present. You did not expect such a one. Now to Vodokty, to Vodokty, to the betrothal and the wedding!"

Further words of Zagloba were lost in the thundering shout raised at once by the Lauda men, under the leadership of Yuzva Footless, —

"Long life to Pan Kmita!"

"Long life!" repeated the crowd. "Long life to our starosta of Upita! Long life!"

"All to Vodokty!" roared Zagloba, again.

"To Vodokty! to Vodokty!" shouted a thousand throats. "As best men to Vodokty with Pan Kmita, with our savior! To the lady! to Vodokty!"

And an immense movement began. Lauda mounted its horses; every man living rushed to wagons, carts, ponies. People on foot began to run across field and forest. The shout "To Vodokty!" rang through the whole place. The roads were thronged with many-colored crowds.

Kmita rode in his little wagon between Volodyovski and Zagloba, and time after time he embraced one or the other of them. He was not able to speak yet, he was too much excited; but they pushed on as if Tartars were attacking Upita. All the wagons and carts rushed in like manner around them.

They were well outside the place, when Pan Michael suddenly bent to Kmita's ear. "Yendrek," asked he, "but do you not know where the other is?"

"In Vodokty."

Then, whether it was the wind or excitement that began
to move the mustaches of Pan Michael, is unknown; it is
enough that during the whole way they did not cease to
thrust forward like two awls, or like the feelers of a May-
bug.

Zagloba was singing with delight in such a terrible bass
voice that he frightened the horses, —

> "There were two of us, Kasyenko, two in this world;
> But methinks, somehow, that three are now riding."

Anusia was not at church that Sunday, for she had in her
turn to stay with the weakly Panna Kulvyets, with whom
she and Olenka remained on alternate days.

The whole morning she had been occupied with watching
and taking care of the sick woman, so that it was late when
she could go to her prayers. Barely had she said the last
"Amen," when there was a thundering before the gate, and
Olenka rushed into the room like a storm.

"Jesus! Mary! What has happened?" screamed Anusia,
looking at her.

"Anusia, you do not know who Pan Babinich is? He is
Pan Kmita!"

Anusia sprang to her feet: "Who told you?"

"The king's letter was read — Pan Volodyovski brought
it — the Lauda men — "

"Has Pan Volodyovski returned?" screamed Anusia;
and she threw herself into Olenka's arms.

Olenka took this outburst of feeling as a proof of Anusia's
love for her; for she had become feverish, was almost unconscious. On her face were fiery spots, and her breast rose
and fell as if from great pain.

Then Olenka began to tell without order and in a broken
voice everything which she had heard in the church, running at the same time through the room as if demented, repeating every moment, "I am not worthy of him!" re-
proaching herself terribly, saying that she had done him
more injustice than all others, that she had not even been
willing to pray for him, when he was swimming in his own
blood in defence of the Holy Lady, the country, and the
king.

In vain did Anusia, while running after her through the
room, endeavor to comfort her. She repeated continually
one thing, — that she was not worthy of him, that she

would not dare to look in his eyes; then again she would begin to speak of the deeds of Babinich, of the seizure of Boguslav, of his revenge, of saving the king, of Prostki, Volmontovichi, and Chenstohova; and at last of her own faults, of her stubbornness, for which she must do penance in the cloister.

Further reproaches were interrupted by Pan Tomash, who, falling into the room like a bomb, cried, —

"In God's name, all Upita is rolling after us! They are already in the village, and Babinich is surely with them!"

Indeed, a distant shout at that moment announced the approach of the crowds. The sword-bearer, seizing Olenka, conducted her to the porch; Anusia rushed after them.

At that moment the throng of men and horses looked black in the distance; and as far as the eye could reach the whole road was packed with them. At last they reached the yard. Those on foot were storming over ditches and fences; the wagons rolled in through the gates, and all were shouting and throwing up their caps.

At last appeared the crowd of armed Lauda men, and the wagon, in which sat three persons, — Kmita, Volodyovski, and Zagloba.

The wagon stopped at some distance, for so many people had crowded up before the entrance that it was impossible to approach. Zagloba and Volodyovski sprang out first, and helping Kmita to descend, took him at once by the arms.

"Give room!" cried Zagloba.

"Give room!" repeated the Lauda men.

The people pushed back at once, so that in the middle of the crowd there was an open road along which the two knights led Kmita to the porch. He was very pale, but walked with head erect, at once confused and happy.

Olenka leaned against the door-post, and dropped her arms without control at her sides; but when he was near she looked into the face of the emaciated man, — who after such a time of separation approached, like Lazarus, without a drop of blood in his face, — then sobbing, rent her breast again. He, from weeping, from happiness, and from confusion, did not know himself what to say, —

"What, Olenka, what?"

But she dropped suddenly to his knees, —

"Yendrek!" cried she, "I am not worthy to kiss thy wounds!"

At that moment strength came back to the knight, he seized her from the ground like a feather, and pressed her to his bosom.

One immense shout, from which the walls of the house trembled and the last of the leaves fell from the trees, dinned every ear. The Lauda men began to fire from pistols; caps flew into the air; around nothing was to be seen but faces carried away by joy, gleaming eyes, and open mouths shouting, —

"Vivat Kmita! vivat Panna Billevich! vivat the young couple!"

"Vivat two couples!" roared Zagloba; but his voice was lost in the general storm.

Vodokty was turned as it were into a camp. All day they were slaughtering oxen and sheep at command of the sword-bearer, and digging out of the ground barrels of mead and beer. In the evening all sat down to a feast, — the oldest and most noted in the rooms, the younger in the servants' hall; the simple people rejoiced equally at fires in the yard.

At the chief table the cup went around in honor of two happy pairs; but when good feeling had reached the highest degree, Zagloba raised the following toast: —

"To thee I return, worthy Pan Andrei, and to thee old friend, Pan Michael! It was not enough to expose your breasts, to shed blood, to cut down the enemy! Your work is not finished; for since a multitude of people have fallen in time of this terrible war, you must now give new inhabitants, new defenders to this Commonwealth. For this I think you will not lack either in manhood or good will. Worthy gentlemen! to the honor of those coming generations! May God bless them, and permit them to guard this legacy which we leave them, restored by our toil, by our sweat, by our blood. When grievous times come, let them remember us and never despair, considering that there are no straits out of which it is impossible to rise, with united forces and the help of God."

Pan Andrei not long after his marriage served in a new war which broke out on the eastern side of the Commonwealth; but the thundering victory of Charnyetski and Sapyeha over Hovanski and Dolgoruki, and the hetmans of the kingdom over Sheremetyeff, soon brought it to an end. Then Kmita returned, covered with fresh glory, and

settled down permanently in Vodokty. After him his cousin Yakub became banneret of Orsha, — Yakub, who afterward belonged to the unfortunate confederation of the
army; but Pan Andrei, standing soul and heart with the
king, rewarded with the starostaship of Upita, lived long
in exemplary harmony and love with Lauda, surrounded
by universal respect. His ill-wishers — for who has them
not? — said, it is true, that he listened over-much to his
wife in everything. He was not ashamed of that, however,
but acknowledged himself that in every important affair
he sought her advice.

VOL. II. — 43

THE END.

9 781589 630192